FOLLOWING THE FLAME

FOLLOWING THE FLAME

A NOVEL

By Greg Lautenslager

—

"Following the Flame," by Greg Lautenslager. ISBN 1-58939-809-2.

Published 2005 by Virtualbookworm.com Publishing Inc., P.O. Box 9949, College Station, TX 77842, US. ©2005, Greg Lautenslager. All rights reserved. No part of this publication may be reproduced, stored in a retrieval system, or transmitted in any form or by any means, electronic, mechanical, recording or otherwise, without the prior written permission of Greg Lautenslager.

Manufactured in the United States of America.

Following the Flame is the debut novel of former world-class runner and college coach Greg Lautenslager, who spent much of his journalism career as a sportswriter for The Dallas Morning News. Lautenslager now coaches runners in Nelson, New Zealand, where he lives with his wife and three sons.

This book is dedicated to
those who have the courage
to follow their dreams.

PART I

OH, I GIVE UP

September 10, 1972

Steve Prefontaine launches from the starting line of Munich's Olympic Stadium and into my den. The light, illuminated from the black and white television, sends Pre through the lens of my black-frame glasses and back into the Olympic 5,000 meters final.

Pre brushes elbows with the world's greatest runners – 10,000 meters winner Lasse Viren of Finland, defending champion Mohamed Gamoudi of Tunisia, Harold Norpoth of West Germany, Nikolai Sviridov of the Soviet Union, Emiel Puttemans of Belgium, and Brits David Bedford and Ian Stewart – all he insisted he would thrash with a surge hotter than the Olympic flame that soars above them. I stare into Pre's intense eyes as a television camera catches his close-up gaze along a turn midway through the race.

A television announcer overpowers the 85,000 spectators with a call that echoes off the paneled walls of my den. Jim McKay describes the scraggly-blond with long sideburns, mustache, navy-blue shorts and spikes, and the wrinkled number 1005 below the red U.S.A letters on his white singlet as "a superbly confident young man. Some say cocky at times. The idol of the state of Oregon. Specifically, of Coos Bay, his hometown, and of Eugene, where he goes to school at the University of Oregon."

Five days earlier, McKay spoke in the same dramatic tone to describe the murders of 11 Israeli team members at the hands of Palestinian terrorists, nearly snuffing the Olympic flame. I sit on the hardwood floor in my white V-neck T-shirt, blue-jean cut-offs, and black high-tops in the fan-cooled room. I am 14 years old and alone on this Sunday morning, mesmerized by the runners gliding along the rubber surface. I watch Pre weave in and out of the 13-man field and wait for the move that could propel him to the gold medal.

McKay says he knows Pre more personally from a conversation a few days before at the Sheraton Munchen Hotel. Pre said, "What I'm gonna try to do is work it out so that it comes down to a pure guts race. And if it is, I'm the only one who can win."

The runners keep jostling, exchanging the lead. McKay says, "It's just like a time bomb ticking."

Boom. Pre bursts into the lead and takes only four runners with him on successive 62-second laps. The crowd noise intensifies. I bite my fingernails and widen my eyes. The thin, bearded Viren takes the lead before a lit "2" on the electronic lap counter. Pre falls to fourth, but rallies on the backstretch.

"Prefontaine is running a gutsy race," commentator Erich Segal says. "This is 600 yards to go and he is trying an all-out kick."

Pre brings the spectators to their feet and the fingers out of my mouth as he leads the blue-vested Viren and the white-clad Gamoudi around the turn. "Go Pre!" I yell.

3

Viren surges back to the front, and only Pre and Gamoudi go with him. The bell for the final lap barely can be heard over the crowd noise. "Lasse Viren is going for his second gold medal of the Games," McKay says as the three runners charge around the turn. "Mohamed Gamoudi is right there with him, and so is Steve Prefontaine! The kid is showing all the guts in the world. He's hanging in there – with the kickers!"

Gamoudi passes Viren on the backstretch, and Prefontaine goes with him. I raise my fists at the screen, "Come on, Pre!"

"Prefontaine going for the lead!" McKay yells. "With Gamoudi! Viren is still there! Here comes Prefontaine!"

Gamoudi holds off Pre as they enter the turn, and Viren cuts inside Pre as they round the final bend. McKay, me, and the rest of the world only can watch – and pray – as the three furiously pumping runners hit the top of the homestretch. Viren accelerates past Gamoudi and sprints into stretch, loping away from his rivals. Pre, his face grimacing, hangs on to third until a resurgent Brit emerges from nowhere in the final 20 meters.

There is a pause. The Brit sweeps by Pre, who almost collapses in the final 10 meters. Viren whips across the finish line, shakes silver-medalist Gamoudi's hand, and raises his bony arms in triumph.

The announcers supply the epitaph on the historic race, which culminated with a four-minute last four laps and an Olympic record time of 13:26.4. "And it was Ian Stewart beating out Steve Prefontaine for the bronze medal," McKay says.

"Pre ran a gutsy race," Segal says. "He gave it everything."

The Olympic Stadium crowd exults Viren on his victory lap. But there are only shocked looks and sobs from Pre's friends and fans in Munich and all over the world. They watch as Pre turns away from the Olympic flame, lowers his head, carries his spikes, looks at his bare feet, and is led slowly to the dark exit tunnel.

I turn off the television and rise from the floor. I rush down the hallway to the light filtering from the screened front door. I shove open the door, march through the yard, step off the curb, and run down the road, toward the sun.

◆◆◆

Uncle Grimsley sat up on his deathbed. His head wobbled like someone smacked him with a two-by-four. He stared around at his basement room, sniffed at the full bedpan, and checked his pulse to make sure he was still alive.

He must have been as cold as a corpse in those black-hooded pajamas, monogrammed with his initials G.I.R. Or was it R.I.P.?

"Uncle Grimsley? Uncle Grimsley," my mother's voice shot through his hearing aid.

On this July afternoon of 1972, two months before the Munich Olympics, Grimsley was in no mood for visitors – not even his 55-year-old niece and her 14-year-old son. With his once-stud body reduced to wrinkled skin stretched over brittle bones and mouth dryer than the stale toast on his nightstand, all Grimsley wanted was to crawl back under his light blue blanket and die.

He hung in there long enough to see Mom, who was clutching black rosary beads with her left hand and stroking his forehead with her right. Somehow in the blur he recognized me, but couldn't remember me. Grimsley tilted his head a bit for a closer look at my black-frame glasses and the Dallas Cowboys' football jersey that covered a body as frail as his.

"Remember your great nephew, Uncle Grimsley?" Mom said. "You know, my youngest son."

Grimsley's mouth opened a little and he pointed his crusty right finger at my scared face.

"J-J-Jonny," I said. "Jonny Langenfelder."

Grimsley twisted his stiff neck toward Mom.

"He's an athlete," Mom said. "Just like his Great-Uncle Grimsley."

That pumped a little life into the 71-year-old man – he looked 91 – and a trickling teardrop down his pale, worn face. He turned away and stared at the tiled ceiling. In that moment he must have been looking back 50 years to the fall of 1922.

He must have seen himself in his red-shouldered jersey, silver pants, black high-top cleats, and leather helmet and sprinting down the Tumbleweed Stadium turf with a football tucked under his left armpit and defenders chasing him toward the goalpost. He must have felt the cold air smacking his gritted teeth and heard the announcer above the screaming 30,000 spectators.

"There he goes! Fifty-seven yards! Grimsley Roeper has just scored the first touchdown in Tumbleweed Stadium!"

Grimsley returned his head to level and looked over to Mom and then at me. He tightened his lips and slowly shook his head.

"I think he's going to say something," Mom said. "What is it, Uncle Grimsley?"

"Oh-h-h." Grimsley strained his raspy vocal chords. "I give up."

I would have given anything to have had the talent of a man whose legacy had grown larger than a West Texas grain elevator. Grimsley Roeper was born in 1901 and broke about every high school state record in about every sport. He broke several more at Caprock State University. He ran 237 yards in one game and scored six touchdowns in another. He also punted a football 80 yards. His senior year, in 1923, Grimsley rushed for 1,733 yards and scored 23 touchdowns. That doesn't include the 199 yards he covered in the Tumbleweeds'

33-6 romp over Georgia in the Cotton Bowl. If there was a Heisman Trophy back then, Grimsley would have won it.

Grimsley also anchored Caprock's 440-yard relay team to the 1923 national track and field title, bowled three perfect games, made two holes in one, starred in several university theatre productions, and dated "Miss Texas." The dashing Grimsley had to choose between professional football and Hollywood. Then something happened that killed his career and eventually confined him to my grandmother's basement at 1721 Lucas Lane, just north of Lubbock.

I was lucky to have lived through my first week. Mom had five children between 1948 and 1953. Then she had two miscarriages and almost lost me in the fourth month. Many novenas later she brought me home after I found daylight on October 30, 1957 to Lucas Lane, where we lived with Grandma and Grimsley. Mom almost lost me again en route to my baptism. Dad caught it on film. Wouldn't this have been great for *America's Funniest Home Videos*? A 40-year-old woman dressed in a pink dress, pink hat, and white high-heels carries her newborn onto the front porch. She forgets about the front step, loses her balance, falls, and watches her baby fly across the yard.

Mom speculated the fall caused my stuttering problem. Or maybe the stuttering was caused by the speed-of-light speech necessary at the dinner table at 2000 Hickory Lane. Mom and Dad moved us into the white two-story wood-frame house in Dallas the summer after I was born.

"H-H-Hey, you g-g-guys, I-got-one. Th-there, there, there was-this-guy..." I was interrupted by my brothers. I eventually finished the joke to Mom long after everyone left the table. My teenage brothers retreated to a bedroom and locked the door. Their kid brother's knock was followed by a, "Stay out!" No doubt they pulled out a magazine from under their mattress and stretched the center-fold across the bed.

I preferred a *Sports Illustrated* and lay on my bed for hours staring at the pictures of the Alabama quarterback in the bright red helmet, the baseball fielder in the pinstriped uniform, and the Boston Celtic in the silky green tank-top and shorts. I turned my house into a training ground for an up-and-coming legend. I threw tennis balls up and down the stairs, on top the roof, and against house bricks. I hung a floodlight above the garage hoop, hit golf balls from the median strip to our front-yard green. I smacked tennis balls with a broken-string racket off the greasy driveway to the garage door. I turned our swing set into a goalpost and hooked a ball through my upstairs window. Dad fixed the glass and me. I watched every televised game and its pre- and post-game show. I retreated to the front lawn to throw the winning touchdown pass in the Super Bowl to myself or sink the winning jump shot in the NBA finals or hit the World Series winning home run. I turned on the hose and pretended a teammate was dowsing me with champagne.

My brothers had as much interest in sports as my first-grade classmates or my neighborhood, which had mostly girls. At recess, I played with the fourth-grade boys on the St. Peter Claver School football field. They took little notice of the boy who came to their waists. Rusty Ridgeway, the Johnny Unitas of fourth grade, designed pass patterns on his palm to his huddled receivers.

"Strickland, you cut across the middle. Halford, go long. Miller, run toward Sister Mary Butt Face and then go to the posts."

The huddle broke, and the toothless first-grader tugged on the quarterback's pants. "Wh-what do you want me to do, Rusty?" I asked.

"You?" Rusty looked over the defense. "Just go out."

Like everyone else I went down field and screamed, "Ridgeway! Ridgeway! I'm open!" I watched a mass of receivers and defenders collide and the ball fall to the worn grass. This went on for months. Then one fine spring day I turned around downfield and saw this brown object spiraling toward me. I put out my arms, closed my eyes, and felt something hit my chest. When I opened my eyes, I saw a football cradled in my shaking arms.

I turned around and spun my little bow legs as fast as they could turn toward the sun-lit end zone. The pursuers' footsteps grew louder and louder. I glanced back to see a big boy lunging toward me. Then I looked down to see the goal line. My teammates picked me up and carried me on their shoulders back to class. I drew a diagram of the play on paper and brought it to the dinner table. "N-N-Now they'll throw the ball to me every chance they get."

They never threw it to me again.

Our trip to Lubbock for Thanksgiving 1966 in our white Pontiac station wagon seemed more like punishment than a vacation. The highway was one long rosary after another for my five brothers and sisters, who mouthed the "Hail Marys" with even less enthusiasm than the prayers they recited with the other parishioners at St. Peter Claver Catholic Church.

By then, at age 9, I was the only Langenfelder child who went to Mass. Had they known, it would have been a major disappointment for the parents who named their four sons Matthew, Mark, Luke, and Jon. (They named me Jonathan Christian, because John already was taken by Mom's sister). Margaret – alias Maggie – arrived between Matthew and Mark, and Catherine – alias Caty – between Luke and me. There are actually eight St. Margarets and eight St. Catherines.

Mom and Dad went to 8:30 a.m. Mass every Sunday, and I piled into Matthew's blue Chevy Belaire with my other siblings for the 11:30. Matthew dropped me off at St. Peter's and drove to Whipple's Donut Shop. Caty renamed it "St. Whipple's." There was also St. Burger Shack, St. Bass Sporting Goods, and St. Chucky's Discount Auto Center. The 18-year-old Matthew picked me up after Mass and asked me who read the Gospel and what the sermon was, in case Mom or Dad asked. Before their conversion to the donut faith, my brothers and sisters spent Mass time whispering jokes. When the lights were turned off one by one for the candlelight Christmas Mass, Luke leaned over and said, "Monsignor forgot to pay the electric bill." As we chuckled, holier-than-thou folks glanced back with a, "Sh-h-h-h."

Another Sunday, after Matthew and Caty played rock-paper-scissors during the homily, usher Patrick O'Malley walked down the aisle with a collection basket and spotted Matthew, whom he had given a car loan in his credit union. As he stretched the collection basket down our pew, the Irishman whispered into Matthew's ear, "Where's that last payment you owe me?"

My brothers and sisters didn't rebel against prayer. They just resented praying hypocrites and nuns like Sister "Baby Face" Malloy and Sister "Slap Happy" McDougall, who sent us home from St. Peter Claver School with bruises on our faces. Mark said such a nun should be behind bars or had a yardstick shoved up her butt, a comment which earned him a belt-lashing from Dad and another family rosary.

It seemed the more we prayed, the more my brothers and sisters sinned. Maggie sneaked out nights on dates with hippies and smuggled beer for Matthew and Mark, who got drunk one night and walked naked around the block at 3 a.m. A neighbor called the police, who lit up the neighborhood with their flashing lights. The frightened, bare-ass teenagers hid behind the station wagon, before hurdling the backyard fence and sneaking in through the back door. A police officer pounded on the front door as Matthew and Mark fled to their room. "Come on outta thar!"

Mom and Dad rushed out of their bedroom to find a police officer with a dark mustache and large silver flashlight. He marched in and demanded a search. My brothers walked downstairs in their pajamas. I had watched their naked escape from an upstairs window and their cover from the top of the stairs.

"What's goin on down here?" said Mark, his breath smelling of mouthwash.

"I saw you." The police officer pointed his flashlight at Mark. "I saw you behind that station wagon. You was buck nekked."

"What'she talking about, Momma?" Matthew said. "We've been in bed since ten-thirty."

The police officer, bracing himself from Mom and Dad's defense and figuring the evidence would not stand up in court, exited with a promise that "the next time there's any trouble on this block, I know what door I'll be knockin' on."

Our return to Grandma's house in 1966 was our first visit since we moved to Dallas. Our former home at 1721 Lucas Lane looked the same with its white picket fence we jumped, the large oak tree we climbed, the porch swing we rocked, and the polished banister and floors we slid down and across. The pounding on the wood floors did not better the mood of Uncle Grimsley, who left the basement only for Thanksgiving dinner.

At first, he looked at his drumstick and grumbled. "Oh, fer gosh sakes."

Dad interrupted Grimsley's turkey-chewing. "I hear you washed the car last week, Grimsley."

"Oh-h-h, fer gosh sakes!" Grimsley's forehead tightened the greasy dark and gray hairs on his head. "Wash the car! Just wash and wax the car til midnight! Yeah, fer gosh."

My brothers and sisters snickered at Grimsley's outbursts as they kept passing food around the table. No sorrow for the man who had a statue mounted in front of Tumbleweed Stadium. Matthew poked Grimsley's drumstick with a steak knife.

"Can I have some of that?" he asked. "I didn't get enough."

Grimsley gulped his turkey chunk and dropped his knife, fork, and napkin on his plate. We laughed as Mount Grimsley erupted. .

"Oh-h-h, meat, meat, meat!" Gravy dribbled down Grimsley's sturdy chin. "I want more turkey, this guy! I want more dressing, that guy! Oh fer gosh. Meat, more meat, more meat! My God, you could kill the bird and then eat half the turkey! For gosh sakes..."

There was silence for a few seconds. Grimsley looked down at his plate and said, "Oh, give up."

Our laughter followed him to the basement, which looked like a jail cell. He had a lumpy mattress without sheets and a pillow without a pillow case. There was a toilet and a sink next to his bed. His 1920's-style suits were hung on a pipe and his clothes were piled in boxes in the corner. His ashtray was a replica of Tumbleweed Stadium, perhaps the only memento of his former life. Grandma said Grimsley, her youngest brother, started going nuts shortly after his graduation from Caprock State. His poor judgement and limited motor skills kept him from holding a job, driving a car, or having much of a relationship with anyone. His body and mind slowly deteriorated. Shit, shower, shave, eat, watch a little television, and read the newspaper had become his life.

He moved into Grandma's basement in 1940, shortly after their parents died. Grandma kept him there so his cigarette smoke wouldn't pollute the rest of the house and in fear of him burning down the place. She must have been scared of Grimsley, who still had enough athletic strength to lift Mark by the bottom of his jeans and shake loose the 10 dollars he stole from the basement. I was not only frightened by Grimsley, but saddened. What a dark, lonely existence for the man who often sang the national anthem before his Caprock State home games.

On our drive home to Dallas from Lubbock that Thanksgiving, Mom declared Grimsley lucky after we finished the rosary somewhere between Sweetwater and Abilene. "He could have gone to Hollywood and lost his soul," Mom said. "Instead, he stayed home and has lived a humble life."

I asked Dad, "What in the devil is wrong with Uncle Grimsley?

Dad pressed the steering wheel of the station wagon and exchanged a curious look with Mom, who was in the front passenger seat. Dad's monotone answer only brought more chuckles from his kids sitting shoulder to shoulder.

"He got hit in the head with a football."

Harley Ruckles Baseball Park is only five miles from 2000 Hickory Lane. But the ride home with Dad in the Pontiac station wagon that March sunset of 1972 seemed like five *hundred* miles.

"How am I going to tell him?" I thought. "Maybe I'll wait till after dinner."

My family was so renowned for its failures that we were often called "Langenlosers." Matthew never failed, only because he never tried anything. Mark entered the seminary after high school, but was kicked out in his first year for having a girlfriend.

Luke spent high school under the hood of his '54 Chevy. I saw more of his butt crack than I did of his face. After two years of work, he painted the car red and added a blue number 7 and lightning streaks. He fired up the engine and took it to the Dallas County Speedway. Luke lost control and rammed into a wall on the pace lap. A wrecker took it to the nearest junk yard, and he never stepped foot in a speedway again.

My sisters competed at dating men with the most facial hair and lowest IQ. Our black mutt Blinkers was the judge. The more hairy and more stupid he was, the more he growled. No one, though, failed more than Dad. The man used pliers to change channels on our black-and-white television set, a coat hanger to keep the oven door shut, black electrician's tape to keep the station wagon from popping out of gear, and tape scissors and a razor to cut our hair. Whatever dreams he had were sacrificed to support his parents and little sister upon dropping out of high school for various welding jobs. He enlisted in the Air Force during World War II to fly planes, but instead welded them.

He moved us from Lubbock to Dallas to work as a welding foreman at Anderson Sheet Metal Company, which went out of business his second day on the job. Dad spent my childhood and early adolescence doing everything from selling encyclopedias to hanging dry wall. He went to umpires' school and spent good money on the chest protector, mask, and shin guards he wore to his first game. He was heckled every ball and strike. After Dad hollered "Steeee-rike-a-three" in the bottom of the third inning, a front row hick hollered, "Leave your glasses at home, ump?"

Dad walked around the fence and threw his equipment at the man. "OK, pal, you umpire." He took me home and never called another ball or strike. Whatever extra money we had went into the St. Peter Claver church basket or a dozen donuts we divided at a donut-and-a-half each. Mom comforted Dad with a Bible verse that claims "it's harder for a rich man to get to heaven than for a camel to go through the eye of a needle."

Mom cooked, cleaned, washed the clothes by hand and hung them on the line, baked cakes and cookies for poor families, shopped at thrift stores, solved most of our problems, read us to sleep with a Bible verse, slept for three or four hours, and woke us every morning before school with a cheery, "Rise and Shine." She had a picture of Jesus Christ on her bedroom wall and her favorite quote engraved in gold on the bottom of the black frame, "I am the light of the world. He who follows Me shall not walk in darkness, but have the light of life."

Mom went to confession every Saturday, and I wondered, "What sins could she possibly have to confess?" They should have opened an express lane – "six sins or less."

Dad didn't have such patience. Every morning he griped about how long it took us to get ready and pushed me from the front door to the car. Every time I stuttered – practically every time I talked – he yelled, "Slow down!" He taught his pigeon-toed son how to throw a baseball by slamming his hand against my shin over and over until I started bawling.

I was cut from five different little league teams, before I finally made the Thunderbirds at age 10 and spent the summer pulling out butt splinters. The only thing worse thing than watching the game from the dugout was having your parents watch you watching the game from the dugout. Down 10-0 in the late innings of a mid-season game and the coach refusing to substitute in a game my parents were assigned the post-game refreshments, Dad grabbed me and the Cokes and drove home.

I talked him into letting me stay on the team. In the season's final game Coach Junior Nesbitt put me in for right-fielder Sparky Lewis, who played more like Jerry Lewis. The dugout seemed safer. I pounded my glove with every pitch, thinking, "Please don't hit to me. Oh, please, please don't hit it to me."

With two outs and the bases loaded in the bottom of the last inning and with a two-run lead, the opposing batsman lifted a fly ball at me. I stood there like a deer in the floodlights. I located the ball in the dark sky and slowly back-pedaled. The ball kept floating, floating and I kept back-pedaling, back-pedaling, my eyes focusing through my black-frame glasses. At the last second, I lost sight of the ball and flung my glove behind my head and heard the ball hit. When I put the glove in front of my face, the ball hung on the tip like a scoop of ice cream. The Thunderbirds had won their first game of the season.

I never played on another youth athletic team – not in baseball, basketball, football, or even soccer. But I had kept practicing and dreaming of playing in the Major Leagues. For Christmas 1971, Dad rigged up this apparatus made out of string hooked onto a metal frame he welded into a square. I spent hours everyday of my eighth-grade year in the backyard, throwing into the "ball trampoline" and fielding each toss. In March of 1972 I tried out for St. Peter Claver's baseball team. I had the starting right-field position sewn up until manager Hal Myers brought in lard-ass sixth grader Timmy Robuski, who didn't field a ground ball all tryouts. Myers tossed a clipboard with the season's roster on the bleachers and said with a smug grin, "If you didn't make it this year, then better luck next year."

I went up and down the list without seeing my name and looked up and down four more times. I walked to third base and walked back for another look. No Jonny Langenfelder. No "next year." I walked to the parking lot in a trance, broken by a smiling Timmy Robuski. "Hey, Jonny, did-ya-make it, did-ya-make it?"

I punched the fat kid in the stomach.

The anger turned to tears on the drive home. But I kept them inside my eyelids. "If I can just hold out until I get home," I thought, "I can run to my room and muffle my cry with a pillow."

Dad steered the station wagon into the driveway, pressed the brake pedal, and turned off the engine. I went for the door handle, but Dad interrupted.

"When's your next practice?" he said.

I looked down and spoke in a hurry. "W-W-Well, you-you s-s-s-see..."

"Slow down!"

Dad's scream opened the floodgates. Tears streamed off my face and wet my blue jeans. I took off my glasses, hid my hands in my face, and went to pieces.

There was a pause.

"You got cut, didn't ya?" Dad said.

I nodded without taking my hands from my face. A few more seconds went by. I could feel Dad's light blue sweater sleeve on the back of my neck. He pulled me to his chest and hugged the pain away.

I had lost my dream of playing big league baseball but finally found the softness of my father's heart.

Mom and I said good-bye to Uncle Grimsley for what we knew would be the last time that summer day in 1972 in the dark basement of Grandma's house. We walked outside in the sunlight to a neighborhood park, where two men played ball with a mentally-challenged boy about my age. I stopped and watched these kind men smile with the boy's every three-foot toss.

"Good throw," one man said with a warm hug.

Tears flowed down my cheeks. "At least Uncle Grimsley had a chance, Jonny," Mom said. "That poor boy doesn't even have that."

I walked away and mumbled quietly enough so Mom couldn't hear me. "I will never, ever give up."

◆◆◆

The afternoon sun reflected off Lanny Hightower's bald scalp and into the eyes of the 1972 Bishop Callahan High School boys cross country team. Hightower looked more like a body-builder than a runner and talked like a bull rider. His biceps filled the short sleeves of his white "Crusaders Cross Country" T-shirt. His hairy chest made the shirt look like an extra small, and his rock hard thighs stretched the nylon of his blue coaching shorts. But the stopwatch and whistle that dangled from his neck to his washboard stomach and the clipboard pressed between his right palm and his hip told me he was The Coach.

Coach Hightower was about to put the three-time defending Texas Catholic Schools state champions back on course on the school's opening day. He looked around at the 19 boys standing on the frying black track in their tank tops, shorts, and suntan lotion. He stopped his eyes on a five-foot, 86-pound freshman in baggy gray sweats, black high-tops, and black-frame glasses.

"I betcha you gotta hop around in the shower to get wet," Coach Hightower said.

The other boys laughed and eyed me up and down like I was their scrawny, new inmate.

"You sure you're in the right place?" Coach Hightower looked at the roster on his clipboard. "What's yer name, pardner?"

I looked down at the track and choked on the opening syllable in my pre-puberty voice. "L-L-L-L..."

"Spit it out, freshman" one of the boys said amidst the giggling.

"L-L-Langenfelder," I said.

"Langen-what?" one boy asked, stirring a pronunciation battery of my surname.

"Langen-flipper."

"Langen-pooper."

"Langen-fucker."

"OK, quiet down," Coach Hightower said. "You ever run before, pardner?"

I stared at the black track. "I started yesterday."

That provoked more laughs and then a roar with my next sentence. "I'd like to make it to the Olympics someday."

"Yeah," a voice called above the noise, "the Special Olympics."

Coach Hightower had to blow his whistle to restore order. He drew his attention away from me to the Crusaders' goal for the 1972 season.

"We want that state title again. We've got it, held it for three years, and let's don't let anyone take it from us. Each one of ya'll has got a job to do. You've put the miles in this summer. Now if ya'll got any balls at all, you'll make the commitment and sacrifice it takes to get the job done.

"So come Dee-cember the fourth, let's bring back another trophy as big as little Langenfeller here."

After a smattering of "Yeahs!," Coach Hightower sent everyone but me off on a six-mile run from the school to Bridgewater Community College and back. The coach watched until the boys were out of sight and walked back toward the locker room.

"Wh-What do you want me to do, Coach?" I said.

Coach Hightower didn't bother to stop. "Just run to Ruckles Park and back. But first, you need to take off them sweatpants, pardner. It's about a hundred-and-ten degrees out here."

"I-I can't."

"Why not?"

"All I got underneath is my underwear."

I jogged a mile and a half to Ruckles Park, took a long drink from the water fountain, turned my back on the baseball diamond, and made it back to school as the other boys were finishing their six miler. That first run felt more like a hike, but I returned the next day.

I had fallen into a pit after my release from the eighth-grade baseball team and Uncle Grimsley's death, a few days after Mom and I saw him. I spent the rest of the summer washing dishes at Bovine's Steak House to pay my high school tuition and staring at my dark bedroom walls and the Dallas Cowboys trash pail filled with torn and crumpled baseball cards.

On a Sunday morning, the day before high school started, I changed channels with the pliers in hopes of finding the *Tom Landry Show*. I stumbled onto the Olympic Track and Field coverage and decided to watch after the pliers broke. I once likened grown men running around a track to watching paint dry. But my eyes couldn't leave Steve Prefontaine in his bid to win the 5,000 meters. I ran a mile up Rolling Hills Parkway from 2000 Hickory Lane and daydreamed I was running down Lasse Viren in the next Olympic Games. I told Mom and Dad over the Sunday pork roast I was signing up for the cross country team the next day at Bishop Callahan High School.

"Cross Country?" Dad said. "Is that with motorcycles?"

Cross country was waking up to "Rise and Shine" every morning at 6 a.m. and running laps around Bishop Callahan High School until the sun came up. Cross Country was taking a shower next to a well-endowed senior who asked why I didn't have any hair on my dick. Cross Country was sipping hot cocoa from my thermos and eating a hard-boiled egg before my first class. Cross Country was loading into the school's bus after seven hours of class and being driven to White Rock Lake by a bald coach singing to a Hank Williams radio tune for a punishing run in triple-digit temperatures.

My first attempt at the eight-mile lake loop ended two miles from the finish. Coach Hightower pried off my black high-tops, checked my pulse, and carried me into the bus. I got lost the next day and hitched a ride back to school on a milk truck. The upperclassmen had no mercy on the freshman whose ribs could be counted on his pale white chest. One day they made me run with my jock on the outside of my shorts. The next day they tied my shoe-laces together after I fell asleep on the bus en route to the lake. I stood up and fell on my face. Later that day, they pushed me into the murky lake and told me the seaweed atop my hair was filled with lice. I washed my hair six times that night.

My teammates made fun of my pigeon-toed running style that made my knees knock together. I heard one say, slowly enunciating every syllable, "I think he is we ta did."

Fifty-four runners, some stretching and some talking, crowded behind a chalk line at Birkenhead Park, on the banks of White Rock Lake, for the season's first cross country race. The morning dew had a scent of heat ointment. I stuffed my white singlet, which had belonged to a shot putter, into my blue shorts, which had belonged to a boxer. Coach Hightower, wearing a blue baseball cap with the white Bishop Callahan insignia, marched ahead of us with his starter's pistol and explained the three-mile course.

"Follow the orange cones straight up the hill, turn left, go through the trees..."

When Coach Hightower finished, I looked up at our senior captain Don Neumann and said, "Where did he say we go after the downhill?"

"Ah, hell, Langenhooper, just follow everyone else."

Coach Hightower took off his hat and raised the starter's pistol. I made the sign of the cross and crouched. A pistol shot sent birds flying from the nearest tree and the runners down the course. I fended off an elbow to the chin and filed in behind Neumann and Bishop Callahan's sophomore sensation Tripp Saxton. I was pumping furiously and in fifth place as we started up the hill. A runner from Fort Worth Westbrook High shouted, "Anyone know a good joke?"

Neumann and Saxton looked at each other and at the same time yelled.

"Yeah, runnin'!"

Ten runners passed me on that hill. Ten more went by on the flat, and ten more on the downhill. At the mile mark I barely could see Saxton, who had broken away from the field. The longer the race went, the harder I breathed, the more tired I became, the more other runners passed me, and the more I questioned if I was going to finish. I kept asking spectators alongside the course, "How far to go?" My blisters were so bad it felt like my black high-tops were trouncing through glass. Stomach cramps and fogged glasses made a tow bar practically necessary to pull me up the hill on the second loop. Ten more runners, including a girl and a chubby guy with leg weights, passed me. As I ran onto the flat, I looked back.

No one was there.

I kept plodding, not knowing how far I had to go and wondering if I would make it. The slower I went, the farther the second-to-last place finisher pulled in front of me. Eventually I lost sight of him, and the faint cheers for the top runners crossing the finish line seemed a million miles away. I hurt so badly, I wanted to walk. But I knew if I didn't make this finish line, I would never make another starting line. So I plodded on.

As I staggered the last 100 meters, volunteers were dismantling the finish chute and the timers had turned off their watches. Many spectators had gone home. Saxton, downing the last swallow of a Coke, had replaced his spikes with training flats and made a date with a Crusaderette. Coach Hightower was patting our top runners on the back and marking their times on his clipboard. I walked away from the finish line, head down, toward the team bus and bumped into Mom.

"Way to go," she said.

What could she be talking about? "I got last place."

"No you didn't." Mom pointed to a boy up the course being carried off on a stretcher. "At least you finished."

Then she did the unthinkable, right in front of the entire team. She hugged me.

I could have quit right there. Some teammates advised it. But for some reason I was back running around Bishop Callahan High School at dawn the following Monday and struggling along White Rock Lake the next afternoon. For some reason I was back suffering another last-place finish the next Saturday. For some reason, I received the only present I asked for on my 15th birthday – a pair of blue suede Dazzler running shoes.

The reason was Coach Hightower. He was there waiting for us every morning, there hollering at us every stride of every workout, there shouting every split on the interval workouts, there helping me lift 40 pounds on the Universal bench press machine, there in his office, listening to a Waylon Jennings' song after the last runner left the locker room every night. Everyday Coach Hightower handed us a results page, cross country training and racing tips, a calendar sheet to log our miles, copies of newspaper articles, course descriptions, or his own account of each meet. The top of each hand-out read, "Callahan Cross Country Catholic State Champs 1969. '70.'71….'72?"

He constantly told us, "The only way to the top is through hard work, you got to give it a hundred-ten percent, you got to pay the price for success," clichés I didn't know were clichés then. My favorite, "When the going gets tough, the tough get going."

I soaked in every word, kept every handout, recorded every mile. I finally beat somebody at the third meet of the season and a few more in the fourth. By the District meet I had passed six runners on the squad and advanced to the number nine spot after three runners quit and another got hurt. The week before the district meet, to the surprised looks and a few claps from my teammates through the bus windows, I ran around White Rock Lake without stopping.

Coach Hightower demanded a clean sweep in the varsity two-mile district race, held the Saturday before Thanksgiving at Birkenhead Park, and slammed his clipboard on the ground after our fifth man, freshman Todd Overbeck was passed in the last 50 yards by Rudy Ruiz of DeSalles. Coach Hightower ordered the seven varsity runners around the lake on their warm-down. What they missed was the ensuing junior varsity race of eight Bishop Callahan and two DeSalles' runners. "The leftovers race," Coach Hightower called it.

For Reese Blankenship, a senior, this was his chance to make varsity for the state meet. "All I gotta do," Blankenship said, walking to the line, "is beat our seventh man's time from varsity."

Blankenship went out hard and built a 100-yard lead on the trailing pack by the first mile. Then he fell into a creek. I wobbled my pigeon toes past him before he could climb out and for the first time ever, I was leading a race. I ran as hard as I could up the final hill. I looked at the finish line 100 yards ahead and glanced behind. No one was there. All those dawn and dusk training runs were worth every agonizing step for the feeling I received when I crossed that finish line. It didn't matter the guys I beat had little talent and less motivation and that Mom and the timer were the only ones there. We celebrated that night by having my favorite meal – waffles and sausages.

At dawn Monday I sat by my locker at Bishop Callahan. I couldn't wait for the workout to start. Coach Hightower handed me a results page.

"Whatcha doin' here, pardner?" he asked.

"Gettin' ready for state, Coach."

"They don't have a JV race at state."

"I-I thought I would be running varsity."

"Where in tarnation did ya' get that idea?"

"My time at district was faster than our sixth and seventh men in varsity."

"So."

Coach Hightower handed the sheets to the other runners, who also seemed surprised to see me. I still sat by the locker when they returned an hour later. "We need strong, experienced runners at state," Neumann said. "Not some wimpy, knock-kneed freshman."

I went out for the basketball team and was practicing in the gymnasium while the cross country team was losing its first state meet in four years. Our sixth man came down with the flu the day before the meet, and Coach Hightower let Blankenship run in his place.

I was shooting free throws on the other side of the gym when the runners walked through en route to the locker room. Coach Hightower, with his stopwatch and whistle dangling from his neck, followed them with a trophy "half" my size clenched into his right hand and his clipboard in his left.

At the Fall Awards assembly the next week, Coach Hightower called the name "Jonny Langenfeller" over the microphone for the winner of the cross country team's Sportsmanship Award. I was perhaps the only one to hear his voice above the 700 chit-chatting boys and girls sitting in the gymnasium bleachers. The chatter turned to laughter as the five-foot freshman with white shirt, wide brown neck-tie, plaid high-water pants, brown penny loafers, and black-frame glasses mended with athletic tape marched to the stage. I wanted to hide under the bleachers after I took my certificate from Coach Hightower at the podium and started walking back to my seat.

"He might be awful small," Coach Hightower said. "But he's got a great big heart."

The boy with the great big heart wanted to crawl into a great big hole at halftime of the Bishop Callahan Freshmen vs. Elam Junior High School basketball game.

"What the hell is wrong with you, Langenfelder?" Al Dinello's voice must have blasted through the rust-stained walls of the visitors' locker room. "You're the best shooter on the team, and you won't shoot the damn ball!"

I kept my black-frame glasses fixed on Dinello in fear of being struck by a folding chair, spit, or the chalk he used to make a Pictionary-like diagram on the chalkboard.

To say I was the best shooter wasn't saying much. Most teammates came from Dinello's freshman football team and shot the basketball like it was a concrete block. Dinello thought he was still coaching football, and perhaps in his native Brooklyn. He constantly interrupted practices to tongue-lash a player who made a bad pass. Dinello would snatch the ball with his hairy hands, demonstrate the pass, and fire the ball back at the player's nose. He didn't mind informing him he was the worst player in school history or simply, "You suck!"

I actually didn't mind the barrage, at first. At least I had a coach who noticed me. He even pronounced my last name correctly when it was preceded immediately by, "Freakin'..." Dinello started me at point guard the first game, against George Washington High of South Dallas, and pumped us up in our locker room. "These black kids got some talent. But they got no team unity and they've only been practicing a week. And we got the home crowd."

Before a crowd of 22, the black kids beat us beat us 92-17. They ran up and down the floor like they were running the hundred-yard dash. They made seemingly every lay-up, hook shot, and jumper in front or behind mid-court. Dinello never sat the whole game. He waved his arms and hollered every expletive I knew and some I didn't know. I played every minute but the last. The next game Dinello replaced me with Ricky Watson, because he said "I liked the way Watson brought the ball up court that one time." Watson was the starting quarterback on the football team and completed even less passes in basketball.

I alternated starts with Watson until the mid-season Elam game. I didn't shoot the ball in fear of Dinello reaming me for not passing it. He let go on everyone at halftime, even though we trailed by only two points. Dinello scribbled some unrecognizable plays on the chalkboard and, with veins popping out of his neck, worked himself up to this:

"Now go out there and eat some butt! Rip their jocks off!"

The first time I touched the ball I threw up a 25-footer that got nothing but air. We lost by five and received everything but a death threat from Dinello in the post-game locker room, on the team bus, and upon our return to Bishop Callahan.

"You'd think we'd committed some sort of crime," I told a teammate.

My sentence was life on the bench. I sat the rest of the 0-25 season and watched the seconds tick down on the last basketball season of my life. I yearned for an eight-mile run around White Rock Lake.

I reported to the track locker room the day after the last basketball game. "Just in time," Coach Hightower said, loading his starting pistol. "You're runnin' the mile this afternoon."

"But I haven't trained in three months, I had three mid-terms today, and it's pouring out there."

"Do the best you can." Coach Hightower didn't take his eyes off his pistol as I walked out the door. "By the way, Langenfeller, it's four laps for a mile."

I slipped and slid around the Bishop Callahan track in my first-ever track race in a time of 5 minutes, 29 seconds. We loaded the bus the next day and traveled to another practice meet, at Cedar Grove. The weather was calm and sunny. I improved to 5:28. I finished eighth in each race in the 10-runner fields, a half-lap behind Tripp Saxton. The Cedar Grove meet on February 21 was the last one I would run for 3 ½ weeks. That doesn't count the 5:18 mile I ran at a freshmen after-school meet. The only other entrant dropped out after the first lap.

Each week Coach Hightower posted Saturday's varsity meet entrants on the locker room door. Each week my name wasn't on it. I was running interval 200's, 300's, 400's after school every day and suffering shin splints so bad it felt like someone was stabbing my legs with a steak knife.

"And for what?" I told Todd Overbeck, the daddy long-legged freshman as we warmed up for a workout. "So I can wait for you guys to come back for Monday's workout? I'm not a track runner, I'm you guys' sparring partner."

"Who are you sparring with?" Overbeck said. "You can't keep up with any of us and you never will."

My chance came after the two-mile was added to the St. Anthony's meet in Fort Worth on March 17. I begged Dad during dinner for the spikes I had drooled over at the Forest Hill Mall. Dad pointed under the table to my faded Dazzler shoes with my dirty big toes sticking out the ends. "What's wrong with those?"

"B-B-But Dad I want the blue ones with the white stripes, the same colors Prefontaine wore in Munich."

"Who's Tree-Fontaine?" Dad stared at the chicken casserole dribbling off his fork.

"It's *Pre*-fontaine."

"Yeah, what sport does he play again?"

For the price of fourteen dollars and 95 cents, or 149 backyard weeds I pulled for 10 cents each, the blue leather spikes with three white stripes were on my feet and grinding St. Anthony's cinder track on the sunny Saturday. I went through the mile in 5:17, a second faster than my previous mile best. I was fourth and 30 yards behind the leader from the home school. I glanced to the infield awards table and winged-foot trophies. I never had won a trophy in any sport. Within two laps I had moved into third, into second, and into the lead. Nothing was in front of me but footprints in the orange cinders and a coach who kept me from staggering to the infield. Coach Hightower had gulped the last bite of his hotdog, jumped the stadium rail, sprinted across the infield, and met me on the backstretch.

"C'me on, Langenfeller, be tough now."

I surged and within a half-lap I no longer heard my panting pursuers. Coach Hightower appeared again as a shot from the starter's pistol started my final lap.

19

"That's it, that's it. Keep pourin' it on."

His call carried me down the backstretch and around the final turn. The spectators, all 35 of them, stood and clapped. I raised my arms and felt the finish line string against my nipples and a whack on the butt from Coach Hightower.

"Way-da-go, pardner."

I hopped to the top step of the awards podium. The announcer called over the public address, "And in first place in a time of 10 minutes, 38-point-6 seconds, from Bishop Callahan, Jonny... Jonny... Langen...uh...uh...Langen-finger."

A cheerleader handed me a blue ribbon.

"Thought I was getting a trophy?"

"Those are only for the fast runners," she said.

The next Thursday I checked the locker room door for the event I was entered at the DeSalles Relays. None. Coach Hightower entered Saxton, Neumann, and Overbeck in the two mile and the distance medley relay. There was no mile. Saxton ran a school record 9:51 two-mile. He skipped Monday's workout and was suspended for the next week's Panther Invitational in Petulia. Coach entered me in his place and handed me a piece of scratch paper between classes. Scribbled were "75, 75, 75, 74" – the splits for a sub-five minute mile.

We loaded the bus at dawn Saturday for a three-hour ride up Tornado Alley, an area near the Oklahoma border with the highest concentration of twisters in the country. A tornado tore the town apart a few years before. I lay around in the bus and fought off butterflies all day, while our sprinters ran the preliminaries. A tornado warning delayed the finals' start to 7 p.m. The mile started at 9:30 p.m. into a wind that blew over an infield tent and with fork lightning as a backdrop. A warning siren went off. Coach Hightower, his windbreaker flapping in the breeze, came by as I put on my spikes. He screamed to make sure I could hear him. "You can forget about breakin' five minutes!"

"Then what should I try for, Coach?"

"Just try to stay on the track!"

I used some big runners as a windshield through unknown lap splits. The storm had frightened off the lap timer. Overbeck battled a local boy for the win and lost by a yard. Neumann followed in third. I dodged a few lightning bolts on the final curve and fought off an opponent and a wind gust down the final stretch.

Coach Hightower back-slapped Overbeck and Neumann. He answered, "What was my time?" by pointing me to the bus and yelling, "Let's get out of this!"

We arrived at school at 2 a.m. following a four-hour ride through torrential rain and lightning. I went to bed with a yellow fifth-place ribbon and without knowing if I broke five.

The next morning's *Dallas Dispatch* carried the top six places. I turned immediately to the Panther Invitational mile. It read: "5. Linganlueger, Bishop Callahan...4:58.6" The Linganluegers had waffles and sausages for breakfast and went to Mass.

On Monday, I asked Coach Hightower after practice if I could run the mile – the longest race – at district in the varsity division. The top three advanced to the Texas Catholic Schools State Meet in San Antonio. A top three would give me four things I never had – a trophy, a varsity letter jacket, a night in a motel, and a visit to the Alamo.

"Sorry, pardner," Coach Hightower said. "We got Saxton, Neumann, and Overbeck. Even if one of them pulled out, they're still two guys from DeSalles and a guy from St. Anthonys and another from Trinity Catholic ahead of ya.' You won't finish in the top six. Just try and win the freshman division."

I asked again the next week, when Neumann dropped down to the 880.

"Nah. I'll just put Blankenship in there."

Blankenship? The guy hadn't broken 5:20 all season. I asked again the next day.

"OK, I'll tell ya' what. If you can break 10:30 in the freshman two-mile at St. Anthony's Saturday, I'll put ya' in there."

I led through more wind and rain and a sloppy track and lapped the field. I ran 10:30.8.

"Close enough," Coach Hightower said. "Run the varsity mile at district."

At dawn the next Monday, a 15-year-old boy stepped off the curb at 2000 Hickory Lane and hammered four miles along Rolling Hills Parkway. I ran every school-day morning and afternoon the next two weeks. If Coach Hightower gave us 10 by 330-yard intervals in the afternoon, I did 12. If he gave us, 20 220's, I did 22. I snuck in another three-miler before my self-imposed 8 p.m. curfew and kept telling myself, "The Alamo. Remember the Alamo."

The harder I trained, the more my shins ached, and the more aspirin I took. I soothed the pain with, "The Alamo. Remember the Alamo."

The talk the morning of district on Bishop Callahan's track was how far Saxton would win by and of young Overbeck's chances of making it to state. I returned home, lay on my bed, and stared at the *Sports Illustrated* cover photo of Pre tacked to my bedroom wall.

My stomach ached. My mind was at battle. "You can do this. No you can't. Yes you can..."

I arrived at the track lit by floodlights and about every star in the universe. It was 70-degrees. The American flag atop the pole was limp. After I jogged a few laps on the infield, Bishop Callahan school record-holder Ben Calloway told me to put on my spikes, lie down, and rest my legs on a hurdle.

"It really relaxes you, don't it." Calloway parlayed his 4:28 mile in 1970 into a college scholarship. I just wanted to go to state and was willing to listen to any goofy tip. I had worked so hard.

But no one gave me a chance, especially after running last in the 12-man field after the first lap. "Don't panic," I thought. "Remember the Alamo."

Saxton and two DeSalles runners separated themselves from the pack on the second lap. I barely could see their shadows as they raced into the night. I passed three runners and moved into ninth. I rushed by four more, including a fading Overbeck, on the backstretch of lap three. Overbeck grunted and didn't try to go with me.

The starting pistol was fired as Saxton and DeSalles' Wesley Conrow battled into the final lap. I looked up at the lap counter card with "1" on it and at the red-clad Rudy Ruiz, Conrow's teammate who was 40 yards ahead of me. I was only 40 yards from the Alamo. I dug hard into the track and halved the deficit by the 200 mark, but I was hurting. Ruiz looked back and ran harder. Calloway screamed into my ear from the infield, "Get 'im, Langenfelder!"

Suddenly, something took over my body. Some sort of spirit. Davey Crockett's, perhaps. It was as if I was above the track and watching this madman burst around the turn and soar past Ruiz like he was running in place. I never looked back in the homestretch and even gained on Saxton, who held off Conrow for the win in 4:35.1. Coach Hightower greeted Saxton and put his stopwatch in his face. I staggered up to them and rested my head on Saxton's back.

"What was my time, Coach?"

"Didn't get it."

As I put on my sweats, I looked down at a large, hairy hand. It belonged to Dinello, an official who was timing the third-place finishers. I grabbed the stopwatch that dangled down his chest and yanked his thick neck forward. The clock hands read "4:41.3," a personal best by 17 seconds. I knelt down, wiped the sweat off my glasses, and made the sign of the cross. Eight months before, I finished four minutes behind Saxton. Now I was close enough to hear him panting after the race.

"Great race, Jonno." Dinello shook my hand, smiled, and let out a little sarcastic giggle. "You're a good runner. But you still suck at basketball."

Dinello and I walked off in different directions. It was such a perfect night that it did not bother me that the announcer called me "Langenfeener" and that no one in my family came to watch me run. I went home, ate my waffles and sausage, and went to bed. I put my winged-foot trophy on the dresser and stared at it until I dropped off to sleep with one thought. "I'm goin' to the Alamo."

Tripp Saxton remembered the Alamo not for the Texas Catholic Schools State Track and Field Championships, but for the 17-year-old girl he nailed the night before the meet. The girl was in San Antonio for a band concert.

"She blew more than her French horn this weekend," Saxton bragged en route to the Holy Cross University track.

I roomed with Saxton and Neumann and their *Playboy* magazines at the Motorway Motel and went to bed at 9 p.m. I could hear Saxton outside the door with the Crusaders' track mob.

"Why the hell is Langenfucker goin' to bed so early? What a nerd."

The next time I heard him, he was dragging me out my motel room door by my light blue pajamas and replacing me with the horn blower. I slept on a pool-side lounge chair, while my teammates stuck their ears to the motel door and listened to a concerto of moans and groans.

The 1973 Texas Catholic Track and Field Championships opened my eyes to more than state competition, where I finished next-to-last in 4:52. My parents told me pre-marital sex was a mortal sin and gave me a soap mouthwash for accidentally reading "Fuck" scribbled on the metal fence of a drive-in movie theater. I didn't know what the word meant until I stayed at the Motorway Motel. At 2000 Hickory Lane all television programs were screened for possible sexual content. "Bless me father for I have sinned, I watched *The Graduate* last week."

Sex education at Bishop Callahan was taught in an all-boys biology class. Father Peter Sorenson stared at his desk with a pained expression and spoke in a shaky monotone to the snickering of his 10th grade pupils. "Let us just say you are at a school function and you are dancing with Gloria Glockenspeel and you get an erection. Tell her you have to go get a Coke or something."

At lunch time we laughed as we compared notes with the other class.

"Look what Father Zorro taught us today," said Saxton, who was repeating the 10th grade.

Father Zorro probably wished he had passed him. During another sex lecture he asked a scientific question. "Father Zorro? Could you, uh, tell us how a penis gets hard?"

Saxton earned another trip to the principal's office after raising his hand during religion class. "Brother Martino? Keaton here, uh, wanted to know if you've ever, uh, uh, balled a girl."

No one asked Saxton that question. He never cared about a girl's looks or her size. "Just as long as she fits into my VW," he said.

The girls were attracted to his messy, long black hair, chin fuzz, cigarette-stained teeth, half-bitten fingernails, and breath that smelled like old beer. He finished a roll in his VW van with "What did you say your name was?"

If Saxton spent as much time running as he did screwing, he would have been an Olympic champion. He hid in the bushes during the morning run, walked up hills, and jumped on the ladder attached to the back of the bus as Coach Hightower drove past us on a lake run. But when the gun went off, Saxton was tougher than a Waffle House steak. That and bronchitis kept me from beating him in cross country in the fall of 1973. I was the anti-Saxton. I recorded every mile on my training log, took notes during Coach Hightower's team meetings, and snuck out of my house at night only to go running. The closer I came to Saxton in races, the worse he treated me. I was singing in the bus on the way home from our first cross country meet, where Saxton beat me by six seconds.

"Hey Langenfucker?"

"Yeah."

"What did ya' do with that 20 dollars?"

"What 20 dollars?"

"That 20 dollars your mother gave you for singin' lessons."

Then there was, "Hey, Langenfucker, why do you part your 'face' down the middle?"

Saxton cracked his whip of a towel on my bare ass in the locker room and called me the Mel Tillis of Track and Field as I held my throat during a stuttering block.

"Choke on them words, Langenfucker."

I had returned my sophomore year with a six-inch growth spurt, a deep voice, and hairy armpits. Saxton did his hill workouts and intervals separate from me. He made a big jump early cross country season, when I missed two weeks with the bronchitis. I tried to make it up by running three times per day. I ran my first 100-mile week, which ended with a 26-mile Saturday and a school dance that night. I sat in the corner and drank punch without asking a girl to dance. Not because I was tired, but because I was afraid to ask.

Still, Saxton beat me every race and by 20 seconds at District in setting a Birkenhead course record. He finished second at state on the DeSalles Preparatory School Course. I was sixth. Our fifth man, Overbeck, faded to 30th, and we again settled for the runner-up trophy behind Houston Marist.

Track season arrived and I improved my mile time to 4:34 in the season's first meet, the Bishop Callahan Invitational. Saxton won the 880 in 1:58.5 and I ran a 4:33 mile the next week at DeSalles and lapped the field in the two-mile at the St. Anthony's meet, breaking Saxton's school record with a 9:48. Saxton got into my face before the following Monday's practice. "I am going to win the mile at district," he said.

It was building into a classic duel. The drinking, partying, loafing Saxton vs. the praying, studying, running Langenfelder. It was Bud Light vs. R.C. Cola. Mick Jagger vs. Pat Boone. The Mod Squad vs. the Brady Bunch.

Coach Hightower entered us in the mile at the Petulia Invitational, where Saxton was in no mood for a duel, "It's too hot and windy this afternoon and there's no one here close to us. Let's just intentionally tie and then get it on at District."

What he was really saying was, "I stayed up all night chasing girls and got about three hours sleep. I have a hangover and a headache and I don't feel like racing."

Saxton and I traded the lead and easily ran away from the field. We slowed down the last lap and crossed the finish line side by side in a track record 4:48. We were called to the press box for a live interview on the Petulia radio station. Saxton motioned to his shot put buddy Arby Lunker.

"Lunkhead," Saxton said. "I got an idea. Go up there and tell the radio announcer that my father was a famous runner who ran the 5,000 and 10,000 in two Olympics and just won the masters division at the Boston Marathon."

"What?" Lunker said. "Your old man's never run a step in his life. He hates having to walk away from the TV to take a piss."

"Just do it, ass-wipe. Then go listen on the radio."

Saxton whispered into Lunker's ear. They looked at each other like two kids about to short-sheet their parents' bed.

"What's going on?" I said.

"You'll see." Saxton grinned.

Lunker walked to the wooden press box, and we followed a few minutes later and sat in the booth with Wynn Collier, who probably did the play-by-play at every Petulia football and basketball game since the 1930's. Collier first turned to me and asked who inspired me to run. I talked between "uhs" into the microphone about Steve Prefontaine and Uncle Grimsley. Collier then put his arm around Saxton.

"Speaking of inspiration, Tripp Saxton's daddy ran in two Olympics and just won the masters division of the Boston Marathon."

"What's the big idea, mister?" Saxton looked down as if he was crying.

"What do you mean, Tripp?"

"How would you like it if your father didn't have any arms or legs?"

I don't know how Saxton could do that with a straight face. I almost burst out laughing on the air. Lunker, Saxton, and I exchanged high-fives under the stands and then sat on separate ends of the bus.

A thunderstorm blew in the afternoon of the district track meet at Trinity Catholic High School on April 25, 1974. It was so cold, wet, and windy that some competitors raced in their sweats. It was the perfect setting for a showdown.

Saxton and I didn't say a word to each other all week. The kids at school took sides, some placed bets. I asked Mom to say an extra rosary.

A wind gust blew off the starter's hat as he fired the gun to start the District mile. Saxton, his blue shirt-tail hanging over of his blue shorts, shot into the lead. He went so fast, and the other eight runners went out so slow, I couldn't even get a wind draft. The rain fogged up my glasses, and the wind made it hard to the hear the smatterings of "Go Saxton" and "Go Langenfelder" as we sloshed through the puddles of the first lap on the hard, black track.

Saxton opened 40 yards by the end of the second lap, but I kept pushing. I looked up on the backstretch and noticed Saxton tiring. I caught him around the turn and tucked behind him on the breezy homestretch. Saxton panted hard and looked like he was about to fall over. When the gun was fired for the final lap, I took off as hard as I could. I rode the wind down the backstretch, but went too hard. My legs felt like Herman Munster's as I hit the turn. In track terms, they call this "a monkey jumping on your back." It felt more like a gorilla.

I could tell from watching Lunker jumping up and down that Saxton was gaining. "Come on, Tripp! "You got 'im, dude!"

I drove my body, gorilla and all, into a final wind gust that probably registered a gale. The finish line through the raindrops on my Coke-bottle lenses looked a mile away. I glanced back and there was Saxton, grimacing and digging his red spikes into the track. I must have looked back a dozen times on the homestretch. Each time Saxton came closer, and the crowd yelled louder. I gave it one last thrust and a lunge at the line. The string hit my chest. Saxton came up a yard short.

I didn't see Saxton the next week. I heard he had been suspended from school, again, for drinking in the parking lot. I also suspected him of stealing my first-place medal, which reappeared on my locker a few days later.

On our return to San Antonio for the 1974 Texas Catholic Schools State Track and Field Championships Saxton and I were more concerned about Houston Marist twins Matty and Marty Rittenbacker and our next door teammates who challenged us to a post-meet water war at the Motorway Motel. Matty Rittenbacker, a junior, the state cross country champion who had emerged as one of the top runners in the country, went solo from the gun on this calm, clear night and won in 4:14.8. I led Saxton on a blast by Matty's brother and Mario Rodriguez of El Paso's Our Lady of Guadalupe in the final 200 meters. I finished second in 4:22.6, and Saxton third in Saxton 4:23.8.

I improved 10 seconds on my time from district and broke Ben Calloway's school record.and I shook hands and returned to the Motorway Motel, where the first water bucket already had been launched into our room. The war ended as Saxton snuck along the outdoor corridor with a trash can filled with ice water. He saw the door ajar on our teammates' room and heard voices. What he didn't see was a bare-chested Coach Hightower standing in the room in his shorts and ordering silence.

Coach Hightower was angrier about our sprint relay team dropping the baton than overjoyed about the rash of personal bests.

"Now I am tellin' ya'll for the last time..."

Saxton pushed the door open and swung the bucket. At mid-heave, he noticed that the muscular, hairy back a yard from him belonged to Coach Hightower.

"You should of seen the look on Tripp's face," Lunker said later, "tryin' to somehow stop the bucket, when he knew it was too late."

Saxton rushed back into the room and hid in the bathroom. Then a "bam! bam! bam!" on the door. I opened it to Coach Hightower with his hands clutched to his hips and water dripping from his bald head.

"If you guys don't cut the shit out, we're loadin' the bus right now and headin' back to Dallas." He slammed the door so hard a picture fell off the wall.

Saxton emerged from the bathroom, walked outside, and returned with a Coke.

26

"All the way down to the Coke machine," he said between sips, "there were these big wet footprints."

We laughed and exchanged jokes until 2 a.m. We turned off the lights of a long night and long, successful season. Finally, I felt I had made peace with this wild, crazy and uninhibited distance runner.

"Good night, Tripp."

"Good night, Langenfucker."

His stride was as long and smooth as I expected. He looked more like he was floating on a cushion of air than pounding the Loos Field rubber track. I had watched him and worshipped him from afar. But on this cold January day in 1975 I wasn't eyeballing him through a television screen.

Steve Prefontaine was one of 23 world-class runners brought to Dallas to participate in tests conducted by scientists at the Institute for Aerobics Research. At the end of three days of being poked and prodded and running to near-collapse on a treadmill, the runners-turned-Guinea pigs were asked to compete in a 24-lap track race. There were Olympians Kenny Moore, Doug Brown, Don Kardong, and Jeff Galloway. I was interested in one man.

Since watching his narrow-miss of an Olympic medal, I followed Pre through every newspaper, magazine, and telecast. I thought of him often, for without him, I never would have taken up the sport. I would be a washed up little leaguer roaming the halls and malls, not knowing where I was going or how I was getting there. Pre gave me hope.

It was written that when Pre talked to you, a glaze came over his eyes. It was like no one else in the world existed. I hoped for such an experience as Coach Hightower and I crossed the track and approached him after he cruised two miles of the six miler for a workout in 8:46.

"That's about the pace I came through last year when I ran 27:43 for the 10,000." Pre straddled a bench in his maroon sweatsuit, smiled, signed autographs, posed for pictures, and chatted to anyone who wanted to talk to him.

I was too afraid to open my mouth. Why would he want to talk to a skinny kid with a Dallas Cowboys toboggan hat and high school letter jacket with awards patches down the sleeve that read such things as "District Mile Champ?" Even if I managed to make a sound, think what awful stuttering would come out. Could I complete a word?

Coach Hightower did the talking for me. "Mr. Prefontaine? I got a boy who I coach o'er here I'd like you to meet. He run a 4:22 mile last year as a sophomore."

Suddenly, time stood still. Pre turned away from freeze-framed fans. Runners finishing the race stopped in their tracks. The public address announcer quit speaking at mid-sentence and the wind died. Pre gazed through my black-frame glasses. I stared back, though wanting to bow my head. I saw the sun glistening in Pre's eyes. Then I felt at ease to study his warm face, his big mustache and sideburns and shoulder-length hair that brought him down to Earth.

"Wow," Pre said, "You ran a 4:22 as a sophomore. I only ran 4:31. You're gonna be a great runner."

Now I froze. Pre took my pen and my souvenir program. On the back he wrote, "Much success in the future. Steve Prefontaine."

I mustered enough courage to utter, "Th-thank you, Pre." Time resumed. Life went on.

My junior year of high school had brought me to a new school, new team-mates, and new adversaries. Coach Hightower took the head coaching job at Forest Hill High School that summer. Rich Buehler, the Bishop Callahan athletic director/head football coach, told Coach Hightower he also would have to help coach football in the fall.

"I ain't coaching no damn football," he told Buehler. "Football's a pussy sport. The real athletes are runners."

Coach Hightower said that, knowing the Forest Hill cross country and track coach just quit and that his top Callahan runner lived within the school's boundaries. At Forest Hill he would make more money, teach fewer classes, and coach at the top classification in the Texas Public Schools. Winning a top division state cross country title could make him realize his dream of becoming a college coach. But he needed me to do that. Coach Hightower proved his recruiting ability by talking Mom and Dad into a transfer. All my brothers and sisters graduated from Bishop Callahan.

"Shoot, Mr.and Mrs. Langenfeller, Jonny'd have a better chance at a college scholarship, if he came to Forest Hill."

Mom must have been thinking, "Wouldn't our little Jonny have a better shot at a scholarship to heaven, if he stayed at Bishop Callahan?"

"I believe your St. Peter Claver parish has religious education courses for public school students." Coach Hightower even had a brochure.

Mom and Dad left the decision to me. I spent 10 years with the kids in the catholic schools. Forest Hill may as well have been in Alaska. I knew a few girls well enough to have the courage to ask one out. Now I would have to start all over. If I sucked as much at running as I did at other sports, the decision was easy. But Coach Hightower was talking sub-four minute mile. A national prep championship. The Olympic Games. I didn't think that was possible for me in high school. But hearing him saying it boosted my confidence. How could I leave a man who once turned on the Crusader Stadium lights, so I could finish a track workout? I needed to follow the man with the shiny head if I wanted to at least win a state title – and a college scholarship. My parents couldn't pay for college. That and lack of ambition kept my brothers and sisters from a post-high school diploma. A track scholarship was my only way out.

Forest Hill High School wasn't what I expected. There was no forest, not even a tree. The only hill was a mogul that banked the track. I thought my name might appear on the marquis the first day. "Welcome Jonny Langenfelder, Texas Catholic Schools Mile Runner-up." Soon I learned you had to tackle a running back or wrestle a steer to gain fame at Forest Hill High School. All anyone asked me in the locker room before our first track workout was, "Is The Stallion here yet?"

That would be Scott Threadgill, a speed wonder who set every city junior high record from the 200 to the 2 mile at Elam Junior High. The Stallion got his nickname from his bronc riding days at a nearby rodeo. I expected a flash of lightning to precede The Stallion's entry into the Forest Hill locker room. I didn't even hear thunder.

The Stallion was a quiet minister's son about my height with broad, bronzed shoulders, short blond hair, and averaged length legs.

"Them legs," a teammate said, pointing, "they's like rockets."

On our 10-mile run to Lake Ray Hubbard that day, The Stallion must have received 20 honks. All I heard was, "Stallion... Stallion... Stallion."

Finally someone honked at me, "Hey you, get out the way. Can't see The Stallion."

I had more to worry about than The Stallion at our first cross country meet, at Oakridge Park in South Dallas, where 125 runners toed the wide starting line. They included my old teammate Tripp Saxton and Kelvin Booker, a tall black runner from Q. Adams High School. I ran past Saxton in warm-up.

"Who's your new coach?" I asked.

Saxton shook his head. "Wish *I* could have transferred?"

As we assembled for the start, the Bishop Callahan team stood in a circle at the side. I heard their new coach from 100 yards away.

"You're the best runners in state! You can take these pussies! Now go out there and kick some butt!"

"Al Dinello must have drawn the short straw," I thought.

Dinello's voice remained within earshot until we ran off into the distance. I threaded through the massive field to the lead pack. Miles and miles of hot summer running put me in super shape and bouncing off the soft grass. I sprinted hard alongside a huge oak tree at the mile mark, surrendering a helpless call from an old rival.

"You bastard!" Saxton yelled. "I knew you'd win it!"

I never looked back the last mile and finished 13 seconds ahead of Booker. Saxton finished 30th and immediately was yanked from the chute. I couldn't hear from where I was putting on my sweats, but Dinello was in Saxton's face, raving - and probably swearing - and using his hands to demonstrate his anger in the aftermath of his team's last place finish. Saxton said probably two words, "Shove it," and peeled off in his VW van. He never ran another step.

During my first period Texas History class on Monday, a classmate asked how I did in the meet.

"I won."

"No you didn't."

"Well, I did."

"You couldn't have beaten The Stallion. Nobody beats The Stallion."

The Stallion finished 12th and was our fifth man. Vice Principal Verne McCormick confirmed my victory during the morning announcements.

"At the, uh, openin' cross countra meet at Oakridge Park, the Forest Hill Rangers and their new coach Lanny Hightower took home the, uh, first place team trophy with 34 points. The overall two-mile race was won in a tam of nan minutes, fort-one seconds by... uh... Jerry... uh... Jimmy... uh... Lingen... uh... Linkenflagger."

"Liar," the classmate said. "That race was won by Jimmy Linkenflagger."

My name was different every announcement. I was Jerry Lagenfielder, Jackie Lingonseller, and Joey Loggenfolder. Everyone at school figured a different Ranger runner won every week.

At the Cowtown Cross Country Invitational in Fort Worth, there were two things I hadn't heard behind me in the last half-mile all season – footsteps and a shrill holler from a coach who sounded like a black preacher losing his voice. "Kill 'im, Kelvin! Kill 'im Kelvin!..."

I glanced back to see Kelvin Booker, the 6-foot-4 senior who finished second in the state mile the previous season. He wore a white T-shirt under his yellow singlet. His head moved from side to side and he flapped his arms like he was swatting flies. I surged and surged but could not escape the footsteps or the incessant call of "Kill 'im, Kelvin" from Booker's coach, Reginald T. Jefferson. "Kill 'im, Kelvin" came louder and louder the closer we came to the finish. In the final 100 meters, Kelvin killed me. As fast as he went by me I thought he must have been Bullet Bob Hayes. Reginald T. met Booker at the end of the chute and hugged his prize pupil like he won an Olympic gold medal.

"Lord All Mighty, you done it, Kelvin. I knew you could." Reginald T. had more gold in his teeth than on his necklaces. "Lordy, lordy, lordy."

Kelvin killed me each week. Midway through the 1974 Texas Public Schools Cross Country Championships in Austin, there were battles on and off the course.

Reginald T. yelled, "Kill 'im, Kelvin! Kill 'im, Kelvin!"

Coach Hightower stood next to Reginald T. and hollered. "Kill 'im, Jonny! Kill 'im, Jonny!"

As we turned into an obscured area behind some trees with 1,200 meters left, Booker caught me with an elbow to the stomach and then kneed me in the hamstring. His awkward style and the narrow course contributed to the mugging. I found it difficult to run with the breath knocked out of me and faded to 32nd. Booker finished second to Lupe Ramirez of El Paso Central. The Forest Hill Rangers, the meet favorites, finished 10th of the 12 qualified teams. The Stallion, who placed fifth at region, complained of an earache and finished 85th. Coach Hightower loaded us in the van, and we were out of Austin before the first trophy was handed out. He didn't say a word all the way back to the Forest Hill parking lot.

He didn't have much to say during track season, either. I returned to Austin for the Texas Relays the next spring with a two-mile best of 9:27 and a dream of becoming the first Texas high school athlete to break 9:00. I was on pace through six laps and gaining on the front-running Matty Rittenbacker of Houston Marist, when I heard the call from the stands, "Kill 'im, Kelvin!"

Booker stormed past me, followed by 10 other runners. I ran the last 880 in 2:55 and finished in 9:40. I was breathing so hard on the last lap that a trackside official offered me a paper bag. At the next week's Indian Relays, as I was being thrashed in the homestretch of the mile by a Class 3A runner, Coach Hightower, screamed, "You baby!"

I talked to no one after the race, not even Coach Hightower. I doubted Coach Hightower's training program. He had us do 10 sprints up the 40 meter-high mogul behind the track and four laps of sprinting the straights and jogging the curves. I hit the showers after the required third set. Coach Hightower turned off my shower and didn't give me time to wash the soap out of my hair.

"Get your clothes back on and run your warm down," he said.

Dad waited in the parking lot, while Coach Hightower watched me jog the four half-mile loops around the athletic fields. I grabbed my stuff and walked to the car.

"Where you been?" Dad said. "I'm missing Andy Griffith."

"I'm feeling like Gomer Pyle, and Coach Hightower is Sergeant Carter. I can't wait for this season to be over."

"Me neither."

Mom suggested I pray the rosary. "Always turn to God in times of trouble, Jonny."

I turned to Pre. I stared at his picture, which had been tacked on my bedroom wall for two years. I looked at the autograph he signed only three months before.

"I'm not giving up, Pre."

I took the autograph to the district meet. The Stallion had improved his mile time from the 4:35 he ran in ninth grade to 4:29. I had a 4:28 best on the season, and classmates figured it was time for The Stallion to take over. There were bets among the student body, but no rivalry. The Stallion and I had become friends and training partners, constantly bitching about the marathon workouts from Coach Hightower. He loved making us run 440's. We did either 10 with 60 seconds rest or 15 with a lap jog rest – all in under 65 seconds

31

and with Dad waiting in the parking lot. As we approached number 13 on a hot windy, afternoon, The Stallion said, "Have you seen a scrotum and two balls lying around here somewhere?"

The Stallion's supporters, who clanged cow bells and chewed tobacco, crowded into the wooden bleachers at Forest Hill High for the District 8-4A meet like it was rodeo. The Stallion and I warmed up together, but that was the last I saw of him. I led the first lap in 66 and the last three in 65's for a personal best of 4:21.9. That quieted The Stallion's fans, whose hero faded to third.

I was the only Forest Hill qualifier for the Northeast Regional meet, held on the same track I met Pre three months before and where Booker recorded a 4:13.5 mile earlier in the season. Only the top two in each event qualified for the Texas Public Schools State Track and Field Championships in Austin. Spectators flocked onto the aluminium bleachers like they came for a Southern Revival Meetin.'

Coach Hightower told me after the prelims to concentrate on finishing in the top two to qualify for Texas Public Schools State Track and Field Championships. I wanted to beat Booker, whose team already clinched the regional title. Reginald T. patted his butt. "Just icin' on the cake, Kelvin. Just icin' on the cake."

Booker stood in the lane outside me and smiled. "I'll talk to ya' after the race," he said.

My fear turned to anger. The stomach butterflies turned into an army. The gun went off, and Booker shot to the lead like he was leading off the mile relay. I stayed on his heels and turned the 6-foot-4 runner into my personal tow truck. He led until 500 yards to go. I flew past him on the homestretch in lane two, careful not to be struck by a flailing forearm. The gun lap began with Booker passing me on the curve and giving the OK sign to a buddy as we reached the backstretch. That infuriated me. I passed him back on the inside and we raced side by side around the final turn – this giant black runner versus a skinny pale kid, six inches smaller and wearing black-frame glasses, held together by athletic tape.

Above the crowd noise, I heard a "Kill 'im, Kelvin!" With that, I accelerated at the top of the stretch and left Booker in my dust. I shot the No. 1 index finger at the finish string and slapped Coach Hightower a high-five after my school record 4:15.6. The Stallion, my only teammate and friend to watch me at regionals, gave me a hug. "Waffles and sausage at my house," he said.

Booker sat on the number two box at the awards stand and stared at the ground. I tapped him on the shoulder, "What did you want to talk to me about?"

The next two weeks Coach Hightower took me to dinner, bought me new sweats, and handed me the workout, four times 440 under 55 seconds with a five-minute interval, between classes. The top of the paper read, "Jonny 'the Champ' Langenfeller." We rode to Austin in Coach Hightower's new Datsun

280Z and stayed in a hotel that overlooked Towne Lake. He bought me a state meet T-shirt and the thickest, most juicy steak in town.

Booker wasn't licking his chops this time. We crossed paths during warm up. He didn't look at me. I wasn't nervous until I looked at the crowd inside the massive Memorial Stadium. It was so hot and humid. I was soaked and stunk of sweat as I completed the warm up. I found shelter from my worries under the stadium. I laced my blue and white track spikes, put my legs up on an old Coke crate, and stared at a little crack in the concrete above me. A small glimmer of light seeped through the little crack. The concrete protected me from the announcer's voice and the crowd's cheers on the other side of the crack. I closed my eyes and opened them to see Coach Hightower, his bald scalp sun-burned, staring at me.

"Stay away from Kelvin Booker," Coach said. "There's no tellin' what he may try, now that a win clinches the team title for his school. When you take the lead, don't let anyone pass you."

I walked to the starting line on the bouncy, orange track, took off the sweats Coach Hightower gave me, and stuck them in my gym bag. I pulled out Pre's autograph and stared at it one more time. The announcer called Jonny Langenfledder to lane 8, and the crowd's quiet was interrupted by the shot from the starter's pistol.

Booker allowed Ramirez, the state cross country champion, to set a conservative pace until taking the lead at the 880 mark. I moved from eighth – and last – to third place on the backstretch. With 500 yards to go, I sprinted as hard as I could and into the lead. Ramirez passed Booker and pulled alongside me as the gun lap began. Booker rallied, and the three of us ran at full steam, three abreast, to a crowd's roar of "Wu-u-u-u!" that carried us down the backstretch. I was tired and hurting and burning from the vicious Texas sun. But I kept telling myself, "Don't let them pass, don't let them pass" as I pumped into the turn.

Suddenly, Booker swatted Ramirez with an elbow and stepped in right front of me. I almost came to a stop. I put my hand on Booker's back to keep from falling. He got away with his dirty tricks behind some trees in cross country, but in the daylight in front of 30,000 spectators and a judge on every corner?

Booker sprinted ahead down the homestretch, and Ramirez passed me in the final 50 yards. Reginald T. Jefferson and the entire Q. Adams track team gang tackled Booker on the infield. They shouted, "We number one! We number one!" Reginald T. hopped up and down. "You killed 'im, Kelvin! You killed 'im!"

The stadium announcer interrupted their celebration. "There is an inquiry on the Class 4A mile."

I looked to the 220 mark at an official holding up a red flag. Runners must be at least two strides ahead while passing, an infraction not overlooked at the state meet. Flogging a competitor with an elbow also is against the rules. Five minutes later, the decision was final. Kelvin Booker had been disqualified.

Booker fell to the turf, planted his long fingers over his face, and cried. The crowd let out a thunderous "Boo!" as Ramirez and I stepped up on the awards podium. Ramirez shot the crowd the finger from the top step and shouted some Spanish words that would have quieted a translator. I was mobbed by reporters. Before I could stutter a word, Coach Hightower pulled me out and rushed me out of the stadium.

A photograph of Booker curled up on the turf appeared on the front of Sunday's *Dallas Star* sports section. The headline above it read, "Q. Adams wins, then loses state track crown."

The story told of the disqualification, his team's disappointment, and then a quote from me. "It was a legitimate call. He's been doing it all year and I'm glad he got disqualified."

I asked Mom, "What does 'legitimate' mean?"

The next quote was from Reginald T. Jefferson. "Langenflabber is lying through his teeth. Kelvin wouldn't do such a thing. I took him to church last Sunday."

We got so many threatening calls from Q. Adams supporters we took our telephone off the hook. Still, I somehow felt sorry for Booker and wondered what it must have felt to win the state title and then have it stripped from you. A foul is a foul, but I still felt bad for him. Mom said I should pray for him. I wanted to do more. He wasn't all that different from me. He trained hard, worked toward his goals, and had a coach who cared about him. I looked up Booker in the telephone directory and called eight Bookers, before I found Kelvin.

"K-Kelvin, I just wanted to say how sorry I was about what happened."

There was a pause. "Thanks, man," he said. "That means a lot to me. I'll get over this, eventually."

The dispute didn't diminish the joy I felt in finishing second in the Class 4A mile with a personal best of 4:15.0. I wondered what Pre would say. I took his autograph and put it back on my night stand.

I went downstairs and sat alone in the den to watch the sports during the 10 o'clock news. I turned on the television to footage of Pre running in the Olympics and at Hayward Field in Eugene and his gold MG upside down on a road.

I turned up the volume. "Prefontaine attended a party last night a few hours after winning the 5,000 meters at a meet in Eugene, Oregon," the sports-caster said. "He apparently lost control of his sports car rounding a sharp curve on a wooded hillside, struck a rock wall, and flipped several times. Prefontaine was expected to be the United States' best hope for a gold medal in the 5,000 and 10,000 meters at the 1976 Summer Olympics in Montreal."

I turned off the television and stared at the black screen.

6

Her name was Holly. She had the body of a centerfold, the face of a movie star, and the voice of an angel. She could flip from the top of a cheerleader pyramid, do handsprings the length of the gymnasium, squeeze her daddy's arm when she was announced Homecoming Queen, hit a tennis ball faster than a highway speed limit, and run the 110-yard hurdles in the time it takes someone to tie his shoes.

I was in love with her.

Holly Ritzenbarger had everything I wanted in a girl, except for that thing on her arm – Forest Hill starting quarterback Chuck Jones, "Chuckster" as Holly and all the football grunts called him. Everywhere I saw Holly, I saw Chuckster. Gymnasiums, hallways, fast food joints, parking lots, athletic fields. They seemed attached by the hip, or make that the groin.

Some boys learn the facts of life from their fathers, some from books, some from films starring a blue sperm and a cute pink egg. I learned from watching Holly and Chuckster between classes. Father Zorro's lessons or Tripp Saxton's exploits couldn't compare with what I learned in the Forest Hill hallway. Holly sent me to the cold showers in that short denim skirt and tight white blouse that outlined her rock-hard nipples. Chuckster pinned Holly against the lockers and drew one hand up her thigh and the other through her curly, blonde locks.

"Get a broom closet," I thought.

There should have been a sign, "No fornicating in the hallway." They were at it everyday, and everyday I found myself wishing I was Chuckster – a dumb ass jock whose brains were in his pants and whose tongue was in my dream girl's throat. Who was I kidding? Why would Holly go for a toothpick, afraid of talking to any girl much less asking one out? What would I say? "Hey Holly, want to come over to my house and read *Track and Field News?*"

I couldn't have said it, anyway. My stuttering was so bad by my senior year I was afraid to say "Here," at roll call, "Hello" when I answered the telephone, and Canuga Falls when Coach Hightower asked me before the first cross country workout of 1975 where I spent my summer vacation. I stomped the floor and gagged on "Ca-Ca-Ca" to my teammates' jeers.

I took up writing for the *Ranger Gazette*, so I could express myself without coughing up words. I was fine until I dialed sports editor Sheryl Fenton. I sat on my bed and practiced, "Is Sheryl there? Is Sheryl there?" Then Sheryl answered.

"Is...uh...uh...Sh...uh...Sh-Sh-Sh..." I turned red and slammed my hand against the wall. "Wait-a-second. Is Sh-Sh-Sh..."

"Sheryl" never came out. I hung up and pounded my face and fists on the bed. "No, No, No, No!

Mom came in. "What's wrong?"

I told her what happened. She said, "Ask God to help you with your stuttering problem."

My speech therapist, for whom I felt comfortable and rarely stammered, said I didn't have a stuttering problem even after a message came out in a special Valentine's Day greeting section of the *Ranger Gazette*. "H-H-Hi, J-J-Jonny. W-W-Will you be my s-s-s-sweartheart?" Sources said Chuckster was behind the cruel joke.

I liked what Holly wrote on the back of a donut box. The cheerleaders were required to show support for the cross country team for the first meet of my senior year. Her words in blue pen were blotched with icing and coffee stains.

> *Jonny Langenfielder is here to stay;*
> *He can win a race any day.*
> *You run through wind and rain and mud.*
> *That's what makes you such a stud.*
> *Jonny Langenfielder, I'd just like to ask,*
> *How in the world do you run so fast?*

The donut box made my bedroom wall, next to the crucifix and my Pre picture. Holly and the goal of winning a state cross country title replaced the disappointment of losing my hero. I did not move from the den for an hour after learning of Pre's death. One moment he was smiling at me and signing his autograph and the next moment he was trapped and gasping for air under his flipped MG with the headlights illuminating the dark road. Finally, I pushed myself off the wood floor and went for a run – down a dark road illuminated by headlights. I know that's what Pre would have wanted.

I had logged 521 miles that summer. The Stallion and I ran around White Rock Lake every Monday, Wednesday and Friday. I spent the other days running solo from Hickory Lane along the fields that flanked Rolling Hills Parkway. Somehow, I felt Pre was running alongside me, pushing me and filling my spirit with confidence and enthusiasm in a household that discouraged stardom. Dad, senior assembler of vending machines at Ross E. Timmons Company, pointed at my district cross country championship trophy on the mantle. "I used to weld junk like this."

Saturday morning meets conflicted with Dad's sleep-in schedule and Mom's daily Mass schedule. Her nooners with Albert Browne fired up the rumor mill at the Olin Browne Medical Supply Company, where Mom worked as a receptionist. She eventually confronted her co-workers.

"Do you know where Mr. Browne and I go every day?"

"Where?"

"To the noon Mass at the Cathedral."

Her prayers for me to quit running went unanswered and her worries that fame would lead me to the darkness of hell or that I would be struck by a car were unfounded. The only road rage I suffered was from fat, lazy rednecks who opened their window with clever comments like "Run!" Or, better, "Run, Mother Fucker!"

I can imagine the talk around their dinner table. "Hey, Momma, we saw this 'ol boy out runnin' on the side of the road, and you know what Billy Bob said? He said, "Run!"

My parents should have been grateful. They had a son who rarely partied, went to bed at dusk, wasn't on drugs, didn't date, and hung around with some nice kids. I was the opposite of their other children, and unlike them, I was going to college. Coach Hightower showed me the path to success in sport and in life. He stressed dedication and discipline, never giving in to temptation. "There's nothing wrong with having sex before a meet," he said. "The problem is staying up all night looking for it."

That was difficult, running by the tennis court and seeing Holly bouncing around in her short skirt. My desire for Holly made me become more desirable. I traded my black-frame glasses for contact lenses. I fired Dad as my hair stylist and let my light-brown locks grow over my ears. I covered my facial zits with gobs of Clearasil. I gave my leisure suits to the Salvation Army, and bought some bell-bottom Levis and wide-collar shirts from the Forest Hill Mall. Perhaps the transition from tall, skinny running nerd to tall, skinny running nerd with new clothes and long hair and my early-season cross country wins could make Holly notice me. She handed me the first-place trophy after our home meet. She grasped the gold plastic with her long, red glossy nails, slid her right hand on my sweatsuit sleeve and pulled me close. "You ran so-o-o good."

I wanted to plant one on those luscious pink lips. But I glanced to the side to see Chuckster folding his arms. The following Monday, Chuckster pushed me against a hallway locker during lunch period. I smelled his burrito breath and stared at his crooked-yellow teeth as he grasped the collar of my blue letterman's jacket. "If I ever see you touchin' my 'ol lady again, I'll mount *you* on a trophy base."

Chuckster showed me his fist. I took out a pen and wrote a column after Forest Hill's 33-0 loss to Eisenhower High.

> *Coach Avery Lockett found him a robot to quarterback the Rangers in Friday's district opener. He cranked him up and watched as the clumsy-looking robot threw each ball into the dirt, into the stands, or perfectly into the hands of an Eisenhower defensive back. Perhaps Lockett should seek a refund.*

The column prompted Verne McCormick to grab a microphone and paddle.

"Attention. I'd lak to see in my office, uh, Jonny, uh, Lankin, uh, Lagen...you know who you are, get down here."

McCormick held the *Ranger Gazette* in his hands. "What do you thank you're doing, boy, writin' this garbage? If it wasn't for this freedom of the press crud, I'd give you 10 licks."

McCormick stared at the hair strands that fell below my earlobes; a violation of the school's grooming policy. "You report back here before the bell tomorrow, boy. If that hair ain't cut, I'm layin' you over my desk."

I ran the next morning with curlers in my hair and tucked inside my hooded sweat-top. I marched into McCormick's office, where he waited with his paddle. "There's a boy who needs a har-cut." McCormick took a closer look. "Oh, dern, you got it cut."

I rushed into the hallway, pushing the hair back below my earlobes. I ran into a gang of grunts, who I easily outran to class.

No one could catch me at the regional cross country meet either. I was the favorite to win the Texas Public Schools State Cross Country meet until I vomited three times in the toilet on race morning. Too many butterflies for breakfast. I felt like fainting even before I crossed the starting line in Austin. I stayed with the front-running defending champion Lupe Ramirez until he surged ahead at the mile mark. I weaved back and forth in the final 200 meters, barely holding off Bobby Baker of San Antonio Lee for second place. I threw up again as The Stallion, third at regional, was finishing 103rd. He said he suffered from a toothache.

Our regional champion Rangers finished last. All Coach Hightower said was, "Why don't you see about gettin' your trophy so we can get the hell out a here."

We were in Temple when the announcer probably was fumbling over my last name. My brother Mark met me at the front door of 2000 Hickory Lane.

"You going partying,' Mark?"

"No. *We* are going partying.'"

A half-hour later, Mark was driving me through the Twilight Zone, a long corridor of Dallas restaurants, bars, striptease joints, and x-rated movie houses known more simply as "the Zone." Mark said he was showing me how the lower half lived. As I locked the door on his light blue '66 Mustang, he said, "I suggest you not wear your letter jacket?"

I was the legal age of 18. But most of what I saw the next four hours seemed illegal, or, at least, immoral. We started at Biff's Pub, where Mark put a shot glass in front of me and said, "This is your warm up."

"What is it?"

"Shut up and drink."

I poured it back and I think smoke came out of my ears. The smoke followed us into The Beachcomber, a discotheque which blared "I'm your boogie man" and other fine selections from K.C. and the Sunshine Band. I sipped a bourbon and Coke and listened through the noise and cigarette smoke to Mark hitting on every cute available and unavailable woman in the place. He wore a silk wide-collar shirt under his black leather jacket and gulped a margarita.

"What's a seminary?" the blonde shouted over the pounding music.

"That's a place you go to study for the priesthood," Mark said.

"You were going to be a priest?"

"Thought about it."

"What changed your mind?"

"My penis."

Mark danced under a silver ball, strung over the dance floor, and led me to the next stop, "T and A's," where I saw my first tits since breast feeding and learned how to fold a dollar length-wise. What a dancer named Bambi was doing to a silver pole was nothing compared to what the actors were doing to each other upon our next stop, The Bone Channel, an adult theatre behind a dark alley in the Zone. I pointed to the screen. "Looks like two pigs wrestling."

Mark gulped his beer and whispered, "That's called mattress polo."

I never blinked the whole film, just sipped. "What did you pay to get us into this hell hole?"

"I don't know," Mark said. "But I think there's two come minimum."

Whatever Holly and Chuckster didn't teach me in the Forest Hill hallway I learned at The Bone Channel. My first night on the town finished with a pitcher and a pool game at Hannigan's, two more shots of jet fuel at Old Yeller's, and another peek at The Bone Channel. Mark said the drunk test would be if I could say Holly Ritzenbarger. It came out "Holy Ribenzarger."

The day ended where it began – with my head inside the toilet. Mom woke me up at 2 p.m., Sunday afternoon.

"That's flu's been going around," she said.

Could Mom have been this naive? Were her nostrils so clogged she couldn't smell my whisky breath or smoky bluejeans? I went for a run, the loud music still blasting inside my skull along Rolling Hills Parkway. What was I thinking, allowing Mark to open my eyes to the Wide World of Filth? Certainly, Uncle Grimsley didn't get to where he was by getting drunk and looking at naked women. Mark welcomed me after my run with a glass of Alka-Seltzer in front lawn. "Have a good time last night, Jonny?"

I took a sip. "Loved it."

I drank only lemonade at The Stallion's New Year's Eve party. His folks left for the holidays, and the Forest Hill track team moved in. We waited for the clock to strike midnight with a game of Twister. I flicked the direction dial and my "Right hand on-" was interrupted by a "Can I play?"

I looked up at a blonde in tight white jeans and pink strapless blouse and better proportioned breasts than Bambi's. "Y-Y-Yeah sure, Holly."

At 10 minutes until midnight the Stallion said, "Right leg on blue." To do that I had to wrap my leg inside Holly's crotch, thus rubbing my hip against her inner thigh as I stared at her face at point-blank range. We were the only contestants remaining in a back room far from the dancing and drinking. Holly squeezed her two legs against my hip, and we met with our shiny blue eyes. Our lips closed in on each other until they were interrupted.

"Hey, you little prick!"

My hand slipped and Holly and I crashed on the big red, blue, yellow, and green dots. Chuckster pulled Holly off and chased me out of the house. I sprinted down the road toward home, hearing the lyrics "Should auld acquaintance be forgot...." on a run from one year to the next, starting a tradition of my own.

◆ ◆ ◆

1

The little crack in the concrete under Austin's Memorial Stadium hadn't changed in the year since I first stared at it. The little crack was my focal point, my comforter from the faint screams above for those whose hopes vanished or dreams realized on an orange, sun-drenched track.

In the time it takes to boil an egg my future would be determined. I win the Texas Public Schools one mile run and go to college, to races around the world, to a life as a writer or a teacher or a banker. My pursuit of the Olympic dream would continue. I lose by bad luck or lack of courage and I spend my life making vending machines, spending summer vacations at a motor camp in East Texas, watching the Olympics on a black and white screen and still wondering.

That was my mindset as I lay on the hard concrete and stared at the little crack and the glimmer of light shining through it. Every time a roar shot through the crowd, another knot was tied in my stomach and the harder I concentrated on the little crack.

I thought about how far I had come since almost being laughed off the track that first day at Bishop Callahan. The lake and track circles Coach Hightower sent me around and around. The fierce battles with Tripp Saxton, Kelvin Booker, and my own doubts. I finished second in the State Catholic mile, second in the State Public Schools mile, second in State Cross Country. This was my last shot.

The 1976 track season had almost ended before it began. At dawn of the first morning workout in January, I drove our white Pontiac station wagon off the driveway and toward Forest Hill High School. The station wagon stalled 10 feet past the Hickory Lane stop sign, in the middle of Rolling Hills Parkway. I looked left, saw headlights 400 yards down the road, and turned the key. I pressed the clutch and accelerator, and the station wagon wouldn't start. I tried again. No luck. The headlights came nearer.

"Surely, he'll stop," I thought. "The speed limit is 30."

I turned the key again and again. Nothing. The headlights were on top of me. "Oh, God!"

I lunged from the driver's seat just before a loud bang. The impact from the Chevy Malibu knocked the station wagon 70 feet into the median strip. I stayed in a fetal position for several minutes until Dad peered through the driver's side door. "What are you tryin' to do, kill yourself?"

I looked up. "Call an ambulance."

When Dad returned to what was left of the station wagon, I was gone. He looked around and saw me jogging up and down the street.

"Are you nuts?"

"No, I just wanted to make sure I'm all right."

I felt dizzy and had a lump on my head from hitting the dashboard. My lower back felt like someone hit it with a baseball bat. Blood trickled down my butt cheeks. I pressed on my spine and almost screamed. Dad went back inside to watch the rest of *The Price is Right*, before going to work in his Ford truck.

Chance Leaming, the other driver, squatted in front of his Malibu and stared at the steam pouring out of his radiator. He shook his head, perhaps wondering, I thought, why he chose to cream me at 40 miles per hour, instead of simply pressing his brake. Leaming wore his black hair slicked back, a sport coat and tie, and about a quart of cologne. The ambulance arrived, and an attendant patched up my wound. A police officer escorted Leaming and I over the broken glass and into the back of his squad car. Officer Lardbutt, or whatever his name was, gulped the last of his coffee and donut and took out a pad and pen.

"OK, what happened." Officer Lardbutt licked the purple jelly from his lower lip and looked at Leaming..

"The kid pulled right out in front of me, Officer. I had no chance to stop. No chance whatsoever."

"Were there any injuries?"

Leaming interrupted me. "Broke my fingernail on the steering wheel."

I wished I hadn't sent the ambulance away, because I felt like beating the crap out of this arrogant jerk. Officer Lardbutt scribbled down some notes, and said, "Looks pretty clear cut. There were no witnesses, right?"

"None," Leaming said.

"W-W-Wait. Don't you want to hear my side of the story."

"No," Officer Lardbutt and Leaming said in tandem.

"Sure," I thought. "No matter what, always believe the suit over the skinny, long-haired kid in sweats."

Lardbutt and Leaming walked back to the Malibu. "Sure hope he has insurance," said Leaming, right before his wife drove up in a brand new red corvette. Officer Lardbutt then offered Leaming his last jelly donut.

As they munched, Fred Nichols, a retired neighbor walked up with Roofy, his miniature Dachsund. Roofy licked the crumbs off Officer Lardbutt's boots as Fred held a limp leash and shook his head. "Can't believe he didn't stop.

The boy must have been stuck in the middle of the road for at least a minute. The fella in the Malibu must've been doin' at least 40, maybe 50."

Officer Lardbutt crossed out his notes and dictated the truth from Fred Nichols. Leaming hid his face in his hands.

X-rays of my back showed nothing broken, but the emergency-room doctor told me to take a month off. I started running four days later, and then spent the next week in bed with the flu. Four days after that, Chuckster sent two of his football grunts to the locker room, where I had finished my shower. One belted me in the hamstring with a broom handle and the other kicked me in the shins. They ripped the awards patches off my letter jacket, threw me out of the locker room in my underwear, and kicked me in the stomach.

"That'll teach ya' for messin' with Chuckster's woman," one grunt said as I spit blood on the concrete.

I reported the incident to Coach Hightower, who relayed it to Verne McCormick. The hit men served an hour of detention. Chuckster didn't serve a second. I missed another four days training. I ran only 12 miles in January. The first day back, The Stallion and I sprinted 10 times 100's on the hard black track. On the fifth one a teammate held The Stallion by his jock, and I fired down the track. I leaned at the finish, looked back at The Stallion, and lost my balance. I tumbled a dozen times. I stood up with blood running from my knees, palms, and shoulders.

"I got it," The Stallion said.

"Like hell you did. I was a good yard in front."

Coach Hightower stared at my wounds. "Put a Band-aid on it and get your butt back here and finish the workout."

While The Stallion was setting personal bests in the 440 and 880 and declaring himself the fastest runner in the school, I was recording personal worsts in the mile and two mile. After finishing seventh in the Texas Relays two mile, Coach Hightower made The Stallion and I run 25 times 440's the following Monday. The first 10 were with a 60-second interval, the next 10 were with a lap jog, and the last five were with a 60-second interval. We jogged a half-mile loop of the practice field between sets. I averaged 65 seconds for the 440's. The Stallion fell off the pace and couldn't finish the workout, but still promised classmates he would win the 440, 880, and mile at district. He won the 440. I led wire-to-wire in the mile in 4:19.1. The Stallion finished seventh in 4:36 and said he would have won had his right shoelace not come undone on the second lap. I dogged the field at the Northeast Regional Meet at Loos Field and let them block the gale-force wind on the backstretch, before running the final 220 in 26.5 and winning easily in 4:24.3.

The state meet preview in the Austin newspaper picked Bobby Baker of San Antonio Lee to win the Class 4A mile with defending champion and two-time cross country champion Lupe Ramirez, who was to be deported right after the race, expected to finish a close second. Baker beat Ramirez to win the Texas

Relays two-mile in 9:02.8 and ran a 4:14.3 mile at his regional. There was no mention of the 1975 state mile runner-up.

Coach Hightower also brought The Stallion, discus thrower Riley Dwyer, and the sprint relay to the state meet. The Stallion was the anchor man. No team in Class 4A had qualified as many athletes to state, and the *Dallas Dispatch* selected us as the pre-meet favorite. Coach Hightower rented a cottage on a lake outside Austin to keep us relaxed. A state title would put him in position for a college job. His hopes faded after Dwyer fouled on every throw and the relay team dropped the baton on the first exchange. I took my eyes off the little crack to watch The Stallion run 58.6 in the 440. He said he stubbed his big toe two days before the race, "or else I would have won it."

My thought as The Stallion jogged the homestretch 80 yards behind the second-to-last finisher: "Oh no, what's gonna happen to me?"

The sun was brighter and hotter than in any race I had run. There was no breeze to push the popcorn smell from the stands, no mute button from the noise of 30,000 Coke-sipping spectators. Somewhere in that crowd Coach Hightower had his finger on his stopwatch, ready to time me one last time. I took off my sweat-bottoms, clutched Pre's autograph, walked to starting line, made the sign of the cross, and stared at the starter.

The gun smoke sent me off the line.

The green-clad Baker assumed the lead with Ramirez on his shoulder. I stayed along the rail at mid-pack, in my neat gold singlet and navy blue shorts, through a 64-second first lap. My hard puffing eased through another 64, and I filed in behind the front-running Baker and Ramirez down the backstretch. I focused on Ramirez's orange shorts around the turn, tuning out the crowd, the announcer, and any thought of losing. I felt so good I wanted to spring into the lead. But I heard Coach Hightower in my head. "Play it cool. Don't go until the final 300 meters."

The gun for the final lap blasted the thought away. At the head of the backstretch, I took off like I was shot out of the starting pistol. By the end of the backstretch I had 10 yards on Ramirez, who passed Baker and chased me around the final bend. I glanced back and accelerated hard into the homestretch. I didn't need to look back again.

The mixture of the crowd's roar, the distant finish line string, and the joy of knowing what I was about to accomplish propelled me through the homestretch. Baker rallied to pass the tying up Ramirez, but he couldn't make a dent into my lead. I took one more look, just to make sure. Nothing in my life felt sweeter than breasting the finish line tape in Memorial Stadium on that glorious May afternoon of 1976.

I looked up at the huge scoreboard that read 4:12.5. Then I knelt down and cried. "Oh, thank you, dear God. Thank you, Pre."

Here, I would like to say that my parents, brothers and sisters, my coach, and my teammates sprinted onto the track and mass hugged me. But they didn't. Dad didn't want to miss *McLintock,* his favorite John Wayne movie. Mom didn't like driving on her own. My brothers and sisters didn't realize I was running in the state meet. Coach Hightower was still fuming over the dropped baton, and my teammates pouted over their poor performances.

I walked over and hugged the starter, who was reloading his gun for the mile relay. "Who *are* you?" he said.

Coach Hightower finally came down, shook my hand, and said, "Good job, pardner." I talked him into letting me stay to accept my medal on the awards platform. Hearing the cheers from the crowd and looking at that bright gold medal ran a close second to crossing the finish line. En route to the parking lot, I took a quick detour to say good-bye to the little crack and to make a quick telephone call. I could hear John Wayne on the television as I gave Mom the good news. She said she prayed the rosary right before my scheduled start.

I was disappointed Mom and Dad already were asleep when I arrived that night. I could hear the national anthem from the television in the bedroom and Dad snoring. On the dining room table was a metal runner Dad welded from a rusty, old vending machine and stuck on a wooden base. Written in Marks-A-Lot on the wood was "State Champ" and beside it a note in Mom's handwriting, "We are very proud of you, Jonny."

I walked through the school hallway with a smile Monday morning and was stopped by The Stallion. "Have you seen the marquis?" he asked.

I threw my books down and ran outside to the front of the school building. The sun reflected off the black letters on the white background. "Congratulations State Mile Champion, Jimmy Lingenfelcher."

Sparks flew everywhere. They shot to the ceiling, bounced off my welding mask, sprayed my thick gloves, slid down my apron, and landed on my boots. I hated every little white speck.

The summer before college provided a frightening glimpse of real life. The only job I could find was spot welder, $2.48 per hour and all the sparks you could swallow, at Ross E. Timmons Company. I worked 8-5, welding these heavy metal parts of vending machines. My office was a 20-by-20 concrete area with an old welding machine in the middle. I held the heavy metal panels in place, stepped on a pedal, and watched these two rods weld the pieces together. Sparks flew in masses and stunk of metal smoke. The odd elusive one found its way to my skin.

"Yeow!" I screamed. The assembly-line welders and cutters went on with this menial repetition without a notice or care. I doubt anyone in there graduated from Harvard. The smartest person there? My father.

I ate lunch with Dad and the men who helped him assemble the vending machines.

"What does you like on a peanut butter sandwich?" I knew this guy's name by his sewn-on nametag – Ed.

"Peanut butter," I said.

"Put jelly on mine, and every once in a while I put a layer of butter on the bottom. Makes it go down real smooth like."

I told Ed about my classmate who was going on vacation to Paris.

"You mean Paris, Texas or Paris, Italy?"

Dad tuned them out by watching *Gilligan's Island* on the lunch room television. Ed didn't watch, because he said Ginger reminded him of his fourth wife. He also said the proudest day of his life was when he was promoted from chief spot welder to senior assistant assembler of vending machines.

That summer I forgave Dad for coming home grumpy so many nights, for sleeping in the morning of my cross country meets, for spending his Saturday nights with a Dino's Deluxe Burger and *The Carol Burnett Show*. I'd rather be dead than work as the senior assembler of vending machines. He had to be proud of me, his only child who made it past high school. Matthew graduated from Bishop Callahan magna cum loser. Maggie was voted Most Likely to marry a man name Moon Dog. Mark wore nothing under his graduation gown. Luke got axle grease on his diploma. The only honor bestowed on Caty during high school was employee of the month at St. Whipple's.

I expected Forest Hill's "Male Athlete of the Year" award after winning state. The school's only other state finalist was a chess player. I was the only male athlete to be offered a college scholarship to a four-year school. When Verne McCormick announced at the All-School Assembly, "And the winner of the school ath-a-lete of the year is..." I started down the aisle toward the auditorium stage.

"Chuck Jones."

I kept walking. "That's Verne's worst mispronunciation of my name yet," I thought.

Chuckster, All-District honorable mention quarterback and Elm Fork Junior College signee, stiff-armed my chest, trotted onto the stage, and lifted the trophy above his head to the grunts of his teammates. I walked head down out of the auditorium into a beautiful woman.

"Congratulations on winning state." Holly had won "Female Athlete of the Year" and "All School Favorite" after finishing third in the state hurdles, fourth in tennis singles, and fifth on the uneven parallel bars. "Got a date yet for the spring sports banquet?"

I never had a date in my life. But I couldn't tell Holly. "Yeah."

Holly half-smiled and walked away. Now I was in trouble. What would everyone think if the state champion walked into the spring sports banquet without a date? I called The Stallion to see if he had any ideas. He came up with his girlfriend's lab partner.

"Trudy Merkle?" I said. "She's a cow."

"She's a girl."

"Good point. Would you call her for me?"

My first date was more like a giraffe than a cow. She was four inches taller than me, had a nose that bent at the end, long red hair, braces, and milk-white skin. Fortunately, her long, yellow dress covered her fat calf muscles. I whispered into The Stallion's ear at the food line. "Thanks for setting me up with the Jolly Green Giant."

I returned to my seat with my date and her trough and watched the other Forest Hill athletes file into the school cafeteria. After long anticipation, Holly made a smashing entrance with a plaid skirt, tight white bare-shouldered top, heart necklace around her bronzed skin, and matching white earrings and bracelet. I only could imagine how her perfume smelled. I looked for Chuckster with his smug smile and tight slacks to escort Holly through the gawks to their seats. But it wasn't Chuckster. It was Trent Babich, a football manager in a purple leisure suit. I kicked The Stallion's leg and dropped my fork on the floor. I met the Stallion face to face under the table. "Where's Chuckster?" I whispered.

"You didn't hear?

"Hear what?

"Chuckster got caught with the Rangerette captain."

"What?"

"He and Holly broke up last week."

I bumped my head on the bottom of the table. I gritted my teeth, looked over at Holly sitting with that dweeb and frowned at The Stallion. He probably knew what I was thinking.

"You idiot. Why didn't you tell me?"

Holly had hinted to me about the sports banquet. She must have thought I turned her down for Trudy "The Wonder Cow." I stared at Holly throughout Coach Hightower's introduction of Forest Hill's Track and Field Athlete of the Year and barely listened to his speech.

"When I first saw Jonny Langenfeller, I thought he was puniest athlete I'd ever seen. He had these thick black-frame glasses, and arms and legs that looked like twigs. He said he wanted to make the Olympics, and I giggled along with the other runners. I never thought he'd make the varsity much less a state meet. But this little kid with the big heart kept provin' me wrong. I've never coached anyone who has worked harder than Jonny Langenfeller. That's why he will continue to reach his goals and follow the path to the Olympics."

I received a standing ovation as Coach Hightower gripped my palm and gave me a plaque. I think I spotted a tear in his eye. It was a great night that would have been perfect, if I only had known Holly and Chuckster had split up.

Holly spent the summer at a cheerleaders' camp and went to LSU on a track scholarship. I also wanted to go far away to college. My first and only choice was the University of Oregon.

I could hear the Hayward Field crowd stomping their feet, "Langenfelder! Langenfelder!" I wrote Coach Dutch Powers every month, telling him how I wanted to run in the footsteps of Steve Prefontaine. I shunned other prospective offers, while I waited for an envelope with Powers' name above the green U of O insignia on the address label. The mailman delivered brochures, letters, and postcards from everywhere but Oregon. I called Powers in late May, told him between the "uhs" and shaky syllable repetitions that I won state, ran 4:12, and was ready to sign on the dotted line.

"What did you say your name was again?"

Powers didn't even offer me a "book" scholarship, and the full scholarship offers from the other colleges and universities had been offered to other athletes. I called every college coach – Rice, Arkansas, Baylor, Oklahoma, Texas - that had offered me a scholarship. But their response was the same. "Sorry, buddy, you're a day late and now about 5,000 dollars short."

Dad suggested I stay at Ross E. Timmons Company, pick up a few hours at Bridgewater Community College, and run some road races. Then the telephone rang.

"Is this Jonny, uh, Langenslusher?"

"Yes."

"This is Coach Fubby Tuppernacker."

It sounded like Elmer Fudd, or The Stallion imitating Elmer Fudd. I returned my own Elmer Fudd impersonation. "Mr. Whippersnacker," I said, "are you looking for that cwazy wabbitt?"

The pause made me realize this was not a prank call, and not even The Stallion.

"Funny name, serious program," said the Head Track and Field Coach at Caprock State University.

Tuppernacker said he did not know I won state, "but I do know that you are the great nephew of Grimsley Roeper. That alone will get you a full scholarship."

Instead of running in Pre's footsteps, I would be running in Uncle Grimsley's shadow. Instead of running in the forests of Oregon, I would be running in the deserts of West Texas. I hadn't been to Lubbock since I said good-bye to Grimsley, and the only person I knew there – my grandmother – was a recluse.

"Where do I sign?"

My running career still looked better than my welding career. Keith Reynolds, the plant manager, told me if I didn't pick up the pace, he would have to let me go. Reynolds transferred me to the metal cutting department. For eight hours I slid a piece of metal into a machine, pushed a lever, slid the metal, pushed a lever, slid metal, pushed a lever. After one day, I handed my one-week notice to Reynolds. "Take your welding mask and shove it. I'm going to college."

Dad resigned before I did. He landed a job assembling wheel parts for Payton's Products in East Dallas. I said good-bye to Dad's working mates my last day.

"Don't know why your old man ever worked with us fellas," Ed said. "Why he's as smart as that professor on *Gilligan's Island*."

Before I stepped off this island, I looked around at the robot-like workers on the assembly lines. Over and over, they slid the metal and pushed the lever. Some had been doing this for 30 years. "These poor old guys," I thought. "I'm going to college and getting myself an education."

The next morning I ran down Rolling Hills Parkway, and a 1973 maroon Mercury Capris rolled alongside me. The driver wore cut-offs, no shorts, no shoes, and had an open Budweiser can stuck in his crotch. "Hey, Langenfucker."

Tripp Saxton drove alongside me as I ran. "What have you been up to, Tripp?"

"Oh, nothin.' Just fuckin' around. You like my new car?"

"It's great."

"Heard you got a full ride to Caprock State."

"Where you going to college?"

"Nowhere. I'm just gonna hang around here and work, pay off my car."

I was about to tell him about the opening at Ross E. Timmons company. But he sped off in the opposite direction, away from the sun.

That night I watched the opening ceremonies of the 1976 Olympics in Montreal. I sat in the den, while Dad watched *Bonanza* on his portable television in his bedroom. Goosebumps grew on my arms and legs as the Americans marched into the stadium, waved to the television cameras, and took their places with the thousands of other athletes and flags on the infield. Then came the Olympic torch, relayed from Athens, Greece, around the track, and up the stadium steps to a huge cauldron.

I smiled as the cauldron was ignited, the flame soared to the heavens, and the Games were declared open. Fireworks lit up the Montreal sky and my dark den.

The sparks kept flying everywhere.

For once, I was loving it.

PART II

FUBBY'S BOYS

July 30, 1976

I couldn't hear the shot from the starter's pistol that sent 14 runners into the 1976 Olympic 5,000 meters final. But I could see the smoke.

It swirled above the starter's pistol and out the television set in my Dallas den.

"Stupid T.V." The smoke was either from rattled television tubes or the dust set free by my banging on the side of the box.

For the next 13 ½ minutes I would sit on the hard den floor in the dark and watch these world-class runners without a word from the television announcers or a cheer from the 70,000 spectators at Montreal Olympic Stadium. Still, I know them. Each one from the pages of *Track & Field News*. Their synchronized stride over a rubber track lit by stadium lights and the Olympic flame is a symphony that ends in a cymbal clash.

The runners take turns at conducting the field through a seemingly orchestrated pace. First, Soviets Enn Sellik and Boris Kuznyetsov and then Great Britain's Brendan Foster, the 10,000 meters bronze medalist who leads a tightly-strung field that includes countryman Ian Stewart, tall, fast-finishing New Zealanders Dick Quax and Rod Dixon, in all black, and the dark-bearded Klaus-Peter Hildenbrand of West Germany.

"Something's missing," I say to myself. I am not referring to the television audio, the boycotting African runners, or my hero, the late Steve Prefontaine. Almost on cue, a thin, bearded man emerges from the pack and takes the lead as he passes the electronic lap-counter lit by the number "7."

Lasse Viren destroyed the 10,000-meter field four days before and is attempting to become the first man to win the 5,000 and 10,000 in successive Olympics. The Finn slows the pace the next two laps, and Foster regains the lead. Paul Geis, a Eugene, Oregon, resident who grew up in Houston, drops off the back of the pack. Quax and Hildenbrand take turns at the lead until Viren takes over with 2 ½ laps remaining.

"Come on, somebody beat this guy." I am now so into the race I don't need television announcers or a crowd's roar to excite me. Sweat drips down my bare chest to my red shorts. I press the floor with my worn-blue running sneakers and grab my ankles.

Seven runners are still in contention as the bell lap begins. Ian Stewart, the man who beat Pre for the bronze medal four years before, starts to drive around Viren at the top of the homestretch. Viren holds him off. Foster, Hildenbrand, Dixon and Quax chase Viren around the last turn. Quax moves alongside Viren at the top of the homestretch, and Dixon sprints in lane three.

"Come on, Dixon! Come on Quax!" I pump my fists for the climax of this grand concerto.

Viren shoves it into another gear. He keeps his head still and his stride smooth in contrast to the Kiwis' wild, over-striding form and holds them off down the stretch. The finish is a flash etched into Olympic history. Viren, head cocked, teeth gritted, three meters ahead of Quax, whose mouth is wide open. Dixon, outside Quax and tying up badly with his head stretched backward. The grimacing Hildenbrand, inside all three runners, and diving ahead of Dixon for the bronze medal.

I stare in awe of the man who has accomplished a feat not even his great countryman Paavo Nurmi could match. Viren's time of 13:24.8 is flashed on the screen. The Finn takes off his spikes, holds them high on his victory lap, and bows to the audience. The Olympic flame forms a perfect backdrop to Viren's glorious moment.

In the paneled den in Texas, the television light shines to no one. I am out the front door and running up Rolling Hills Parkway before Viren's victory lap is completed and the evening sun fades off the Dallas horizon.

I signed up for the Caprock State "track" team. But after running, walking, and staggering halfway up a mountain on a trail of rocks, dirt cracks, and paw prints I feared from a grizzly bear or mountain lion, I wondered if I had signed up for the Caprock State "trek" team.

"Come on ya' bloody losers, get your butts up here." Rupert Wade had no mercy on an 18-year-old freshman whose steepest hill climb was a 200-yard rise along Rolling Hills Parkway in Dallas, Texas. My trails were along flat roads, median strips, and golf-course fairways. On this warm August afternoon of 1976, somewhere in North Central New Mexico, I kept climbing.

"Now I know why they call this the 'Rocky' Mountains." My pun went unnoticed to fellow back-of-the-packer Mitch Hansby.

"Fucking Rupe," Mitch said. "Why don't you go back to the fucking Outback where you belong?"

I'm not sure Mitch's question was heard by Rupe, who pushed his runners like he was driving slaves in a ship gally. "Come on, Hansby, Langenfelder, your mates are kicking your ass. Only a few more miles to the top!"

"Fuck you, Rupe!" Mitch made sure Rupe heard that.

Two days before my mountain climb I had loaded my Samsonite and duffle bag onto a Trailways Bus headed for Caprock State, where my great Uncle Grimsley set so many records. Under the guidance of Coach Filbert "Fubby" Tuppernacker I could rewrite Caprock's track record book, win national titles, make the Olympic team, and have a statue of me mounted next to Grimsley in front of Tumbleweed Stadium. I would be the Pre of Caprock State. On my runs along Rolling Hills Parkway in 100 degrees, I dreamed of people filling Tumbleweed Stadium and clapping in unison as I circle the track and race toward another victory, "Langenfelder! Langenfelder!"

The eight-hour bus ride took me to the southern Panhandle of West Texas past miles of flat farm and ranch land and desert and oil rigs and grain elevators and on top of a ledge known as "the Caprock." A few tumbleweeds blowing on the highway and the smell of cattle fields told me that Lubbock was near. I couldn't wait to hear Coach Tuppernacker's voice as I called his office from a pay phone at the Lubbock bus station.

"C-Coach Tuppernacker, it's Jonny.

"Jonny?"

"Yeah, Jonny Langenfelder."

"When ya' comin'?"

"I'm at the bus station." I had sent him my itinerary. I was surprised he didn't greet me as I stepped off the bus. "Can you come get me?"

"Well, no, I'm, uh, busy fillin' out some important enrollment papers. Just grab a cab."

He hung up before I told him the $212.85 to my name was on a bank check. I had dropped my only other dime into the pay phone. Fortunately, the Samsonite had wheels. I slung the duffle bag over my shoulder, dodged a few tumbleweeds, and lugged myself and my belongings toward Caprock State. The three-mile journey took more than an hour as I pulled the Samsonite along the cracked sidewalks and over curbs and shaded my eyes from the sun and an occasional dust devil. Scouring the streets for loose change and thumbing pickup trucks for a ride was not the grand entrance to college I had envisioned.

I took a break half-way and sat on a curb, talking to myself. "What's with this Fubby Tuppernacker guy? This is no way to treat the future of Caprock State distance running."

I felt like going back to the bus station and getting on the first bus back to Dallas. But I plodded onward. I stopped again at University Savings, where the marquis read "104" degrees, to open an account and beg for and then receive $20 of my own money.

My next stop was Uncle Grimsley's statue, in front of Tumbleweed Stadium. What a magnificent sight, the sun reflecting off the black bust of a running back sprinting toward the goal line with his left arm carrying the football and his right about to stiff arm a defender. At an adjacent practice field the Caprock State football team ran drills to the whistles and shouts of their coaches. I gave Uncle Grimsley a thumb's up and dragged my luggage through campus and to the head track and field coach's office at Tumbleweed Coliseum.

I stood in the office doorway to see Tuppernacker sitting and talking on the telephone. He squeezed the telephone between his ear and his shoulder. He used his right hand to shove a greasy burger into his mouth and his left to lift a 32-ounce soft drink glass to his mouth. Dusty old running trophies sat on his desk and on his file cabinet. Dirty spikes were piled in the corner. His framed diploma from Saskawany State College, Class of 1951, hung crooked on the wall in front of him. There was no sign of any enrollment papers. On the wall behind him were a fox head and a squirrel stuffed and mounted. I stared up at the squirrel and down at Tuppernacker.

"It's funny," I thought. "Coach Tuppernacker and the squirrel look a lot alike."

Tuppernacker looked at me leaning against the door well, but did not acknowledge my presence in the last 20 minutes of a telephone discussion about the best time and place to hunt quail. He may have continued the telephone conversation had Caprock State basketball coach Oscar Raintree not brushed past me and sat on the little office sofa. The two coaches talked about basketball tickets for 10 minutes, before Coach Raintree stared me up and down.

"Boy, you stink." Coach Raintree whiffed the cigarette smoke the bus passengers blew on my jeans and the perspiration that soaked my light blue tennis shirt.

"Coach Raintree, this is Grimsley Roeper's nephew Jonny, uh, Langenpooner."

"That's Langenfelder," I said. "Grimsley was my *great* uncle"

I shook Raintree's hand, and the two coaches resumed their basketball discussion. They were interrupted by a man with wire-rimmed glasses that hung over his long, pointy nose and under his brown wavy hair. "Langenloober, this is Rupert Wade, he'll be coaching you distance runners this year."

"I thought you were the coach."

"Well, uh, I'm so busy doing all the travel plans, budgets, and coaching all the other athletes that I hired Rupe here to coach cross country."

I turned to Rupe, whose sly smile showed the thin gaps between his crooked teeth.

"You're mine," he said.

At 6:30 p.m., only 12 hours after I had boarded the Trailways bus in Dallas, I was sprinting up 72 rows of bleachers at Tumbleweed Stadium in Lubbock with 10 other runners who wondered the same thing.

"Why in the hell are we doing this?"

"Bah, this is an easy workout." Rupe stood on the top step. "Back in Australia, Darcy had us running up and down sand dunes in 120-degree weather."

"Who in the sam hill is Darcy?" I asked.

My new teammates were breathing and concentrating too hard to answer. After 30 minutes of bleachers, Rupe led us on a three-mile run around campus.

I gulped a steak in the dining hall and crashed in my new bed in the Rutherford Hall dormitory. I awoke in a dark room and to the knock, knock, knock on the door. I didn't know where I was until I opened the door to see my new coach and the same sly smile.

"Get dressed, mate, and meet in the lobby for the morning run."

It was like a morning race and just past dawn when we finished the five-miler. By dusk we had driven eight hours through a New Mexico highway so desolate that Rupe drove a school van 100 miles per hour and on the other side of the road. Tuppernacker followed Rupe in his brown station wagon, filled with me, four other runners, his wife of about two tons, Mitzie, and their six-year-old bawl-a-minute daughter, Millie. "Rupe thinks he's back in Australia."

"Wish he was," someone said from the back.

I was tying my sleeping bag to the top bunk in my camp cabin, when Rupe ordered us out for an eight-mile run on a gravel road. We stopped only to throw rocks at an angry German Shepherd. We felt like throwing them at Rupe, after he said, "We'd go on runs in Australia, and Darcy let a pack of Dobermans out the back of his truck and told us to outrun the bastards?"

"Who's Darcy?" I asked.

We left the camp early the next morning with a warning from Tupper-nacker, who stayed behind. "Stay together."

A mile up the mountain trail, Rupe threw in a surge that dropped Mitch and me. We eventually lost sight of Rupe as we winded up a trail that tucked beneath pine trees and seemingly had no end. We considered turning around until we saw light through the trees and heard laughing. We jogged up the final grade and put our hands on our knees as we reached the mountaintop.

"About bloody time," Rupe said.

Mitch was breathing too hard to utter another "Fuck you, Rupe." Rupe wouldn't let me enjoy the stunning view of the rows of mountains and forests.

"We got up here in two hours, 30 minutes. It took you mates an extra 20." Rupe stood with his hands on his hips below his gray cut-off T-shirt. I looked down at the dirt that was caked to his shins and turned his white Wooosh training shoes brown.

"Where did you learn to run up a mountain so fast?" I asked.

"Darcy."

"Darcy?"

"Darcy."

Rupe and I sat on a tree log. He told me about Darcy Ellard, the "toughest runner and the greatest coach ever to come out of the Australian Outback."

"Darcy once raced a horse 10 miles and beat it," Rupe said. "He finished fourth in the 10,000 meters at the 1948 and 1952 Olympics. In the marathon at the 1956 Games in Melbourne, he staggered into the stadium and collapsed in the sweltering heat 300 meters from the finish line.

"Did he finish?"

"As the capacity crowd of countrymen and countrywomen sang "Waltzing Matilda" Darcy crawled to the finish line on his hands and knees and then passed out. He never ran another race."

Darcy returned to the Outback with a group of young runners and used his rigorous training methods to develop them. Rupe left his home in Brisbane to become one of "Darcy's boys." He earned a scholarship to Houston Christian University, where he won the 10,000 meters and marathon titles at the NAIA Championships. He accepted the graduate assistant position at Caprock State to pursue a master's degree in psychology. Or was it reverse psychology?

"OK, you pack of losers, get off your lazy bums and head back down the mountain." Rupe hit the trail like he was running the 100-yard dash. Everyone chased him but Mitch and me, still recovering from our upward journey. I left Mitch, who took a mountaintop nap in the sunlight. About five minutes into my downward run, I stopped and stared at the steep bank.

"What a great idea," I said to myself.

I left the trail and went straight down the mountain. "I'll be waiting for these wimps back at camp," I thought.

I ran down the steep grade, dodging pine trees and jumping over mountain streams. I kept running and running and suddenly realized I had no earthly idea where I was. I was lost in a jungle of Christmas trees. I walked and ran and all I could see were trees and rocks. Would I still be here in the dark and cold of night with grizzly bears and mountain lions prowling for food?

"Help!...Help!...Help!..." Only an echo replied. I prayed the rosary. Nothing. Then I slid 20 feet down an embankment. I opened my eyes and saw dirt.

I knelt and made the sign of the cross. "Thank you, God, for putting me back on the trail."

I made it back to camp dirtied from head to toe and with cuts on my elbows and knees. Tuppernacker passed by without noticing. "Hey, Langenflogger."

I felt safe inside my sleeping bag in the darkness of the cabin that night. We stayed up talking until midnight. Mitch, who was in the bunk below me, told me how Fubby Tuppernacker became the head track coach.

"Fubby came to Caprock State with Mitzie, who got a teaching job in the Home Ec Department," Mitch said. "She became friends with the athletic director's wife, who talked him into giving Fubby a part-time job as an assistant track coach."

"Who'd he coach?"

"Nobody. He mainly did some recruiting and hob-nobbing with the A.D. at football and basketball games."

"But I read in the media guide that he was a state cross country champion."

"In North Dakota. There were 11 runners and the other 10 got lost in the blizzard."

"And the bit about being a champion college runner?"

"He won the intramural cross country race."

"At Saskawany State."

"Yeah, that's my point."

I stopped for a second in the darkness to take this all in. "Obviously none of this came out when he interviewed for the head job."

"What interview?" Mitch said. "When the old coach retired, the A.D. called Fubby."

"But doesn't the athletic director care about building a great track power."

Mitch laughed along with the other runners. "You got a lot to learn about college athletics, Langenhooch."

"Langenhooch? someone said.

"Yeah, that's his name," said someone else said, giggling. "Langenhooch."

I turned over and started drifting off to sleep until a "Bang! Bang! Bang!" and white sparks shot off the wooden floor.

"What was that?" I said.

"The old firecracker under the door trick," said Mitch, popping out of his bunk. Mitch rushed to the door, yanked it open, and was splashed by two water-bucket wielding teammates from the adjacent cabin.

"We'll get you for this!" Mitch's scream was interrupted by Tuppernacker, who marched to our cabin with his flashlight.

"What's all this racket?" Tuppernacker wore long underwear and hunting boots. "You woke Mitzie and Millie. You guys get your asses back in bed and shut the hell up."

Tuppernacker slammed the door. Mitch walked back inside. "Let's get Fubby."

The next night both cabins brainstormed a plan to terrorize the head coach, whom everyone called Fubby. "Calling someone 'coach' requires respect," Mitch said.

Sophomore Boyd Turner, a New Mexico state mile champion, masterminded the plot. Shortly before midnight, Boyd crawled on the rooftop of Fubby's cabin and dropped three lit bottle rockets down the chimney. Fubby didn't take time to put on his boots. The explosion sent him running toward our cabin, which had the lights and the radio on. Yet, no one was in it. The door was ajar. Fubby pushed it open and had his long johns soaked from the water bucket that was leaned atop the door. As a bonus, the bucket hit him on the head.

We hid in the pitch-black distance, struggling not to laugh. Fubby stubbed his toe, went back for his flashlight, and walked the grounds. He walked right by me and didn't notice. Then he shined the light in Mitch's eyes.

"Hi Fubby," Mitch said.

Everyone howled.

"You, you, you guys get your butts in bed!" Fubby yelled. "We're leaving first thing in the morning!"

Back at Caprock State, my roommate had arrived and stocked his side of room 907 as if readied for inspection. His books were placed alphabetically in his desk shelf. His bed couldn't have been made better at the Holiday Inn. His clothes hung in the closet in the order of coats, shirts, pants above his polished black loafers. He brought a 13-inch color television that sat atop his little refrigerator, which was stocked with fresh apples and pears. A glamor picture of his girlfriend sat on his desk, next to an open Bible.

The door opened, and in walked a young man out of the pages of GQ. He had jet black hair and not a pimple on his movie star face. "Hi, I'm Jack Walden." He smiled with those perfect white teeth and gripped my hand with his well-manicured fingers. "You must be Jonny Langenfelder."

Jack introduced me to Julie Tomkowicz, his girlfriend. Julie looked at a college catalogue, while Jack and I sat and talked about ourselves for an hour. He told me about growing up in the northern Texas Panhandle, winning the 220, 440, and long jump at the State Class 2A meet, his brother who goes to Dartmouth, and his desire to one-day marry his high school sweetheart and work in his father's law firm.

"Walden, Walden, and Walden, how does that sound?" Jack picked up his framed glamor shot of Julie, set it back on his desk, and put his arm around her. "I'm sure going to miss you."

Julie pecked Jack's cheek with her red lipstick. He escorted her to the elevator and to the parking lot, where his parents waited by their white Ford pickup. I looked out my window as he shook his Dad's hand, hugged his mom, smooched his sweetheart, and waved until the truck was out of sight.

Jack returned to the room and set some ground rules. "Everything that belongs to you – including yourself – stays on your side of the room. No watching television when the other person is studying. No lights on after 11 p.m. One last thing - if you pick up a girl, put a red tack on the door so I don't walk in on you."

"You got nothing to worry about, Jack."

I asked Jack if he wanted to go with Mitch, Boyd, and me to watch *Rocky* at the Caprock Four Theaters.

"I've already seen it," Jack said. "Besides, I have a prayer group meeting tonight."

Rocky fired me up. I couldn't wait for Rupe's next workout and to discuss the film with Jack. Just as I was about to put the key in the lock, I spotted a red tack on the door. I put my ear up close and heard panting.

The woman: "Oh baby, oh baby you're the best."

The man: "I know, I know. What's your name again?"

I slept down the hallway on Boyd's floor every night that first week and did some heavy breathing of my own during Rupe's workouts. We went to a golf course and sprinted from tee to green on the "36" hole course one day, a 10-mile time trial on a flat, dirt farm road with no turns the next day, and 20 sprints up a 300-meter-long hill the following day.

I joked in the shower, that "yeah, I could have done another 10 hill sprints."

"Bullshit, Langenhooch." Senior Ward Andrews turned off his shower and grabbed his towel. "I bet you can't even do 10 atomic sit-ups."

"Betcha I can. What are atomic sit-ups?"

I dried myself, wrapped the towel around my waist, and lay face-up in the middle of the locker room floor with my hands behind my neck. Ward lay a towel over my face. "OK, Langenhooch, when I lift the towel, you sit up as fast as you can."

The towel was yanked from my face. I lifted my chin to my knees and back down on the hard red carpet. Mitch, Boyd and my other teammates also draped in towels, yelled "One!" I lay back down, and the towel was draped over my face. The towel was removed. I drove my chin up. "Two!" I continued like that to number nine. On number 10, the towel was lifted, I rose up and my nose collided with Ward's butt cheeks.

I don't know who laughed harder, me or my teammates. "Told you ya' couldn't do 10," Ward said.

I got them back at our first cross-country meet, the University of Amarillo Invitational. We nicknamed Amarillo the University of Nairobi, because five of its seven runners were from Kenya. There were three other schools, including Central New Mexico and their top runner John Kiplagat. I thought I was skinny until I saw Kiplagat.

Rupe advised me not to go out with the leaders. Good advice, seeing their first mile was faster than what I ran to win the state meet. The 28-year-old Kiplagat, who probably would have won a medal in Montreal had Africa not boycotted the Games, broke away from Amarillo runners Julius Butai and Phillip Murambo and glided to victory. After the race, a reporter asked Kiplagat how far the race was. He didn't know.

"Four, five, six miles," he said. "It does not matter to me."

Kiplagat was a mile ahead of me, and I still finished fourth. Mitch Hansby and I ran with Amarillo's third man, Charles Rotich. Striding up a grade, halfway into the four-mile race on the University golf course, Rotich said, "Let's work on them."

"Work on 'em?" Mitch said. "We can't even see 'em."

I outkicked Rotich for fourth. Mitch was sixth, Ward Andrews 10th, Boyd Turner 12th, and junior college transfer Renny Vasquez 15th. We finished second, 14 points behind Amarillo. Rupe walked over, smiled, and said, "Do a six-mile warm-down and let's get the bloody hell outta here?"

I never finished the team's No. 1 man again that season. The second meet, on a cow pasture in Central Oklahoma, saw the return of Niles Whitney, a fifth-year senior athletically and a first-year med-student academically. Niles' said his studies prevented him from working out with the team. He allotted himself one hour for training per day. The athletics department paid for Niles' flight to Oklahoma, so it wouldn't ruin his study time. His one-hour flight and my eight-hour ride in a track van in bad need of shock absorbers and seats is why Niles finished second at Oklahoma and I finished 32nd. The backseats were replaced by lawn chairs. Every time Rupe hit the brakes, all runners and chairs smashed into the front seats.

The race was so tough that Mitch, who finished 33rd, threw up on my back in the finish chute. After we staggered through the chute, Niles walked toward us with a smile and a towel around his neck.

"How did you fellows do?" he said, adjusting his sunglasses.

"Fuck you, Niles," Mitch said.

Mitch the Bitch was fuming still about his scholarship of books, tuition, and fees. It was a good boost for an average high school runner who walked on at Caprock State. But not satisfying to beat teammates who were on full scholarship. Even Vasquez, who finished 63rd at Oklahoma, was on a full.

"If I get half a scholarship, then I should work out half as hard?" Mitch reasoned.

Rupe didn't care if you were on a "book" scholarship. He put on a devious grin every time I asked what the workout was. "You're gonna run until you drop."

We literally did drop that Monday after finishing a promising second at the TCU Invitational. Rupe sent us to the Tumbleweed Golf Course in the pouring rain and made us run 20 times 880 yards on a loop that finished on a steep hill. Rain poured off Rupe's glasses and dripped into his mouth as he pressed his stopwatch every time we struggled up the muddy hill.

"Come on, ya' pack of losers! You're slowin' down right toward the top!"

"This would be a good time to hang it up." Mitch was so cold, he barely could talk before the start of the 15th 880.

Niles showed up then, breezed through the last six, and drove off in his Volvo. We crawled to the van in our soaked sweats and turned on the heater. Rupe opened the door.

"Bah, what the bloody hell is this? You guys get back out there and do five more."

Following that workout, Mitch came down with what he termed "Tungsten Steel Hamstrings." Ward came down with mononucleosis. Boyd became anemic and couldn't run for a week. I caught a horrendous cold and coughed up green phlegm. Renny Vasquez quit the morning of the Caprock State Invitational. Rupe and the team filed into Renny's dorm room as he packed his bags. Mitch crawled under the covers of Renny's bed.

"Renny, are you really going back to Arizona?" Mitch waited for Renny to nod. "Then can I have your scholarship?"

After the Austin Invitational, where we finished 14th out of 17 teams, Rupe didn't say a word during the eight-hour drive to Lubbock until he slammed on the brakes 10 miles from campus.

"You losers get your butts out of the van and run back to campus." Within seconds, we abandoned our lawn chairs for a sub-freezing run on a highway lit only by occasional headlights. I couldn't wait to crawl into my warm bed. But there was a red tack stuck in my door. Again, I spent the night on Boyd's floor.

"I'm gonna have to start attendin' those prayer group meetins," Boyd joked.

I wrote a letter to Lanny Hightower the next night.

Dear Coach Hightower,

I came to college thinking college coaches would be a level above high school coaches. At Caprock State I have found college coaches who are a level "below" high school coaches. It took me to come here to appreciate you so much...

Your ex-runner,
Jonny

A letter arrived in my dormitory mailbox a week later.

Dear Jonny,

Thanks for the compliment, pardner, but I am darn sure those guys have an idea of what they're doing. Keep hangin' in there and I know you will become a great college runner. No one there has the dedication you have. Don't let them get you down. Keep working hard and you will be what I've always known you to be – a winner...

Sincerely yours,
Coach Hightower

Rupe called me anything but a winner after my 38th place finish at the Southwestern Conference Cross Country Championships in Houston. He had less mercy on Mitch, who was 41st, and attacked him before he even exited the finish chute.

"Piss poor, Hansby. Piss poor."

Rupe made us run hill sprints for our warm down and didn't say a word all 10 hours of our drive back to Lubbock. He didn't say much else after the NCAA Region VI Meet in Austin, where I finished 45th and 35 places from qualifying for nationals. Niles finished third and became the first Caprock runner to qualify for the NCAA Cross Country Meet. Niles' performance saved Rupe his job. Fubby was too busy watching basketball to realize Rupe wasn't really coaching Niles. Ward Andrews attempted a team revolt, if Rupe was not fired. But Fubby called his bluff and ended a heated discussion with, "We'll see."

Niles flew to Fort Worth for the NCAA meet, which was to be held the Monday before Thanksgiving. Rupe and Fubby drove the lawn chair van on Saturday morning, and Mitch and I talked them into letting us go to support Niles.

"We're stowaways," Mitch said.

Fubby wanted to make Fort Worth in time to watch the Caprock-TCU football game, but he also didn't want a speeding ticket. So he made Rupe drive.

Fubby interrupted Rupe, who bragged about Niles. "He's an animal. He'll go out with the leaders and make All American..."

"I've driven this road for 20 years and I've never seen a cop."

Rupe pressed the gas pedal and took it off when police lights flashed in his rearview mirror. Rupe took the ticket from the police officer and flung it at Fubby, "Bloody hell. No cops, Fubby?"

Mitch and I snickered from our lawn chairs and laughed harder, when Rupe was pulled over again 30 minutes later. "Can't bloody, fucking believe it! Bloody fucking hell!"

Fubby took the ticket from Rupe. "You won't have to pay these fines."

"What do you mean?"

"Once you go back to Australia, there's nothing they can do about it?"

"Bloody hell. And you two losers quit laughing back there."

Niles' 232nd place finish didn't help Rupe's case. Niles flew back to Lubbock. Mitch went to his girlfriend's house in Fort Worth. Fubby went on a hunting trip, and I left with Mom for Thanksgiving.

As I walked off, I saw Rupe sitting in the van, alone, studying a map and the fastest way back to a place where everyone hated him. Only 2 ½ months before, we felt lost without him. Now, we felt lost with him.

It just so happened we had been following someone who didn't know where he was going in the first place.

◆ ◆ ◆

10

The indoor track at the University of Amarillo was not a track. It was 30 small orange cones set around the green rubber basketball court that formed a 220-yard oval. The turns were tight. The stretches were long and less than two lanes wide. Only one person could pass at a time. If you went too wide or forced outside, you could ram into the concrete wall in front of the backstretch stands or into a padded wall on the homestretch. The start/finish line was set in the middle of the straight, making a last-ditch victory rush nearly impossible.

Also deemed not possible was a 19-year-old freshman from Dallas beating a 29-year-old junior from Nairobi. I came to the University of Amarillo that February night of 1977 to disprove the theory.

No one in the packed stands in Amarillo believed it. Their beloved Kenyan, Julius Butai, held every school record from 800 to 10,000 meters. He qualified for three straight NCAA Cross Country Meets and never had been beaten on his home court. He led his team to the last two victories in an Amarillo-Caprock State duel meet called "the battle for the Panhandle Cup," which looked so much like a frying pan it was nicknamed "the Panhandle Pan." Butai's picture was on the front of the meet program. That made me want to beat him even more.

Rupert Wade, who had talked Fubby Tuppernacker into letting him stay as the distance coach, had labeled me "the Kenyan Killer" after my first two college track meets. I returned to Lubbock off five straight 101-mile weeks during the Christmas break. The 100 mark was in jeopardy on New Year's Eve, when Mom said I wasn't allowed to do my second annual run from one year to the next.

"Too dangerous," she said. "Someone might shoot a bottle rocket at you out their car window."

Mom went to bed and prayed a rosary through the new year, and Dad fell asleep on the sofa during John Wayne's *Westward Ho*. I snuck out for a two miler and snuck back in before Mom said her last Hail Mary.

Rupe's first track workout at Caprock State was three times 990 yards. I went through the 880's in 1:58, 1:57, and 1:56 and blew away my teammates, who doubtfully ran a step before or after New Year's. After the second one, Niles limped off the track and back to medical school for good.

At the Lubbock Indoor Meet, held on a converted airplane hanger's concrete track, I stunned NAIA champion Richard Cheptimboi of Southern New Mexico. I burst up the final banked turn and flew past him in the final five meters for victory in the one-mile run. A picture of me waving to the crowd appeared the next morning on the front page of the *Lubbock Ledger*. The headline read, "Grimsley's ghost haunts champion Kenyan." The story noted that Grimsley Roeper still held the school's 440-yard dash record.

The next week at the Oklahoma Indoor, James Motua of Oklahoma Junior College must have thought *I* was a ghost. All he heard as I went by on the final lap of the mile was the pounding of the board track. My introverted style more than my rising celebrity captivated my teammates, especially my roommate.

"Damn, Langenhooch," Jack Walden had said the night before the duel with Amarillo as I sat up in bed, reading *Track and Field News*. "You don't cuss, you don't drink, you don't party, you don't screw women. All you do is run, go to class, eat, sleep, and read those damn track magazines."

I turned the page and looked at this *Charlie's Angels'* worshipper who had a red bikini-clad Farah Fawcett poster tacked to the ceiling above his bed and removed it only when his girlfriend came to town. I thought, "You don't go to class, you don't train, you cheat on your girlfriend, and that desk Bible is open to the same page as the day you arrived."

I told Jack I wanted to lose my virginity on my wedding night, to have four or five kids, and live in a house with a white picket fence.

"Wife, kids, house? You gotta get a date first, Langenhooch."

I told Jack about Holly Ritzenbarger, about how I was in love with her. "That's who I want to marry."

"Where's she now?"

"LSU on a track scholarship. She's also a cheerleader."

"You'd have a better shot at making it to the sun. You better try for someone local – or at least that fat cow who sends you letters from Dallas every
week."

"Trudy? You saw the picture she sent of herself."

"Must have been taken with a wide angle lens."

I went back to my magazine. Jack kept after me. "I think you should go
for the fat chick."

"You kidding?"

"It's all the same once you get down there. You just have to ask for the directions."

I finally chuckled. "If I took her to a movie theater, I'd have to get her two
seats. One for each bun."

Jack didn't laugh. "Well, at least she would be a date. One thing for damn
sure, you ain't gonna get a date lyin' there readin' *Track and Field News*."

Nothing could distract my focus the next night at the indoor meet in Amarillo.
Not the graffiti I saw as I changed in the restroom stall – "flush twice, it's a
long way to Lubbock." Not the sly smiling coach who escorted me to the starting line for the one mile run – "he's bloody fast, Langenhooch. Make sure he
doesn't lap ya', mate." Not the thin, legs-up-to-my-chest Kenyan, who took a
victory lap "before" the start of the mile.

The starter's pistol barely could be heard over the crowd noise. All I could
hear was the thumping of my heart. All I could smell was the heat lotion lath-
ered on the legs of Butai's teammate Phillip Murambo who ran second to his
front-running countryman. I was last, behind my teammate Boyd Turner, as
the four of us whipped around the tight bends. With three laps to go, a gap
formed between the two Kenyans, and I filled it, sneaking between Murambo
and the wall.

Butai picked up the pace, and I went with him. The crowd chanted "Boo-
tay!" Boo-tay!" as we raced past the smoke on the final lap. My adrenalin
soared through the roof as I sprinted up to Butai's shoulder on the backstretch.
Around the final turn, Butai swung wide. But not wide enough. I had just
enough room between his shoulder and the padded wall to match strides with
the Kenyan. We leaned for the finish line, neither knowing who won. There
was no finish line photo, only a hometown finish line judge intimidated by a
crowd of Kenyan worshippers. He gave it to Butai.

"That's b-b-bullshit." I started walking toward the judge, but Rupe pulled
me away.

"Bah, don't waste your energy, mate. Save if for the two-mile."

I rested my legs in the empty natatorium next door and kept telling myself
"I'm gonna get that Kenyan."

Rupe walked with me to the starting line. "Go past him on the backstretch.
Don't wait until the homestretch. There's not enough room."

Butai went to the lead again, and again I went into last, behind Mitch
Hansby. Butai surged hard at the mile mark, and I sprinted after him. With six

laps to go, Butai and I had broken from the field. I stared at his smooth black calves and waited. The more he pushed the pace, the faster the crowd chanted "Boo-tay!" Boo-tay!" and the better I felt.

"Just wait, just wait," I told myself. "I'll surprise him on the final back-stretch."

Breaking me the last four laps wasn't going to happen. This was a last lap sprint, and this time I was ready. The pistol shot for the last lap echoed off the gymnasium walls. I revved up as we approached the turn and accelerated atop the backstretch. My lightning-quick burst was about to devastate Butai until he chopped me across the chest with a forearm. I slammed into the concrete wall with a "Ohhh" from the crowd and staggered around the turn holding my ribs and a middle finger. "You cheater!"

Rupe grabbed me as I came within a stride of Butai. The Kenyan escaped me again. "We will race again," he said.

"How about tonight? In the parking lot!"

Everyone but the hometown officials saw Butai's well-landed forearm. Now I knew what those scribbled words on the bathroom wall meant.

My outburst surprised my teammates as much as my drinking a beer with them in the van lawn chair back to Lubbock. Jack was shocked I had my first date. It came the week after the Southwestern Indoor Conference Meet in Fort Worth, where I finished fourth in the two mile in 9:12. Mitch informed me during a post-workout shower that he had found me a date for his Kappa Alpha frater-nity party. I fumbled the soap, when he told me I had to call her.

"C-C-Call her? On the telephone?"

Mitch turned off his shower and grabbed his towel. "Is there a problem with that?"

The last call I made to a girl ended in a major stuttering block, and this name was worse than Sh-Sh-Sheryl. This was Ka-Ka-Karina.

I paced the dorm hallway for an hour. "Is Karina there? Is Karina there? What's so hard about that?"

Jack pushed me into the room and ordered me to dial the numbers. The telephone rang for five seconds. It seemed like five hours. A girl answered, "Hello." My heart was in my throat.

"Hello, is Karina there, please?" I could not have said it more calmly or more smoothly.

"Sorry, you have the wrong the number."

Another 30 minutes of pacing followed, and I got the right number and a break. She answered, "Hello this is Karina. Is this Jonny?"

Mitch and I picked up our dates at T.R. Rust Hall, which he had renamed "Tits R Us Hall." I hugged the backseat door more than an arms-length from Karina, a smilie, short-haired brunette who wore a crucifix on the gold chain over a pink corduroy sweater. Mitch started the conversation as he drove by Uncle Grimsley's statue.

"Karina, did you know that Grimsley Roeper is Jonny's great uncle?"

"Oh really? That's exciting."

"Y-Y-Yeah. Nice statue, isn't it?"

"There's an old saying 'round here," Mitch said. "If a virgin ever graduates from Caprock State, 'ol Grimsley's statue will fall down?"

"Is that true?" Karina said.

I glanced at Karina and turned my eyes back toward the street.

Grimsley's statue cracked a little after my first date. Four hours of talking track and the worst-ever John Travolta impersonation got me a peck on the cheek. Mitch put his arm around my shoulder as we walked back to Rutherford Hall. "What were you tryin' to do out there on that dance floor, Langenhooch, stomp roaches?"

Fubby also had a heavy foot, on the accelerator of his brown station wagon. He threatened triple digits halfway into our 12-hour trip to Laredo for the Border Relays. His new CB radio gave him the confidence to break the law.

"Break one nine, for The Quail Hunter." Fubby sounded more like Buford T. Justice than the Bandit. "You got a smoky report?"

A trucker's voice cracked over the static of Fubby's CB. "Yeah, you gotta smoky down 'ere just past mile marker 321."

Fubby looked at a green sign with the white number 321 along the four-lane highway and ahead to a police car sitting in the median strip. Fubby slammed on his brakes. The station wagon lifted onto its front wheels, almost dragging the front bumper to the road. We skidded past the police officer at 85 miles per hour. Fubby waved. The police officer must have been too stunned to chase us.

Fubby rarely had both hands on the wheel. The other hand was used to stuff a burger in his mouth, hold his cards in a poker game, or flip the page of his newspaper. He often looked and conversed with someone for 20 seconds before returning his eyes to the road. Just ahead, Rupe drove the lawn chair van filled with sprinters and *Soul Train* hits. A real train rolled along next to the highway and caught Boyd Turner's attention from the back of the station wagon.

"I think I'll moon this train," Boyd said. Within seconds, Turner's butt cheeks were pressed against the side window in full view of train passengers.

Fubby's eyes left the road for at least 30 seconds. "Put your clothes back on."

I did a Boyd the next morning to the Border Relays crowd. I was so nervous I forgot to put on my shorts. I realized this when I dropped my sweatpants on the starting line as the announcer introduced me before my mile preliminary.

"In lane three, the 1976 Texas Public Schools State High School one mile champion and Caprock State's top runner indoors. He's on his way to being a great one, ladies and gentlemen. Welcome Jonny Langenfelder."

I struggled around the cinder track in second to last place in my tank top and sweatpants and wishing the announcer had flagrantly mispronounced my name like I had grown accustomed. I kept running past the finish line to the exit, past Rupe, Boyd, Mitch, and Jack.

"I don't know who that guy was behind me," I said. "But he'd better hang it up."

I talked Fubby, against Rupe's wishes, into entering me in my first-ever three-mile track race that night. "You're not a three miler," Rupe said. "But you better run hard or we'll leave you back in Lubbock the next meet."

I turned to Mitch. "I hate these last-minute pep talks."

I passed the first 220 yards behind the herd of 42 runners and tried to tune out the track announcer. "They just passed the 220 in 31 seconds. They are on 12:24 three-mile pace. That's a world record, ladies and gentlemen!"

His loud voice and the crunching of cinders below my spikes kept me going through the mile. "Look at these runners cruising around this track on a glorious night for racing, ladies and gentlemen! Wouldn't you like to join them?"

I broke away from last place in the second mile and kept passing runners every lap. Boyd, Mitch, Kelvin Booker of Houston, Mario Rodriguez of UTEP. I ran in lane three and passed four more runners on the gun lap and finished fifth in 14:08.6, a school record by 10 seconds and 15 up on Rupe's lifetime best.

"Not a three-miler, eh, Rupe?"

Rupe shook his head.

"I'll make the Olympics at that distance. Just like Pre."

"You'll never make the Olympics."

"Not while you're the coach."

Rupe put me through some hard 300's and 400's every other day that spring. I looked for a sub-14 three mile at a four-way meet in Austin and for LSU freshman hurdler Holly Ritzenbarger. En route to Austin I told my teammates the story of Holly and I and our close encounter on New Year's Eve and the mix-up at the Forest Hill sports banquet. We left a Lubbock dust storm for the cool spring air and green grass of Austin. I spotted Holly in the Memorial Stadium stands as I warmed up for the three-mile that night. Whatever ounce she gained was muscle and in all the right places.

"Why don't you go over and talk to her?" Jack said.

"Can't. I'm warming up."

Jack introduced himself to Holly as the starting gun set me off in the three mile. A few laps later, which Jack disclosed the next day to my disbelief, Holly pointed to the track, "You see that tall, skinny guy from Caprock State running near the end of the pack?"

"Yeah."

"Didn't he go to Forest Hill?"

My second-place finish in the near-NCAA qualifying time of 13:51.43 unclogged her memory. She gave me a hug on the infield, "Way to go, Forest Hill," she said.

Then somehow the words fumbled from of my mouth.

"Y-Y-You want to go for ice cream after the meet."

"Sure," she said. "Where you staying?"

"The Roachside, I mean the Roadside Motel. Room 208."

"I'm right down the road at the Hilton. I'll come by your room."

I raced back to the motel and set a school showering and blow-drying record. I put on my red tennis shirt with the little silver Caprock State insignia and paced the outdoor corridor in front of my room below the starlit sky. She never showed up.

I took a bus to Dallas for spring break the next morning and reported to Forest Hill High School on Monday with Rupe's workout schedule. Coach Hightower crumpled the piece of paper and tossed it into the infield. I was so sore from racing The Stallion on all out 220's and 330's all week that Butai beat me by a straightaway in the Caprock Invitational 1,500 meters. In the Texas Relays 5,000 meters I was safely in second-to-last until the last lap, when the runner behind me dropped out. As I rounded the final turn, two meet officials in a show of compassion started to put their hands together.

"Don't clap," I pleaded.

I anchored the distance medley relay to seventh place the next day and arrived back at Room 907 that night to the sound of a film projector and college guys yelling, "Oh yea baby, you know you like it! Do it! Yeah!"

I opened the door to a white sheet strung on the wall above my bed and illuminated with two naked women and a man with a very long tongue.

"Sit down, Langenhooch and enjoy the film."

I barely could see Jack through the darkness. He and his three friends sat and sipped their silver beer cans without taking their eyes off the make-shift screen. It was the first time anyone made love on my side of the room.

"Isn't that your girlfriend, Holly?" said Jack, who didn't make the Texas Relays travel squad.

"No," one of Jack's friends said. "It's his mother."

"Funny," I said without laughing. "You could at least lock the door."

"Relax, nobody's coming." Jack took a quick swig. "Except this guy in the film."

About two seconds later during the film's and actor's climax, Wendell Timmons, a 400-meter hurdler and the team rep to the Christian Athletes Association, walked in. He looked at the screen, shouted, "Oh, Golly!" and rushed out.

"Don't you knock?" Jack shouted.

The next morning, there were scripture quotes underneath our door. I took Jack's Bible and looked them up. They mentioned adultery and fornication, but nothing about *watching* adultery and fornication. Jack scribbled a passage of his own and slipped it under Wendell's door. It read, "Jack 1:1 - mind your own fucking business."

We found out later Wendell called the campus cops, who told them they had better things to do than arrest a few horny college kids.

"They were probably too busy watching their own porno film," Jack said.

Jack could star in his own film. During a jock raid by Tits R Us Hall residents, he wrote "Mr. Big" and his telephone number on a jock and tossed it down. The telephone rang five minutes later. I didn't see him the rest of the night. Jack could pick up a girl at Disco Dick's faster than it took me to get the nerve to ask one to dance.

He showed no guilt about two-timing his girlfriend, who wore his high school letter jacket in the stands at the Pampa Relays. I ran the three-mile and sat on University of Pampa star Duncan Frost for 11 and three-quarters laps, before blowing by the Canadian in the homestretch. The crowd booed, and Frost and his coach came after me.

"What was that all aboot, ya' show boater?" Frost yelled.

"Sour grapes," I said, grinning. "Sour grapes."

The win gave me confidence to take the Southwestern Conference three-mile title with this sit-and-kick tactic and make the NCAA qualifying standard of 13:45. Rupe had another plan. He interrupted my focus on the little crack under Austin's Memorial Stadium an hour before the race that night in mid-May.

"Follow the leaders through the first mile, mate." All I could see were his teeth in the darkness under the Memorial Stadium stands. "Then take the lead with a 62."

"You want me to run like Prefontaine."

"No, like Darcy. He would get far ahead and then crawl to the finish line if he had to."

I jogged for ten minutes on the turf infield for warm up that night in May, and my T-shirt and warm-up pants were drenched with sweat. I put on my spikes and motioned Rupe from the stands. "The temperature and humidity are each triple digits. I'll die if I go for it at the mile mark."

Rupe grabbed my T-shirt collar and pulled me to within an inch of his clenched-teeth. "Bloody follow the plan, Langenhooch or I'll make sure Fubby cuts your scholarship to books next semester."

As I walked to the start, Fubby hung over the rail. "Beautiful night for runnin,' Langenfelster."

I looked in the stands at Rupe beating a folded up a program against his palm. I made the sign of the cross and whispered, "Help me, Pre."

Rice's Ramon Savage, the defending champion, and Arkansas' Sean O'Malley blitzed the first mile in 4:30 and broke all but five of the 30 starters. I barely could stay up, much less take the lead. But I did, and my 64-second lap broke no one. I followed with a 66 and then a 69. Savage passed me, then O'Malley, and eventually everyone in the field, after successive laps of 75, 78, 81, 85, and 90 that got me nothing more than a pity clap.

I did feel like Prefontaine – dead.

I sat in the stands long after the jumping pits and flags and starting blocks were taken away and the stadium lights were turned off. I stared at my red and silver Wooosh track spikes and then at the dark track and pondered the outcome had I not listened to Rupe. I closed my eyes and fantasized about hanging with Savage and O'Malley and blowing past them in the final homestretch to the roar of the crowd en route to the NCAA qualifying time of 13:43. As I grabbed the finish line string in my fantasy, someone grabbed my arm. I opened my eyes to Rupe gulping from a Fosters beer can and looking out at the track.

"Ya' gave it your best shot, mate."

"I finished last."

"Bah, that's not the important thing. Ya' stuck to the plan and ya' made 'em work. I found some sand dunes, 40 meters high, just west of Lubbock. I'll have ya' runnin' them 40-50 times. They'll make ya' so strong, nobody will touch ya,' mate. When you're a senior, runners will be flocking to Caprock State. They will be calling themselves 'Rupert's Boys.'"

Rupe chugged the last of his Fosters, crushed the can with his right hand, tossed it onto the track, and walked under the stands into the darkness.

I never saw him again.

◆◆◆

"Tuppernacker" was scribbled above the red and silver Caprock State return address on an envelope addressed to me. I took the letter to my 1977 summer job at J.B. Bowers, Inc., where I worked – well, sort of – in a warehouse office. It was Payton Products until J.B. Bowers bought the company at the beginning of the year.

Dad worked upstairs, assembling wheel parts, and heard the warehouse foreman, Bud Gribbon, needed help to rearrange the huge warehouse of wheels, axles, screws, bolts, and other accessories from the production line. Bud gave me a stack of papers to file and then went on his two-week vacation. J.B. Bowers made it a permanent vacation within two minutes of Bud's return. As Bud was packing his things, I asked, "What am I suppose to do now?"

"I don't know," he said.

I pretended to work the rest of the summer, hoping no one – especially J.B. Bowers – would ask what I did. Frankly, I did not know.

Reading Fubby's letter looked like working.

Dear Tumbleweed Cross Country Runner:

As you all know, Rupert Wade went back to Australia and I've been looking for someone to coach the cross country team. After a long search, I am very proud to announce Neil Horsvall as the new cross country coach.

"Neil Horsvall." I kept staring at the name and saying it over and over. "Neil Horsvall. Neil Horsvall." This was the 47-year old Boy Scout leader/Sunday school teacher who kept showing up at our track workouts. He never read the rules posted on the gate – "joggers not permitted between 3 p.m. and 6 p.m. and are not allowed in lane one" – and refused to move from the first lane even when we hollered "track!" He ran with his head on a pivot and arms flailing so low he could scratch his ass. He yelled, "Looking good, ladies" every time we passed him and then hung out after our workout to tell us how he would conquer the four-hour marathon.

Neil Horsvall, Caprock State head cross country coach? There was silence in the warehouse office until I looked up at the large man with a suit, tie, and a frown.

"C-C-Can I help you?"

"I'm J.B. Bowers."

This is the man who fired three 30-year company veterans and six others within four months of buying the company. He would fire Dad two months later, because he felt like it.

"I just came to tell you what a good job you've been doing for us this summer," he said. "Keep up the good work."

My $3.10 per hour job was secure. I wasn't so sure about my sophomore cross country season. I had written Fubby early in the summer and suggested Coach Hightower. Fubby's offer of $2,000 and free tickets to all Tumbleweed home football games was not enough. Neil Horsvall would have done it for the tickets. I ran 101 miles per week that summer, despite 41 straight days of triple-digit temperatures and living in a house without an air conditioner. I refrigerated my pillow until it was time to go to bed. I saved enough money to buy from Matthew's ex-girlfriend a yellow VW beetle, just large enough to fit my belongings.

Mitch the Bitch, Boyd Turner, and I made a pact to return fit. We didn't want to remain the conference laughing stock, which was inevitable at first glance at our new coach. Neil Horsvall showed up for the first workout wearing a purple baseball cap with ear covers, a white v-neck night shirt, brown knee-length bermuda shorts, black socks, and sandals.

"This is the guy who is going to lead me to the Olympics?" I thought.

My teammates weren't going to lead us to a conference title. Fubby invested most of his scholarship money on throwers who couldn't throw, jumpers who couldn't jump, and runners who wouldn't run. He signed a 1:52 half-miler who we only saw at registration. He signed Brandon Sowerby, a 4:15 miler with talent, but without balls. We nicknamed him "Scrotum."

The rest were walk-ons, or, more accurately, crawl-ons. We never knew them by their real names. One was called The Woodpecker, because of his long nose. There was Rocky, who came from some mountain shack in Colorado. Don Ho from Honolulu. Kar-oom, from somewhere no one knew. David Bedford, whose first name was really Clarke. We renamed him, in mock sarcasm, after the great English runner. Finally, a pale little guy we simply called Thad.

Horsvall was the ultimate crawl-on. "O.K, ladies," he said. "I am Neil Horsvall, your new cross country coach. We are going to have loads of fun this season and do really, really good."

I whispered in Boyd's's ear, "Will we be having milk and cookies in the locker room after workout?"

Horsvall continued, "I would like for every member of the team to call me Coach Horsvall. I want you to wear red socks when we race. And anytime you feel any kind of pain I want you to stop..."

As we jogged to Prairie Dog Park, I asked Mitch, "Did he actually just tell us to stop every time we felt pain? If I did that, I'd never finish a run."

Horsvall drove by us in his chartreuse green pinto and yelled, "Looking good, ladies." He made us stand in a circle at the park and yell out a letter for each jumping jack until we spelled Tumbleweeds.

"That will scare you're opponents," Horsvall said.

"All it scares 'round here is prairie dogs," I whispered to a snickering Boyd.

Horsvall then told us all to join hands, bow our heads and pray.

"What did you pray for, Mitch?" I asked.

"I prayed that a prairie dog would jump out his hole and bite Horsvall on the nuts."

Horsvall then had us do "pursuit running." He set off each runner at 20-second intervals and told us to catch the guy in front of you.

"Now when you pass your teammate, yell 'Iron, '" Horsvall said.

"Iron?" I said.

"Yes, and then the runner you pass yells, "Tummy."

"Iron tummy?"

"Yes. Or for variety, you can yell tummy and the other runner can yell iron."

"Tummy iron?"

"Hearing those words will bring us together as a team, make us tough."

We took off on Horsvall's orders and ran around the park. I passed several crawl-ons without uttering "Iron." I ran by Horsvall in his black socks and sandals and pivot head. He yelled, "Tummy!"

I cut the pursuit training, ran back to campus, grabbed my clothes from my locker, and went back to Rutherford Hall. Over dinner that night I called for a boycott of Horsvall's workouts. "I'm not running another pursuit drill for Coach Iron Tummy."

The next afternoon while everyone else was pursuing each other at the park, I was doing hill sprints up a ramp at Tumbleweed Stadium. That night, the telephone rang in Room 907. "Langenfolker?"

"Yes."

"Coach Tuppernacker. I need to see you in my office right away."

Fubby and I talked for more than an hour. I told him about the pursuit drills, the Iron Tummy, and the stopping every time you feel pain. I turned away from Fubby and stared at the new stuffed raccoon on his office wall. "If we carry on with these workouts, we'll get dead last at conference."

The next afternoon Horsvall and I sat in the stands, alone. "Jonny, you're one of the best runners in the state and I think you can be one of the best runners in the country."

This was the first thing he said that made sense. "So to keep you happy and on the team, I've devised a plan."

Horsvall let the runners decide each day's workout. That meant one day we would run 20 times 220's, a 10-mile time trial the next day, and hill repeats the next. We were destined to finish last in conference.

I knew who had returned the afternoon I opened my favorite stall door in Rutherford Hall's ninth floor bathroom, pulled down my shorts, and slipped off the toilet. The old Vaseline on the seat trick had been perfected by my roommate, Jack Walden.

Within the first week Jack spread a glob of peanut butter on the telephone ear piece and called me from another room, short-sheeted my bed, dumped salt under my covers, and poured Tabasco sauce in my lemonade.

"What's with you, Jack?" Everyone laughed as I drank my fifth glass of cold water.

"His squeeze graduated from high school early and enrolled at Caprock," Boyd said.

"Worse than that, " Jack said, "she's residing next door at Tits R Us Hall and she joined the women's track team."

"We have a women's track team?" I asked.

"It's more like a club?" Boyd said.

"It's bunch of lesbians throwing a spear and a ball with a chain on the end of it," Mitch said.

"What event does Julie do?" I asked.

"How the hell should I know?" Jack said.

Julie's arrival kept me from having to sleep on Boyd's floor. Julie was a virgin and proud of it. Jack, whom she thought was likewise a virgin, shook his head. "She's saving it for her marriage."

"Did you know," Boyd said, "that you are not considered to be having sex if you use a condom?"

Jack rushed out of the dining hall. I watched television for an hour in the dormitory lounge and walked back to my room. Still, no red tack.

I saw red at our first cross country meet, in Amarillo. Horsvall wore red socks with his sandals and red Bermuda shorts and a red T-shirt with silver letters that spelled "Caprock State Cross Country" on the front and "Iron Tummy" on the back. His red cap covered the gray streaks atop his balding scalp. He made us march like soldiers onto the University of Amarillo golf course and stand in a circle for callisthenics. Horsvall put a tumbleweed in the center as we yelled letters during our jumping jacks. Only the crawl-ons wore the red socks. Julius Butai jogged by and laughed with his teammates. He must have said "idiots" in Swahili.

Butai probably giggled through his 4:22 first mile. I went out in five minutes and slowly picked my way through the pack. At about two miles a flash of red crawled out of the bushes and yelled at Boyd and me from the side.

"Go Iron tummy!"

"Dorky sumbitch," Boyd said between puffs.

Horsvall must have thought his Iron Tummy crap worked. I outkicked Phillip Murambo for second. Boyd finished fourth, and Mitch fifth. The freshman, Scrotum, was tenth. Ka-room was the top crawl-on in 28th place, about three minutes behind me in the four-mile race. The other crawl-ons brought up the rear, leaving Ka-room our only hope at keeping us out of the conference cellar.

Ka-room looked like Gandhi before the hunger strike and received his nickname from a pre-workout routine in which he knelt on top of a picnic table, closed his eyes, raised his arms, and brought his hands down to the table while chanting, "Ka-r-o-o-m." He spent the seven-hour trip to the Oklahoma Cross Country Classic meditating and raised his palms over his meal of salad, carrots, and bean sprouts.

"What are you doing?" Mitch asked.

Ka-room kept his eyes closed. "I am energizing my food."

Boyd whispered in my ear, "I need to get me one of them energizers."

Ka-room spent more time meditating before the race than jogging. As he walked to the line, he said to himself, "My name is Anton, my name is Anton." He went out with Boyd and me the first mile and as we surged away from him, he hollered, "Go Anton."

We finished last of the 15 teams. "The planets must not have been aligned properly, " Ka-room, the 91st place finisher, said.

Mitch slammed his spikes to the ground. "Then damnit, why don't you go back to Pluto and straighten 'em out? "

On the way back to Lubbock, two chubby girls in a banged up brown convertible Le Baron drove alongside our van and whistled.

Boyd whispered from the next lawn chair. "Let's moon these fat chicks, Langenhooch."

"Don't know. Horsvall is religious. He might get pissed and tell Fubby when we get back."

The chubby girls kept whistling, "Whew! Whew!"

Boyd and I, nodded to each other, dropped our sweatpants, and parked our cheeks on the glass. Horsvall looked back from the driver's seat and laughed so hard he almost crashed into the Le Baron.

"He don't get out much," Mitch said.

Horsvall laughed even harder when I got a cramp in my left hamstring and fell to the floor.

This team was in serious trouble. We needed a crawl-on to step forward, but Ka-room was the only one who showed up for workout everyday. I asked Rocky, a 36-minute 10K runner, why he came to Caprock State. He said, "I was going to go to Washington State, but I didn't want to run in the limelight of Henry Rono."

On a group run Don Ho asked, "You guys mind if we all sing a song while we're running?"

"I got one." Mitch broke into song. "Hit the road, Jack, and never come back for more, no more, no more, no more. Hit the road, Don Ho..."

We all sang what turned out to be Don Ho's swan song.

Thad never had to run a step in his life before that season and it showed. When a 50-mile-per-hour dust storm forced us to jog laps on the hard six-lap-to-a-mile concourse around Tumbleweed Coliseum, Thad did intervals. He jogged a lap with us, rested a lap, jogged a lap and so on.

David Bedford only showed up on the easy days and surged away from us after the halfway mark. We formed a posse one afternoon and blew by him six miles into a 10-mile campus run. David let out a loud, "Oaf" as we stormed by. Boyd drew a picture of David lying on the side of the road on the locker room chalkboard. The caption above it read, "When the going gets tough, David takes a bus."

Our team had no discipline and no leader. The "what the hell are we doing today" program put me in the worst shape of my life. Jack came up with this analogy over dinner:

"The cross country team is like joining a spa. You come in, do some weights and a little run, sit in the whirlpool, take a shower, get dressed, tell a few jokes, and go home."

"So, Jack, you must have a lifetime membership." My burn brought a "Whew" from Boyd, Mitch, and Scrotum. Jack did Fubby's workouts when either of them showed up.

"Fubby's program is like 'workout bingo.'" Jack said. "You pull a work-out out of the jar, and that's what you do. That's why The Blob was runnin' the hurdles instead of throwing the shot, and why I was throwing the javelin."

I wanted to throw up the morning of the Southwestern Conference Cross Country Championships in Waco. Horsvall showed up in his Boy Scout uni-form, complete with the string tied from the hat's bill around his throat. He was off on a scouting trip right after the meet. He stood before the line of run-ners on the starting line with both fists raised and clenched.

"Iron tummy, Iron tummy! Go-o-o Iron tummy!" He jumped, and I was afraid he would do a herky. Everyone laughed but the Caprock State runners. We hid our heads and pretended we didn't know him.

Rice's Matty Rittenbacker, the race favorite, slapped me on the arm. "Hey, is that your coach? Good luck."

Horsvall was all over the course. The slower we ran, the more he yelled. Mitch and I, struggling for a top-30 finish, ran by him at five miles.

75

"Looking good, ladies! Get after 'em! Go Iron Tummy!"

"Shut the fuck up!" Mitch yelled.

Mitch finished a few strides ahead of me in 30th place. Scrotum placed 25th and proclaimed himself Caprock's top runner, even though it was the first time he was in our top three. Boyd finished 36th. Ka-room over-meditated and finished 54th. The Woodpecker fell on his beak and was 60th. Rocky finished about a minute behind the second-to-last-place finisher for the cellar dweller Tumbleweeds.

Horsvall gave us warm pats at the end of the finish chute. "Good job, ladies. You really did good."

Mitch turned his back. "Fuck you, Horsvall."

I still hoped to qualify for nationals at the NCAA Region VI Meet in Austin on a Monday. Only Mitch, Ka-room, and I were going. We met with Horsvall in Fubby's office a few days before the meet. Horsvall said he couldn't leave until 1 p.m. on Sunday.

"No good," I said. "We won't get there until 9 p.m. and won't see the course. We need to leave no later than eight."

"Can't do it," Horsvall said. "I have to teach Sunday school."

"Then why the hell are we goin'?" I yelled. "If we can't leave first thing in the morning, get down there and run the course and do things right, then what's the point?"

No one said a word until Horsvall stood up. "Is that the way you feel, Jonny?"

"Yep."

"Then we'll leave at 8 a.m.," Horsvall said just before the door handle hit him in the butt on his hasty exit.

We arrived in at the Roachside Motel in Austin and flipped coins to see who would share a room with Horsvall. Mitch and Ka-room both landed on heads and mine on tails. I threw the coins against the wall.

"I've had it up to here with Coach Iron Tummy all season, and now I have to share a room with him?"

Mitch put his finger on his lips. "Horsvall is right next door and just heard everything you said."

"Who cares?"

Horsvall dropped us off at the course just before dark and returned two hours later.

"Where you been?" Mitch asked.

"Thought you fellas would jog back to the hotel."

The hotel was six miles from the course. Mitch and I looked at each other in our lawn chairs and shook our heads. We gave Horsvall his own room. Mitch slept in one bed, I slept in the other, and Ka-room sat on the floor all night with his legs crossed and his palms raised.

We bundled up in our warm-ups in the near-freezing conditions and took them off just before the start of the race. We looked at Horsvall who stood there, arms folded, in his Bermuda shorts, sandals, red socks, and a tank top.

"What a fucking idiot," Mitch said.

Mitch and I ran in the lead pack for two miles until Arkansas' Sean O'Malley sprinted down a hill and yelled, "Hog, S-o-o-o-ey!" in thick Irish. That broke my concentration more than a "Go Iron Tummy." Mitch finished 21st and I finished 23,rd thus ending the coaching career of Neil "Coach Iron Tummy" Horsvall.

The week after Thanksgiving, Mitch, Boyd, and I were on a campus run and saw Horsvall in front of us and running 10-minute miles with his chubby running buddy. Horsvall's head went from side to side, his red socks flapped in the breeze, and his hands swung low and scratched his ass. I couldn't resist at the moment we breezed by him.

"Looking good, ladies!"

◆◆◆

12

Jack Walden called them my "midnight snacks." After my third helping of steak or shrimp or mash potatoes, I always returned to the food line of the Rutherford Dining Hall for cookies or brownies or cake. What I didn't eat, I wrapped in a napkin and smuggled to Room 907 for a midnight snack.

After dinner our second day back in 1978, I returned to the dorm with a stack of books and a midnight snack of sugar cookies. I walked into our floor's restroom and carefully placed the midnight snack on top of the books, lowered my jeans to my ankles, and sat on the toilet. When I finished, I stood and pressed down the silver flush handle atop the long silver pipe and wham! I was smacked in the eye by a water blast. A bolt had been removed below the handle. The water exploded from the bolt hole and blinded me. Water kept spraying from the pipe. At first, I thought the water was coming from the bowl, and I was having a piss and poo shower. I jiggled the stall door handle. It wouldn't open. I couldn't go under or over the door and stood there another 10 seconds.

The water stopped moments after I shoved the door open with my shoulder. I hopped out, while sliding my books along the flooded floor and with my pants still at my ankles. I looked like I had jumped into a swimming pool, a hysterical sight to the ninth-floor residents who pointed and held their stomachs. I picked up my midnight snack off the floor and squashed it in my hands.

In the middle of the howling hooligans was the culprit, Jack Walden.

This was the work of a sexually frustrated young man. Jack couldn't convince Julie pre-marital mattress polo was all right, and he couldn't escape her either. He returned to Caprock State for the winter term and declared war on his scapegoat. He sprayed me with his water pistol if I didn't hit my alarm clock within three seconds or if I came in late from studying. Jack slept half the day and plotted the other half.

At bedtime one night while I was in the bathroom down the hall, Jack hid Boyd Turner into the narrow space between my bed and the wall and under a six-foot long shelf. Jack turned the lights out and pretended to be asleep. I returned to my room and crawled under my blanket. About 10 minutes later, this cold, bony hand came seemingly out of the wall and grabbed my neck. I was so scared, I couldn't scream. At least 10 other ninth-floor residents with their ears glued to the door outside in the hallway rolled around laughing.

"You all right Langenhooch?" Boyd asked.

I caught my breath. "Y-Y-You're a dead man, Walden."

The battles that semester were not limited to Room 907. Fubby threatened to replace the distance runners with Kenyans, if we didn't perform well that spring. No one was more infuriated with that threat than Boyd, who clenched his teeth with every syllable at our table in the Rutherford Hall cafeteria. "If he takes away my scholarship, I will take a stick, walk over to his office, and beat every last hair off the sumbitch."

Boyd would do this, and not just for a prank. He normally was a fun-loving guy. But when it came to the foreigner debate, his faced turned red and he gritted his teeth on every "F" word. I wrote a story for the *Daily Tumbleweed* on the recruitment of foreign athletes. I interviewed Boyd, but couldn't quote him.

"Fuckin' foreigners. How do they expect 18-, 19-year-old kids to compete against these world-class assholes in their late 20's and 30's?"

I asked about a possible age restriction.

"Fuck that. There shouldn't be any foreigners, period. Them sumbitches are takin' our scholarships. For every scholarship you give a foreigner, an American kid can't go to college."

The foreigner subject ate at Boyd as the lawn chair van zoomed toward the University of Amarillo for our annual duel meet, the battle for the Panhandle Pan, in their two-lane gym and with their hometown officials. From his lawn chair, Boyd read out loud a quote from Julius Butai's in the *Amarillo Daily News*: "We will take Caprock again. No problem. They are afraid of us."

We were greeted by a gaseous layer of heat ointment, a banner that read, "Blow away the Tumbleweeds," and a crowd that booed us on our warm-up jog. Boyd shot them the finger. Our team callisthenics included a drill displaying the use of an elbow and a forearm. If needed, I would use it on Butai.

Halfway through the mile, I couldn't reach him or his pacer Phillip Murambo with a slingshot. The Kenyans slowed from the four-minute pace the next three laps of the eight-lap race and I reeled them in. At the gun, I flew by them. Butai caught me on the backstretch, but I held him off.

"I've got 'im," I thought between pants and amongst the ear-splitting crowd noise.

I accelerated around the final turn and, then, I felt a knee on the heel of my right spike. I stumbled, and Butai steamed around me for the victory in a track record 4:06.3.

I slapped my hand against the blue pad on the homestretch wall and started after Butai, who was jogging his victory lap and waving to the crowd. An Amarillo sprinter stepped in front of me.

"Let me by."

"No way, man. That sheet happens."

I didn't take off my spikes. I sat against the far wall with my teammates and watched our top sprinter, Tyrus Blue, clothesline Amarillo's Jesse Marshall in the 200. Fubby and Amarillo coach Dean Hughes restrained their runners. Blue, who was disqualified and ejected from the meet, clenched his fists at Marshall and yelled above the crowd boos and jeers. "Come own, Mo-Fo!"

"This is better than Saturday night wrestlin'," Mitch the Bitch said.

As I walked toward the start of the two-mile, Boyd pulled Tuppernacker aside.

"Enter me in this race, Fubby"

"But you just ran the thousand."

Boyd wiped the sweat off his forehead and panted. "Get me in that fucking race!"

The gun went off, and Boyd sprinted after Butai. He stayed on his heels for three laps. As they turned the corner onto the homestretch, Boyd tripped Butai and pushed him to the green rubber track. Boyd held his fists over Butai. An Amarillo shot putter squeezed Boyd from behind. Butai hopped up, got back into the race, and won in a track record 8:47.6. I finished a half-lap behind in fifth. Mitch and Scrotum both beat me. Butai didn't stop running until he was face to face with Boyd against the back wall of the gymnasium. Athletes from both teams gathered. Spectators leaned over the railing.

"What did you do that for?" the Kenyan asked.

"Because you've been doin' it to us for four years, sumbitch, and I'm fuckin' tired of it."

Fubby stepped between the two runners. "Come on, Boyd, he just wants to make peace."

"I want a piece of him."

Dean Hughes escorted his runner off, and the crowd settled in for the last event. We trailed Amarillo by a point. The mile relay winner would take the Panhandle Pan, which was placed on a table in the middle of the gymnasium. Fubby's relay strategy was to run the fastest man first and the slowest man last. The slowest man was Jack, who finished last in the 600 and then disappeared.

"Where the hell is Walden?" Fubby screamed.

I walked down a hallway and found him peeking through a glass door at an aerobics class. I peeled Jack off the door. "You can't run the mile relay with a boner."

The race started with the crowd chanting, "The Pan stays put! The Pan stays put! The Pan stays put!..."

Athletes in the red and silver of Caprock and the maroon of Amarillo stood on the infield shouting for the runners, who sped around the gymnasium. Jack took the baton with a 30-yard lead, which Amarillo anchorman Jesse Marshall erased the first lap. The crowd noise drowned the gun lap. Jack held off Marshall on the penultimate turn. But Marshall fired his engines and started to go by down the backstretch. Without looking, Jack swung the red baton in his right hand and whacked Marshall in the face. Marshall grabbed his left eye, and Jack sprinted through the finish into the arms of the triumphant Tumbleweeds. The Amarillo competitors hollered and charged at us. Spectators jumped over the rails.

"Oh, shit," Boyd said. "Mitch, grab the van keys."

I grabbed Jack, Scrotum, and the Panhandle Pan and sprinted for the exit. Everyone stopped pushing, shoving, and slugging and chased us.

"Come back here with our pan!" someone yelled.

Mitch drove through the parking lot and slid open the van door. We jumped in and crashed into the lawn chairs as Mitch slammed the gas pedal. I looked out the back window at a cloud of maroon chasing us down the snow-banked streets of Amarillo. But soon we were gone, laughing and drinking all the way back to Lubbock.

The night's only casualty was Mitch, who pulled his hamstring sprinting to the van. Fubby red-shirted Mitch and made him the distance coach. Mitch coached every runner but me. I had a training program sent from Coach Hightower, who wrote me a strong diet of 220's and 330's. Mitch had his runners doing interval 440's, 880's, miles, and 10-mile time trials.

Our weekly snowstorm sent us inside the old airplane hangar, where my legs were deadened on the concrete track. Then I was almost killed by a snowball thrown from an upper floor window of Rutherford Hall. I saw stars and heard a familiar laugh. I rushed to the elevator, down our ninth-floor hallway, and knocked on the door.

"This is the campus police," I said in a deep voice. "Open up right now."

"Get in here, quick," Jack said.

He stood at the window with a trash can full of snowballs he chunked at innocent bystanders. "I just hit a fat, bald guy," Jack said. "I love it when their legs buckle."

Julie came by later that night and announced she had become a little sister at the fraternity Sigma Alpha Phi.

"You joined the Sap-heads?" Jack said. "Those guys are animals. At frat night, they get drunk and beat each other up."

The untrustworthy Jack couldn't trust his girlfriend – even with me. Attacking my speech made me less of a threat. To a repetition of "I-I-I...," he replied, "Who are you Ricky Ricardo? 'I Yi-Yi, Yi-Yi.'" To one of my daily stuttering blocks, he said, "What's that, S.O.S? 'Dee-deet-dit, dee-deet-dit. '"

Jack said, "Jonny won't stop stuttering until he loses his virginity."

Julie slapped him on the leg, "Now don't be mean, Jack."

I returned to speech therapy, where therapists' prescribed me to talk before a speech therapy class. I made students laugh with my 10-minute speech about our track team and our near brawl in Amarillo. One student asked, "What are you in speech therapy for?"

Apparently to humiliate myself. Dr. Roz Rubello made me walk around campus and ask cute girls, "Wh-wh-what t-t-time is it?" Then I spoke to another class and, as ordered, purposely went into a stuttering block and made myself come out of it.

I wanted to snap my fingers and disappear from the students' pity. The exercise succeeded, but not how Dr. Rubello planned. I quit speech therapy. In the middle of holding my throat and choking on a syllable, I decided, "What the heck? If I stutter, I stutter. What's the big deal? People will either accept me for who I am or they won't."

Jack kept an eye on Julie by pledging with the Sap-heads, whose initiation ended in what was called Hell Night. Julie snuck me into the Sigma Alpha Phi house. We peeked from the basement door at the Sap-heads, dressed in black hooded robes, and Jack and the other seven naked pledges. The Sap-heads sprayed Nair on the pledges' chest, pubic, and under-arm hair. They sprayed the pledges off with a hose and splattered them with honey. Each pledge was blindfolded and thrown into a vat of cornflakes they were told was broken glass. The pledges' shrill screams echoed off the basement wall.

"I can't believe this," Julie whispered.

After another wash and rinse, the pledges were divided into two teams for the Oscar Meyer Relay. The naked contestants passed off – or rather, assed off – their weenies and yelled "Hoy!" in the exchange zones. They were then mummified with athletic tape, carried to the back of a pickup, and dropped off 30 miles from Lubbock on a farm road. Jack found his way back to the frat house, where a Sap-head welcomed his bare ass with baseball bat, sawed and shaved into a paddle.

Jack limped into Room 907 about 4 a.m. and fell on his bed. "Ohhh."

I raised my head off my pillow.

"You all right, Jack?"

"You saw it, didn't ya?"

"Yeah. How does it feel to be a Sap-head?

Jack put his hand under his sweatshirt and scratched his hairless chest. "I quit.

"What do ya mean?"

"Julie was so offended by what she saw that she left the Sap-heads and ordered me not to have anything to do with those, as she called them, 'Satanic pranksters. '"

81

"So?"

"So I stuck a weenie up my ass for nothin'!"

My sophomore indoor track season finished with a seventh of the eight finalists in the Southwestern Conference Indoor Mile. Arkansas' Sean O'Malley, a fifth-year senior, won in 4:05.8. O'Malley also anchored his team to victory in the distance medley relay, won the 1,000-yard dash, and overcame a 50-yard deficit on the two-mile relay to overhaul Baylor in the homestretch for his fourth victory of the night.

After all that, the headline in the next morning's *Dallas Star* read, "Jones wins 60."

I timed my own workouts with a hand-held stopwatch to the jeers of Mitch, who told my teammates I was on the "I don't know what the hell I'm doing program."

I finished second to last in the mile final at the Border Relays in Laredo and entered the 5,000-meters at the quad meet at Memorial Stadium. I focused on the little crack under the stadium that night and then on the crack in the shorts of Texas' Bradley Borlan. With two laps left, Borlan and I had broken clear of the pack, and the announcer tried to excite the crowd of 423 in the 80,000 seat stadium.

"Here they come, ladies and gentlemen, around the turn and into the stretch with a lap to go!" The announcer, the same one who called the Border Relays, continued as the gun was fired. "It's going to be a dogfight! Down the backstretch, it's Borlan leading Langenfelder! Now the final turn! Borlan holding off Langenfelder! The final homestretch...."

Boom. My final 100 meters may have placed in the sprint. I put four seconds on Borlan to the announcer's, "It looks like he had a little bit left, ladies and gentlemen."

I returned to Lubbock, where winter snowstorms gave way to spring dust storms. I wore ski goggles on 10-mile campus runs that made me feel like I was pushing a blocking sled and left my face black. I resorted to 40 times 200 meters for track workouts. The wind subsided at the Caprock State Invitational, where Butai put five seconds on me in the last 200 meters of the 1,500 and qualified for the NCAA meet in Eugene, Oregon with his 3:44.7. I was the anchor mile of the distance medley at the Texas Relays, but never got the baton. Jack was elbowed, spiked, tripped, and knocked down in the first 100 meters of lead-off 800 meter leg. He never got up.

We went the next week to the UTEP via Carlsbad Caverns. The walk toward the center of the Earth deadened my legs. "Carlsbad Cave Legs," Mitch called them. I finished 11th in the 1,500 in 3:57.4. Driving to the University of New Mexico the next week, Tyrus Blue lit up a joint and passed it around to his fellow sprinters in their lawn chairs. The passive toking gave me a headache and a 4:02.5 for the 1,500.

My high was the lowest point of the track season. I missed school exams both Fridays and my professors purposely made the make-ups impossible to pass. The highest grade I could make in any class that semester was a C. Then there were the ongoing rumors that Fubby was recruiting a Kenyan to take my scholarship. The only consolation was the letter I received from Holly Ritzenbarger. I had consoled her with a hug and a letter after she finished last in the 400 meter hurdles at the Texas Relays. I ran up nine flights of stairs and ripped the envelope open on my bed. Out fell a four-page letter on LSU stationary.

It began, "Dear Jerry."

"Jerry?" I crumpled the letter and threw in the trash pail.

Jack wasn't doing to well, either. He was flunking out of everything – running, school, and his relationship with Julie. On a women's track trip to Arkansas, the same weekend we went to New Mexico, a half-miler started talking about Jack and the nights he spent with her roommate last year without realizing Julie was in the back seat. Julie told Jack she never wanted to see him again.

"BOHICA," Jack said, as we relaxed in our beds in Room 907 the night before the Pampa Invitational.

"What does BOHICA stand for?"

"Bend Over, Here It Comes Again."

Jack bent over and pulled a box of fireworks from under his bed. "Want to have some fun?"

Jack stuck a bottle rocket in a Coke bottle and aimed it out the window at a campus cop who was writing a student a ticket in the parking lot. Jack lit the fuse and the bottle rocket soared to within a few feet of the cop. I told Jack that wasn't a good idea. He lit three more and came closer each time. Jack then lay on his bed and laughed until we heard a knock on the door.

"This is the campus police. Open up right now."

"That's just Boyd," Jack said. "Come on in."

The door opened, and a campus cop as tall and wide as our door stepped inside.

"Somebody up here's been shootin' bottle rockets, and we think it came from here."

Jack shook his head. "Not us officer. We've been studying."

"On a Friday night?"

I looked down at the officer's right boot. A foot away was the Coke bottle with smoke swirling up from it. The smell of popcorn from next door overpowered the smoke. Jack saw the Coke bottle, gulped, and pointed up. "I heard some racket from up above us, officer."

The officer nodded and closed the door upon his exit. We exhaled. Jack rushed to the door and yelled down the hallway, "If I'd have been shootin' bottle rockets, I'd have hit ya' right in your big fat ass!"

Jack was a better aim the next Monday in the locker room shower, where he splashed me with a bucket full of ice water. Jack dropped the bucket, which was still half full. I grabbed it and chased him into the locker room. Everyone else scattered, leaving a naked runner and fully dressed one to fake and juke. Jack made his move for the exit. I led him perfectly and drenched his new silk shirt.

Fubby had proclaimed my season finished after New Mexico. Mitch heard him refer to me as a "washed up, aged quail that needed to be shot out of the sky." Fubby asked me, "Are you sure you're related to Grimsley Roeper?"

At Pampa, Fubby entered me in the 5,000. "I can't go back to the 5," I told him. "I've been training for the 1,500."

Fubby scratched the back of his scalp. "I just wanted to save you the embarrassment of running against Butai."

Another "Butai beating" were Fubby's words I took with me on my warm up in Pampa. I heard the announcer's voice while I sat in the Port-A-John, "Final call, 1,500 meters."

I ran from the Port-A-John to the starting line with a long piece of toilet paper stuck to my spiked shoe. Fubby had given me the wrong starting time. Butai had his sweats off and was doing his final stride down the black Reslite track. My first stride was the first 100 meters, fast enough to put me on Butai's heels. I followed Butai through laps of 62, 63, 63. Suddenly, I realized, "I'm not tired."

Butai surged on the backstretch, and I covered it. I waited for the final 100 meters and sprinted past in lane three, too wide for Butai to throw an elbow. I grabbed the finish line string in 3:49.8, five yards ahead of Butai. Now I was tired.

Jack and Boyd, who had run the 800, patted me on the back 10 yards beyond the finish line. I put my arms around their shoulders and let them help me walk off the track. I can't believe it," I said. "I finally beat him."

Butai, running his last race in West Texas, met me on the infield with an extended hand. "You are a very good competitor," he said. "I hope to see you in Eugene."

My Hayward hopes went wayward after leading the Southwestern Conference 1,500 finals field through a 61-second first 400. Arkansas' Dirk Redmond strung the eight-man field with a 55 on the second lap of the Memorial Stadium track. I went from first to last within 100 meters and stayed there to watch Rice freshman Trent Granger reel in a faltering Redmond in the final few meters in 3:42.1.

Boyd paid the price for his personal best 3:46.8 for fifth place. When I finished 13 seconds later, Boyd still lay on the finish line. "Langenhooch," he said. "My asshole's been turned inside out."

I helped Boyd up, and he headed home to New Mexico for the summer. Fubby went to the country to hunt quail and out of the country to hunt Kenyans. Jack went to jail. He was charged with attempted assault. One night the week before conference Jack strapped firecrackers on a tape roll, lit it, and flung it from Room 907 into a group of football players sitting in front of Rutherford Hall. They scattered and noticed that our room had the only light on. Jack told the campus cops I did it. But I had an alibi Jack never could use.

I was out running.

Jack was thrown out of Caprock State. I received a letter from him in early June. He apologized for all the crap he gave me, but said it was all in good fun. He said Julie forgave him, and they planned to marry in September. "No need for any more red tacks," he wrote.

Jack gave up running and his dream of becoming a lawyer. He said he wanted to be a plumber. I thought it suited him, since his life, like my running career, was slipping down the drain.

◆ ◆ ◆

13

"Breathe."

The word fell out of Father Arthur Litzke's mouth as easily as the air floated out of my lungs.

I sat with my eyes closed and barely noticed my running sneakers tucked under the chair in Father Litzke's candlelit den. He paused for several seconds, allowing me to listen to my slow, deliberate inhale and exhale. Father Litzke was not a hypnotist, a psychiatrist, or a psychic. He was simply a Zen master trying to save my running career.

"Feel the feeling." Father Litzke spoke even more gently. "Feel your feet on the carpet, your hands resting on your thighs, your back resting against the back of the chair."

He then instructed me to smell the smoke from the candle and listen to his calm voice. "Now again, feel the feeling. How do you feel today? Are you nervous, angry, agitated? These are all unconscious concepts. If you react to them, you are down in an unconscious state. It is like being trapped in a basement with your darkest fears. Feel the feelings and breathe. Rise above to the conscious level, and live."

"The miracle," Father Litzke said, "is to walk on Earth."

After two discontented seasons of college track and field, I needed a miracle to put me back on the path toward the Olympic Games. There seemed no way out of Uncle Grimsley's shadow. I felt like quitting.

Dad turned off *True Grit* to offer his opinion. "You've been going at it for two years, runnin' every day, and look where it's got ya,' pilgrim. You can't run your whole life. You graduate in two years, and then what are you going to do?"

"Hopefully, still run."

Dad turned *True Grit* back on. Mom suggested I sit in church and ask God what I should do. I asked Ka-room. I had told him at the Roachside Motel after my Conference bomb how I got so nervous I couldn't eat before races and how my mind would drift in the middle of them.

"I spend the first two laps talking myself into it. I go back and forth like a tennis ball, 'You can do this. No you can't. Yes you can. No you can't.'"

He suggested Father Litzke, a pastor of a small parish north of Dallas. Ka-room learned of Father Litzke in his yoga class in Lubbock.

"Jonny, he will help you to see."

"See what?"

Ka-room smiled. "You will see."

I saw a little priest in his late 60's with white hair and a pleasant smile. He lived in a small apartment in back of the St. Francis of Assisi Catholic Church. He offered me a piece of home-made bread and a glass of water. I told him about my desire to run in the Olympics.

"The secret," he said, "is not to run to make it to the Olympics. The secret is to run just for the sake of running."

Father Litzke said it is much like washing the dishes. "You don't wash the dishes to get them done. You wash the dishes to wash the dishes.

"When you run, you feel each stride. You feel one foot hitting the ground, then the other and then your arms working in perfect harmony with your legs as you glide around the track. All this, while you are watching your breathing."

"If you can see," he said, "you can act rightly."

Father Litzke told me to take five more breaths and open my eyes. The candle's flame illuminated the grin on Father Litzke's wrinkled face. I smiled back and floated home with his parting words, "Blessed are the single-hearted for they shall see God."

The next day I did not run 10 miles up and down Rolling Hills Parkway to get it done. I ran only for the sake of it, to feel my feet touching the grassy median, my legs bouncing me down the road in perfect cadence with my fluid arm swing and the air that flowed from my lungs. I could see that I needed to quit my $5 an hour summer job driving a fork-lift in the Mason-Edwards Paint warehouse to focus on running. I could see that I needed to leave Coach Hightower's program.

I had learned in the spring of 1978 it wasn't Coach Hightower's program that made me a good runner. It was Coach Hightower. If he was not there to guide me, to motivate me, it didn't matter what program I was on. I explained it to him at his backyard pool that summer. He responded by handing me a beer.

"Beer's good for ya,' pardner," he said. "I couldn't tell ya' that in high school for obvious reasons. But not bad havin' one now and then."

By the look of Coach Hightower's belly and the trash can full of empty silver bullets, he was having more now than then.

"You're a great coach, because you are a great coach," I said to Coach Hightower, who stared at the pool and sipped his silver bullet. "It just doesn't work long distance."

It also didn't work for The Stallion, who left Ozark University at midterm of the spring season. The Stallion was homesick for Dallas and for high school sweetheart Bonnie Benton, whom he married in June. I was a groomsman at The Stallion's wedding. Coach Hightower spent the reception at the bar. The Stallion said our failures stung Coach Hightower, who failed to qualify a team or individual for state for the first time in his coaching career. His private life remained a mystery. The Stallion also gave me the scoop on Holly. Jack guessed wrong. She was not dating the entire LSU football team, only the starting backfield. Still, I worked up the courage to dial the first six digits of her telephone number. Then I hung up.

In July I received a letter from Fubby Tuppernacker confirming that Mitch Hansby would coach the cross country team that fall. I later learned that Mitch the Bitch was in Lubbock plotting against me. He called Boyd Turner and said, "When Langenhooch comes back and says he's doing his own program, I'll tell him to do his own thing, and never show his long, skinny body in the locker room again."

My thought on those long, hot runs along Rolling Hills Parkway was this: "The only time I ever ran well was when I did exactly what the coach told me to do. Mitch is a pretty smart guy. Why not do what he says and see what happens?" This was the higher ground Father Litzke talked about.

A bigger concern was a new roommate. Fubby said he had someone in mind. "He's quiet and very serious about life."

That's what I wanted to hear, but not what I heard as I walked toward Room 907 with my duffel bag slung over my shoulder. A loud voice sang along with the music monotone that blasted down the hallway.

"We are not men, we are Devo. We are not men, we are Devo..."

I opened the door to a purple cloud of incense and a bare-chested punk rocker with a black afro, an earring, paint-stained shorts, worn black tennis sneakers, and no socks. He jumped up and down on his bed and kept playing his air guitar even after he saw me. I looked to make sure this "was" 907 and marched in and hit the off button on his boom box.

"What the hell you doin, man? I was jammin."

"Who are you?"

"I am Jose Rafael Medina, uh, the third."

There was a short pause and the words I feared from the man who left his razor and toothbrush at whatever nut house turned him loose. "I'm your new roommate."

I threw my duffel bag on my bed and ran to Fubby's office. Fubby extended his hand. Mine stayed on my hip.

"I ask for a good roommate, and you give me Funky Joe Medina?"

"Best I could do, Langendelfer. Just be thankful you got your scholarship back"

I looked at his walls to see a few new stuffed faces. "Looks like huntin'season was better here than in Kenya."

I checked with the front desk at Rutherford Hall for a private room. Full. I was stuck with Jose Rafael Medina III. Before I opened my door, I took a deep breath and exhaled. Then I opened it and saw Funky Joe tacking huge Devo posters on his side of the room.

"You want one for your side?"

"No thanks. I've got Prefontaine."

"Prefontaine? Never heard of that group."

Funky Joe helped me unload my VW beetle and move in. Then he opened the refrigerator. "Cervesa?"

"No thanks." I stared at the 18 beer bottles he somehow stuffed into the tiny refrigerator.

He took out a beer, used his desk as a bottle opener, took down half the cervesa on one guzzle, and burped.

"You wanna hear some more Devo?"

"No thanks."

"How 'bout The Talking Heads?"

I shook my head.

"What kind of music do you like?"

I cupped my hand over my mouth. "Barry Manilow."

Funky Joe laughed. "I could have sworn you said Barry Manilow."

We settled on the Beatles, another of Funky Joe's favorites. We went for a run on campus that evening with Boyd and Scrotum, and Funky Joe swerved toward every cute coed and sang "She loves you yeah, yeah, yeah" into their faces.

"Sumbitch is nuts," Boyd whispered to me.

"Yeah, and he's my roommate."

The next day, a Saturday, Mitch marched into the locker room for our first official workout and into my face.

"Ten-mile time trial," he said.

I stared back. "OK."

We filed into the van. Funky Joe arrived just in time and wearing brown cut-off shorts that hung to his knees and looked like they had been eaten by rats. He had on a stolen gray T-Shirt with the guy's name, "Jensen," printed in Marks-A-Lot on the back.

"Who's the fucking freak?" Mitch said.

"My roommate."

I hammered the 10-miler on the flat dirt roads, north of Lubbock, in 53:26. Boyd ran 54:20, Scrotum 54:38, and Ka-room 54:46. Funky Joe arrived with a beer he scarfed from an "amigo" he met along the road in 55:06.

On Monday, Mitch returned to my face. "Twenty times 440's on the track in under 70 seconds with a 220 jog interval."

"OK."

88

Wednesday. "Seven miles of fartlek, up and down the Caprock Country Club fairways."

"OK."

"You have to run through that muddy creek and up that steep hill."

"You mean that creek where I once lost my shoe?"

"That's the one."

"Fine."

On the ensuing Saturday, Mitch thought he came up with the word that could send me back to my solo workout on the Tumbleweed Stadium ramp.

"Wuffalo."

"Wuffalo?"

"Wuffalo."

Wuffalo was our nickname for Buffalo Lake Park, a 6.5-mile road that looped a lake at the bottom of a canyon. The hills that went up and down the canyon were 600 meters long and steeper than a black-diamond ski slope. Any workout on that course was sure to make you "Wuff" your guts.

"OK," I said. "Wuffalo."

My 41:55 eight-miler convinced Mitch I was on his program. I did everything he threw at me. I finished second to Amarillo's new Kenyan, Samson Kibet, in the first three meets and won my first college cross country race, a low-key meet in Lubbock.

I used Father Litzke's meditation technique to keep my life simple and resist temptation and a roommate without a curfew. Blueberry muffins were my only weakness. Darla McGee, the women's track manager, invited me to Sunday brunch at her apartment. Darla said she would whip up another batch of muffins if I asked her to the homecoming football game, causing a stir on the next day's campus run.

"Langenhooch got him a squeeze," Boyd said on an easy run around campus.

"Balled her yet?" Funky Joe yelled from the back of the pack.

Mitch, the pack leader, answered by saying he's got money riding on the fall of Grimsley's statue upon my graduation. He laughed when I told him I wanted to marry a virgin.

"They don't make that model anymore, Langenhooch."

Mitch told us he picked up a girl at a bar that summer and spent the night with her. When he dropped her off at her apartment the next morning, he asked if she wanted to get together later that day.

"No thanks," she said. "I'm getting married this afternoon."

I remained a virgin, proud to uphold the sixth commandment and the third by going to Sunday Mass at the Caprock Campus Catholic Center. I asked Funky Joe if he wanted to go with me to "Father Gino's 30-minute miracle on Broadway."

"Father Gino has a stopwatch in his pocket," I said.

"What makes you think I'm Catholic?"

"You're Mexican."

"Not all Mexicans are Catholic."

I returned from church and the hymn "Holy God we praise thy name" to "Whip it."

Funky Joe, wearing purple glasses he made out of construction paper, stood on his bed and sang to the music.

"Whip it, whip it good...You must whip it...Break your mother's back...Crack that whip."

He jumped to the floor and snapped an imaginary whip. "Crack that fuckin' whip!"

Then he looked at me in my Sunday sport coat, shirt, and slacks and turned down the music. "How was church?"

"Muy bueno," I said.

Funky Joe tore off his purple paper glasses. "What does that mean?"

"You don't know?"

"Just because I'm Mexican, doesn't mean I speak Spanish."

I stared at Funky Joe. "You're not Catholic. You don't speak Spanish. Are you sure you're Mexican?"

Funky Joe leapt like a cat from his bed to mine. I broke his fall with my ribs, and we wrestled each other off the bed. We rolled around amongst the dirty clothes and debris on our lime shag carpet and grunted and laughed until the Resident Assistant's knock broke it up. As I went for the door Funky Joe struck my calf muscle with his patented double-barrel thump, in which he used his thumb to release his well-coiled fore and middle fingers.

I fell on my bed and stared at the welt growing on my calf. "That felt like you hit me with a ruler."

We played thump poker on the 10-hour lawn chair van ride to the Southwestern Conference Cross Country Meet in Fayetteville, Arkansas. Thumps, instead of coins, were the ante. Each hand's winner thumped the loser's palm, sometimes bursting a minor blood vessel. We wanted to thump Fubby for stopping in Oklahoma City to watch the junior college football game coached by one of his hunting buddies. The detour put us in Fayetteville at 11 p.m. I missed Mass, a tour of the course, and my desired eight-hour pre-race sleep.

I used Father Litzke's breathing technique and finished 11th place to lead the team to a sixth-place finish. Fubby, who bet several coaches I would win, said he wasn't taking me to the NCAA Region VI meet.

"How do you expect to qualify for nationals, if you can't finish in the top 10 at conference?"

Mitch answered. "Don't worry about missing the basketball opener, Fubby. I'll take Langenhooch to Austin."

Darla didn't want me to go either. She had concert tickets.

"I'm running regionals that day," I told her during the third quarter of the Tumbleweeds' homecoming football game against Baylor.

"The hell with your running," she said.

We never made it to the fourth quarter. I put my energy into training the next week with a remarkable hill workout on the golf course and took a minute off my eight-mile best at Wuffalo. At the NCAA Region VI Meet I breathed comfortably and freely along the rolling 10,000 meter route in Austin. I was focusing so much, it was 5K before I realized I was in the lead pack of five runners. The other four broke away, and I was passed by another three in the final mile. But that didn't matter. My raised arms at the finish told Mitch that I was going to the NCAA Cross Country Championships in Madison, Wisconsin.

Mitch called the press table at Tumbleweed Coliseum and asked for Fubby, who almost choked on his hotdog. "I knew he could do it."

Fubby had my result called out over the loud speaker at halftime. He did a radio interview, which Mitch and I heard through the static in the lawn chair van on the drive back to Lubbock.

"Jonny Langenfetcher is one of the finest runners I've worked with over the years," Fubby said to the announcer. "I drew up a good program that would peak him for the regional meet."

Fubby's comments almost sent the van into a tailspin. "Fuckin' Fubby," Mitch said.

"Well, he did do one good thing," I said.

"And that would be?"

"Hiring you."

Fubby bought airline tickets to Wisconsin for only himself and me. Before my eight-miler at Wuffalo, I told Mitch I wouldn't go to Madison without him.

"You've worked too hard for this, Langenhooch," he said. "When you came back here, I was convinced you were going to do your own thing. Then you shocked me. You did everything I threw at you. Now you're going to nationals."

"But what about you?"

"Don't worry. I've got a date with a nympho this weekend. Some chick named Darla."

I wasn't sure if I would be doing cross country running or cross country skiing at the Madison Hills Golf Course. Ankle-deep snow covered the course for the NCAA Meet in Wisconsin. For once I could take advice from Fubby, the North Dakota native. But I couldn't find him. That morning he went ice fishing. I took a cab to my first national meet.

I wore three pairs of sweats, two pairs of socks, wool gloves, and a toboggan hat. A Michigan runner interrupted my warm-up, "Hey Texas, this is called snow, sucker!"

I was so cold I had a spectator tie the shoelaces of my spikes on the starting line. I wore a red T-shirt under my red singlet, white painter's gloves, and Vaseline to cover my face, arms, and legs. I looked across the starting line at the 234 other runners in so many different colors from so many colleges. I closed my eyes, made the sign-of-the-cross, and took a deep breath. I opened my eyes to a distant starter, whose pistol blast sent a herd of the world's best runners down a white fairway. It took two miles for my feet to thaw as I crunched the snow with my gold Wooosh spikes. I not only could feel my breath; I could see it. I kept running and passing and re-passing some runners in tights and others in panty hose between a narrow, roped-off lane of scream-ing spectators. My goal of finishing in the top 100 was replaced by the goal of finishing without frostbite.

I could hear Father Litzke as I raced along the course. "Feel the feeling. Feel the snow under your feet, the cold air in your lungs, the strain in your muscles. Run right here. Breathe."

I passed 20 runners in the last mile not for a good placing but a quicker exit from the blizzard. The five-minute wait in the finish chute was brutal. I ran from the end of the chute to Dean Hughes' rental car and put my hands over the heater.

"Where's your coach?" said the University of Amarillo coach, who es-corted Kibet to nationals.

"Back in Lubbock."

"No, I mean Tuppernacker."

"Who cares? Let's get back to the hotel."

Fubby returned to the hotel to see me running up and down the hallway in my sweats.

"Langenfopper?" he said. "You got 48th place, and third runner from the region. That's only nine places from All American."

It took several minutes for the number 48 to melt my cold veins. Finally, I could breathe.

Skooner Gold was the scapegoat for the hiccup in my college track and field career. Skooner Gold congested my head, infected my ear, inflamed my throat, flooded my lungs, soured my stomach, and emptied into my stinging, aching shins.

Boyd Turner iced a case of Skooner Gold in our hotel bathtub before the finals of the 1979 Oklahoma City Indoor Meet. I did not desire a Skooner Gold until our track coach turned a potential triumph into a travesty.

It started after I strained my hamstring in blowing away Samson Kibet in the mile of our annual and surprisingly quiet duel with Amarillo. I told Fubby I was scratching from the two-mile.

"What?" Fubby contorted his face and pointed to the starting line. "Lan-gennacker, you get your ass out there or you ain't goin to Oklahoma City next week."

I jogged the two mile in 11 minutes. Fubby blamed me for having to return the Panhandle Pan to Amarillo and entered me in the two-mile relay at Oklahoma City. I felt sorrier for Scrotum. Fubby promised to take him to Oklahoma City if he broke 9:20 in the two mile in Amarillo. Scrotum ran 9:18. But Scrotum was replaced on the chartered 21-seat, 1942-style bus by team manager, Howie Mercer, who threatened to quit if he didn't go. Fubby told us how much Howie was needed in Oklahoma City. Howie sat on his fat ass all weekend, popping his facial zits.

Fubby pulled Boyd out of the mile, even though he won his morning heat, and scratched Funky Joe from the three-mile to go fresh for the two-mile relay. Levon Wright, a high-hurdler who never had run an 880, led the first 440 in 56.5 and finished with a 76.5 on the second 440. Funky Joe, who chugged his first Skooner Gold before he left the hotel, ran 2:09 and got lapped. Boyd didn't even take the baton. We retreated to the hotel for the Skooner Gold. Mitch the Bitch, our teammate/coach who finished last in the 1,000 meter final, joined us in a Skooner Gold toast.

"To Fubby Tuppernacker," Boyd said. "The worst coach in the history of college track and field."

I passed out on the floor in my Fruit-of-the-Looms after seven Skooner Golds. My drinking buddies carried me into the hallway, laid me in a service elevator, and sent me down to the kitchen. I awoke to some old ladies preparing breakfast. I jumped up, pushed the elevator, and yelled "Boomer Skooner!" as I was lifted back to my floor.

Fubby couldn't sleep, so he decided to leave at 6:30 a.m. in an ice storm. I had two hours sleep and a hangover. Each word from a teammate's mouth seemed to come from a bullhorn and the roller coaster-like ride on the old bus turned my stomach into a washing machine. Then the heater broke. My thin sweats were not enough to keep my teeth from chattering at the end of our 11-hour trip. I awoke Monday morning with a throat so sore I couldn't swallow my Rice Krispies. I showed up for the departure to the Southwestern Conference Indoor Meet in Fort Worth the next Thursday with a smoker's cough, burning lungs, a nose dripping like a tap, a migraine, and a temperature of 102. I recommended that my lawn chair be given to another athlete.

"You'll be all right once you get there," Fubby said.

I was worse. I had an earache, diarrhea, and a nauseous tummy. I stopped my warm up for the first of the five events in which Fubby entered me and called a guy named Earl.

As I screamed "E-a-r-l" into a garbage can along the track, Fubby walked over and said to Mitch, "He'll be all right. He's just a little nervous."

I turned away from the garbage can and threw up on Fubby's black cowboy boots.

"You don't have any guts, Langenhacker."

"You're right. They're in the bottom of this garbage can."

I couldn't run for a week, and Fubby threatened to red-shirt me if I didn't run the opening outdoor meet of the season, at the Northeast New Mexico State Open in Clovis. He entered me in the 3,000 meters steeplechase.

"I can't walk and chew gum at the same time." I glared at a smirking Fubby in his office chair. "How do expect me to jump over a barrier the size of your ego?"

Fubby and several teammates took lawn chairs from the van and sat next to the water pit. It was so cold that ice formed on the edge of the pit. I led, despite landing on top of each barrier and the ground with both feet. The water felt like it had been shipped from Alaska. The third time over the water pit, my right foot smacked into the barrier. I did a belly flop into the Arctic water. I tried to get up, but slipped back to the bottom.

Fubby and the others laughed so hard, they fell out of their lawn chairs.

"Y-Y-You guys shut up." The cold caused me to stutter, not the excitement. I went from first to last on that spill and stayed there.

The cold dip caused a relapse. As we ate in the dining hall the night before leaving for the Border Relays, Funky Joe noticed I was shaking. "F-F-Feels colder in here than it did on that old bus," I said.

"I don't feel cold." Funky Joe wore cut-off jeans and a gray T-shirt with the name "Howell" marked on the back. I wore red cotton sweats. "Maybe you're thinking about the steeplechase."

Funky Joe walked back to room 907 to find his teeth-chattering roommate snuggled under three blankets.

"Tell Fubby I'm not going to Laredo."

By morning, the chills gave way to the aches. It felt like someone was stabbing my shins with an ice pick. I couldn't even walk to the medicine cabinet for aspirin. I could reach for the phone, but everyone was either en route to Laredo or to the Ruidoso Ski Resort.

I crawled to my VW beetle the next day and drove to the emergency room of St. Mary's Hospital, where after three hours of tests and evaluations and $135, a doctor with four years of medical school and 20 years in the field determined I had the flu.

That week Caprock State trainers strapped electrodes to my shins, took them off, and sat me in the whirlpool. I started running by midweek with padded white straps on my shins and ordered to run on even surfaces. Boyd called me "Seattle Slew," and Mitch said I was the new poster child for Jerry Lewis. Fubby called me a red-shirt.

"Cash in yer chips for this year!" Fubby yelled as I jogged nine-minute miles around the track.

"I'll be running at the Quad meet in Austin in two weeks!"

"They don't have a cripples division there!"

I went round and round on that track all week in both directions, often losing count of laps on the hour or so runs, and took the straps off that weekend. I made a deal with Fubby to let me run the 5,000 in Austin. NCAA rules allowed me to run one race and still red-shirt. Fubby said he would cancel my red-shirt orders only if I won.

Fubby really didn't care if I won or not. That winter he had signed Sammy Alcola, a 1:47 half-miler from the Bahamas via Miami Junior College. Sammy looked like a black version of Mr. Potato Head and had a voice lower than The Uncola Man. We simply called him The Franchise.

Fubby figured he could ride The Franchise to national championships and make it look like he was actually doing some coaching. It was a rough ride, though. The first indoor meet, in Lubbock, Fubby entered The Franchise in the sprint medley relay without telling him the legs were 220, 220, 440, 880. After seeing the first two runners go one lap of the eight-lap-to-a-mile track and the third runner go two laps. The Franchise figured he was supposed to anchor with a 440. He ran 47 and raised his arms at the finish line. Fubby ran onto the track and motioned him to go two more laps, which The Franchise staggered on for 90 seconds.

He grabbed his knees at the finish line and then Fubby's collar. "Don't do that shit to me again, man."

The Franchise recovered to win the conference indoor 600 meters and took Fubby to the NCAA Indoor Meet in Detroit. The Franchise had a program from his coach in the Bahamas, but Fubby pressed his stopwatch and called splits anytime a reporter came for an interview. Every newspaper story on our team that spring centered on The Franchise.

As I stared at the little crack under Memorial Stadium in Austin on St. Patrick's Day night 1979, I breathed and visualized a win. The Father Litzke exercises were essential for a runner still recovering from a Skooner Gold hangover.

Mitch took his shot at beating his pupil by running the first mile in 4:35. Texas' Eric Reed, a Canadian with a diamond stuck in his pierced left ear, surged to the lead and broke all but Mitch and me. He and Mitch traded the lead, and I ran in their shadows of the well-lit track. With three laps to go and Reed leading, Mitch flicked my shoulder.

"Take the lead, Langenhooch."

"Nah."

I finally took the lead – at the head of the final homestretch. It wasn't the four-second romp of the previous year. But I ran 14:34.8 and won by 15 meters over Mitch, who held off Reed for second. Fubby was so pleased with the team's second-place finish, he let us have the lawn chair van that night. We started at Brohm's Beer Garden, where green beer was flowing and flooding the concrete floor. The Blob, our 300-pound shot putter/discus thrower, chugged a pitcher with his left hand and poured another pitcher into our glasses with his right.

"Drink up little fellas," The Blob said in a voice suited more for a choir boy. I never had seen so many drunken athletes in one space in my life, and I loved it. The Blob kept pouring. Mitch, Boyd, Scrotum, Funky Joe and I kept drinking. On the drive back to the Roachside Motel, Boyd took a detour to Memorial Stadium. He drove inside the gate and pointed under the stadium.

"I wonder how fast we can go under there?" he said.

"No way?" Mitch said. "You're gonna get us arrested."

"Or killed," I added.

Boyd planted his foot on the accelerator and peeled out under Memorial Stadium like it was a drag strip. I closed my eyes as Mitch yelled, "70 miles per hour!" and opened them as Boyd hit the brakes. We skidded on the front wheels and came to a stop a few inches from the black iron fence at the other end of the stretch. A shot put rolled off the seat and landed on Funky Joe's foot.

Fubby still debated my red-shirt status, especially after Boyd thrashed me in the 1,500 at the Caprock Invitational the next week. The three by 660 workout in 1:21, 1:24, 1:23 with Boyd and Mitch convinced him to enter me in the Texas Relays. Boyd, Mitch and I could all run 1:52 for the 800, and The Franchise was good for 1:46.

"The Franchise is gonna win us a watch," Boyd said to Fubby, as we jogged past on our warm down.

He almost won us two. The Franchise reeled in Iowa State's anchorman down the stretch with a 1:46.3 on the anchor leg of the 4 x 800 meter relay, and led off the next afternoon's distance medley in 1:47.0 in a driving rainstorm. The lead was 40 meters when Boyd handed me the baton for my 1,600 meters anchor leg. I had asked Fubby to holler my splits from the stands. I hauled the first lap in 56 seconds without knowing it. Fubby forgot to start his stopwatch. I kept hammering and looking back to see the hungry running mob behind me. I still had 40 meters as I hit the final turn, where someone placed a baby grand piano on my back. I must have looked back 20 times on the world's longest homestretch. The harder I ran, the farther away the finish line string seemed. Ten meters from the line, three runners went past me.

The crowd moaned as I took three steps past the finish line and collapsed like I had been belted with an uppercut. My face turned colors more quickly than a chameleon. When I awoke, all I saw were fingers. Two fingers from the Texas trainer, who asked me how many there were, the fingers clasped together in prayer from a local priest, and the middle finger from Fubby.

My teammates consoled me. The Franchise told a reporter, "I was pissedoff, man, when he got beat. But when I saw him change to the color of death, I was just glad to have my buddy back."

I didn't say a word all the way back to Lubbock and only a few words until our return to Memorial Stadium for the Southwestern Conference Outdoor Meet five weeks later. I ran my fastest 1,500 of the season of 3:54, five seconds off my personal best and nine seconds off the NCAA Qualifying standard, in finishing third in my heat. As the gun sounded for the last lap of the 1,500 final the next evening, I looked up at the seven other finalists and thought, "I can win this thing."

Rice's stud sophomore Trent Granger led into the backstretch. I went wide, but not wide enough. Milt Molonky of Texas A&M cut me off, and I braked. The leaders sprinted, and I was gone. Granger won in 3:45.1. Boyd was third in 3:45.8. Still, my personal best 3:47.0 for seventh convinced me I could run the 3:45 qualifying standard. Howie the manager knocked on my door at the Roachside Motel that night with a huge white duffel bag.

"I'm not turning in my uniform," I said. "I'm gonna try to get into that Tri-Conference meet here next week, so I can qualify for nationals."

"No way, Langenhooch. Coach Tuppernacker said if you wanted to run anymore meets, you'd have to run in your own stuff."

I called Fubby from 2000 Hickory Lane on Monday and begged him to try to get me into the Tri-Conference Meet in Austin.

"Sorry, Langendropper. They only take two or three from each conference, and there already is Boyd ahead of ya.' So no point in callin."

What he was really saying was, "I've already got my ride to nationals with The Franchise. I don't need any extra baggage."

I drove my VW back to Austin the next Thursday in hopes they would let me in the race. I went to the meet director's office and looked down at his desk. "S-S-Sir, what would I have to do to get into the 1,500 meters tomorrow night.

"I'll tell ya' what," he said. "If you can spell your name correctly, I'll let ya' in the race."

Some of the race entrants didn't even make the conference 1,500 finals, and Fubby couldn't even make a simple telephone call.

I stood on the starting line next to the finest runners in the Southwest in their red, blue, and green college uniforms that Friday night after I meditated under my little crack at Memorial Stadium. I wore faded red workout shorts and a sleeveless white T-shirt cut above my belly. I didn't care if those fancy-dressed runners beat me. I came to Austin to run 3:45.0.

I did all I could to hold the pace of 59, 2:00, set by Kenyan Thomas Mungai of New Mexico. I went through 1,200 meters in 3:00 and sailed down the backstretch, alongside Boyd in his Caprock colors. Boyd looked at me like "What are you doin' here and what are you wearing?" We raced side by side into the homestretch with Boyd inching ahead at the finish. Boyd finished fourth in a school record 3:42.9. I ran 3:43.0. We embraced.

"I can't run any faster than that," I said. "I just sprinted a mile."

I think I was happier for Boyd. He was quitting after this his senior season, marrying his high school sweetheart, and leaving only with the memories of this great night. I intended to have many more great nights ahead.

Fubby saw to it that there was nothing great about our first NCAA Track and Field race. He put The Franchise on a three-hour flight to Champaign, Illinois. Boyd and I took a 23-hour ride with Fubby, his fat wife Mitzie, and loud-mouthed daughter Millie in his brown station wagon. Fubby said he didn't have enough money to fly us up there. We later found out that Fubby had bought us plane tickets with the track budget, got a refund, and used the money to pay for his vacation. Fubby and his family stayed at the Executive Suites Hotel, where The Franchise also stayed. Boyd and I stayed in Nightingale Hall on the University of Illinois campus. The only time we saw Fubby was the night before our 1,500-meter heats, when he came to our dorm room. He had the heat sheets and a look of desperation.

"Langenheeper, you gotta run the race of your life."

I ran the worst race of my life. As 50 yards of green rubber lay between the lead pack and me on the homestretch before the final lap, a girl started to bring the finish line string across.

"Oops," she said, "there's one more guy out there."

I ran 4:01.5 for last in heat one. Boyd ran 4:03.2 for last in heat two. We jogged our warm-down to a strip of bars near the University of Illinois campus. We bombed on the track and got bombed in town. About halfway into our third pitcher, Boyd looked under the table.

"Langenhooch?" he said. "You're still wearing your spikes."

Boyd and I drank until they kicked us out and went to a convenience store, where Boyd bought a six-pack. We zigzagged through the dark campus, drinking beer concealed in brown paper bags, and throwing the empties on the front lawn of the administration building. We walked to the dimmed lights of the stadium, where I swigged a mouthful and looked at the beer label.

Immediately, I spit it on the track and hollered over Boyd's high-pitched laugh. "Ohhh, no! Skooner Gold!"

◆◆◆

The curb where I launched my running career in 1972 is the same curb where I began my drive for the 1980 U.S. Olympic Team.

Exactly one year from that lonely run along Rolling Hills Parkway, I would shock the 20,000 spectators at Hayward Field in Eugene, Oregon and a live television audience at the U.S. Olympic Track and Field Trials with a desperate finishing dive to claim the third and final spot on the U.S. Team to Moscow, Russia.

It was only a dream. But it kept me going for a summer of mile after mile, through grass and weeds that turned my red Wooosh training shoes black, in heat that dried a wet T-shirt within four miles, past motorists who called me a pussy and family members who thought I was wasting my time.

Perhaps my family was right, as I thought on my out-and-back Thursday night 14-miler that covered Rolling Hills Parkway, the Cross Creek Golf Course, and the access road of Highway 72. The turnaround point was the gas pump at the Shell Station. Only 4 ½ years before, Steve Prefontaine remarked how my mile as a high school sophomore was nine seconds faster than his time at that age and that I was going to be a great runner. By age 21, Pre had won five NCAA titles in cross country and track and almost an Olympic medal. Now 21, my best was a minute behind the NCAA Cross Country winner and 20 seconds behind the second-to-last place finisher in my NCAA 1,500 meters *heat*.

But how many titles would Pre have won if his college coach was Fubby Tuppernacker? How well would he have run under an Australian Outback idiot who called us a pack of losers or a running nerd who yelled "iron tummy" every time we went by? I trained along flat farm roads that allowed you to see a mile into the distance. Pre ran along steep mountain trails surrounded by meandering streams and fir trees. Pre's teammates were four-minute milers. Mine were drunks, womanizers, and slackers.

Father Litzke taught me to rise above that, to listen to my breath, to focus on my goal. "Go straight along the path," he said, "and let no one deter you."

I sometimes needed a flashlight to find the path along Rolling Hills Parkway. Running 131 miles per week often required three runs per day and spending the summer of 1979 in a jock. Dad gave me a new nickname that summer – "Miles."

"All you do all day is run," Dad said as I tied my laces in the den for my third Saturday run. "Why don't you get a job?"

"What do you call running 20 miles per day?"

"I don't know. A waste of time?"

Mom didn't mind unless I ran at night. I ran at 9 a.m., 2 p.m., and 8 p.m., except for the night The Stallion took me to a Texas Rangers' game that went 14 innings. I snuck out for a five-miler at 1:30 a.m. The only headlights I saw on Rolling Hills Parkway were from the 1968 Chevy Impala my parents adopted from my ailing and still-reclusive Grandma, who wouldn't even allow a visit to 1721 Lucas Lane from her nearby, Grimsley-wannabe grandson. Mom had awoke to find my bed empty and my Wooosh running shoes gone. She woke Dad. When I reached the finish line curb, I saw Dad on the front lawn in his long plaid pajamas and with his arms folded.

"What in the world do you think you're doing, Miles?"

"Had to get my run in." I put my hands on my hips and stared Dad from his plaid slippers to his frown.

"At this time a night? You don't know what kind of creeps are out there?"

"But the only car I saw-"

"I don't care. We *don't* want you running at this time of night. Period. Understand?"

The more our voices raised, the more neighbors' lights came on. The louder we yelled, the less we looked at each other.

"I have to get my run in no matter what."

"You can skip a run now and then."

"If I skip one run, I'll skip another run, then another run, and then another run. Then where will I be? I'll never make the Olympics."

Tears trickled under my eyelids. "You never understood my running, Dad. You never even tried. All you do is watch television. You'd rather watch John Wayne's horse than me. Why can't you watch *me* run for a change?"

Dad's face, worn from raising six kids and working so many jobs he hated, was illuminated by a porch light. He half-smiled with one side of his face, walked to the front door, and turned around just before turning the knob.

"I did watch you run tonight, Miles. You looked pretty good."

I don't know why Mom and Dad worried so much. Their other sons and daughters went out "drinking" at 2 a.m. Did Dad ever go looking for them? Imagine him walking into a bar in his plaid pajamas? Running 20 miles per day kept me out of the bars. It kept me out of strange girls' beds. It kept me away from my family. I didn't mind eating cold meat loaf and watching Johnny Carson's monologue before collapsing in bed and waking at dawn to do it all again. I figured to be following the Spartan lifestyle of the Great Grimsley, whose ghost I had been chasing for three years.

I rolled my VW beetle out of the 2000 Hickory Lane driveway after a mega-mileage summer that put me back on the Olympic path. I waved, honked, and sped down Rolling Hills Parkway with Dad's faint call sending me toward Lubbock.

"Get after 'em, Miles!"

I made the commitment for my final college cross country season not to date or drink and to devote my life to running. A top-20 finish in the NCAA Cross Country Meet would propel me closer to a start in Moscow.

My first night back in Lubbock I sat and talked to a statue.

"They say you'll tumble when the first virgin graduates, Uncle Grimsley. Looks like you're comin' down, ol' pal. Ohhh, I give up."

Funky Joe returned to Room 907 with a case of beer and his Devo tapes, but with a vow to run and go to class every day. Just coming back was an accomplishment. Caprock State, his fifth college, was the first to welcome him back.

Not back was Mitch the Bitch. He grabbed his diploma like it was a baton and sped to Midland to work for an oil company. Boyd Turner returned with his new bride, the portly, yet sweet Beverly Turner, to finish his physical education degree and serve as the graduate assistant in charge of cross country. Boyd agreed to use the previous season's workouts, which I had documented in my training log.

We had three new runners that season – a farm boy, a Kenyan, and a spoiled brat. When Garrett Toms reported for the first workout, Fubby told him, "Just do whatever these guys do"

Boyd drove us to the dirt roads for a 14-miler. No one knew that Garrett, a state champion 800 meter runner who played cornerback and saddle bronc rider at Bromlee High School, never had run more than two miles. On the drive home, Funky Joe asked, "Where's the farm boy?"

We found Garrett walking down the dirt road like he had been walking through the desert for five days. We drove Garrett back to campus and never saw him again.

Fubby's new find, Kenyan Kip Wonjoie, arrived the next day. He sat at our table in the dining hall and mauled a steak the way a lion finishes off some of his countrymen. The guy could eat corn-on-the-cob through a picket fence.

Bart Harris, our new track manager, pointed to Kip's white bucks carving at the meat. "Those teeth were made for eatin,'" he said.

Wonjoie looked nothing like the starving University of Amarillo Kenyans who ran away from me in cross country. He had short legs and looked like he woofed down a few too many T-bones. He didn't speak a word of English and was nicknamed, "Cheese Omelette" by the breakfast servers in the dining hall. He went through the serving line his first day, wondering how he could tell the servers what he wanted. He decided to say whatever the sleepy-eyed 6-foot-10 basketball player in front of him said. The basketball player muttered, "Chee-amet," and was served a cheese omelette. The server asked Wonjoie what he wanted. Wonjoie smiled and said, "Chee-amet."

"What?"

"Chee-amet."

"Come on, man, I ain't got all day. Speak up."

The server finally figured it out, and Wonjoie ate a cheese omelette every morning.

Wonjoie showed up for his first run at Wuffalo with a pair of red cotton sweatpants, no shirt, and running shoes he had no clue how to tie.

"It's a hundred frickin degrees out here." Boyd motioned to Wonjoie to remove the pants. The Kenyan shook his head.

"All he's got underneath is a jock strap," Funky Joe said.

We finished our eight-miler and waited 15 minutes for Wonjoie, who succumbed to the heat and discarded the sweatpants. All that was left was the jock strap.

"Where's his spear?" Scrotum hollered.

"Imagine," Boyd said, "looking out your lake house window at three-thirty in the afternoon and seeing a naked African running down the road."

After several workouts, Boyd conferred with Fubby over lunch on his talent-less Kenyan. "Where did you get him?" Boyd asked. "Rent-a-Kenyan?"

"I was told he's run 3:46 for the 1,500 and 7:58 for the 3,000." Fubby looked over at Wonjoie, sitting by himself in the corner and beating his hand on a ketchup jar. "The important thing is I got me a Kenyan."

As we walked to the starting line of the Amarillo Invitational, the season's first meet on a late Thursday afternoon, the barefoot Wonjoie uttered his first recognizable English word. "Toilet?"

I pointed to my watch and then to the starting line. "No time for toilet, Kip." Then I whispered in Funky Joe's ear. "I think our Kenyan's a little nervous."

As Amarillo coach Dean Hughes raised the starter's pistol, Wonjoie came up out of his sprinter's crouch and wandered in front of the starting line. He pointed at Hughes as if to say, "Wait a second," pulled down his shorts, and watered the grass.

Wonjoie relieved himself and every runner of his nerves.

"I can't believe this," Funky Joe said. "His dick is even longer than his toenails."

I giggled two miles into the four-mile race along the flat fairways of the University of Amarillo golf course. When Amarillo's Samson Kibet surged from the lead pack, I went with him and stayed on his heels until I surged the final 100 meters, an all-out sprint that whisked me past the Kenyan for my second college cross country victory.

I raised a No. 1 at the finish line and hollered, "U-S-A! U-S-A!" Our only Kenyan finished about the time of my last question from the veteran *Lubbock Ledger* sports columnist Wade Moore. "Where's Wonjoie?"

Wonjoie looked like that knee-bandaged, dead-ass-last Tanzanian marathoner, who finished in the darkness of the Mexico City Olympics. Nearby, I could hear Fubby talking to Hughes, a frequent visitor to Kenyan running tribes.

"Don't know what's the deal with this Wonjoie character. He can't run a lick."

Hughes squinted his eyes toward the struggling Kenyan. "That's not Wonjoie."

"Whaddaya mean?"

"I've seen Kip Wonjoie. And that is definitely not Kip Wonjoie."

Wade Moore overheard the conversation. The headline of Moore's column in the next morning's newspaper read, "Imposter fools coach, but not rivals."

The lead:

> *Kip Wonjoie ran superbly into the glow of a Nairobi sunrise Friday morning about the same time a countryman of the same name lumbered into a fading Amarillo sunset.*

Using Swahili interpreter Kibet, Moore uncovered how the fake Wonjoie forged the real Wonjoie's signature on the NCAA letter of intent and boarded a Texas-bound jet with the passport of his much faster countryman. Asked how he could have been fooled by the Kenyan con man, Fubby said, "No comment."

Fubby steered clear of Moore since the previous spring column entitled, "Where's Fubby?" Moore wrote of Fubby's frequent absence from track workouts and of his dissatisfied track and field athletes. Moore quoted Scrotum, "If there's a drop of rain or if the temperature is less than 50 degrees or if a flock of quail has been spotted within 50 miles of Lubbock, you can guarantee Tuppernacker is nowhere to be found."

Scrotum lost his scholarship with that comment. He protested by not running a step all summer and running backwards across the finish line at the

Amarillo Invitational, not far ahead of Wonjoie. The Blob also got the axe for echoing what everyone else called "The Caprock Handicap."

"You come here as a 52-foot shot putter and under Fubby's guidance you can be sure to be throwing 42 feet by your senior year."

The Blob smashed Fubby's office door with his fist and took a job as a bouncer at Disco Dick's to pay his tuition. The success of the The Franchise, for which Fubby took full credit, saved him from the A.D.'s axe. But he was warned that "laughing stock coaches don't last long at this school."

Opponents only could chuckle at a cross country team whose No. 2 man arrives at meets with a boom box blaring "The best of Devo," whose third man kneels and bows on the starting line, and whose fourth man The Franchise, trains by jogging around campus in the moonlight with blonde coeds.

Then there was fifth man Denny Noonan, whom Fubby recruited from his native North Dakota. Denny wore to class his green high school letter jacket, complete with white track wing patches with such honors as "All District Cross Country" on the sides and track medals on the front. He brought more board games than books to college and made up teams with players on his "All Star Baseball Game," held a tournament with himself, and kept statistics. I felt sorry for Denny and offered to play with him. He drank chocolate milk and ate Oreos as he rolled the dice. Every time Denny rolled a home run, he shook his fist at the ceiling and yelled, "Baby! Baby! Baby!"

Denny slammed the game on the carpet and stomped on it after my game-winning grand slam in the bottom of the ninth. I never was invited back to this dorm room with posters of Tom Seaver and Carl Yastrzemski on one side and with posters of Cheryls Tiegs and Ladd on the other.

"The guy's a fuckin' boy scout," said Bart, Denny's roommate. "The only time he leaves the room is to do his laundry or take a shit. How can I screw a bitch in here with a guy playin' with himself and yellin,' 'Baby! Baby! Baby!'"

I put my effort into trying to win cross country races and passing the toughest journalism class at Caprock State. I had avoided Dr. Hugh Werrimer, the professor every journalism student called "The Werminator" for three years. But I needed Editing 303 to graduate in the spring, and The Werminator was the only one who taught it. That's a tough task considering The Werminator hated two things - athletes and sportswriters. Tougher considering the first words The Werminator spoke to our class. "Last semester I gave out one B, eight C's, 3 D's, and 5 F's – and that was the best editing class I ever had."

The Werminator looked more like a worm than a terminator. He was 5-7, as bony as a skeleton, and had gray hair and a long gray beard. He spoke more like someone who would grease an axle than conjugate a verb. The Werminator hadn't given an A in three years. I was praying only for a D. He crushed us with writing assignments he returned with red marks and lines all over the paper. He spent an hour pelting us with questions from the textbook and screamed if we couldn't answer it.

He was the best teacher I ever had.

I got more nervous before an editing test than a race. Samson Kibet was a cinch after a week with The Werminator. I even became a front-runner that fall and won two more races as we headed to the Southwestern Conference Meet on the hilliest golf course in Houston.

I paid my airfare to Houston, instead of riding for 12 hours in lawn chairs. I led this race, too, but not to copy Pre. I just felt more comfortable leading. The tactic eliminated all but five of my rivals, including defending champion Hamish Nalley of Arkansas. The three Razorbacks attacked first and dropped me to fifth by four miles. But I fought back and passed all three and Rice miler Trent Granger on the final steep ascent. I was catching Granger's teammate, fifth-year senior Matty Rittenbacker, up the homestretch and lost by four seconds. I exchanged a high-five with Boyd, who coached Caprock to its best conference finish in 30 years. I was followed by Funky Joe in 19th, Ka-room in 21st, Denny Noonan in 32nd, and Scrotum in 35th. The Franchise finished 47th. Wonjoie – we still called him that, because Fubby forgot his real name when he sorted things out with the INS and NCAA – even beat a TCU runner. Fubby congratulated us on our fifth-place finish and announced the end of the season for everyone but me and him, before driving off for a hunting trip.

Boyd was so pissed he drove from Houston to Lubbock in nine hours with one-hand on the wheel and the other on a Budweiser. Boyd spoke his only sentence somewhere between Austin and Abilene. "That sumbitch. I don't take any credit for this season, so why the hell should he?"

"Fubby's just trying to keep his job," I said. "He sees I can become the first cross country All-American in school history and he wants the A.D. to think he actually had more to do with it than booking a motel room at nationals."

Fubby booked the room in Bethlehem, Pennsylvania after my fifth-place showing at the NCAA Region VI meet in Austin. He also booked a flight to New York, instead of Philadelphia, taking advantage of the free travel to see the Statue of Liberty, the Empire State Building, Wall Street, Times Square, and Uncle Elroy. Fubby's 68-year-old uncle never married, never cleaned his apartment, and seemingly never washed the dishes. We stayed at Elroy's rat-infested apartment in Queens two nights before my attempt at history. My bed was a lumpy sofa that stunk like dirty underwear. After three hours of tossing and turning and holding my nose, I lifted the cover off the sofa and found a pair of Elroy's dirty underwear.

We arrived in Bethlehem the next day too late to run the course, because Fubby preferred driving the New York City Marathon course and then got lost in New Jersey. He borrowed $20 from me to pay one of the 15 tolls on the route and kept saying, "Langentrotter, tomorrow you're gonna be the little star of Bethlehem."

Upon arrival at the meet hotel Fubby pointed to a sale of meet T-shirts. "Langencrocker, I'll buy you a T-shirt."

Fubby paid the girl and handed me the shirt. "Now I only owe you 10 dollars," he said.

The next morning I didn't care that I spent four hours trying to get to sleep amidst Fubby's snoring. I didn't care that Pennsylvania in November was hotter than Texas in September. I didn't care that Fubby woke me up with, "Good morning, little star of Bethlehem". I went to the rolling course along Lehigh University to make the top 20, All America, and a name for myself.

The gun was fired and 246 runners shot down the field like we were being chased by the Pamplona bulls. I hit the first mile in about 40th place and to a split timer's shout of "4:21."

"Felt like a sprint," I thought. "Keep running hard, watch your breathing and these guys will start coming back."

Instead, they started passing me. I was in 60th through an 8:53 two mile and kept falling back into the sea of no-names.

The only good thing about finishing 165th is that Fubby couldn't take anymore credit for my success. All he said on the flight back to Lubbock was, "Can I have your peanuts?"

After Thanksgiving, I had a bigger challenge in trying to pass editing. I never wore my Caprock letter jacket to class and made sure my by-line never appeared in the *Daily Tumbleweed*. The Werminator's final was a marathon of writing, editing, essays, and multiple-guess questions. It was harder than the NCAA Cross Country Meet. I only could wait to see if I guessed right enough to graduate in the spring or spend another breathless semester with The Werminator.

My sobriety ended the night before I left for Christmas vacation. We threw a farewell party for Boyd, who was leaving the next day for a teaching job in East Texas. I also celebrated the proudest "C" of my academic career. Somewhere amidst the beer chugging and the Tequila shooting, Boyd created "Fubby's Theme Song" to the tune of Pink Floyd's "We don't need no education." Boyd's version went:

> *We don't need no shitty track coach.*
> *We don't need no workout bingo.*
> *No zones or presses in the track room.*
> *Hey, Fubby, go coach ping pong!*
> *All in all, you're just A 'nother prick with no balls.*

We sang in unison throughout the party and on our drive to a 24-hour convenience store for toilet paper and white shoe polish. Boyd, Funky Joe, Bart, Scrotum, and I filed out of Boyd's four-seat blue Datsun onto the snow of Fubby's front lawn. Within 10 minutes, Fubby's yard was full of Charmin and his station wagon was covered in Boyd and Funky Joe's shoe polish graffiti, "Flush twice for Coach? Tuppernacker," and "Hey Fubby, Saskawany State is hiring."

The telephone rang in room 907 at dawn the next morning. Funky Joe answered before the second ring.

"Hello."

"Hi, Fubby. How are you this mornin'?"

The groggy-voiced Funky Joe answered every question straightforward, as if he forgot the events that led to the demolition of Fubby's front yard.

"Last night? We had a blast. We threw a farewell party for Boyd. Drank some beer, danced, sang songs. It was a great time. Sure wish you could have been there."

Funky Joe's answers must have confused Fubby and left him only to wish him a Merry Christmas.

Funky Joe said, "Feliz Navidad to you too," hung up the telephone, and snuck back under the covers. I looked at Funky Joe, winked, and went back to sleep.

16

That wasn't Devo blasting down the ninth floor hallway of Rutherford Hall that winter afternoon of 1980. It was the slow, melodious voice of Neil Diamond.

> *Holly holy, dream*
> *Dream of only you*
> *And she comes –*
> *And I run, just like the wind will*
> *Holly holy*

That wasn't Funky Joe lying on his bed in Room 907 and singing with the music from his clock radio. It was Funky Joe's roommate.

I kept singing the "Holly Holys" after Funky Joe walked in, sat on his bed, and opened his mouth wide enough to stuff a taco.

"I like this song," he said.

This from a man who likes songs about whips, chains, and snakes.

"You do?"

"It's a great song." Funky Joe stood and changed face when Neil Diamond sang another Holly Holy. "About 10 fuckin' years ago!"

That remark and my hyenia laugh also carried down the hallway, drowning Neil Diamond. After the final Holly Holy, I said, "O.K., man, then let's hear some real music."

Funky Joe, sporting a taller Afro and a fuller Fu Man Chu, stuck a tape in his boom box. The chorus went, "Gonna raise hell, gonna raise hell, gonna raise hel-l-l!"

Funky Joe cranked the volume. When the chorus came again, we sang along to the top of our lungs. On the final "gonna raise hell" we picked up our Wooosh running shoes and fired them into the Venetian blinds. After the third crash and chorus, a door knock over-powered the hard rock. Funky Joe turned the volume down as I opened it to Resident Assistant Rory Arnsperger, who leaned against our door well.

"Would you like to come in?" I picked at my peach fuzz and shoulder-length hair, which hadn't been washed in three days.

Rory looked at our dirty underwear, *Track and Field News*, Coors Light cans, chicken bones, and *Playboy* magazines scattered amongst our floor debris. He whiffed at an odor combined of dirty socks and stale beer.

"No."

"I guess you want us to keep it down a little."

Rory half-grinned and retreated down the hallway.

"Is he gone?" Funky Joe asked, sitting on his bed mouthing the chords.

"Yeah."

"Then crank that shit back up."

I didn't lose my mind along the street lamp-lit Rolling Hills Parkway as the clock struck a new decade. I had just had it with Fubby, with school, with the pressure of living up to my great Uncle Grimsley, with running the soles off my feet for the sole purpose of reaching a goal that seemed unreachable.

Funky Joe and I sat on our beds that first night back in January 1980, sipping Silver Bullets.

"I gave up drinking and dating for what?" I said. "To get 165th in the NCAA Cross Country Meet?"

"You're right, Langenhooch. We need to get you laid."

Was sex the answer? I pondered that on a campus bus ride to the first class of the last semester of my life. I stared at the honey-blondes and the long-legged brunettes and the sun that glistened off their wet lips and soft cheeks. Was I so wrapped up in a Holly fantasy, an Olympic pursuit, and church law that condemned pre-marital mattress polo to not notice these beautiful women my eyes were undressing before me? Would a warm woman in a cold dormitory bed really cure my stuttering? Or would she dry up all my dreams?

"I will have no chance of knowing," I thought, "if I don't at least ask one out."

First, I had to tend to business. Mitch the Bitch returned from a dry and washed up oil business in Midland to tackle the M.B.A. program at Caprock State. Fubby reinstated him as the distance coach. I was elated until I found that Mitch spent the fall reading Darcy Ellard's new book, *Run like a Cheetah*. He had switched from Lydiard to Ellard. From January 13th until March 29, I ran 11 straight weeks of more than 120 miles per week. The appetizer was a freezing five miler at dawn, the entrée a track workout in the afternoon, and for dessert a three-miler around campus at bedtime. The eleventh week, the first week of spring, was typical. The scribble in my log book did not include the 3-mile warm-up and warm-down.

Sunday: 17 miles
Monday: a.m. 5 miles; p.m. 8:48 two mile and 12 x 440's in 62.5
with 1 ½ minutes interval; nightcap – 3
Tuesday: a.m. 5 miles; p.m. 52:40 10-miler on the dirt roads, night-
cap – 3
Wednesday: a.m. 5, p.m. easy 10 on campus
Thursday: a.m. 5, p.m. 8 x 880's in 2:12 with a 3-minute interval,
nightcap – 3
Friday, easy 10 on campus, 12 x 100-meter strides.
Saturday, Tumbleweed Invitational, first in 1,500 (3:59.5), first in
5,000 meters (14:18.2, meet record) – wind 35-40 mph, dusty. Later
– 5.

First places had been hard to come by during the winter of 1980 after winning the mile and two mile in the indoor duel with Amarillo. I won the mile at the Oklahoma City Indoor, but was disqualified. The announcement echoed off the coliseum roof and sent me into Fubby's face in the stands. "The guy tried to push me onto the infield concrete. If I didn't elbow him, I would have been off the track. Aren't you gonna protest?"

"Nah."

Funky Joe, Mitch, Bart, and I protested by drinking a case of Lite beer, putting the empty cans in a large brown paper bag, and leaning it on Fubby's hotel door. The next week we got drunk en route to the Southwestern Conference Indoor Meet. I lay on my bed at the old downtown Fort Worth Statler Hotel and noted the political correctness in our new Tumbleweed Track and Field Media Guide to Mitch and Bart, who watched a Tumbleweed basketball game on television.

"We have 26 guys on the team, 13 blacks and 13 whites."

Funky Joe, passed out on the next bed, came to life. "What did you say?"

"Oh, sorry, 13 blacks, 12 whites, and one Mexican."

Funky Joe sprang from his bed, landed on top of me, and did a vampire on my neck. I screamed over Mitch and Bart's laughs. Fubby charged into the room to see Funky Joe and me wrestling on the bed.

"What's going on here?"

"He bit me! He bit me!" I yelled.

Funky Joe took his fangs out of my neck, looked up at Fubby, and slowly spoke every word.

"He called me *white*."

Fubby scratched his head. "You guys just stay in your rooms, and keep it down."

As soon as the door slammed we walked next door to a bar next to a law office, where an attorney was batting a typewriter through midnight. He was still there when we exited the bar. Mitch tapped on the glass, pulled down his Wranglers, and planted his cold flesh, leaving frosty cheek marks on the glass. We ran back to the hotel, where our howls were met by Fubby and his purple silk pajamas in the hallway.

"I told you guys to keep it quiet." Fubby's whisper was loud enough for curious teammates to crack open their doors. "If you don't shut up, I'll send your asses back to Lubbock."

Mitch slid off his trousers and pointed to his behind. "You mean this ass?"

I finished second the next night in the mile final to the lightning finisher Trent Granger of Rice and ran 133 miles the next week, despite frequent interruptions. Fubby asked me to help move the pole vault pit midway through my 12 times 660's workouts and the next day tried to tell me a joke as I gasped on my 10 times 440's with a one-minute rest workout that nearly required an oxygen mask. Fubby became such a nuisance we considered moving workouts to the evening. We liked it better when he *didn't* show up for training.

There also was no relief from a roommate who apparently gave up shaving, cleaning, bathing, and studying for lent and pinned a race number to the back of his robe. Something stunk in Room 907 for weeks, and it wasn't just Funky Joe's feet. Dusting behind the television set one Sunday afternoon, I found a bowl of moldy potato salad with green hairs growing out of it.

I held my nose as Funky Joe chunked it out the window and said, "When we leave this dorm room, they'll give it over to the biology department to check for specimens."

I took a shower after our 12-mile run and dropped the towel to answer the telephone. Funky Joe had warned me several times to stop walking around nude. After I said hello to Mitch, Funky Joe snapped me with a double barrel thump that dropped me to my knees. "Ugggh!"

"You all right, Langenhooch," Mitch said.

"No. Funky Joe just thumped me on the head."

"Is there a welt on your forehead?

"That's not the head I was talking about."

I woke up the next morning to Funky Joe lying face down on his pillow. His arms were stretched over the bed, and his Afro was covered with grass. I didn't know what time he had come in. He lay in the same position when I returned from my morning run.

"Funky Joe, you better get up."

I took a shower, and my roommate still hadn't moved. He made a noise and turned his head the other way. I shook him, and he barely moved.

"Funky Joe, you better wake up or you're gonna flunk out of school."

He turned his head around, shook some grass out of his Afro, and pried open his eyelids.

"I'm not gonna flunk out of school, D-U-D-E!"

Funky Joe showed up for workout with a cigarette and blew smoke in Fubby's face. He showed up for our departure to the Border Relays in Laredo in a three-piece suit, black high-top sneakers, and no socks. He sat down in his van lawn chair and started his watch.

"What are you timing? Bart asked.

"How long I can go without takin' a piss."

Funky Joe held off until Cattleman's Family Style Steak House in some remote hole-in-the-wall only Fubby could find. The Tumbleweeds' head coach couldn't coach, but he sure knew where to eat. At Cattleman's, we stuffed our guts with all-you-can-eat sirloins and T-bones. The Blob put three steaks on his plate and hid two on a plate under the table. Wonjoie carved into his steak with his buck teeth and came up for air only long enough to yell, "More meat, more meat!"

"It's up my ass!" Bart hollered. "You want it now!"

Wonjoie learned enough English to tell us about his girlfriends. He sat in his lawn chair van as Mitch drove toward sunset.

"I have a chain of women," he said. "We like to do all the different styles."

"You mean positions," Mitch said from the driver's seat.

Bart stared toward the Kenyan, spit a wad of tobacco into a cup, and spoke a language only Texans could understand. "What kinda bitch would suck Wonjoie's dick?"

Mitch muttered to himself without taking his eyes off the road. "The Kenyan's more full of shit than Thanksgiving turkey."

Bart then looked to Funky Joe. "How ya' doin' over there, hoss?"

"Six hours, 42 minutes," Funky Joe said.

"You haven't taken a piss in "six hours 42 minutes?"

"Si, senor."

Bart shook his head. "I think we need to order some beers, Mitch."

Mitch pulled alongside our other van, looked at the front passenger seat, and pretended to drink an invisible beer. Reefer Jones, a hurdler who was driving the other van while smoking his nickname, and Mitch pressed their accelerators until their speedometers hit triple digits. Fubby, who trailed in his station wagon, was no longer in sight. The drivers did not want Fubby to see the two vans pull to within an arm's length, and the passengers of Reefer's van passing two six packs to Mitch, who somehow managed to keep the lawn chair van on the road.

Funky Joe chugged a Silver Bullet, a tactical error for a man trying to set a record.

"Mitch, you gotta pull over."

"Why?"

"Cause I wanna set a new kind of record."

"What's that?"

"A record for world's longest-timed piss."

"Fuck no, I ain't pullin' over. If I wasn't willin' to stop for beer, why the hell would I stop to watch you take a piss?"

Funky Joe kept pleading. Mitch kept refusing.

I offered Funky Joe my empty can.

"I'm gonna need a lot more than that," he said.

The Blob manuevered out of the front passenger seat and escorted Funky Joe to the back door. Funky Joe undid his zipper. The Blob opened the back-door. The wind blew over the vacant lawn chair and the dandruff out of Funky Joe's afro. The Blob held Funky Joe by the back of his belt as he sprayed the highway.

"I wrote 'Fuck you, Mitch' in yellow on the road," Funky Joe yelled.

"And it's in Wonjoie's handwriting," Bart said.

Funky Joe kept drinking and pissing until the start of the next day's 5,000 meters in Laredo. I crouched at the start in my typical butt up pose and looked down the line at Funky Joe in a running back's stance. Funky Joe lasted about two laps before collapsing in lane six on the cinder track.

I led into a 30-mph wind that kicked dirt and chalk and hot dog wrappers into my face. I broke everyone but two real Mexicans, who also were real runners. Armando Chavez and his Mexico City teammate Ricardo Gamez spoke Spanish to each other, probably something about kicking the skinny Gringo's ass. With three laps to go, Chavez and Gamez went by me and waved to spectators, who waved Mexican flags. A Mexican band played and someone outside the stadium was roasting a pig. Gamez had 20 meters on me, and Chavez had 50 at the start of the gun lap. It stayed that way until the 200 mark, where Mitch and Bart stood with angry looks.

Mitch's call of "Run, you son of a bitch!" was echoed by Bart and sent me around the final turn like I was shot out of a cannon.

I flew past Gamez and gained on Chavez, who looked back, and sprinted with the strong tailwind into the homestretch. The announcer did play-by-play in Spanish, "Chavez y Langenfelder, Chavez y Langenfelder, Chavez y Langenfelder."

I passed Chavez in the last five meters and was met by a meet official who did not understand the announcer's call or a puffing athlete's inability to talk five seconds after a race.

"Name por favor."

"Langenfelder," I said between breathes.

"Como?"

"Langenfelder."

"Como?"

I took a deep breath and yelled, "Langenfelder, you idiot! Do I look like Chavez?"

The race launched a string of seven straight wins, including four within seven days over NCAA Cross Country "All American" James Motua of Kenya and now at Oklahoma State. I outkicked him in the 1,500 and 5,000 at TCU and in the mile at SMU. In the SMU three mile I led Motua by 20 meters as I approached the final backstretch. Mitch sat in the stands with his arms folded.

"Any time, Langenhooch, any time," he hollered.

No way Motua dare pass me. After the meet, I pulled alongside Motua as we walked into the parking lot and smiled. He squinted his eyes like he didn't know who I was. I walked ahead and patted my butt. "Now do you recognize me?"

I was so confident after my perfect March that I asked out Kirsten Peters, the roommate of Mitch's girlfriend. We double-dated the day after the SMU meet and laughed through dinner and danced until Disco Dick's bouncer, The Blob, tossed us out. The short brunette had the credentials to replace Holly as my dream girl, and the lip-lock we exchanged on her dormitory doorstep indicated that Grimsley's statue might survive after all.

Back in Room 907, Funky Joe was planning strategy.

"Don't call her for three nights."

"Why not?"

"You gotta make her think you don't want her."

"But I do want her. Why can't I just call her up and be honest – tell 'er that I had a great time and wanna see her again?"

Funky Joe laughed. "Man, you got a lot to learn about women."

I waited until Tuesday night, and the conversation from my end went like this:

"Hi, it's Jonny."

"Langenfelder."

"The guy you went out with Sunday."

"The tall, skinny guy with the slight stammer."

I asked if she wanted to go for ice cream.

"I have to wash my hair," she said.

"How 'bout tomorrow night?"

"I have to let it dry."

I kept pursuing Kirsten, though she didn't come watch my double victory at the Tumbleweed Invitational and ducked my telephone calls. Finally, she answered. I asked her to accompany me to the Tumbleweed Athletics Banquet. She said no before I even finished the sentence.

"Then let me just ask ya' straight, Kirsten. Do you have a boyfriend or do you simply hate my guts?"

"I don't have a boyfriend."

The crushing blow sent me walking to the Grimsley statue, where I often went in times of distress. I sat there for two hours that night. My workouts sucked that week, which worried Mitch on our ride to Austin for the Texas Relays.

"Women weaken legs." Mitch borrowed that line from Rocky Balboa's trainer as he looked over from his lawn chair.

I stared at my reflection on the side window. "I'm just a tall, skinny geek with zits and no other interest other than running. What girl would ever want a guy with a picture of Steve Prefontaine on his wall?"

"A girl who's after a winner, not a whiner," Mitch said. "Here you've won seven races in a row and got a shot tomorrow night at qualifying for the

NCAA and the Olympic Trials, and you're gonna blow it because of some little bitch."

I looked nothing like Pre – I couldn't even grow sideburns or a mustache – but I ran like him the first four laps of the Texas Relays. The more I thought of Kirsten Peters, the harder I pressed the pace. I led through the mile of the 5,000 in 4:25, and then watched all 15 competitors go by in one lap. I summoned all of Father's Litzke's breathing techniques. But it was Mitch's and Bart's call from the backstretch stands that resuscitated me. "Kirsten Peters! Kirsten Peters!"

The name propelled me past my competitors like an angry bull. They yelled louder each lap, "Kirsten Peters!" until I worked myself into fifth place and crossed the finish line in an NCAA qualifying time of 13:51.4. I just missed the Olympic Trials 5,000 meters qualifying time of 13:50 and expressed my intention of making that standard at the Penn Relays on the return drive to Lubbock.

"Penn?" Fubby turned his head from the steering wheel and stared at me in the lawn chair. "We ain't goin' there. That's not in the budget. Go for it next week at Howard Payne."

"Howard Payne? Fubby, I am running '5,000' meters, not '500' meters. I need people to run with and cool weather. I won't get that at Howard Payne. And could you please put your eyes back on the road."

I was convinced Fubby put Howard Payne on the schedule, only because of the great barbecue restaurant in Brownwood. He entered my hotel room at the crack of noon in the next week with barbecue sauce on his chin and opened the blinds to a day that offered sunshine and a temperature of 95. "It's a great day to get that Olympic Trials qualifier," he said.

I switched to the mile for a personal best of 4:05.9. Fubby surprised me at my locker the next Monday with airline tickets for me, him, and The Franchise to the Penn Relays. The school was paying for he and The Franchise, and an anonymous donor in Dallas was paying for mine.

"Coach Hightower." I thought. "He must have gotten my letter."

The gift gave me a final shot at the 1980 Olympics. The Trials, in Eugene, Oregon, were seven weeks away, and chances of qualifying in the heat of Waco at the Southwestern Conference or Austin at NCAA were against me. This was my last chance to finally run in Pre's footsteps at Hayward Field. Once I was on that starting line, I would have as good a chance as any other runner to see the Olympic flame soaring into the Moscow sky.

My coach seat assignment allowed me to avoid Fubby, who sat in first class with The Franchise. He booked a room at the Executive Suites in Philadelphia. I stayed in a dorm attached to the old wooden bleachers of Franklin Field. The separation helped me stay positive and focus on a silver rail that lined the green rubber track on a cool, calm Thursday evening. I went to the lead from the gun and towed the 32-man field of college runners through laps of 65 and 2:11. Adam Larkin of Michigan State took over and maintained the pace. By the mile in 4:23 Larkin, Wake Forest's Bret Cox and I had broken from the pack. Larkin and Cox traded the lead through an 8:51 two mile.

I never had been out that fast before and never felt so strong. I wanted to shout, "I'm goin' to Eugene!"

Larkin sprinted past Cox just after the gun for the final lap sounded, and I chased him down the backstretch. I couldn't catch the feisty little runner and missed out on a Penn Relays watch by two seconds. As I jogged a cool-down around the track, I focused on the large, dark scoreboard. I kept my eyes there as I put on my red sweats and sat on the infield. Holly could have walked naked in front of me without a blink. Finally, the scoreboard lit up with the 5,000 meter results and my face with the numbers I worked so hard for.

"2...Langenfel...13:44.1."

◆ ◆ ◆

The story in *The Philadelphia Leader* the morning after my Olympic Trials qualifier told of the renewal of an old rivalry between Michigan State's Adam Larkin and Wake Forest's Bret Cox.

It told how Larkin and Cox battled each other in high school and waited three years to meet again at the Penn Relays. It told how they exchanged leads in the 5,000 meters and dueled into the late stages without a mention of the Caprock State runner also vying for a Penn Relays watch. The story even said Larkin finished first, and Cox was second.

I was so upset I spilled my orange juice on the sports section. When I glanced at the headline on the front page of the newspaper, I almost spewed my pancakes:

"Carter calls for Olympic boycott."

Eight years of running up and down hills and around and around a track for the privilege of having a peanut farmer-turned-president pull the plug on my Olympic dream. I sat staring at the newspaper and wondering how pulling out of the Olympics would somehow make the Soviet Union pull out of Afghanistan. I shook my head until Fubby, sitting next to me at Balboa's Pancake House, shook my arm.

"Hey, Langenflupper, could you pass the comics?"

My return to Lubbock went through New York. Fubby rewarded The Franchise for his 800 meters victory with a Saturday night tour through a dark city street lined with hookers, dope pushers and dealers, illegal immigrants, drunks, and hobos. Every 30 yards someone walked by and whispered, "Loose joints?"

I looked at a clock atop Times Square that read, "3:20 a.m." and thought, "I've walked 10 miles through dried up vomit and piss and haven't been stabbed once. Amazing."

Fubby reasoned that it was all right to pull an all-nighter, because "it's daylight savings time and we're gonna lose an hour of sleep anyway."

The only sleep I had on the dawn flight back to Texas was in my non-reclining coach seat between a Sumo wrestler and a woman who was nine months pregnant. I collapsed upon arrival to Room 907. My alarm at 7 p.m. was the telephone.

"Langenhooch?"

"Yeah."

"Get your butt out of bed and meet me on the track in 30 minutes."

Thirty-five minutes later I was rounding a track lit only by the headlights of Mitch's silver corvette parked at the head of the homestretch. When I finished the five-mile time trial, Mitch's watch read 23:41. I went back to bed and returned Monday afternoon for my eight times 880-yard interval workout in perfect conditions. Mitch said he wanted them all under 2:10. I ran the first one in 2:18, the second in 2:21 and the third in 2:29. Mitch pointed me off the track after I came through the first 400 of the fourth one in 80.

"I think you're a little flat there, Langenhooch."

I returned to the dorm and crashed onto my mattress. What was the point, I told Funky Joe, of training for the Olympics if there wasn't going to be an Olympics.

"You need some good pussy," he said. "Let's hook you up with one of Wonjoie's whores."

Mitch drove me the next day to Wuffalo, where he opened the door of his silver Corvette two miles into an eight-mile time trial."

"Get in," Mitch said. "Eleven minutes ain't gonna cut it."

Mitch gave me a week off. I resumed training with a 15-miler on Sunday and 20 times 440's in a 65 average on Monday. Mitch took his copy of Darcy's Ellard's *Run Like a Cheetah* to Austin, where I won the 1,500 in 3:54.7. Mitch must have just read the chapter entitled, "Run them until they drop."

"You didn't run hard enough," he said.

"I won."

"You didn't run hard enough."

After the mile relay and the unplugging of the Memorial Stadium lights, Mitch had me run 12 times 400's. En route to Waco for the Southwestern Conference Meet, Mitch pulled the van to the side of a two-lane highway and made Funky Joe and I do a five-mile morning run in a thunderstorm. The storm followed us to Waco and into a track workout. By the fifth 600, the track was flooded. Mitch had me run the final three 600's in a mall parking lot late that night. I led the conference 5,000 field two nights later through a 66 first lap and then faded to third in 14:23.

"What's wrong with me?" I asked Mitch. "I run 13:44 at Penn, and now I lose conference to some Aggie I never heard of who runs 14:09."

Mitch mentioned nothing of the 98-degree heat, the 11 weeks of triple digit mileage, or the weekend meet doubles. Evidently, Darcy Ellard did not cover this scenario in his popular book. Funky Joe's solution was simple.

"Let's get drunk."

Mitch, The Blob, Bart Harris, Reefer Jones, Funky Joe, and I piled into the lawn chair van. We used up the rest of our per diem money to each buy a $1.99 a six-pack of Stony Lager beer and found a Baylor party. The Waco runners laughed as we entered their apartment party chugging down cold Stonys. "We didn't know you Baptists were allowed to party," Bart said. "I heard the reason ya'll never have sex standin' up is 'cause you're afraid people will think you're dancin.'"

Funky Joe was in a Beatles mood. He played "Sergeant Pepper's Lonely Heart Club's Band" on the tape player. He used a table as a stage and encouraged everyone to sing along. Funky Joe talked in an "English" accent.

"I've got chewing gum on my shoe and keep stickin' to the stage!" he yelled.

The Waco girls looked at him like, "Wow, a Mexican with an English accent. That's pretty cool."

The Baptists kicked us out at 2 a.m. Funky Joe and I strolled from the motel parking lot to our room, singing "It's been a hard day's night, and I've been workin' like a dog..." until someone banged on the door. Fubby walked in wearing blue-plaid boxer shorts and a large bump on his head.

"Which one of you guys stuck a shot put in my pillow?" he asked.

"Don't look at me," I said. "I don't throw the shot."

Fubby looked around the room. "Where's Funky Joe?"

"He's lying in state against the wall."

"You keep the noise down, stay in your room, and go to sleep," Fubby said. "This is your final warning."

"Where was our first warning?"

The door slammed behind Fubby. I crawled over Funky Joe's bed and looked at him on the floor next to the wall.

He opened his eyes and smiled. "Let's go."

Funky Joe and I zigzagged down a desolate Waco highway to a John Deere dealer. We each climbed atop a tractor and pretended to be racing. We made dragster tractor sounds with our lips and pulled the gear shift back and forth until Funky Joe broke his lever in two and cut his forearm

I watched the blood trickle off Funky Joe's hand. "Amigo," I said. "I think we better call it a night."

I returned to Lubbock to save my senior season. The NCAA meet started in 10 days, and the Olympic Trials – if they would be held – began four weeks after that. Mitch was more worried about Grimsley Roeper.

I overheard Mitch talking to Funky Joe in the shower. "Langenhooch graduates in two weeks. If we can't get him laid, the statue's fallin' down."

Funky Joe was so taken by the cursed statue that he offered a reward of $300 to the first woman who got me in bed. All of Funky Joe's past and present girlfriends who called me received the same answer.

"Gotta go run."

I was too wrapped up in the NCAA and my last final exams to be tempted by some whore who shared sheets with a punk rocker who blew his sweaty underarms with a blow dryer. Fubby left for a hunting holiday without leaving Mitch the locker room key. I couldn't get to my spikes and ran track workouts in heavy training shoes with holes at each toe.

I never saw Fubby at the NCAAs in Austin and very little of The Franchise, whom I shared a dormitory room on the Univeristy of Texas campus. He spent more time in the women's dormitory. Rumor has it, The Franchise nailed the girl who handed out the medals in a lower deck stairwell between the shot put and high jump prelims. It must have been his warm down after winning his 800 meter heat.

I led my 5,000 meters heat in Memorial Stadium that night and fell apart after the first mile. I regrouped the last mile and surged into seventh. But only six qualified for the final, and six Africans, with an average age of 28 and average 5K PR of 13:28, were 70 meters ahead as the gun lap began. UTEP's Manfred Sambewi, the great Tanzanian runner who was listed as age 29 as a freshman and now 26 as a senior, jogged the final bend in sixth place and looked back at the helpless first non-qualifier. He smiled and pointed at me as if to say, "Na, Na, Na-Na, Na. I'm making the finals, and you're not."

I lifted my right middle finger, grabbed my right bicep with my left hand, and held that pose down the final homestretch of my college career. I kept running, in my spikes, out of the stadium to my dorm room. I showered, ate dinner, wandered around campus for two hours, and fell asleep under my little crack at Memorial Stadium. I dreamed that I made the Olympic team, Carter lifted the boycott, and I went to Moscow.

The sun, shining through the little crack, woke me up the next morning. I returned to my room, put on my Wooosh trainers, and floated 11 miles around Towne Lake. I tagged along with The Franchise to the Dazzler Shoes, Inc. hospitality suite that featured a leather sofa, fruit baskets, open bar, and shoe boxes lining the wall. Tanner Hudspeth, the Dazzler Shoe rep, shook The Franchise's hand.

"Good race last night, Sammy." Hudspeth looked back at me. "Who's your friend?"

"I-I-I'm Jonny Langenfelder. I ran the 5,000."

"OK." Hudspeth turned his back and showed The Franchise the Dazzler line of shoes. I waited through The Franchise's 30-minute shoe and apparel fitting and snuck out the door without anyone noticing – like anyone did anyway.

I went with The Franchise, after his fourth-place finish in the 800 final the next night, to a post-race party held at a fraternity house just off campus. There were four kegs that never stopped pouring, music so loud you could barely hear yourself talk, and sexy women in halter tops and tight jeans pulling the athletes to the dance floor.

"This is a great party, man!" The Franchise touched his plastic beer glass with mine and squeezed through the traffic of boobs and butts. I didn't see The Franchise for about 45 minutes. He returned about 1:30 a.m. with a girl, who looked like she was about 17 on his arm. She went to the bathroom with her cute friend, whom I had been dancing with. The Franchise walked over to me.

"Where you been?" I asked.

"In the van humping that girl on a lawn chair."

The Franchise sipped his beer. "How about I ask her and her friend to come back to the dorm with us? I think she likes you, man."

I said, "Yeah, sure," trying to act like bringing a girl home wasn't new to me.

The Franchise downed his beer, crumpled the plastic cup, and tossed it away. "O.K. man, here we go."

The girls followed our lawn chair van back to the dorm, and we escorted them to our room. My girl's name was Amy. The short, curly blonde wore a white, cut-off tank top that showed her bronzed belly, faded jeans that fitted nicely on her tight butt, a necklace with a dangling heart, and no bra. Amy sat on my bed and planted red lipstick on my cheek. "You are such a stud," she said, giggling.

"How old are you? I asked.

"Old enough not to know better," she said.

The Franchise left with his girl and gave me a thumbs-up sign just as the door closed. I was alone with a beautiful, half-drunk girl who didn't follow the stud runner back to his room to play gin rummy. Amy smiled and laid spread eagle on my bed and gently stroked my palm with her long, red fingernails.

"Care to join me?" she said.

I looked into her blue watery eyes and at the hard nipples outlined on her shirt. I closed my eyes. In one ear I heard Funky Joe. "Now's your chance, Langenhooch. Fuck her brains out." In the other ear I heard Father Litzke, "Rise above the temptation. If you can see, you can act rightly."

I opened my eyes to see Amy lying there in nothing but her panties. I leaned over to the bedside lamp and rested my finger on the light switch.

Two nights later, in the lights of the Tumbleweed Coliseum, I walked toward the stage in a red cap and gown in front of hundreds of other men and women in the same garb. I looked around at the massive crowd to see Mom and Dad sitting together, smiling at their only child to graduate from college. I reached for my diploma following the call from the oratorically-gifted dean of Arts and Sciences.

"Jonathan Christian Langenfarber."

I walked from the coliseum to Rutherford Hall via the track to say fare-well to the room that was my home for four years. I grabbed my last suitcase, took my Prefontaine picture off the wall, smiled, and shut the door on some bizarre but great memories. I met Mom and Dad in the parking lot, thanked them for coming, and said I would meet them in Dallas. I crammed my suit-case and Pre picture into the backseat of my VW Beetle and cruised through campus – one last time.

"I'll say good-bye to Grimsley, and I'm out of here," I said to myself.

I played an 8-track tape of the Tumbleweed marching band as I ap-proached the statue that stood tall through decades of rain, hail, tornadoes, and 60 mile-per-hour dust storms. But on this Saturday afternoon in early June, the Earth shook as I grabbed my diploma.

This time ol' Grimsley had been sacked for a loss.

◆◆◆

18

I had run around this track hundreds of times – in my mind. Everytime, the clapping and foot stomping echoed from the green-wooden bleachers on the backstretch and carried me around the yellow rubber oval and in front of the large, covered grandstand packed with track and field fans from around the world.

Maybe that's why the grand sight of Hayward Field that sunny Saturday afternoon of June 27, did not send me to the toilet as I marched to the starting line for the 5,000 meters final of the 1980 U.S. Olympic Track and Field Tri-als.

In only minutes, a gunshot would send me onto the footsteps of Steve Pre-fontaine. My spikes would touch the same holes he made in this surface en route to an American Record and touching off a thunderous chant of "Pre! Pre! Pre!" heard from the surrounding green hills to the rocky Oregon coast. I took a breath and closed my eyes as I reached the starting line. For a moment, I felt like I was home.

119

I had returned to 2000 Hickory Lane after graduation and spent the rest of the week logging miles up and down Rolling Hills Parkway. I turned my Olympic hopes to the one man who could restore my confidence.

"Who cares what happened at conference or the NC2A's." Lanny Hightower sipped beer from a can, while sitting on his concrete pool bank and splashing his legs alongside me. "There's no reason in the world you can't go up to Ory-gone and run with those fellas."

"B-B-But these guys have run in the Olympics, in Europe, and set American records."

"So what's your point?"

Coach Hightower had me running short hill sprints and laps of 50 and 100 yard dashes and 220's with a 40-second jog across the infield at Forest Hill High School. His repetition of "lookin' good, Champ" made me believe that I was good, and that I had a chance to make the Olympic team.

I visited Father Litzke, who told me in his soft voice as I sat, eyes closed, on a wooden chair in his den and listened to my breathing, "You are going to the Olympic Trials not to win a race, but to run a race. You run just for the sake of running."

Dad asked me the next day, during a commercial, why I was even running the trials. "Even if you made the team, Miles, I wouldn't want you runnin with a bunch of Commies."

Coach Hightower drove me to the DFW airport. He bought me a "good luck" beer in the airport bar and sent me down the gate tunnel with a "get after 'em, pardner."

The no-shows from runners who lost hope in the United States going to the Olympics or the faith in their own condition forced officials to cancel the 5,000 meter preliminaries. I went for an easy run on Pre's Trails. I drew strength from the Great One as I floated on the 10K path of wood chips that wove through a fresh forest of Douglas Fir and along the meandering Willamette River. The temperature was cool and crisp, unlike the boil and fry conditions of Texas.

I walked to the stadium that Saturday so focused I barely paid attention to the man in the brown hunting cap at the gate.

"Is it dove season here in the state of Oregon?"

Fubby Tuppernacker half-smiled and adjusted his cap. Somehow he had talked the Caprock State A.D. into sending him to Eugene to be with a runner he had never coached. What I didn't need was a pep talk from a man who now sounded and *looked* like Elmer Fudd.

"How you think you're gonna do, Langenloofer?"

I brushed past Fubby and showed my Olympic Trials credential to the ticket taker without looking back. "Don't know. Left my crystal ball in Lubbock."

Pre's track seemed to breathe life into my over-raced legs. I walked to the starting line without paying attention to the faces I had watched on television or saw in *Track and Field News* and in *Sports Illustrated* for the past eight years. There were University of Oregon standouts Armando Rojas and Rocco Toller, both who had run faster than Pre. There were three former U of O runners, including U.S. champion Mac Wilcox of Team Dazzler. Three-time Olympian Marv Lenzi, representing Lenzi's Locker and running the last race of his career, spent the winter training with Darcy Ellard in the Outback. The other 10 runners in their sparkling club and school colors seemingly all had run in the Olympics, set an American record, or won an NCAA title. The only other entrants not mentioned in the front page advance in the *Eugene Record-Times* were my Penn Relays combatants Adam Larkin and Bret Cox.

I was sandwiched on the starting line next to the dark-bearded and slightly graying Lenzi, who refused to shake my hand, and Wilcox, who elbowed me while flexing his well-toned and tanned shoulders.

The crowd was quiet only for the starting gun. Then they went clap, clap, clap, clap for 12 ½ laps. The excitement swept me to the shoulder of the front - running Rojas, who blitzed the first lap in 64 seconds and the mile in 4:20. The loud rhythmic clap almost overpowered these thoughts as I followed Rojas' green shorts and yellow singlet past a "6" on the lap counter: "I'm more than halfway through the Olympic Trials 5,000, and I'm not even tired. These guys are world class runners and I'm hangin' right with 'em. I don't seem to be breathing as hard as them.

"Maybe I should go for it like Pre did here in the 1972 Trials and bury these studs."

Rojas threw in a surge, and I covered it easily. We breezed past the "5" on the lap counter, and the crowd's clap echoed louder off the old backstretch bleachers to the line of spikes tapping the sunlit track. The stadium announcer's call was a mere mumble as I focused on the empty track in front of me. I rounded the turn and pulled alongside Rojas before the massive rows of track and field faithful who must have reached for their program to see who was wearing race number 1419.

The number "4" dangled from the distant lap counter. I lifted my knees, swung my elbows harder, widened my eyelids, and accelerated slightly. Just as I was about to make my "Pre" move, I glanced over my right shoulder to a three-time Olympian with a white grin amongst a black beard.

"Boo!"

The veteran Lenzi scared me off a lead that lasted a moment and elbowed me as he breezed past me. Rojas regained the lead. Toller and Wilcox went with him. I fell back to fifth on the turn, sixth on the backstretch, and eighth on the homestretch. One by one, they went by, and there was nothing I could do about it. Lenzi woke me from my Olympic dream and to the reality of big-time running. With the lap counter at "1," a big roar carried the leaders down the backstretch. I had a good view from the other side of the track as Wilcox sprinted past Rojas and Lenzi on the final turn. As Wilcox was waving to the crowd in the final 20 meters, I was being passed for last place on the final curve by Bret Cox. I looked back once in the homestretch, hoping to see

121

someone else. Nobody. Several seconds and a few pity claps later, I finished the longest season of my life.

Then everything seemed to go silent and in slow motion as I sat on the track. Wilcox smiled and dodged photographers and reporters as he began his victory lap. Rojas and Lenzi hugged each other. The other 13 runners shook sweaty hands and patted each other's shorts.

The volume and pace resumed. The glimmering sun was a spotlight for the three runners who jogged along to the clapping of standing spectators and their souvenir programs they begged them to sign.

I kept running, also, out of the stadium, through campus, across the main road, to Pre's trails. No matter how far or fast I ran, I could not escape the crowd's roar or the humiliation of finishing dead last in the U.S. Olympic Track and Field Trials.

My spikes pierced the wood chips of Pre's Trails as I followed the winding path through the shadow of the dark woods. Suddenly, it occurred to me. "I don't know where the heck I'm going."

PART III

HOLD THE PICKLES, HOLD THE LETTUCE...

August 1, 1980

To a Russian sitting in the 100,000-seat Lenin Stadium, the 12 athletes lined up for the 1980 Moscow Olympics 5,000 meters final look ready to run the world's fastest time.

But to a college graduate, whose black-and-white images have been beamed via satellite to a blurred television screen in West Texas, the runners look like they are about to run on the moon.

I need no translation from the Russian television announcer for a pistol sound that sends the runners around a rubber track and in front of the Olympic flame. I sit alone on the soft carpet of a friend's den and figure out who's who from the only words I can understand.

"Yifter... Kedir... Coghlan... Nyambui... Treacy... Maaninka...," runners I have watched on television, seen in running magazines, or competed against in college.

I watch Miruts Yifter, the 33-year-old balding Ethiopian with the small frame and giant strides, lead the field through the first kilometer. Yifter destroyed the 10,000-meters field which included two-time defending Olympic champion Lasse Viren of Finland, five days before with his devastating kick.

I have no favorite. There are no Americans and not even a single returnee from the Olympic 5,000-meters final in Montreal. Still, I cannot turn my eyes from the smooth-flowing athletes on a fuzzy screen. Everyone stays in contention through eight laps, after Yifter and his countrymen Mohammed Kedir and Yohannes Mohammed take turns leading. Eight runners are in contention at the bell, barely heard above the crowd's whistles and cheers in support of Soviet Aleksandr Fyedotkin.

Ireland's Eamonn Coghlan ruins the Russian's bid with a backstretch burst that puts him in gold medal position. Coghlan glances right to check if anyone will challenge and then left to see Yifter soar by him on the inside. Yifter sprints free on the final 200 meters. Tanzania's Sulieman Nyambui passes Coghlan on the turn and chases, in vain, the fleeing Ethiopian. Finland's Kaarlo Maaninka charges wildly on the homestretch to win the bronze, just ahead of the Irishman.

Yifter "the Shifter" has won his second Olympic gold medal in the moonlight of Moscow and in the faded light of a West Texas television, switched off by its lone viewer. I have left Moscow and my friend's den for a mid-day run that seems much closer to the sun.

125

19

What do you do when you fail miserably in the U.S. Olympic Track and Field Trials and have 1,440 days before your next try? What do you do when you have no coach, no club, no job, no girlfriend, no family support, and no idea how you are going to pursue your ultimate goal?

You run. And run, and run, and run.

Most Caprock State graduates of 1980 spent their late summers and fall traveling, looking for their dream job, or actually doing their dream job. I spent them along Rolling Hills Parkway, pounding mile after mile and running once, twice, three, and even four times per day with the gentle melody of Simon and Garfunkel spinning inside my head.

Hello darkness my old friend. I've come to talk with you again
Because a vision softly creeping, left its seeds while I was sleeping
And the vision that was planted in my brain, still remains – within
the sound of silence.

When I had arrived at 2000 Hickory Lane fresh from my failure in Eugene, Oregon, I didn't run a step for four weeks. Mom and Dad figured I would retire.

"I know you're disappointed," Mom said after praying over her welcome-home meal of meat loaf and mash potatoes. "Maybe it's for the best. Maybe you would have made that Olympic team, gone to Europe, become a famous runner, gotten into God-knows-what, and lost your soul."

"If I was real lucky," I said, cutting my meat, "maybe someone would have hit me in the head with a football or a shot put. Then for sure I would make it to heaven."

"No way to answer your mother, Miles." Dad, now sold on his new nickname for me, didn't look up from his meat loaf. "Maybe now you can forget this foolish running nonsense, get a job, and get on with your life. Pass the ketchup."

"But I want to keep running, try and make the 1984 Olympic team."

"That's four years from now. Pass the salt."

"Making the Olympics is my goal, my dream. I want to know what it feels like to walk down the tunnel of the Los Angeles Coliseum, parade in my red, white, and blues alongside my fellow American athletes and in front of the whole world, and compete before the flash of cameras and in the glow of the Olympic flame. I will sacrifice anything to have that."

Dad sliced a piece of meat loaf with his fork and stuffed it in his mouth. "I hear they've advertised for a sportswriter at the Muskegan Weekly News. Pass the pepper."

The conversation was the same, no matter if Mom made meat loaf, turkey, chicken, pork, or fish sticks. I spent my days tossing a tennis ball against my bedroom wall and my nights staring at the same wall and pondering when I would run again and my dream girl, who would not leave my daydream. Holly Ritzenbarger had graduated from LSU and without an MRS degree. But how could fate bring two people together, when one person has locked himself in his room. I needed something to wash out my thoughts and put me back on the road to reality.

The telephone interrupted roast beef on a Wednesday night, and I leaped from the dining room.

"Langenhooch, its Bart Harris. Mitch the Bitch is comin' to my house this weekend for the first annual washed up Tumbleweed runners' reunion. Whattaya say to a little trip to Gilmore."

Gilmore was a dust-driven dot on a West Texas map. It had no movie theater, no bowling alley, no traffic light, and one nearby honky-tonk frequented by every buck-tooth redneck in town. I looked over at the gravy sliding down Dad's chin as he read a television guide.

"I'll be there."

Within one minute of my arrival in Gilmore, there was a cold Lone Star in my hand. I drank 18 Lone Stars on Bart's ski boat at Lake Gilmore on Friday afternoon.

The lather of suntan lotion glistened on Bart's flabby chest as he studied the brown choppy water. "If it wasn't for skiin' or drinkin' or chewin' tobacco, there'd be nuttin' else to do in Gilmore."

Mitch slid his sunglasses down his nose and pointed his Lone Star toward Bart's pink bikini-clad and well-tanned and toned girlfriend, Raeleen Moss. "I can think of somethin' else you can do in Gilmore."

The thought was on all our minds after several pitchers that night at Merle's Country and Western Disco, where I learned how to chug a glass of Hillbully Lager while doing the Cotton-eyed Joe with Raeleen's 17-year-old sister Rhonda Sue. We slow-danced through cigarette smoke to the dagger stares from Merle's C & W patrons, who made visitors without cowboy boots or a cowboy hat as welcome as a banjo at a Bach festival.

"Let's git before we get the shit kicked out of us." Bart led us past the mosquitoes buzzing around the C&W's outdoor floodlights and between puddles of vomit and urine to his red Pontiac Grand Am. We heard "Picked a fine time to leave me, Lucille..." from the juke box as we spun out of the gravel parking lot.

Bart drove 24 miles back to his parents' house along the two-lane, no-light "Gilmore Expressway" with one hand on the wheel and the other around Raeleen. Rhonda Sue, wearing blue jeans and a halter-top, sat in the backseat between Mitch and me. My 23rd beer of the day released my inhibitions and made me sing along to a crooner's chorus from Bart's tape player – "Let's get drunk and screw..."

I put my hand on Rhonda Sue's knee and carefully slid it up her thigh. Just as I approached the sweet spot, I hit another hand.

I looked over at Mitch, who smiled as if to say, "Beat ya' to it, Langenhooch."

Bart dropped off Raeleen and Rhonda Sue at their house and drove back to Bart's house before remembering his and his girlfriend's parents were out of town. Bart and Mitch beat me out the door and to the Pontiac. I rolled off the hood and hit the concrete. My Wranglers got caught in the front bumper, and I was dragged down the driveway. I hobbled to the front lawn and collapsed.

Bart rushed to my aid. "You all right, hoss."

"Yeah, I think so."

Bart was back in the Pontiac and driving toward Raeleen and Rhonda Sue's house before I said, "...so."

Mitch woke me up an hour later in Bart's den, where I had passed out with an ice bag on my swollen ankle. He was huffing and puffing like he had just run a 5K. He did.

Mitch said he walked into Rhonda Sue's room, sat on her bed, looked up and down her nightie and into her eyes, and said, "I am gonna screw your lights out."

Then they heard somebody opening the front door. Rhonda Sue said, 'It's my daddy. Quick, out the window. He's got a shotgun.'"

I looked at Mitch's feet. "You ran all the way back here in your cowboy boots?"

"I got one hell of blister on my foot."

"Thanks to Rhonda Sue's parents, you're now gonna have one on your hand."

Mitch, Bart, and I limped into the den the next morning. Mitch pointed to Bart, who swigged Alka-Seltzer from a glass. "I ran 5K in Cowboy boots. Langenhooch got dragged down the driveway. What's your excuse?"

"Raeleen and I snuck out the back door and did it in a park."

"How could that be so painful?" I asked.

"Cactus."

Bart and Mitch met Raeleen and Rhonda Sue for lunch, while I went through the cable channels until I found the Moscow Olympics. I did my first run since the Olympic Trials and returned to 2000 Hickory Lane to a huge box of running shoes, sweats, shorts, socks, and singlets from Wooosh Athletics, Inc., which agreed to sponsor me. I loved the smell of a new pair of running shoes. Mom loved throwing my old fungi-filled trainers in the garbage.

Within a month I was up to 141 miles per week. That required three-a-days Monday through Friday. On Saturday I started with a 10-miler, then followed with four-hour breaks sandwiched between runs of five and eight miles. My final five- miler finished at 11:30 p.m., just in time for the television show *Dance Fever* and the hamburger and French fries Mom left in the warmer drawer.

The final five-miler in the darkness and quiet of Rolling Hills Parkway was peaceful, the easiest run of the week and always capped with a clenched fist at the finish-line curb. I sometimes was offered things on my runs from smartass drivers. A can of Budweiser, which I opened and swigged to the passengers' delight. A joint, which I declined with "I don't need that to get high."

One afternoon a teenager, showing off his newly-purchased used red Gremlin to three female passengers, rolled down his window. "Hey, buddy, why don't you get a shirt?"

"Hey, buddy," I snapped back. "Why don't you get a car?"

The girls laughed. The teenager honked. "Fuck you, you skinny bastard!"

Sundays I ran an easy 10-miler after 11:30 a.m. Mass and finished just before the Dallas Cowboys kick-off. Mark greeted me at the curb before the Cowboys-Redskins game with a water-splash from his coffee mug. He refilled it and chased me around the front lawn. The handle broke off and the jagged edge struck me in the lip. I stood in the front lawn with blood pouring down my chest, shorts, and legs. Dad marched out the front door, stared at me, and shook his head. "That's what you get for horsin' around."

I got four stitches in my lip and missed the Cowboys' dramatic comeback win over the Redskins. The busted lip discouraged me from calling Holly, who had returned from a summer cheerleader camp. The Stallion, on a rare non-solo run at White Rock Lake, suggested I not wait until my lip healed.

"She'll think you're a bad ass," he said.

"No, I want Holly to see me for who I really am."

"You're an unemployed college graduate who runs 140 miles a week and spends his afternoons watching soap operas. Where ya' gonna take her? For a run around this lake?"

I picked up the pace and again was running alone. I called back to The Stallion before disappearing on the winding road that looped the lake. "It's a hundred and forty-*one* miles per week!"

I didn't have to call Holly. I saw her during bench press reps at Hercules Health Spa the day after my lip stitches were removed. She wore a sleeveless T-shirt, cut-off sweatpants, and the firmest, bronzed muscles this side of Baton Rouge. I grunted on my 12th 90-pound repetition, strapped on a weight belt to make myself look less scrawny, and walked to a well-loaded squat bar next to the tall mirror Holly used to watch herself stretch. She saw me in the reflection, rushed to me, and hugged my bones hidden by a "Caprock Invitational" T-Shirt.

I did not want to let go until I looked down at her left hand squeezing my left shoulder "Is that a glass door knob on your finger or an oversized diamond?"

Holly looked at the ring and blushed. "I'm getting married in January. Isn't that exciting?"

Slugging me in the eye with that huge rock would have hurt less than using the "M" word. I acted like I was happy for her. "Who's the lucky fella?"

Holly Ritzenbarger would become Holly Rogenberger. "I barely have to change my name."

"Or you could call yourself Holly Ritzenbarger-Rogenberger."

I never did a squat. I left Hercules Health Spa knowing my dream girl had vanished into the rock-hard arms of Coach Rodney Rogenberger, LSU's assistant weight coach. It's a wonder what motorists along Rolling Hills Parkway thought that evening of the runner slapping himself in the forehead and muttering, "Way da go, Langenloser. One phone call. Just one phone call. All you had to do last year or the year before or the year before was make one little phone call. Just one lousy phone call."

I did not appreciate The Stallion's sarcasm during our lake run the next evening, "Trudy Merkle is still available."

I channeled my anger into hard-as-you-can-go 10-milers on Mondays, 14-milers on Thursdays, and eight-milers on Saturdays. I tuned my brain into Simon and Garfunkel again on a dreary night run in early December.

In restless dreams I walked alone, narrow streets of cobblestone,
'neath the halo of a street lamp. I turned my collar to the cold and damp,
when my eyes were stabbed by the flash of a neon light, split the night,
and touched the sound of silence.

I was extremely fit with nowhere to go. I wanted to return to Eugene and run for the famed Wooosh Track Club. I had written a letter to Wooosh general manager Taylor Markham before the Olympic Trials and told him I wanted to run as fast as Steve Prefontaine and of the obstacles I overcame at Caprock State to run 13:44. I wrote: "If I can find a coach, runners to train with, good places to run, and high quality meets, there is no telling how fast I might run. Markham wrote back: "I will watch you run at the Trials and call you, if we think you are the right caliber to join our club."

I never heard from him.

Coach Hightower insisted I stay in Dallas, get a part-time job, and train with him. But there were few elite races for post-collegians in Texas, and I couldn't imagine running eight-minute miles alongside zit-faced boys who didn't even know who Steve Prefontaine was.

Marv Lenzi invited me to Atlanta to run for his Lenzi's Locker. Marv gave me the name of the *Atlanta Daily Mail* sports editor, who said I had a better chance of throwing the paper than writing for it.

The best offer came during a baked chicken dinner in early November. Mom answered the call, and I took a chicken wing to the telephone.

"Langencalper, it's Coach Tuppernacker."

"Oh no," I thought. "He must want my uniform back."

"How would you like to run for Caprock State this winter?"

Fubby explained that my Skooner Gold illness earned me a red-shirt for the 1979 indoor season. He offered me a full scholarship that included a private room at Rutherford Hall to run four or five meets. The only catch was I had to enroll in nine graduate-school hours. I hated school and, after 16 years, I would have preferred a root canal. To me B.S. was the initials for "Bull Shit". M.S. stood for "More of the Same," and Ph.d was "Piled Higher and Deeper."

Mitch solved that problem. "Don't go to class. The drop date is the Monday after conference."

Fubby took the phone back from Mitch and said, "And, while I'm thinkin' about it, bring your uniform back."

The decision to go to grad school satisfied Mom and Dad, who saw it as getting on with my life and out of their house. They encouraged me to spend time with my ailing 93-year-old Grandma, whether she wanted to see me or not. I traded much of Christmas with my brothers and sisters and their latest girlfriend or boyfriend for a 20-miler and played penny poker at The Stallion's apartment on New Year's Eve. I brought a large pickle jar half-full of pennies, which became fuller after winning with a straight.

The Stallion passed me a beer and dealt the cards to the four players.

"I heard that if you had put a penny in a jar every time you had sex the first year of marriage, and then took a penny out every time you had sex after that first year, you'd never get to the bottom of the jar," said one of the players.

"Probably true," I said. "In fact, I got this jar of pennies from my parents' bedroom."

I continued my New Year's Eve tradition with a half-drunk three-mile run at midnight in the sleet that welcomed the year 1981 and iced a bridge along Loop 480. I took my foot off the accelerator on that bridge, a mistake that sent my VW Beetle into a center guardrail at 50 miles per hour. The car was totaled, and I wasn't sure what condition I would be in after calling Dad from a motel pay phone at 3 a.m. and asking him to leave his warm bed for a freezing cold highway. Dad arrived at the crash site at 3:30 a.m., drove me home, towed the VW to the nearest car graveyard on New Year's Day, and co-signed on my rusted 1973 Mustang. He never said a lecturing word about my accident.

A week later, I drove that same highway in the other direction, toward Lubbock. I backed the Mustang down the driveway at 2000 Hickory Lane and waved good-bye to Mom and Dad about the same time Holly was walking down the aisle at Forest Hill Fellowship Church.

"Maybe I'll be like Dustin Hoffman in The Graduate," I thought. "I'll tap on the glass outside the church. 'Holly!...Holly!...Holly!' She stiff arms Rogenberger, bars the door with a crucifix, runs away with me, and rides off, wedding gown and all, into the sunset in my yellow Mustang."

Forest Hill Fellowship Church and the bride and groom were left in my exhaust cloud before I finished the daydream. I stuck my Simon and Garfunkel tape into my 8-track player and sang along, leaving Dallas with my own words to "Mrs. Robinson."

"And here's to you Mrs. Rogenberger, Jonny loves you more than you will know. Wo-wo-wo. God bless you please Mrs. Rogenberger, heaven holds a place for those who pray.

"Hey, hey, hey...hey, hey, hey..."

◆◆◆

20

Four offensive linemen, "crowbarisms" we called them, crowded a small table on a January afternoon that frosted the Rutherford Dining Hall windows. I don't know what was bigger, the milky white flesh that hung off their biceps or the blood-drenched steak they stuffed between their lips.

Crowbarisms are unique creatures. They wear thong sandals, gym shorts, and tank tops in sub-freezing conditions. They have more zits than hair on their back, butt, and shoulders. They take courses like Fun Machine 101 not to learn to play an instrument, but to stay academically eligible. They call each other "Dude," high-five their buddies after taking a massive dump, and greet each new day with, "Uhhhh! I feel good today."

Mitch the Bitch pegged them crowbarisms a few years back, after one came by his dorm room and asked, "Dude, you got any lighter fluid. Uhhhh!"

After the dude left, Mitch said, "He looks like someone hit him in the face with a crowbar."

Mitch stared at the crowbarisms at their tiny table and then at his skinny distance runners at our big round one. "I betcha if you totaled all four of those guys G.P.A.'s, it still wouldn't add up to a four-point."

With Mitch's blessing, my G.P.A. didn't add up to a point that semester. I enrolled in three management courses he was taking, so he could use the books the scholarship paid for mine. I felt no guilt for taking a scholarship and not showing up for class, because otherwise the scholarship would go to waste. How many of the football team's 80 scholarships did the crowbarisms use? I figured the university owed me after winning 26 races and making the dean's list seven of eight semesters.

I returned to Caprock, because I had nowhere else to go. I could escape Uncle Grimsley's shadow by winning a Southwestern Conference title in mid-February, drop the classes the following Monday with a "withdrew passing," and leave Lubbock without anyone knowing the difference. Marv Lenzi promised me a spot on his Lenzi's Locker team and a few trips after indoor season.

The least-pleased with my return were the University of Amarillo fans, whose track coach, Dean Hughes, had left for Arkansas Southern and had taken the Kenyans with him. The pre-meet advance for the duel battle for the Panhandle Pan in the *Amarillo Daily News* read, "...and Jonny Langenfielder, who it seems has been running in this meet for 10 years, will attempt a rare distance triple in the 1,000, mile, and two-mile."

I hadn't raced since the Olympic Trials. But the shocked look on Mitch's face after my 10-mile time trial on the dirt roads showed how fit I was. "I think the watch is broken," he said as I sipped water from a farmhouse hose. The split timer read 48:59. Funky Joe, who finished next, clocked himself in 53:12. Mitch's watch had the same time. The same handy watch caught me in 39:13 on an eight-miler at Wuffalo the next week.

"I don't know if anyone in the world could run that fast on this course," Mitch said as I grabbed my knees and spit on the road.

"Maybe, I should be running a marathon."

Instead, I was running and winning three events in Amarillo and being booed every step, especially after I lapped the field in the meet finale two-mile. The boos followed me and the Panhandle Pan out of the gymnasium.

At the next Saturday's *Dallas Star* Indoor Games at the packed Reunion Arena I followed Manfred Sambewi, the recent UTEP graduate and Olympic 5,000 finalist, through the first mile of the two-mile in 4:21. With "8" laps to go, the card on the lap counter read "9." We yelled at the officials every lap over the crowd's cheers and the thumping blue board track. Still, they didn't correct it. Figuring on an extra lap, I dropped off the pace.

"This will be great," I thought. "These guys are thinking the race is over. Then as they stagger through the bonus lap, I'll blow by them."

Up the homestretch and 30 meters behind Sambewi and the two runners tucked behind him, the lap counter read "2." As Sambewi passed the start/finish line, an official noticed the mistake, changed the counter to "1" and clanged the bell. I sprinted only in vain and settled for fourth place in a school record 8:45.7. Sambewi did the extra lap, a victory lap.

I won the mile in 4:08 at Oklahoma City to break Uncle Grimsley's career school record for individual track-and-field victories with 30. My success worried Mitch after I completed five times per mile in 4:22, 4:21, 4:21, 4:20, and 4:16 with a four-minute jog interval the following Monday.

"What happens if you qualify for nationals in the three-mile at the Astrodome this week?" Mitch said as I sat naked in front of my locker alongside he and Bart Harris, who were bundled in sweatsuits.

"You think I can qualify for indoor nationals?" I asked.

"With that workout and running on a five-lap to lap mile track?" Mitch said. "Heck ya."

"Great."

"Not great considering the negative publicity we'll get once you get kicked out of school for not goin' to class. The professors are seeing your name in the paper and already are starting to talk."

"What should I do?"

"First, put some clothes on. Then go beg the professors for forgiveness and go to class?"

I turned to Bart. "What do you think?"

"I agree," Bart said. "I think you should put dad-gum clothes on."

I disagreed about the forgiveness part. I had promised myself if I graduated I'd never return to class. I loved waking at the crack of noon for my morning run. Then it was lunch, soaps, afternoon workout, dinner, and *Monday Night Football* or *Happy Days* or another prime time show. I read *Track and Field News* until I fell asleep at midnight or so. The only difference between me and fifth-year crowbarisms is that I graduated from college.

"I'll worry about it after the Astrodome Meet," I told them as put on my jeans.

The next morning brought an Arctic front and a wind-chill factor of minus 30. Mitch brought more bad news to lunch. The Astrodome meet was canceled due to a sponsor's withdrawal, leaving the Southwestern Conference Indoor as the last chance to qualify. I bit into a ham sandwich and stared over at the crowbarism table, which had added a fifth person. The new guy had a shaved head, a tattoo of a Tiger on his left shoulder, and a blond goatee. "Who's the new crowbarism?"

"The new strength coach," Bart said. "Coach Roge they call him. He's from LSU."

I knocked over my lemonade. "You mean Rogenberger?"

I explained who he was to Mitch, Bart, Funky Joe, and the other runners at our table.

"You lost your dream girl to a crowbarism?" Bart said. "He must have a big dick or somethin'?"

"No way," Mitch said. "Crowbarisms all take steroids. It shrinks the dick so much that it gets hidden in the bush."

Funky Joe scraped at his face stubble. "I wouldn't care about having a little dick if drugs made me run faster."

Mitch sipped his Coke and explained that three things can happen when a runner takes drugs before the race. "One, you go out and run like crap. Two, you run great. Or three, you run great. But not on the track. You're out running a record pace in the stands or the parking lot."

"The Franchise definitely ain't taking steroids," Bart said.

"Why's that?" I asked.

"The guy could model for Gooch Sausages."

Funky Joe smiled. "I think you been hangin' 'round the locker room too much, amigo."

A blonde in a short skirt and high heels interrupted our conversation. Everyone stared at her sitting on Roge's lap.

"Can't believe she married a crowbarism," I said.

"They must have Monroe shock absorbers on their bed," Bart said.

Holly walked to our table, took my hand, and led me to the crowbarisms. "Honey, this is Jonny Langenfielder - my good friend from high school."

Roge devoured a chunk of steak, glanced at me, turned back to the other crowbarisms, and said, "Uhhhh!"

Later that afternoon Mitch drove Funky Joe and me to the dirt roads north of town despite the 20-below wind-chill factor. Funky Joe was angrier about my 45-minute warm-up than Mitch making us do a 10-mile time trial.

"It only takes me 20 minutes to get warmed up, Langenhooch."

"I run 13:44 for the 5,000 and you run 15:44. So, who do you think is doing the right warm-up?"

We never warmed up on that 10-miler. The cold air congested my lungs so bad I couldn't run for two days. I struggled through my next workout, two times two miles in 9:06 and 9:08 and spent the rest of the week in bed. I was diagnosed with the Bangkok Flu by a doctor who looked like he was from Bangkok and advised me not to run conference. I think that's what he said.

Advice not taken, I stepped into the lawn chair van and waited 30 minutes for our departure to Fort Worth. The Franchise arrived in his white cowboy hat, sunglasses, and with a big-breasted brunette who wore his Caprock State sweatshirt. Fubby opened the station wagon's front door for The Franchise, the only athlete he ever waited for. We stared from our lawn chairs.

"You guys think that girl is a virgin?" I asked.

Funky Joe pulled the tab on his first Silver Bullet before we left the Lubbock city limits. "Some teams go to a meet and drink on the way home," he said. "At Caprock State, we get drunk on the way *to* the meet."

Funky Joe didn't mind drinking in the lawn chair van, because he was buying it right after the trip.

"Can't believe you're buying this piece of shit," Bart said. "It has like 600,000 miles on it."

Funky Joe took out a Beatles tape. "But it's got one hell of a tape player."

We drank and sang along with John, Paul, George and Ringo for five hours. Funky Joe directed us to join hands during the chorus of "Hey, Jude" er rather, "Hey, Dude."

We raised hands and swayed back and forth as we reached the Fort Worth Downtown Hotel. Fubby peered through the foggy side window, saw the lawn chair party, and started screaming. The music was so loud all we could see were his lips flapping. We locked the door so he couldn't get in.

The Silver Bullets proved good medicine and helped me to a 4:11 mile anchor and a third place for our distance medley relay on the Friday afternoon. That night my college career ended, this time for good, with a fifth-place finish in the three-mile. Mitch was more peeved about my breaking, by a half-second, his indoor school record of 13:56 than relieved I now could drop out of school with a "withdrew passing."

I went Monday morning to the School of Business, where I was informed by a woman in a three-piece suit that the drop date had been changed to the previous Friday.

"What happens now?"

The woman smiled. "You're fucked."

Three professors in the School of Business descended on the athletic department that week to make sure I was given a dishonorable discharge. As I lifted
a chicken drumstick to my mouth in the Rutherford Dining Hall, someone
grabbed my forearm.

"Make this bite a good one, Langenweanie. 'Cause it's gonna be your last
one."

Athletic Academic Counselor Paul Booner, a former Caprock lineman and
crowbarism, decided to make an example of me. He told me to pay back the
athletic department for the meals I ate and called a special meeting of the Athletic Council.

Mitch and I pressed our ears against the wooden door of the meeting room
at the Tumbleweed Coliseum the next evening. Paul Booner, president of the
local chapter of the Christian Athletes Association and proud father to three,
went after me like he once did a defensive tackle or a prime rib.

"Jonny Langenfelder is a disgrace to this athletic department and to the
name of his late great-uncle, Grimsley Roeper. He used this athletic department for his own gain and didn't care who he hurt or what lives he destroyed."

"Lives I destroyed?" I whispered to Mitch. "How do you destroy a life by
running around a track or leaving an empty seat in a classroom?"

I yearned for someone to tell the council how I graduated in four years,
made the dean's list, represented Caprock State in national competition, and
inspired the athletes who ran in my footsteps. The next voice we heard was
Fubby's.

"I've known Langenfooner for five years now. I recruited him, signed
him, and coached him."

"Coached me?" I whispered.

"Sh-sh-sh." Mitch said.

"I thought he was a first-class individual. But he proved to be a problem,
and out of my good graces I decided to keep him around. He lied to me about
going to class. Mr. Booner is right. Langenfrowner is a disgrace to my track
and field team and this athletic department. I will go along with any action
taken against him."

I stood with my mouth open.

"What a fucking weasel?" Mitch whispered almost loud enough to be
heard through the door. "He's just trying to protect his own ass."

I didn't know whether to cry or take one of Fubby's hunting rifles and
chase him around campus. I marched into Fubby's office the next morning and
shut the door. He stayed on the telephone for 20 minutes without acknowledg-
ing my presence, which made me angrier. I looked on his office wall and
imagined his stuffed head hanging there next to his quail.

Fubby hung up. "I put a good word in for you last night. Hopefully the
A.D. will go easy on ya. '"

"Does a good word include calling me a disgrace to the track team?"

"You were listening?"

"To every word. You know how much I've done for this athletic department. I'm one of the few track guys to graduate in four years. I'm the first athlete in this university to qualify for two-straight nationals in cross country. I set a school record for track victories. I ran the top 10 fastest 5,000's in school history. I ran in the Olympic Trials. I made the dean's list."

"That's beside the point."

I stormed out of Fubby's office and slammed the door so hard his stuffed racoon fell off the wall. I was met at my dorm room by Head Resident Theo Dickson, who stood there until my bags were packed and placed on a trolley. He escorted me and my belongings out of Rutherford Hall to my yellow, rusted Mustang.

"This your car?" Theo said.

"Yep."

"Looks like a Big Banana."

I stuffed my belongings in the trunk and backseat and sat in the driver's seat. I leaned my forehead atop the steering wheel, looked down at my Wooosh running shoes, and considered my options. I couldn't go to Dallas and face my parents' shame. I couldn't go to Atlanta or Oregon, because I didn't have any money. I couldn't go to my brothers' or sisters' houses, because they would discover I was a loser just like them. I couldn't go to Grandma's house, because she was under the care of a hospice nurse and preferred no visitors.

I lifted my head from the steering wheel and gazed at the dark clouds that covered the sun. "I've got it. I'm goin' to Fat Doug's."

21

The bell that clanged at 10 minutes until 6 p.m. on Wednesday, March 25 was not for the last lap. It was for the last call for Happy Hour at Fat Doug's.

The bargain beer guzzlers lined up for their last $1.50 pitcher. I scraped enough pennies and nickels from the ashtray of the Big Banana. The Blob, the track team's token crowbarism, had enough money and time for two more pitchers. The first one he chugged to the foot-stomping chant of "Blob! Blob! Blob!.." Then he let out a "Uhhhh!" and got back in line.

"What are all those scratches up and down his arms?" the barmaid asked me.

"He's on the Caprock track and field team."

"Isn't he a shot putter or discus thrower?"

"Between throws he catches javelins."

"So why the scratches?"

"I didn't say he was any good at it."

Fat Doug's became my home after my dismissal from Caprock State. Funky Joe and I started and finished our 10-mile run there on Monday, Wednesday, and Friday. Mitch the Bitch and Bart would meet us for $1.50 pitchers and the complimentary bar snacks of pretzels, nuts, tacos, and meat pies that qualified as my dinner. We shot some pool, threw darts, and made fun of Fubby. The four of us clinked our last full beer mugs and yelled FUBAR!, before chugging every last drop.

"What's FUBAR?" a woman asked from the next table.

"That's the name of Caprock's new post collegiate track club," Bart said. "Fucked Up Beyond All Recognition."

FUBAR didn't go to the Texas Relays to compete. Funky Joe drove his newly purchased lawn chair van, complete with its dented fenders and bumpers and rusted turquoise exterior. He pulled the van off a country highway en route to Austin, set his Bud bottle on the floor board, and walked to the back of the van. I looked above the hanging dice in the rearview mirror to see him holding the van's tailpipe like a hot potato. He heaved it into the pasture and drove back onto the highway with smoke billowing out the back.

He then revealed that he is "not really Mexican."

"I have about one-fifth Mexican and rest Spanish and European."

"You're a Heinz 57," Mitch said.

"Nah," Bart said. "He's just plain weird."

In Austin we went to a basement bar that featured a punk rock band called "The Croakin' Devils." Funky Joe claimed them the best band he ever heard and set sail for the dance floor. "I'm gonna ask the ugliest, fattest girl in the bar to dance." The ugliest, fattest girl turned him down.

The next day I sat in the Memorial Stadium stands and looked over at this long-haired guy smoking a cigarette and watching the meet.

"Don't you know who that is?" Bart said. "Or were you too FUBAR'd?"

I took a closer look. It was the lead singer of the Croakin' Devils.

I walked under the stands and looked up at the sun that glimmered through my little crack in the concrete. "What the heck am I doin' here?" I thought. "I should be on that track, instead of nursing another hangover."

I drove the lawn chair van back to Lubbock, while Mitch, Bart, and Funky Joe sat in the lawn chairs and drank a case of Old Milwaukee. I thought, as the headlights illuminated the darkness, of how my life had gone to pot.

After my first visit to Fat Doug's, I had stored my stuff in Funky Joe's apartment attic and slept in his lawn chair van. I cleaned out the beer cans and fast-food and condom wrappers and made a bed out of loose foam from the pole vault pit. There was more room in the van than in Funky Joe's apartment, which was in an alley behind Fat Doug's. My Caprock track buddies smuggled food out of the dining hall, and Funky Joe brought it back for me. I did my shit, shower, and shaving in the Caprock track locker room.

About two hours from Lubbock, Bart gulped his beer. "Hey, Langenhooch, whatcha thinking? '"

"I'm thinkin' about qualifying for the U.S.A. National Track and Field Championships."

"You got the background for it," Mitch said. "We just need to put in some good track workouts and find you some races."

I remembered something Father Litzke said, "Your life is like driving a car. Don't look sideways or stare into the rearview mirror. Look out the windshield and focus on the lit path ahead of you."

On Monday, I called Marv Lenzi from Funky Joe's place to see about the meets he promised to send me to. Lenzi's first words were, "How's Sammy Alcola doing?"

He said he had several meets he wanted to fly The Franchise to. I explained that the school would be paying The Franchise's way to those meets.

"When he finishes the NCAA meet, we're gonna take good care of that young man."

Lenzi almost hung up, before I could ask him about me. "Run some fast times, and we'll send you to a meet or two."

No meet within a 500-mile radius of Lubbock allowed post-collegians until the Caprock State All Comers Meet, five weeks away on May 9. Fubby, whom I had not spoken to since our last confrontation, pulled me aside after a Tuesday 10-miler around campus. He said he had found me a place to live and a job in the sports department at the *Lubbock Ledger*.

Fubby's hunting buddy Walker Clements, who occasionally flew him in his private plane to hunting trips in Canada, had a one-room apartment behind his mansion next to the Caprock Country Club. The place was small, had dirt caked to the tile floor, a dripping tap, a gas leak, and a twin mattress less comfortable than the pad in the lawn chair van. But for 12 weekly hours of yard work on Clement's property, it sure beat sleeping behind a bar. The newspaper job was taking results over the telephone and re-writing press releases. Sports Editor Wade Moore said if I did a good job he would let me write a feature in the summer.

Within a week I was running eight 880-yard intervals in under 2:10 and was back under 40 minutes for the eight-mile time trial at Wuffalo. Lubbock's spring weather was unseasonably calm and cool without one dust storm. For the Caprock All-Comers' 5,000, I recruited recent Kenyan arrivals Barnabas Budet and Solomon Udo from New Mexico Junior College. They both were looking to go sub-14. The weather forecast was sunny with light winds. I awoke Saturday morning to branches smacking against my roof and a dark orange sky. By race time, wind blew sand at gusts of 40-45 miles per hour. The skinny Africans were not much of a wind block. I beat them in the last 220 in a wind-unaided time of 14:31.5.

I trained harder, improved to 14:19 on a time trial two weeks later, and then turned my best 440 workout of the season. The efforts convinced me I could run under the U.S.A. qualifying standard of 13:52, but not Marv Lenzi.

"We only have enough travel money in the budget for our top runners," Lenzi said over the telephone at the *Lubbock Ledger* the Monday afternoon of May 25.

"B-B-But you promised me a trip, and I need to go to Tempe, Arizona next week for a chance to qualify."

"What do you want me to do about it? I tell you what, if you qualify for nationals, we'll fly you there."

"B-B-But I need a trip in order to qualify."

Lenzi hung up before I got out the "but." It was too late to find another club. My only chance was Funky Joe, who loaned me the lawn chair van. I had enough money for gas, but not enough for a motel room. I could sleep in the van at a rest stop and in Arizona. I filled the gas tank, packed my bag in the van, and turned the key. Nothing. I tried for an hour. Nothing. A mechanic tried for an hour and all he could charge up was a $50 service call.

I walked into my apartment and threw my running shoes into the trash can.

During the next nine weeks I never ran, never watched a televised track and field meet, never read a *Track and Field News*, and had nothing to do with Mitch, Funky Joe, Bart, Fubby, or anyone who had anything to do with track and field.

I worked at the newspaper, mowed the millionaire's lawn, played slow-pitch softball, and attended Happy Hour with fat sportswriters at Fat Doug's. I begged Wade Moore to let me write a story. Finally, he said, "OK, I've got one for you that's close to home."

Moore stuck his lit cigarette in the ashtray and leaned back on his office chair. "Caprock State is kicking off its football season with Grimsley Roeper Day on Saturday, August 29th to commemorate the 60th anniversary of Tumbleweed Stadium and the first touchdown. You still have several weeks, so I want you to dig deep and interview your relatives and old Caprock players and write a feature on Grimsley's life. If it's good, we'll run it on the front page."

The assignment angered Brandt Cooney, *The Ledger's* college football writer who wanted the story. I overheard Cooney from Moore's glassed office. "The kid hasn't written a story since he's been here. He'll write the same bullshit "glorifying Grimsley" story we've read over and over the past 60 years."

I set out to prove Cooney wrong, and my main source was Grandma. She had all sorts of health problems that left her pale, weak, and dying. She didn't want anyone to see her that way – not even the grandson who followed so closely in her little brother's footsteps. The interview was my chance to see her and learn more about Grimsley. Grandma obliged.

It was my first visit to 1721 Lucas Lane since the last time I saw Uncle Grimsley. Running, classes, weekend trips, and her reclusive nature kept me from visiting her during my college years. Mom only visited her one summer. I quickly was reminded how beautiful Grandma's place was. Located north of Lubbock and along a winding, rolling back road, the Colonial two-story with large oak trees and white picket fence and Bermuda lawns looked like a bed and breakfast in Vermont. A large, tree-lined park across the street made it more difficult to believe I was in West Texas. But this was, indeed, the house that had been my first home.

I checked my shoes by the front porch swing and slid on the polished wood floors past the oak staircase to the living room, where Mom's sister Aunt Gracie and Uncle Terry sat on the sofa. I told them about my story on Uncle Grimsley and how sad his promising career ended in such freakish manner.

"Whatcha talkin' about?" Uncle Terry, a Caprock State football fanatic whom we nicknamed "Tumbleweed Terry," set his beer can on the coffee table next to the other empties and stood next to Grandma's embroidered and framed "Home, Sweet Home" picture on the wall.

"You know," I said. "How he went nuts after getting hit in the head with a football."

Tumbleweed Terry laughed. "Who told you that?"

Aunt Gracie pinched her husband's leg, "Shush, Terry."

Terry continued. "What happened was Ol' Grimsley got himself a bad case of V.D."

We all looked at each other. Aunt Gracie shook her head and left. Tumbleweed Terry continued. "He was engaged to Miss Texas. When they broke up, Grimsley chased every skirt in Lubbock. He had deals set up in Hollywood, professional football, everywhere. But he gave that all up once he heard he had it."

"Had what?"

"V.D. There was no penicillin back then. He knew it was just a matter of time before his brain would get all deteriorated and stuff."

My immediate thought: "What a scoop. This will show those hotshot writers at *The Ledger* and expose the 'great' Grimsley."

Aunt Gracie returned and led me to Grandma's bedroom. She didn't respond to my "Hi Grandma" and looked so pale I thought about checking her pulse. She patted my arm with her bony fingers and smiled.

"My little Jonny boy. All grown up. And you're writing a newspaper article about Grimsley. How nice."

I pressed record on my tape recorder. Grandma reflected, in somewhat distorted detail, on Grimsley's first touchdown in Tumbleweed Stadium, his 80-yard punt, his great romp through collegiate football and track, and how much he was loved and respected by the people of West Texas. Then I said. "Gr-gr-grandma, I heard something about Uncle Grimsley getting a venereal disease or something?"

Her wrinkled face turned stern. She raised her eyebrows, lifted her head from the pillow, and grabbed my T-shirt sleeve. Grandma seemed never more alive. "Yes, Jonny, it is true. But you must promise me. Promise you won't mention a word of it. Not a word of it. It would ruin his reputation. Promise me, Jonny. Promise me."

Grandma put a death grip on my arm. "OK, Grandma. I promise."

Grandma kissed my cheek, and I sped to Lubbock, at sunset, to find as much dirt as I could on Grimsley. Old teammates said Grimsley was quite the boozer and womanizer, often missing team curfew on road trips. The night after he scored the first touchdown, he also scored the coach's 18-year-old daughter.

"Grimsley got more ass than a toilet seat," said 80-year-old Clyde Tuttle, Grimsley's college roommate. "When we heard he got V.D., we thought that stood for Vicious Dick."

I stayed up until 4 a.m. on Friday, August 14 scripting the quotes from my tape recorder. At 7 a.m. my doorbell, which sounded like a buzzer at an old gymnasium, lifted me from the bed. I opened the door to a gray-haired man with a shiny-gold belt buckle, cowboy boots, slacks, plaid shirt, and a frown. Without my contacts I barely could make out Walker Clements, my millionaire landlord.

"How long you plannin' on stayin' in this here apartment?"

I stared at his alligator-skinned cowboy boots. "I-I-I don't know."

"I want you out by Monday."

I had not seen Clements since I moved in three months before. I cut his football-length lawn with a crapped-out mower, raked leaves, trimmed his bushes, pulled weeds, and washed and polished his Cadillac.

"My wife and my maid say they haven't seen you do nothin.'"

I choked on my reply. "W-W-W-W..."

"Well, you owe me a hundred hours of work. So I tell you what. You come up with 400 bucks for the time you owe, and I'll let you stay."

I went back to bed, but couldn't sleep. I cleared my mind by retrieving my Wooosh shoes from the garbage can and running to the Caprock State campus. I looked at Grimsley's statue, so well repaired and repainted that no one could tell there were cracks inside.

I knew what I had to do.

On Monday morning Clements rang the buzzer to an empty apartment. All I left was a trash pale full of pizza boxes, T.V. dinner trays, Coke cans, and mud-stained gardening gloves.

If I wanted to make the Olympics, I needed meets and places to run and people to train with and a coach who trained world-class runners. I needed to go to Eugene, Oregon. I saved enough money from working at *The Ledger* all summer to make the move. I gave Wade Moore my notice and moved back into the lawn chair van. I didn't know how I was going to lead the Grimsley story until the telephone rang at *The Ledger* late Tuesday, August 25

"Miles?" The tone of Dad's voice told me what he would say next.

"Grandma passed away this morning."

A thought precluded the tears that landed on my typewriter keys. "I guess now it won't matter how I write this story."

After Grandma's funeral Mass that Friday night at the country church near her house, I drove back to Lubbock and filed my story on Uncle Grimsley. Wade Moore read it and said, "You've got a very bright future in journalism."

I met Mitch, Bart, and Funky Joe for one last pitcher at Fat Doug's. We looked through the crowd to a table of crowbarisms, which included Paul Booner and Rodney Rogenberger. Two girls prepping for a wet-T-shirt contest sat on their laps and licked lime juice off their flexed biceps.

Mitch said, "Langenhooch, as a farewell present, what can I do to these guys?"

I thought for a second as I stared at the foam dripping down my glass. "Just one simple request. Call Roge's wife?"

Mitch returned from the pay phone.

"Talk to Holly?"

"Yep. I asked for Roge."

"What did she say?"

"She said he went to a Christian Athletes meeting with Booner."

"Should I ask her to come down here?"

I looked at Roge squeezing the girl's thigh. "Nah."

Mitch, Bart, Funky Joe and I did a final toast.

"To Fubby?" I asked.

"No," Mitch said. "To Jonny Langenfelder and his Olympic quest."

"Thanks, Coach."

We tapped glasses, yelled "FUBAR!" and chugged for the final time to a Mac Davis song on the jukebox, "Happiness is Lubbock, Texas in the rearview mirror..."

The next morning, Mom, Dad, and I said good-bye to Grandma as she was laid to rest next to Grandpa and Uncle Grimsley in a cemetery not far from her home. Then I said good-bye to Mom and Dad. They were too distraught over Grandma's death to question my move to Oregon. They walked with me from her grave to the Big Banana, crammed with my belongings. I sat in the driver's seat with the window rolled down and started the engine. Suddenly, I realized I wasn't moving across the state. I was moving across the country. There was no telling when I might see them again.

Mom looked at me with the tears of losing her mother and her youngest child on the same morning. She kissed my cheek and said, "No matter where you go, Jonny, always go with God."

I extended my hand to shake Dad's hand. He put his arms around my shoulders, scratched my face with his whiskers, and squeezed me. He didn't say a word.

I cried all the way to the Texas-New Mexico border.

Meanwhile, the celebration for Grimsley Roeper had begun at Caprock State and the *Lubbock Ledger* was being delivered all over town. Tumbleweed fans were particularly interested in the story by Jonathan Langenfelder on the front page of the sports section:

Grimsley Roeper ran through the dust of Lubbock and into the hearts of Caprock State sports fans. His endearing spirit has survived 60 years, even though his body and mind succumbed to a tragedy many never knew about.

Grimsley Roeper, the greastest sports legend in Caprock State history, got hit in the head with a football...

◆◆◆

22

I woke up one morning and found myself in Eugene, Oregon. Track capital, U.S.A. Home of the late great Steve Prefontaine. The city with miles of endless trails and a who's who of world-class runners.

I showered and shaved. I popped a zit and a few blackheads and put on my work clothes of brown slacks, brown shirt, and brown hat with a monogrammed, flame-broiled Bopper Burger. I stared into the mirror and shook my head.

"Oh-h-h, no. I look 16 years old."

Sixteen was the average age of my colleagues at the Bopper Burger on the Eugene outskirts. The average wage was $3.35 per hour, and the average stay of employment was about two months. I wasn't sure I would last that long.

I made Boppers, hundreds of them, from noon until 2 p.m. every weekday.

How do you make a Bopper? You put a frozen patty on a revolving chain that carries the meat through a sizzling flame and deposits the burger in a silver pan on the other end. You stick the meat in a toasted bun and hand it to some teeth-wired geek, who slaps it with onions, pickles, lettuce, and tomatoes and sprays on mayonnaise and ketchup. Within 30 seconds, a 300-pound trucker is munching the greasy sandwich and proclaiming it to his lumberjack buddy as "the best burger I ever eat."

I asked that same Bopper-making geek what he likes about working here. "The best thing? After your shift, you get a free Bopper."

Time stood still at Bopper Burger. I looked at a digital wall clock that read 1:02. I put a dozen frozen patties on the chain, ran five meters to collect the flying fat, slammed them onto buns, rushed them to the geek, and tossed a dozen more on the chain and in the buns and back to the geek. I looked at the clock again. It read 1:03.

All this to the piped in broken-record jingle, stolen from another fast-food chain, "Hold the pickles, hold the lettuce, special Boppers don't upset us," overpowered by the whining schoolgirl announcing a customer's order over a microphone, "Bopper ...Coke...chocolate shake...f-r-i-e-s..."

I was anything but looking forward to work the morning I almost cried on a mirror streaked with zit pus. A man in a white Honda Prelude cruised by the Big Banana, as I entered the freeway. He rolled down his sunroof and shot his grimy middle finger into the sky. I wound down my window faster than I could make a Bopper and countered with a bone of my own. Each driver held their stubborn finger in the cold winter breeze for four miles, until I made the exit to Bopper Burger.

In August 1981 I had driven the Big Banana loaded with mostly running gear 2,000 miles from Texas in search of runners' heaven. What I found was rain that pelted me every day for five months from the instant my steamy radiator crossed the California-Oregon border. I found a city that broke a national record for unemployment rates. I found runners who heard my 5,000 PR of 13:44.1 and laughed.

I was lucky to find a place to live. I walked, a little bent over, into the Wooosh Eugene store. I had slept five straight nights in the drivers' seat at roadside rest areas in New Mexico, Arizona, Nevada, California, and Oregon. I told a Wooosh sales clerk I moved here to pursue my dream of making it to the Olympics.

"You and everyone else in town." He shook his head as he stocked Wooosh rain suits on a shelf. "Lookin' for a place to live?"

"Yeah."

"There's a girl who works here whose housemate just split for New York. I'll give her a call for you."

That night, in pouring rain, I transferred the contents of the Big Banana, into an old two-story house a few blocks from the University of Oregon. As rain dripped off my eye-length locks after the final load, my new housemate Penny Weaver brushed her wet hair and read me the house rules by heart.

"Your rent is $109.67 per month, payable on the first. We split the electric and water bills three ways and pay $40 each every other month for heater oil. Write down your long distance calls on the pad by the phone. Your room is upstairs on the left, and you share the bathroom with Reid, our other house-mate. Do your own dishes, don't eat anyone else's food or drink anyone's beer, and keep the noise down if you come home late."

Penny walked into her downstairs bedroom and walked back out, strangling the top of her robe. "And one more thing," she said right before slamming her door. "I am not sleeping with you."

I had more of a hard-on for Hayward Field than for Penny Weaver. I ran 5,000 meters around the track in the pouring rain that night and awoke the next morning to more rain. I put on my rain suit, walked outside, and it stopped. I took it off and it was raining again.

I put on the suit for good and ran through the puddles of Pre Trails. "Sure beats dust storms," I thought.

The weather guy's forecast on the six o'clock news that night was "clouds, rain, hail with a slight chance of sun."

Penny walked through the doorway to her room. "Found a job yet."

"A job? I haven't even been here 24 hours."

There was a better chance for sun. The *Eugene Record-Times* newspaper already hired its sports grunts for the season. The Wooosh running store had a stack of running nerd applicants 100 deep. The editor of a local running magazine said he didn't hire runners. The manager of a radio station said he didn't hire stutterers, even if I never talked on the air. The only thing I could get was food stamps.

Autumn nearly passed before I found a job or met my other housemate. Reid Rampton was in his first year at law school, where he spent 16 hours per day. I knew he wasn't sleeping with Penny, because it seemed like he didn't sleep. The first communication I had with Reid was a note he left next to a dish tray. "These dishes are not clean. I can see egg stains on this plate."

One morning I heard him and Penny talking about me downstairs. "All he does is run," Reid said.

"Yeah," Penny said. "That's all there is to life – running?"

That's all there is when you have no job, no track club and no mail. I was rejected by the two track clubs in town – Oregon Striders and the Wooosh Track Club. The Striders 5,000 standard was 13:44.0. I pleaded with Striders' manager Adrian Brumley as I splashed alongside him at Pre's Trails. "You can't give me the tenth?"

"You'll have to earn it."

I wasn't exactly welcomed at the Wooosh training complex, either. "Another California dreamer," the club's general manager Taylor Markham said. "We get guys like you in here all the time. Just run some of the local road races and all comers meets."

"Could I just work out with the team?"

"We don't have a walk-on program."

Or a crawl-on program. The only break I caught was from Amigos, perhaps the only Tex-Mex restaurant in the state. A total of 412 people, most from the closed-down timber mills, applied for jobs. I landed a waiter's job, because I was the only Texan applicant. There was no Mexican applicant.

Restaurant owner Harley Frohm had less patience than my customers and demoted me to dishwasher. As I scraped tacos and bean dip off a plate I thought about hanging my diploma above the towel rack and sending a line to the Caprock State Alumni Magazine. "Tammy Smith, Class of '78, is an account executive for Dalkins Advertising Firm in Houston. Thomas Jones, Class of '79, is a news reporter for WFRT in San Antonio. Jonathan Langenfelder, Class of '80, is washing dishes in Eugene, Oregon."

I became perhaps the first college graduate to be laid off from a job washing dishes. Frohm said he made a few calls and traded me to Bopper Burger for two busboys and a cook to be named later. That's where I spent Christmas

Eve. I spent my first Christmas Day away from my family with a church group, singing carols at several retirement homes. I worked at Bopper Burger until 11:30 p.m. New Year's Eve and did my run from one year to the next, in my all browns, in the pouring rain.

The year 1982 started with a routine of eat, run, make Boppers, eat, run, eat, sleep. I often wondered how long it took to run 20 miles. This is how long. One afternoon Penny was playing mattress polo in the room below me as I tied the laces on my Wooosh trainers. In the time I was gone she showed her playing partner to the door, showered, blow dried her hair, put on a skirt, went on a date with another partner to a restaurant, returned home, drank a glass of wine, and played polo with him. The game was reaching its climax when I finished the run.

Running 20-milers around an evergreen city of fir trees relieved me from the housemate in the thin floor below and the other housemate who taped a note to the shower curtain asking me to "not hang your soaked running gear over the shower line." It kept me from looking at Lubbock and Holly Ritzenbarger in the rearview mirror. It helped me stave off the "who's this nerd" looks from the Wooosh running pack I frequently passed on my solo runs along Pre's trails. It gave me the confidence to enter the Oregon Striders' 10-miler the first Sunday of February along the Willamette River bike trails. It was my first race in eight months.

I worked the 6 p.m. to midnight shift at Bopper Burger and had six hours sleep. I warmed up in my red and silver Caprock State cotton sweats and crossed paths with several Wooosh runners in their sharp red and white Lycra suits.

"Look out for that guy," I heard one say with a chuckle. "He's got a tumbleweed on the front of his sweats."

The Wooosh runners were still snickering along the cloud-covered starting line also toed by the top Oregon Striders, some University of Oregon and Oregon State runners, and NCAA steeplechase champion and former Virginia runner Jonas Kiprono, who was training in Eugene for the Commonwealth Games. I wore a new pair of green Wooosh racing flats, green shorts, white ankle-high socks, and a white singlet.

After the starting gun was fired, the only person in front of me was the pace cyclist. Behind me, the Wooosh runners and the Oregon Striders were discussing the previous night's Portland Trailblazers' victory. The first mile felt like seven minutes. The split timer yelled, "4:50."

I blazed my own trail through consistent low 4:50's splits that quieted the trailing pack and brought me through five miles in 24:15. Then I surged, slowly forming a fading single file of world class huffers and puffers. I dropped all but Kiprono as I ran over a bridge and raced down a trail toward the finish line. The harder the Kenyan breathed, the harder I ran.

"One good surge," I thought, "and I've got him."

147

I hammered the eighth mile in 4:45, and all I could hear was the spokes of the lead cyclist. I looked back with a mile left and saw no one. I looked ahead and saw, finally, the sun breaking through the clouds.

The pace cyclist pulled off a wet leaf road a half-mile from the finish. "I don't know who the heck you are," he said. "But you just made a name for yourself in this town."

His words carried me to the finish line and to an announcer who struggled to find my race number in the program. "Here comes the first runner...in a race record 48:26...Jonny, uh, something or other."

I knelt at the end of the finish chute and made a little fist. I didn't know whether to cry or pray. I did a little of both. I won a *Chariots of Fire* sound-track album and a bottle of red wine. More important, I won some respect. Wooosh's Gary Hicks, the three-time Olympic steepler who finished third, said, "If you'd run that in a race back East, you'd have won a lawn mower and a Cadillac." Another Wooosh runner, Dave Stubblefield, invited me to a party at his house the next Friday.

All I hoped as I walked into Stub's house in my jeans and Wooosh tennis shirt that Friday night is that I would be recognized as the man in the red and silver tumbleweed sweatsuit and not the man in the brown Bopper Burger one.

Actually everyone wore jeans and Wooosh tennis shirt and introduced themselves by what they did in their last good race.

"I'm Jonny Langenfelder."

"Who?"

"The guy who won the Oregon Striders10 miler."

"Oh, I know who you are."

"And you?"

"Wayne Snyder, I finished second in the U.S. Cross Country Champion-ships."

I followed Snyder to the garage, the party's most popular room. That's where the keg and the male runners were. (The women mostly congregated in the kitchen with their wine glasses.) It seemed if you wanted to say something, you had to pump the keg first. I didn't pump, so I didn't talk. Finally, Chicago Marathon runner-up Trace Alcott stared at me sipping foam from a plastic cup.

"Aren't you the guy who won the 10 miler last Sunday?"

I pumped the keg. "Yeah."

"Do you know who he looks like?" said Ken "U.S. vs. USSR 5,000 me-ters winner" Harwick. "He looks like someone who would work at McDon-ald's."

"Or rather Bopper Burger," Hicks said. "I've seen you there in that brown uniform."

"No you haven't."

"Yeah, I have. I took my kids there for lunch last week."

"So? I'm Jonny Langenfelder, the fastest Bopper-maker in town."

"Langenfelder?" Harwick said. "It's more like Langenbopper."

I was no longer the guy who won the 10 miler. To a runners'choir belting out. "Hold the pickles, hold the lettuce, special Boppers don't upset us," I was now Jonny Langenbopper."

"Where you from Langenbopper?" Hicks asked.

"Dallas, Texas."

"That's a good place to be from," Harwick said.

Stub pumped the keg and refilled my cup. "There seems to be a lot of stupid people in Texas, Langenbopper. Why is that?"

"Three reasons," I said. "One, because of the way they talk and how slow they talk. 'Hey, me and 'ol Billy Bob is goin' down to git a beer at the mini mart.'

"Second, because the media often portrays a Texan as some dumb old guy ridin' through the country in his pickup with horse manure on his boots."

"And the third reason?" Stub asked.

"Because there really are a lot of stupid people in Texas."

We stood in the cold, beer stench of a garage until only foam poured from the keg. The party was over. As I opened the door of the Big Banana, Snyder invited me to share a Wooosh party ritual on the way home. Moments later, I was following the Wooosh runners on a joy ride through the hills of Hendricks Park. It wasn't until I drove around a sharp bend and saw a rock in my headlights did I realize what I had done. The chalk-like inscription read, "Pre, May 30, 1975, R.I.P."

"My God," I thought. "I've just driven the Prefontaine Memorial Loop."

I felt this was a peculiar way to honor a hero. But it was more of a tribute to our fellow runner, our brother – and a way of keeping his memory alive, of saying hello to a friend. It was a reminder that life could be taken from us anytime and that we, like Pre, should live our lives to the fullest.

The next week Wooosh coach Graham Hutton met with me in his office at Wooosh headquarters. He had just returned from New Zealand, where the 34-year-old Brit won a marathon and – according to Wooosh runners – "drank the country dry and the left the Kiwi women smiling."

"I-I-I would like you to train me, but Mr. Markham said Wooosh doesn't take in walk-ons."

"Don't listen to Markham," Hutton said. "He doesn't know bloody shit about runnin.' If you can drink with these guys, you can bloody hell train with 'em."

The problem is "these guys" didn't spend their afternoons making Boppers. They were paid a monthly stipend of $600 dollars and up, provided new shoes every week and a massage every other day, given free medical care, and flown to meets anywhere they wanted. I received limited equipment from Wooosh and competed in the Hayward Field All-Comers Meets, held in the morning before the pre-University of Oregon duel meets. I won a 5,000 at 9 a.m. in 14:15 one week and finished second in a 3,000 in 8:12 the next before an empty grandstand.

Those stands were full of foot-stomping, hand-clapping spectators for duel and invitational meets. Unlike crowds at Texas meets, the fans didn't go for a hot dog as the field for the women's 5,000 was announced. The crowd was there to watch Armando Rojas, who won the Boston Marathon a month before, beat me soundly in the Oregon Twilight Meet 5,000. But my fifth place 13:59.61 gave me the confidence to drive the Big Banana to Vancouver, Canada the next week and attempt to run the U.S. qualifying standard of 13:50.

First, I went to The Duck Pond. The campus pub across from the University of Oregon overtook The Pad, where Pre was once a bartender, as the official runners' hangout. There, the Wooosh runners exchanged conquest stories about the girl in Sweden or Finland or England or Italy or New York or Los Angeles. I never heard a story about a girl in Eugene.

"Eugene?" Snyder, a former Penn Stater with a slick, black mustache, poured me a watered-down beer from his pitcher. "There ain't no girls in Eugene. Just runners. Maybe a few road whores now and then."

"What's a road whore?" I asked.

Harwick, a former Arizona Stater and the only Eugene runner with a tan, pulled his beer mug from his lips and smiled. "That's a whore you tell to hit the road right after you've done her. Leave any of them behind in Texas?"

"No. There's too many good lookin' ones in Texas."

"We had one Oregon girl who made the cover of a magazine," Stub said.

"What magazine?" I asked.

"National Geographic."

The joke from the Cornell grad prompted a barrage of Oregon women bashing.

Snyder: "To an Oregon girl, make up is something you get when you miss a day of school, and Mary Kay is Danny's sister."

Harwick: "The only things that get laid here are eggs and carpets."

Stub: "You know why it's so embarrassing taking an Oregon girl to dinner?

"Because she chews her cud."

I interrupted. "My mother always told me beauty is only skin deep."

"Yeah," Snyder said, "but ugly goes straight to the bone."

I drove home via the Prefontaine Memorial Loop and met the runners again Monday for 12 times 440 at Hayward Field. Graham Hutton stood in the infield and blew a whistle every 100 meters to make sure we were on pace. His precise training methods showed why he came within two seconds of the world 5,000-meter record, competed in the Olympics and Commonwealth Games, and was an adversary of Darcy Ellard.

"The guy's a bloody idiot," Graham said of Darcy. "If he was coaching ya', he'd have ya' running twenty-four 440's in hiking boots."

At the Vancouver Games, there was nothing under my feet but air. I left after my Bopper Burger shift on Friday, and the Big Banana and I crossed the border for the first time. I slept on the floor of Stub and Snyder's hotel room. The next afternoon, below the cool pines of an adjacent park and on a springy red rubber carpet, I followed a Canadian and his rabbit through an 8:20 3,000. As soon as the rabbit dropped out, I popped into the lead and ran three consecutive 66-second laps that separated me from everyone but Stub. I put my last contender away with a surge down the penultimate backstretch and won by 40 meters. I pumped my fist at the time 13:44.3 that flashed on a screen just past the finish line and with these super thoughts.

"U.S. qualifier! Two-tenths off the PR. Four more seconds and I'm on the Wooosh Track Club."

My first cash prize paid for my gas back to Eugene. I prepped for the Prefontaine Classic with a fourth place at the Oregon State open 1,500 in 3:45.5. The pre-party for Pre was a bachelor party starring rookie Wooosh runner Donnie Forster and special guest, Sheena, in Stub's living room. Forster was so wasted on beer and tequila shots, he probably didn't remember the stage show for his running buddies and his coach. Sheena, whose name was tattooed on her right buttocks, wasn't exactly a school teacher. But she did give her subject an oral exam before the entire class.

I hoped Forster didn't recite at his wedding, "I, Donald Charles, take thee, Sheena...I mean Priscilla, to be my wife."

I warmed up the next day with Hicks, who had stayed home with his wife and kids.

"It was a wild bachelor party last night," I said.

"Yeah? Graham said it wasn't that wild."

"To Graham it wasn't that wild. To this Texas boy, it was very, very wild."

Even wilder was the pace Rojas forged at the Pre Classic. I ran on his shoulder through a 62 first lap and then watched 17 guys pass me and my dream of a sub-13:40 vanish. I finished 42 seconds behind Mac Wilcox, who beat Rojas and the American Record with his 13:12.77. I sat on the track and watched through bleary eyes the top runners posing for photographers and smiling and waving to fans who cared less if I was there. I returned to my room to find my bed covered with dirty dishes and leftover spaghetti and garlic bread crumbs. Reid didn't need to leave a note.

"When's that dipshit going back to Texas?" I could hear Reid's voice downstairs later that night. "Did he run in that Pre Classic thing today?"

"I was there watching the meet," Penny said. "I didn't see him."

"Just what I thought," Reid said.

I boxed up my belongings that night. I was out of money and food stamps. My rent was $109 per month and my monthly pay check from Bopper Burger was $110. I had exhausted my attempts at finding another job. My only hope was to break 13:40 at the U.S. Track and Field Championships in Knoxville, Tennessee and acquire a stipend and a spot on the Wooosh roster.

I tossed my brown hat on the Bopper rack and sent it through the flame. Wooosh promised me an air ticket to Knoxville, but not a dorm room at the University of Tennessee. I slept in the television lounge. I walked the green track the night before the race and devised a plan that countered Graham's suggested tactic of sit and kick. With five laps to go, I would surge into the lead and hold it as long as I could – just like I did in Vancouver.

One night later I looked at the starting line below my Wooosh spikes and didn't care that these were 23 of the best distance runners in the United States alongside me.

I didn't care that I was 22nd after the first mile. I had a plan, and I was sticking to it. With the electronic lap counter at seven and the field tightly bunched, I flew past eight runners in the third lane on the backstretch and six more on the homestretch. As I cruised the next backstretch and glided around the turn, I looked into the stadium lights and the three runners ahead of me. I felt strong and fresh, ready to commit to a move that would elevate me from Wooosh walk-on to World wonder. I moved alongside the tall, broad-shouldered Wilcox, who was running second. I glanced at the lap counter, spotlighted with the number "5." It was go time.

I crossed the line and sprinted as if it was the gun lap. Right as I roared into the lead, a flash of red and white went past me. Harwick cut me off on the curve, turned around, spit in my face, and yelled, "Let's go, Fuck Face!"

If he had said, "Let's go, buddy" or "jerk" or "dude" I may have survived. But no amount of concentrated Father Litzke breaths could combat "Fuck Face" at that precise moment. A train of runners went by, leaving me as the caboose.

I didn't see Harwick, who finished fourth, until later that night at The Gun Lap Tavern. "Why'd ya have to call me 'that'?"

"Because I was hurtin' and you got in my fuckin' way, Langenbopper."

Harwick turned around, and Stub stopped me from pouring a pitcher of beer over his head. Instead, I poured it down my throat. The pitchers kept flowing at The Gun Lap, overtaken by runners, jumpers, and throwers who set personal bests for alcohol consumption. All inhibitions were lost in this den of indecency. Runners, male and female, took off their shirts and danced on tables, while chugging a beer and singing along to the top of our lungs to whatever rock and roll song blasted off the walls.

It took the Knoxville police to remove us from the bar, splattered with beer and broken glass, 45 minutes past the 2 a.m. closing time. The pissed-off cops chased piss-drunk 10-flat 100 meter men and sub-four milers, still screaming rock songs, down the main road back to campus.

"Come on you fuckin' pigs!" someone yelled.

I staggered and zigzagged, alone, along the dark, winding campus sidewalks, through practice fields and between buildings, at the end of a fiery season that put me back on a straight path.

23

The smoke from a starting pistol sent me and 47 other runners off the starting line at Hayward Field for the 1983 Oregon Opener Track and Field Meet. This was my first race since being called "Fuck Face" and the first 10,000 meter track race of my life.

I came armed with 20 straight weeks at 141 miles per week and an appetite to prove I could run any Wooosh runner into the ground. I ran wide around the first backstretch to avoid the crowd and set my new white-and-orange-striped Wooosh shoes behind the leader. The pace felt like a training run on one of my 28-mile Saturdays, so I took the lead. I cruised along in the same green shorts and white singlet I wore in my 48:26 10-mile one year earlier. The yellow rubber track felt like a trampoline until I heard the worst sound in track and field.

"Twenty-four laps to go."

Then it was "23" and "22" and "21." By "16" I realized I may never hear a bell. One runner passed me. Then another. Then another. Then another. I wondered how long it would take before all 47 would go by. I had 15 laps to wonder how it all went wrong, how I spent eight months away from the place I wanted to be, and the people I wanted to be with.

On the flight to Dallas from the 1982 U.S Track and Field Championships in Knoxville, I had smelled of the beer and sweat I wore at The Gun Lap Tavern. I slept for one hour on the dormitory lounge floor and somehow woke up an hour before my flight.

Dad met me at the baggage claim area at the DFW airport and sniffed my wrinkled white Wooosh shirt like a dog looking for dope. "Little party last night, Miles?"

Two hours of stop-and-go on a freeway-turned-parking lot and with a driver who went through John Wayne's *Rooster Cogburn* scene by scene made me want to hop out and thumb a ride to Eugene. Hitchhiking was all I could have afforded. I arrived in Dallas with all 77 dollars and 42 cents to my name in my wallet. The Stallion invited me to dinner at his apartment. Tanya Pertle, Bonnie's old roommate who showed up uninvited, insisted we go out to dinner.

I ate a four-dollar hamburger and drank a glass of water. The short, dark-haired Tanya with her caked-on make up and padded bra had a shrimp appetizer, filet mignon, chocolate mousse dessert, and three wine coolers. The bill came to 80 dollars and 25 cents. When the check came, Tanya looked the other way.

"Oh no," I thought. "She's not going for her purse."

The waitress stared at me and the 40 dollars and a quarter The Stallion lay on the tray. I couldn't believe I was about to pay 40 dollars for a hamburger without cheese. After the movie and popcorn, again at my expense, I had 17 dollars and 42 cents.

The Stallion asked the next day, "Why don't you ask Tanya out again?"

"Again? I didn't ask her out in the first place."

"Just tryin' to help you out, man. You're not still pining for Holly are ya?"

I couldn't ask out Tanya or Holly or anyone. With $17.42, I couldn't even take a date to Bopper Burger.

It didn't cost a dime to run up and down Rolling Hills Parkway. I returned to my midnight home burgers on Saturday and life in a jock until my oldest brother Matthew came for a Sunday roast dinner. He didn't say anything until Mom and Dad left the table.

"Still sitting on your ass all day, Jonny?

"I don't call running 20 miles a day sitting on my ass. I have a goal of making the Olympic Games. How about yourself?"

"I work my ass off roofing houses, hanging dry wall, carrying shit to the junk yard for the goal of paying rent and the rest of my bills. All you're doin' is sponging off Mom and Dad. You're just usin' them. Dad's retired now. He can't afford to keep feeding you off his pension."

"They haven't said anything."

"They haven't said anything, because the Catholic Church says you aren't supposed to send your spoiled brats out on the street. Good Lord, Jonny, you're the only one in the family who went out and got a college degree. And look what you're doin' with it."

An hour later, Dad walked into my bedroom to see me finish packing my bags.

"Where you goin,' Miles?"

I didn't look up, just kept packing. "Eugene."

"How you getting there?"

"Hitchhiking, I guess."

"You don't like your Mom's cooking anymore?"

I turned around, sat on the bed, and stared at the carpet. "It's not fair."

"What's not fair?"

"Not fair that I live here, eat your food, and take advantage of you like this."

Dad sat next to me. "I don't know what Matthew told you, but your Mom and I like having you here. I don't exactly understand what you're trying to do with your life more than I do your brothers and sisters. But this is my house, and I'll be the one to tell you when to leave."

I unpacked and found a job stringing Friday night high school football games for *The Dallas Star*. I made $40 per game for phoning in the stats and a three- paragraph story, leading with something like, "Billy Jack Boswell ran for 172 yards and three touchdowns to lead Forest Hill to a 42-10 victory over Groverton."

By the end of football season I had 497 dollars and 42 cents, enough for a bus ticket and a first month's rent. I couldn't wait to go back to a city with a running and cycling lane in the street, where you could run without some jerk in a pickup calling you a "faggot," and where an old friend's first question isn't, "You still runnin'?" I missed the Catholic Student Center, where I could hear a Sunday sermon related to modern life without the words "Jews" and "Gentiles." I missed my new friends and running buddies and being called "Langenbopper."

Stub, who was storing the Big Banana and my stuff in his garage, called me one night after *Dance Fever*. He shouted over a background of loud music and howling runners. "Whatcha doing, Langenbopper? Why aren't you at my party?"

"Just got back from a run. I'm getting into shape, so I can come back and kick your butt."

Stub said autumn in Eugene was like one Gun Lap Tavern party after another. "Road whore heaven" he called it. He also told me Graham Hutton was so angry that Wooosh sent Taylor Markham instead of him to Europe that he quit and went back to England. He was replaced by Jocko Girelli, a loud-mouthed New Yorker who coached 17 NCAA champion runners at Manhattan College.

Thanksgiving dinner was to be my last meal at 2000 Hickory Lane. After three slices of whipped cream-lathered pumpkin pie and a Dallas Cowboys' victory, I went for an easy 12-miler. At the finish curb I heard "Good run, Miles." I looked up at Dad in his navy blue parka standing on a branch in the tree, trying to remove a stuck football. "I could see you from about a half-mile down the Parkway. You run like a deer."

"Be careful, Dad."

As Dad reached for the ball, the branch snapped. He fell 20 feet to the cold, hard ground and landed on his side. I rushed to him and patted his shoulder. "You all right, Dad."

He didn't move.

As the paramedics put Dad on a stretcher and Mom started on her second rosary, I did a John Wayne impersonation, "O-K, there, pil-grim. Ya' better wake up. There's a good John Wayne movie on tonight. Wa, hah."

Dad's eyelids creaked open. The sun glistened off his brown pupils. He let out a little smile as he was lifted into the ambulance.

I cashed in my bus ticket and spent the next three months helping Dad recover from broken ribs and a dislocated shoulder. I helped him walk to and from the bathroom and changed television channels. Come February of 1983, Dad told me during a commercial. "You remember when I said I would tell you when it was time for you to leave."

"Yeah."

"Well, go. Get out of here and go make the Olympics or something?"

I bought a cheap airline ticket and arrived at Stub's house the night before the 10,000 meters track race. I told Stub, "After I win tomorrow, I'm just going to do my own training."

"I don't know, Langenbopper, Jocko's a pretty good coach."

"I need this town. But I don't need him, and I'll prove it tomorrow."

As I passed the "8" card on the lap counter, all I proved was what a "Fuck Face" I really was. I wanted to drop out.

"But if I drop out," I thought, "I'll get back on a plane to Dallas tonight and never set foot on a track again."

I finished 27th, but it felt more like 37th. Then I realized that 10 runners actually lapped me. I didn't wait to find out I had run 30:38. I ran up the backstretch bleachers and sat next to Jocko. He was talking a mile-a-minute with his thick, black mustache flapping and too absorbed into the women's 10,000 to notice me. I extended my hand, but he didn't shake it.

"I'm J-J-Jonny Langenfelder."

"I know who you are." Jocko didn't take his eyes off the track.

"Will you coach me?"

"Yeah, sure."

I went to Jocko's office at Wooosh headquarters with my stack of log books Monday morning. I barely could see him beneath the cloud of cigar smoke. Before I could say a word, Jocko went off about Annie Riley, the freckle-faced Boston Marathon favorite he coached in New York.

"Annie's in ah-some shape. She'll blow through the Heartbreak Hills like they're pancakes. She's so smooth and tough. If she was a man, she'd have balls like grapefruit."

Jocko rambled on like that about five more of his athletes, before I interrupted.

"About my workouts?"

"Let's go for a run and we'll tahk about it."

Jocko spiked his cigar in a coffee mug. He put on a pair of blue Lycra tights, tied his Wooosh running flats, and led me out the door. He coughed and continued on with how great his athletes are as we ran down an industrial road. A passenger in a dump truck honked and yelled, "Hey, you faggots!"

Jocko flipped him a bone. The truck stopped, and out rushed a lumberjack of a man in jeans and work boots. Jocko stopped and waited. The guy went to throw a punch. Jocko, a former Navy boxer, blocked it and hit the guy with four quick body blows. As the guy lay on the sidewalk, holding his stomach, Jocko looked at the guy's buddy in the driver's seat.

"You want some of this, too."

The driver sped off and left his buddy on the sidewalk.

We continued our run, and Jocko talked more about the athletes he trained 3,000 miles away than the one three feet from him. With Graham Hutton, I spent 10 minutes and left with a typed schedule that told me what I was doing the next 10 weeks. With Jocko Girelli, I spent three hours without knowing what I was doing the next day.

For sure, I knew I couldn't keep sleeping on Stub's sofa. I feared I would end up like one of the many bums that slithered around the streets of Eugene. The bum I met on Monday after the meeting with Jocko didn't ask what time it was. He asked what "day" it was. Then he asked for three dollars and said, "Look, I'm not gonna lie to ya' and tell ya' I'm hungry. I just wanna get drunk."

My apartment and job hunting that day was a bust with a series of "no vacancy" and "never hiring" signs." The *Eugene Record-Times* had a hiring freeze. I went to the 15th Street Quads, where the manager was moving his things from his apartment to his car. He told me he had been receiving free rent and $50 per month and gave me an odd look when I told him I might like to replace him.

"You want to live – and work – here?"

I drove to the management company and within 30 minutes I had a box of keys, files of lease agreements and 30-day notices, a job, and a place to live. But no place to sleep. The first night my next-door neighbor threw an all-night pot party. I barely could see Brick Guthrie through the marijuana smoke, after he opened his door with a cough.

"Wow, man. We like woke you up?"

The second night a transient passed out before the doorway of an apartment. I called the police at midnight. A police officer arrived and whacked the bottom of the bum's boots with his night stick. The bum woke, saw the cop above him, and threw a slow-motion punch. That gave the cop permission to yank him up by his scraggly hair, slam him on top of his police car hood, hit him three times in the hamstrings with his nightstick, and cuff him. My tenants cracked open their doors to witness the Rodney King-style beating.

"You're a fucking asshole," the bum said.

"That might be so. But you're goin' to jail, mother fucker."

The third night there was a loud knock on the door at 2 a.m. I opened it to an unshaven thug and a pregnant teenager.

"We're lookin' for a place to stay for the night," the thug said.

"This is an apartment complex, not a motel."

Now I knew why the old manager called this the "Midnight Express" apartments.

They were referred to as quads, four small rooms, surrounding a communal ant-covered kitchen and enter-at-your-own-risk bathroom I shared with a dope head, an ex-con, and some guy I never saw. Earl Weatherby, the ex-con, wore sleeveless white T-shirts and had tattoos of snakes and naked women up and down his meaty white arms. I asked him why he went to prison.

"'Murdered my landlord." There was a frightful pause and then Earl's cigarette-stained smile. "Just kiddin.' You don't have to worry 'bout me. I is totally reformed."

Not exactly. He skipped town without paying rent and with fifty dollars of food he stole from the refrigerator and kitchen cabinets.

The guy I never saw finally turned up – at the psychiatric hospital. I did a lawful entry into his apartment and found rows of radar equipment. I think he was trying to contact Mars.

I wanted to evict Dusty Travers, a reddish-haired and bearded bum with freckles, no teeth, a monthly disability check, and a barbecue grill in his room. I don't know what smelled worse, the smoke on his ripped plaid shirt and jeans or the whisky that blew out of his mouth. If I lit a match, he would have caught fire. But Dusty always came to my door the first day of every month with a check and a smile.

"Sure am glad you let me stay here, boss. This here's the best place I ever lived."

I looked out my window at midnight to see Dusty pacing back and forth for hours in the parking lot, while scratching the back of his head.

Sleepless nights didn't affect my training or my social life - only because I had no social life. I could imagine myself picking up a girl and saying, "Hey babe, your place or yours?" Or "would you like to come over for a ménage a quad?"

Jocko put me through some long interval sessions at Hayward Field. His favorite was five times per mile with a two-lap jog. He hollered split times with a cigar stuck in the corner of his mouth. I traded leads with the Wooosh runners and by April I was running and winning the 3,000 at an All Comers Meet in 8:09 and the 1,500 at the Twilight Meet in 3:47. Jocko wangled a Wooosh deal that sent me to Knoxville for the Tennessee Relays. The problem was I had to share a room with him and his cigars and hear all his moaning and groaning all night about his bad back, the cut in pay he took to come to Eugene, and the alimony he owed his ex-wife in New York. The 5,000 was moved up from the cool of the night to the 90-degrees of the early evening, in fear of predicted showers that would have made for good conditions. I finished third to last in 14:20.

That left me only three weeks to run the U.S.A qualifying time of 13:50. I ran the following Thursday at the Oregon State Open in Corvallis against a dozen University of Oregon walk-ons in their last ditch attempt at the NCAA qualifying standard and three-time Olympic steeplechaser Gary Hicks, who said he was using the 5,000 as a "training run." The Prefontaine-wannabes in their yellow and green tanks and shorts traded the lead the first six laps at a pace well off any standard. I followed their shadows on the dimly-lit track and lost my patience. I did a Pre move that dropped the Ducks and upset Hicks' training run. Hicks surged past me with three laps to go and I re-passed him down the backstretch with 600 meters left, only to lose the lead at the bell.

Hicks sprinted to a 10-meter lead. With 200 meters left, I dug deep and collared the arrogant Wooosh runner in the homestretch and won by five me-ters. I walked back to shake Hicks' hand and he refused it.

"Fuck off, Langenbopper," he said.

My time was 13:50.7, and my last mile was run in 4:12 in what Jocko called "one of greatest fuckin' duels I ever saw." He told me I had balls like grapefruit.

Nine days later I entered the Prefontaine Classic. I needed to shave seven-tenths of a second to qualify for nationals in Indianapolis, where a top per-formance could land me in Europe and increase my chances for a berth in the 1984 Olympics. Qualifying seemed a certainty as I strode into Hayward Field that early Saturday evening with my black Wooosh spike bag and the sun glaring off my sunglasses. It didn't matter that I spent the previous night breaking up another midnight pot party and turning away another prospective bum tenant at 2 a.m.

I hid my bag, which contained my Wooosh spikes, in the yellow equip-ment shed at the head of the backstretch. I felt strong on my warm-up jog and strides on the grass field behind the track. I couldn't wait to get into my spikes. I walked into the shed and reached for my bag. It wasn't there. I looked all over the shed, checked the other bags, and pushed javelins, shots, hammers, and discuses out of my way. No bag. No spikes. The 5,000 meters was 10 minutes away.

I ran into the athletes section of the stands. "You wear size 10 spikes? You wear size 10 spikes?" No size 10. I saw Jocko staring at his stopwatch. "I need some spikes."

Jocko took the cigar out of his mouth. "Did you see what Annie Riley ran in the women's 5,000?"

As they introduced the 19 other 5,000 meter entrants, I scrounged the track like a hobo looking for a quarter. I found a pair of size 9 dripping wet steeplechase spikes on the infield. I arrived at the line just in time for the starter's smoke. I ran through the mile in 4:22 to the beat of the clapping, shoe stomping bleacher bums.

"That's not bad," I thought. "But these one-size-too-small shoes are killing my big toes and weigh a ton."

I hit the two mile last in the large chase pack in 8:48 but ahead of the qualifying pace even with huge blisters scraping my big toes. "You can do this," I thought. "Listen to your breath."

As I ran past the shed on the curve, I saw Hicks with my bag on his shoulder. I thought about yelling from the back of the pack, "You jerk! You took my bag!"

I tried to regain focus and hold onto the pack. But all I could think about was how bad my feet hurt. Around a turn by the steeplechase pit, I stopped, tore off the shoes, and tossed them into the water. Bloody blistered toes and all, I regained my rhythm. With a lap to go, the timer called "12:50." I needed to break 60 seconds to make nationals on brittle feet that made the track feel like broken bricks. I passed two runners on the backstretch and sprinted into the homestretch. I fell across the finish line and was helped up by Stub and Wayne Snyder, who finished right in front of me.

"Langenbopper ," Stub said. "Those got to be the ugliest toes I've ever seen."

The 5,000 meter results were announced over the Hayward Field speakers as I wiped the blood off my aching toes with a rag in the equipment shed. "Come on," I whispered. "Thirteen forty-nine, oh please, thirteen, forty-nine."

The announcer called 13.47.83 for 14th place, Dave Stubblefield, and 13:48.57 for 15th place Wayne Snyder. Then the call echoed off the old green bleachers for "16th place, Jonny Langenfelder, unattached..."

I closed my eyes and squeezed my sore toes with the rag.

"Thirteen, forty-nine...no, excuse me...Thirteen-fifty, point forty-one."

I opened my eyes to see two feet dressed in Wooosh training shoes. I looked up at Hicks holding my bag with his two hands. He dropped it on my lap.

"Here's your fucking bag, Langenbopper. Mine looks just like yours. Now what did you do with my spikes you stole."

I stood and rested my hand on a stack of javelins. I felt like taking one and harpooning the asshole who just ruined my track and field season and perhaps my career.

"Borrowed, you pompous prick!" I yelled, pointing to the track. "They're floating in the steeplechase pit with blood all over them."

Hicks pushed me over a cart that sent shot puts rolling around the shed. I grabbed an opened sack of powder that officials use to line the shot and discus area and shoveled it at Hicks, who braced himself from the chalk shower. He tried to joust me with a high jump bar, but he couldn't see me through the white smoke and dust that covered his face. I escaped, but not before clamping the padlock on the shed door. Hicks pounded his fists inside the shed, "I'm gonna kill you, Langenbopper!"

I made one last bid for nationals the next Friday evening at the Oregon Last Chance Meet in an empty stadium and with three other 5,000 meters competitors who had no prayer of qualifying. Stub, whom I talked into becoming my "rechargeable rabbit," led me through the first mile in 4:25. He rested for two laps and then jumped back in and led me for two more laps to some claps of a few "real" wine-guzzling bleacher bums who couldn't afford to watch any other meet in the famed stadium. Leading me the last two laps was like dragging a wounded mule. I finished my fourth 5,000 in 20 days in 14:12.

I thanked Stub and walked to the parking lot in my spikes. I drove the Big Banana toward the Midnight Express apartments with bandages on my toes, past a coach who talked like a New York City cab driver, to tenants who owed me rent, and away from a beloved track I wouldn't touch for another seven months.

24

Big Bucky wasn't so big. But in terms of his ego and his appetite for ladies in skirts or tight jeans, Big Bucky was huge.

A summer 1983 rent reduction at the Midnight Express Apartments drew characters from all over the region to my front door at all hours. The leasing company installed a peep hole I looked through with a "Men at Work" tune beating through my head:

Who could that be knocking at my door?

Go away; don't come here no more...

Among the faces in my peep hole was Chang Wao, a chinese busboy who knew only one English word – "key" – and locked himself out of his apartment every night. There was Charlene Easley, a well-breasted barmaid who snacked on her fingernails and asked me with a wink, after a night of sipping the merchandise, to come fix her plumbing. I told her I didn't know how. There was rent evader and eventually evicted Lonnie Himmell, who left grease stains on the beige shag carpet from the engine he was rebuilding in his room. There was Victoria Owens, a University of Oregon home economics student who came by every evening with a list of complaints or things needed to be repaired or replaced. She showed me one light bulb that was brighter than another light bulb, to which I said, "Life is rough."

There also were prospective tenants, including a man with a beard that hung to his waist. His backpack was tied to his matted hair. I opened the door at 11 p.m. and closed it faster than I could say, "No vacancy."

One afternoon I peeked through my peep hole and saw another eye.

I opened the door and stared down at a stocky punk in faded blue running shorts, a sleeveless, purple tie-dyed shirt, and sandals he probably bought at the supermarket.

"Howdy and hello, I'm Buck Brody. But you can just call me Big Bucky."

I gazed at his blond crew cut and at his packed VW van with South Carolina license plates, personalized with "BBucky."

"What can I do for you, Big Bucky?"

"I drove straight here from South Carolina, and I need me a pad. This place looks pretty good. How are the chicks?"

"If you drove here from Carolina looking for chicks, you came to the wrong place."

"No, no, I came to train for the Olympics. My Dad gave me $5,000 and said 'go find you the best place in the world to train.'"

I felt like telling Big Bucky they didn't have skateboarding in the Olympics. "What sport do you do?"

"Running. I'm a marathoner."

"What's your best time?"

"Two twenty-seven. But I was on 2:13 pace at 12 miles."

I rented Big Bucky the apartment above me, and he told me about a bikini contest at the Grumpy Mule. I went to look at the babes, but instead watched Big Bucky. He approached every hot woman with or without a date. He bought some women drinks; some women bought him drinks. By the end of the bikini contest, he had won the hearts of the gold, silver, and bronze medal winners. He drove Bronze to the Midnight Express apartments and made his van rock in the parking lot. Silver arrived at his apartment an hour later and made his walls shake. He spent the rest of the night at Gold's place. He bragged the next morning that the Earth moved.

Big Bucky carried on this itinerary every night to the amazement of me and the Univeristy of Oregon college students, whom he shared the kitchen and bath. He showed us photographs from South Carolina his old girlfriend took of him having intercourse with his new girlfriend.

College boy number one said, "Big Bucky, you make love more than I masturbate."

"What's masturbate?" Big Bucky asked.

"You know, flog the log," College boy one said, initiating a round of more AKA's from himself and the other two College boys.

"Slam the ham."

"Choke the chicken."

"Spank the monkey."

"Never done that," Big Bucky said.

"Never?"

"Never had to."

Every time I went to a bar, no matter where I went, Big Bucky showed up. I timed how long it took before he had his arm around a girl.

"Fifty-three seconds," I told Dave Stubblefield that night at The Duck Pond. "Personal best."

He talked to this stranger for 45 minutes. "What could they possibly be talking about for that long?" I said.

"Probably about making the Olympics, running a four-minute mile, having a 10-inch dick, or any other bullshit he can think up," Stub said. "He's a legend in his own mind."

His Midnight Express quad mates couldn't pick up his rejects. I never tried. I saw Big Bucky as a young Uncle Grimsley. Spending your nights picking up women and the mornings watching the sunrise was no way to make the Olympics – unless you're trying out for the mattress polo team.

The closest I came was one night after Big Bucky left the Grumpy Mule. Bikini gold medalist Lori Capps and I slow-danced, sat, drank a beer, and talked. The college boys gawked at me with green eyes. Eventually I walked Lori to her Datsun pickup and watched her drive off. As I drove the Big Banana toward the Midnight Express, I thought of a plan. Instead of sliding into my reserved manager's parking space, I parked three blocks up the street and walked to my apartment. I left my parking space empty, making the college boys think I followed Lori to her place. When the college boys came home and saw the space empty, they drove to Lori's apartment to see if my car was there. They were so consumed with the idea that I was sleeping with the bikini champion, and one of Big Bucky's conquests, they stayed up all night discussing the possibility.

The next morning I heard them talking about it above me in Big Bucky's apartment. "You think he'll tell us, if he fucked her," a college boy said.

I replaced my pajamas with the clothes I wore the night before, snuck out through the apartment behind the kitchen, and drove the Big Banana back to my parking space. The college boys and Big Bucky followed me into my apartment.

After several minutes of prodding and pleading for the story, I gave them one. "I followed Lori back to her place and parked around the corner of the crowded parking lot. We went in, drank a beer, and talked. She walked to her bedroom and returned wearing a black nightie."

The wide-eyed perverts slouched on the floor as I sat on my bed and continued in a straight-faced monotone. "I walked to the kitchen to get another beer. She followed and met me by the fridge. I turned around, and she hugged me. I could feel her hard nipples against my chest."

I now had my audience members' full and, I presumed, upright attention. "Then she led me to her bedroom, dropped her nightie, and tore off my shirt. I pulled down my jeans and fell with her on the bed. She slipped off her black panties. She kissed me passionately, reached down, and started pulling on my leg – just like I'm pulling on yours right now."

The college boys and Big Bucky sat there with their mouths open. Big Bucky laughed. A college boy let out a, "Ohhhh! You Son Of A Bitch."

I was still a virgin with a secret wish of losing the label on my wedding night. It meant cold showers and sticky pajamas. But I didn't want to end up like Uncle Grimsley or Big Bucky, who went through his Daddy's money in three months and left Eugene and his Olympic dream in his VW van, at sunset, with three road whores and likely some sort of disease.

That autumn of 1983 my only grunts and groans came on a rope during Monday night's circuit training in the Eugene Community College gymnasium, on Tuesday's hill session in Hendricks Park, on Friday's tempo run along the Willamette River bike trails, or on Saturday's 20-miler that capped another 121-mile week.

In November, Jocko sent Stub, Wayne Snyder, Ken Harwick, and I to the Autumn Classic 10K in Phoenix. I wasn't sure if 10K stood for 10,000 meters or 10,000 runners. I was awed by the sound system blaring rock music, an aerobic warm up, a pace motorcycle, hospitality tent, refreshment tent, and take-a-number Port -A-Johns that lined the mall parking lot. I refused to stand in a 10-deep line of joggers for a hold-your-breath toilet and parked my cheeks between some bushes and an office building.

I ran like what I left on the glass window and left Phoenix wondering how I possibly could go from finishing 42nd in the Autumn Classic road race to third in the U.S. Olympic Track and Field Trials in Los Angeles in just seven months and with a coach who treated me like number 42. I was a lonely number one, eating a shaved Turkey sandwich for my Thanksgiving supper and watching the Cowboys on my black and white television. I was so desperate to talk to someone that I knocked on Dusty Travers' door. He didn't answer. I hadn't seen him pacing up and down the dark parking lot for several days and worried when he didn't pay rent the first of the month as he always had. My late notices and eviction order stayed taped to the door, forcing me to use my master key to see if he was still alive. I opened the door to a cloud of smoke and a bearded man sitting on his bed and drinking a bottle of whiskey.

"I done screwed up, boss." Dusty scratched his beard and smelled like someone who spent the last week in a Port-A-John. "I got drunk and spent my

entire disability check on a bus ticket to San Francisco to go see The Grateful
Dead. Could ya' just let me skip a month. I'll git my next check around
Christmas. Could ya' do this for me, boss?"

I scratched the back of my head. "S-S-Sorry, but if the leasing company
found out I let you stay, they'd kick both of us out."

"Wow-K, boss, I understand."

I told Dusty I'd give him a lift to wherever he needed to go. Within 15
minutes he had packed all his belongings in a duffel bag and was riding in the
Big Banana. I asked him if he would be staying with family or a friend until he
found a new place. He said he hadn't spoken to his father in 15 years. His
mother was an alcoholic who traveled from man to man. He had no brothers or
sisters, no close friends. He gave me directions to a government housing complex for people with mental or emotional illnesses. The old building looked
like it needed a good wrecking ball. He said he would live there – probably
share a padded room with the rats and cock roaches.

Dusty opened the passenger door. "Thanks for puttin' up with me, boss.
You been real decent to me."

As Dusty walked toward the building with his army-green duffel bag
slung over his shoulder, I realized I had just thrown a man out on the street. I
rested my forehead on top of the steering wheel and watched the tears land on
the floor mat.

"At least I have family and friends I can turn to," I thought. "This poor
soul has no one."

I honked the horn, and Dusty walked back toward the car.

"What is it, boss?"

"Get in, I've got a better place for you to live?"

I handed Dusty the key to his apartment and started a "Save Dusty" campaign. The Midnight Express dwellers contributed enough to pay his December rent and enough left over for a bottle of Christmas whisky.

I had just enough money for a plane trip to Dallas. When my flight was
canceled in Eugene, I had only one option to avoid Christmas with Dusty and
a whisky glass. I took a bus to Portland at 1 a.m. Christmas Eve. I arrived at
the Portland Airport at dawn to a flight that was to have the Houston Rockets
aboard. The millionaire basketball players slumped in the waiting area. I asked
them, "Who won last night?"

They shook their heads. "Sheet, man," said Shambo Rolliston, the Rockets' 7-4 Sultan of Sweat. "Git da' fuck outta 'ere."

They presumed I was rubbing it in. They thought everyone in the world
knew they were defeated 124-78 by the Portland Trail Blazers. Did they consider someone could be awake for 46 hours and so preoccupied with trying to
get to his family for Christmas that he didn't have time to read the sports
page? I worried about missing the connection in Denver. But Republic Air-
ways officials delayed the flight to accommodate the Rockets and fill the first
class section. I walked up to Shambo Rolliston at the head of the ramp and
asked for his autograph. He didn't bother reaching for my pen. "Git on da'
plane, man."

I flew to Houston, took a six-hour bus ride to Dallas, and arrived at 2000 Hickory Lane at 10:30 p.m. to a table of dirty dishes and a living room with a fake Christmas tree and opened presents. Mom said my brothers and sisters couldn't wait and made other plans for Christmas Day. Instead of going to midnight Mass they went to a midnight movie.

I slept through Christmas Day and spent the rest of the week – like always - sleeping, eating, and running up and down Rolling Hills Parkway and into an Olympic fantasy. I returned to the Midnight Express on New Year's Eve. I slid through the snow and ice on my five-mile run from one year to the next to and from Hayward Field. Dusty greeted me with his rent check and a whisky flask. "Happy New Year, boss!"

Dusty did not resolve to stop drinking. I resolved to stop eating sweets. It seemed like half my food stamp money went toward Butterfingers, Hostess Cup Cakes and Snowballs, Peanut M & M's, Coke and Dr Pepper, and chocolate chip ice cream. I would eat the packet of Oreos on the way home from the supermarket, which I regretted on my evening run.

I gave up beer, parties, and chasing women – or at least the thought of chasing women – and running for the Wooosh Track Club that season. Taylor Markham told me he was not adding any new runners so close to the Olympics. The next day, Jocko introduced us to new Wooosh runners Adam Larkin of Michigan State and Herby Gimble of Rutgers.

Two months of the no sugar, women, or alcohol diet put me back on track – Pre's track. Jocko hammered his Wooosh runners with five to six miles of intervals at Hayward Field every Tuesday and hills or a tempo run on Friday. In the cold rain in February, we ran a ladder of 440-880-1,320-mile and back down. We started to take off our spikes, when Jocko yelled, "Two mile."

"Fuck it, I ain't doing it," Snyder said.

"Me neither," Stub said.

I retied my laces and jogged to the starting line. "You pussies." I ran 9:15 and caught up with the others on the warm down.

"What's with this John Wayne bullshit?" Harwick said.

"I'm just trying to do everything right, make the Olympic team."

"How does it make us look, a Wooosh walk-on showing us up? I get tired of going into Jocko's office and hearing 'Langenbopper is looking ah-some.'"

I turned and ran in the other direction from runners whose workday ended after the warm-down. While they were relaxing with dinner and television, I was fixing a leaky toilet or calling such references as a parole officer or a psychiatrist for a prospective tenant or answering my telephone with "Midnight Express Apartments, Vacancies 24-7."

"I'm calling about an apartment."

"Yes sir, it's a small room, and you share the kitchen and bathroom with three other people."

"Do you have one with a private bathroom?"

"No, you share the bathroom with three other tenants."

"Well, do you 'have' one with a private bath?"

Click.

The Midnight Express had the largest turnover rate in Eugene. The problem was guessing what four people could share a kitchen and bath without killing each other. I guessed right with my quad. I left Brick's old apartment vacant and picked Gilbert Simms, a study-a-holic engineering major for one room and Blanche Bosworth, a tall, stocky PE major who only dated her volleyball teammates.

I guessed wrong in a quad that contained Jasmine Hayes and Roddie Collins. Jasmine preferred soul music and quiet reading. Next-door neighbor Roddie liked hard rock, getting high, and punching holes in the wall. Roddie one night threatened to punch a hole in Jasmine's face. Dusty informed me of the loud quarrel. I entered the kitchen just as Jasmine reached into the drawer and pulled out a butcher knife. I grabbed her forearm as she lunged at a white-faced Roddie, who retreated to his room. He cranked a Led Zeppelin tape on full volume, but still not enough to over-power Jasmine's, "I'm gonna kill that honky bastard!"

The police broke up the disturbance about midnight.

On the next afternoon's warm up Larkin complained about his $670-per month stipend to his four Wooosh teammates and his sparring partner. "That's barely enough to pay for my rent, my food, and gas for my 280Z. I barely have enough money to buy tapes for my VCR."

"What an insensitive jerk," I thought as we jogged through the U of O campus. "This guy gets a stipend, unlimited travel, medical and dental coverage, daily massages, physiological testing, and as many shoes and socks he can shove into his condo. Meanwhile, I get a couple pairs of shoes and bus fare to Portland."

Gimble added this: "I really don't like runnin.' I'd rather be back in West Virginia buildin' tractors. I only came out here, because Jocko talked me into it."

I took my anger to Hayward Field for the U of O Opener. Larkin, Gimble, Stub, Snyder, Trace Alcott and several other Wooosh runners were entered along with some U of O guys and several other post-collegians, seeking the U.S. Olympic Trials 10,000 meters qualifying time of 28:40. I needed to cut two minutes off my PR to qualify.

The sharp red-and-white-clad Wooosh runners traded the early lead. I followed at the mid-pack of 50 in my white singlet and skimpy maroon shorts I nicknamed "the loincloth." We went through the 5,000 in 14:25. The pace increased on Jocko's call from the backstretch bleachers, "What's this – a fuckin' funeral procession?"

I was not about to sacrifice myself this time. I stayed in the procession and covered every surge and waited for every Wooosh runner to drop off the pace. With three laps to go Larkin shot into the lead, and I filed behind him. We had broken everyone by the start of the gun lap. As we hit the head of the back-stretch, Jocko hollered, "You got it, Adam!"

Immediately, I stabbed my spikes into the rubber and burst by my spoiled training mate on the backstretch. I lapped six runners, including Gimble, around the curve and two more in the homestretch without checking back to see by how much I had destroyed Larkin and the other Wooosh runners. I grabbed the finish line string in 28:32.1 and ran my first victory lap of Hayward Field to a few claps from Dusty, Gilbert, Blanche, Blanche's girlfriend, and a few other Midnight Express tenants, and a Brooklyn cheer from Jocko, "Way-ta-go, Langenboppa."

I won again in a University of Oregon All Comers 3,000 and again in the 1,500 at the Oregon State Open. I asked the Wooosh shoe company for a ticket to the Mt. Sac Relays in Los Angeles, but was rejected. Instead, I drove the Big Banana back to Vancouver for my one and only try for a 5,000 qualifier. A race-week flu bug weakened me so badly I couldn't even walk to the door to see what scumbag stood behind it. I recovered and finished fifth in Vancouver in an Olympic Trials qualifier. I waited to hear from the announcer if I had finally beaten my PR of 13:44.1, which I rode for four years. "...and in fifth, Jonny Logginfaylor...13:43.8."

I clenched my fist. "Yes."

No. The result I read in the newspaper over an Egg Bopper sandwich and en route to Eugene the next morning was 13:44.6. Still, I was feeling good again and rounding into form only a few weeks before the Olympic Trials. I quit my job at the Midnight Express Apartments to the dismay of my tenants, who said farewell with gas money for my road trip to the Olympic Trials in Los Angeles. Dusty gave me a hug the morning I stuffed my belongings in the Big Banana and pulled out of the manager's parking space for the last time. Dusty smiled through his reddish beard, "I'll be watchin ya' in the Olympics, boss."

I stopped halfway to Los Angeles at the Sacramento Howard Johnson's for the Wooosh Heat Training Camp. Life at Ho-Jo's was a morning run, pool lounge, afternoon workout, cable movies, and restaurant meals – all complimentary of Wooosh. You could play the Rocky Theme "Gonna Fly Now" to my one-arm push ups, crunching sit-ups, dawn five-milers, lightning-fast track intervals with the cigar-jawed Jocko yelling the splits, late night runs down city streets, and a Sunday 14-miler to the top of a mountain that overlooked Lake Tahoe.

The music climaxes with a loud "Gonna Fl-y-y-y" and with me sprinting to the summit with my arms above my head, my feet bouncing my slim frame, and my eyes staring into the distance as far as they could focus, seemingly to Los Angeles.

25

Allpo Vaartanen had hands that felt like rocks, steel knuckles, and an elbow that could carve meat. He dug into my calves, hamstrings, and buttocks like they were dog food and did not respond to "Stop, you're killing me!"

I should have learned the Finnish word for "ouch" before Allpo's brutal one-hour massage two days before my 5,000 meters heat at the 1984 U.S. Olympic Track and Field Trials. Wooosh brought the world renowned masseur to Los Angeles to work on brave runners who needed some final kinks worked out before, during, and after the Trials. Allpo, a balding man in his 60's with a gray goatee, was said to be psychic. He raised his hands above the massage table and sensed the condition of each towel-draped runner.

"Vardy good, yaa," he told Ken Harwick, during his massage. "Yar vardy fine boody. Gewd shape. Vardy fit, yaa. Yar will do vardy gewd."

Then I undressed, strapped a towel around my waist, and lay face down on the padded table. Allpo closed his eyes and took a deep breath. He moved his hands back and forth above my body and said, "Oh shit."

I was a bit tired and dehydrated from the long drive from Sacramento in the Big Banana, which had no air conditioner. But I was invigorated by the magnificent ocean view along Highway 1 and the incredible workouts I ran at the camp. My final workout was a mile in 4:12 and four 440's with a lap jog interval in 59, 59, 58, and 53.6. Jocko looked at his stopwatch and took his cigar out of his mouth. "Holy smoke! You just made the Olympic team with that workout, Langenboppa."

I would be the only Olympian, other than a Southern California resident, who drove to the meet. The Olympic Trials committee paid travel expenses only for 5,000 meter qualifiers who ran under 13:44, and Wooosh said it only would reimburse me if I made the Olympic team. I also was eligible for a Wooosh bonus of $5,000.

"That's a dollar a meter," Stub said over a spinach salad at the University of Southern California dining hall the night before the heats. "How would you spend it?"

"I would trade in the Big Banana for a red Firebird the morning after the Trials and cruise back up Highway 1 toward Eugene with the T-tops down."

"Would there be a Playboy model in there with you?"

"No. Not until after the Games."

I figured my six-month abstinence from women, beer, and sugar gave me a chance to make the Olympic Team. I was so fit that making the Games would seem a miracle to everyone but me. I decided to forego the 10,000 meters and save myself for the 5,000, which had heats Thursday, semifinals Friday, and finals Sunday.

My Olympic dream was interrupted at 6:30 the next morning by a harsh scraping noise outside my dormitory window. I walked from my bed to see a Mexican in white overalls on a ladder scraping paint off the building. Of all times, USC housing officials chose dawn of my Olympic Trials 5,000 meters heats to paint the place.

"I undid the latch and pulled up the window."

"What the hell are you doing?"

The man kept scraping and rambled off in eight seconds about 50 Spanish words, of which I only understood, "No Ingles." I motioned for him to get lost. He kept scraping. I closed the window, pulled the covers back over my head, and tried unsuccessfully to tune out that "scrape-scrape, scrape-scrape, scrape-scrape."

I jumped out of bed, threw open the window, and stuck my middle finger between his eyes. "Comprende?"

I slept for an hour until my 300-pound roommate lumbered through the door. Burke Plunker was just coming in after celebrating his hammer throw victory the night before. His footsteps sounded like the Incredible Hulk's, and when he dropped on his bed, the walls shook. Immediately, he started snoring.

It was a rough morning, but I kept telling myself, "It's just a heat, it's just a heat."

Through breakfast and lunch and time spent in the television lounge, the butterflies scraped my stomach like the Mexican scraped the dormitory walls. I took a deep breath. "It's just a heat. It's just a heat."

I returned to my room and to Plunker's snoring and the Mexican's scraping and tried to have a nap. Then the telephone rang. "Hello."

"Langenfumper?"

"Yeah."

"It's Coach Tuppernacker."

"What do you want, Fubby?"

"I came to watch the meet and see you run. How do ya think you're gonna do?"

"I don't know, Fubby. Why don't you go ask Allpo?"

I put on my racing uniform and sweats, grabbed my spikes, and jogged my two-mile warm-up on a loop from the dorm to the Los Angeles Coliseum. It turned into a four-mile when I took a wrong turn and ended up in Hollywood Harlem. The spiked shoes I carried in each hand felt like my roommate's hammers by the end of the longest warm-up of my career. I kept telling myself, "It's just a heat, it's just a heat."

I met the runners in my heat in a small tent outside the Coliseum. I took one look at the 11 others, looked away, and breathed. "Think what Father Litzke would tell me to do. OK, feel the feeling. Feel the scraping against my stomach. Feel it. Just a heat."

The grim-faced officials handed me the race numbers to go on the front and back of my white singlet and the sides of my shorts. They escorted us down the dark tunnel to the light as I struggled to fit the little side numbers on my maroon loincloth shorts. When I looked up, I was standing in the Los Angeles Coliseum. I stood with my mouth open for a minute, soaking in the enormity of this great, historic stadium with huge arches along the curve where the Olympic flame would stay, 100,000 seats, huge scoreboard, and two Jumbotrons with instant replays. Here was where they played the first Super Bowl, filmed *Heaven Can Wait*, held the 1932 Olympic Games, and where they would hold the Olympics again in six weeks.

"Will I walk back up that dark tunnel and never return?" I thought. "Or will I come back in a red, white, and blue suit, march around this red track with thousands of athletes from all over the world, wave to the television cameras and standing room only crowd, and revel in the Olympic flame soaring into the night sky?"

I jogged to the starting line and tied the shoelaces of my white Wooosh spikes. Looking around at the half-empty Coliseum helped remind me that this was, indeed, just a heat. Still, I had to finish in the top six or have one of the next six fastest times to keep my Olympic dream alive. I did two little strides along the curve, made the sign of the cross three times, touched my toes, and took my position in lane six. The runners' names, their affiliations and career highlights echoed through the stadium.

Then the announcer came to lane six. "Running unattached, Jon Langenfelder."

I closed my eyes, felt my breath and the rubber under my spikes. I opened my eyes and the race already had begun. I was standing alone at the starting line. I could be awakened by a Mexican painter and a drunk hammer thrower, but not a starter with a loud pistol.

"Oh shit."

I ran around the Coliseum track that late afternoon like I was asleep. I never woke up to a mid-race surge or the gap that grew between me and the next-to-last-place runner. This was more than just a heat. This was a race, and I was never in it. I stared ahead at the different colors of shorts and singlets, the sweat glistening off arms and backs, and the bottoms of spiked shoes tapping the rubber surface almost in rhythm. Ten minutes before, I would have given anything to be in concert with these runners. Now, struggling to keep them on the same straightaway, I could care less. I did pass some college kid in a bikers' hat from Montana or Minnesota or Missouri, some place. Still, I was no place with two laps left.

I crossed the finish line 11th of 12 runners of heat two in 14:09.4. Four years of training, dreaming, sacrificing, hoping. Just like that, it was over.

I refrained from looking at the other runners standing in the sunlight, patting each other, shaking hands and asking, "Did ya make it, did ya make it?" I was down the tunnel.

Within 10 minutes I was in the USC dining hall and chomping on every cupcake, fudgesicle, ice cream sandwich, glazed donut, chocolate chip cookie, and brownie in the building. The dining hall servers heard the *Jaws* music as I walked through the door and took cover. I yelled to no one as crumbs flew out of my mouth, "I went six months without chocolate-covered graham crackers to get 11th in my heat?"

A brave cafeteria server tapped me on the shoulder, "'Cuse me, sir," the black gentleman said. "We don't mind you going through our dining hall like a pig going through slop. But could you please remove your spikes?"

I sat there for an hour, eating, staring at the red and gold drapes, and moaning. "No guts. No glory. No Holly. No Olympics. Congratulations, Langenloser."

The next afternoon, still suffering from a Hostess Twinkie hangover, I joined Trace Alcott high in the Los Angeles Coliseum bleachers along the backstretch. Alcott, the Prefontaine Memorial Loop creator who had finished seventh in the Olympic Trials Marathon a few weeks before, helped some friends sneak a small keg into the stadium. They had stuffed it in a huge Wooosh bag and wrapped towels around it. They told the ticket guy they were Carl Lewis' trainers and they had a large ice bucket.

We took turns putting the small, black tap in our mouths and pouring beer down our throats. I sobered only long enough to watch the semifinals of the 5,000. Alcott pointed to the runners bouncing along the starting line. "Better hurry Langenbopper. Your race is about to start."

The starting gun was fired, and I slipped the tap back in my mouth.

The next day I saw Mickey Mouse, a taping of *Dance Fever*, and the Playboy Mansion. Alcott drove me in his black Porsche to Hugh Heffner's house that night, and begged whoever was listening to the security camera at the front gate. "Look, we just made the U.S. Olympic Wrestling Team and wanted to see if Hugh would let us come in and celebrate."

The camera moved but not the gate.

I ate and drank my way through Olympic Trials 5,000 final the next night. I wiped my tears and went to a better event – Wooosh's Olympic Trials Party. I danced with almost every finalist in the women's 3,000 meters. I did tequila shots with three women shot putters and chugged Miller Lites with the only guy I beat in the Olympic Trials.

"A toast," I said, "to that fricking wetback who painted my dormitory at 6:30 Thursday morning."

I continued dancing, drinking, chugging, but stopped remembering. I don't remember urinating on a tree outside the night club or the USC campus cop chasing me inside the building. I came to, about the time a black Barney Fife was slamming me against an outside wall and slapping handcuffs around my wrists. "I gots you, Stringbean. I gots you for indecent exposure."

Larkin and Stub looked at me from the window, laughed, and sucked down a beer. Ken Harwick, who captured the final Olympic spot in the 5,000, smiled as he walked toward the entrance. "What ya' done now, Fuck Face?"

Following him, three girls I danced with simply snickered. Jocko walked from the other direction and didn't even notice the handcuffs through his cigar smoke. "You watch Harwick in that 5,000? He was ah-some."

Jocko was followed by Allpo Vaartanen. "Sorry, sorry. Yar, no speak English."

As I was being escorted from the premises I summoned Marv Lenzi, who was escorting an attractive Wooosh representative to his car.

"You know dis guy," Black Barney said to Lenzi.

"No, I don't know the kid."

Black Barney grabbed my bicep and led me away, despite my desperate cry for help. "Marv, you know me. The guy you promised could run for your track club. But you wouldn't give me a dime or the time of day. Don't you know me, man?"

My voice faded into the distance. "Help me, Marv! Help me, man!"

Black Barney led me to the campus police station. He pushed me into a small, dark holding cell that reminded me of Uncle Grimsley's basement and slammed the barred door. Outside the cell another campus cop was eating a donut and watching reruns of *The Andy Griffith Show*. In this episode, the real Barney Fife stuffed Otis, the town drunk, into the Mayberry jail.

"Whatcha got tonight, hotshot?" the campus cop said to Black Barney.

"Got me an indecent exposure."

I looked back at the other campus cop. "I exposed a bush."

The cop returned his eyes to Andy Griffith and chuckled. Black Barney lifted the telephone and dialed the Los Angeles Police Department. The thought of sharing a urine-stained cell in downtown L.A. with a tattooed freak named Bubba sobered me up for a moment. "Gentlemen, please, I ran in the U.S. Olympic Trials. I ran terrible. I used alcohol to cover my pain. I regret it. I just want to go back to my dorm and sleep it off."

Black Barney told whoever was in charge at the LAPD how he caught me watering the garden. I looked at the light in the corridor, "Oh God, please help me."

The response from the LAPD came over the campus station's speaker phone. "Big freaking deal. I got officers out chasing murderers and rapists and drug dealers, and you want me to sacrifice a man to come pick up some drunk kid who peed on a tree?"

Black Barney unlocked the cell and my handcuffs and escorted me back to the party at 2:30 a.m. "You lucky this time, Stringbean. Next time keeps your little dick in your pants."

I saluted the officer and opened the door of the club. It was empty. The party was over, and so was the Olympic Trials.

I staggered down the dark road toward a dormitory at a location I couldn't remember and over the thought of four days and four years I would rather forget. At dawn I would be heading back to Eugene in a yellow rusted out Mustang, not a red T-topped Firebird. I had four hours to find my room and four more years to find my dream.

PART IV

HEARTBREAK HILL

August 11, 1984

Al Michael's voice was heard 'round the world the night the Americans defeated the Soviet ice hockey team en route to the gold medal at the 1980 Winter Olympics in Lake Placid, New York:

"Do you believe in miracles? Yes!"

The only miracle I want while watching the 5,000 meters final at the 1984 Summer Olympics is to leap through the color television screen to the starting line in Los Angeles. Four years of bad luck, poor timing, and lack of support has planted me on a friend's black leather sofa in Eugene, Oregon, 1,000 miles north of the Los Angeles Coliseum.

I sit in my sky-blue Wooosh running shoes, dark-blue Wooosh shorts, and white Wooosh T-shirt, as 13 of the 14 contestants hope for their own miracle – to beat the heavily-favored Moroccan Said Aouita.

The firing of a gun starts Al Michael's race call and sets two Portuguese runners off as if they are running *500* meters. Ezequiel Canario looks like a rabbit for his speedier teammate, Antonio Leitao, and runs at near-world re-cord pace for the first kilometer. The white/green streak pulls a train of re-nowned runners, including 5,000-meters world-record holder Dave Moorcroft in the British all-whites and former mile-record holder John Walker in the New Zealand all-blacks. In red, white and blue, American Doug Padilla digs into the red track on a pace hotter than the Olympic flame that burns above them.

Leitao takes over from his teammate on the third lap and leads the field to the fastest, yet dullest, 5,000 meters in Olympic history. From here until the final lap, there are no surges, no lead changes, no breakaway attempts. Only a swift, methodical pace from a Portuguese runner, shadowed in green and red by the much smoother striding Aouita.

There is no reason for Al Michaels to make his voice echo off a television in Eugene, where I gaze off to an Olympics 12 years before.

"This is the pace Pre needed." I talk only to myself in the shade-drawn apartment near my late hero's training ground.

For the next nine laps, there is no change on the color television screen and on the Jumbotrons that sandwich the Olympic flame at the L.A. Coliseum. Padilla and Walker and Moorcroft, rarely ever in the picture, are dropped from Leitao's torrid pace survived only by Aouita, red-clad Markus Ryffel of Swit-zerland and surprising Brit Tim Hutchings.

175

Hutchings' fade at the bell decides the medals. To a packed crowd in Los Angeles and a lone man in Eugene, the gold medal also has been decided. Halfway down the backstretch, Aouita drives his white Nikes into the track and sprints past Leitao. Ryffel chases on the final turn, but Aouita accelerates and charges into the homestretch as the clear winner.

He barely has crossed the finish line in an Olympic record time of 13:05.59, when I burst out the front door of the apartment. As Aouita jogs his victory lap in the sunset of Los Angeles, I run a lap around Pre's trails in the sunset of Eugene.

I keep running until the sun gives way to the moon and to the glowing path that lights my way to a miracle.

26

I thought how you become a world class runner was to train your butt off. To run 141 grueling miles per week and interval upon interval until your lungs burn, your knees ache, and your legs buckle.

But after 12 years and total career training mileage that would scale the Earth, I found running off at the mouth just as important. "I let my running do my talking for me" didn't cut it for a young man who needed more than a loud-mouthed coach. I needed a few trips away from Hayward Field and a shoe contract that would keep me from washing dishes or making burgers for my keep. In the mid-1980's you had to press the right buttons, or at least the telephone buttons. There was no room for phone-a-phobia, no tolerance for the worries over the possible stuttering blocks. I touched each button and tapped my fingers on the receiver until someone finally answered.

"Thunderbolt Shoes."

"H-H-Hi, I'm calling about getting a shoe sponsor."

"I will connect you with Leonard Mills, our elite athletes' representative. One moment, please."

The moment turned into minutes and seemed like months.

"Leonard Mills."

"M-Mister. Mills. This is J-Jonny Langenfelder from Eugene, Oregon. I competed in the Olympic Trials last June for the second time, and I was looking, hoping for a shoe contract. I qualified in the 5,000 and 10,000 and my time ranks in the top 30 in the U.S. in both events."

"What did you say your name was?"

Any hope of a contract ended with that question, asked by all five shoe company reps I called. Perhaps they saw me run in the post-Trials Canadian Tour. In Saskatchewan I was so far off the lead pack in the 5,000 that I started watching the race from the other side of the track. I looked down with a lap to go and I was in lane eight.

Some Canuck spectator in a Montreal Canadiens' jersey must have poked his buddy. "That American hoser must have drunk too much Moosehead before the race, eh?"

I returned to Eugene, which turned into a ghost town during the Olympics. It seemed like I was the only person *not* in Los Angeles. Wayne Snyder let me stay at his apartment and watch the Games on his color television while he watched inside the Coliseum. Wooosh fully accommodated the club's non-Olympians and gave them tickets to the track events. That meant Adam Larkin, who ran his 10,000-meters heat slower than the winner of the women's exhibition 10,000, was sent to watch the Olympics. So was Herby Gimble, who didn't even qualify for the Trials. All that money spent to watch a meet, and Wooosh wouldn't spend a dime to send me to *run* a meet. I went to the Wooosh Headquarters the week after the Games. Everyone looked at me like *I* was a ghost.

Gary Hicks, who competed in his fourth Olympic Track and Field steeplechase, did a double-take. "What are doing here?"

"I live here."

"We figured you'd go back to Dallas."

I was 26 years old. I had at least four more years in me to reach my goal. Age 26 is still young for a runner. I sat down in Taylor Markham's office and asked to join the club.

"Too old," he said. "We want young guys, fresh out of college. Guys we can mold and train to become world-record holders. What is your name again?"

Four years before, Markham said I was too young. He said they wanted more experienced runners. Now I'm too old? Was Markham at the hot dog stand when 37-year-old Carlos Lopes entered the Coliseum en route to his marathon victory?

Wooosh wanted guys like Purdue's Doug Wicker, who finished eighth in the NCAA 1,500 final and eighth in his Olympic Trials heat. They wanted Villanova's Karsten Phelps, who ran a 4:01 mile in high school and not a tenth faster in college. They wanted Northern Minnesota's Zac Groves, who won four straight NCAA Division III cross country titles and no track titles. Northern Minnesota didn't even have a track team.

I walked five meters from Markham's office to Jocko Girelli's office. Jocko sat back in his chair with his feet crossed and propped up on his desk. He took long, savoring puffs on his cigar and stared through his window to a rare blue Eugene sky.

"Jocko, I don't think it's fair that guys I beat every race like Larkin and Gimble are getting six or seven hundred dollars a month and unlimited travel, and I don't get anything. I get as much from this sport as some jogger who wins the Colder 'N Hell 10K every year in Fargo, North Dakota."

Jocko kept puffing, staring. "Did you watch Annie Riley win the bronze in the Olympic Marathon?"

I needed a job and a place to live. I found work, finally, at the *Eugene Record-Times* sports department. Lyle Hester, the sports editor, also thought I was too old. But his staff writers persuaded him to hire a man with a journalism degree, newspaper experience, and the persistence to apply for the fifth time over a 20-year-old frat rat, who had changed his major for the fifth time. I made $4.92 per hour for answering the telephone and typing results from some hoarse high school coach calling from some static-line phone booth in Nowhere Oregon.

The return of the runners and students left me homeless. When Wayne Snyder returned, I went to Larkin's place. When Larkin returned, I went to Stub's place. When Stub returned, I went to Ken Harwick's house. I asked Ken if I could pitch a tent in his backyard.

"Then where are you gonna piss, Fuck Face?"

"I got nowhere else to go. It's a good thing I've got so many friends in this town."

"Keep imposing on everyone and you're not going to have any friends left. People are going to start calling you Langenlodger."

Harwick laughed. "Yeah, that's it. Langenlodger."

I walked through town, wondering where I was going to live, and bumped into a bum.

"Watch where you're goin' there, boss?"

I took a closer look and a better whiff. "Dusty?"

He was so drunk on whiskey he didn't recognize me. I found out later that my replacement at the Midnight Express Apartments cleaned house and tossed Dusty onto the street. I could see myself sleeping on the concrete slab next to him, or at a trailer park in the Big Banana.

My last hope was Trace Alcott, who was on a U.S. road racing tour. He had a two-bedroom condo in an industrial section, near the railroad tracks. I dialed from a pay phone at The Duck Pond for the race headquarters at the Philly Half Marathon and found him.

"Sure, stay for a week until I get back. Get the key from the neighbor across the driveway. She's been coming in to water my plants. Make yourself at home and keep your hands off my Porsche."

I drove from the phone booth to the neighbor's doorstep. Trace's driveway was like a separation of the haves from the have nots – Trace's modern upstairs condo from a run-down duplex. A chubby girl with braces, red stringy hair, freckles upon her freckles, and an oversized gray T-shirt answered my knock.

"Is your mother here?"

"My mother? She lives up in Portland. What do you want?"

"I need the key to Trace's apartment."

"What for?"

"He told me I could stay there."

"He didn't say anything to me about it."

"Look, he's my training partner. I called him in Philadelphia, and he said I could stay at his place until he gets back next week. Are you going to let me in or not?"

Her answer left me sleeping in the Big Banana in the driveway. I returned to The Duck Pond and dropped a handful of coins into the telephone box.

"I forgot to mention the girl had charisma bypass surgery," Trace said. "And she's rather a track groupie."

"What, is she like 14?"

"More like 21 or 22. But she acts like she's 12. Don't worry. Kimmy's harmless. I'll call her and tell her to let you in."

Kimmy Culversen was doing more than watering Trace's plants. She was using his washer and dryer, playing tapes on his VCR, sleeping in his bed, and driving his Porsche. She didn't even have a driver's license.

"He told me I could house-sit," she said, taking a jar of peanut butter from Trace's cupboard. "And who the hell do you think you are to question it? I've known Trace a lot longer than you have. Besides, he's my coach."

"What sport?" I thought. "Mud wrestling?"

I slept on the sofa the next six nights and spent the next six days trying to find a place to live. The only place I could find was an $80-per-month sewing room in the back of a one-bedroom duplex. The only problem was the bedroom was occupied by Kimmy. It was better than sleeping in a backyard tent, but not much.

I stored most of my belongings in Trace's attic. I barely had enough space in the sewing room for the double mattress I pulled from a nearby alley and the milk crates I used as a dresser, a mattress side table, and a T.V. stand. I broke down a cardboard box and used it as a window shade. My room had the only carpet, perhaps history's first shag. The den and kitchen had the light brown tile found in most mid-1900's elementary school hallways. There was no shower, only a bathtub with a rubber spray stuck to the spout. I don't know what Kimmy's bedroom looked like, because I never went near it.

She entered my room one morning and asked if I needed an extra milk crate. I said no, and then later changed my mind. That afternoon she returned with, "Where's my milk crate?"

"I decided I needed it after all. Did you need it?"

"Yeah, about an 'hour' ago!"

The telephone rang that night and my tan hand beat her milky-white arm with connect-the-dot moles to the receiver. As I was saying, "Hello," Kimmy was yelling, "You know, I might be expecting a call, too! You aren't the only person who has friends!"

If looks could kill, Kimmy would be a mass murderer. The telephone rang again an hour later. I let her answer it. I walked to the kitchen and into a frown. "It's your mother."

Trace came over a few days later to look up a woman's telephone number from the University of Oregon telephone directory I borrowed from the den.

Kimmy opened my bedroom door, smiled and said, "Oh, hi Trace," ripped the directory out of my hands, and stormed out with words louder than her door slam. "I've been looking for this for the past five hours!"

Trace half-smiled. "Sounds like she's practicing to be a bitch."

"Practicing?"

Trace said he never told her she could house-sit or go anywhere near his Porsche. I suggested a train from the adjacent tracks may have stormed by, and Kimmy did not hear him say, "Get the hell out of my condo!"

Trace also made no claim to be her coach. "The girl runs an hour 10K. If I'm her coach, I suck."

He advised me to find somewhere else to live without offering me his spare bedroom. He said other runners were asking if Kimmy and I were "living together," even after I told them she was nothing more than duplex-mate who rarely left the duplex. I hid in my little room and waited for her to finish cooking before I dared enter the kitchen. I tacked a red-and-silver Caprock State blanket over the den entrance, so I wouldn't have to look at her. I told her the blanket kept the kitchen warm.

I spent as much time away from the duplex as I could. If I wasn't running 20 milers or doing drills or typing results of a cross country meet or football game at the newspaper or going to church, I was closing down The Duck Pond or the Grumpy Mule or a Wooosh bash. After Wayne Snyder's Lycra tights party, I climbed into the backseat of Trace's Porsche with two U of O track girls and put my arms around them. One girl asked, "Can this thing get up to a hundred?"

"You asked for it," Trace said.

He sped up the highway ramp at 3 a.m. and hit 130 miles per hour with my backseat cheer, "Triple figures! Triple figures!" Trace finished with the Prefontaine Memorial Loop.

I was lucky to get one girl into the Big Banana. I met Veronica Bartlett, a cute brunette, at my 7 p.m. candlelight Mass at the Catholic Student Center. We held hands during the Our Father and she hugged me during the sign of the peace. Turning to God and a God-fearing woman, instead of a six-pack and a stack of *Playboys*, seemed the answer to my post-Olympic Trials blues. A relationship with a devout, abstinent Catholic like myself would keep me whole and away from Kimmy.

After Mass, Veronica agreed to go with me for ice cream. I tried to open the passenger-side door of the Big Banana, but it was stuck. After my 10th yank, I turned to Veronica and said, "Are you limber?"

"What?"

Veronica's laugh was either peculiar or pity as she crawled over the driver's side seat and sat on a burger wrapper and a used ketchup container. Then the car wouldn't start. I smiled. "Don't worry. I'm used to this. In fact, I keep the jumper cables here in the backseat."

I summoned Father O'Leary from the rectory to give me a jump. We finally reached Schooky's Ice Cream Parlor, where I chose chocolate chip of the

36 flavors on the menu. Veronica, licking her triple-scooped almond double-fudge, called me a "plain-Jon."

"I always have liked chocolate chip," I said. "I don't see how another flavor could beat it."

I paid the bill from the dimes, nickels, and pennies I had scraped out of my car ashtray and escorted Veronica back to the Big Banana. I slapped my palm against my forehead. "Oh, no. I locked the keys in the car."

Veronica was not impressed that I opened the car with a coat hanger in less than four minutes. She crawled back into her seat. I twisted the key in the ignition. Nothing. I walked three miles with Veronica back to her apartment in a freezing rainstorm. She didn't ask me to come in or thank me for a lovely evening. In fact, I never saw her at the candlelight Mass again.

All I wanted for Christmas in 1984 was a midnight Mass in Dallas and an escape from the duplex-mate in Angel's garb with a Christmas tree stuck up her ass. Dad made that possible two days before Christmas, when he offered to pay for half of a round-trip plane ticket. The problem was finding a ride to the airport on Christmas Eve in a city with a taxi strike and vacated by runners and students.

My only lift was the 5:30 a.m. daily airport shuttle from the Emerald Hotel. I lugged my suitcase a mile from the duplex to within 50 meters of the shuttle bus, when it took off 10 minutes early. I chased and waved 200 meters down the road until the bus lights faded into the darkness. I turned around to see distant headlights coming toward me. The light blue Ford four-door pulled to the side. A police officer stepped out and wrote me a ticket for soliciting a ride in the roadway.

"But officer, that was my only ride to the airport. Now I'll never make it home."

The police officer finished writing the ticket, handed it to me, smiled, and said, "Merry Christmas."

I lugged my suitcase back to the duplex, stuffed it in the Big Banana, drove 12 miles to the airport, put my suitcase in a storage locker, bought a plane ticket for the later flight at 11 a.m., drove back to the duplex, and ran to the airport. That night I was eating turkey at 2000 Hickory Lane, exchanging running socks, and sleeping on Mom's shoulder at Midnight Mass while she sang "Silent Night."

The year 1985 began with a tender groin muscle I pulled after a slip on the icy Rolling Hills Parkway on a frigid five-mile run from one year to the next. I returned to Eugene unable to run and to a duplex-mate unable to smile.

"I thought you were going back to Dallas for good." Kimmy looked like she gained a few pounds over the holidays, but no charisma.

"I showed six cute guys this room for nothing."

Now I *was* thinking about going back to Dallas, leaving this silly Olympic dream and this town that endears champions, not losers. The next afternoon, while I was rubbing ice on my sore groin at Wooosh Headquarters, I heard a voice from the other side of the locker room.

"Works better with Vaseline." Zac Groves sat next to his locker and tied his training flats.

"I got a pulled groin. Gotta put ice down there three times per day."

"Sounds like an excuse to me."

Zac walked toward the door. "Let's like go for a run on the McKenzie River Trails. It's beautiful out there. Just like Minnesota without the snow."

"You deaf. I've got a pulled groin. I haven't run in a week. I have to go to work tonight. I haven't had lunch."

An hour later Zac and I were weaving through the forested trails, wading through streams, and bounding up and down the small rises. We chased rabbits along the trail and pulled salmon out of the cold river. Zac found a cure for my groin. He also found my laugh.

He came to my duplex on a sunny Saturday. We looked out the window to see Trace lying under his Porsche and changing the oil. Trace had set his telephone atop the long outside staircase in front of his condo to avoid missing an important call, probably from the beautiful blonde or brunette he met the night before. Zac dialed Trace's telephone number from my kitchen and watched him pull himself from under the Porsche and jog up the concrete stairs. As soon as Trace answered, Zac hung up. Zac waited for Trace to lie under the Porsche and dialed again. Trace sprinted up the stairs only to a dial tone.

The third time, Trace lay under the car as the telephone rang 20 times. Finally, he raced up the stairs. Zac hung up. Trace slammed the telephone and was about to pull it out of the wall. He saw us in the window, holding our stomachs. We could read Trace's lips as he shook his wrench at us, "You assholes!"

After lapping Gimble three times at the Portland Indoor finale three-mile, Zac crossed the finish line and grabbed the microphone from the announcer. As the spectators were leaving the arena and with Gimble still rounding the track, Zac hollered over the speaker, "Hey, Gimble, could you get the lights when you're done there?"

I heard Zac short-sheeted every woman's world cross-country team member's bed in Portugal, hid a pair of girl's panties in the dirty laundry of Gary Hicks' suitcase, and put on a female voice to ask Hicks' wife for her briefs back. He reported to a Jocko workout, puffing a cigar, and yelling in Jocko's New York cab driver voice, "O.K. yuhs fuckahs, we're doin 10 times a two mi-la."

Zac saw Kimmy's things-to-do list in my den, while I changed in my bedroom for our tempo run on the Willamette River trails. Kimmy had scribbled in vertical order, "Do the laundry, take books back to library, study for biology exam..." Zac added "Fuck Jonny" to her list.

I didn't know what he had done until we returned from our run. Kimmy had tears in her eyes as she threw the pad and pen at me. "I can't keep anything around here without you messing with it!"

My running was rounding into form about the time I re-injured my groin muscle doing 100-yard strides on a cold, wet track at Hayward Field the day before the 10,000 meters at the U of O Opener. I stood in the bleachers - instead of on the starting line - with Zac and Jocko, who kept warm with the use of a cigar and a flapping mouth.

"Gimble is in ah-some shape. He'll knock out a 28:30 like he's fallin asleep – even in this shitty weather."

The gun went off and so did every one of the 43 entrants, but Gimble. He couldn't get his red cotton sweatpants off. Jocko threw down his cigar, jumped over the wooden rail, tackled Gimble, and pulled his sweats so hard that his shorts came off with them. In a flash, Gimble had his shorts on and was off chasing the pack with Zac singing like Ray Stevens, "Oh yeah, they call him The Streak, the fastest thing on two feet..."

It took Gimble 45 seconds to cross the starting line and 14 laps to catch the last-place runner.

It took a month before I could do a track workout. I did my distance runs with a handkerchief tied around my groin and without sympathy from a duplex-mate who called me an ice hog. My groin injury was nothing compared to her ulcer, overactive thyroid, sore throat, menstrual cramps, and every strain of flu known to man. I escaped to The Duck Pond, where Wooosh runners were sharing pitchers and planning their European track tour.

"My agent is flying me to Oslo to run the 10,000," Trace said. "My frequent flier plan will give me a free first-class trip to Hawaii."

I refilled my glass. "I've got a frequent mileage plan."

"What do you got, Langenlodger?" Stub asked.

"Greyhound-plus. After 5,000 miles, I get a free trip to Fresno."

"Yeah," Zac said. "One way."

Actually, I was thinking about going to Dallas and bagging the track season. But Zac's stories about riding the train from Portugal to the Cinque Mulini race in Italy fired me up. I awoke at dawn the next morning and hammered a solo 12K time trial along the Willamette trails in 36:12. I ran some long intervals with Zac and Stub and successive 3,000-meter races of 8:13 and 8:04 at the Oregon Relays and the Oregon Twilight. My one and only hope of qualifying for the 5,000 at nationals was the Prefontaine Classic, which was held on the 10th anniversary of Pre's death. I begged Jocko to get me into the race.

"The bad news," he said before Tuesday's track workout at Hayward Field, "is the race director wouldn't let you in. The good news is that he wouldn't let Zac or Stub or Snyder or Gimble in either. They're bringing in Kenyans and people from all over the place."

"How is that good news?" I asked.

"They're putting on a special 5,000 at the developmental session in the afternoon. You guys can get together and run a fast time."

I was so nervous about the race I wanted no reminder of it. I returned to the duplex after workout to see a Pre poster hung on the den wall. I moved it outside to the bathroom hallway. I went out for dinner and returned to see it back in the den. So I hung it on the opposite, blank side.

I was in the bathroom when Hurricane Kimmy blew open the front door.

"B-a-s-t-a-r-d!"

It sounded like a woman who had found her husband in bed with another woman. I opened the bathroom door to a 22-year-old woman with braces and tears and fortunately no butcher knife.

"I spent five dollars for that poster at the bookstore, and now you've wrecked it. You've been nothin' but a nuisance ever since I was stupid enough to let you move in here."

I felt like crying in my beer that night at The Duck Pond. I looked around at Zac and Trace. "I drove this girl all over the city, loaned her money to pay rent, spent hours hearing about her latest ailment. And not once did she ever say thanks."

"She's a bitch," Trace said. "Don't worry about it."

Zac had a different take. "You don't know where she's come from. You at least had parents who stayed together and loved you. Have you ever like asked this girl about what she's come from?"

The next day I had Kimmy's hero Annie Riley autograph a new Prefontaine Classic poster, which I presented to her the night before the meet as she ate macaroni and cheese out of a pan. She said her mother and father divorced when she was two. Her mother worked as a barmaid in a bowling alley, leaving the youngest of her three daughters to fend for herself. Her father committed suicide four years before, and her mother was suffering from manic depression.

I stood in the pouring rain at Hayward Field the next afternoon and looked at my competitors, none who could break 14:30. I whispered to Gimble, "where's Zac and Stub and Snyder."

"They talked their way into tonight's fast section."

I outkicked Gimble in the last 200 meters in a winning time of 14:22. I drove the Big Banana to the duplex in my spikes and returned to watch the rain stop, wind die, and 18 runners finish the 5,000 under 13:45.

My season was finished, and I was flying to Dallas the next day. First, I got drunk at the Prefontaine Classic party and finally set a personal best – at the world's longest timed piss. I bet Zac I could pee for three minutes and held a steady stream for 3:12 as he stood at the urinal with a stopwatch.

"My goal someday," I said, "is the four-minute piss."

Our next piss was a group effort in the garden Kimmy planted outside the duplex. "If Kimmy ever like offers you a salad," Zac said, "turn her down."

Then Zac, Stub, Snyder, and I took off the rest of our clothes. We cut holes for our eyes in paper bags, put the bags over our heads, and snuck up Trace's steps and sang "Happy Birthday." Trace's girlfriend from England yanked open the door. "It's bloody 3 o'clock in the morning."

"No it's not," I said. "It's only 10 till."

By 3 a.m., Trace had joined the four of us for a naked mile run on Pre's trails to salute my hero on the 10th anniversary of his death. I put my clothes back on, jumped in the Big Banana, and drove the Pre Memorial Loop about the same time Pre did 10 years before. I sang along to Elton John's "Rocket Man," the same song Pre listened to when he crashed, as I passed the fateful, engraved stone.

The song hummed in my head on my flight to Dallas the next morning. I told Kimmy I was sorry that things didn't work out between us. She said it was OK and handed me a bag full of oatmeal cookies she baked the night before. I breathed a deep sigh of relief as I cookie-munched and looked down at the clouds. As the plane descended into Texas, I felt sick. I grabbed a vomit bag and filled it up.

"It's the cookies! It's the cookies!"

◆ ◆ ◆

27

The slow strum of a guitar and Cat Stevens' voice followed me somewhere on a 14-mile run along Rolling Hills Parkway on a 92-degree day:

Miles from nowhere, guess I'll take my time. Oh yeah, to reach there.
Look up at the mountain, I have to climb. Oh yeah, to reach there.

The mountain seemed like Mount Everest after the worst season of my running career. I had returned to 2000 Hickory Lane to regroup, re-evaluate my goals, re-think my future. Dad flooded his Sunday roast beef and potatoes with gravy, when I announced plans to end my running career.

"I'll run another three years, until I'm 30, then that's it. If I can't come close to making the Olympic team, then I don't see any point in continuing. I'll go on with my life."

"Good to finally hear it, Miles. I was afraid you'd be a running bum the rest of your life."

Mom made the sign of the cross and looked to heaven like another prayer had been answered.

Dad carved at his meat with more enthusiasm. "So what are your plans now?"

"I'm training for the San Diego marathon."

Dad gulped. "A marathon. How fars it?"

"Exactly 26.2 miles."

185

"Twenty-six miles? That's as far as it is from Dallas to Fort Worth."

"Precisely."

"What do you wanna do that for?"

"For about 10,000 dollars. That's first prize."

A month after my return to Dallas, I found myself miles from nowhere in Gilmore, Texas for the Second Washed Up Tumbleweed Runners' Reunion. I maintained a marathon theme that weekend with Bart Harris and Mitch the Bitch. In two days I ran 26 miles, played 26 holes of golf, and drank 26 beers. I was the only unmarried, unemployed reunion guest and stepped onto the Greyhound bus with three parting words from the tobacco-chewin' Bart Harris. "Give it up."

I intended to. But not until I ran a marathon and took another shot at the Olympics. I became very serious about my running in the summer of 1985. How serious?

During the middle of one of my 126-mile weeks Funky Joe Medina met me at Arlington Stadium for the Rangers-Blue Jays game for free beer night. We were drunk by the second inning. I don't remember who won or lost or driving back to 2000 Hickory Lane. I woke up at 4 a.m. on the bathroom floor and went for a five-miler. I could have been pulled over for RWI.

How serious?

The Stallion called me the late afternoon of a 28-mile Saturday. "A friend of Bonnie's is a flight attendant and she has four flight attendant friends in town tonight who want to party with you."

"Can't. Got a 10 miler tonight."

Lord my body has been a good friend, but I won't need it when I reach the end!
Miles from nowhere! Guess I'll take my time, oh yeah, to reach there.

Reaching there is not what Father Litzke taught me on my return visit that summer to his candlelit den. I closed my eyes and breathed, meditating to his soft, slow words.

"A marathon is a concept, a word that conjures images of a struggle to the finish line. Those images exist only in the unconscious level. All that exists in the conscious level is your breathing.

"You don't run a marathon to finish. You run just for the sake of running it. You don't run with the thought of reaching the finish line. You run right there. Stay in the present, focus on your stride and how you feel, and don't realize the finish line until your foot crosses it."

I continued breathing, focusing on my posture in the chair, and smelling the smoke from the candles. Father Litzke continued.

"Life is no different. Do you only think about death? If you did, you wouldn't be living. Live your life with each moment, each breath, doing the right things, knowing that God will be waiting for you at the end. Your struggle is not with the marathon, it is with yourself."

In the marathon, the struggle is what I worried about. I recalled the story of Darcy Ellard crawling to the finish line of the marathon at the 1956 Melbourne Olympics. I read about the disoriented Dorando Pietri being pushed across the finish line by officials at the 1908 Olympics and then later disqualified. I watched in horror at the 1984 Olympic telecast as Gabriela Andersen of Switzerland staggered from side to side in the homestretch like a mule looking for water in the desert.

Marathon training that summer was fine, as long as I stayed off the Cross Creek Golf Course. Six miles out on a Wednesday 10-miler, a Doberman named Taffy darted out of her unfenced backyard along the 13th fairway at sunset and took a bite out of my shin. Bobby Joe Jimmerson heard my scream and called off Taffy. From the slur of his words and the swerve of his Ford pickup driven toward the nearest emergency room, I could tell Bobby Joe had a few after-dinner drinks. "Ol' Taffy never done that before. She sat thar all the time watchin' the golfers without a peep."

The doctor cleaned the wound and stuck a long needle in my arm. Bobby Joe paid the bill and said he was sorry. As I trotted out the door, he asked, "Where you goin'?"

"Home. Taffy bit me four miles from the finish line, and this hospital is exactly four miles from my house."

The next afternoon some hacker airmailed the par three 16th green. His Titleist 3 hit me in the right butt cheek as I ran by. He didn't yell "fore," and perhaps thought I was the flagstick. If I had bent over, it would have been a hole-in-one. The following night I tripped over a foot-high rope at the 17th tee and fell on a cart path. I bruised my shoulder, elbow, hip, buttocks, thigh, and knee. The rope was strung across the cart path, so people wouldn't slip on the wet concrete and hurt themselves. The next day I completed my 28-mile Saturday and my eighth straight 126-mile week.

I returned to Eugene in September and found an attic apartment at the house of Eugene Community College athletic director Griff Townes. My two-dollar-per-hour raise and extended hours at the *Eugene Record-Times* helped cover the $160 monthly rent. Jocko Girelli mapped out a plan similar to the one he devised for Annie Riley before the Olympics. It began with many quick loops of Pre's trails and Pre's rock memorial.

I trained with Zac and Trace by day and partied with them by night. Zac rated his alcohol consumption rate on the 1-10 Goon system. The drunker you are, the higher the goon. A 10 goon meant you are passed out, also considered one-fifth dead. The higher the goon the harder it was to distinguish the Oregon girls from the non-Oregon girls. We also rated girls on a scale of Kimmy Culverson to 10, considering Kimmy was a one. A 10 was Adam's Larkin's girlfriend, Andrea Lefaber, who followed her boyfriend from Michigan. We drooled over her long legs and long dark hair. Trace told us Larkin played around when he traveled to races, and that Andrea played around while he was away.

187

Zac and I stayed at parties too long, reasoning that as long as there was one girl left there was a chance. We left with an eight goon and without a woman for either the "Chief Dunking Donut" shop or the "LHOP", the only places open at 2:30 a.m. The Indian with the long pony tail and apron always shrugged when we entered the donut shop. Zac pointed to a huge cinnamon twist behind the glass, "Hey Geronimo, like how much for Moby Dick there?"

The LHOP was an International House of Pancakes we renamed the Losers' HOP. If you didn't score at a club or a party, you ended up with plate of scrambled eggs and sausages alongside truckers who were driving a rig to Billings, Montana and all the other losers. The biggest loser was Doug Wicker, the 1,500-meter runner who hurt his knee the first week he arrived in Eugene in January and hadn't run a step since. Still, he received a monthly stipend from Wooosh.

"Steee-rike three again tonight, Wicker?" Zac stared at the blueberry pancakes Wicker dowsed with maple syrup.

Wicker had returned from Indiana, where he had abandoned his high school sweetheart a few months before to run for Wooosh. She wanted to get married, but Wicker didn't.

"So I dumped her. But after sitting there in that dark, dingy apartment with nothin' to do, I kept thinkin' about her. I seen this movie called "St. Elmo's Fire," where the guy is in love with this woman and drives up to this resort in the snow and tries to woo her.

"After I seen that, I done the same thing. I drove all the way to Indiana in two days and two nights."

Wicker stuffed pancakes in his mouth. Syrup stuck to his brown mustache. "I went right to her door in the middle of the night. I stood there under the porch light with a bouquet of flowers and a smile."

"What happened?" I asked.

Wicker stared at his pancakes. "She threw the flowers at me and told me git lost. Then I seen this guy who looked like a bear runnin' down the hallway. It was her new boyfriend. He chased me down a dark alley, and I got the hell back to Ory-gone."

No matter how high the goon or how late we stayed up, Zac was always at my doorstep at 9 a.m. Sunday morning for a trail run along the McKenzie River. I was exhausted from those two-hour runs and Jocko's interval sessions and tempo runs, but ready for the San Diego Marathon on December 8.

I creep through the valleys and I grope through the wood... 'cause
I'll drink to you my baby, I'll drink to that, I'll drink to that.

The hard training and my work at the *Record-Times* required an afternoon nap interrupted one day by a ringing telephone. I pulled off the covers, crawled out of bed, stubbed my toe on the dresser, and tip-toed across the cold kitchen floor to the telephone.

"Langenlodger, its Wicker. My car broke down again. Can I use yours?"

"What for?"

"To get some milk and a birthday card for my mom."

"There's grocery store two blocks from you."

"But there's special place across town that has really cheap cards."

I was too tired to figure it out. "Just ride your bike over here."

Ten minutes after crawling back under the covers, the telephone rang again.

"Langenlodger, its Wicker. Gimble called and wants to come over and play whiffle ball. So I'll just borrow his car."

Two minutes after laying my head back on my pillow, the telephone rang again.

"Langenlodger, it's Wicker."

"Now what?"

"Forgot to ask. Did you want to play?"

The week before the marathon, I pulled the telephone cord out of the wall. The only telephone I talked into was at the *Record-Times*, where I chased coaches after high school football playoff games the Friday night before Sunday's marathon. The phone crew often called the local bar if a coach did not call in the scoring summary and statistics of his game. The Friday night before leaving for San Diego I needed Pleasanton's summary, and the coach was nowhere to be found.

"Anyone know who the Pleasanton coach is sleeping with these days?" I asked.

"He's banging the cheerleading coach," said a co-worker.

I looked up the cheerleading coach in the telephone directory and called her house. The woman handed the telephone to the coach. "You're not gonna tell my wife, are you?" he said.

"I don't care about your personal life. I just want the frickin' score of your football game."

I spent the rest of the night answering the same question in the sports department. "How fast you think you can run a marathon?" Non-runners don't know times. I could say "one hour, 50 minutes" and they'd respond, "Pretty good."

Running a marathon at least would shut up the first question asked when someone finds out you're a runner. "Ever run a marathon?" Then you explain to an "I don't get it" look that you are a 5,000 meters runner."

I went to watch the 1982 Dallas Marathon and counted 14 people at the race site who asked me why I wasn't running. That accounts for 14 explanations why I don't run a marathon. Then I returned to 2000 Hickory Lane to my sister Maggie who asked, "Why didn't you run that marathon today?"

Once you are training for a marathon, marathoners come out of the woodwork to give you advice – anything from what type of pasta to eat the night before the race to how to drink from a cup while running. Trace, who was running his 15th career marathon at San Diego, should have advised me this: always travel two days before the race and keep your specialty water bottles in your carry-on bag. That's in case the airline loses your luggage, so you aren't up until midnight trying to recover them.

Actually, an airline rep came to my hotel room door at 11 p.m. But I stayed up until midnight pouring half-in-half replacement drink and water into the plastic bottles with a spout and taking them to the room of the race official in charge of delivering them to the aid stations.

"Shouldn't you be in bed," he said.

I struggled until 1 a.m. to go to sleep. At 1:10 the fire alarm went off and the hotel was evacuated. My 5 a.m. wake-up call came at 5:30, leaving me no time to eat breakfast. I grabbed a banana and a muffin from the hospitality suite and caught the shuttle bus to the start of the point-to-point course. I jogged a mile and snuck into the bushes for a pre-race whiz. I told the runner squatting next to me, "Got arrested for doin' this at the Olympic Trials." Then I realized the other runner was a woman.

The starting gun was fired as the sun broke over the horizon and sent 2,000 runners on a winding road toward a finish line in downtown San Diego. I tucked my new ultra-light white and blue Wooosh singlet into my maroon loincloth and filtered into the rainbow of running colors. At the end of the rainbow, was a first-prize pot of $10,000. Each mile was marked by a large digital clock, whose numbers blurred as the race drew on.

"*4:58.*" The first mile felt like a jog. "I can't go any slower," I thought.

The lead pack of a dozen – it also included a Canadian, Mexican, Kenyan, Brazilian, Dane, Scot, Swede, and Trace Alcott – maintained the clip on the calm, 45-degree morning. We grabbed our drinks from the table at 10K and cruised down the road.

"*49:54.*" I was as comfortable at 10 miles as I was at one. The rolling highway was a conveyor belt that carried me toward the finish line. I nudged Trace.

"How do you spoil an aggie party?"

"How?"

"Flush the punch bowl."

Trace: "Why did the aggie put the ladder on the bar?"

"Why?"

"Because he heard the drinks were on the house."

No one else with whom we rubbed greasy elbows laughed. They were too tired, didn't know what an aggie was, or didn't understand English.

"*1:05:23.*" Halfway there and on a pace that would net one of the fastest debut marathons ever, I looked around to see the lead pack dwindle to eight. By 14 miles, it was six. By 15 it was four – only the Canadian Braden Anders, the Mexican Jose Jiminez, the Scot Nigel Edwards, and myself. I was feeling no pain. My gold Wooosh racing shoes bouncing on the road like it had springs under it.

"*1:24:51.*" At 17 miles, the Canadian surged. The Scot went with him. I dropped to third, alongside Jiminez, who rallied past me to join the two leaders. I felt a cramp in my right hamstring, then a cramp in my left hamstring. Then my calves. I had nine miles to go.

"*1:30:21.*" I covered the 18th mile in 5:30. The 19th in six minutes, and the 20th in 6:30. One by one, they went by me. The Kenyan, the Brazilian, the Dane, Trace Alcott.

Trace patted me on the butt. "What do you call a German virgin?"

I was breathing too hard to respond.

"Guten-tight."

The punch line faded into the wind. This marathon was a cruel joke. The question I wanted answered? Where's the finish line?

> *Miles from nowhere, not a soul in sight, oh yeah, but it's all right...Lord my body has been a good friend, but I won't need it when I reach the end.*

"*1:56:49.*" I ran the first mile in 4:58 and couldn't go any slower. I ran the 22nd mile in 6:58 and couldn't go any faster. The finish line was four miles away. I was low on gas and quickly losing my will to live. I was tired and cold and starving. I would have pulled into a Bopper Burger drive thru, if I had put a couple of dollars in my shorts. Two things kept me from dropping out. One. I had never dropped out of a race in my life and swore I never would. Two. There was no other way to the finish line.

"*2:10:37.*" The Canadian Braden Anders waved to the crowd as he crossed the finish line in course-record time. A $2,000 bonus was added to his $10,000 first prize.

Meanwhile, 2.2 miles behind, I picked up a cup of water at the aid station and tried to throw it in my face. I missed. I had a hallucination of my mother standing along the sidelines saying, "Bless his heart."

A well-proportioned blonde in a tight, white blouse and red skirt yelled through the crowd, "Great legs." I ran to the side and got her telephone number. That also was a hallucination.

"*2:26:07.*" I barely could read the numbers atop the finish-line chute through the sweat and pain in my eyes. I couldn't hear the crowd or their pity clap. The only way to know I finished 29th was if the finish card was in Braille. Other runners had told me of this great excitement that rushed through them at the finish of their first marathon. All I felt was, "Let's get the hell out of here."

First, I went to the refreshment area where a woman served tomato soup and a roll on a ceramic plate. After wolfing down my fourth roll, she said, "You mean you want another one?"

"I just ran a marathon."

"We have to save some for the other runners."

Trace, who finished eighth in 2:16.08, hobbled to me in an aluminum cape. "You look like death," he said.

"Feel like it."

I was shivering even after I bundled into my heavy sweats. Trace pointe to a shuttle bus across the street. "Let's catch that bus."

Neither of us could run. When I got to the curb on the other side of the road, I tripped over it.

That night Dennis Gladstone, a race official and a husband and father of five grown children, drove Trace and me to a dance club called "Castaways." I asked Dennis what he did for a living. "I work for the FBI," he said. "I kill people for a living."

I think the FBI he worked for was Federal Bureau of Intoxication. As we walked into the club, Dennis said, "I am going to make sure you guys get laid tonight."

The FBI guy kept bringing women over to us. "Ladies, this is Jonny Langenfelder. He'll make your teeth chatter."

Trace whispered in my ear. "We gotta lose this guy."

Trace met two local women on his own and told them he and I were from Denmark. "Yah, I am Hans. An dis is my friend Jorgen."

The girls looked at us like we were from Saturn. "What... brings... you... to... San... Diego?" one said.

"We run marathon dis morning. Yah," Trace said.

I just nodded.

"Would...you...like...to...dance?" her friend said over the pounding music.

Dancing was more of an effort than running. I was John Travolta on stilts. I abandoned the dance floor for a barstool. My dance partner sipped a Long Island ice tea.

"Do...you...like...it...here?"

I gulped a half glass. "Look, my friend is full of crap. I'm from Dallas, Texas."

I blew our cover. The FBI guy maintained his cover – a balding, overweight slob trying to pick up the barmaid. "It's scary," Trace said. "This guy is defending our country."

The girls drove us back to the hotel, where they borrowed our shirts and shorts and joined us in the hot tub at 2 a.m. Sally Johnson pulled back her shoulder-length, dark hair and kissed my shoulder. Then there was a splash of hot spa water. I opened my eyes to hairy, flabby-chested FBI guy.

"It's time to go to bed," Trace said.

Trace escorted his lady back to his room. Sally, wearing only a towel and sweat beads, went into my room and lay on my bed. She looked at the results of the women's race on the nightstand.

"These are the top finishers?" Sally asked.

"Yep."

"These are all women."

The small talk went to a discussion of last names.

"Langenfelder," she said. "Is that Russian?"

"No."

"Hungarian?"

"No, it's German."

"How about Johnson? Swedish?"

Sally sat up on the bed. "My father is black. Are you prejudice?"

My thoughts were running 26.2 miles around my head. "It's 3 in the morning. I ran a marathon. I'm on an eight goon. It's a holy day, the feast of the Immaculate Conception. Maybe I won't lose my virginity to Holly. But I am sure as hell not going to lose it to someone who acts like Wicker's sister."

I showed Sally the door, kissed the back of her hand, and went to sleep. The next morning my legs were so sore I walked backwards down the stairs of the airplane in Eugene. Zac greeted me at the gate with a smile.

"Hey, you ever run a marathon?"

Later that night, I walked to the street in front of my attic apartment with the intention of going for a run. I moved my arms, but my legs would not follow. I stood there flapping my arms and going nowhere.

A boy rode up on his bike and stopped next to me. "Oh, I get it mister, you're a helicopter."

I gave up the run and walked three miles down a cold, damp road, alone, to a store for a box of chocolate-covered graham crackers and some time to ponder my cloudy future.

Miles for nowhere, guess I'll take my time, oh yeah, to reach there.

◆◆◆

The Oregon All-Comers Meets were the worst. I awoke at dawn after a hard night of working or drinking, put my bare feet on a cold tile floor, ate a bruised banana and a dry piece of toast, and drove to the empty bleachers of Hayward Field.

It was the first race of 1986, the first since my marathon exploded like a shaken beer can. It was cold and windy and wet. It was 9 a.m. My competitors were U of O crawl-ons or post-collegians who, like me, had no sponsor and little hope of running at Mount Sac or Drake or Penn or anywhere else. All I wanted to do was run my 3,000 meters and get back to my attic apartment in time to watch *American Bandstand*.

The wind and rain dampened my spirits and tempted me to abandon the track for the comfort of the Big Banana. Only a voice calling from the green backstretch bleachers kept me sloshing through the puddles. "Come on, Jonny! Drive into the wind! Look up! Get that guy in front of you! Now!"

I thought, "This guy wants it more than I do."

That voice, that inspiring voice kept me in that race and in my career. I pushed past the leader from the Oregon Striders on the final turn and held on in the homestretch for my first victory in two years.

The voice grew louder as I jogged toward it. "You are the man, Jonny!"

Zac Groves smiled. "Wasn't so bad, was it?"

"8:17?"

"Hey, you won."

"Don't you got a race in Switzerland or Italy or somethin' else better to do?"

Zac had returned the previous night from the World Cross Country Championships in Switzerland. He must have been jet-lagged out of his mind. Still, he set his alarm clock and came to watch this dinky meet. Zac always seemed to be there when I needed him.

He had given me $100 to help pay for my flight to Dallas for Christmas and pounded on the door of my attic apartment late New Year's Eve in sweats and gloves.

"What are you doin' here?"

"I like came back for the New Year's Eve run from one year to the next?"

"Pretty damn cold in Minnesota, eh?"

"Like 20-below. Hard to run with three layers of sweats and through snow up to you're A-hole."

Zac and I ran the Prefontaine Memorial Loop through the dark hills of Hendricks Park. Fireworks went off, and cars honked as we ran past the stone where Pre crashed. "It's 1986, Zac."

I could see Zac's cold breath as we ran down the hill. "Let's make it a memorable one, Jonny."

The run back to my apartment was the only good one in January. The marathon hammered my body and shattered my confidence. When I wasn't taking a basketball result over the telephone from a stat nerd in Portland or Pendleton, I was running around Pre's Trails with Glad Wrap around my hamstrings or standing in the corner of a party with a longneck in my palm. I watched the young men and women laughing and talking and presumed they were talking and laughing about me. I ended up buying a cinnamon twist from Chief Dunking Donut or a short stack at the LHOP. Wicker always saved me a spot in his booth.

"You want to come to my birthday party tomorrow night," he said. "I've invited a girl I met from the personal ads."

"How about I bring Zac, Trace, and a few other runners with me?"

"Don't do that?"

"Why not?"

"The girl's bringing a chocolate cake. I like to slice it up, freeze it, and a take a slice out every week or so. That way I can celebrate my birthday all year long."

Wicker wanted his cake and eat it to. I barely spoke to anyone the next five days. I wasn't scheduled to work. I didn't run with anyone. I saw *Rocky*

III at the dollar theater by myself. The only thing I said in those five days was to Bernice, the checkout lady at the all-night grocery store. "Got a coupon for that oatmeal there."

I was like Clubber Lang, the boxer who pounded Rocky for the heavyweight title. "I live alone. I train alone. I win alone."

The next afternoon the telephone rang. "I'm like running by your apartment in five minutes. Be ready."

I barely tied my left shoe when Zac cruised down my street.

"Let's go, dickhead!" he yelled.

The next hour Zac raced cyclists along the road, intercepted a football in a pick-up street game, jumped on top of three car hoods that blocked intersections, threw in two 1000-meter surges on the Willamette trail, hollered "I think you're cute; my name is Jonny Langenfelder" to four coeds on the U of O campus, and hurdled six headstones in a cemetery. It was fartlek, Zac style. "Zaclek," he called it.

A few Zacleks put Zac on the U.S. cross country team and me out of my slump. I followed my 3,000-meter win with second-place finishes, a 14:02 5,000 in the next week's All Comers meet and a 28:56 in the 10,000 at the Oregon Relays – all to the crescendo of Zac's backstretch cheering. After the 10,000, I shared pitchers at a large round table at The Duck Pond with Zac, Trace, Stub, Harwick and three runners on the U of O women's track team. Trace decided on his version of spin the bottle. Whomever the bottle pointed toward had to ask a question that required everyone to answer. Stub spun. The bottle pointed at Trace, who asked, "What is the name of the first person you had sex with?"

Names flew out of mouths faster than a spinning bottle until it was my turn.

"Come on, Langenlodger," Harwick said. "What's your sister's name?"

"Shut up." I hollered the first name that came to me, "Floretta."

The next morning Zac took me for a run on the Oregon coast. The waves crashed to shore as we ran barefoot on the beach.

"Floretta?"

"Yeah, Floretta."

"Sounds like a made up name."

"No, I met her a few weeks ago."

"Like what happened?"

"I was out running, and she stopped her little Mazda truck in front of my apartment. She turned off the engine, rolled down her window, and we talked for about an hour."

"Was she cute?"

"Yeah. Curly auburn hair. Big breasts. I asked her to the dollar theater that night?"

"And?"

I glanced at the ocean and then stared at the sand. "Well..."

"Well, what?"

"Well her butt was so big she barely could fit into the Big Banana. I had only seen her from the waist up, when she was inside her truck."

Zac laughed. "Come on, Jonny. That's just a little more cushion for the pushin.'"

"There was no pushin'."

We finished our run and threw rocks at the waves. "There's nothin' wrong with being a virgin, Jonny?"

"Are you?" I asked.

"You kidding. I'm from Northern Minnesota. There's like nothing else to do, and you can only throw so many logs into the fire."

I chucked a rock as far as I could and waited for a splash. "I am proud to be a virgin and I have this foolish fantasy of losing my virginity on my wedding night to Holly, a married woman who's barely ever given me the time of day. But I realize I can't hold out forever."

Zac fired a rock into a wave. "Sounds like you've got DSB"

"DSB?"

"Deadly Semen Backup. Your first time, be careful where you aim that thing."

On the highway back to Eugene, Zac looked over from the steering wheel and asked me where I saw myself in 20 years.

"I see myself by a roaring fireplace with a woman who truly loves me and a son who's become the little brother I never had. Yourself?"

"Coaching runners at my old high school in Minnesota. Married with eight kids and a Golden Retriever and time to like go hiking through the woods. I want to live everyday like it's my last. There is never anything wrong with dreaming, Jonny."

The next Friday, Zac and I found ourselves at Wayne Snyder's pajama party. I wore red boxer shorts and a white football jersey with Caprock State in red letters and a silver number 7 on the front and back. About 1 a.m. Andrea Lefaber, in pink silk pajamas, pulled me onto the living room dance floor. She kissed my cheek as we slow danced to Bread's "Baby, I'm a want you."

"What about Larkin?"

"He's at a meet in Ohio. Two-thousand miles away."

"When's he coming back?"

Her answer was to lead me by the hand to Snyder's bedroom. Zac winked at me as we disappeared down the hallway. I sat on the bed and stared at Andrea's silk-covered knees and smelled her perfume in the room lit only by a full-moon. "I've always liked you," she said. "You have sort of this shy, boyish charm about you."

"L-l-look, you're a beautiful woman and all," I said as Andrea kissed my neck. "But there are people right outside, and you *are* Adam's girlfriend."

Andrea massaged my thigh as she aimed her lips at my mouth. "Let's just forget about Adam for a minute."

She remembered him at the moment our lips met, and we heard Zac's warning in the hallway. "Hey, look! Adam is here!"

I broke the lip-lock and hid under the bed. Adam assumed my position on the bed. He told Andrea that he couldn't wait for the morning flight to be with her. She told him how much she missed him, and their love was rekindled one foot above me.

The next heavy breathing I heard from Larkin was the Oregon Twilight 3,000, where I rolled by him with 500 meters to go and into the lead pack of six. I flew past Zac and two other runners on the backstretch and held on for third place in a nine-second personal best of 7:54.17. Zac slapped me a high-five. Jocko took his cigar out of his mouth long enough to give me a thumb's up.

I was back on the line a week later for the Oregon Invitational 5,000. This was my chance to qualify for the U.S.A Championships, also at Hayward, to break through my 13:44 jinx, and prove that the 7:54 was no fluke. Midway into the race, Canada's Sean LeDoux threw in a surge. Zac patted me on the butt. "Let's go, Jonny."

I couldn't. LeDoux won it 13:38.6, a few strides ahead of Zac. I struggled home in 14:13 and didn't stop until I got to my car. As I put the key into the ignition of the Big Banana, I looked down at my white Wooosh spikes and then to the tapping on my side window. "Don't worry about it," Zac said. "You were just flat tonight. You'll do it at Pre. I guarantee you. You've got like two whole weeks."

I wasn't sure I could get into Pre. Jocko said Jerry Fredricks, the meet director, was bringing in more high quality foreigners and wanted me to be the rabbit.

"What good is that going to do?" I said before the Tuesday track workout at Hayward Field. "I need a qualifier."

Jocko had a back-up plan of flying me to Boston for a big 5,000 there. So instead of traveling three miles for a race, I would have to go three-*thousand* miles. My legs felt like two-by-fours the rest of the week, but Zac kept insisting they would come right. On the Monday before Sunday's meet Zac and I ran 10 times 440's on the track at Hayward Field in 61 seconds or less with a 90-second jog interval. We breezed through our last one to Jocko's call of "Fifty-seven-five" and Zac's immediate response, "You're back, Jonny, you're back."

As we warmed down around campus, Zac said he would call me the next day for an easy 10 miler on Pre's Trails. I told him, "I don't know where I would be without you, Zac. You're gonna be a wonderful coach someday."

"Yeah, I sure hope so."

The sun, sneaking through the blinds of my attic apartment, woke me late the next morning, June 3. I washed my face, brushed my teeth, put contact lenses in my eyes, did some pushups and situps, ate oatmeal, watched *Days of our Lives*, and looked forward to the phone to ring and for Zac's voice, "Be outside in five minutes, dickhead."

The call came about noon. I spoke first, "I know, I know, you're on your way. I'm tying my shoes, and I'll be out there."

There was a pause.

"Zac?"

"No, it's Lyle Hester."

"Need me to work today?" I asked the *Record-Times* sports editor.

"No, I need you to tell me what you know about Zac Groves – where he's from, what college he went to, when did he come to Eugene-"

"You writing a feature on him?"

"Uh, no. I guess you haven't heard."

"Heard what?"

"Zac died this morning."

I laughed. "Good impersonation," I thought. "I didn't even know Zac had met Lyle Hester."

"Come on, Zac. Quit screwin' with me. Let's go run."

There was silence, not snickering on the other end of the telephone. I looked at the breeze blowing the curtains of my open window, the clouds stretching into the sky, the eerie quiet of my neighborhood street.

"Sorry, Jonny," Hester said. "Zac collapsed in the locker room at Wooosh headquarters after a training run this morning. They think it was some sort of a brain aneurysm. They tried to revive him, but, uh, now about that information I needed."

"You'll have to excuse me, Lyle. I need to put the phone down for a few minutes."

I walked to my chair, sat, and shook my head. "That's so typical of you, Zac. Never can wait for me to get my butt out of bed to go run."

I gazed at the light coming through my kitchen window for a few minutes. Then I finished tying my shoes and ran to Pre's Trails for some Zaclek that would make my running buddy proud.

Running was the only thing I could do that week. I had to, because I knew Zac wanted me to. I knew how much he wanted me to beat my personal record 13:44. I didn't want to travel 3,000 miles to do it. I wanted to run it at Hayward Field at the Prefontaine Classic, where Zac and I were suppose shake hands at the starting line and then run the race of our lives. I couldn't believe Zac, the one person who seemed to care more about my running than anyone else, was gone. I asked to see his body. But the guy at the morgue said, "Sorry pal, he's already been shipped home."

On Friday, Zac's family and hundreds of other runners he had inspired gathered in Northern Minnesota at a cemetery next to a wooded trail on which he ran thousands of miles. As Zac was being laid to rest in the red, white, and blue uniform he wore to represent his country in the World Cross Country Championships, I was eyeballing Jerry Fredricks in the Emerald Hotel hospitality suite.

"I am running the 5,000 on Sunday."

"I still want you to rabbit."

"I am running the 5,000, and I am running it for Zac."

The next day a Memorial Service for Zac was held at the Millbrook Methodist Church, where Zac never missed a Sunday service when he was in Eugene. It was the first time I saw runners in suits, dresses, and tears. I sat next to Jocko, who had spoken at Zac's funeral in Northern Minnesota. He told me Zac complained of headaches for several weeks. But Zac told Jocko he felt so good early Tuesday morning that he went for a run on his own. In his log book, Zac wrote, "Easy 10. Felt great. Look out, sub-13:30 at Pre."

Zac came in from his run, waved at the cigar smoke, said "Jocko, man, when you gonna like give up them ropes," and walked to the locker room to take a shower.

Jocko wiped at his eyes with a handkerchief. "I walked in a few minutes later and found him on the floor in front of his locker, naked, curled up in a ball with his eyes staring at the skylight."

I learned more things about Zac during the service from Stub, Harwick, Larkin, the minister, Zac's sister, and a masters' competitor he inspired to take up running. Zac wrote letters to runners at his old high school in Minnesota. He talked to inmates at the Oregon State Penitentiary and got them on a running program. He went to a different school every week to talk to students about the dangers of drugs, alcohol, and drunk driving. Jocko and every athlete who spoke about him at the service were so broken up they failed to finish their speech.

Then it was my turn. Before I met Zac, I wouldn't even think about standing before a hundred people and talking. I spoke to only a few people after Zac died. But Zac once told me, "What difference does it make if you stutter? People don't care how you say it, just as long as you say it."

I looked down at the speech I intended to carry to the pulpit. The minister asked the congregation, "Is there anyone else who would like to say something?" I couldn't move.

"Oh well," I thought. "Guess I'll find another way to honor him."

Twenty-four hours later, I was on the starting line at Hayward Field alongside 16 of the finest runners in the world. I tucked Zac's blue Northern Minnesota singlet into my maroon loincloth shorts and fixed my eyes on the starter, who roared his command, "Set..."

The starter's pistol blast sent my elbows into the runners' guts on either side of me and onto a world-class pace. "Sixty-five!... 2:10!... 3:15!... 4:20! the lap timer shouted."

My eyes never strayed from the runner's back in front of me. I was as strong and powerful as the grandstand clapping and pounding. There was no way I was going to back off a pace I tried and failed to run so many times before. Not with that voice only I could hear along every backstretch. "Come on, Jonny! Drive into the wind! Look up! Get that guy in front of you! Now!"

I moved past stragglers after 8:42 at two miles. Nothing could keep me from slowing down. I just kept going and going and going until I sprinted the final straight with every last ounce of courage I could muster. When it was over, I didn't know or care about my place. All that mattered is that I ran the race of my life, and I ran it for Zac. I kept jogging around the curve and down the backstretch into Jocko's leather arms. As he squeezed me, I looked over my shoulder and read the stopwatch clenched in his hand.

"13:33.94."

I put on my training flats, jogged for a few minutes, and drove the Big Banana back to my apartment. I dropped my bag on the kitchen floor, sat at my little dining table, and pressed my hands over eyes. The tears dribbled off my chin and splattered the ink on the words I intended to speak at Zac's funeral.

The last time I ran with Zac Groves was on a three-mile warm-down around the University of Oregon campus. As we approached the track, we spotted a golf ball lying in the soft green grass. We lunged simultaneously, trying to surprise one another. As I scooped for the round, white object, Zac caught me with an elbow and sent me flying. He helped me up, and we laughed until we reached the track.

"This is crazy," I said. "Here we are fighting over a golf ball, and neither of us plays golf."

We grabbed our spikes and headed in different directions. My departure was interrupted by a familiar voice, "Hey, Jonny, turnaround!"

Zac stood along the rail at the head of the backstretch. He pulled the golf ball out of his bag, grinned, and tossed it into the infield. I picked it up and started to say, "Thanks, Zac. You're a great guy."

But when I looked up, Zac was gone. He already had climbed the bleachers and walked into the distance.

So long, Zac. God speed.

My first sight in Boston was a young woman's ass.

Megan Mallard arrived at the airport and dropped her keys as I departed the gate ramp. Her ass was firm and thin and rather inviting. Megan also had a smile – on her face. "You must be Jonny. Welcome to Boston."

I had no intention of moving coast-to-coast after my emotional race at the Prefontaine Classic. My encore was a next-to-last place performance at the U.S. Track and Field Championships two weeks later at Hayward Field. I jogged to Jocko along the backstretch after the race. "Why does 14:30 hurt more than 13:30?"

Two days later, Wooosh, Inc. announced it was closing the Wooosh Headquarters in Eugene and dividing into four regional clubs: Wooosh West out of San Francisco, Wooosh East of Boston, Wooosh North of Chicago, and Wooosh South of Atlanta. Taylor Markham was transferred to the Wooosh, Inc. office in Portland, Oregon to oversee the clubs. Jocko was sent to direct the Boston club. I decided I needed Jocko and a new adventure. I figured Eugene would be left with ghosts and Oregon women.

My last race in Eugene was the Prefontaine Memorial 10K Road Race, which started and finished at Hayward Field and incorporated a loop around Pre's Trails. I wore my green shorts and white singlet, the same I wore in my first race in Eugene, and led from start to finish for a 10-second victory over Dave Stubblefield in 29:33. I donated my first-prize case of Coke to Father O'Leary, who wore his race number on the back of his vestment at my last Mass at the Catholic Student Center.

I shared a final pitcher with Stub at The Duck Pond that night. Everyone else was racing in Europe, except Gimble and Wicker, whose contracts expired along with their running careers. Stub did a final toast to "Langenbopper, Langenlodger, and Fuck Face." I clinked his class and said, "To you my friend, and to Graham Hutton, Snyder, Harwick, Trace, Kimmy, Wicker, Larkin and his lovely girlfriend, and to my buddy who resurrected my running career – Zac Groves."

I packed the Big Banana that night, slept a few hours, and departed Eugene via the Prefontaine Memorial Loop. A picture of me crossing the finish line was on the front of the *Eugene Record-Times* sports section. The headline read: "Rojas finishes sixth in first race since stress fracture."

I had driven first to Dallas, because I didn't think the Big Banana would make Boston. The Big Banana made it. I didn't. My roll-down-the-window air conditioner left me dehydrated and throwing up at a rest stop in Nowhere, New Mexico. I somehow made it to Gilmer, Texas, where Bart Harris offered me a Budweiser in bed.

"You're 28 years old, still, runnin' and still a virgin," Bart said. "I'm gonna rent you a whore for your next birthday."

"I've taken my share of cold showers."

"After 28 years, Langenhooch, I'll bet the crack of dawn is startin' to look pretty good to ya.'"

Dad used the power button on the television remote as a temptation blocker, clicking off the scantily-clad and well-limbered Solid Gold Dancers. "That's how Jimmy Swaggert got started," he said.

I wondered how many cold stream dips Jesus had taken. I realize He was perfect, but He was a man and surely tempted. Hopefully, God realizes it's much tougher for men 2,000 years later. Back then, women didn't take bubble baths. They didn't wear halter tops or hot pants or ankle bracelets. They didn't paint their lips or fingers or toenails pink. There was no *Playboy* centerfolds, no Cheryl Tiegs, no MTV. Certainly, men of the 20th century would be judged on a sliding scale. Mom suggested I pray harder – or get married.

I prayed that Holly had divorced the philandering crowbarism Rodney Rogenberger and would take refuge with her old high school running chum. Bart said Roge still was playing hide the salami with the Caprock State cheerleaders. I intended to find out at the Forest Hill Class of 1976 Ten-Year Reunion.

Most former classmates I met that night already were married, divorced, and remarried. I spent the reunion at the Forest Hill cafeteria hiding from Trudy "Moo" Merkle, explaining to 250-pound former teammates that distance runners don't reach their peak until their late 20's and early 30's, hearing fire-fighter Chuck Jones embellish – er, rather lie about – his high school football career, and keeping my eyes peeled for Holly's arrival.

I was on my third margarita, when I saw this perfect face and blonde locks through a crowd of premature bald men and starch-exploded women. I made three people spill their drinks and stiff-armed Trudy the Wonder Cow as I weaved through the former classmates and their wallet pictures of their stepchildren and prize poodles. Finally, Holly and my eyes met and she ran to me faster than she once went to the net. She wrapped her arms around me, left pink lipstick on my cheek, and rammed my stomach with a thud. I looked down and closed my eyes. Any chance of leaving that cafeteria that night – or perhaps any night – with my arm around my beloved Holly ended at that awful moment.

"When are you due?"

"Next month."

"Does it belong to Coach Rogenberger or Coach Tuppernacker?"

"Jonny, you are as funny as ever."

"Where is Coach Hercules? Parking the car?" Or, as I thought, "Parking the porpoise?"

"Caprock started football drills today."

I spent the rest of the evening parking my eyes at a bulge on the greatest body this side of New Mexico and the glory days gridsters-turned-plumbers and electricians each asking my dream girl the same question. "You got an eight-pound football in there? Uhhhh."

The oven bun sighting crushed my ridiculous wedding night fantasy and made me realize another more humiliating fact. The only two virgins in that cafeteria were Trudy Merkle and me.

I returned to long runs along Rolling Hills Parkway, to meditation sessions with Father Litzke, to covering high school football games for *The Dallas Star*, to drinking beer and reminiscing with The Stallion and Coach Hightower, to selling the Big Banana. The first respondent to the newspaper ad looked at the rust spreading like cancer on the yellow paint. "How much?"

"Two-thousand dollars."

"Give ya' 50."

"Sold."

Most of my belongings arrived on a carousel at the Boston airport. I am not sure if the people there were more depressed about the baseball that rolled between Billy Buckner's legs in the sixth game of the 1986 World Series or the downpour that canceled game 7.

Megan Mallard apparently liked balls going between her legs. Megan, a Wooosh East runner who volunteered to let me crash at her apartment, helped me load my bags on a trolley and push it to the parking garage. She was typical Bostonian, which requires its natives to talk like JFK and say "cah" instead of "car" and 'pahk' instead of "park." En route to her car, Megan told me she had "PSDS."

"PSDS?" I thought. "Is that like AIDS?"

She was trying to say "pierced ears."

I loaded my bags into Megan's rusted Ford Granada, and she started the car and the scraping windshield wipers.

"You can just call me, Mal."

"As in malfeasance or malfunction?"

Mal stared at me from toe to head and winked. "Mal-fucking."

Mal spent the drive to her high-rise apartment in Brookline talking about the different sexual positions she enjoys and the men she screwed that month. She scored more in October than Mr. October. I tried to change the subject.

"I see you got a little bruise on your bumper in the back?"

"Yeah, I got rear ended last night."

"Does he have insurance?"

"Oh, you were talking about the car."

Mal parallel parked her Granada and led me and my bags up the elevator to her seventh-floor apartment. I put the bags next to the sofa, where I assumed I would sleep. Mal showed me her bedroom with bare-chested rock stars on the walls and prophylactic sponges on the dresser.

"I'm going for a run," I said.

"In the pouring rain?"

"Heck yeah, it's just like Eugene."

I opened my Wooosh bag, and my maroon loincloth shorts fell out. Mal picked it up by the crotch.

"These are disgusting. I can't believe you run in these."

That night I wore a rain suit on my run to Harvard University and back. Mal met me at the door. She was wearing the loincloth. Her ass in that loincloth immediately excused her sailor's tongue and eliminated whatever shrinkage the cold rain caused. After a cold shower, Mal introduced me to her deep-voiced roommate and Wooosh East teammate, Ellen Glickmann. Ellen was more suited for my boxer shorts.

"What event do you do, Ellen? Shot? Discus? Hammer?"

203

"I'm a distance runner."

The next day Mal showed me the hidden track where our club trains, Heartbreak Hill, the Wooosh East Running Store, Harvard Square, Fenway Park, Boston Garden, and a downtown runners' bar called Boston Bully's. The first question from Ellen upon our arrival: "Found an apartment yet?"

What I found was a woman with a gorgeous body, dirty blonde hair, thin face, and the ability to make a stranger feel like a long lost lover. The Thursday after my arrival, Mal rubbed her butt against my jeans at Hagland's ice cream counter

"Cross Country meet Saturday, you runnin?" she asked.

"Nah, I'm not really in shape?"

"You slacker."

"Slacker?"

"Yeah, slacker. Jonny Langenslacker."

"Don't call me that."

"Yeah, yeah, Langenslacka."

"Please."

"I tell you what. If you win the race on Saturday, I won't call you Langenslacker."

"You're on."

Mal took her ice cream cone and twirled her tongue around the tip of the upper swirl scoop. "Ellen's going to Albany to be with her boyfriend this weekend."

I bit at my chocolate chip scoop. "So I can sleep in her bed."

"Sleep anywhere you want."

Mal took Ellen to the airport Friday night and returned at 11 p.m. to find candles burning and me with my back on the floor, eyes and feet propped on the sofa.

"What are doin', Langenslacker?"

"Meditating over tomorrow's race. I want to run well so I can lose the 'slacker.'"

"You're weird, Langenslacka. You are weird."

My eyelids popped opened. I tackled Mal by the jeans and wrestled her to the carpet. She struggled for a while and then let me pin her. I pushed my chest off her and stared at her face, illuminated by the candlelight. Mal slowly undid each button on her shirt. I looked down at her juicy lips. All I had to do was lower my lips to hers, a move that certainly would lead us to the fresh white sheets of her bed. Then I looked at the burning candle and thought with a different head. "My race is at 9 a.m. tomorrow. If I start this now, I'll be up all night. There's always tomorrow night. I want my first time to be somewhat special, even though it's not with someone special."

By the time I finished thinking, Mal had buttoned her shirt and gone to bed, alone. I must have been the first man in history to give up sex for sleep.

I arrived at the Franklin Park course and found Jocko. I asked when the organized workouts would begin. He took his smelly cigar out of his mouth and told me he took a coaching job at Pickering College, an NCAA Division

III school on Long Island. He said he was fed up with Wooosh and that Pickering paid better. By mere coincidence, Jocko insisted, the former lingerie model he met on the flight from Oregon to New York lives on Long Island. I had moved across the country for a man who went from coaching American record-holders to high school record-holders.

My day got worse. I wore half-inch spikes on a course that was 30 percent concrete and finished sixth. I felt like I was running on needles. The fifth-place finisher was Evan Waynewright, a Wooosh East runner who was going to Harvard Business School. Mal introduced me to Evan as Jonny Langenslacker and invited him to a party near Boston College.

Mal and I took a cab to the party. We chugged beers with the other Wooosh East runners, danced, and locked lips on the balcony. I went back to a bedroom to chug more beers with the Wooosh East runners, while Mal and Evan talked in the kitchen. Louis Cannoli smiled at me. "Hey, who was the idiot who wore spikes on that course today?"

I stared at Louis. "I beat you."

At 1 a.m., Mal asked if I was ready to go back to her place. We walked out the door. Evan followed.

"Evan is giving us lift home," Mal said.

I sat in the back seat of Evan's Audi and counted down the seconds to the end of my virginity. I was on an eight goon, and the DSB had reached a dangerous level. "In less than 30 minutes," I thought, "I will be in a warm bed with a very warm body. Sorry, Holly. I can't wait for you any longer."

Evan parked in front of the apartment building. He followed us into the elevator. He walked us to Mal's apartment. Mal opened the door, and they walked into her bedroom and shut the door. The little slam noise was like a kick in the groin.

I couldn't bear hearing another kind of slamming in that room. I walked the streets of Boston for three hours, while drinking Molson Goldens and singing to the lonely streets an R.E.M. line over and over, "That's me in the corner. That's me in the spot light..."

Somewhere I hit my head on a lamp post and asked, "Why, why, why, Langenloser, did you turn down a game of mattress polo with a woman who has the body of death?"

Later that night I followed some residents and a case of beer to the penthouse of Mal's apartment and drank until dawn. I awoke on Mal's sofa to the same back I followed through the finish chute the previous day. Evan sat in front of the television eating a bowl of Wheaties and watching the New York City Marathon. Mal walked out in a T-shirt and panties and sat next to her boyfriend. She suggested that Evan take me out on a 20-mile run.

"No way," I thought. "This preppie, stuffed shirt prevents me from my first night of passion, and now I have to spend two hours running with him?"

Seconds after Grete Waitz crossed the finish line in New York, Evan and I left Mal's apartment for a run along the banks of the Charles River. He told me about everyone he knew on the Wooosh East track club. He told me the best places to run and to drink, gave me leads on apartments, and suggested newspapers I could hit up for a job. He told me how he and Mal had been dating off and on since high school. He laughed at my stories about my dad, Uncle Grimsley, Fubby, and the Midnight Express Apartments and listened to my recount of Zac's death. By 20 miles, I could see what Mal saw in Evan. But what did Evan see in a foul-mouthed slut besides well-proportioned breasts and a tight ass? The cold showers and lumpy sofa forced me to find my own place in a hurry. Ollie Dillworth, a Wooosh East running store clerk from Florida, pointed up. The store was located on the base of Heartbreak Hill at the 17-mile mark of the Boston Marathon. Ollie had moved out of the apartment above the store and told his roommate I was moving in.

The night before I moved in, I shared several rounds of beers at Boston Bully's with my Wooosh East clubmates Ollie, Evan, Phil Bentley, and Wooosh East store manager "Bobby Mac" McKenzie. After the third round, they told me about the plot to trick my new roommate. Ray Coster regarded himself as "the black guy from Vermont," because as Ray put it, "I might be the only black guy from that state." Ray had tattoos of an eagle on one arm and a woman on the other. "Bobby Mac" told Ray that I might be gay.

Ray told Bobby Mac. "I ain't rooming with no faggot"

The next morning I walked into the apartment, gave Ray a soft handshake, and paraded around the lounge with my hands on my hips. "Oh, I just love these draperies. Such a fabulous color."

Ray looked at me like I was from another planet. "You ain't movin in here."

"Why not?"

"Because I think you might be gay?"

"Well, I think you might be black?"

Ray scratched the hair on his chin to consider this idea. If I was a racist, then that made him a homophobe. Ray smiled. "You havin' me on, ain't ya."

We shook hands and laughed. From that day onward – in our own mock sarcasm of the ridiculous racial and homophobic undertones that permeated the mid-1980's and out of mutual respect for each other - he called me "Faggot," and I called him "Nigger." We liked yelling at each other, knowing neither of us was serious. "Hey, Faggot," Ray looked through the kitchen cabinet. "You been eating my potato chips?"

"Yeah, Nigger. That's because you ate the rest of my tuna casserole last night."

Ray must have giggled when I called him the N-word, because he knew that underneath his hostile and sometimes perverted exterior he was far above that demeaning label. He had run for the University of Vermont and worked as a porter at the Taft Hotel in downtown Boston. His goal was to be the first non-African born black runner to win an Olympic medal in the marathon.

But the Wooosh East runners, like Ray, were mostly legends in their own minds who came to Boston to run with a legend. Boston native Nick Loman won the 5,000, 3,000 meters steeplechase, and 10,000 meters in successive

NCAA meets for Boston University. He finished eighth in the Olympic 10,000 final in 1984 and ran 13:18 for the 5,000 and 27:41 for the 10,000 in Europe in 1985. The runners figured if they trained with Nick, they too would run these times.

In reality, Nick used these guys as training jockeys and ran them into the ground. I didn't have a coach, but I wasn't going to let Nick Loman dictate my running career. Ray poked my shoulder at 6:45 a.m. my first day in the apartment. "Get up, Faggot, Nick's coming by here at 7 for the morning run."

"So?"

"So get your ass up. We will be running at 7 a.m. and 3 p.m. today. Nick says."

"Jonny says he is getting up at 10 and doing his runs at 10:30 and 4:30."

I ran solo in a city that surprised me with more places to run than Eugene. I could go east and run Heartbreak Hill, the climax in a series of hills in Newton from 17 to 20 miles of the Boston Marathon, and loop a pond at Boston College. I could go west to Wellesley and run on a trail that led to a lake along the all-women's Wellesley College. From there I could run past million-dollar homes in Weston and around a reservoir along a forest trail with autumn leaves crunching under my feet.

My only occasional running partner was Evan, who was too busy studying or chasing Mal, to be bothered chasing Nick Loman. Evan and I ran a fartlek workout on a golf course covered with ankle-high snow and waist-high snow drifts. I fell down six times, somehow managing to stop my watch each time. I finished seventh in the New England Cross Country championships in Rhode Island and 44th in the U.S. Cross Country Championships in San Francisco. I was the fourth man on our fifth-place Wooosh East team. Nick Loman finished second. He was followed by Ollie in 28th, Bobby Mac in 38th, Evan in 41st, Louis Cannoli in 58th, Phil Bentley in 61st, and Ray in 73rd.

I didn't train with the Wooosh East guys. But I partied with them in San Francisco, at Boston Bully's, and at whatever blow-out was on each Saturday night. Our Christmas party was held at the Wooosh East store. Bobby Mac shoved the apparel and shoes aside to make room for the dance floor. The keg was flowing non-stop in the stock room. The windows were fogged from the loud laughter and the dirty dancing.

Evan skipped the party for a family function in Connecticut. That allowed Mal to be my dirty dancing partner. I slid up and down her legs and between her thighs. She pecked my cheek and used the same procedure on her next dance partner.

Also getting into it was Donna Gorman, a tall dark-haired track groupie with legs that wrapped around me like a snake. When the keg ran dry, the Wooosh East partygoers frolicked upstairs and flooded Ray's and my apartment with popcorn, beer, and shaving cream. I sat on a chair in the living room. From what I remember, Mal sat on my right leg and Donna sat on the left. I put my arms around each woman's shoulders. I felt Mal's right breast with my right hand, and Donna's left breast with my left hand. I took turns making out with Mal and then with Donna and, at some point, lost consciousness. I woke up in my bed, alone, about noon the next day.

On New Year's Eve, Bobby Mac rented a 40-seat bus for 40 drunk runners to wave at drunk partygoers on a tour of downtown Boston. I jumped out five minutes before midnight for my annual run from one year to the next in jeans, a wool sweater, and Wooosh tennis sneakers. I ran through Boston Common and caught the party bus in front of the Paul Revere House in the North End. I jumped on board and yelled, "The British are coming! The British are coming!"

"They aren't the only ones," said Mal, who welcomed 1987 by trying to swallow my tongue.

"Where's Evan?" I asked.

"Pissing on a lantern."

Mal rubbed her hand up and down my thigh and whispered in my ear. "You remember that night at my place when we almost...?

"Yeah."

"Well, we will."

Evan returned to the bus, and Mal winked at me.

Several hours later, around 10 a.m., New Year's Day, Evan and Mal and Bobby Mac and Ollie and Phil and Louis and anyone else not too hung over ran eight miles from the Wooosh East store to Boston Bully's. We showered in an upstairs hotel room and returned for a day of dancing, eating, drinking, and watching college bowl games. Donna, a mysterious absence from the bus tour, followed me all over Boston Bully's. She followed me back to my apartment and took over where we left off after the Christmas party.

Donna followed me the next afternoon through the snow to an indoor track with rubber boards and Daytona-like turns and timed my workout. She followed me to the pizza parlor after workout and on long runs that required her headlights to show me the way. She followed me to the Princeton Indoor Invitational in New Jersey.

Donna became my girlfriend, whether I wanted one or not. She turned my mind into a battleground over my virginity. One side won the night before the 3,000 meter race, when I declined an invitation to her hotel room with, "I have a race the next day."

"But you don't run until noon."

I finished fourth in 8:13. I watched Mal in her 3,000 in her bun huggers, which looked even better than the loincloth. Evan ran the 1,500, and the four of us shared a pizza and a pitcher in the lounge of the Princeton Inn. Evan said he had a class in the morning and was driving back to Boston. He offered me a ride. "Come with us," Mal said.

Donna looked at me with her puppy dog eyes, put her hand under the table, and rubbed my thigh. "Jonny, sweetie, I'm in no condition to drive five or six hours in the snow back to Boston tonight. Could you please, please go back with me tomorrow?"

"I'll drive," I said.

"You're in no condition either."

We said goodbye to Mal and Evan and went to Donna's small room with a comfortable queen-size bed and a sunset view of a frozen pond and a snowy hill that faded into the night. I took a warm shower, put on a pair of running shorts, and a T-shirt and walked out of the bathroom. Donna, illuminated by a bedside lamp, sat on the bed with her soft dark hair resting against the wooden headboard and her long muscular legs stretched atop the white duvet. She wore a white sleeveless shirt that came to her belly button, black panties, and a thin layer of perfume.

I stood and stared at this woman three years older than me and many years more experienced lying there with her juices flowing for the man she wanted for so long. Donna motioned me with her long glossy nails to the bed. I couldn't stop myself. I slid under the sheets and pulled the covers over Donna's warm body.

Then I turned off the lamp.

◆ ◆ ◆

30

Max Steiner lit a cigar and sat behind the sportswriter, who was banging his head on the computer screen. Inflicted with a massive midnight writer's block, the sportswriter took refuge in Steiner's office at the *Cumberland Express-News*.

"Tell me about it, Jonny." Steiner, the Express-News' assistant sports editor, relaxed in the padded chair and puffed his cigar.

"I've got two hours until deadline and I haven't written a word," I said.

"Come on, this is Cumberland North High School, not the Celtics. Tell me what's going on with you."

I looked ahead at the blank screen and spoke as if I was in a confessional. "I met this woman, Donna, and we spent the night together at a hotel after an indoor meet at Princeton eight weeks ago. We kept seeing each other, even though I found out she has a live-in ex-boyfriend, Gus, who has his own bedroom. Gus runs on my Wooosh East Track Club, but we've never met.

"Then, there's Mal, also a member of Wooosh East. Mal has been after me since the moment I stepped off the plane. I resisted her until three weeks ago, when Donna went out of town for a week. Mal knows I've been seeing Donna, but Donna doesn't know I fooled around with Mal.

"Now here comes the tricky part. I would rather be with Mal. But her on-and-off boyfriend, Evan, also runs for Wooosh East and is one of my best friends. Then two weeks ago, Mal gets kicked out of her apartment and moves in with Donna and Gus.

"I was still trying to hook back up with Mal, but she fell in love with Gus. And I've never met Gus."

I looked behind me at Max, sitting straight up in the chair with his mouth wide open and a half-burnt cigar dangling from his thumb and forefinger.

"Jonny, Jonny. I'm a married man with two kids. I've heard about things like this and saw it on television. But I didn't know it existed. Jeez, I thought you were this nice, quiet kid."

"I used to be. Now all of a sudden I've got three girlfriends."

"*Three* girlfriends?"

"There's also Nancy Grimes."

Max stood up, dropped his cigar in the trash pale, and said, "Finish writing your story" before walking out.

The story had picked up the morning I woke up at the Princeton Inn. Donna went downstairs for breakfast. I ran a 10-miler through the snow of the Princeton campus and down this icy, desolate road. I thought I would feel guilty, ashamed, different. I didn't feel anything. I was the same guy. I still stuttered, still put one foot in front of another. What I did in that queen-size bed the night before was no big deal. At least, that's what I thought.

Donna took that night as an invitation to drop by my apartment anytime she wanted, which I didn't mind. She timed my workouts, cooked me dinner, cleaned my apartment, and screwed my brains out. Who was I to say no?

She called one late night after I returned from covering a high school hockey game. "Hi, it's me. Want some company?"

I wanted to go to sleep. Then I thought, "I'm hungry, horny. The apartment is a mess."

"Sure, come on over."

Donna was getting three hours sleep, going to work, taking care of two apartments. But who was I to say no? I slept until noon, squeezed in two runs or an indoor track workout before going to the newspaper. Life was good.

Then came "the relationship" talk. "I really like you," Donna said over another midnight dinner. "But you never take me to a movie, to dinner, to a party, anywhere. All we do is fuck?"

"What's wrong with that?"

I looked myself and my shoulder-length hair in the mirror that night and tried to convince myself I was the same shy person who one year before was living in Eugene, Oregon without a date. I was ashamed that I didn't feel ashamed for breaking the sixth commandment and my streak of abstinence. I tried to use Father Litzke's breathing technique, but that only led to heavier breathing. I was a mattress polo rookie, who played like a veteran and got bored playing with the same partner. I ran 13:57 for third at the Harvard Indoor 5,000 meters. Two weeks later, after Donna went to Chicago for a graphic arts convention, I won the mile at the Brown Invitational in Providence with a 4:08. Mal drove me back to Boston and gave me a goodnight kiss that steamed up the windows of her Ford Granada.

"Aren't you going to invite me in? she asked.

"I'm kinda tired. Come by tomorrow for dinner, if you want?"

Mal arrived at 9 p.m. the next night to a dimly-lit apartment, a cold bucket of chicken, and two Budweisers. She sat on my sofa and shot-gunned her Budweiser. I pointed to the chicken and asked for a breast. Mal removed her sweater and gave me what I asked for. She also removed her jeans and gave me a thigh. Who was I to say no?

Mal was a drive-through window date. It was cheap. I didn't have to dress up. I got what I ordered, and we were finished in 20 minutes. I asked Mal to stay the night, but she had another date.

Ray came in a few minutes later, and we finished the chicken. I told him about Mal, and asked him if what I had done was wrong. I looked at Ray with grease over his face and realized that was like asking Jeffrey Dahmer if it is wrong to eat fried chicken. Ray was on what he called the "lard circuit." The condition he had for picking up a woman was that she had to fit through the front door.

"I like playing the odds." Ray picked up a chicken thigh and chewed. "What are the odds of picking up a good looking chick at a party? Pretty slim. But the odds for a fat, ugly one are great, because they aren't used to being hit on. They'll take whatever they can get. I figure I'm doing them a favor."

"So it's like charity work?"

"You could say that."

"Do you like white meat or dark meat?"

"Black, white, Chinese. It don't matter. I'm not prejudiced."

"I was talking about the chicken."

Ray's charity work and my late night rendezvous with Donna and Mal gave us a nickname for our apartment – "Ramrod estates." Ray put so much into his charity one night his bedroom walls were shaking. He finished his effort with two words, "Get out."

Then he walked into the kitchen in his white bathrobe. "This place is a mess," he said. "When's Donna coming back?"

When Donna returned from her trip, I left for the U.S. Indoor Track and Field Championships in New York City's Madison Square Garden. In New York I slept on a downstairs sofa in a Wooosh-owned apartment in lower Manhattan. The night before the 3,000 meters I met Ollie and Bobby Mac for some dark beer. I staggered into the apartment at 3 a.m., brushed my teeth in the upstairs bathroom, filled a plastic cup with water, and stumbled down the stairs. Miraculously, I didn't spill a drop. I woke up with a large bump on my shin and limped through that night's 3,000 meters on an 11 lap-to-a-mile track that made me feel like I was I running around my living room in next to last place in 8:11. On the drive to Boston the next morning in my 1981 silver

Honda Accord I purchased early in the year, I told my passenger Bobby Mac I was breaking it off with Donna.

"I told you she was a leach," he said.

"It's not that," I said. "She's getting serious. She's telling Gus he has to move out of the apartment. I'm using her for the sex, and that's not right. I don't want to end up like Ray. I had a great uncle like him. If we keep going the way we are going, I'm just leading her on. I'm telling her tonight."

Donna was house-sitting for a friend in Natick. I drove to the house, and sat down with her on the sofa. She gave me a kiss, and before I knew it we were back in the master bedroom. I stayed the next six nights.

On the Sunday night, I prayed hard at my candlelight Mass at St. Thomas Chapel in downtown Boston. The girl seated next to me shook my hand during the sign of peace and said she liked my voice. I went with Nancy Grimes, a Boston University nursing student, for a cup of tea after church. I needed to turn to someone else, especially after Donna told me Mal was moving in with she and Gus. I realized Mal had too big a mouth not to tell Donna what happened the night after the Brown meet. Nancy was good company. But she had an annoying Wisconsin accent, and with a few more pounds she could be considered a charity.

After two weeks of girl juggling, I showed up at Nancy's apartment on an April 1st night that reached zero. A blizzard moved in after dinner and a movie, and Nancy and I used an hour of passionate sofa necking to keep warm. Then Nancy said, "My roommate is out of town. Do you want to spend the night?"

"Sure."

Nancy went to her bedroom to slip into something more comfortable. She returned in a long, white granny gown and with a blanket, sheet, and a pillow she dropped on the sofa.

"Sleep here."

I didn't care how cold it was or how much snow was on the road. I wasn't sleeping on that sofa. I couldn't be into someone who wasn't into polo. My silver Honda slipped and slid all the way to Donna's apartment. Mal cracked open the door.

"Where's Donna?" I asked.

"She's out with Gus."

"Can I come in? It's freezing out here."

Mal opened the door wider but blocked my entrance. "She knows about you and me."

"How did she find out?"

"I told her."

"Bitch."

Mal slapped me on the face, a blow that knocked the icicles off my hair. "Because of that, she went back to Gus. Now I'm stuck with Evan."

Mal slammed the door and left me in the cold. I went back to my Honda, parked on the side of the road. My hands were so cold, I couldn't twist the key in the ignition. I shook my hands and blew into them. I twisted the key, and the car wouldn't start. I had worn down the battery. Frostbite suddenly was brought into the equation.

A car's lights went past and were dimmed around the corner. Donna, looking quite cozy in a fur-lined coat and gloves, walked toward her apartment and was followed by a silhouette in a long, dark coat. I hollered, "Donna, my car won't start!"

I barely could see her through the blizzard. She called back. "I've got some jumper cables."

"You do?"

"April Fool's."

I felt like a fool running five miles home in a sweater, jeans, tennis sneakers, and a dirty pair of socks I used for gloves. I felt like a fool for losing my virginity to a woman I didn't care about and chasing a woman who didn't care about me. Even Nancy deserved better than a guy with his brains in his pants.

My foray into love and sex left me with a bruised shin, a pulled groin, and a month in which I totaled only 127 miles and no track workouts. And I expected to be racing Olympic medal winners in Europe in three months?

In troubled times I always turned to running. When the snow melted, I returned to the track. I researched my old running logbooks and devised a plan based on the workouts from Coach Hightower, Mitch the Bitch, Graham Hutton, and Jocko Girelli that would put me in peak form for the European season in July. I didn't run with anyone in April, especially not Evan. He broke into Mal's diary. One day she listed all the people she had slept with. The three-page list included half the Wooosh East Track Club, several members of his high school cross country team and band, his college coach, his brother, his minister, and two women. Evan either was too embarrassed or too mad to consider running with me.

So I ran, around and around an empty if-you-built-it-at-least-one-person-will-come rubber track in a forest west of Boston. It was owned by Central Massachusetts University, an NCAA Division II school which dropped its track and field program a week after the track was completed. I covered games, meets, matches, and tournaments anywhere from Wellesley to Worcester for the *Cumberland Express-News*. I listened to Ray brag about his track workouts and how his training partner, Nick Loman, was going to run away with the Boston Marathon.

I learned much about this Boston running community the week of The Marathon, which is to Boston what Steve Prefontaine is to Eugene. Boston is Clarence DeMar, Johnny Kelley, and Bill Rodgers. Prefontaine would have had to win Boston to have become a legend in Boston. The week of Boston, 57 people asked me if I was running The Marathon. Some just assumed it. "You running Boston?"

When I said no, I had to explain to dumbfounded athletic ignoramuses that I'm training for the 5,000 meters on the track. In Boston, if you run, you run the Boston Marathon. On my 20-miler up and down Heartbreak Hill the day before the race, 14 people honked and wished me good luck for The Marathon. I thought, "Why would a guy be hammering up Heartbreak Hill the day before the Boston Marathon?"

My wake-up call on Patriots' Day was, "Marathon Monday! Marathon Monday!" Ray couldn't wait to assist Nick. I went for my out-and-back morning run from the 17-mile mark to the 14 ½-mile mark and deflected the same call from people who set up their lawn chairs and barbecue grills along the course, "You're going the wrong way!"

During the next five hours, spectators lined up five deep from Hopkinton to Boston and cheered runners to the finish line. I watched The Marathon from atop the Wooosh East Running Store with Bobby Mac, Ollie, Phil, Louis, and a few others. Nick asked Ray to buy a large sponge, wet it, and hand it to him in front of the store. Nick came by with the lead pack of nine runners and grabbed the sponge from Ray. What neither knew was that Ray had bought sponges with the soap already on it. Nick had soap suds dribbling down his hair and back as he faded on Heartbreak Hill. He finished 17th in 2:18.

I took the subway downtown to catch Ibrahim Hussein's winning kick and wrote a column for the *Express-News*.

I battled my temptations to hook back up with Mal or Nancy or Donna. I took Mal out for a pitcher and pool game at the Mass Pike Bar and Grill. I went to the bathroom and returned to find her flirting and shooting pool with two crowbarisms. I drove home without her. Nancy kept calling me and sent me a letter, telling me I was the nicest and most considerate man she'd ever been out with it. "You're so kind, Jonny," she wrote. "I feel so relaxed around you. You make me happy. I haven't felt that way in a long time."

I never called her again.

I didn't want Donna, either. But I didn't want anyone else to have her. It was like digging out my old toy truck from the garbage can, not wanting the snot-nosed kid across the alley to play with it. Finally, I called Donna and asked her to lunch one Sunday. I made the mistake of asking her how she felt about me. I returned to my apartment in a shell-shocked gaze and found comfort in an unexpected source.

Ray turned his head from a televised Boston Celtics game. "What's wrong with you, Faggot?"

"You won't believe what Donna called me."

"A scum-sucking, male chauvinistic pig who doesn't give a shit about anything but himself and his over-exaggerated penis."

"How did you know?"

"I get that shit from women all the time."

I went to the Sun Devil Track and Field Classic in Phoenix in mid-May to run my first outdoor race of 1987 – my first outdoor meet outside of Hayward Field since the 1984 U.S. Olympic Trials – and to forget my girl problems. Wooosh East paid for the flight that stopped over in Denver to pick up a passenger list that included the University of Northern California track team. The first question I asked Chaz Steward, Northern Cal's stud 800-meter man who sat next to me in the window seat, "Who's the beach girl sitting two rows up and staring back at me?"

Kelli Fuller and I stared at each other throughout the next day's meet. When I finished ninth in the 5,000 in 14:10, she was there at the finish line in her cut-off jeans. When she finished seventh in the collegiate 1,500 a few hours later in her tight bun huggers, I was there smiling at her from the rail. We smiled at each other upon her arrival at a post-race party near the Arizona State campus.

"Hi, I'm Kelli." Her teeth looked whiter against her smooth bronze skin and her bleach blonde curls. There was a minty scent to her breath.

"Hi, I'm Jonny Langen..."

"I know."

I once spent parties, staring at other people. I wanted to crawl in a hole. Now I was in the spotlight, talking and laughing with Kelli and dancing in a living room with no designated dance floor. A well-built and groomed pole vaulter looked at me like, "What she doin with that tall, skinny dweeb?"

A crowbarism thought about it too much. I stuffed his cut-in attempt as Kelli and I slid against each other's jeans on our makeshift dance floor.

"Do you mind?" I said.

He did. He picked me up and tossed me onto the front lawn. I escaped to the bushes on the side of the house. Kelli found me and renewed our dirty dance until we drank the party dry and Chaz Steward called to drive her and two other NorCal runners back to the Coronado Hotel. Kelli held my hand and led me to the velour backseat of the rented Buick, which Steward and all other passengers abandoned in the hotel parking garage. Kelli and I spent the next four steamy hours in that backseat. She wrote Kelli heart Jonny on the back window mist left by our passion. Above that she drew the Olympic rings.

"Perhaps, one day we will be in the Olympics together," she said.

We exchanged telephone numbers. I etched hers in my brain.

Chaz knocked on the backdoor at dawn, as we swiftly put our clothes back on. I opened the door to see Chaz with his suitcase. "We're discussing the 1988 presidential race – Bush versus Du-Cock-us."

I gave Kelli one more passionate lip-lock and promised I would call her in California as soon as my plane landed in Boston.

I could have floated back to Boston. My girl troubles were solved by the most lovely running beach blonde in the country. I couldn't wait to drop a roll of quarters in the pay phone just outside the gate at Logan Airport and hear her sweet voice.

I ran from the airplane door down the ramp to the nearest telephone and pressed every number by heart. I heard a dial tone, and a woman's voice resonated through my ear.

"The number you have dialed has been changed or disconnected. Please check the number before re-dialing."

31

I woke up in a strange bed in a strange place that afternoon of July 3, 1987. Looking at the gray-haired woman shaking my shoulder, I thought it possible I was still asleep.

"Aufwachen, Herr Langenfelder. Achtung!"

I didn't fully awake until the woman pumped her arms in a running motion and spoke her first two words of English, "Athletics meeting."

I glanced at my watch and realized it was 45 minutes until my first European race. I almost knocked over my German hostess en route to the bathroom. Within five minutes I stuck in my contact lenses, slipped into my Wooosh East track uniform and sweats, tied my training shoes, grabbed my spikes, and ran out the door. I didn't stop until I covered the two-mile distance to Rolf Schmidt Stadium in Dorfenheimer, West Germany.

I yawned as I toed the starting line for the 3,000 meters race. I glanced across at the blurry images of my competitors from Germany, Switzerland, Kenya, France, and England. The shot from the starter's pistol woke me up for good.

The Americans wondered what I was doing in Europe. I had followed my 14:10 in Phoenix with a 13:53 for 11th at the New England Outdoor Championships at the Central Mass Track. The following Monday I called Taylor Markham in Portland, Oregon from my Boston apartment and asked him to enter me in some European meets.

"Europe?" he said. "Why are you going to Europe when you can't even qualify for the the U.S. Champs?"

I answered with some sizzling track workouts the next two weeks. I ran three times per mile in 4:16, 4:18, 4:15 with a two-lap jog interval. I averaged 2:06 for six times 800's with a lap jog. I ran eight 400's under 61 with a 200 jog interval. I was more determined than ever to make a name for myself in Europe and to show Markham I belonged there and Kelli Fuller that I wasn't just another roll in a rented Buick.

After paying two months rent and for my round-trip airline ticket from Boston to Dusseldorf and a Eurail pass, I had 198 dollars in my bank account. Bobby Mac gave me a telephone number of Bernhard Schlotter, the meet director in Dorfenheimer, where he ran the previous year. I called Schlotter, who spoke very little English, about coming to his meet. I would not have gone if I had known the meaning of the German word he kept saying over and over: "Neun."

A contingent of American sprinters and jumpers was on the flight to Dusseldorf. As we waited at the baggage carousel at the Dusseldorf Airport, I asked the athlete next to me if he was going to Dorfenheimer and how he was getting there?

"Some German dude from the meet's pickin us up," he said.

"You think he could give me a lift?"

"I suppose. Who's your agent?"

"I booked the flight myself."

"Shit, man, not your travel agent. Your track and field agent."

"I don't have one of them either."

The athlete looked at me like "What are you doing in Europe?"

"Just follow us," he said.

A man drove us in his van through the German countryside to the small village of Dorfenheimer and dropped me off at the home of Rudolf and Anna Busselmann, who had volunteered to billet an athlete. Rudolf showed me to my room and said, "You schleep alone."

I thought, "This guy must know my reputation."

I spent the next three days sleeping. I awoke only to eat, to run seven miles with the Busselmann's teenage son Rudy, and attempt to communicate with the Busselmanns. They looked at me funny when I asked, "How do you say 'jetlag?'" They taught me two similar words, "mude," which means tired, and "schlafen," which means sleep.

I felt extremely mude early in the 3,000 meters in a packed stadium with spectators cooking sausages on the surrounding grassy banks and an announcer spitting his German words into the microphone. I was 15th in a field of 16 through a four-lap split, hollered in German. I clung to the runner in front of me, trying to keep myself awake. I crossed the start/finish line, where an official held up two fingers and hollered, "Zwei! Zwei!"

I remembered what that meant from Sergeant Schultz on *Hogan's Heroes* counting the prisoners at Stalag 13. There were "two" laps to go. I passed six runners down the backstretch and four more on the homestretch. It was like I passed every country in the world in one lap. The bell carried me by two more. I was in third place, trailing only a Kenyan and a dark-haired guy with a mustache with 200 meters to go. The dark-haired guy passed the Kenyan at the head of the homestretch, and I went after him. We raced side by side with the crowd carrying us down the straight. I never could get a chest in front and lost by a half-meter.

As I jogged around the turn, I was mobbed by 50 schoolchildren who stuck pens and programs in my face. "Bitte! Bitte!" they said.

I signed them all and spoke, even though I barely could talk and they couldn't understand a word. "The last race I ran, in Boston, there were about 50 spectators and they all stood in lane seven."

I warmed down back to the Busselmann's house, where Rudolph and Rudy met me with a smile and a second-place garment bag. "Vunderbar," Rudy said.

I didn't go to the awards ceremony, because the announcement was made in German. "Danke." I pointed to my stopwatch. "Do you know what my time was?"

Rudolf wrote, "7:57.09" on his meet program and showed it to me. Then he wrote the winner's name. "Tomas Wernsperger, 7:57.01."

"Wernsperger? You mean the German National Record holder?"

Rudolf and Rudy nodded.

I sat with the American sprinters and jumpers at the post-meet reception at a long table with several pitchers of beer. The Americans, one by one, walked into a back room and returned with a roll of American dollars in their hand.

"What's the money for?"

They stared at me like the naive runner I was. "It's called appearance money," a high jumper said. "Gotten yours yet?"

"Thought I was just getting a garment bag."

They laughed. LaRoy Jasper, who won the 100 meters, put his arm around my shoulder and taught me the facts of European racing. He told me you make your deal with the meet promoter before the meet and you never leave the meet without your money. He doubted Schlotter would give me a cent, or even a pfennig. "I missed beating their national hero by the length of my dick," I said. "If I would have had a hard on, I would have beat him. I'm going in."

I sat on a back room chair with only a thin table separating me and Schlotter, who looked like General Burkhalter. He looked at me like, "Who in the Yankee Doodle are you?"

"Langenfelder, drie-thousand meters?"

"How much?"

"Uh, I don't know. Four hundred?"

"Marks."

"U.S."

Schlotter slapped four Ben Franklins on the table. I had successfully negotiated my first under-the-table appearance fee over the table. Back at the long table, I poured myself a beer and smiled at the big-busted fraulein and her friend sitting across from me.

"Sprechen sie Englisch?" I asked

"Neun."

"You got big tits."

The Americans laughed. I turned to the frau's friend. "Would you like to have sexual intercourse?"

She smiled. "Not right now, thank you."

The Americans laughed harder. "Oh, you got busted," LaRoy said.

Then I got drunk with the German girls, Margita with the big tits and Brigitte (pronounced Bri-GEET). I called it quits about the time I fell down en route to the bathroom. Brigitte was still chugging away. "How old are you," I asked.

Brigitte burped. "Seventeen."

I staggered around the village until I found the Busselmann's house at 3 a.m. I opened the door, and all three Busselmann's – Rudolf, Anna, and Rudy – were waiting for me.

"Where you been?" Anna said. "Ve worry about you."

I giggled. "Sorry, Mom."

The telephone woke me up the next morning. Brigitte invited me to join she, Margita and two more of her female friends on a 10K bike ride to a castle, where I drank and danced in the style of my forefathers. I could have been pulled over for BWI on the ride back to town. I passed out on the Busselmann's sofa and again was awakened by the telephone.

"Hello, Jonny. Dis is Brigitte. Would you like to go to the pub tonight?"

I met Brigitte and more of her friends at a bar called Schultzie's. I told them, "This isn't the Germanfest. This is Mardi Gras."

Brigitte drank more beer than any person I ever met. I liked that in her. I also liked the way she laughed and the way she asked her friends to keep the conversation in English. I also liked how she volunteered to help me get into the next meet in Geneva, Switzerland.

"Could you talk to Schlotter? Perhaps, he could talk to the meet director in Switzerland?

"I can do this"

"Thanks, Brigitte. Do you know Schlotter?"

"Yes, very much. He is my father."

I was using the 5,000 in Switzerland as a tune-up for the 10,000 in Paris. The starting line looked like an Olympic final. There stood Heinrich Hoffmeister, the Swiss National record holder and three-time Olympic finalist in the 5,000 meters. There was Italy's Dani Mazzari, the 10,000 meters European Champion and bronze medalist in the 1983 World Championships, and Hungary's Hugo "Buy a Vowel" Cryzk, the former world record-holder in the two mile. The average personal best of these three runners, whose credentials on the scoreboard lit up the night sky and the Swiss crowd, was 13:16.

The only face I recognized in the glistening stadium lights on this cool, calm night was my Wooosh East teammate Louis Cannoli, who lied his way into the race. I had met Hoffmeister in a little room under the stadium, where I tried to relax before warm up. Hoffmeister looked more nervous than me and then relieved when he asked me my name.

"Langenfelder. Jonny Langenfelder." He probably feared I would say Doug Padilla or Steve Scott or Nick Loman.

Hoffmeister's look turned to surprise when he glanced back after an 8:41 through 3,200 meters at the unknown American in the breakaway group of five runners. "Why are these guys slowing down?" I thought.

I felt like my spikes were barely touching the track. As we ran down the homestretch toward the three laps to go sign, I thought, "There's three of the greatest distance runners in the world – Hoffmeister, Mazzari, and Cryzk – and I'm gonna kick their asses."

The best part wasn't kicking their asses. The best part was *knowing* I was going to kick their asses. Hoffmeister surged down the final backstretch and I covered him. He surged again around the bend. I matched him stride for stride, dug my spikes into the red track, and whipped past him entering the home-stretch. I accelerated into the final 100 meters and never looked back to see Cryzk pass Hoffmeister for second or Mazzari fade to fifth.

None of those studs shook my hand, and Hoffmeister yelled something I doubt translated to "fiddle sticks." I jogged to the 200 mark to retrieve my spikes. Louis, who had been peeking at the race from the other side of the track, dodged an airborne javelin on the infield after he finished and sprinted into my arms.

"I love it, man. I love it." I took off my spikes and put on my sweats. "Easiest fricking race of my life."

And the fastest. My time was 13:29.34, four seconds faster than the Pre race – and it earned me a berth in the 1988 U.S. Olympic Track and Field Trials, in Indianapolis. If the pace had been faster, I felt I could have gone under 13:20. I won a Swiss watch and foot-tall Swiss chocolate bear, which I ate in the shower under the stadium. When I came out, everyone was gone but a Swiss official who was picking up the flags around the track now lit by only one stadium light. I asked him for a ride to the post-race party, and he said, "OK, but you help clean up, first."

I put the flags in his trunk. En route to the party he asked if I ran in the meet.

"Yes, the 5,000."

"What place? Eighth? Ninth?"

"First."

"First? Oh, you that guy who beat Hoffmeister. You very gude runner." The official took two bottles of beer from a cooler in the backseat. We clinked bottles and drank on the dark road. We walked into the party. I grabbed a tray of food and stood at a table that seated Louis, LaRoy, and several other shocked Americans.

"Mazzari sucks," I said, showing off my Swiss watch. "He's the European Champion? He can't even beat me."

At the next table was the meet director. I pulled him aside. "I was told there was a twelve-hundred dollar first prize. Where is it?"

The meet director looked down at my Swiss watch. "You're wearing it."

I protected the watch on a night in which Louis, LaRoy and I walked through town drinking beer. We put our thumbs on the bottle tops, shook them up, and watched the suds explode into the night like rockets, while singing "Born in the U.S.A." About 2 a.m., I told Louis and LaRoy I was walking back to my hotel.

"No fucking way," LaRoy said. "You ain't walking down the street at this time of night with a $1,200 watch on your wrist. You'll get mugged."

"This is Geneva, not Manhattan."

My American pals wrestled me into a cab and pointed the driver to their hotel. "You sons of bitchs," I said. "I wanna sleep in my own hotel. Shit."

The driver mocked me. "Shit. Son of a beech. Ha, Ha, Ha!"

The next morning I thanked Louis and LaRoy for protecting me and letting me crash in their hotel room. I went to the bathroom, put the contact lens on the counter in my eye, and wished them a safe trip to Italy. I figured my hangover blurred my vision as I walked to the bus that would take me back to my hotel. As I put one foot in the bus, I squinted into the distance at Louis hollering and running toward me. He was more blurry than ever, when he pulled me off the bus.

"Langenslacker, you idiot. You put the wrong contact lenses in your eyes."

My vision was 20/20 now that I had emerged as a world-class runner. I returned to Dorfenheimer and to Brigitte. I thought about her constantly in Switzerland. I wondered how I would make a move on the meet director's daughter, a German girl still in high school and 12 years my junior. How did Elvis pursue Priscilla?

I couldn't get anywhere with a girl I couldn't get alone. Every night she was accompanied by four or five friends. I don't know if that was a German custom or just a custom to protect herself from a horny American. The last night before I left for Paris she picked me up and then Helmick and Hans and whoever else she could fit into her convertible sports car. A song from Heart that goes, "How do I get you alone?" blasted on the car radio. I sat on top of the back seat and sang as we whizzed through the village streets, "How do I get you alone, Brigitte?"

Answer: you don't. After a final drink at Schultzie's, Brigitte dropped me off at the Busselmann's house with less passion than the fat Swiss girl who kissed me on both cheeks after winning the 5,000 in Geneva. I looked into Brigitte's eyes, "You never know when and where I might pop up. Auf Weidersehen."

At least Brigitte was a good agent. She talked the French into letting me into a 10,000-meter race with world-class runners and into the country without a visa. No one asked for the visa and no one showed up at the Paris train station. I spent three hours at the station trying to find someone who could speak – or willing to speak – English. I showed a cab driver the name of the meet hotel, scribbled in German on a notepad, handed him some funny colored French bills and he somehow found it about midnight. My dinner was a microwave hamburger from a convenience store.

The next morning I met with the Paris meet promoter, Enri Coutier, about an appearance fee. "We did not expect you, Misseur Langenfeljour," he said. "You are fortunate to be in the race."

I felt like slapping the smirk off the Frenchman's face. Courtier pointed to his eyes with his index fingers. "I see you. If you somehow happen to do something, then we talk about it."

That seemed remote, considering the chronic fatigue I suffered in the eight days following Geneva and what it took to make Paris. I fought to stay up with the leaders through a string of 68-second laps on the warm, cloudy afternoon in the French capital. Every time someone dropped off, I thought, "Oh no, I've got to pass another one."

In Geneva, I floated on air. In Paris, I waded through mud. Britain's Stu Slattery tossed in a 62 with seven laps to go to separate himself from the lead pack of six. I clung to that pack for dear life, and then came to life at the bell. I passed two Portugese on the backstretch and a West German on the final turn and somehow found the energy to run down Hoffmeister for second in final 10 meters. Hoffmeister rushed toward me with his middle finger and called me "a Yankee Doodle Pansy." He took a breath and pushed me, moving my hands off my knees. "You fucking Americans come over here and make us do all the work."

I pushed the arrogant Swiss backward. "I was just trying to hang on to the pack."

Hoffmeister and I threw a couple of slow-motion punches at each other, before realizing we were too exhausted for an all out brawl. After all, I had just run 28:04.16, a personal best by 28 seconds and the 12th fastest time in world so far that year.

That night, after dinner and several glasses of wine, I marched into Coutier's hotel suite. I sat on a leather sofa and put my wine glass on the side table. Coutier shook his head, "What do you want, man?"

I smiled, "One...Thousand...Dollars."

I took the grand and an extra night's stay in the hotel. I was keen to see the Eiffel Tower and ran 5K from the hotel. I stared up at the incredible site, said "that's great," and ran back to the hotel. I was the rabbit in the 5,000 me-ters in Amsterdam two days later and then finished fourth in rainy, blustery London in the two-mile in 8:31.83. I ran a 4:08 last mile.

It was my third straight personal best. I was beating some of the best run-ners in the world. I wrote in a postcard to Mom and Dad: "I have made my mark in Europe. I am making a few bucks, a few friends, and have proven I can run with anyone in the world. I'm on my way."

Those last weeks in Europe I didn't see much. The most excitement came from a London cab driver, who had blue hair and tattoos below his rolled-up black sleeves. He told filthy jokes as he balanced a cigarette in his lips and raced around the narrow streets like a Grand Prix racing driver. When an ambulance screamed past us, he tucked in and blew past cars stopped in the other lane.

I gave him a two-pound tip at the airport. "In America, we have to go to an amusement park to have that much fun."

Such rides would be disappointing to most Americans who would ask upon my return, "Oh, you went to Europe. What did you see? London Bridge? Windsor Castle? The Vatican?"

"I saw the airport, the train station, the hotel, and the track."

In Stockholm, my last race in Europe, I saw a beautiful blonde sprinter. I met Hillary Swain, a Welsh sprinter, the night before the meet at a pizza restaurant next to the meet hotel. I sat at a round table with Hillary, four other female competitors, and LaRoy. I made them laugh with tales of my European adventures. Hillary followed me back to the empty hotel lobby, where we talked and laughed for another hour. I liked Hillary, but I did not like the large diamond on her left ring finger.

She said I was the skinniest shot putter she ever saw, a crack that started a wrestling match on the lobby sofa. I held her arms back and stared at her smooth face, her well-toned breasts and inhaled her perfume. The next step was inevitable, but erased by a momentary lapse of catholic guilt. "I can't do this. She's married."

The next day I made the mistake of watching Hillary run the 200 meters. She wore a white one-piece suit with briefs stretched along her butt like a thong bikini. Her legs were like rocks. She probably could crack a walnut with those thighs. As I put my legs up on a chair under the stadium and visualized my race, Hillary came to wish me good luck. "Go away," I thought. "I can't run with a boner."

After the race, she was there to console me after a disappointing European finale – 11th in 13:46.23 – and there at dinner to share an ice cream sundae. She was there at the disco in downtown Stockholm to slide her tight leather skirt down my jeans on the dance floor, buy me drinks, laugh at more of my stupid jokes, and lift me on her shoulders and carry me out at closing time. We took a cab back to the hotel. Hillary jumped out and yelled to everyone in the lobby, "Party in my room! Party in my room!"

Thirteen track and field athletes – mostly men who had been away from their girlfriends or wives far too long – crowded into Hillary's room. I walked into a quick realization: "This woman is going to sleep with someone tonight. It might as well be me."

I made a perfect strategic strike. I jumped into her bed and pulled the clean, white sheets over me, forcing Hillary to either pull me out or crawl in with me.

32

The telephone rang at my Boston apartment a month after my return from Europe. It was Mom, calling from Dallas.

"A postcard from Rome arrived for you today, Jonny."

"Who's it from?"

"Let's see here. It says, 'Love, Hillary.'"

"Don't read it, Mom. Please forward it. Immediately."

The last time I had seen Hillary was at the London Heathrow Airport after our flight from Stockholm. I stood behind Hillary in her tight white jeans and pink top at the baggage carousel. Quincy Mitchell, a tall 400 meter runner who stood beside me, whispered, "I'd like to go to bed with her."

I looked up at Quincy and smiled. "I did. Last night."

Hillary leaned to grab her suitcase off the carousel, and I grabbed it for her. Another hand grabbed the other side of the handle. I looked left and straight into the eyes of Richard Swain, Hillary's husband. I pulled away and gave a farewell wave to the happy couple.

Now, she writes me from the World Track and Field Championships to the address I gave her after our rendezvous.

I put the telephone down, fell back-first on my bed, rested my head on a pillow, stared at my Prefontaine picture, and tried to figure out how I had become what I had become – a world-class runner and a world-class boozer and womanizer. A year before, I was cutting cut out oatmeal coupons. Now I was writing "condoms" next to toothpaste and peanut butter on my grocery list, comparing the beer prices on the 12-packs, and checking the newspaper for the lastest research on AIDS. Was my guardian angel replaced by Uncle Grimsley? Why was I telling the person behind me in line for the confessional, "You go first, I might be in here for a while?"

Mom and Dad treated my worldly success like the grain of salt we become through eternity. In a letter Mom reminded me of a Bible passage that reads, "What good is it to gain the whole world, if you lose your soul?"

Did she expect me to give up fame and fornication? Did my recent mattress polo pursuits give me the confidence to achieve the fame? Was I really even famous?

Melvin Arbuckle didn't think so. Melvin called me from Oshwash, Iowa the week of my return from Europe and introduced himself as the director of the Iowa Camp of Champions.

"We're holding our 12th annual camp next week," Melvin said. "We have 212 kids enrolled in the camp and we desperately need a world-class runner to speak. We pay for all travel and expenses and a speakers' fee."

"Sounds great."

"So Jonny, we were wondering..."

"Yes."

"If you had Nick Loman's phone number."

Taylor Markham definitely didn't think I was famous. I received a letter the next week that read, "Congratulations on a nice season that ended with a few good races in Europe. We would like to offer you our Wooosh-plus program, which is equipment and one trip."

I wrote Markham back. "Thank you for your offer. But that basically is what I have received from Wooosh the past seven years."

I settled for equipment, two trips, a $3,000 stipend, and a bonus schedule that included $1,000 if I were to make the 1988 Olympic Team. I ran the third fastest 10,000 in the country in 1987, and athletes like Nick Loman who ran slower than me that year were making 10 times as much. While I was writing stories for the *Cumberland Express-News*, Loman was reading what I wrote in his sauna after a hard workout. On my 30th birthday I ran four times per mile up and down a hill in the windy 45-degree temperatures in Lincoln. I ran my last mile in 4:14, jumped into my silver Honda, drove 40 minutes to Framingham, covered the first half of the high school football game, ran my two-mile warm-down at halftime, covered the second half, interviewed coaches and players, drove 30 minutes back to the newsroom, wrote a 20-inch story, and worked in the office until 11 p.m.

When I arrived at my apartment, Ray asked me how old I was. "I'm 29. Or make that 30, uh, today."

I was dirty-thirty. After finishing sixth in the BusterBurger 10K Road Buster in Charleston, West Virginia, the race director invited several athletes to his house that night. I took my 10th bottle of Bud to a backyard hot tub that included Charlotte Busby, a 36-year-old divorcee who served as the elite athlete coordinator, and two other female runners. I shared my Bud with Charlotte, who put her hand on my knee under the bubbling hot water and winked. "Honey, I'd like to ball your brains out."

My teeth lit the darkness. "That can be arranged."

I went for a 12-miler with Ray up Heartbreak Hill the next Monday. "How's your body after the BusterBurger? he asked."

"Everything is good, but my dick is a little sore."

I finished 41st in the U.S. Cross Country Meet and fifth man on the champion Wooosh East team at the famed Van Cortland Park Course in New York City. I roomed with Seth Standiver, who actually read the hotel Bible in the bedside drawer the night before the race. The night after the race every Wooosh runner but Seth did the Manhattan bar tour. I finished at 3 a.m. with two shots of Johnny Walker Red with Ray and Bobby Mac. Teri Mac, Bobby Mac's girlfriend, helped us to her two-door Mazda. Bobby sat in the front passenger seat, and Ray and I bracketed Terry Mac's pudgy 20-year-old sister, Traci, in the backseat. The three guys took off our clothes as we went through a toll booth.

Traci followed me to my room at the Bronx Best Eastern Hotel. New York is the city that never sleeps. Neither did we. I looked at Seth on the team van ride to Boston that required two Alka Seltzers and an aspirin. "Sorry if I woke you up last night, man," I said.

"It wasn't 'you,' who woke me up."

Three days later, the telephone rang in my apartment. "Hi Jonny, it's Traci."

I paused for a second. "Let's see. Traci, Traci. Oh, you're that fat chick I slept with the other night."

I remembered the next telephone caller a little better. Her sweet voice trickled down my ear and wrapped around my heart.

"Kelli?"

"How are you, Jonny?

I was infuriated Kelli Fuller gave me the wrong telephone number and never called or wrote to acknowledge our steamy Phoenix rendezvous. "I'm doing well."

"Sorry I waited so long to call you."

"No problem, Kelli. It's just great to hear your voice."

The conversation seemed to last until mid-December. We called each other every week, and arranged to meet in Tulsa, Oklahoma on Dec. 21. She was going to her grandparents' house in Tulsa for Christmas. My brother Matthew was visiting his fiancée, Eileen, in Tulsa and was driving to Dallas on Christmas Eve. Then I would spend the first two months of my pre-Olympic Trials build up on Rolling Hills Parkway.

"Can't wait to see you walk off that plane." Those were Kelli's final words after I hung up the telephone two nights before my Boston departure.

I told Ray as he drove me to the airport, "This could be the girl who could kick me off the one-night stand circuit and make me forget about Holly for good."

I left Boston the afternoon of the 21st with a new haircut, a navy P-coat, matching slacks, a red tie, a bottle of champagne, and two wine glasses in my carry-on Wooosh bag. I checked my hair in the airplane mirror one last time before landing. I strutted down the gate ramp and walked and walked and looked around at all the hugs and kisses going to every passenger but me. I waited 30 minutes and kicked over a metal ashtray stand. "I ripped a quarter out of my pocket, slammed it into a pay telephone, and dialed Kelli's grandparents. Kelli answered.

"Where are you? I just kissed three blondes at the airport gate before I realized none of them were you."

Kelli giggled and explained that she was tired from her flight the day before and decided to spend the night with her "Popo and Momo." I spent the next two hours sipping champagne and waiting for Matthew to pick me up. His advice: "I wouldn't walk away from that relationship. I'd run."

Kelli called me at Eileen's apartment after my 10-mile run late the next afternoon. "I'm bored, Jonny. Let's go do something."

Within an hour I had shaved, dressed, and driven Matthew's Honda Prelude to Popo and Momo's house. Kelli looked even better in Oklahoma than she did in Arizona. We ate, drank, and were told to "Get a room" at Cole's Steak and Suds. We got a backseat in the parking lot and took over where we left off in Phoenix. I dropped Kelli at Popo and Momo's house at 2:30 a.m., a departure sealed with an "I can't wait to see you again" kiss.

I called Kelli as soon as I awoke the next morning. This is how Matthew heard my end of the conversation from Eileen's kitchen.

"Say babe, what's happening..."

"Jonny..."

"Langenfelder..."

"Tall, skinny guy from Dallas. Slight stutter. You promised last night to take Christmas shopping this afternoon?..."

"Do I have the right number?"

I wondered how many tall, skinny stutterers she had been out with that week. She said Popo and Momo had guests coming over.

"You can come over later, if you really want to," she said.

I arrived at Popo and Momo's house and to a den full of cakes, cookies, eggnog, and Kelli's former neighbors, the Gillihans. Rance Gillihan was all grown up and appeared ready to renew their childhood game of "Show me yours, and I'll show you mine" with Kelli.

"Rance, do you remember when we were little and you played Santa Claus." Kelli walked to Rance, sat on his lap, and put her arm around him.

Rance smiled into Kelli's eyes. "Ho, Ho, Ho, what do you want for Christmas little girl?"

I wanted to shove a fake Christmas tree up Santa's flabby ass. Instead, I changed the subject. "So Rance, have you lived most of your life in Oklahoma?"

"Tif, Tif, I've lived all over the world. Just like my little Kelli, Kelli." Rance tickled his giggling lap lounger's tummy and kissed her neck.

I grabbed my coat, thanked Popo and Momo for the eggnog, wished Kelli a Merry Christmas, and shut the front door with a firm slam.

I drank more eggnog, filled with bourbon, alone, at Eileen's apartment. I picked up an early Christmas present for our five-hour drive to Dallas on Christmas Eve. Matthew let Eileen in the front seat, and looked at me and my six pack of Miller Lite in the backseat. "You can drink all those beers, if you want. But I ain't stoppin.'"

I broke the four-minute piss in the backyard at 2000 Hickory Lane, before going inside for more eggnog.

My run from 1987 to 1988 was a 13-miler along the icy, snow-banked streets and Christmas lights that lit Rolling Hills Parkway. No matter how hard I ran, I could not escape the heartache Kelli gave me for Christmas. Maybe this is what I deserved for the womanizing turn I had taken in 1987. Maybe I would be punished for my behavior at the Olympic Trials or, worse, suffer a fate worse than Uncle Grimsley's. Maybe Kelli was my punishment. I wish I could have snapped my fingers and returned to the pre-Boston Johnny Langenfelder.

Just before midnight, I came to a highway overpass nine miles into the run. I slid into an intersection at a four-way stop. All I saw were the headlights of the pickup truck that accelerated from the stop sign and knocked me to the pavement.

I was out for a moment. But I awoke to total peace. My worries and troubles vanished. Perhaps, I thought, this is what death is like.

I put my head inside the pickup and told the trembling driver. "Don't worry about it, mister. Next July, when you are drinking a beer with your buddies and watching the Olympic Trials, you can say, "See that fella there. I ran over him with my truck."

I glided to 2000 Hickory Lane amidst the New Year's fireworks. The next morning I told Mom and Dad my swollen wrist resulted from a fall on Rolling Hills Parkway. Fearing another fall on the ice, I drove to Hercules Health Spa where the carpeted indoor track is 21 laps-to-a mile. I did 210.

The sun returned, the ice melted, and I flew through January and February at 121 miles per week. I did weights three times per week and went to Father Litzke, who said I was controlled by the unconscious throughout my episode with Kelli. I was too embarrassed to tell him about the other women and saved those sins for an unknown priest behind a screen.

"When we rise above the unconscious level, we are conscious and have complete control to make the right choices." I closed my eyes and breathed as I sat in a chair and smelled the burning logs from the fireplace of Father Litzke's den. "After you awoke from your fall, you were fully conscious. You were totally into the present, because all the worries and fears from before had vanished."

I looked at Father Litzke, his warm smile spotlighted by the fireplace flame. "So I had to be knocked unconscious to regain consciousness?"

"That's right. Remember this: Yesterday is history, today is a gift, and tomorrow is a mystery."

Father Litzke said I should run not just with my feet and legs and my whole body, but with my whole spirit. I understood this on my first timed effort, a four-mile tempo run I cruised in 18:47 at White Rock Lake on February 29. I told Mom and Dad over spaghetti and meatballs that night, "I wish the Olympic Trials were next week."

My workout schedule, which I conceived and wrote on a Kleenex in bed the night I returned to Boston, indicated I was on the path to Seoul. Every Tuesday I ran five to six miles of intervals, alone, on the Central Mass track. Every Friday I ran a tempo run, alone, in Lincoln. Every Sunday I ran, alone, on my Heartbreak Hill loop, an 18 to 20 miler capped by a sub-five-minute mile. I also was sleeping alone. I spent my spare time writing for the newspaper or watching television.

Ray, who kept bugging me about this Marvin Hagler-Sugar Ray Leonard bout, wasn't even a distraction. I bet him a pizza that Leonard would beat Hagler. He bragged for two months about how Marvelous Marvin was the greatest fighter who ever lived, and how Leonard didn't stand a chance. The bout was not carried in our living room, only reports from the local sports anchor. Each report favored Hagler, and Ray kept putting in his order for an extra large mushroom and bacon pizza just as he did all week. Finally, the decision.

"And the winner was..." Ray smiled and shook his fists. "Sugar Ray Leonard..."

Ray shut his eyes, dropped his head, and walked back to his room while uttering two words right before he slammed the door, "Hagler sucks."

I finished 11th in 48:44 in the Capital 10 miler along the Potomac River, a mass urinal for pre-race contestants. Then I finished 10th in 29:11 in the Freedom 10K in Boston. I treated myself to one party, at the downtown Boston condo of Lenny Hargrove, who celebrated his ninth place finish in the Olympic Marathon Trials.

Teri Mac intercepted me on my way through the door. "Is this going to be another one of those all-out Langenslacker liquor nights?" she said.

"No way. I am in serious training for the Olympic Trials, and I have an important workout tomorrow. No way would I jeopardize my chances at making the team. I am in complete control."

Nine beers and four shots of tequila later, I elbowed Lenny on the street and drove my Honda through downtown Boston. I kept my car on the road without knowing where I was going. At 3:30 a.m. I pulled over at some college in Nowhere, Massachusetts, opened a map, and tossed it in the backseat. "Hell, I can't even see that."

I ended up in a town called Mayfield and found my way home from there. I arrived at dawn, as the Sunday newspapers were being delivered and Ray was going out to meet Loman for their long run. I awoke at noon and put my feet on the carpet. "Time for my run," I said to myself staggering toward the bathroom. "Run? I can't even walk."

For once, getting drunk was good. I felt stale in my training and needed a day off. But I refused to take one. The hangover forced a rest day and infuriated me on Monday's morning run. "Here you are trying to make the Olympic Team, Langenloser, and you go out and get drunk."

I retaliated with second-place finishes at consecutive Northeast Twilight Meets on the Central Mass track in early June, 7:59 for 3,000 meters and 13:39 for 5,000. Three weeks later, I returned to Eugene and the Prefontaine Classic. I ran un-Pre-like, hanging back in the pack and covering every move after a sluggish un-Prefontaine Classic 5K-like pace. The 9:03 for 3,200 was a mere jog that set up a 55.3 last lap that ignited a crowd roar and propelled me past U.S. 10,000 champion Marty Ashford in the homestretch. My 13:50.84 was the slowest winning time in Prefontaine Classic history.

I smiled and waved on my victory lap as the grandstand spectators continued their stomp and romp support. I was so on a roll that I set a record for delivering a urine sample in the post-race drug test. "This drug testing is great," I said to the nervous-looking testers. "You get free beer, just for letting a guy watch you pee into a bottle."

I was never more fit or ready to take a shot at making the Olympic team. In 13 days I would toe the line for my heat of the 10,000 meters in Indianapolis. That night I attended the post-race party at the Emerald Hotel. I sat at the bar and shook hands and talked with my fellow running rivals. Then I heard a sexy voice and smelled even sexier perfume from the barstool behind me.

"How you been, Jonny?"

I did not want to turn around, but I did. I nodded at the women's 3,000 meters competitor in her tight blue jeans and tighter white shirt. She crossed her legs, sipped a margarita, and smiled those sterling blue eyes through me.

"Hello, Kelli."

"You looked awesome in that 5,000."

"I only caught the start of your race, but you looked pretty good too."

"I've really missed you, Jonny?"

The bartender interrupted. "Ma'am, can I get you another margarita?"

"Sure."

"And for you, sir?"

I eyed Kelli from the heels of her black ankle-high boots to her pink, wet lips. Then I looked at the bartender.

"I'll have a Coke."

◆ ◆ ◆

I did not march into The Indianapolis Track and Field Stadium on opening night of the 1988 U.S. Olympic Trials. I marched into a war zone.

Runners from heat one of the 10,000 meters lay unconscious at the finish line. Paramedics rushed to the backstretch to a runner who passed out on the last lap. Another runner was taken out by stretcher and with an I.V. in his arm. The survivors staggered to the exit with wet towels over their heads, smiled at the heat two entrants, and offered a sarcastic, "Good luck."

It made sense the Olympics would be held in Korea, because the setting for the Olympic Trials looked like a M.A.S.H. unit.

I had entered my third Olympic Trials in the best shape of my life and with a Prefontaine Classic title under my belt. But my only thought as I stood on a starting line in triple-digit temperatures and triple-percent humidity was, "Do I really want to do this?"

Amber Shields didn't. She creamed the first barrier in her 100 meters hurdles heat and attempted to escape humiliation by jumping off the Hoskins Bridge, less than 400 meters from the stadium. The Olympic Trials not only broke Amber's spirit. It broke her back.

A shot from a starter's pistol sent me off a starting line in the 10,000 meters, heat two. For 25 laps, I felt like I was falling off a bridge. But the other contestants fell faster. When the bell lap clanged in the distance and sweat flooded my Wooosh spikes, I passed a runner who had passed out. I ran alongside a paramedic on the backstretch and dodged a medical cart on the final curve. At the finish I won a berth in the Olympic Trials 10,000 meters final, the opportunity to go through all this again in three days. The survivors gathered for their third straight meal of spaghetti without meatballs in the Creighton Suites dining room.

"All you got to do to make a final in this sauna is stay on the track." I set my tray on the round table next to other 10,000 meters survivors and mauled a roll of starch. "Too bad the U.S.A. track officials couldn't have chosen a warmer climate. Maybe Miami or Cancun. Maybe they could put some heaters on the track."

"The officials are probably laughing at us," one of the other survivors said. "They're probably saying, 'What's wrong with these distance runners? Can't believe they come to the U.S. Olympic Track and Field Trials so unfit.'"

I stuck my fork into a plastic salad and gnawed. "If I get a PR this week, I'll need CPR."

No matter how I looked at it, the road to Seoul went through hell. Three women, vying for the third and final Olympic spot in the 3,000 meters the day before my 10,000 meters final, collapsed in the final 30 meters. The third-place winner crawled to the finish line ahead of the other two and collapsed again. My trials' suite-mate, Rick Cauley, loved it. Cauley won my heat in 29:35 and walked into the living room with a beer and a Hawaiian shirt. I ran 30:00.01 and grabbed the sixth and final automatic berth.

"Pretty cool out there tonight, wasn't it, Langenslacker? It's normally a hundred and five when I train in Fort Lauderdale. What's it normally like in Boston?"

The battle the two days before the finals was with my nerves. I tried meditating, but it was too hot in my room. I took refuge in a Winn-Dixie. I stocked up on ice and broccoli, which my fellow finalist and shopping buddy Tad Drummond said was good for helping you recover from a hard race. I stood in the produce aisle and shook a head of broccoli at Tad. "I never thought 16 years ago, when I started this sport that I would be in a supermarket buying this."

The day of the 10,000 final began with an 8 a.m. telephone call from someone with a deep voice.

"Hello, Jonny?"

"Matthew?"

"No."

"Mark?"

"No."

"Dad?"

"No."

"Well, who is it then?"

"It's your Aunt Judy."

Aunt Judy called to tell me – or rather, warn me – Mom, Dad, Matthew, and Mark left her house in Terre Haute bound for Indianapolis. Dad thought this was his last chance to see me run, because I told him several years before I would run until I was 30. He called two weeks before the Trials and said he wanted to go to John Wayne's birthplace in Winterset, Iowa en route to Indiana.

I ran for 10 minutes the morning of the 10,000 final to relieve butterflies and then daydreamed over a stack of pancakes about making the Olympic team that night and jumping into the stands to hug Mom and Dad and my older brothers. The IHOP waitress brought me back to reality.

"You seem kinda nervous."

"I'm in the Trials tonight."

She dropped the check on table. I barely could hear her on her way back to the kitchen. "I'd be nervous, too, if I was on trial."

Eighteen finalists assembled at the starting line that night of July 18. A rain shower an hour before the race dropped the temperature to 97 degrees. I looked into the crowd, but only saw a mass of colors, some people waiting for the start and others heading for the exit. "Jonny" never followed the call of "Go" from the loved ones who traveled hundreds to thousands of miles for this once-in-a-lifetimer.

I closed my eyes, took a long, deep breath, made the sign of the cross, and fixed my eyes on the black raised object. The smoke set us off on a battle of wills and willingness to endure 25 laps of pain. The early pace was a funeral procession. No one dared to test the steamy elements, lest he leave the stadium in an ambulance or a hearse. The first mile went in 5:03, slower than the women would go in the first mile of their 10,000 meters a few nights later. I ran near the back of the procession, hoping the jog continued until the gun lap. If it came to a 400 meter dash, I was on the Olympic team.

The big finish line clock read 9:57 at eight laps, a wake up call for the normally fast-starting cross country champion Brad Bostick. The long-legged Californian ran the next four laps in 4:41, a surge which broke absolutely no one. We reached the halfway mark in 15:14, and the pace slowed even more. My broccoli buddy Tad Drummond took the lead. I picked my way to mid-pack and focused on the shorts in front of me. For the first time, since I had moved to Boston, I was running with Nick Loman.

"Stay with this guy. Stay with this guy," I kept telling myself over and over. Ray told me what kind of shape Loman was in and his Pre-like plan in the final eight laps.

The stadium lights glistened off the track dampened by the pre-race shower. Desperate "Go" calls for Nick, Tad, Ken, Brad, Rick, Marty – everyone but me – rang from the crowd. Cauley raced past Drummond at the eight-laps-to-go sign. Harwick and Bostick moved from the pack to Cauley's shoulder. I followed Loman, who looked poised to pounce. Down the homestretch, my brain pilot went to work, "You are strong. You are powerful. Stay with Loman. Stay with Loman. God, this is exciting."

Around the turn just past the seven sign, Loman took off like he was running the 200 meters. Cauley chased him down the backstretch. So did Harwick, Bostick, and Ashford. I stayed within my comfort zone and watched men of courage race for glory and men of lesser ability go by me like a fart in the breeze. Within a finger snap, I was out of it. I wasn't tired. I wasn't winded. No paramedic or priest needed my attention. I didn't even reach Purgatory.

A half-lap down and one to go, the gavel had struck. They don't let pussies on the Olympic team.

The pain of watching the victor, Nick Loman, hug Ray and his other Boston training mates, who rushed down from the stands, and then join his fellow Olympians Harwick and Bostick on a fan-waving victory lap hurt more than any of the 50 laps I ran on this track the previous three days. An attendant draped a wet towel over my head. I tore it off and flung it against the fence. I grabbed my black Wooosh bag and walked out of the stadium toward the hotel, my spikes grinding the sidewalk. "Way to stay with 'im, Langenloser."

The path to the hotel took me over the Hoskins Bridge. I stopped and looked over the railing at the long drop to the shallow creek. I felt a tap on the shoulder, and turned around.

"What are doing here?" I said.

"Came to watch you make the Olympic team. So what happened out there, Langenhooch?"

"Lack of fan support."

"I was yelling for you."

"Didn't hear you."

"I kept hollering, 'Run, you son of a bitch!'"

He wasn't Dad, but Mitch the Bitch was the comfort I needed. He drove me in his silver Corvette to the LHOP. The same waitress served us.

"How your trial go?"

"I was found guilty?"

"Oh yeah, what's your sentence?"

"Bacon and eggs at LHOP and 37 and a half more laps of the Indianapolis track."

I invited Mitch to stay in my room. First, we joined the other 10,000 meters losers for 50 cent beers in the hotel lounge. The cast included eighth-place Marty Ashford, ninth-place Tad Drummond, 11th place Rick Cauley, 12th place Jonny Langenfelder, 16th place Ollie Waynewright, and last place in the women's 3,000 meters, Paige Downing. We filled our glasses, clanged a losers' toast, and ordered the waiter to bring beer faster than we could drink it.

Cauley became especially friendly with Paige, an amazing feat seeing that her husband was seated next to them. At 2 a.m. we took the party poolside. I put on my trunks and sunglasses and reclined next to Mitch and a large Coors pitcher.

Paige sent her husband back to his hotel and joined Cauley for a moonlight dip.

Mitch and I retired to the suite at 3 a.m. and were followed by Cauley and Paige. Cauley gave up his room to his coach, thus giving Mitch and me a live floor show in the lounge. I heard Paige say, "I can't do this, I can't do this," followed by "It's wonderful."

I cracked open my room door to see Cauley and Paige going at it. Mitch, now a proud husband and father in Odessa, Texas, crawled under the covers. "I've never heard anyone fuck before."

We heard it all night. They stopped long enough in the morning to tell me I had a telephone call. Paige draped a sheet over her and went to the bathroom as I answered the telephone.

"Hello, Jonny?"

"Aunt Judy?"

"No, it's Matthew."

"You guys find something better to do than to come watch me run in the Olympic Trials?"

"Yeah, instead we decided to take Dad to the hospital."

Before Paige came out of the bathroom, Mitch and I had driven off in his Corvette. About 30 miles out of Terre Haute en route to Indy the day before, Dad had felt a pain up and down his arm. He returned to Terre Haute, where doctors determined he suffered a mild heart attack.

Mitch dropped me off at the hospital and drove back to Texas. Dad lay in his bed with wires hooked up to him and a machine that kept beeping and making graphs of his heartbeat. Mom sat at his side with a rosary dangling from her wrist. Matthew and Mark had gone to the movies.

"So how was John Wayne's birthplace, Dad?"

Dad smiled. "Pretty good, Pilgrim."

"Seriously, how are you feeling?"

"Not good, Miles. I missed your last race."

I didn't want to tell him I was running the 5,000, because he might try and escape the hospital. I didn't tell him that I hadn't decided to retire, because that could give him another heart attack.

"You didn't miss much."

"What place did you get?"

"Twelfth."

"Twelfth out of the whole country? That's a good way to finish." Dad slurped some water with a straw and shook his head. "Sure wish I could have seen you run."

I stared out the fourth-story window at a large park and told Dad to look out there. Five minutes later, he saw me wave and then run around the park for 30 minutes, about as long as he would have seen me run in Indianapolis. I returned to Dad's hospital room to say good-bye.

"You've see John Wayne's birthplace and you've seen me run."

Dad smiled. "Well, then I guess I can die now."

I returned to Indianapolis via Greyhound to the silence of my suite. Cauley gave up the home field advantage and spent the next two nights in Paige's suite. He returned the next evening. I told him we were in the same heat in the 5,000.

"Langenslacker, we've run two races together and the score is two-zero."

I tied a light blue handkerchief around my neck. "You see this. This is my lucky hanky. I have never lost when I wore this in the warm up."

"I guess you have to look good for your last race."

The U.S. track officials made us run heats to drop two of the 26 entrants. To make the next night's semifinal, heat three runners only needed to run faster than 14:35. I looked at Cauley next to me on the starting line and grinned. "Dead meat."

Cauley and I traded the lead throughout the race. Well under the required pace to qualify for the next round, I slowed around the final curve and jogged in fourth place. Cauley roared past me. In a finger click, I hollered, "you sonuvabitch," and went after him. I sped past four runners and Cauley at the finish line."

We slapped hands and laughed to the exit. "It's 2-1 Cauley. Look out."

There was no laughter the next night. Only the top five in our first semifinal heat were guaranteed spots in the 5,000 meters final. My heat had "Amercian" record holder and naturalized citizen Rafeg Motulo. The Algerian native who attended the University of Wyoming and married an American had a personal best of 13:02. Three other runners had run under 13:30 and four others under 13:40.

That night it did not matter how hot the pace or the weather. Nothing could keep me from the final. I felt stronger and smoother than in my Geneva victory. I moved from mid-pack to the leader Motulo's shoulder on the final backstretch. I looked back on the final turn to make sure no one was gaining, and then ran stride for stride with the American record-holder to the roar of the homestretch crowd. Motulo let up in the final 10 meters, and I leaned ahead for the semifinal win in 13:57.36. I slapped a high-five with a paramedic, jogged to the athletes' tent, and put on my training flats. Cauley staggered in and sat next to me.

"You make it?" I asked.

"By the skin of my teeth." Cauley wiped his face with a towel. "Man, I'm beat. I ran along there, thinking, 'I need sleep.'"

I almost was too excited to sleep. If I felt this good in the final, I was going to Seoul. Nothing could distract me from my goal.

Not Kelli Fuller, who reportedly slept with half the distance runners at the trials. I told Cauley, "I thought I was a stud until I found out I was the caboose."

"What does it take to get her into bed?" he asked.

"'Hello' will do it."

Not Mal, one of the many hangers on who laid out in a bikini at our pool every afternoon. Her Trials ticket came from Jocko, whom she was shacking up with at the nearby Motel 6.99. I told Jocko I might need a priest to administer the last rites. He told me he would leap out of the stands and give me mouth-to-mouth, if necessary.

"I'd be willing to do that," Mal said.

"That's OK," I said. "You stay in the stands."

Not Fubby Tuppernacker, who called as I walked out my door to the track on the afternoon of July 23.

"Langenlapper? It's Coach Tuppernacker."

"You in Indy, Fubby?"

"No. Lubbock. I'm watching the Olympic Trials on television. How do you think you're going to do?"

"I tell you what, Fubby. Why don't you watch "The Outdoorsman" on Channel 5 and tape my 5,000 final. Then I will call you and let you whether it's worth watching the tape."

I felt like I was in an oven as I warmed up in the mid-afternoon of Indianapolis. Five minutes of jogging is all I could stand. I walked to the athletes' tent to see Mal standing in a purple bikini top.

"Put some clothes on, Mal."

"Fuck you, Langenslacker."

235

Cauley said the same to Paige the night before. He said his lust turned to love and then to hate, when she chose to spend the night with her husband. As we waited to file onto the track, Cauley made a headband out of a piece of white cloth and wrapped it around his head.

"What is that?" I asked.

"Paige cut off the bottom of her singlet before her first race last week. This will blow her away, when she sees me wearing it."

If Indianapolis was an oven, the track was a stove. I marched with the other runners down the backstretch to the start, where an official uttered the worst sound a 5,000 meter finalist could hear at that point. "Ten minutes!"

The television people held up the race, so FloJo could tell the world what outfit she would wear in Seoul. The 10 minutes was an eternity. I sat in lane three and fried like a burger. Finally, I stood up and ran a stride around the curve. The television cameras focused on the starting line, and the starting gun put the television announcer's lips and 16 pairs of legs in motion.

My suite-mate in his silly, ragged headband led through the first lap in 63 seconds. I stayed back in 15th in the long line of rail huggers. Motula led through the 1,600 in 4:20, and then Cauley surged to another 63.

The pack split in half like the Titanic. I panicked and passed six runners on one turn and three more on the next. I sprinted down the backstretch to reach the back of the lead pack. Then I fell apart and drowned in a sea of sweat and also-rans. I crossed the finish line, after 87 ½ laps and almost 22 miles of racing in nine days, in 10th place in 13:59. 93 and put my hands on my knees. Someone in a white suit draped another wet towel over my head. I looked up to see Cauley, who finished second to Motulo, take off his headband and fling it into the crowd in Paige's direction.

Television cameras and microphones flocked to the three Olympians – Motulo, Cauley, and resurging Oregonian Rocco Toller. I walked behind them and a television technician yelled, "Get the hell out of the way!"

Thirty minutes later, I jumped spikes-first into my hotel pool. I felt like staying at the bottom.

Four years of gut-wrenching work that brought me to a world-class plateau was shattered on a world-watched stage. I was knocked off and into a hotel pool that seemingly was filled with more tears than water. I needed a lifeguard to save me from myself or at least the two things that could make me, at least for a moment, forget my pain – a beer and a woman.

I held my breath at the bottom of the pool and then opened my eyes. A vision, slim and sweet, elevated me to the top. She wore loose running shorts, a crop top, and an ankle bracelet.

"Need a life preserver?" she asked.

"Not when I have you."

Cindi Carver, a recent Indiana University grad, came up to watch the Olympic Trials finals. Now we watched each other from point-blank range.

"Going to the Wooosh party?" I asked, as I sat on the side of the pool alongside Cindi.

"I don't have a ticket, and I'm with some friends from Bloomington."

"If you get bored, just go to the Wooosh party and ask for Jonny Langenfelder. You can be my guest."

I spent the first two hours of the Wooosh party, held in downtown Indianapolis, at the bar. The place was wall-to-wall runners. Mal and Kelli asked me to join them on the crowded dance floor. I opted for another beer and another shot. I swigged the shot and looked out the window to see Cindi walking down the street with her friends. I elbowed my way through the crowd to the exit and went to three taverns before I found Cindi at a dive bar called "Ike's."

"You're coming with me, Cindi-rella." I took her hand and led her to the Wooosh party and to a dance floor of winners and losers, who guzzled beer from glass bottles and discarded their shirts and their inhibitions. Cindi tore off my white beer-soaked shirt and ran her hands down my back as we danced and howled with my fellow finalists. I slapped Cauley a high-ten and hugged his lover, who wore a lucky headband.

I shouted in Cauley's ear, "Where is her husband?"

"Who gives a shit?"

The wild dance went until midnight or about the time I went to the urinal for another four-minute piss. I returned to a dance floor taken over by locals. There was no sign of Cindi. Not even a glass slipper I could have used to sip the remaining drops of the keg behind the bar. A bouncer carried me to the exit at 2 a.m., and I ran alone on a route to my suite that had a track and bridge on its path. I staggered into the dark stadium and completed 12 ½ laps to make it an even 100 for the nine days.

I plodded out of the stadium for the last time through the debris of water cups and past a row of folded medical tents and miniature American flags the Olympians carried on their victory laps. As I staggered down the road, I fell atop the Hoskins Bridge and propped myself up to the railing. I stared down into the deep, dark pit and watched as my tears and sweat dripped into the water like a leaky faucet.

Whatever pain I felt on any of the 100 laps could not compare to the pain I felt at that moment.

PART V

LAST GO-ROUND

October 1, 1988

It is midnight in a basement apartment at the bottom of Boston's Heartbreak Hill. Cardboard boxes are everywhere.

Some boxes are duct-taped shut. Others are ripped open, spilling debris onto the dirty carpet. There are race numbers from meets in Germany, Switzerland, England, Norway, Greece, and from three U.S. Olympic Track and Field Trials. Running shorts, shirts, socks, and sneakers. Rosary beads, a Bible, a crucifix, and a packet of condoms. *Track and Field News, Sports Illustrateds,* and a *TV Guide.*

Pizza boxes are piled up in the corner next to crunched beer cans and empty potato chip bags. The only piece of furniture in the bare-wall apartment is the sofa sleeper the tenant uses only as a bed. The only light comes from a street lamp funneled through the small, rectangular window and from a color television I have not taken my eyes off in two weeks except when I slept.

The last individual track race at the 1988 Seoul Olympics is difficult to watch. The fifteen 5,000-meters finalists, some I raced and a few I beat, stand at the starting line and before the world.

"I should be in there." A shot from a starter's pistol interrupts my comment heard by no one.

The rainbow of runners breaks the line and into a pace the high-pitched expert analyst Frank Shorter dooms, "Tactical."

As if he could hear Shorter in the press box, Kenya's John Ngugi surges from the back of the pack to a 20-meter lead with a sub-60 second lap after the first 1,000 meters. The faster Ngugi runs, the more his lead expands, the higher Shorter's voice becomes, and the more I drift toward Seoul.

I see myself loping in the back of the pack ready to pounce on a laboring Kenyan. I think of Steve Prefontaine and how he would have admired the Kenyan's bold move or the courage of Portugal's Domingos Castro, who chases Ngugi in the final five laps.

"I'd be right there." I point to Castro's shoulder. "I'd wait until the last 300, and, 'boom,' I'd catch the Kenyan in the homestretch."

Instead, Castro fades. Ngugi is carried down the homestretch by the voices of Shorter, who calls the race a "wonderful display of front-running, gauging your effort," and throaty play-by-play man Charlie Jones, who need not spill a word but does after West Germany's Dieter Baumann and East Germany's Hansjorg Kunze sweep past Castro in the final 10 meters. "Castro's going to be shut out. Oh, what a disappointment!"

241

Castro sits on the track and sobs. Ngugi takes a red, white, green, and black flag and jogs around the track.

I lift from the sofa sleeper and trudge through my debris. I burst out the door and onto a roller coaster hill, illuminated by stars and street lamps.

◆◆◆

I've woken up to beautiful blondes and brunettes, but never to a bald man with whiskers, muscle shirt, sledgehammer, and a "I heart Momma" tattoo on his fat, hairy shoulder.

The workman stuffed his chest through my opened bedroom window and stared down at me.

"You movin' out today?" A droplet of spit flew between the gap in his front teeth and landed on my chin.

"What are you talking about?" My morning breath didn't faze him.

"You were given a 30-day notice to move out, and this is the 30th day. By 5 p.m. this here apartment will no longer be an apartment."

Thirty days before, I was in Europe on a post-Olympic Trials tour known to other Trials losers as "The Consolation Tour." I did not know the building owner decided to demolish the apartment and the adjoining space above the Wooosh Store and turn it into shops. Within six months, women would be shopping for lingerie in my living room.

I was so jetlagged on my return from Europe I didn't realize Ray had moved out or see the note he left on the kitchen counter. "Faggot – Our asses have been kicked out of here. Get your shit and go."

Good thing I returned that night. The next day all my belongings, like the walls and the plumbing, would have been rubble.

I had gone to Europe to salvage what was left of my 1988 track and field season. The five races and 87 ½ laps in nine days at Indy had demolished my body. Bobby Mac took one look at me and asked if I was anorexic. I jogged 30 minutes easy each day on the grass and couldn't finish a 100 meter stride at week's end.

I used my last Wooosh trip to fly to Dallas with an option of flying to Zurich. I wanted to check Dad's recovery from his heart attack and let Mom fatten me up. Dad was fine. When I told him I would devote another four years to training for the Olympics, he yelled and shook his fists without any sign of another attack. My legs felt dead, even after several runs along Rolling Hills Parkway. I called Coach Hightower, who had learned massage therapy from a blind man in Flagstaff, Arizona. He put life back in my legs with his strong thumbs and knuckles, and the next day I rounded the Forest Hill track like my old self. I told Coach Hightower to write down my times on the ladder work-out of 400, 400, 800, 1,600, 800, 400, 400 and not tell me what I ran until I finished. Still breathing and sweating hard, I looked at the times.

"I'm going to Europe."

I started with a personal best of 7:50.83 for fourth in the 3,000 meters in Geneva and a personal worst of 14:17 for the 5,000 six days later in Heidel-berg, Germany. Motivation was difficult on the Consolation Tour. While many opponents were building for their Olympics in four weeks, my Olympics wouldn't be possible for another four years. Meet promoters cut my appear-ance fees to not much more than a handshake. A little girl asked for my auto-graph before the Heidelberg race and if I was running in Seoul. I smiled and shook my head. She snatched her pen and paper from my hand and walked away.

The Athens meet promoter offered me no appearance fee. I griped about it to my roommate, Wes Ashford, in my Heidelberg hotel room, and then re-versed myself. "What an asshole I am. A guy offers me a free round-trip ticket to Athens, Greece with a hotel room and free gourmet meals, and I'm bitching about an appearance fee?"

I slept through my alarm the next morning and missed the bus to the Frankfurt airport and my flight to Athens. All that was present at the Air Greece counter was a red telephone. I picked up the receiver and told the Greek attendant I missed my flight.

"You did what?" the man yelled.

I pulled the phone from my ear. "I missed my flight to Athens."

"What do you expect me to do about it?"

"Isn't there a later flight?"

"No, there's no other flight! You must come back tomorrow!"

He slammed the telephone down, before I could ask him what time the flight was. Now I was stranded. I had checked out of the hotel in Heidelberg, and a large convention left Frankfurt without a vacant hotel room. I called Brigitte in Dorfenheimer. Her younger sister, Lilli, told me in attempted Eng-lish that Brigitte had moved to Wiesbaden and had no telephone. I had her spell out the street address and the town, which I noted was only an hour train ride from Frankfurt.

Brigitte returned from work that night to a surprise guest on her apartment doorstep. We immediately broke out laughing. Brigitte remembered the last thing I told her when I left Dorfenheimer. "You never know where I might pop up."

We picked up where we left off, eating strudel and drinking pitchers of beer. I slept on her floor that night without an attempt to crawl into her bed. Brigitte was my drinking buddy, and nothing more. Besides, I wouldn't want a relationship with someone who speaks in a foreign tongue. I like to know what my girlfriend is yelling at me.

I said "auf wiedersehen" again the next morning and took the train to the Frankfurt airport, where a Greek ticket agent stood at the Air Greece counter and talked on the telephone with presumably her boyfriend. After about 10 minutes, I started looking at my watch and banging on the counter. She kept talking. I interrupted. "M'am, I have a flight to catch?"

She hung up five minutes later. I told her I had a pre-paid flight to Athens and showed her my passport. The woman checked her computer. "Nothing here for you."

"What do you mean? I have a pre-paid flight from the Athens meet promoter."

"Nothing here for you."

"Can you check again?"

"No!"

I sprinted to the nearest pay-phone, slammed down several marks, called Athens, received confirmation from the meet promoter, and sprinted back to the ticket counter. I waited in line for 15 minutes, while the woman took another telephone call.

"Look, ma'am, I just got off the telephone with the meet promoter, who assured me there is a plane ticket for me here. Could you please check?"

The woman looked at my passport and typed on her computer.

"Nothing."

"You sure?"

"Look, there is nothing here under your name. Come back when you have some money to pay for a flight."

I barely had enough for another telephone call to Athens, but no time to make my flight. I returned again to the counter, this time armed with the pre-paid flight authorization numbers. The woman typed them into the computer, and my order popped up. I leaned over the counter to see the screen and that she had misread my passport. She thought my first name was Jonathan and my last name was Christian.

"You gave me the wrong name," she said, grinning. "So you miss your flight again. Ha. Ha."

My hands formed a grappling pose. I looked at the ceiling and whispered, "Just one, Lord, just one. Please, just one around the neck."

I shared a room that night with three zero-English-speaking Polish runners I met in the airport. They wore Poland national track and field sweats, and we communicated by pointing to each other's names in the *Track and Field News'* 1987 Annual Rankings edition. I finally arrived in Athens the next day, walked the Acropolis, ran a lap around the old Olympic Stadium track, and met a group of athletes at the practice track. They laughed as I told them about my travel misadventure in Frankfurt.

Then I smiled, turned around and stepped into a water sprinkler hole. Water shot out of the hole and sprayed up my shorts. I escaped the blast but not the embarrassment from the athletes, who held their stomachs and fell to the grass. I smiled, jogged off the practice track, and felt the golf-ball size lump on my leg. "Ohhh! I think I broke my fricking leg."

I finished fourth in the next night's 5,000 meters in 13:54.87 and was welcomed back to Boston by a two-ton wrecking ball. Wally and his working crew wouldn't wait to let me pack. When I returned with cardboard boxes and duct tape from the Wooosh store, sledgehammers already were breaking through the walls. I tossed my things in the boxes and lugged them through chunks of plaster and crowbar-wielding workmen and downstairs through the pouring rain to the Wooosh van in the parking lot. By 2 p.m., caked in wet sawdust and perspiration, I returned for the bag of groceries I stuffed in the refrigerator before I went to bed. I opened the refrigerator. Empty.

I knocked on Wally's hardhat. "Where's my food?"

"We ate it." I could see a piece of fresh ham between Wally's teeth. "Sure was good."

I returned later that night to a gutted second floor. The toilet, which had been ripped from the wall and abandoned in the center of where our lounge used to be, was all that was left. As a farewell to my favorite apartment and a thank you to Wally and the crew, I sat on the toilet one last time and left a stinker of a surprise on the dry linoleum.

Two days later, I found a basement apartment in an old lady's house near the Wooosh store. It was small and had noisy pipes running along a ceiling, only two feet above my head. There was no shower or kitchen. I had a toaster oven, hot plate, and a refrigerator barely big enough for a 12-pack. I washed the dishes in the bathtub. But it was cheap by Boston standards and all I could find in two days.

I expected Wooosh to give me a raise, which would allow me to find a better apartment. I wrote Taylor Markham and pointed to my victory at the Pre Classic, my PR in Geneva, and my five races at the Trials. Markham returned from the Olympic Games with a new Wooosh consultant, Darcy Ellard, the run-until-you-drop Australian whom he met in Seoul. Markham wrote back: "From the advice of Mr. Ellard, we have decided to confine our paid athletes to only those who ran in the Olympic Games. However, we will keep you on our Wooosh-plus program."

I tossed the letter in the garbage can, hung my clothes on a pipe, and made myself at home. I called Max Steiner at the *Cumberland Express-News* and booked myself for the remainder of football season. I bought my first answering machine, making sure I didn't miss "the" call from my new dream girl. The morning after the Trials party Ray had located an Indiana University runner who told him Cindi Carver's address. Ray wrote it on a condom wrapper. I sent Cindi a postcard from Europe and a letter from my new apartment with my new telephone number. Every telephone ring, I hoped it was her. Every letter I received I wished she sent it. I knew very little about this girl, yet I would sit in that basement for hours, staring at the walls and thinking about nothing but her. It was an even worse obsession than Holly.

To take my mind off all women, I resorted to running. Training was never more difficult. Chasing that Olympic dream was like climbing a giant tree. As I reached for the top branch, I fell to the bottom. Now, only days before my 31st birthday, I had to start all over again. Every run was agony, knowing the next Olympics was four years away. Jocko Girelli didn't ease the pain. He quit his job at Pickering College, moved to Boston, and demanded to be coach and king of Wooosh East. He somehow had stayed on the Wooosh payroll as a consultant.

I decided to give him a chance that fall, but he was either an hour late for workout or wouldn't show up at all. He would tell me to be warmed up and ready to go at the Harvard playing fields at 3 p.m. I would be cooled down by the time he turned up.

I ended my coach/athlete relationship with Jocko after his famous "mystery whistles" workout. He blew the whistle and I kept running hard until he blew it again. I jogged the interval, and sprinted when I heard the whistle. Jocko would blow the whistle after 20 seconds, 40 seconds, or two minutes of hard running. I ran as hard as I could after another whistle blow and kept running hard around fields filled with Harvard football, lacrosse, and field hockey players. I ran and ran five, six, seven minutes. I went into my atomic breathing. Lactic acid shot through my veins. I ran slower and slower until I collapsed on the grass after nine or ten minutes. I stared into the distance at Jocko, who was smoking a cigar and talking with the Harvard women's cross country coach. He forgot to blow the whistle.

Markham flew to Boston several weeks later to meet with the 31 runners of Wooosh East. We had a closed-door meeting at the Wooosh East Running Store, but we knew Jocko had his ear to the door. We smelled the cigar smoke seeping under the door. Markham told us Jocko requested to become the coach and chairman of Wooosh East. Mal presented a roster that included the members whom Jocko coaches.

"He already coaches 23 of the 31 runners anyhow," Mal said.

I snatched the roster from Mal and saw a check by my name. "He doesn't coach me. Does he coach you, Ray?

"Hell no."

"How about you, Ollie?"

"No way."

My count showed Jocko coached only three runners – Mal, her friend Bea Wakelin, and Pickering College graduate and Jocko's prize pupil Robbie Bolt. Mal wanted to inflate the numbers, so Jocko could take charge and give travel money to lazy runners, like her, who least deserve it. The club ran fine without Jocko, who abandoned us two years before.

Ray then yelled above the chatter. "It's obvious what's happenin' here! Mal's screwing Jocko, and she wants to do the same to everyone else!"

Mal charged at Ray with her fists and four runners pulled her off him. Markham screamed for order. "I've heard enough," he said. "I'll take your comments into consideration and make a decision next week."

The decision was to appoint a committee of coaches outside the club to administrate the club. The five coaches chosen were Jocko's buddies, who gave Jocko the power to do whatever he wanted.

The turning point of my training came on a Friday night in which I needed a 10-miler to stay on pace for my first 101-mile week of the season. It was cold, dark, rainy. Lenny Hargrove was having a blow-out party downtown. I lay in bed, wanting to do anything but run. Somehow I threw the covers off, put on my raingear, and slugged through the 10-miler. The next day I ran 18 miles to complete the 101-mile week and did 121 the next. I felt great from then on.

On a fall run, as I crunched the leaves along the trail at the all-women's Wellesley College, it occurred to me that I had gone all of 1988 without a game of mattress polo. My focus on Olympic Trials training and a possible relationship with a woman I met once and never answered my letters had returned me to a celibate lifestyle. You not only get horny living in a pit, but you get downright lonely. Uncle Grimsley took residence in Grandma's basement in his 30's and never left. I didn't know how long I could hold out for Cindi, so I made myself a deal. "I will send Cindi a Christmas letter in early December. If she doesn't respond by the strike of midnight January 1, then any woman in my sight is fair game." I wrote:

Dear Cindi-rella,

Been to any lavish balls lately? Or have you been knee-high in paperwork in some Indiana office, consumed with marathon training on some cold, lonely road, befuddled with cleaning and cooking chores in some dark, dingy apartment?

Truly,
Prince Jonathan

I told Ray about the deadline and the letter at the Christmas party hosted by he and his house-mates Bobby Mac, Louis, and Phil. "Fireworks ain't gonna be the only thing explodin' on New Year's," he said.

"I'll hear from her."

Every day I checked the mailbox. Nothing. I checked my answering machine. Nothing. Christmas passed. Nothing. Finally, I suited up in my tights and turtleneck for my New Year's Eve Run from one year to the next. I waited until 10 minutes before midnight. Nothing.

I hammered the eight-miler on the winding, snow-banked roads, leaving the thought of Cindi-rella and 1988 behind. The next morning I ran with my running buddies from the Wooosh East store to the annual New Year's Day party at Boston Bully's. I hit on every woman in the joint. Mal told me she had broken up with Jocko, wrecked her car on New Year's Eve, and resolved to not have sex in 1989.

"So what are you doing next New Year's?" I asked.

Ray pulled me aside. "Whatcha doin,' Faggot? I thought I taught you better than that. This is a G.U.E night, my man."

"G.U.E.?"

"Go Ugly Early. You got to go for a big, fat ugly one. Play the odds, just like I taught you. You're not still holding out for Cinderella, are you?"

"No, I just don't have a place to take a G.U.E. She may not fit in my basement?"

"Don't be worrying about that. We'll pick up two ladies and bring them to my place. You can use Bobby Mac's room. He is the visiting team at Teri Mac's."

Ray demonstrated G.U.E. to perfection and found two women who could play offensive tackle for Boston College. The more we danced and drank the more they began to resemble fashion models, not tent models. As we escorted them to the exit, Bobby Mac pulled me aside. "Langenslacker, you can use my room. Just let me know if I need to change the sheets."

A few minutes after I nudged my G.U.E. date out of bed with my bare feet and heard her and her friend drive off, I staggered out of Bobby Mac's bedroom and into the kitchen. I wore nothing but a blanket. Ray busted out laughing after I wrote a note on a napkin to Bobby Mac, "Change 'em."

I went back to sleep and arrived at my basement apartment about noon to a blinking message light on my answering machine. I pressed the button, marked "play message."

"Happy New Year, Prince Jonathan. It's Cindi-rella."

The Florida coastline stretches about 500 miles from Key West to Jacksonville, inviting cruise ships and tankers from all over the world. A running dot next to the Atlantic Ocean grew more familiar the closer I came that Saturday afternoon in February of 1989.

Cindi Carver and I wrote each other every week in January, and now it was time to become more than pen pals. The Daytona 15K was an opportunity to stab the pens in the sand and roll around in the waves.

I ran harder the closer she came. I couldn't wait to take this petite runner in my arms and carry her to the hotel. I spread my arms wide and smiled as she approached to within a football field. Down to the 50, the 30, the 20, the 10. Cindi ran right past me into the end zone.

"Cindi? Cindi-rella."

Finally, she stopped. "Sorry. Didn't recognize you, Jonny. Must have been thinking about tomorrow's race."

I went to give Cindi a kiss, and she shook my hand. We ran back to the hotel and made plans to eat together at the pre-race pasta dinner. She didn't show up. Instead of dining with a cute runner, I sat with a veteran woman who said her goal was to break two hours in the next morning's race.

I was lucky to break an hour. I ran 4:30 the first mile in the lead pack that included 18 Mexicans. I felt like Davy Crockett at the Alamo. I suffered a similar fate, finishing 27th in 46:54. Cindi finished not far behind me. We warmed down together and agreed to go to the post-race luncheon. She didn't show up for that either. I called her room a dozen times, all with no answer. I told my roommate, "This woman is driving me crazy. I spent a month exchanging letters and telephoning her. I arrange to meet her in Florida for a race and romance, and now she wants nothing to do with me. I feel like jumping off the hotel."

My roommate replied, "Como?"

Cindi finally appeared at the awards ceremony. She explained that her parents drove from Indiana to watch the race and she wanted to spend some time with them. That night she agreed to go with me and other runners to a lively bar called The Sand Dude. I wore my black designer jeans, black shirt, and black leather tie. Cindi showed up in Cinderella attire – faded jeans, plaid colored shirt, pink sweater, and hair begging for a brush. She also wore something on her sleeve I didn't like – another guy.

"Hi everyone, this is Jamie. He's a friend from Indiana who works at DisneyWorld."

"Another pen pal," I thought.

I flooded Jamie with a tidal wave of jokes and old running stories that had Cindi and the runners who understood English laughing in their beers. Cindi, who minored in Spanish, interpreted for the Mexican runners, who also laughed. We took several photographs, one of Cindi sitting on my lap. The group walked back to the hotel and piled into the elevator. I left Jamie smothered in Mexicans and followed Cindi to her room. She put her key in the door, gleamed up at me, and said, "I had fun. I'll see you for a run tomorrow morning at eight."

"Not even a handshake," I thought.

I found Jamie riding up and down the elevator and joined him for a nightcap in the hotel lounge. He explained the thrill of operating a ride at DisneyWorld and his desire to become Mickey Mouse.

"He's got a small brain after all," I thought.

Cindi and I went for a 10-miler along the beach the next morning. En route to the airport, I went to her room to say good-bye, which I figured would be more like farewell. She had just showered and wore a white cotton robe. Her wet hair sparkled in the sun that splashed the windows. She had breakfast of orange juice and blueberry muffins set for us. I looked at my watch and at her and thought about missing my flight.

"You'd better go." Cindi embraced the love in my heart and kissed me on the cheek.

One peck is all it took to keep the infatuation alive. I wrote her a letter on the return flight to Boston. I told her I already missed her and looked forward to her coming to visit me in Boston. Louis picked me up at the airport. As we waited by the baggage carousel, I said, "I'm gonna marry that girl."

February passed without a letter from Cindi, but with the best training of my life. I carried 112-mile weeks with a weekly tempo run and long intervals on the roads in Lincoln or the Harvard indoor track. I wanted a fast 10K, but needed a warmer climate. I received a free airline ticket to Houston for the Texicon 10,000. I left a week early for the Ranger Run, a 10K that started and finished outside Arlington Stadium.

I ran the day before the race on Rolling Hills Parkway in shorts and no shirt. I awoke the next morning to an ice storm.

"Guess you won't be running today," Dad said.

"It's a road race, not a baseball game."

"It's 20 degrees out there."

It felt like minus-20 on the starting line next to runners dressed like Eskimos. I psyched out the field, when I stripped to singlet and shorts. My 4:45 first mile easily broke the field, but failed to warm me up. Ice formed in the perspiration in my hair and eyebrows. My fingernails turned blue. My testicles froze. I finished in 30:33, out of sight of the second-place finisher, and jumped into the backseat of the press Cadillac.

"What did you think of the course?" asked *The Dallas Star* reporter, who sat next to me.

"Can't talk, can't talk."

"You mean no comment?"

"No, my jaw is frozen. I really can't talk."

The next day's story in *The Dallas Star* read:

> *Jonny Langenferder has run in some cold places – a snowstorm in Wisconsin, frigid showers in Oregon, and in Boston blizzards. But the coldest place? How about yesterday's Ranger Run in Arlington, Texas.*

Beth Mahoney read the story and asked me out. She was the youngest of the eight red-headed, freckle-faced, wire-toothed Mahoney girls of the St. Peter Claver Parish. I obliged, reluctantly, and found a college-aged woman without freckles and braces and with short blonde hair and the charisma Cindi lacked. We talked for hours over dinner and drinks in that huge phallic symbol in the Dallas Sky, known as the Reunion Tower. We talked about growing up in strict catholic families, Sisters Buttface and Slap Happy McDougall, and the dress code at Bishop Callahan.

The next afternoon Beth biked alongside me on my 10-mile run around White Rock Lake and had dinner with me and my parents. I kissed her on the lips the day before my departure to Houston, but that's as far as I wanted to go. I was saving it for Cindi. Besides, those Mahoney girls are fertile. Beth had 27 nephews and nieces. I was told you could get a Mahoney pregnant by blowing in her ear.

I finished 16th in 29:30 at the Texicon 10,000 in a field that looked like an Olympic final. My disappointment was eased by a race director who handed me a beer in the finish chute. Red Wooten, an oil executive, spoiled his elite runners with a pre-race feast at our Glass Towers Hotel and a post-race feast at his mansion in West Houston. Then we piled into Red's van with two kegs in the back for a tour of Houston. One runner pumped the keg, while another put the tap in his mouth. We washed our throats with beer for three hours. At dinner, the foreigners sat on one side of the restaurant and the four Americans sat in the corner. So we lit up. Tad Drummond blew cigarette smoke out of his nose and circles out of his mouth. I mostly coughed and scoffed at the foreigners who made fun of us.

I returned to my basement apartment in Boston and couldn't wait to read my mail that had piled up for 10 days. Certainly, there would be a letter from Cindi. Nothing. I went through the mail twice. Nothing. I went through my telephone messages. Nothing. Then I went for a 10-miler with Louis on Heartbreak Hill.

"Sounds like this girl Beth is more suited for you," he said.

"But I'm in love with Cindi."

"What's the longest conversation you've had with Cindi?

"About 10 minutes."

"And Beth?"

"Several hours."

"See my point?"

"Yeah, love is pretty messed up."

I decided a new deadline for Cindi-rella – the 1989 Boston Marathon, April 17. I wrote Beth a letter and left the bottom blank. If Cindi called or wrote, I would sign the letter to Beth. "Your friend, Jonny." If Cindi didn't call or write, I would sign it, "Love, Jonny."

After watching runners climb Heartbreak Hill, I returned to my apartment and an empty mailbox. I signed the letter to Beth, "Love, Jonny" and sent it. The next day I received a 14-page letter from Cindi on pink and blue stationary. She had been writing a diary to me everyday and waited to surprise me. She enclosed pictures from The Sand Dude, and signed her letter "Love, Cindi."

Two weeks later, I received a letter from Beth. She signed it, "Your friend, Beth."

The letter writing campaign continued between Bloomington and Boston. I scripted clever words on scratch paper and re-wrote them on Wooosh stationary. I wrote one letter with subliminal messages and another in cut-out pictures and letters from magazines. She promised to watch me run at the Notre Dame Distance Festival, where I won a tactical 5,000 meters with a last-lap surge. There was no hug or kiss at the finish line. Just a handshake from runner-up Jed Mortimore of Michigan State. I spent the evening with a box of chocolate-covered peanuts and a hotel movie.

I wanted to blow off Cindi. But I couldn't stop thinking about her, no matter how little we had in common or how reluctant she was to see me. I organized an airline ticket through the Maine Half Marathon race director to bring Cindi to Portland. She rejected my plan to spend a few days in Boston after the race. I went up anyhow to watch her win $1,200 for second place. She sent me back to Boston late that night with another peck on the cheek. Tears rolled down my checks on the dark drive home, alone, in the silver Honda and with a Lionel Ritchie song that didn't help me take my mind off Cindi.

Hello, is it me you're looking for?
'Cause I wonder where you are.
And I wonder what you do.
Are you somewhere feeling lonely or is someone loving you?
Tell me how to win your heart,
For I haven't got a clue.
But let me start by saying, I love you.

The next night Max Steiner caught me banging my head on his computer again at the Express-News.

"How many girls you got this time, Jonny?"

"One, and she's driving me nuts."

I told Max the story while watching him smoke a full cigar. His take? "Maybe she's anorexic."

"What?"

Max referred to a recent story a woman wrote for the news section. Cindi had all the symptoms – the bony features, the oversized and ragged clothing, sunken eyes, bruised fingers, and her constant withdrawal from social interaction. Then I recalled the race in Maine. "Cindi ran a half-marathon and the only thing she ate after the race was a few of my French fries. I found tiny, high-powered laxatives on the bathroom counter, and she played audio tapes of Karen Carpenter."

"Scary," Max said. "It's worse than having the three girlfriends."

I consulted the writer of the story on eating disorders. She said the girl needed desperate help and to be confronted. She said Cindi probably would deny she had a problem, and the laxatives were put into her toilet bag by accident. I called Cindi, who said she didn't have a problem and laxatives were put into her toilet bag by accident. My next call was to Phil Bentley, whose fiancée was anorexic. "What should I do, Phil?"

"Run for the hills. Once she's anorexic, she'll always be anorexic. You'll be planning something for weeks. Then at the last second, she'll cancel. The Fine Young Cannibals wrote a song about her called, 'She drives me crazy.'"

"Then why do you stay with her?"

"Because I love her. I guess."

I took Phil's advice. I ran. Through all the wasted motion over a girl who wanted to be – and couldn't be – anything more than a pen pal, my training still went well and on target for a European season sure to vault me to the world's elite. Wooosh's crack European agent Brian Brennan entered me in the World Games 10,000 in Turku, Finland and promised me at least seven other European races. I sold my silver Honda, intending to put my European appearance cash into a brand new Firebird – with T-tops, of course.

I bypassed the U.S.A. Championships to remain fresh for Finland. My last U.S. race was the 5,000 at the New England Championships at the Central Mass track. The field also had Nick Loman, Rick Cauley, Brad Bostick, Jocko Girelli's golden boy Robbie Bolt, and 16 of the best runners along the Northeast seaboard.

Loman set off at 13:20 pace and turned the track into a single file of also-rans. I was 60 meters off the lead at the halfway point and 80 meters behind with four laps left. I kept passing runners the last mile and chopped Loman's lead in half at the bell. I flew past four runners down the backstretch and Loman with 200 meters to go. There was just one runner to beat – Robbie Bolt.

Jocko sprinted through the infield, took his cigar out of his mouth, and shouted in Bolt's ear on the final turn, "Here he comes, Robbie! Sprint!"

Robbie and I burst into the homestretch, with Jocko's primal scream carrying us to the tape. He edged ahead, then I edged ahead. He edged ahead, then I edged ahead. In the last few meters, I dug just deep enough to keep the edge.

I went to shake Bolt's hand, and he said, "Fuck off."

I walked with Louis through the parking lot after the race. An old man marched up from behind us.

"You guys watch that 5,000? I never seen anyone run like that."

The old man looked me in the face without realizing he was talking about me. "He kept passing people one by one and came from a mile back."

I nudged Louis, encouraging him to play along. "Yeah, he was incredible. Wasn't he, Louis?"

"Oh yeah, that guy can really run," Louis said. "What's his name?"

"Langensticker or Lingensnapper. Something like that?"

The old man walked past us. "Whoever he is, he has a great future."

The victory made me forget Cindi and other heartbreaks on and off the track. The beer and the gorgeous brunette at Bobby Mac's party also made me forget. I shunned the G.U.E tactic and introduced myself to the 3,000 meter runner.

"My name's Jill, I'm from Indianapolis. You been there?"

"I ran 87 ½ laps there last summer."

"Congratulations."

Loman walked by and whispered in my ear, "Nice try, Langenslacker."

Jill shot down nine other nice, decent-looking bachelors in favor of Loman, who escorted Jill out the door and tested the shock absorbers on his family station wagon 50 meters from the party and less than a mile from where his wife and daughter were asleep in his house.

Two weeks later, I was far removed from the Jills and Cindis of this world. I used a third of the money from my Honda sale to buy a ticket to Finland for the World Games. Brian Brennan arrived the day before the meet with a briefcase full of 100 dollar bills. Wooosh athletes dropped by Brennan's table in the restaurant, shook his hand, and left with a Ben Franklin tattoo on their palm. All I got was a flesh mark.

"You said I would get my ticket from the U.S. paid for."

"If you break 28 minutes," Brennan said.

"That was never a stipulation."

"It is now."

I didn't argue, because I knew I could break 28 minutes. I knew I could run with the top Kenyans, Italians, Ethiopians, Moroccans, or anyone thrown onto the track. The Turku newspaper the morning after the race proved it. On the front page was a picture of me running in lane two alongside Italy's Gustavo Antonelli and Ethiopia's Berube Marfu. The only problem was that I was being lapped. They set off on a 27-minute pace, and with three laps to go I had the courtesy to pull out and let them by.

I didn't even break 29 minutes. That left me empty-handed with Brennan. I asked him about the other races he had entered me in Europe. He said, "What other races?"

I chased meet directors that day and called places all over Scandinavia. They all said the same thing, whether in Finnish or Swedish. "Vat did you say your name was?"

I went for one last plea with Brennan. He opened the door of his hotel room at 9:30 p.m. "Please, Brian. I need you to get me into a race somewhere, anywhere – a 3,000, a 5,000, anything. I've trained so hard this season. I barely have enough money to get back to the States. Please."

He slammed the door in my face.

The next night I found myself on a ship in the middle of the Baltic Sea, not knowing where I was going or how I was getting there. My fare was just above what a stowaway would pay. I slept in a room with bunks extended to the ceiling and with the loudest snoring Finns, Swedes, and Norwegians in Scandinavia. I tied my Wooosh bag to my leg, so no one would steal it. I awoke in the night to a bearded man who shined a Bic lighter in my face.

I spent the next day along the deck, looking at the miles of endless sea and the waves that crashed against the ship. I went to Europe, hoping to cruise home on the Queen Mary. Instead, I was on the Poseidon.

◆◆◆

A snowdrift of mail piled up in my basement apartment during my eight day-European misadventure of 1989. If the tour had gone as planned, my entrance would have started an avalanche.

Still, I had enough mail to fill my trash can. A tire sale at Penske Automotive. Albert Gruden for City Council. Fourth of July Blowout at Towsend Sporting Goods. The telephone bill. Race brochures for the Firecracker 5K, the Summer Sizzler 10K, the Beat the Heat Five Miler, and the Run for the Homeless in Santa Barbara.

I plopped myself on the sofa, wadded each piece of junk mail and flung it toward the trash can. I swished each one but the Run for the Homeless flyer, which rimmed the trash can and fell to the floor. It would stay there for several weeks.

Then I hit the message retrieval button on my answering machine.

"Beep! Hi Jonny, it's your Dad. Just wanted to see what you were doing."

I pressed the erase button. "Didn't you get my postcard, Dad?" I said to my apartment walls. "I'm in the Baltic Sea and swimming for Boston."

"Beep! You can save up to 25 percent on your telephone bill by..."

I hit the erase button again.

"Beep! Hi, Jonny, it's your Mom. Just called to see what you were doing..."

There was no call or mail from Cindi or Beth or any other available woman, which was fine for me. I just wanted to sleep. I woke up in time for Lenny Hargrove's Fourth of July party atop the roof of his downtown condo building. We lay back in our lawn chairs, drank a few of his so-called "beverages," and watched fireworks color the night sky before falling like my love life and running career into the Boston Harbor.

"Look at that one." Lenny pointed to the sky. "It went up, made a boom, and fell away."

"It's a dud," I said. "Just like my summer."

"You still whimpering over that anorexic chick," Ray said. "Why don't you call the one you did on New Year's?"

"You mean the woman who's never met a dessert tray she hasn't liked?"

"At least you know she's not anorexic."

"Actually, she is battling anorexia and winning quite handily."

I watched another rocket soar into the sky and flash purple, before turning to smoke. "I am giving up women indefinitely. I want to concentrate on running. If a woman I find attractive crosses my path, fine. Otherwise, I'll just keep running my path."

Ray put down his beer bottle and laughed. "Shit, Faggot, a bitch will cross your path on the drive home."

Bobby Mac turned his head from the sky. "If you had a choice, Langenslacker, would you rather have a path that leads you to the Olympics or to the altar?"

"Right now, they both look about as far away as one of these fireworks."

"Go ahead, choose."

"Why do I have to choose? Why can't I have both?"

The sky crackled, and Bobby Mac pointed to the fireworks streaming across the horizon. "You see yourself in the Olympics?"

"I see myself marching down the stadium tunnel in a red, white, and blue suit next to the other athletes and onto the track with the American flag ahead of us and the people in the stands screaming 'U.S.A.! U.S.A.! '"

"And marriage?"

"I see myself standing on the altar at St. Peter Claver Church in a black tuxedo and watching a beautiful blonde escorted by her proud father walk up the aisle in the prettiest white wedding gown ever designed."

We turned again to a skyrocket's ascent. This one didn't even make a boom.

"Another dud," I said.

I returned to my basement and scraped up enough money for a plane ticket to the Motor City Five-Miler in Detroit, where the winner would receive a new Ford Probe. I needed a car, because I sold mine with the intent of buying a new one with the appearance money I intended to make in Europe. I needed a win, because I needed to restore my confidence. I needed a right hamstring, because I pulled mine in the warm up.

I didn't even watch the race. I went right to the bar across from the start and was drunk by the time the first runner crossed the finish line and hopped into the new car I intended to drive back to Boston.

Now I had no car, no girlfriend, a bum leg, and just enough change for happy hour. I rehabilitated on a night out with Ray, Louis, and Lenny. We met at Boston Bully's and did 13 bars before closing time. We went to a XXX-rated club called the Hell Hole. I went into a viewing booth that required the patron to put a quarter in a slot. I allotted myself one quarter, absolutely one, and dropped it in the slot. A little screen slid open, allowing me to view a live naked woman lying on a round floor and thrusting her hips in an upward motion. The screen went down, and I went for my pocket. "Where's another quarter? Quick, where's that quarter?"

We went next door to Audie's Adult Theater. At the film's climax, the projector cut off and lights came on. I yelled, "OK, all you perverts, get out of here."

We retreated to the Boston Surf Club, where we met some borderline G.U.E.'s and danced until closing time. We followed them to a 24-hour diner, we nicknamed "The Night of the Living Dead." Every customer was either hungry, horny, drunk, stoned, or deranged – or a little or all of the above. One guy staggered to our table and looked at one of the women, "You want to come back to my place."

"Sorry, "she said. "I have a live-in boyfriend."

"What a coincidence," he said. "So do I."

We escorted the women outside, and they said, "Goodnight." Ray, Louis, and Lenny walked in one direction, the women walked in the other direction. I sat down on the sidewalk. Dierdre came to my rescue.

"You guys aren't going to help your friend up?"

"You're not falling for this, are you?" Louis hollered.

"He's drunk off his ass," Dierdre said. "We just can't leave him here."

"I've seen him drunk," Lenny said. "This ain't drunk."

"He's a faggot," Ray said. "You won't get anywhere with him."

Dierdre drove me back to her apartment and offered me half her bed. When I started to cross the border, she read the ground rules. "You stay on your side of the bed. If you touch me, you're out the door."

While I waited for Dierdre to fall asleep, I thought, "What kind of woman would bring a complete stranger home from "The Night of the Living Dead" and let him sleep with her?"

At the first snore, I sneaked out of bed and limped seven miles back to my basement apartment. It took two weeks of light jogging and Teri Mac's elbow, knuckles, and long fingernails digging into my flesh for the hamstring to come right. I entered the Nantucket Nine Miler, where I maintained a nine goon for most of the weekend. A local doctor, Hayward Abernathy, and his family billeted Ollie Dilworth and me. I never slept in my assigned bed.

The first night Ollie and I were ejected from a bar called Captain Bly's for talking too loud. Two mid-packers from the women's field, Janine Throckmorton and Sabrina Crawford, pushed me into their convertible. They drove down the street with my feet dangling out the side of the car and me yelling, "Help! I'm being kidnapped!" I spent the night in their hotel room, tied to a bedpost.

I spent the next day rowing the Abernathys' boat through Nantucket Sound with Dr. Abernathy's 18-year-old daughter, Shelly, and the night rolling around in her bed. I finished 37th in the next morning's race and went from the chute to The Boat Dock Bar and Grill, about 50 meters from the finish line. Bobby Mac bought me beers and introduced me to Linda Powell, the winner of the women's masters division. I intended to sleep at Dr. Abernathy's house the last night, but never made it past Linda's bed and breakfast.

257

My performance at Nantucket – not the one on the race course – was lauded at the Season Ending Party the next Friday night at the Wooosh East Running Store. Ray slapped me a high-five.

"After that effort, I am heretofore on this day never again calling you a faggot. You are the balls. Three bitches in three days?"

"Four."

Megan Mallard walked around a T-shirt rack and sat on a Wooosh director's chair. "I think it's disgusting."

"Look who's talking." I planted myself in a purple bean bag chair. "You've been laid more times in a week than I have in my life."

"I doubt that," Mal said. "But tell me, Langenslacker, why is it that a guy who screws four girls in three nights is considered a stud, and a woman who screws four guys in three nights is considered a slut?"

"I don't know. Luck?"

As I slapped Ray a low-five, two other women pulled up a chair and joined this politically incorrect roundtable – Donna Gorman and Traci, Teri Mac's sister. Traci gave me a little wave. "Hi, remember me, I'm that fat chick you slept with."

"Which one?" Ray asked.

Bobby, Teri Mac, Louis, and Ollie joined the group. I pulled Bobby's ear to my lips. "You ever have a nightmare you go to a party, and every girl you slept with is there?"

"It's kind of like a sex intervention," he whispered.

Teri Mac said she was content in being in a monogamous relationship. "I think every time you sleep with somebody different, a part of you dies."

Mal pointed to my crotch. "I know one part that's very much alive."

Donna, who was now in a serious relationship with her psychologist, quieted the laughs. "I just want to say something. I think Jonny is a fantastic guy. He's just a perpetual adolescent. Someday, when he least expects it, he'll find the right woman, someone who can share in his happiness."

"Or his misery," Mal said.

"Wait a second." I stood up and held my Heineken bottle in my right hand. "You girls are the ones who screwed *me* up. I'll have you know I came to Boston as a virgin."

A long pause and stare was followed by a longer laugh.

"Yeah, right." Donna said. "I can guarantee everyone at this party, Jonny was no virgin."

Deep down, I had the last laugh and that echoed Mal's point. If I was a woman, they could have believed I was a virgin. But a man, no.

"Let's drink a toast," Mal held up her wine glass. "To Jonny Langenslacker. He loves us, he leaves us. We really would love it, if he would just leave us alone."

As the three women clinked glasses, Louis whispered in my ear. "You nailed Teri Mac's sister."

"I picked her up after the national cross country meet two years ago."

"What did you use, a forklift?"

258

That night I stumbled back to my basement apartment and decided to clean myself up. I took a bath, shaved, said a rosary, washed the dishes in the bathtub, changed sheets, and picked the garbage off the floor. I took the wadded race brochure next to the trash can and unraveled it.

"Run for the Homeless," I thought. "Unless I start winning, this race will be benefiting me."

Then I read the race director's note attached to the brochure: "Jonny, I wanted to invite you to participate in this year's Run for the Homeless. We have a $10,000 prize purse and will pay for your travel and expenses to and from Santa Barbara."

I called the race director the next day and secured my spot in the race. I doubted I could win any money. But how could I refuse a free trip to Santa Barbara?

I flew coast-to-coast to the Labor Day event, which began with a beach party for the sponsors and athletes two days before the race. I checked out the sponsors and the elite women and stopped my eyes on a blonde in a yellow halter top, black leather skirt, black high heels, and bronzed legs more suited for a high jumper. She was a dead ringer for the bride I described in my fantasy for Bobby Mac. The sun's glare off the ocean couldn't stop me from staring at her.

Suddenly, I realized she was staring back.

I did not formally introduce myself to Jacqueline LaFleur. I placed myself in a circle with 10 other runners and would-be suitors, drinking margaritas and watching the sun descend into the ocean. We returned via limousines to the Grande Resort Hotel and to a dinner of filet mignon, shrimp, and chocolate mousse.

"This doesn't seem right." I looked around the table and then to Jacque, who sat next to me, and the other runners. "Here we are sipping fine wine, eating whatever we want in a room with pillars and pink table cloths, and staying in suites with a turn-down service and white bath robes all complimentary of the race promoters. And what is this race called? Run for the Homeless?"

Jacque laughed. "It is a touch hypocritical. Waiter, could I have another glass of Chardonnay?"

"When my steak arrived, Jacque looked at the red juice pouring out. "That's doesn't look done."

I poked it with my steak knife. "You're right. 'Moo, Moo.'"

When we finished the chocolate mousse, I sensed that Jacque was drawn more to me than other 10 drooling runners. I had gone against all the rules of G.U.E. But, now, I was playing the odds. I looked only at Jacque and said, "Anyone want to come up to my room and watch some television?"

Everyone understood that I wanted to be alone with Jacque but the Kenyan Sam Chirgat, who followed us up to my room and wouldn't leave. He sat on the other bed alongside Jacque in his oversized sport coat and buckteeth, while we watched MTV. Several times, while Jacque looked away, I stared at Chirgat and motioned my head toward the door as if to say, "Scram, buddy." Instead, he lay on the bed, reading my *Track and Field News*.

Finally, Jacque announced her departure. She smiled and thanked me for a pleasant evening, and Chirgat followed her out the door.

"So much for that." I clicked off the television. "Fricking Kenyan."

The telephone awoke me the next morning. I answered.

"Hi Jonny. It's Jacque. You want to go to breakfast?"

We had breakfast and lunch and hung out with each other all day. We went for a run on the beach and sat down and watched the waves crash ashore. I told her about my life, and she talked about hers. She told me how she grew up in Vancouver, Canada and slowly developed into a national champion in the 3,000 meters, competed in the Commonwealth Games and the World Cross Country Championships. Like me, her goal was the Olympics. But injuries and illness always seemed to get in her way.

At sunset, we decided to return to the hotel for dinner. I stood first, grabbed her hand, and helped her up. She bounced into my arms and hugged me. We locked lips and did not disengage until the sun gave way to the moon. It felt like the Fourth of July.

We walked to dinner hand in hand and returned to the beach. She told me about her parents' divorce when she was 12, her abusive boyfriend in college, her longtime coach who decided he wanted to be more than a coach, about falling in love with an American cross country legend and following him to Lake Tahoe, and about unrequited love. I told her about my less than supportive family, my many coaches, my infatuation with Holly, Kelli, and Cindi, and my heartbreak in three successive Olympic Trials. We could have talked until sunrise. But we opted for a few hours sleep.

"You know there is a race in the morning," Jacque said.

"What race?"

I walked Jacque to her room and gave her a passionate good-night kiss. As I turned to walk to my room, I thought about the wadded race brochure that rimmed my trash pale and fell to the floor.

"Sure am glad I missed."

"Missed what?"

"Never mind." I smiled and walked the path back to my room.

Jacque LaFleur stood 10 meters from me along the starting line of the 1989 Run for the Homeless. It seemed like 10 miles.

The passion from only several hours before was channeled into an attempt to win a 10K race. Still, her love cushioned my suffering along a rolling road that stretched through the hills of the point-to-point course through Santa Barbara. Sam Chirgat finally took my order to scram. He hit the first mile in 4:30 and created a single-file chase group. I remained patient for four miles and then gradually passed those who succumbed to the brutal pace, hills, and heat. I went from sixth to second in the last two miles and actually saw Chirgat from atop the final hill.

I crossed the finish line $500 richer and waited for the first woman. It wasn't Jacqui. It was Kelli Fuller, who drove from Northern California. Jacque entered the chute in seventh. I didn't approach her as she stood there about to collapse.

I walked to the food tent wondering, "Will Jacque do what Kelli did? Will she blow me off and pretend yesterday didn't happen? Will she, like Cindi, say I can't wait to be with you and then make an excuse for not seeing me? Or is she like Mal with a coastline of boyfriends she likewise professed her love?"

I put on the race tie-dyed T-shirt that read "Run for the Homeless" and picked up a yogurt cup. Jacque stood 50 meters away by the bagels. Kelli stood halfway between us at the sliced oranges. I smiled and waved to make Kelli think I was saying hello to her. As Kelli waved back, I walked past her and into Jacque's arms. In one clever strike I got revenge on one woman and validated my love from another.

Jacque and I jogged our warm down on the beach. "Are you going to write me every week?" she asked.

"I can do better than that. I could go back to Lake Tahoe with you?"

"You can do that?"

"If the airline will let me change my ticket. Besides, there's another 10K just north of San Francisco on Sunday."

An hour later, Jacque answered my knock on her hotel room door. She wore only a towel wrapped around her hard, tanned body. When I told her the airline agreed to change my flight plans, the towel dropped to the carpet.

That night, following an eight-hour ride we hitched from a masters' competitor, I was in a beautiful woman's apartment shadowed by pine trees, mountains and a majestic lake. One week I was running alone on Heartbreak Hill and the next with Jacque through the forest trails in the mountains above Lake Tahoe on a crisp September morning. We spent the week shopping, dining, and talking freely about our pasts. She received letters and calls everyday from guys who wanted what I was getting. A Scot sent her a letter in a bottle. A Swede sent her a letter on ticker-tape. A Japanese sent her a letter in his native language with the English translation written below. Stanley Wymon, a local blackjack dealer who just turned 20, sent her chocolates and music he recently recorded.

I asked Jacque, "You can have any guy in the world. Why me?"

"I don't know, there's just something about you. I immediately was attracted to your little stutter and your kind face." Jacque pointed to my heart. "I think there is a very special person down there."

Me special? Jacque wrote letters to friends all over the world. She volunteered at the local children's hospital. I watched her help an old man across the street and carry a grocery bag for a woman with a broken arm. She drove me in her maroon Honda Civic three hours to San Clarenta for the North Harbor 10K, even though she didn't compete. She apologized for making a wrong turn and getting me to the start only 20 minutes before the race.

My warm up was a jog through the horde of entrants to the registration tent and a 4:28 first mile. I made up my mind the night before I would not let Chirgat go this time. With every surge, I kept saying to myself, "I'm not letting you go. I'm not letting you go." He slowed down in the fourth mile and I took the lead in the fifth. He burst by with 800 meters left and ran hard to the finish, but not without an American's shadow. The people of San Clarenta lined the village streets as the two runners approached the final 100 meters. The Kenyan attacked first, but U.S.A. responded. I sprinted past him hard and left him in my tracks as I raised my arms at the finish line. I clocked a road personal best of 29:08 and pocketed my biggest pay check of $1,000. Second place didn't even get a backslap.

As Jacque and I walked away from the awards area, Chirgat sat on a curb with a green garbage bag that contained probably most of his belongings. "He looks like the guy on the front of my Run for the Homeless T-Shirt," I said.

"You need a ride somewhere?" Jacque asked.

"I fly home to Kenya tomorrow. I use last week's winnings to pay for air ticket."

"Where are you sleeping tonight?"

"Probably in airport."

"Nonsense, you're coming with Jonny and me. We'll give you some money tomorrow for bus fare to San Francisco."

I hoped Chirgat refused, thus allowing me to spend a relaxing evening with my new girlfriend. Instead, I spent the night staring at Chirgat's buck-teeth. Still, I had another glorious four days at Lake Tahoe. I told Jacque I would rather stay with her than fly to Dallas for my sister Caty's wedding. "My family doesn't care whether I come or not."

"Yes, they do." Jacque put her hand on my shoulder as I sat up in bed. "This is a very special time for your family."

I held Jacque in my arms. "Trying to get rid of me?"

"Of course not. I wish you could stay another two weeks, two months, two years. I just think it's important for your mom and dad to have all their children there."

Jacque drove me to the Reno airport and said good-bye with a carton of my favorite chocolate-covered graham crackers and a warm kiss and embrace. She stood at the window of the gate and waved until my airplane reached the end of the runway.

I changed planes in Denver, where I saw an older couple saying goodbye to each other with tears in their eyes. The man sat next to me on the flight to Dallas. I looked at the gold ring on his wrinkled finger. "Been married long?"

"Thirty-seven years." The man took off his white cowboy hat and set it on his lap.

"What's kept it going?"

"Trust, I would say. Absolute trust."

I finally looked forward to Dallas about the time the plane landed at the airport. That night was a backyard barbecue at 2000 Hickory Lane for the families of the bride and groom. I couldn't wait to show everyone pictures of my new girlfriend. I walked the ramp and into the gate where, as usual, no one was there to greet me. A honey blonde – probably a Dallas Cowboys Cheerleader – greeted the man in the white cowboy hat with red lipstick on her sugar daddy's cheek. Watching the man kiss her and rub her butt, told me that unless they were from Arkansas this was not his daughter.

I waited at the airport for three hours and used 10 quarters to leave 10 messages on Mom and Dad's answering machine. Everyone must have been too busy eating chicken or a hamburger to answer the telephone. Or perhaps they couldn't hear it ringing through all the backyard laughter.

At dusk, Caty finally answered.

"Hi Jonny, we're having a par-r-r-tee."

"Put Dad on the telephone."

"Where the heck you been, Miles?" Dad asked. "You were supposed to call here when you got in at noon this afternoon."

"Got Alzheimer's, Dad. I called last night and told you my flight arrived at 5."

"Why didn't you call at 5 then?"

"Check the machine. There are 10 messages on there. Are you coming to get me, or do you expect me to run 32 miles from the airport while dragging my luggage?"

"Oh, stop being so selfish. We can't leave Caty's new in-laws. Take a cab or book a room at the airport and someone will pick you up in the morning."

The next sound Dad heard was a receiver smashed against a pay phone. I picked up my bags and threw them against the wall.

"Frigging asshole!" I gave dagger looks to those who stopped and stared.

I picked up my bags, lugged them to the airline ticket counter, and slapped my plane ticket in front of the ticket agent.

"When's the next flight to Boston?"

The next flight would have cost a thousand dollars. Instead I paid ten dollars for a rescue call to The Stallion and airport beer.

"You going to the rehearsal dinner tomorrow?" The Stallion asked.

"I'm not even going to the wedding."

"But it's your sister's wedding. How many weddings do you have in your family?"

"This is probably it. Matthew and Maggie each went to a justice of the peace. Luke is married to his '54 Chevy, and Mark goes through women like I go through running shoes."

"What is bugging you, man?" The Stallion motioned to the bartender for a couple more beers.

"Don't know. My life, I guess."

"Your life sounds great. You just met the girl of your dreams. You're running well again."

"After all the women and booze I've been through the last couple years, I don't know if I deserve Jacque. Why couldn't I have met her 2 ½ years ago?"

"Two-and-a-half years ago, you were still obsessed with Holly and you didn't even know how to talk to a girl. Life is all about timing."

"Maybe you're right."

A 10-hour sleep in The Stallion's guest room and an afternoon of watching soaps and reruns did nothing to change my mind about the wedding. The Stallion came home from work to see me in my jockey shorts and T-shirt and lounging on his sofa with a bag of pretzels.

"Wanna run in the Fab 5K tomorrow?" he asked.

"You kidding? My season ended last Sunday. I haven't run all week. There's no fricking way you are going to get me out for some podunk 5K tomorrow morning."

"Hundred dollars for first place."

"OK."

The Stallion said I could cruise 15:00 and win by a minute in a race that attracted 83 locals. I led through the mile in 4:43, and someone passed me. I tried to take the lead, and he held me off. For the next two miles of asphalt pounding, I kept thinking, "Who is this guy?"

I tried going by him with 200 meters left. What saved me was a woman who screamed in the final 80 meters, "Come on, Jonny, you can beat him out!"

I won in a lean. The runner and I staggered through the chute, each throwing up. I shook his hand, and said between puffs, "Who are you?"

"Bo Hoffman. I ran for Wisconsin. I'm in grad school here."

Hoffman also came to the Fab 5K for an easy 100 bucks. He also had the recurring thought, "Who is this guy, and why can't I shake him*?"*

I told Bo my name and asked him how many dollars he would get for second place.

"Seventy-five."

"You mean we ran our nuts off for twenty-five bucks?"

I turned around to see the woman, whose voice pushed me to victory. She wore a beige raincoat, brown slacks, and a rosary.

"Hi, Mom."

"I figured this is where I could find you."

"What are you doing here?"

"Jonny, your Dad is too proud a man to admit it. But he feels really bad about what happened at the airport. We all want you to come to the wedding this afternoon. Please. We want everyone there."

I dressed in my blue suit and escorted Mom down the aisle at St. Peter Claver Church. Maggie, the maid of honor, was followed by Dad, who escorted Caty and took his seat next to Mom. He stretched his arm in front of Mom and shook my hand.

"Good to see you, Miles."

"Good to see you, Dad."

I got champagne drunk with my brothers at the reception. We danced with the old ladies of the St. Peter's Parish, beat up the D.J., and ran naked up and down the dark hallways of our old school. I went to Mass the next morning with Mom and Dad, returned home for breakfast of waffles and sausage, and showed them pictures of Jacque.

"She looks darling," Mom said.

Dad took me to the airport the next morning, bragged about how he had seen every John Wayne movie but one, sat with me during a flight delay, and started another "when you gonna give it up" conversation. "I'll try for Barcelona in '92. Whether I make it or not, that's it. I am going on with my life."

Dad took a breath and looked out the window at my airliner docked at the gate. "I hope you get this thing out of your system once and for all. I hate seeing all the pain you've gone through. All the disappointments. It's your life; it could end in a flash. I want to see you enjoy yourself and have some contentment."

Dad looked at me, and I stared at his tired eyes. He was wearing the same light blue sweater I cried on that day I got cut from the baseball team. "I'm going to make those Olympics. You'll see."

My boarding call broke up our conversation. We walked to the entrance ramp. I went to shake Dad's hand, but he hugged me. "God bless you, Miles."

"You too, Dad. I love you."

More mail greeted me upon arrival at my basement apartment in Boston. I dug through the pizza ads to the letter with a Lake Tahoe return address. "God, please don't make this a Dear John letter."

It was a "Dear Jonny" letter:

"You've only been gone for an hour, and I'm already missing you like crazy..."

I shook my fist at the letter. "Yes!"

There was a "Dear Jon" letter in the stack of mail – from Taylor Markham at Wooosh Headquarters:

"Because of your lack of creditable performances in 1989, we regret to inform you that we can no longer support you in the form of travel and equipment..."

I shook my fist at that letter, too. "You asshole! How could I run creditable times when your fricking agent left me stranded in Europe?"

The other letter from Markham made me more infuriated. It read that in order to remain on Wooosh East, I had to be trained exclusively by Jocko Girelli. I called Bobby Mac, who said he and half the guys on the club quit. I called Jocko's house, and Mal answered. She said she was back with Jocko, even though she maintained her celibacy resolution. I went to the Wooosh store and told Bobby Mac, "I can't be coached by a man who's going out with a celibate, unstable woman. That makes him a celibate, unstable coach."

I compromised with Jocko, who agreed to consult with me on my training program. I drew up my schedule for the year, and took it to Jocko's apartment. He glanced at it through the cigar smoke and said, "Looks good to me."

The $1,600 I won on the road race circuit saved me from being evicted from my basement apartment. Jacque called and said, "I am not going to date anyone else. I might go out for a meal now and then, but that's it. I've found my honey."

I dittoed those remarks, and we exchanged "I miss yous" and "I love yous" and a chain of letters, complete with photographs and those little o's and x's. I stayed away from the nightclub scene and told Ray in a rare visit to my basement apartment I was off the lard circuit. He took one look at a photo of Jacque in her white bikini and said, "You done struck gold."

I still couldn't afford a car, so on Saturdays I ran to whatever football game Max Steiner assigned me and ran home and wrote the story on my little Tandy laptop computer. I earned enough money for a Christmas plane ticket to Vancouver, not Dallas.

"You selfish asshole," Matthew said, when he answered the phone at 2000 Hickory Lane on Thanksgiving night. "I can't believe you would spend Christmas with some bimbo, instead of your family. You know Dad's health hasn't been real good. What are you thinking?"

"Dad's fine. I got him a pair of Wooosh shoes for Christmas. That will encourage him to exercise. I'll come for Christmas next year and bring Jacque with me."

That meant Mom would put us in separate rooms, as far away from each other as possible. Not so in Vancouver. Jacque's mother and stepfather showed me and my bags to Jacque's room. They conveniently went out to dinner that night, allowing Jacque and I to renew our romance. That Christmas season was full of peace and love. New Year's started with a war.

I had left my date inside her favorite Vancouver nightclub, Russeau's, for 10 minutes until midnight for my annual run from one year to the next. This one was one decade to the next. "You're going to run with a tie and in your good shoes? Jacque asked as the band tuned up to play "Auld Lang Syne."

"Want to run with me?"

"In high heels?"

The swift two-miler through an industrial section on the near freezing night finished a minute into 1990. But the bouncer would not let me back in.

"Too many people."

"Look Crowbar Face, I just ran out 10 minutes ago and my girlfriend is in there."

I tried to rush by him, but he grabbed my collar and flung me into the parking lot. As I sat there wiping the blood off my right eyebrow, a black high heel stepped on my fingers. Jacque may as well have kicked me in the groin.

"I've never been so embarrassed in my life. Right after midnight, all these strange guys came up trying to kiss me."

"I told you about my tradition. Then this lard butt bouncer wouldn't let me back in."

"It's the dumbest tradition I've ever heard of."

We didn't say a word to each other on the drive to her parents' house. I walked to her dark bedroom and said two simple words that put our love affair back on course, "I'm sorry."

I stayed in Vancouver another three weeks, running 121 miles per week through the forests and along the glorious coast. Her mother and stepfather took a holiday, leaving the house to us for our last two weeks. I returned to Boston in late January to prepare for track season. Jacque stayed in the warmer Vancouver climate to gear up for the World Cross Country Championships in France. That summer Jacque promised we would tour Europe together and "make love in London, Paris, Zurich, Rome, and Vienna."

The romantic letters and telephone calls kept me warm through a frigid February. On March 2nd I said good-bye to Jacque, who was leaving for a Canadian training camp in France. She would fly back to Lake Tahoe after the World Cross Country Championships in late March, and I would meet her there a week later. I could look forward to postcards from France and Italy and more perfumed letters signed "Love, Jacque" in lipstick. I went to the mall and looked at engagement rings in a jewelry store window.

I finished a 20-miler on a Heartbreak Hill loop the next afternoon, when I heard the telephone ringing from my basement apartment. I rushed to it thinking, "Is this call from London, Paris, or Monaco?"

It was from Dallas.

"Matthew? How's it going?"

"Dad suffered another heart attack early this morning."

"Oh my God. How's he doing?"

"Not so good, Jonny. He's dead."

◆ ◆ ◆

That wasn't Dad lying in the casket at McGinley Funeral Home. It was a frame of skin and bones and the three-piece suit and mascara an undertaker used to make him look like a person.

Dad used this body for 76 years to walk and talk on the Earth. Staring at this silent, breathless facade in a pine box made it clear that Dad was gone. His spirit had been evicted, and all that remained were memories.

Maybe that's why I didn't cry at the funeral home. I felt no relationship between me and the stiff. I felt much closer to the brisk breeze that swept past me on the playground swing I straddled a half-hour after Matthew had spoken his fateful words. Maybe I didn't cry at the funeral home, because I emptied my eyes as I sat on the swing for three hours trying to recall every moment I spent with Dad and trying to block those devastating words that pounded through my head with a cymbal clash on every syllable. "Not so good, Jonny. He's dead."

I needed a real body to hold. But my girlfriend was somewhere in Europe, an eternity from the pain I suffered. The only comfort came from the hug I gave Dad the last time I saw him and the last thing I said, "I love you."

But did he love me – his last and sometimes forgotten son he often called by a sarcastic nickname and never bothered to watch race no matter if it was in Denmark or Dallas? I had pondered the question on my $800 flight from Boston the next morning and the three days leading up to his funeral.

For sure, Dad loved John Wayne. He saw all of the Duke's 175 films. Dad died after watching John Wayne's final film, *The Shootist*, the only one he hadn't seen. Wayne played an aging, cancer-stricken gunslinger who spent his last days looking for a way to die with minimum pain and maximum dignity. The film paralleled the life of Dad's hero, who died of lung and stomach cancer three years after his final film.

The Shootist was aired after the 10 o'clock news. Mom went to bed, and Dad relaxed on the sofa with a bowl of popcorn. Mom reckoned the end for Dad came shortly after "The End" appeared on the film.

"That long, monotone beep from the network's sign-off signal woke me up." Mom sat on the same sofa and looked at the drapes as she talked. "I came out of the bedroom to see your Dad sitting still with his mouth open, and the television light glaring off his eyes. Somehow, I just knew he was gone."

A better way to tell if someone has died is by looking at the food piled atop the dining room table. Ham, chicken, roast beef, pizza, casseroles, cakes, cookies, brownies, chocolates, cinnamon rolls, donuts. The smell of coffee permeated inside 2000 Hickory Lane as, one by one, people we hadn't seen in 20 years came by to offer their condolences and an apple pie. They were either trying to kill us with their kindness or with the high fat foods that killed Dad. For some folks, it probably went like this.

"Hey, Pa, I heard George Langenfelder died."

"Who, Ma?"

"George Langenfelder."

"Then what are we waitin' for. Let's get over there and get somethin' to eat."

My favorite guest was Coach Hightower. He brought beer. He hugged Mom and took me and a six-pack for a drive in his jeep down Rolling Hills Parkway. Coach Hightower leaned his massive forearm atop the steering wheel.

"How are things at your house, pardner?"

"Crazy. If I have to hear one more person tell me they know how I feel, I'm gonna stuff a drumstick down their throat."

"How's your running going?"

"Good until Matthew called yesterday. I haven't run since, and I don't know when I will again."

"You got to get back on the horse, Jonny. Your Dad would want you to."

I wasn't so sure. I told Coach Hightower about what Wooosh did to me and about making me train under Jocko.

"That's a pile of crap. Why don't you move back here and let me coach ya'? I guarantee I can get you into those Olympics."

I didn't run the next day – just ate, drank, and shook hands with old men and women next in line for a burial plot. I asked my brother Mark, "Why is it that you see mostly old farts at funerals?"

Mark bit into a chocolate chip cookie. "Because it's the only party they ever get invited to."

The next night I walked Mom up the same St. Peter Claver aisle I escorted her up five months before at Caty's wedding. Dad's open casket sat in front of the altar. I knelt in front of it one last time. Then I felt Mom's hand on my shoulder. "He sure was proud of you, Jonny."

Her words confused me as much as the relationship between Dad and me. Matthew asked everyone to read a touching letter we wrote to Dad as part of the eulogy. The only words I remember writing Dad were, "How 'bout them Cowboys?"

Finally, I dug deep into a file of old letters Dad kept in a box and came up with a card I sent him on his last birthday. My words echoed off the St. Peter's pews.

"Dear Dad. I'll never forget that night I wrecked my VW Beetle at 3 o'clock in the morning of New Year's Day. I was half-drunk and frightened to dial my home number. But you answered my call without a complaint or a three or four-day lecture on the evils of drinking and driving. You got out of your warm bed, drove me from the cold highway, towed the VW to a junk-yard, and helped me look for a new car. You were there when I needed you. I am thankful to have a father like you."

The handkerchiefs came out and stayed out until my family followed Dad's casket down the aisle and everyone sang the recessional hymn:

You shall cross the barren desert, but you shall not die of thirst.
You shall wander far in safety, though you do not know the way.
You shall speak your words in foreign lands, and all will under-
  stand.
You shall see the face of God and live.
Be not afraid. I go before you always. Come, follow me, and I will
  give you rest.

I kept walking until I smelled perfume and felt long, fingernails on my shoulder. It was "my friend" Beth. I turned around to hug the next person without seeing who it was. She felt warm, firm, familiar.

"Jacque.?"

We pushed apart. "No. Holly. I'm sorry about your Dad, Jonny."

Holly said she had moved to Fort Worth, where Rodney was the strength coordinator at TCU. The Stallion called her and asked her to come cheer me up.

Holly, Beth, The Stallion, Coach Hightower, and a few other old high school running mates were about the only people who didn't follow my family from the church to 2000 Hickory Lane, where more food and "I'm sorrys" were unloaded. I escaped to the darkness of my parents' closet. I turned on the light and looked at Dad's wardrobe and all the Wooosh sweats and sneakers I had given him for his birthdays, Father's Days, and Christmases. I went through some photo albums and found a scrapbook, marked "Miles" in Dad's handwriting. I opened it to find dozens of newspaper articles, everything from the results of my first district cross country meet to winning the state meet to running in my third Olympic Trials. He underlined my name in the results no matter how badly they butchered it. I stared at the closet light. Suddenly, I felt Dad was with me.

To honor him, I went for a run at 2 a.m. All I saw on that run along Rolling Hills Parkway were the headlights of a car that slowly passed me. We buried Dad's body the next morning at Holy Cross Cemetery atop a hill on Rolling Hills Parkway. Mom whispered, "Now Dad can watch you running up and down the road."

I whispered back, "He can watch me run anywhere, anytime he wants."

I stayed at 2000 Hickory Lane for five more weeks, leaving me suspended from Jacque and her postcards from Europe. She returned to Lake Tahoe from the World Cross Country Championships the night of March 25, and I called her the next morning. Her roommate, Colleen Randall, answered.

"No, she's not here. Who's this?"

"Jonny."

"Wait. I think she might be back in her room."

Three minutes later, Jacque answered. "Hi, I was sleeping on the sofa."

There was a pause.

"Jonny, can you call back in an hour?"

No one answered when I called back. I kept calling until Jacque answered at 10 p.m.

"Sorry about this morning," she said. "Colleen was expecting a call from her boss any minute, and I couldn't stay on the phone. I hated doing that and I tried calling you in Boston 30 minutes later."

"I'm in Dallas."

"What are doing there?"

"My dad died of a heart attack the day after you left."

"Oh Jonny, I'm so sorry."

"It's been tough."

"Wish I could have been there for you, honey. I've missed you so much. You'll have a stack of postcards from me when you get back to Boston."

"Well, if you don't mind, I would like to come to Tahoe first like we planned."

Jacque, who finished 67th in the World Cross Country Championships, said it wasn't a good time to visit. She was helping Colleen prepare for her wedding. But I insisted. I could use the $250 I hoped to win at Saturday's Wildflower 10K for a red-eye flight to Las Vegas and a bus ticket to Reno. Jacque finally agreed.

"I can't wait to see you," she said.

Gale-force winds greeted me at the Wildflower 10K, which I won by three minutes in 30:27. As I entered the homestretch, the wind carried a voice from the sidelines. "Good race, Miles." I ran back from the chute to see who yelled that. No one was there.

I said good-bye to Mom on Easter night, April 15. She asked what I wanted of Dad's.

"Just one thing. His light blue sweater."

"That's what he was wearing when he died."

That's what I wore at the end of an 18-hour trip to Reno. Jacque's last words in her sympathy card were, "I can't wait to see you step down off that bus."

I brushed my hair one last time as the bus pulled into the Reno bus station. I walked the aisle and out the door and stood there in the bus fumes looking for Jacque. I waited for 30 minutes, gave up, and went to a casino next door and won enough money from a slot machine to cover my bus ticket to Tahoe and cab fare to Jacque's apartment.

Colleen answered the door. "Jacque went to Reno to pick you up."

"Then where the hell is she?"

I sat and sulked in the living room for another two hours. Jacque arrived at 9 p.m. "Jonny, I'm so sorry. I must have got the arrival time mixed up."

I smiled. "That's OK. You're worth waiting for."

Jacque and I picked up where we left off on my planned three-week visit that would conclude with Colleen's wedding. On the morning of my fourth day, a Monday, I ran, showered, and shaved. As I pulled the little trash pale under the bathroom sink, it fell over and spilled garbage onto the floor. I put each piece of trash back in the pale. I stopped when I came to a small plastic, rectangular box with a middle compartment.

"What's this?" I thought.

Suddenly, I realized, "It's a home pregnancy test."

The pink-tinged compartment confirmed that the test was negative. I sorted through the rest of the garbage and found the pregnancy test box and the receipt.

Jacque returned that afternoon to my packed bags in the living room.

"Where are you going?" she said.

"Boston."

"Why?"

I held up the pregnancy test in my left hand. "I found this in your bathroom. I know it's not Colleen's, because her fiancé has been stationed at an

Army Base in North Carolina the past three months. A woman with her moral standards wouldn't fool around three weeks before her wedding."

"Well, what difference does it make? It's pink."

Then I held up the receipt in my right hand. "It's dated April 16th, the day I arrived."

Jacque hid her eyes in right palm. A deathly quiet came over the room. Jacque obviously had worried about missing her period. But I couldn't have gotten her pregnant. We had not seen each other in three months. A woman, like Jacque, who had regular cycles, would not wait for her third missed period to take a pregnancy test. Why would she buy it and use before I even arrived?

Tears dribbled down Jacque's forearm. She said, "Sorry, Jonny," rushed out the door, and drove off.

Did Jacque screw around in Europe? Did she sleep with Stanley, the blackjack dealer who picked her up at the airport? Had she been sleeping with Brad Bostick, the cross country runner she had a crush on the past year? I took the first flight out of Reno and was back in my basement apartment in Boston that night. I didn't read any of the postcards with foreign stamps and "I love yous." I did read the letter on pink stationary that arrived three days later.

Dear Jonny,

Where do I start? Maybe with this. I love you more than any guy I have ever known, and knowing what I did to screw up our relationship hurts more than the thought of losing you. All I can do is tell you the truth.

I remained faithful to you, as I promised, until the night I arrived back in Lake Tahoe. Stanley had offered, before I left, to pick me up at the airport in Reno. That's a pretty good drive down the mountain. He met me at the gate with a bouquet of freshly picked flowers and took me to dinner. He bought me lobster and my favorite bottle of wine, must have spent over $100. He carried my luggage into the apartment and put on a tape he recorded especially for me. He was so nice. I felt like I owed him something. But I was strong. I called you and got your answering machine. I hadn't talked to you for a month and my imagination ran wild. I was drunk, lonely, and hadn't been with a man since I last saw you. Stanley put his arm around me, and I felt like I couldn't say no.

I blew you off the next morning, because Stanley was in the bedroom. That night I took him to dinner and told him I didn't want a relationship with him. The stupid thing I did was not using protection that night. I was so relieved my pregnancy test was negative.

Oh Jonny, all I can say is how sorry I am. I made a horrible, horrible mistake. If you come back to me, I promise you this will never happen again. I will be faithful to you forever.

Love always,
Jacque.

I did not respond to the letter. I did not drown my sorrow in a case of beer. I did not go back on the lard circuit. I did not watch porno flicks. I turned into a recluse. I prayed the rosary. I went to Church. I asked Dad for strength. I stared at my Prefontaine picture.

And I ran. Boy, did I run. Heartbreak Hill and the Central Mass track became my best friends. I spent more time with them than with Bobby Mac, Louis, Phil, or Ray. I took off on the 5,000 at the New England Championships at the Central Mass track like a madman. My pace killed everyone but Robbie Bolt, who clung to my heels and snuck by me in the homestretch and won by 10 meters in 13:40.46. Jocko tackled his prize pupil as he crossed the finish line, burnt Robbie's arm with his cigar, and escorted him on his victory lap. The next week I finished third in the mile at the Central Mass All Comers meet in a personal best 4:02.31.

I arrived in Los Angeles for the U.S. Track and Field Championships in late June in no mood to have Robbie Bolt, Jocko Girelli, and Taylor Markham as roommates. Jocko did not reserve enough rooms for the club. He and Markham crashed in our room on Thursday night and expected me to stay there upon my arrival Friday and breathe cigar fumes.

I asked Jocko, "Why don't you guys get your own room?"

"No more left."

"You know, there are other hotels in Los Angeles."

I think Jocko had a hard-on for Bolt, and Markham didn't want to bother looking for another place. I went to dinner and told Bolt, "When I get back, those track fags had better be out of here."

I returned at 9 p.m. to a dark room clouded with cigar smoke. Bolt slept in one bed, Jocko slept on the floor, and Markham was in my bed.

"Just grab the other side of the bed, Langenfelder?" Markham said.

He didn't even save me a pillow. I didn't say a word. I gathered my things and walked to the lobby. "Do you have a spare room?"

"Sure," the clerk said. "Who do I bill it to?"

"Jocko Girelli."

I ran two miles the next morning and spent the rest of the day psyching myself up for that night's 5,000 meters. The top four runners in the race would represent the U.S.A. in a duel meet vs. Great Britain. It was my only chance for Europe. I used up all my money flying to Dad's funeral and to and from Lake Tahoe.

Nothing could distract me as I ran my warm-up strides on the UCLA track that night. Nothing, but a blonde who leaned over the railing to wish me good luck as I walked to the starting line. Of all the race courses and stadiums and tracks all over the world, she had to show up at my meet.

Instead of concentrating on the race, I kept thinking about Jacque and why a Canadian would come to a U.S. national meet. I heard her voice every lap I struggled to stay in the lead pack and every lap I struggled to stay out of last place. I forced myself not to look across the track at the race for the top four spots. I stared at the track and contemplated a summer off the European circuit.

I kept running past the finish line and through the night, six miles back to my hotel with a Wooosh bag on my shoulder and on spikes that made dents in the sidewalk and blisters on my feet. I went to the hotel bar and slammed a whisky shot and three Heinekens, before staggering back to my room. I turned the key in the lock and stood in the doorway in shock. Jacque was lying under the covers of my bed and sipping champagne. Her bra, panties, shorts, and halter top were scattered on the carpet. She wore nothing but lip gloss and a tan. Her perfume overwhelmed the stench of my dirty socks.

"How did you get in here?"

"I told the front desk I was Mrs. Jonathan Langenfelder. Care to join me?"

"I'd rather sleep with Taylor Markham."

Jacque looked at my feet. "You're still wearing your spikes?"

"That's what I do when I lose concentration, after the girl who screwed around on me shows up moments before the most important race of my life."

I turned around as Jacque gathered her clothes and put them back on. "Did you get my letter?" she said.

"Yes."

"Why didn't you respond?"

"Because I'm trying to forget you."

"But Jonny, we love each other."

I turned back around as she tied her halter top around her neck. "So much so that you sleep with someone else?"

"I explained that in the letter. I felt I had to thank Stanley for being so nice to me."

"Maybe a handshake, a peck on the cheek, or a card. But wham, bam, thank you Stan?"

Jacque started crying. "Why can't you just forgive me?"

"I can forgive, but I can't forget. You destroyed the trust. How do I know you weren't screwing other guys in Lake Tahoe or Vancouver. How many guys did you sleep with in Europe?"

"None. I swear it. How many girls have you slept with, since we met."

"None. I swear it."

As Jacque wiped at her runny eyeliner, I continued.

"You lied about Stanley. How do I know you aren't lying about everyone else? If we got back together, I'd spend the rest of my life suspicious of the milkman, the plumber, and pizza delivery boy. Do you see my point?"

Jacque didn't answer. I kept going.

"The damage for me is that I don't know if I will ever trust *any* woman again. You are no different from my roommate in college, the Welsh sprinter I met in Europe, or the old fart with the white cowboy hat I met on the plane in Denver. Is there anyone outside my Mom who doesn't cheat? "

Jacque wiped her eyes once more and picked up her purse. "What do expect me to do now?"

I thought of Clarke Gable's last line in *Gone With the Wind*, but came up with a better one. "I suggest the next time you meet a nice guy, someone you think you could spend the rest of your life with, don't fuck the blackjack dealer!"

Those were the last words I spoke to Jacque, who walked out the door and out of my life. I took off my spikes, tossed them in the trash can, stripped off my shorts and singlet, and took the longest, coldest shower in track and field history.

◆ ◆ ◆

On June 25, 1990, Lanny Hightower received a telephone call that saved his life.

On the flight back to Boston from the U.S. Track and Field Championships, somewhere over the clouds and the Rocky Mountains, I had decided to re-route my life. I no longer could run for Wooosh East. Jocko Girelli severed my club travel funds. Jocko had pointed to Robbie Bolt as we waited for our boarding call at the L.A. Airport. "We need to put our money into the young up-and-comers like him."

I did not want Jocko as my coach – or me. I wanted someone I could rely on. Someone who would pat me on the back after workout and say, "Good job, man."

Every move I had made since watching Prefontaine run in the Olympics was geared to realizing that same dream. At age 32, time was ticking down on my running career. When the airliner landed at Logan Airport, I knew what I had to do.

"How you doin' there, pardner?" Coach Hightower was either very happy to hear my voice over the telephone or he was drunk. "How'd it go at nationals?"

"You probably saw the results in the paper."

"I looked, but didn't see your name."

"Didn't even make the agate, which is the reason for this phone call."

"What's on your mind?"

"You told me when we went driving around in Dallas last March that you could get me to the Olympics in 1992."

"Yep, I recall saying it."

"I'm going to give you that chance."

There was a long pause. I didn't know whether Coach Hightower had fainted or was in shock. I continued.

"I would like to finish my career in Dallas, where it all started, under Coach Hightower, who started it."

"Jonny, that's fantastic, the best news I've heard in months. I would be honored to coach you into the twilight of your career. I will do everything I can to get you to the Olympics."

Mom cried when I told her I was moving back to Dallas. Bobby Mac said it was a good move, especially if I strayed from the long distance relationships and found a steady cowgirl. Or as Louis put it, "Go local or go left-handed."

Ray said, "You might as well go to Dallas. You've been through all the chicks in Boston."

Lenny Hargrove offered a blow-out going-away party at his apartment, but I opted for a low-key night at Boston Bully's with a few buddies and beverages. The next morning I ran a farewell 14 miler on the Heartbreak Hill loop, packed the auto driveway Dodge, and drove south without one glance in the rearview mirror.

En route to Dallas, I finished eighth in the Boardwalk 10K in Atlantic City, New Jersey and sixth in the Big Rock Run in Little Rock, Arkansas. I earned enough prize money to pay for my gas and expenses. I arrived into Mom's arms on Saturday, August 7th and escorted her to St. Peter Claver at 8 a.m. the next morning. She said going to Mass everyday got her through the struggle of losing Dad.

"I didn't realize how much I needed him until I lost him," Mom said, as we sat at the dinner table after Mass and ate our waffles and sausage.

"How do you live without him?"

"By knowing he is with God. That was his goal, Jonny. And he acheived it."

"How do you know?"

"Because he always stayed close to God, no matter what. He didn't earn a million dollars. He earned something better. Your Dad's in heaven is not something you know; it's something you feel."

I took one more trip to Santa Barbara for the Run for the Homeless 10K, before calling an end to my 1990 season. I rushed through the first mile in 4:40, looked back, and saw no one behind me. I thought, "Did they take the prize money out of this race?"

I won by two minutes and received $1,000 for first and a $1,000 bonus for breaking the course record with my 29:21. The $2,000 check was my biggest payday, but not one to celebrate after watching Pete Sampras win the U.S. Open Tennis title on my hotel room television later that afternoon. The 19-

year-old Sampras won $200,000. At the awards ceremony, photographs were taken of me and the women's winner, Kelli Fuller. I drank a beer with Kelli and told her about Jacque and my move to Dallas. She said she was sorry to hear that and invited me to visit her at her Popo and Momo's house in Tulsa.

"No thanks," I said. "Been there, done you."

I didn't figure on doing anyone in Dallas, where size mattered most to most eligible women. Dallas women wanted to know how big was your wallet, how much money you spent on your BMW, and how many square feet were in your condo. I had no job, no car, and lived with my mother.

According to Father Litzke, that's what it took to make the Olympics. "Keep your life simple," he said in his usual soft manner in the quiet of his den, "and keep your eye on the prize. Remember what I told you. Happy are the single-hearted, for they shall see God."

According to my brother Matthew, on a lunch stopover to Hickory Lane, my move kept Mom from seeing God too soon. "She spent hours wandering from room to room, wallowing in her loss and with only her rosary to keep her company. You have given her something to live for, someone for whom to cook and clean and express her feelings. For once, Jonny, you did something without thinking of yourself."

According to The Stallion, my return gave Coach Hightower "someone" to live for. "He had so many beer cans in his garage, he had no room to park his jeep," said The Stallion, as we sipped ice-tea on his porch. "He poured whisky down his throat like it was Gatorade. I didn't light a match in fear of his breath starting a fire."

The Stallion said Forest Hill High School had been taken over by gangs, racists, and drug addicts. "That was the benefit of bussing."

"Coach Hightower struggled every season to field a team. The kids were making fun of his bald head and his washboard stomach-turned-beer belly. They called him Coach 'Lowtower.' After last track season, he quit. He applied for 40 other coaching jobs without one interview."

He also broke up with his girlfriend, whom he had dated for almost 20 years. After my call from Boston, The Stallion said Coach Hightower decided to live off his savings – and cashing in his recyclable beer cans – and put his energy into coaching me.

"He's working out some grand scheme to put you into the Olympics in two years," The Stallion said. "If he does that, he figures he can go after a college coaching job again."

The Big Plan was unveiled one month after my return from the Run for the Homeless. Coach Hightower took me to dinner at The Longhorn Steakhouse. He smothered his prime rib with horse radish, clasped his hands and then pointed at me. "The program is this."

Coach Hightower looked around at the restaurant and whispered like it was top secret. "Twelve miles in the morning. Twelve miles at night."

I wrinkled my forehead. "Twelve miles in the morning. Twelve miles at night."

"That's right. Twelve miles in the morning. Twelve miles at night."

"Everyday?"

"Everyday."

I wondered how many Lone Stars or Jack Daniels it took Coach Hightower to come up with this program. But I decided not to question it. Every time I steered from a coach's program I failed. "Besides," I thought. "What do I got to lose?"

"When do I start this 12 miles in the morning, 12 miles at night."

Coach Hightower shoved a piece of steaming prime rib in his mouth. "Tomorrow."

I looked down at my sirloin steak and thought, "I am coming off my annual running break and haven't run in three weeks. Before that, I averaged 40 miles per week since track nationals. The most I ever ran in a week is 151. Maybe, at age 22, I could have eased into it and survived. But at 32? One hundred and sixty-eight miles per week right off the dock will kill me."

"I'll get started tomorrow."

That first 12-miler up and down Rolling Hills Parkway on the Sunday morning wasn't bad. The second 12-miler that night flattened me.

My alarm clock blared for 20 minutes the next morning, before I shut it off. Somehow I crawled out of bed, crawled 12 miles, and crawled back to bed. A loud whistle in my ear woke me up the next afternoon. I dreamt that Coach Hightower was standing over my bed in a baseball cap, white T-shirt, and coaching shorts. I opened my eyes and realized it wasn't a dream.

"Let's go, pardner. Time for your 12 miler."

He drove me to White Rock Lake and insisted I run with him. I abandoned his 10-minute per mile pace and finished the around the lake loop in 90 minutes.

"How ya' feel," Coach Hightower said, as he finished 10 minutes later.

"About as bad as the first time I ever ran around the lake."

"Am I going to have to carry you to the jeep?"

"Not that bad."

On the drive home, Coach Hightower took two beers from the cooler in the backseat and passed me one.

"I know this is going to be tough, Jonny." Coach Hightower took off his sunglasses as dusk settled over Dallas. "That's why I recommend you get some supplements. I used to take them when I was doing my weight training. I really bulked up. I know a doctor who will give them to you."

I knew exactly what he was talking about, but this was the one piece of advice I would ignore no matter who coached me.

"I don't think so." I took a swig of beer. "That's sort of cheating."

Coach Hightower took a drink and put his beer can between his thighs. "Everyone else is doing it."

"You don't know that. But more important, I wouldn't feel right about making the Olympic Team if I cheated. Besides, I don't want to drop dead in five years."

The subject never came up again.

I wondered if I would drop dead by the end of the week. I felt like someone stuck a two-by-four down my thighs and sliced my calf muscles with a razor blade. I walked part of the Thursday night 12 miler. On Friday night, The Stallion drove by Rolling Hills Parkway in his pickup at about the seven-mile mark and rolled down his window.

"Come on you pussy, you'll never make the Olympics at that pace."

I hollered back, "You don't have any spare supplements on you, do ya'?"

The Stallion drove to 2000 Hickory Lane and waited for me in the front lawn. I tripped on the curb, lay in the grass for half an hour, and stared at the stars. The Stallion sat down next to me.

"Stallion, has Coach Hightower lost his mind? I'm out there running eight minutes a mile and can't go a lick faster." I pointed at the sky. "I think I'd have a better chance making it to Pluto than the Olympics on this program."

"You know he always was an advocate of LSD."

"I always felt Long Slow Distance made for Long Slow Runners."

The Stallion helped me into the house, where Mom kept my dinner warm. I walked and jogged the 12 miler the next morning and slept until 10 p.m. I started my final 12 miler of the week at 10:15 and wondered if I would make it home by midnight. I did. I made 168 miles – 12 miles in the morning, 12 miles at night.

On Sunday, I couldn't run a step.

I did the best I could through the following weeks. Some weeks I made 168 miles, others I was lucky to make 80. On Friday nights I covered high school football games for *The Dallas Star* and struggled to make it up the bleachers to the press box. I had no trouble making it down during halftime of my assigned Forest Hill Homecoming game to the woman sitting in front of the cheerleaders – Holly Rogenberger.

Holly didn't take her eyes off the cheerleaders, who yelled through their megaphones "Give me an F, give me an O, give me an R!..." as I told her I had moved here and reunited with Coach Hightower. I waited for the cheerleaders to yell, "What does it spell? Forest Hill!" for Holly to answer.

"That's great. I bet he loves having you back here."

"So how's motherhood and marriage?"

"Motherhood's great. Hannah is four and a bundle of joy. The marriage, well, it could be better."

"What's the problem, if that's not too personal."

I waited for the band to finish playing "Hail to Forest Hill High School."

"Rodney's never home. He spends his days on campus and nights with all the coaches and TCU buddies, playing cards or throwing darts or whatever. I hardly ever see him. I feel more like his maid than his wife."

I told Holly about Jacque and Cindi, although I don't know if she could hear me over the drums and tubas. I gave her a little hug, wished her luck, and climbed back to the press box.

By the end of the base-training phase of 12 miles in the morning, 12 miles at night and a football season running up and down the bleachers, Coach Hightower started his second training phase. It included running up and down the bleachers. Three days per week I ran five miles from my house to the Forest Hill football stadium. Coach Hightower sat on the top step in his woolen coat and gloves as I went up and down and up and down – there were 56 rows, I counted them – for as long as it took him to finish his thermos of coffee. Then I ran home and soaked my knees in an ice bath.

My New Year's Eve Run from one year to the next was more like a hobble from 1990 to 1991. I was almost out of energy, motivation, and shoes.

My move should have been an easy transition from the Wooosh East Track Club to the new Wooosh Texas Track Club, which was run by Mick Flannery in Houston. I sent Flannery my resume. He wrote back: "In order to join Wooosh Texas, you must first establish some times in Texas," quite an insult seeing that I had run the fastest-ever times in Texas. I suspected that Flannery, like Jocko, didn't want to take travel funds away from his own athletes. I wadded the letter and flung it against the wall. I pulled out my Swiss army knife and sliced the Wooosh stripes off each shoe, physically and symbolically ending my 10-year relationship with the shoe company.

I wasn't sure how long my relationship with Coach Hightower would last, either. January saw more miles, more bleachers, and more injuries. My toenails were black, my ankles were blue, and my eyes were bloodshot. The coach's elbow massages only made me more sore. I begged him for a day off after another bleacher session.

"Sure," he said. "You can take next Friday off."

"Thanks."

"That way you'll be rested for the half-marathon on Saturday."

I needed a month off after finishing ninth in the Tyler Half, in a race almost slower and more painful than the last half marathon of my San Diego Marathon fiasco of 1985. Coach Hightower helped me to the jeep.

"It's all right, pardner. You got the work in. We'll get you there."

"Where?" I thought. "To the funeral home?"

The Stallion helped me into a booth that night at the Backstreet Bar. He looked at me as I sucked the foam off a frosted mug. "You look like shit."

"Thanks."

"How's your training going?"

"Let's put it this way. How do I go about firing Coach Hightower?"

"That bad?"

I took a sip. "Let's put it this way. I'd rather be training under that idiot Australian Darcy Ellard than Coach Hightower."

The Stallion motioned the waitress to bring us another round. "Actually Jonny-my-boy, you are being trained by Darcy Ellard."

"What do you mean?"

"Coach Hightower must have got rid of all his Lydiard books. That day I went to his house, he was reading Darcy's *Run Like a Cheetah, Volume II*."

"Stallion, I got to fire this guy first thing Monday morning. I don't care how much he means to me."

"Jonny, you can't."

"Why not? I won't make even make the Olympic Trials on this program."

"But Coach Hightower has nothing left in his life. He's got no wife, no kids, no family. Coaching is everything. You're all he's got."

I decided to give it another try, when I recovered from the half marathon. That was about mid-March. I met Coach Hightower at the Forest Hill track. He drove his jeep to the starting line and unloaded an old tire, a rusty bicycle, and a long rubber tube. He tied one end of the rubber tube around the tire and the other end around my waist. Moments later, I was dragging the tire 100-meters up and down the hard black track. Then he untied the tire and strapped the tube to the bicycle and pulled me around the track

Coach Hightower pedaled hard and glanced back at me running harder and gasping for air. "Come on, Langenchamp. No pain, no Spain."

I barely could stay on my feet. He pedaled faster. "Think how fast you could run a 5,000 like this."

By the 12th interval 400, Coach Hightower was pulling a dead horse. I unwrapped myself and drove to The Stallion's house.

"That's it, Stallion. I got to cut the guy loose. I felt like a fricking chariot racer out there today."

"Now Jonny, you got to give him another chance."

"No way. My hamstrings are tighter than steel. My feet feel like they've walked through a field of rusty nails. My back feels like someone whacked it with a sledgehammer. My left leg goes dead after a mile, and I spit up blood after every workout. The guy just stands there with sunglasses on, scratches his head, and repeats, 'When the going gets tough, the tough get going.' And I'm going nowhere. At least not with him."

Bonnie, The Stallion's wife, placed a full cookie jar on the kitchen table and then left to put their son and daughter to bed. "Jonny, we just got to sit here until we come up with another plan."

Two hours later, The Stallion took a bite out of the last Oreo and smiled. "I've got it."

That week The Stallion and I wrote to about every NCAA Division I, II and III school and every junior college and NAIA school in the United States. We told them of this great track and field coach in Dallas, Texas with "a fountain of knowledge and a mountain of running experience." My letter of recommendation stated, "Without Coach Hightower I would not be the runner I am today, and more important, I would not be the person I am today." It was the only truthful sentence I wrote.

281

"Next," The Stallion said. "You have to go into secret training, by faking an injury."

"What do you mean fake it?"

I told Coach Hightower I couldn't run and then trained late at night along Rolling Hills Parkway and on the Bishop Callahan track. I was slowly working myself back into shape, when Coach Hightower called and asked me to come to his house one afternoon.

I knocked on the door, and no one answered. I walked around the back, and heard some clinking noise in the garage. I pulled the garage door open to see Coach Hightower, bare-chested and with sweat dripping from his bald head to his shorts, lying on a padded bench and pumping a bar full of weights. The concrete floor was swept clean, not a beer can or whisky bottle in sight. I looked around at the garage wall, a picture memorial to all the great high school runners he coached. In the middle of them all was a poster-sized color print of me with my arms raised and crossing the finish line at the state high school meet in Austin.

Coach Hightower set the bar on the metal stands on either side of his bulging biceps and sat on the bench. "Jonny, I wanted to give you some news."

"What's that, Coach?"

"I received a call last week from Haven County Community College in Northwest Kansas. They are starting up a cross country/track and field program and asked me to be the head coach. They want me up there next week. I wonder what you thought about it?"

I don't know if the tears in my eyes were because I finally was freed from this run-until-you-drop running program or because this good, deserved soul finally achieved his goal. I clasped his sweaty palm. "Coach, I'm sure going to miss you."

"Would you consider coming with me? I promised I would put you in the Olympics."

I scratched my head. "Thanks for the offer. But I need to stay here with my mom. The Stallion will look after me."

"OK, but just remember the secret, 12 miles in the morning, 12 miles at night."

The Stallion and I stood next to a front yard "For Sale" sign a few days later, on May 2, and waved until Coach Hightower drove his sun-drenched jeep off his driveway and into the distance. During the past seven months I had learned how little Coach Hightower knew about running, but how much he cared about me.

"You feel bad about shipping him off to a junior college in the middle of nowhere?" The Stallion asked.

"Nah. He'll just go up there and ruin some Kenyans."

40

As Cody Bexler, the college kid across the street, stuck a rag into a can of car wax and started polishing his red Mitsubishi Mirage, I stepped across the curb from 2000 Hickory Lane. When I first trotted from that curb 20 years before, I was a foot shorter and 50 pounds lighter. Richard Nixon was president, John Denver's "Rocky Mountain High" was a big music hit, and Cody Bexler hadn't even been born.

I had run 70,000 miles, competed in 21 states and nine countries, and failed miserably in three U.S. Olympic Track and Field Trials. For me, the Olympics were like Cody Bexler's car – a mirage.

Making it from the curb to Barcelona seemed improbable for a runner who never finished in the top 10 in the NCAA or U.S. Championships, ran under 14 minutes for the 5,000 meters only twice in the past three years, and spent much of the summer dragging his left leg around the track. If I made it to New Orleans and my fourth Olympic Trials, I would be 34 years old.

Nine months of Coach Hightower's repetition 12 milers, bleachers, and tire dragging had left me an unfit, physical wreck. I felt like I was dragging a tire in my workouts and races, leading to the U.S. Track and Field Championships. I went to San Jose, anyway, and dug my stripe-less spikes in the middle of the lead running pack in hopes of a miracle top-three finish and a berth in the 1991 World Championships in Tokyo. I said, "Sayonara" to the lead pack after a 4:25 first mile. I wasn't tired. My left leg went dead, a numbness that forced me to carry it around the track for the final eight laps and limp across the finish line 17th out of 19 competitors in 14:21.

European track races were out. Doctor visits were in. I spent the summer being poked, prodded, x-rayed, and forced to run naked up and down office hallways in front of clueless doctors and peeking nurses. I received only educational guesses from men who spent half their lives receiving an education. The orthopedist reckoned the problem came from my hip. The chiropractor said it was my back. The podiatrist said it was my feet, and the psychologist said it was all in my head.

I listened to the shrink and was passed by a runner with one arm en route to a 12th place finish at the Firecracker 5K in Jacksonville, Florida on July 4th. Two weeks later, a chubby guy with glasses outkicked me at the Harry Moss Run in Fort Worth. I felt like Harry Moss, who ran across the United States on one leg to raise money for cancer. I couldn't even make it around White Rock Lake. I didn't run another race in fear of being overtaken by Harry Moss.

Then I received a telephone call from Ike Regan, the coach for the South squad at the National Sports Festival in Los Angeles. He asked me if I would run the 5,000 meters on August 10. Somehow the word, "Yes," slipped out of my mouth.

I called The Stallion. "What am I going to do? I'll be hopping around the track like a kangaroo."

"Didn't Coach Hightower once talk about some clever blind guy who taught him massage somewhere in Arizona?" the Stallion asked.

"Flagstaff, I think. Coach Hightower gave me his card, but it's hard to read."

"Why's that?"

"It's in Braille."

Malcolm's Gould's neighbors thought he was God. Not because of the athletes he cured, but because of the primal screams heard down the block from his torture chamber. "Oh God! Oh God!" they yelled.

Still, I showed up at his doorstep, willing to endure whatever pain the blind man would inflict. The day before my Sports Festival 5,000 in Los Angeles I did a stopover in Phoenix, rented a Nissan, bought a six-pack, and drove three hours north to Flagstaff. I thought I could mask the pain by getting drunk.

I rang the doorbell four times. A stocky, gray-bearded man with a face of a 70-year-old and the fit frame of a 30-year-old opened the door.

"I heard you the first time," he said. "I'm blind, not deaf."

Malcolm led me upstairs and through a dark hallway to a sunlit room with a well-padded table, a small window, and nothing else.

"You been drinking?" he asked.

"You smelled my breath."

"No, I heard you trip on the steps. I don't even do that."

I lay on the table, and Malcolm heard me taking off my running shorts.

"Oh, you're one of those nudists. If you want soft music, candles, incense, and beauty oil you came to the wrong place."

"No sir, I came here to get fixed."

"Then you came to right place."

It was difficult to tell Malcolm was blind. He didn't wear sunglasses or use a cane. His T-shirt and shorts were wrinkle-free and his rock-hard hands went right where he aimed them. I closed my eyes in the headrest and braced for the pain as Malcolm felt up and down my spine.

"You're spine is like the Himalayas," he said.

"Yeah, and the rest of my body is like the San Andreas Fault."

Malcolm pressed up and down my spine a few times. "OK. You're fixed. Pay me 20 bucks and run your butt off in L.A."

"That's it?"

"You had a vertebra out in your back, and I put it back in place. That's probably from lifting or pulling something. It was pressing on a nerve, and that made your leg go dead."

"Just like that, I can go."

"Yep, unless you want me to tickle you for another 20 bucks."

"Wow, I didn't feel any pain at all."

I finally saw a smirk on the old man. "Guess you got drunk for nothing."

I was still a non-believer on my drive to Phoenix and flight to L.A. If all the doctors with all their degrees couldn't fix me, how could I expect to be cured in 10 minutes by a blind man without one framed certificate on his wall?

I lined up the next evening on the UCLA track next to seven other runners who also failed to qualify for the World Championships. I ran in the back of pack and waited each lap for the left leg to go dead and the leaders to leave me behind. The leaders left, but the leg survived. There were tremors, but no earthquake. I finished in 14:03.16 and probably the first fifth-placer in Sports Festival history to take a victory lap.

My next run was the out-and-back seven miler from the curb at 2000 Hickory Lane in late August. I took two weeks to rest and formulate a master plan that would put me in the Olympics. I etched it in my head by the time I returned to the curb and as Cody Bexler was waxing the final red panel on his Mirage.

I completed 60 miles that week and added 20 miles each week. By October I was running 121 miles per week and doing weights and plyometric drills with only my Olympic dream and Prefontaine picture to keep me company. My biggest supporter was Mom, who prayed what she called her "Olympic novena" and defended me against Matthew's complaints about not painting the house to pay for my room and board. "Dad wanted him to get into those Olympics. So I'll do what I can to get him there," Mom said over a Sunday pot roast.

The Stallion called me Langenhermit and set me up with Karen Stapleton, Bonnie's friend. Our first and only date was to the high school football game I covered on a Friday night. Bonnie's report was not good.

"You took her on a date to the press box?" The Stallion threw noodles from Bonnie's chicken casserole at me.

"It's the only weekend night I could go out. I run three times on Saturday. Did she say she enjoyed the game?"

"Yeah, until you accused her of flirting with the scoreboard operator."

"I've had a hard time trusting women since Jacque."

Bonnie poured me a glass of wine. "Perhaps, Jonny struggles with commitment?"

"Oh, here we go with the perpetual adolescence thing again," I said.

"No Bonnie's right," The Stallion said. "You think a permanent relationship will distract you from making the Olympics."

I went to take a bite of casserole and stopped. "Then why did I insist on covering the Forest Hill homecoming game this year?

The Stallion also put his fork down. "Not the Holly thing again. You've been dreaming about her about as long as you've been dreaming about the Olympics. Give it up."

I took a sip of wine. "Well, get this. Holly told me she finally found out that Coach Roge was cheating on her with about every Horny Frog cheerleader on the squad. She is thinking about leaving him."

The Stallion put a spoon-turned-microphone to my mouth. "So where does that leave you, Jonny Langenfelder, Vaseline spokesman and bachelor of the century?"

The commitment I wanted in the fall of 1991 was from a shoe company. My last pair of Wooosh training flats looked like a hobo's sneakers. I begged shoe companies and received "What was your name again?" replies from Thunderbolt and Dazzler. Then I tried Spyridon International Shoe Corporation out of Seattle and got, "What size?"

Six days later a box arrived with four pairs of trainers, two pairs of spikes, sweats, T-shirts, shorts, hats, gloves, socks, and a pair of sunglasses. I was a new member of the Spyridon Track Club. I tried on my new shoes with gold wings etched on the sides.

"The Lord has answered my prayers." Mom said. "I asked him to put wings on your feet."

The new gear came in handy during one of Dallas' coldest winters. A 14-miler was threatened by ice and snow and a wind-chill factor of minus-20. I turned around at the seven mile mark into a Siberian-style wind that blew the icicles off my eyebrows. I knew there was only one way to survive – to hammer as hard as I could. The furious pace kept me warm.

"Come on, you fricking cold wind!" I hollered on a deserted Rolling Hills Parkway. "I am kicking your ass!"

I crossed the curb with the shake of a fist. Then I staggered into the house and fell like an ice block on the sofa. "Oh, Oh, Oh."

Mom sat beside me. "Jonny, you all right."

"Fr-fr-frozen extremity."

"Your finger?"

"Guess again."

"Maybe you should wear a sock on it."

"Nah, Mom. I'd require a knee sock."

I kept training through Christmas and New Year's and Easter and no matter if lightning made me hide under a bridge or if torrential rains forced me to wade through a flood or trudge through a mud bath. I kept training through recurring colds, flu bouts, diarrhea, and sore and strained muscles. I walked to the starting line of the Downtown Dash in my best March form in four years.

A bullhorn-wielding race director stood before the front row of elite runners and motioned every baby jogger to the front. I said to the runner next to me as the three-wheeled carriages were manuevered through the pack of 4,000 runners, "Somebody – runner, kid, or parent – is gonna get hurt."

The baby joggers were given a one-minute head-start, just long enough for the real racers to juke, dodge, and weave through the Chariots of Tires. The babies cried as boogey men swarmed in every direction. One woman simply stopped, allowing herself to be rear-ended by an Olympic hopeful in his brand new Spyridon racing flats. I looked up to tires, spokes, and the bottoms of every brand of running shoe on the market. Some gentleman, probably the men's 70-and-over winner, helped me up. I re-dodged the baby jogger brigade and worked my way past the masters and women's leaders and eventually into an out-of-the-money fifth-place finish of 24:36 for the 8K race.

I picked the gravel out of my road rash and returned to the Forest Hill track, where old men in their slippers and middle-aged women in their cross trainers performed their daily lane-one ritual. It took more than "track" screamed in their ear or an elbow across their belly flab to direct them to lane two. One man in baggy plaid shorts and black loafers dared to rebut my plea with "Why cain't you just go around?"

I had enough breath left on the second to last of 12 interval 400's to fill him in on the etiquette of track running. "Because it's courtesy, asshole!"

More runners got in my way in the 40 degrees of Austin, where I revisited the little crack under Memorial Stadium that Thursday night in early April. I flew around them on the final lap of the 5,000 meters and stormed the long homestretch for a Texas Relays triumph in my first race on that beloved track in 12 years. I called Norm Girard, Spyridon's elite athlete representative, on Monday. I told him of my victory in 14:06.08 and asked him for travel expenses to run the 10,000 at the Penn Relays. He said, "How much?"

My Olympic Trials qualifying attempt at 10,000 meters fell 16 seconds short with my seventh place 28:56.43 in a 57-man race, where lapped runners also failed to yield lane one. If I had to run any farther outside, I would have been in the Franklin Field bleachers.

Two weeks later I returned to Austin for a 1,500 meters, figuring on the endurance of the 10,000 and the speed of the metric mile as a perfect combination for my bid for a 5,000 meter Olympic Trials qualifier. I marched into Memorial Stadium and checked the entry list to see which lane I was in. No lane.

Denise Howarth, the University of Texas women's coach and director of the Longhorn Open, closed me out with a "you're not fast enough" without asking me how fast I was. She told me to show up on the starting line and gave me a stand-by status for the 3¾ths flight around the orange rubber track. I took a lane from a no-show and proved Howarth wrong with a third place 3:46.8.

By mid-May, I was fit enough to qualify for my fourth U.S. Olympic Trials. But I needed a cooler climate and a hotter group of competitors than I could receive in Dallas. I traded my frequent flyer miles for a plane ticket to Eugene, Oregon, where I also was greeted by a "you're not fast enough" from Prefontaine Classic director Jerry Fredricks. He forgot about the emotional 13:33 I ran for Zac Groves in 1986, and even argued that I did not win the 5,000 in 1988.

I made a deal with Fredricks over the telephone a week before the race. "If my name is in the program as a former winner of the 5,000, you let me in the race. If my name is not in the program, I will never bug you again."

He let me in, but without the travel expenses or the Emerald Hotel suite my competitors enjoyed. I stayed in the Motel 6.99 in Springfield and took a cab to Hayward Field, where a record was broken before the meet even started. At 93 degrees, it was the hottest day in meet history. I stared at the green backstretch bleachers of Hayward Field and the spectators in their shorts, tank tops, halter tops, and sunglasses and thought, "I could have stayed in Dallas to compete in this kind of heat."

Still, I had no choice. If I didn't qualify here, I would be thumbing a ride to Canada for a Last Chance Meet. I needed only a lap of the practice track to break a sweat and a second lap and a stride to be fully warmed up. I realized my chance at running 13:47 had no margin of error.

My march to the starting line was a reunion call from my old Eugene buddies – former runners and backstretch bleacher bums Dave Stubblefield, Wayne Snyder, and Trace Alcott. "Good luck, Langenbopper," one yelled.

I felt like a bopper, frying on the starting line. To run 13:47, I needed to use everything Father Litzke taught me. "Feel the feeling" meant feeling the sun beating down on my scalp, feeling the sweat pour down my face, feeling the blisters scrape the hot rubber of the red track." I literally would have to walk over burning coals to make the Trials.

I felt the starter's gun echo through my head and a swift jolt off the starting line. As the leaders disregarded the conditions and raced for the pole, I stayed back on the pace I needed to qualify. I needed to run 66.1 per lap, and that's precisely what I ran no matter how far I trailed or how many heat exhausted runners I passed. The lap timer yelled "8:48, 8:49" as I passed eight laps. I was strong, but struggling in the heat that made cowards of an international row of competitors who didn't have to bet their way into the race.

I swept past the slow motion track-tappers and into fourth place with two laps to go. I ran by a Canadian champion on the backstretch and a famed Frenchman on the homestretch. I could not see the leader and only looked through the sweat drips on my contact lenses at the scoreboard clock as I heard the clang for the bell lap. The time read 12:46.

"I need a 60," I thought. "I am hurting so badly that I don't want to hurt this badly again in six days."

I pushed hard around the final lap, harder than I or perhaps Pre ever pushed on this hollowed ground. If the crowd roared, I didn't hear it. I just ran harder and harder until the finish line came and I didn't have to run anymore. I staggered like a boxer after the 15th round to an infield official with a headset. I somehow managed to speak between breaths and with my hands tucked against the back of my neck. "What was it? What was my time?"

"What's your name?"

I pulled the man's mouth-piece to my foamed lips. "Langenfelder, 5000 meters."

I dropped my hands to my knees as the official nodded his head and put his hand on my back. "Thirteen, forty-six, point-forty-one."

My hands went from my knees to my eyes, turning the sweat into tears. "Thank God."

◆ ◆ ◆

41

The butterflies arrived when my airliner touched the runway at the New Orleans International Airport. They swarmed my stomach like bead hunters on Bourbon Street and refused to leave until my sweat-stained Spyridons jabbed the finish line for the final time in the 5,000 meter run.

Father Litzke taught me that extermination attempts would be futile, to feel the feeling, and accept the butterflies as part of me. Were they my friends or the enemies trying to destroy my confidence and keep me from attaining a lifelong goal?

There were more butterflies for the 1992 U.S. Olympic Trials than in any other event I entered for good reasons. Three Forest Hill track sessions that followed my dramatic Olympic Trials qualifier proved I was in the best shape of my career and capable of running with anyone. I ran 10 times 400 meters in 60 seconds or less with a 200 jog interval on one workout, four times 1000 meters in 2:36 with a lap jog on another, and three 800 meters in 1:57, 1:55, 1:54 with two-lap jogs on the other. I ran some easy 200's three days before my 5,000 meters heat and looked so strong and powerful that the walkers and joggers surrendered lane one without a fight.

I planned this to be my last chance to make the Olympics. If I failed here, I would take it to my grave.

I thought about that grim prospect as I looked over the railing outside my room of the New Orleans Renaissance Hotel to the courtyard 17 floors below. I told my roommate, hurdler Tramone Davis, over dinner, "These Olympic Trials officials are trying hard to kill us. They make us run in one of the hottest places on Earth and then tempt humiliated and discouraged failures by giving them a room with a death view."

Tramone almost choked on his sliced ham. "You let me know if you fixin' to jump, Langenleaper, or whatever your name is, so I'll make sure you don't land on me."

No butterflies fell over the railing. They multiplied and grew more intense the more the minutes clicked down to my competition. They eased a bit over a restful night in the luxury hotel and after a look at the 5,000 meters heat sheet over my breakfast oatmeal. Eleven runners were listed in each of the three heats. The top four in each heat and the next four fastest times advanced to the final two nights later. There would be only seven in my heat, because one runner was injured and three others ran the 10,000 with no intention of doubling. Only one of the seven had a faster personal best than mine.

I stepped off the hotel shuttle on that Wednesday night to Tad Gormley Stadium and marched to the check-in area, where the first word I heard awoke the butterflies in my hollow stomach. "Redraw."

The new draw had me in heat one with 15 other runners, including eight runners with faster times than mine. I stuffed my black Spyridon bag in the athletes' tent and started a slow, lonely jog that became lonelier as I marched onto the well-lit track with the other heat one contestants and endured the "Go get 'em" calls from their friends and relatives from long rows of filled bleachers.

There were no calls from the Jonny Langenfelder section. There was no such section. That's what happens when you remove yourself from a social climate in favor of a self-centered approach to realizing a dream your friends, relatives, and potential soul-mates and polo partners could care less about. I bounced around on the starting line and stared at the moths swirling around the giant scoreboard that lit up the name "Langenfel."

The smoke from the starter's pistol filled my lungs like one of Jocko's old cigars, making it tougher to breathe the stale, humid air through a 4:29 first mile. Brad Bostick, who finished fifth in the 10,000, duplicated his pace on the second mile to the rhythm of Aaron Norwood, Iowa State's NCAA cross country and track champion, who ran on his shoulder to the Norwood section chant of "Go Aaron, go! Go Aaron, go!"

I ran on the left shoulder of the second-to-last place finisher in an attempt to keep myself in the game. At 3,200 meters I filled a mid-pack gap that put me in contention, just behind 1988 Trials roommate Rick Cauley, and shook off my lethargy. Bostick's surge with 600 meters to go dropped all but six other runners, who charged past the bell. I was in seventh as we sped the backstretch. "All I have to do is beat one guy, and I'm automatically in the final," I thought.

I sprinted through a gap on the turn and entered the homestretch in fourth place and in lane four. I eased up as the finish line approached and checked back to see two runners gaining on the outside. I dug my spikes into the red track and leaned ahead of a blanket finish in a 57.2 final lap. Only two-tenths of a second separated the first seven finishers, and I wasn't sure I had won until I saw "1. Langenfel 13:54.6" on the huge scoreboard.

I was a second faster than heat-two winner Ned McClaren, the ex-Villanovan who won the U.S. Championships 5,000 in 1990 and 1991. Ken Harwick, going for his third Olympic team, and Robbie Bolt jogged the final homestretch to easily qualify out of heat two.

I awoke the next morning and figured I had swallowed a few stadium moths. There had to be more than butterflies swarming inside my stomach in a room that became more of a prison than a luxury suite. For the next day and a half, I was confined to the fear of failure and the seemingly impossible reach to Barcelona.

I escaped that afternoon to a restaurant in the French Quarter, where I sipped cold lemonade and calculated triumphant possibilities. "None of these guys are more acclimated to this heat than me," I thought. "That 13:46 in Eugene was worth at least 13:36 in normal conditions, and now I am in better shape."

I returned to my Renaissance Hotel cell and the doubts and despair that only a 17-floor plunge could destroy. I jogged for 10 minutes on Friday morning, June 26th with only one recurring thought. "Let's get this thing over with."

The butterflies by now unpacked their bags and turned my sour stomach into a fleabag motel. Each of the 16 finalists sat at a separate table for a lunch of ham sandwiches, chips, or whatever else I could eat without vomiting. I refused to look at any of their faces in fear of them recognizing my fear. I retreated to the 17th floor, where my pre-race nap was interrupted by a wake-up call from Lubbock.

"Jonny Langenfowler?"

"Fubby Tuppernacker?"

"I just called to see-"

"I know, I know. You wanted to know how I am going to do."

"How did you know that?"

"Because, Fubby, I'm a fortune teller and a pretty damn shitty one. I ain't got a fricking clue what's going to happen on that track tonight."

I slammed the telephone down, knowing I just cut off the only person who seemed to give a damn about my bid to make the 1992 U.S. Olympic team. I crawled out of bed, flipped a light switch, and dressed into my white and yellow race armour. I said good-bye to my luxury cell and rode 17 floors to the lobby. I checked my key at the front desk and was handed an envelope that read, "Jonny Langenfelder, Spyridon Track Club."

I didn't open it until the shuttle bus was halfway to the stadium. Inside was one fax from The Stallion and another from Mom. I used the passing street lights to read The Stallion's fax: "Coach Hightower and I are bursting with excitement over your win in the 5,000 meters heat. We're pulling for you tonight."

Mom's fax was signed by every member of my family and contained a scripture quote read in the film *Chariots of Fire*.

God giveth power to the faint, and to them that have no might, He increaseth strength. But they that wait upon the Lord shall renew their strength. They shall mount up with wings as eagles; they shall run and not be weary; and they shall walk, not faint.

Mom wrote, "You have the advantage. Dad's up there telling them to put some more wings on your feet."

The wings, in gold on my Spyridon track spikes, stepped to the starting line alongside the colored stripes and white laces of 15 other Olympic hopefuls and before television cameras and a packed stadium. I made the sign of the cross, closed my eyes, and opened them to a 5,000 meter run that I hoped led to a 5,000-mile journey to Spain.

Bostick resumed his front-running chore, just as I took my usual position in the pack's rear. His 63-second opener set the field in a single file spread 25 meters from first to last. I held on like a water skier to a speedboat as Bostick kept stinging us with 65-second laps and a 4:18 first mile. He finally succumbed to his own pace and the 92-degree temperature. The pace dropped. But not until four runners, including Robbie Bolt, had fallen off the pack.

The lead pack remained at 12 to the whistles, shouts, and the return of the "Go Aaron, go" chant. My crowd was there in spirit and in my heart. Harwick took the pole with the number "4" flashed on the lap counter and slowed the laps to 69 seconds. I didn't notice the pace reduction, only the 11 runners who were in front of me and wanted to ruin my Olympic hope. As we approached the lit "2"on the lap counter, Ned McClaren made his Olympic bid with a burst that put him in the lead and eliminated Bostick and Cauley. I countered with a move down the backstretch that put me in sixth place atop the curve. Into the homestretch with 500 meters to go, I moved again into fifth, then fourth, then, yes, third. Adrenalin shot out my ears. My heart pounded harder than the clanging bell.

McClaren led Norwood around the turn as I wound up to sprint down the final backstretch. I wound and I wound and I wound and soared only like the dud I once saw from atop a Boston rooftop on the Fourth of July.

With 300 meters to go, someone pulled the plug.

My slow-motion Spyridons pounded into the rubber track as I watched the fast-turning heels of McClaren's and Norwood's spikes grinding away from me. Harwick flew past me at the end of the backstretch without having to call me "Fuck Face." One of the next three runners should have yelled "track" as they rushed past me on the final turn. I didn't look at the homestretch, that long lane of bodies separating me from the fulfilment of a life-long pursuit. I couldn't have seen, even if I had desired, McClaren's and Norwood's arm-raising salutes at the finish or the surprising miler-turned-5,000 Olympian Darren Greenwell, who swept past Harwick in the final five meters for the third and final spot to Barcelona. I was blinded by sweat, tears, and disbelief.

I was the 10th person across the finish line and first person down the tunnel. I sat on a bench in a holding area under the stadium and stuck a white towel in my face, shielding my eyes from the reporters who took quotes from the Olympians and the children who wanted their autographs. The butterflies were dead and buried in an empty stomach. I continued to sit with a face-planted towel and waited for the inevitable pain that accompanies a broken heart.

After my competitors left for warm hugs and a cold brew, I dropped the towel and walked, head-down, out of the stadium and into the chest of a teen-age souvenir hunter.

"Excuse me, sir." The boy looked down at my Spyridons and their broken winged stripes. "Can I have your spikes?"

I bent down, untied the laces, took off each shoe, stuffed them in my black Spyridon shoulder bag, and walked barefoot past the empty-handed teenager.

PART VI

FASTEST WRITER IN THE WEST

Twenty televisions, all tuned to sporting events, surround the patrons of Cowboys All American Sports Bar in Dallas, Texas. Nolan Ryan strikes out a Cleveland Indian on the big-screen TV in the dining room. Hale Irwin sinks a birdie putt on the television above the pool table. A.J. Foyt roars past two stock cars on the set next to the rest rooms, marked "Cowgirls" and "Cowboys."

On the smallest television, the 13-incher above the bar, 16 men toe the starting line in Barcelona, Spain for the 5,000 meters Olympic final. I sit there on a barstool without taking my eyes off the screen. The TripleCast cable coverage of the 1992 Olympic Games allows me to watch every step without commercial interruption for the first time since Steve Prefontaine ran in Munich. But I can't hear it. The bartender refuses to turn up the volume in fear of drowning the play-by-play of the Rangers' game.

I sip from my beer mug as the runners crouch for the start. The starting gun goes up, and the beer mug goes down as Kenya's Dominic Kirui sets off at Olympic- record pace. He keeps surging, stringing the field of runners into a single file around Estadi Olimpic's red track, lit by stadium lights and the Olympic flame atop Montjuic.

I press my denim shorts into the barstool. I have two television sets in my head. One shows replay-after-replay of my U.S. Olympic Trials disappointment and the other a "What if" tape of the ongoing Olympic final.

"If I was in there," I say without attracting the bartender's attention, "I would be at the back, carefully working my way to the front."

Back to the real coverage, Kirui leads the field through a 4:12 at 1,600 meters and surrenders the lead to countryman and reigning world champion Yobes Ondieki midway through the race. At 3,000 meters only one non-African, 1988 Olympic silver medalist Dieter Baumann of Germany, remains in the lead pack of six.

I turn off the television in my head, take another beer sip, and focus on the small screen. "Baumann will kill these guys with his kick," I say to myself.

The bell for the start of Happy Hour clangs simultaneously with the bell for the final lap. Baumann runs into an African box down the backstretch and remains trapped as Kenyan Paul Bitok sprints to the lead. I take my right hand off the mug handle, clench my fist, and pound it on the bar. "Come on Baumann, drop back, and go around them."

Baumann does just that. He sprints past Ondieki on the turn and chases the three leaders into homestretch. He passes Morocco's Brahim Boutayib on the inside and then Ethiopia's Fita Bayissa. Twelve meters from the line, Baumann catches Bitok and powers past him. Baumann's moment of glory – his head cocked, mouth open wide, and right arm stretched skyward – is witnessed by thousands of spectators and millions of television viewers.

No one leaves their seat as Baumann runs his victory lap. But there is an empty barstool in Dallas, Texas. I have chugged the remains in my beer mug and trot out the door to a summer glow that ignites an otherwise dim afternoon.

Clare Eggers said she would follow me anywhere. It didn't matter if it was across the street for a Coke or across Europe for a meet. She would follow me back to my home in Texas or to her home in the Outback.

That's what the native of Moose Junction, Australia said after 10 German beers at Schultzie's Pub in Dorfenheimer, Germany. On the 11th beer, to my astonishment, she called me handsome.

I took Clare's beer mug away. "Darlin,' I think you've had one too many."

"Hasn't anyone ever called you handsome before?"

"Yeah, once."

"Who?"

"Some gay hair stylist on Newbury Street in Boston."

Clare laughed at that and my every attempt at humor. She smiled no matter how rude or selfish I became. She sat at a restaurant table and sipped her beer, while I went on for hours about the struggle and demise of my running career. And we only knew each other a few hours.

I had returned to 2000 Hickory Lane from the Olympic Trials, locked myself in my room, and kept pounding my head against the wall, "No brain, no Spain, Langenloser."

I lay up days and nights, unable to shut off the tape in my head. Worse, I was sent a videotape of the 5,000 final. I played it 127 times, and each time it ended the same. But in my mind, it ends differently. I move into third with a lap to go, cling to the leaders like cellophane, and hold off Darren Greenwell in the homestretch to make the Olympic team. Then I opened my eyes, and I was not at the Olympic training center. I was in my upstairs bedroom at my mother's house.

Mom's comfort attempt of "Everything happens for a reason, just like it did with Uncle Grimsley" failed. I tortured myself with "If I had done this" or "If I done that" for two weeks until I found an out. I announced to Mom over Friday supper that I was going to Europe.

"What for?" Mom dipped her fish stick in tartar sauce. "I thought you were retiring."

I slid my fork under my white rice. "I am, but I need some way to cap off my career. Maybe a sub-four-minute mile or 5,000-meter PR or marathon victory. Something."

Spyridon's Norm Girard rewarded me for a fine season with a round-trip ticket to Frankfurt. I couldn't wait to touch down in Europe. Once I did, I couldn't wait to leave. Carrying a 50-pound bag around my shoulder and pulling a suitcase trolley while trying to read a German map along a cracked sidewalk in a carbon monoxide fog, I wondered, "What in the Adolf Hitler am I doing here?"

For two days I stayed in a concentration camp-turned-athletics center. There were three bunks and five athletes per room, which forced us to sleep in shifts. The floors were concrete, as hard as the breakfast toast.

I announced to my cell mates, "I am making a complaint to the Geneva Prisoner of War Convention."

Wolfgang Kuntz, probably a WWII Gestapo or head cook at Stalag 17, directed the Franfurt meet for the refugee runners, throwers, and jumpers. We were surprised Wolfgang didn't put barbed wire and guard dogs around the compound. The day before the meet I woke 1,500-meter runner Russ Adkins. "They've got a huge breakfast this morning. We're talking pancakes, sausage, scrambled eggs, buttered toast, freshly squeezed orange juice, and hot chocolate."

Russ rolled out of bed and followed me to the mess hall and a breakfast of cheese, stale bread, and luke-warm tea.

"Not exactly your Grand Slam Breakfast, is it?" I said.

Russ scraped the mold off his cheese. "Grand slam? This is more like a bunt."

Later that morning, we asked Wolfgang when he would give us our appearance fees. He laughed.

We escaped that night between the Frankfurt search lights to Dorfenheimer, where meet director Bernhard Schlotter provided shelter and a start in his meet. He said his daughter Brigitte would have traveled home from university in Cologne, if she knew I was coming. I told him I didn't know I was coming until a few hours before.

Warming up for the 3,000 meters two nights later, all I wanted to do was go back to Texas or at least to the nearest pub. There were no nerves, no hope for a personal best, and no medal at the end of the race. I grabbed my knees at the finish line and slouched until someone poked me on the arm.

"Can I help you, fraulein?"

"Yeah, mate, you can move your bloody ass off the track so we can start the women's mile."

I put on my sweats and watched Clare's little Aussie ass finish dead last to German and French women, who looked twice her size. As she walked through the infield, I poked her shoulder. "Too bad you weren't in that much of a hurry in the race."

She stared at my feet. "Why are you wearing your spikes? You running the 4 by 400 relay?"

Clare and I did a beer relay that night at Schultzie's Pub with several athletes and locals. She couldn't drink as much as Brigitte, but close.

"There's probably nothing else to do in Moose Junction, Australia," I had said a few rounds before she called me handsome.

"Bloody hell. There's heaps to do."

"Like what, wrestle alligators?"

"Crocodiles, you wanker."

The conversation switched to the bus that would transport the athletes the next morning across Germany to Rosenheim, a small town about 50 miles south of Munich. There was no mile or 5,000 meters there. Just the 3,000. I didn't care. I just wanted to finish.

"It's my last track race," I announced to the stunned athletes, before taking a long drink.

"You mean for the year," Clare said.

"No. Of my life."

Adkins, who was only a year out of Georgia Tech, asked, "Why are you retiring?"

"Are you still going to be running when you're 34 years old?"

Everyone had a horrified look but the 26-year-old Clare, who said she wanted to compete until she was 40, or even 50. "You got at least another four years in ya,' Langenwanker."

I barely had another four days. My life for 20 years had been "the next run, the next run." I wanted off the roller coaster and onto the merry-go-round, free to ski or play coed softball and touch football without worrying how it might affect my running career. I wanted a job as a sportswriter and a salary that would allow me to buy a car from someone who spoke English, take a date to a restaurant without a drive-through window, and rent an apartment that didn't have my mother as the landlord. The last polo game I had was with Jacque, more than two years before. Clare was right to call me a wanker.

No telling what she called me as we staggered out of Schultzie's Pub, emptied garbage pales onto the village square, and knocked over a row of chairs at an outdoor cafe. We picked up the large pieces on the outdoor chess game and put them in compromising positions. The king was doing the queen, and the rook was getting friendly with the horse. Clare asked what I had planned for the bishop I held in my hands.

I threw it in the fountain.

We laughed back to her hotel, where I said good-bye. With a hug? A kiss? I was too drunk to remember.

300

"You have fun back in Moose Junction"

"You'll come visit me?"

"Yeah, right."

I wished Clare sat next to me on the bus to Rosenheim, instead of the Russian shot putter who smoked cigarettes the entire eight-hour trip. I asked if she was throwing in the Olympics.

"No," she said. "I have operation."

"Sex change operation," I thought.

There was no women's distance race in Rosenheim and no woman who shaved her legs or armpits or owned an electrolysis machine. I just wanted to run 3,000 meters, visit Munich and the stadium where Prefontaine ran the Olympics, and leave Europe and yesterday behind.

The clouds darkened that Saturday afternoon in Rosenheim over a stadium not much bigger than the stadium I ran my first track race. It was hard to believe as I looked at the Kenyans, Germans, Austrians, and Swiss along the starting line that this was it. One final gun and one final gun lap. I didn't want to go through the motions and finish fifth or sixth. I wanted my last track race to be special. That's why the butterflies returned and why I tied my spiked Spyridons three times.

The three Kenyans didn't know or care that it was my last race. They ran 61 seconds on the first lap and then picked it up, quickly separating themselves from the field. I hung onto a chase pack of bearded Europeans who probably didn't even qualify for their Olympic Trials through a 4:19 first mile and then went after the Kenyans, who probably didn't qualify for their Trials either. They laughed and joked the next two laps and didn't look back to see me coming.

I ran as hard as I could and caught them on the final backstretch. Then one Kenyan said something to the others and they left me in no man's land on my final, final homestretch. The finish line could not have come soon enough. I jogged across the infield, grabbed my sweats, and ran through the gate toward the hotel. The clanking of my spikes on the sidewalk was overcome by a distant call.

"Hey, Langenwanker!"

I turned around to see a petite, young lady with dark blonde hair and a smile running after me. "You wanker, come back here."

"I thought you'd be back wrestling a crock by now, Clare."

"Were you too drunk to remember what I told you?"

"That you'd follow me anywhere? Thought you were too drunk to remember saying it."

"No, I meant it."

"Does this mean you will follow me to Munich?"

"Good on ya,' mate."

Munich's Olympic Stadium was more spectacular than I imagined. I could see the glass canopies as Clare and I walked through the Olympic Park past the swimming pool where Mark Spitz won seven gold medals, along a quiet lake, and over a shaded hill that provided a view of the track I saw on the television in my den at age 14.

We stood and admired the sight until sunset, when I decided to find a way into the stadium. I found a gate Pre must have unlocked. We walked through the same tunnel Pre exited in his disappointment. Then I felt the rubber below my Spyridon running shoes, grabbed Clare's hand, and ran around the track. I looked up at the rows of empty seats and visualized them filled and me as Pre, battling Viren and Gamoudi on the gun lap to Jim McKay's race call I echoed off the stadium, "The kid is showing all the guts in the world! He's hanging in there – with the kickers!"

"You're crazy," Clare said.

"Just crazy about you, honey."

I sped around the turn and into homestretch and stopped 15 meters short of the finish line.

"This is where it happened."

Clare put her hands on her hips and stood on the finish line. "Where what happened?"

"Where Ian Stewart passed Pre for the bronze medal."

I staggered, as Pre did, in the final meters and into Clare's arms. I opened my eyes to the waning sunset and into the eyes returning my pleasure. I hugged Clare and kissed her moist lips. I never felt more at ease, more at home in a place I dreamed about for so many years. We made love on the soft grass beside the start/finish line and then ran naked, like children, a victory lap Pre would have enjoyed.

My next run came moments after Germany's Dieter Baumann gunned down the Africans in the homestretch of the Olympic 5,000 final in Barcelona. I ran six miles in denim shorts, tennis shirt, and Spyridons in 100-degrees away from Cowboys All-American Sports Bar to 2000 Hickory Lane. Trying to catch my breath, I announced to Mom I was running the Dallas Marathon in December.

"I've run my last track race. This will be my last running race."

"Where's my car?" Mom asked.

"Oh, it's back at, uh. I'll go get it."

I changed into running shorts, slapped some sun screen on my bare chest, and ran back to the bar. I stayed in shorts and Spyridons the next three months. I promised Mom the marathon, for sure, would be my last race. Then I would pursue full-time sports writing, rent an apartment, and pay bills like everyone else in their mid-thirties.

There was no better way for a runner to leave a long career than by running the longest race of his career. The Dallas Marathon route would take me past Harley Ruckles Park, where I played my first little league baseball game. It would go by Birkenhead Park, where I ran my first cross country race, and around White Rock Lake, which I circled hundreds of times in training. The finish line was Dallas City Hall. I would walk 100 meters from the chute to a small graveyard, where I officially would declare my running career closed.

I ran up and down Rolling Hills Parkway, building my mileage to 126 per week in September. I covered high school football games, including the Forest Hill Homecoming game on Oct. 2. I was intercepted en route to the press box that crisp Friday by a blonde with a good tan, great body, and no wedding ring.

"The divorce will be final December first," said the woman who soon would return to the name Holly Ritzenbarger. "Then I will be on the dating market."

I summoned all the nervous energy I wasted in my youth over the words that stammered from my lips. "W-W-Well, then, Holly. C-C-Could I have the great honor of being your first date."

A smile was followed by a wink. "You certainly may, Mr. Langenfeller."

I returned to the press box. I drifted from the game to an improbable dream date that finally would take place the same day I would end my running career. I envisioned a limousine, dinner and champagne at Mario's, and a stroll through Highland Park.

"You're gonna need that $3,000 first prize to pay for the date," said The Stallion on an easy run around White Rock Lake the next morning. "What about that gal you met in Europe?"

"Clare? I don't know. She stayed in Europe for a while and went to Barcelona to watch the Olympics with her coach. She sent me postcards every week, saying how much she enjoyed being with me. The last correspondence was postmarked 'Moose Junction, Australia – September fifth.' I haven't heard from her since."

I figured Clare had hooked up with her coach, a disappointed runner in the Barcelona Games, or a crocodile hunter back home. It probably was for the best, now that I finally had landed a date with Holly. Also, I don't know if I wanted to be with a runner. I intended to burn my running shoes immediately after the marathon. The pain of watching someone pursue my Olympic dream could be unbearable. In her last letter Clare said I should reconsider retirement. She quoted a line from her favorite film, *Ice Castles* – "Not trying is wondering your whole life if you quit too soon."

My body was telling me I was quitting too late. I suffered back spasms on a 10-mile tempo run along Rolling Hills Parkway, a calf pull on interval 400's, and a heel bruise on a Sunday 20-miler. Mom tried to cheer me up on my 35th birthday by putting on 25 candles. She had to help me blow them out.

"Twenty-five? I feel like *eighty*-five."

Marathon training was impossible. I mean, how do you train to run 26.2 miles? I ran 20 miles in training for the 10,000 meters, thinking "That's more than three times the distance." For the marathon, you have six miles to go at a faster pace. To assimilate the effects of hitting the wall I ran 15 miles, stopped, strapped on leg weights, and ran another five miles. No non-runner could conceive of putting his body through such torture. A copy editor at *The Dallas Star* called and asked if I was home. Mom said, "No he's out on a run. He'll be back in two hours."

Two hours? For most swivel chair-potato-sportswriters, a run is 10 minutes.

By mid-November, I wasn't sure if "I" could run 10 minutes. I never dropped out of race in my life. With the San Andreas Fault rumbling through my over-trained and under-nourished body, this was a possibility. My only hope was a blind masseur. I returned to Malcolm Gould's house in Flagstaff, two days before the Autumn Classic in Phoenix. This time I wish I had drank a *case* of beer. Malcolm drove and twisted his elbow into every sore muscle of my body, and called me a pussy every time I hollered, "Oh, God, that hurts!"

"If I got a dollar every time you screamed, I'd be a millionaire," he said.

It was worth it. I ran down the hallway of his house without pain. "Good as new," I said. "I just have to make it through the next two weeks, and then I won't have to worry about such agony ever again."

"Why quit?" Malcolm said. "You are a very fine, fit specimen. I can see you running at your best for another eight years?"

A blind man seeing into my future? An obvious figure of speech.

I returned to Phoenix and to the office window I used as a personal Port-A-Jonny in 1983. I finished 12th in 29:58 and without pain, giving me hope of a farewell victory. Mom cooked me pre-race spaghetti and prayed the rosary with me. She drove me to City Hall the next morning and took my sweats in front of a crowd of about 3,000 marathoners.

"You remember the first race you took me to 20 years ago, Mom? I think I'll beat a few more this time."

Mom made the sign of the cross and kissed me on the cheek. "You've done well, Jonny."

The starting line of the Dallas Marathon had a front row of running nerds, who doubtfully ran in high school. They were either on the chess or debate team. They started running in college as stress release from their aeronautical engineering classes. These guys stand in line for three hours at the pre-race expo to have their picture taken with Bill Rodgers and wear their race T-shirt to the awards ceremony.

I doubt many of these guys could run five minutes for one mile, much less 26. I figured they would be intimidated by my PR's of 13:29 and 28:04, listed under *The Dallas Star* headline "Langenfeeber favored to win marathon," in Saturday morning's sports section.

But as the starting gun was fired, and we threaded through the downtown skyscrapers, I realized most of these guys only read the business page. Some guy with a beard, glasses, and a singlet from "Bernstein's Bagel Run" surged from the lead pack and into a 300-yard lead by the five-mile mark. Some kid in Highland Park probably looked out his mansion window and reported to the breakfast nook, "Father, some geek is running through our neighborhood."

Soon, the neighborhood was invaded. By the half-marathon, the geek had at least doubled his lead. One of the guys in our five-man chase pack said, "Let's go get him."

"Go get him?" I said. "We can't even see him."

The Stallion handed me a water bottle along White Rock Lake at 15 miles and said, "He's a half-mile ahead, but looking tired."

I was feeling tired, and let go of the pack at 18 miles. I looked across the lake at downtown. It seemed a million miles away. "I just hope I can finish," I thought.

I left the lake at 20 miles for a two-mile stretch of hills that stuck steel rods up my hamstrings and jagged rocks into my calves. I distracted myself from the pain by recalling the memorable moments of my career – winning state, beating the studs in Geneva, running a victory lap at Pre – and looking ahead to that night's date with Holly. I took my last water bottle from The Stallion at 22 miles. "You're closing," he said.

"On who?" I thought. "The first cripple?"

In the next two miles I passed one guy who was lying on the sidewalk and another who was being helped into an ambulance. I blew past a runner walking down the course and another standing at an aid station and drinking Gatorade. Then I looked into the distance and spotted the press truck. Suddenly, I knew there was a geek ahead. I pushed hard toward city hall, and though I felt like I was running on stilts, the running dot was growing larger. I erased my mind of Holly and focused on the man who probably bought his racing flats at K-Mart.

The geek looked back at 25 miles and ran harder. Every muscle in my body was tighter than a tennis racket string in a Siberian winter. Still, I gained. A light fog that crept through downtown and the sweat that covered my contact lens could not obscure the leader's back. At 26 miles, I realized my last race would come down to a 385-yard sprint. Then, as I looked ahead at the finish line banner and the overhead timer and the spectators jumping up and down in slow motion and the geek turning his head back and forth like a jack-in-the-box, I realized there is no such thing as a sprint at the end of a marathon. No matter how hard I tried, I wasn't going to catch this guy and spoil the greatest moment of his life.

The final steps went in even slower motion. I could hear my heart thumping over the crowd's cheers. I waved, as if saying good-bye, at the finish line. I staggered through the chute, stopping a few times to grab my knees and for a lady volunteer to hang a finisher's medal around my neck. I limped through the fog toward the graveyard, the official burial ground of a 20-year running career. Ten yards from the opened iron gate, a voice stopped me.

"Hey, Langenwanker!"

I looked up and around and then to a woman in a white tracksuit, walking toward me.

"What are you doing here, Clare?"

"I read the paper. I knew this is where I could find you. I need to talk to you."

I wiped the sweat off my forehead. "Not a good time."

"Jonny, I have to talk to you. How about tonight?"

"Really not a good time." I shook my head. "Look, I've just run a marathon. Why don't you go back to Moose Junction and chase crocodiles or something?"

"Not until I talk to you."

"Forget it." I turned around and walked toward the graveyard. A yard from the gate, two words stopped me for good.

"I'm pregnant."

◆ ◆ ◆

I remember when I was six, telling Mom I belted a baseball through the bathroom window. Or when I was 12, the D in arithmetic. Or at 16, her favorite coffee mug I dropped on the kitchen floor.

Now, at 35, how could I tell her the one thing that would break her heart? She thought of her baby son as a model of virtue, even called me pure amidst my sexual prowess in the late 1980's. It was easy confessing to a priest behind a black screen that I busted the sixth commandment. But how could I tell Mom face to face at point-blank range that I got a girl pregnant?

Those were my thoughts as I soothed my battered, worn out body in a bubble bath after running 2:21:47 at the Dallas Marathon and the earlier humiliation suffered at the awards ceremony. I had shaken the hand of a smiling bearded man in a marathon race T-shirt and asked, "Are you one of the volunteers?"

"No, I am Corbin Huxley. I won the race."

Corbin said he would use his $3,000 first prize for computer software. I wanted to use my $1,500 second prize for a down payment on a Pontiac Firebird and a deposit on an apartment. Now I looked at spilling the wad at Kids R Us.

A reporter asked me, "When did you hit the wall?" Off the record, I hit it when Clare told me she was pregnant. Paramedics should have checked my pulse. I told Clare I wanted a pulse inside her stomach.

"You don't believe me? Bloody hell." Clare helped me walk from the awards ceremony to a vacant boardroom in the convention center, where we sat at a long table.

"I barely know you. If you really are pregnant, how do I even know it's my kid?"

"You just have to trust me, mate."

"Trust you. Trust you?" My voice must have carried through the closed door. "I trusted Mal and Kelli and Jacque and how many others? How do you expect me to trust you? How do I know you didn't screw your coach or an athlete at the Olympic Games or an alligator hunter in Moose Junction?"

"Crocodiles, Jonny. How many times do I have to tell ya'? We have crocodiles, not alligators."

I planted my elbows on the table, put my hands over my eyes, and shook my head. Maybe, I was being a bit harsh. But I had just run a marathon, the last race of my career. The words "I'm pregnant" kept spinning through my mind. I didn't know what to think or say or do. But I was too tired and beat up to argue anymore. We walked to the parking lot, where The Stallion waited to drive me to 2000 Hickory Lane. I introduced him to Clare as an Australian friend who needs a ride back to her motel.

"That's a long way to come to watch a marathon." The Stallion exchanged smiles with Clare and let her into the front seat of his family station wagon and closed the door.

"She's cute," The Stallion whispered. "Is she the one you-"

"I'll tell you about it later."

The Stallion dropped Clare at the Motel 6.99 en route to my house, and I took her place in the front seat. We made plans to meet in her room later that night and said good-bye. The Stallion drove back to the freeway.

"Thought you were going out with Holly tonight."

"I think I'll have to cancel."

"What?" The Stallion almost hit the guardrail. "You are canceling your dream date. The date you have dreamed about for 17 years? Just because you're a little sore from a marathon?"

I told The Stallion to pull onto the exit ramp and pointed to a Bopper Burger. I ordered two Boppers, fries, and a large chocolate shake. We brought our food to a corner table next to a window, where The Stallion asked why we were there.

"First of all, because I'm hungry as shit. All they had at the marathon were bagels, cut up bananas, and yogurt. Second, because I didn't want you to crash when I told you."

"Tell me what?" The Stallion bit into his Bopper.

I looked out the window at the toddlers at the Baby Bopper's playground. "Clare's pregnant."

The Stallion choked on his burger and sipped his Coke. "You're gonna be a dad?"

Hearing the word "Dad" and watching a man helping his two-year-old son down the slide outside, it finally hit me. The Stallion swallowed the rest of his Bopper. I stared at mine.

"Could it be true?" I thought. "I didn't use any protection. I hadn't had sex in two years, so I must have had enough sperm to populate China. I don't know Clare very well, but she doesn't seem like a manipulative person."

"You're obviously not thrilled about this," The Stallion said.

"More like stunned. Here I finish my last race. I finally can look forward to life without running. I am free to date Holly and any other woman I want, and now this. Why now?"

"Do you love this girl, Jonny?"

I took that question to the bathtub at 2000 Hickory Lane and then back to the Motel 6.99. I had called Holly and told her I couldn't go out, because the marathon had temporarily paralyzed me. This wasn't far from the truth. Getting out of the bathtub and driving to the motel was an effort.

Clare opened the door of a cramped room with cigarette-stained walls, vibrating bed, no television, and the roar of traffic from the adjacent highway. She called it cozy.

"There are motels in the Outback that don't have indoor toilets," Clare said.

I smiled. "I guess that's why they call it the Outback, because to use the bathroom you have to go out back."

Our laughter eased the tension. Clare said she found out she was pregnant in September, the day after she returned to Moose Junction and the day after she sent me her last letter. She said she couldn't write it in a letter or call me. She had to tell me in person to convince me the child was mine and give me the option of raising the child with her. She scraped whatever money she had from races and working at the Moose Junction Dairy, the town's only convenience store, to travel to Dallas.

I left that night telling her I didn't know what to do and thanked her for not having an abortion. As I walked out the door, she said, "Jonny, believe it or not, everything I said in those postcards is bloody true. It's exactly the way I feel about you."

After Mass the next morning, I sat with Mom at the dining room table. I couldn't keep this secret from her forever and I couldn't keep Clare and her unborn child in that smoky motel room. I said it as I had rehearsed it to my bedroom wall 37 times the night before.

"Mom, I don't know how to say this."

"You say anything you want to me, Jonny?" Mom took a sip of hot tea.

I almost chickened out. I wasn't sure a 75-year-old widow could take this from her youngest son. What would I do if she fainted? "This is very hard for me."

"Just tell me what's on your mind."

"Do you remember seeing me talking to a young woman after the marathon, right before you left?"

"Oh, yes. She was cute."

"Yeah, well," I took a deep breath and let it out, "she's pregnant, and I think I might be the father."

Mom looked more relieved than stunned. "Thank God. I was afraid you were going to tell me you were going to keep competing."

"No, no, Mom, I'm not joking. This is serious. I didn't know how to break it to you. It has to be the worst news you've ever heard."

Mom smiled, hugged me, and sat back in her seat. "Are you kidding? How about this, 'Marie, your brother's plane was shot down over Germany.' Or 'Sorry, Mrs. Langenfelder, you've had a miscarriage.' Or 'We tried everything we could, ma'am, but we couldn't revive your husband.'

"Jonny, I think I can handle this one."

Mom amazed me with her compassion, her composure, and her kindness. A million Hail Marys will do that to a person. She insisted on Clare staying at the house until we worked things out and welcomed her with a Sunday pot roast and steamed potatoes. She took her shopping for baby clothes at the Forest Hill Mall and showed her how to make enchiladas for dinner on Monday night.

I did something that night I had never done with a girl. We watched a Dallas Cowboys game together. Clare shared popcorn and Cokes with me and cheered the Cowboys to a 27-10 victory over the Vikings on Monday Night Football.

"This is almost as exciting as watching the rugby," she said.

The rest of the week Clare helped Mom with the meals and dishes and spoiled me with brownies and chocolate chip cookies. We stayed up late talking about running, Australia, our faith in God, and everything but the baby. She massaged my hamstrings and calves, still aching from the marathon. I rubbed her back after her daily bout with morning sickness. Clare even watched an entire episode of "Days of our Lives" without telling me it was a waste of time. I was falling in love with the possible mother of my child until Matthew stormed into the den on Friday afternoon and turned off the television.

"So where's this girl you knocked up?"

"She and Mom are out buying groceries."

"You mean Mom is buying the groceries that you and your girl from down under are going to eat."

"We'll pay her back."

"With what? You've been retired from running for almost a week and look at ya.' How many jobs have you applied for? How many apartments have you looked at? Do you expect Mom to pay for the delivery of the baby and then support all three of you?"

"I don't know what I'm gonna do. But Clare has been really spoiling me."

Matthew laughed. "Of course she's spoiling you, dumb ass. She wants a father for that kid whether it's yours or not. She'll do or say anything to get your money."

Matthew often threw such shit in the air. But this time some of it stuck to the ceiling. I stayed up all night long thinking about it. The questions swayed through the darkness like a pendulum swinging in rhythm to the ticking of my bedside alarm clock.

"What if she was trying to butter me up, so I'd marry her and support the baby? Maybe she wants U.S. residency and will dump me as soon as she acquires her green card? Maybe she only made love to me in Munich, so she could get pregnant? Or perhaps someone else got her pregnant but won't claim it? Maybe she has no idea who the father even is? Maybe she is some wacko

309

and not even pregnant. Did I confess to Mom that I am not a virgin for nothing?"

Clare interrupted the thought process at dawn. She snuck into my bedroom and under the covers. She wore nothing but white silk panties.

"We can't do this?" I whispered.

Clare rubbed her hand up my thigh and kissed me on the cheek. "Why not, Misseur Langenwanker?"

"The baby."

"The baby won't hear us."

"Yes, but my mother might. Her bedroom is right below us, and she's a light sleeper."

Clare kissed me on the forehead and returned to her room. She woke me three hours later with a breakfast tray that contained a plate of pancakes, link sausage, hot syrup, a glass of orange juice, knife and fork, a napkin, and a little glass vase with a yellow rose in it. I sat up in bed and put the tray on my lap, while Clare sat on my bed in her white robe and sliced my pancakes. Mom had gone for her Saturday morning shopping, leaving Clare and me alone. Clare stabbed a slice of pancake with her fork and lifted it to my mouth. I took a bite and then spit it out. I pushed the tray aside and stepped away from the bed. I put my hands to my hips, hidden by my T-shirt and pajama pants, and pointed at Clare.

"I know what you are trying to do?"

"Feeding my boyfriend breakfast?"

"I'm not your boyfriend. I'm some sap you're trying to con into becoming the father of your child."

"No, Jonny. You *are* the father of my child. I swear it. Do a DNA test, if you don't believe it."

"You're bluffing. I think the father is somebody you met at Barcelona. Probably an Olympic medalist who will never claim paternity."

"Like who?"

"I don't know. Dieter Baumann?"

"Dieter Baumann? The closest I got to him was the upper deck of the Olympic Stadium. You think I jumped over the rail and had it off with him right there on the finish line?"

"It wouldn't be the first time you did that with someone."

Clare ran out of my room and slammed the door. I was so stressed I did something strange for a recently retired runner. I went for a run. I ran 10 miles amidst the snow flurries that bounced off my toboggan hat along Rolling Hills Parkway. My thoughts were as clear as my breath in the freezing air as I coasted on the white-coated fairways of the Cross Creek Golf Course:

"What if this girl is genuine? I might never find someone like this again. She'll spend the rest of her life selling Camel cigarettes and Foster Lager cans to greasy, tattooed Aussie men who haven't had sex since the 70's. And what of this child, spending his or her life in Moose Junction, Australia without a father and a bunch of no teeth Australian Outbackers to bring him or her up.

Who's going to be there to protect him or her from the alligators or crocodiles, snakes, or whatever deadly creatures they have crawling around down there?"

I recalled each postcard Clare sent me from Europe with the little "I love you" bear stickers and the final words of her last letter. "Jonny, I miss you more than you can imagine. There is no bridge from Australia to Texas. But there is one linked to our hearts."

I finished my run at the curb of 2000 Hickory Lane stress-free and with the understanding of why non-competitors still run. I walked upstairs, tapped on Clare's door, and walked into the room to find Mom sitting on the bed. Clare's suitcase was gone, and so was she.

"I got back not long ago, and saw an airport shuttle pulling away from the curb." Mom looked around the empty room. "You two have an argument?"

I paced up and down the room for 30 minutes and then walked to my room and stared at the breakfast tray with syrup dripping off the cold pancakes and the yellow rose wilting from the glass vase.

"What are you going to do?" Mom said.

I grabbed my check book and Mom's keys and drove her Chevy Impala through Dallas like a Grand Prix driver and not caring how icy the roads were. I made one pit stop – at the Forest Hill Mall – en route to DFW Airport. I parked the car in the "loading and unloading only" zone. I ran through the International terminal dodging stares from passengers who acted like they never before saw a man in a yellow toboggan hat, red sweat-top, blue tights, white Spyridons and smelled like a gym rat soaked in perspiration. I searched at every ticket counter, every gate, every news stand. Then, finally, there she was, standing in the boarding line for Air Australia's non-stop, no-looking-back flight to Sydney with bus service to Moose Junction and all deserts north.

"Clare!" I yelled, as she was about to hand her boarding pass to the flight attendant.

I hurdled a row of chairs, ran to her, tore off my hat, grabbed her boarding pass, and stared into her watery eyes. "Where do you think you're going?"

"Home, wherever that is."

The flight attendant stopped taking boarding passes, and the passengers watched as I pressed Clare's head under my sweaty chin. "Clare, I'm so sorry. I've been so mixed up and confused the past week."

Clare pushed away. "Jonny, I don't have time for this bloody nonsense. I have to get on this plane."

"Not without this." I took a black veldt box out of my sweat-top pocket and knelt on one knee before her. I opened the box. A small diamond sparkled off her eyeballs. I did not stutter a syllable in a proposal witnessed by a crowd of passengers and airline crew who surrounded us.

"Clare Eggers, would you be willing to struggle through life with me?"

Clare put her hands to her face without taking her eyes off the diamond. Tears dripped from both eyes to my forehead. She ignited a rousing applause and barrage of "Oh, how sweet" from our audience with her answer and ensuing bear hug.

"You bloody wanker. Of course, I will."

The future Mrs. Jonny Langenfelder waved from the window of the Air Australia 747 until the jumbo jet, bound for a 14-hour flight to Sydney, vanished from the gate. With the flight attendant's permission I had escorted Clare onto the aircraft, kissed her good-bye, exchanged "I love yous," and told her to start planning the wedding.

Meanwhile, I was planning the bachelor party.

I chose my brother Mark to be my best man not because he was the only person I knew, other than Clare and Mom, coming to the wedding. But because I couldn't think of a better person who could stage a bachelor party. Mark frequented the Dallas striptease circuit so often he knew the dancers by their real names. He planned the party for Saturday, December 26, because I was leaving on the 28th for Australia. The wedding was January 23, 1993, which Mark said would give me enough time to recover from the bachelor party.

Clare wrote to tell me about the little Catholic Church in Moose Junction, the hall where we would have the rehearsal dinner and reception, and the priest who would perform the ceremony. Mark called to tell me about the porn theater he discovered in West Dallas, the VIP suite he arranged at Club Down and Dirty, and the blonde bimbo who would perform a special striptease.

I lay off the Christmas eggnog and wore a Santa hat on what Australians call "Boxing Day" to a downtown Dallas bar and grill appropriately called "The Outback." Mark summoned the guests to the large wooden table with the crocodile shaped ashtrays. Seated around the table were Mark, The Stallion, Mitch the Bitch, Bart Harris, and surprise guests Funky Joe Medina and my brother Luke. Matthew's wife threatened divorce if he attended the party.

I slapped high-fives with my brothers and buddies. Mark ordered a large Foster's for everyone and shots of tequila. I held my shot glass in the smoke-filled air. "Gentlemen, let the games begin."

Mark ordered another round of shots before we threw back our first one. He ordered a pitcher before we finished our Fosters. Bart lit a cigar and passed it around the table.

"So Langenhooch, I take it you are no longer virgin?" Bart's question ignited laughter that rolled through the night.

"I'm surprised your gun didn't go off in the holster," Mitch said.

The Stallion poured beer in everyone's glass. "Obviously, it went off in Clare's holster."

I shook my head. "I've been with 12 women in the last six years."

"I've been with 12 women in the last six *weeks*," said Funky Joe, the whiskered-face punk rocker.

Luke, who looked like he just got off work at the garage and did, didn't laugh or speak. Just drank, smiled, and burped.

We threw back another shot, before I opened my wedding presents. Funky Joe gave me a whip and a leather bikini with a frontal pouch for the baby. Mark gave me a glow in the dark condom. Mitch and Bart pitched in for a year's subscription to *Playboy*. The Stallion gave me a jar of Vaseline and a box of Kleenex. I threw the wrapping paper off the table. "Once I get married, I'll never look at another woman."

The married guys – The Stallion, Mitch, and Bart – laughed. "Langenhooch?"

Mitch said. "You know what the best method is for abstinence?"

"What?"

"Marriage."

The Stallion took a long puff on the cigar and blew smoke in my face. "If you're getting married just to get laid, then you need to think twice about it."

Mark held up his beer glass. "I get laid more often than all three of you guys combined and I'm not even married."

The waitress walked over, set another pitcher on the table, and asked us to keep the noise down.

Mark kept pouring. "Keep it down you guys. The cook is trying to sleep."

That was our cue to leave. We chugged our beers and marched single file out of the The Outback Bar and Grill into the cold parking lot singing to the Men at Work song Mark ordered from the juke box:

We came from the land down under. Where beer does flow and men chunder.
Can't you hear, can't hear the thunder. You better run, you better take cover.

Mark led the procession of drunk drivers to West Dallas and a four block section of bars, striptease joints, and adult theaters and book stores known as "Death Row." The merry bachelor partiers strolled into the theater called "Behind the Green Gate" singing "'Tis the season to get wasted, fa-la-la-la-la, la-la-la-la."

We each grabbed a bottled beer, sat at a table, and eyed the screen. "What's this movie called?" I asked.

"The Orgasm on 54th Street." Mark joked.

Mitch was impressed with the well-endowed male lead. "He could use that thing for a baseball bat."

Bart pointed at the screen. "You guys didn't recognize me up there?"

"No," I said. "But I did recognize Funky Joe's mother."

Funky Joe hopped on me like a wild cat. I hollered, "He bit me! He bit me again!" as the bouncer picked us up off the floor by our collars.

"He called my momma a slut," Funky Joe said, right before the bouncer shoved us out the door.

We crossed the street and to the door of Club Down and Dirty. "OK, you assholes," Mark said. "We've been to two clubs. We've been kicked out of two clubs. We're running out of clubs."

Mark walked us through the striptease joint past dancers on the stage, at the bar, and on the tables. They said, "Hi, Mark" as he escorted us through the crowd of bimbo worshippers to the VIP suite and bought another round of tequila shots. Mark held up his shot glass.

"A toast to my little brother, Jonny. I didn't think he had it in him. Now I'm afraid she's got it in her."

The round of cheers was followed by rounds of drinks and lap dances. Luke sat in the corner, sipping his beer. I took my wallet out of my back pocket.

"What are you doing?" Mark said. "The groom doesn't pay for anything."

"Just one thing." I took out a 10-dollar bill, handed it to a large-breasted dancer named Candi, and whispered something in her ear. Candi strutted to the corner, removed her top, straddled Luke, and gave him the lap dance of his dreams.

"Look at him," Mark said. "He sits there with that scraggly beard and axle grease under his fingernails and doesn't say a word. Sometimes I wonder if he even likes women."

I pointed to the crotch of Luke's oil-stained Wranglers. "Yep, I guess he does."

When Candi finished, she took my arm and led me out of the VIP suite through the cigarette smoke to the main stage. She sat me in a chair, and two other dancers walked out to Donna Summer's "Hot Stuff" that blasted off the mirrored walls. The dancers stripped and then, to the whoops and hollers of the perverted patrons, unbuttoned my shirt button by button and unzipped me. By the end of the song, I wore nothing but my Fruit of the Looms and the two dancers who sat on either leg and kissed my cheek. I put my arms around them and accidentally gripped their breasts, a violation that got us expelled from our third bar of the night.

We also were tossed out of the next-door club, The Boob Trap, for drunk and disorderly conduct. I don't remember much of The Boob Trap. The Stallion told me I drank several shots, performed a table dance for one of the strippers, and crashed on the floor. A waitress said to Mark, "Aren't you gonna buy the groom another drink?"

"What do you expect me to do," Mark said, "prop a funnel in his mouth and pour the drink down his throat?"

I do remember Luke helping me to the lighted parking lot, giving me a warm bear hug, and finally breaking his silence. "I love ya,' little brother."

I passed out in Mark's RX-7 on the drive back to Mom's house. I woke up in the driveway and ran for the nearest toilet. I made it to the stairs before leaving my mark on the walls that led to the upstairs bathroom. As I buried my head in the toilet, Mark poked me on the shoulder. I raised my head, turned, and was struck in the face by a banana cream pie. I sat there with bananas and cream and vomit dripping from my face to the toilet and started to cry.

"What's wrong?" Mark said.

"I miss my dad."

I woke up at 3 p.m. the next day and only for an Alka-Seltzer. Mark came to my bed to pay his respects.

"I told Mom you had the flu," he said.

"Did she buy it?"

"I don't know, but she cleaned up all the vomit."

I grabbed Mark's arm. "That had to be the best bachelor party a best man has ever thrown. But you were wrong about one thing."

"What's that?"

"No way I'll be recovered by my wedding day."

The trip from Dallas to Moose Junction, Australia didn't help me recover from my hangover. I sat next to a fat woman with a baby who screamed, shit, and spit up for 14 hours. "I'm traveling halfway around the world so I can have a wife and a kid who does that?" I thought.

The bus to Moose Junction took longer than the flight and it didn't have a non-smoking section for the three of the forty-two passengers who didn't smoke. The other two were crying babies. I quickly grew accustomed to down under driving on the opposite site of the road, because there seemed to be no other cars. The seemingly endless stretches of straight desert roads alongside donkeys that seemed to go faster than the bus carved another thought into my mind. "If I have to go through all this, I must really love this girl."

Another reason to love her is that Clare was the first person I saw as the bus pulled into the curbside bus depot. She stood in her cut-off jeans, white maternity top, and a sign with large red letters "Welcome, Jonny Langenwanker." The diamond from her engagement ring sparkled off the mid-day sun. I stepped off the bus through a wave of perfume and into the arms of Miss Moose Junction. Clare eschewed her parents' house that New Year's eve afternoon and took me to Moose Junction's Oasis Lodge, where we made love until a quarter til midnight. Then Clare joined me on a moonlit run from 1992 to 1993.

The soothing rest stop is what I needed to face my future in-laws. I had a dream that night of a very large Australian man with buckteeth and a shotgun. "You the bloke who got my little girl pregnant?"

The reality was a man in a green brimmed hat with corks dangling off the sides to keep the sand flies away from his red, wrinkled face. He wouldn't have to worry about the flies if he would repair the hole in the screen door of this two-bedroom shack. I couldn't tell how tall he was, because he wouldn't leave his worn, duct-taped sofa seat in fear of missing a bowl in the Australia vs. Pakistan cricket match that blared from his black and white television topped by movable aerials with aluminum foil. He turned his eyes from the screen only for a moment to shake my hand.

Fortunately, he tuned out my first question, "Are you Clare's grandfather?"

Eldon Eggers sat there all afternoon, mumbling, "Bloody hell" for every hit wicket and "Good on ya,' mate" for every run a batsman scored. His head didn't even turn when I asked, "Why do they call it Moose Junction? There's no moose and there's no junction."

Clare's dad was Crocodile Dundee without the charm.

There was more movement from Clare's mother who walked back and forth from the kitchen table to the stove to pour herself a cup of tea every half-hour. She also made dinner that included overcooked ham, overcooked potatoes, and overcooked carrots.

"Yummy ham, Mum," Clare said of the meat that tasted like leather. It took me three minutes to chew each slice. I almost choked when Fiona Eggers said, "Yip, this is what I will be serving at the wedding reception."

We discussed the wedding over dessert of canned peaches and melted ice cream. Clare brought out a notepad, on which she had organized the details from the photographer to the flowers. On the long flight I had written the readings from combined Bible passages of Isaiah and the letters to the Corinthians, Philippians, and Timothy, which Mom helped me pick. I read one aloud.

"Every athlete in training submits to a strict discipline in order to be crowned with a wreath. That is why I run straight for the finish line in order to win the prize, which is God's call through Christ Jesus to the life above. I have done my best race, I have run the full distance, I have kept the faith. And now the prize of victory is waiting for me."

I looked up and no one was there. Clare was doing the dishes, Fiona was making a cup of tea, and Eldon was watching cricket. When the first day of 1993 was almost over, Eldon went to his bed in the camper outside the door. Fiona slept in one bedroom, and Clare and I in the other. The rotating fan did little to discourage the sand flies or cool the hot, stuffy air. I woke up to Eldon watching the second day of the five-day cricket match and Fiona drinking a cup of tea. The only way to escape the boredom was to go for hour runs along dirt roads that led to nowhere and help Clare with the wedding plans.

No wonder Clare developed into a runner who would win a berth in the 1990 Commonwealth Games. "What else is there to do in Moose Junction, but run?"

"That's not why," Clare said. "A coach saw me running at an athletics meet in Darwin when I was 16 and encouraged me to leave home and join his running group. Without him, I don't know where I would be."

"Probably married to some guy who likes cricket."

Our tour of the wedding sites told me my wedding would not be the fairy tale I once dreamed. Christ Savior Catholic Church looked more like a manger than a cathedral. The hay and the sheep were there. All it lacked were camels and the three wise men. The town hall made me wonder if there would be square dancing at the reception. I was living Clare's dream, a wedding she visualized all her life. So I freed her to help her mother bake the wedding fruitcake and sew an extra large pink dress for Melody Aitkin, her life-long pen pal-turned-maid of an honor. The best man arrived via the Mustang convertible he and Mom rented in Sydney. I arranged a room for the three of us in the air-conditioned Oasis Lodge.

Mom first wanted to see the Church. Mark wanted to see the women.

"There's only one cute girl in the town, and I'm marrying her," I said.

We drove 90 miles north to Wallonby Creek. We didn't find women, but we did find a tuxedo rental shop, a golf course, and the Crocodile Pub. The manager at the golf club asked us if we had our own sticks and trundlers.

"Huh?" Mark said.

"I think he means clubs and golf carts."

We carried our rented rusty sticks around a nine-hole course and bounced our Titleists off the sheep and cows that roamed the course and ate whatever grass was left on the fairways. I couldn't find the ball I sliced off the sixth tee.

"I think I saw it up a cow's butt," Mark said.

"No, that was Titleist 1. I was playing a Titleist 3."

We saw more cows, called "Sheilas," at the Crocodile Pub and several cans of Fosters. "You ready for this marriage thing?" Mark asked.

"No. I feel it is more like a rush to the altar. I still haven't been around Clare enough to know if I really love her. But she is a good woman, nice to everyone, and she spoils me. Also, with the baby I feel an obligation – even though I'm not a hundred percent sure I'm its daddy."

Mark took a long swig. "You could go through a lot more women and not find one like that. Maybe Clare is the best you're gonna do."

I could find better in-laws. Eldon showed up at the rehearsal the day before the wedding and told me there wouldn't be a Mass.

"Too bloody long," he said. "I want to get the bloody thing over, so I can watch the last day of the Australia-New Zealand test."

Father Henry Mulligan, a red-faced Irish priest who ran both churches in Wallonby Creek and Moose Junction and looked like he spent some time at the Crocodile Pub, agreed. "There are only three Catholics, the rest Protestant, and no air conditioner. No one would survive a Mass."

The other bad news was Eldon switched sights for the rehearsal dinner, so he wouldn't miss day four of his cricket match. I went to the Eggers' shack to see tables and chairs in their garage.

"Give me your fricking keys," I told Mark. "When I get back, these tables and chairs better be out of the garage."

I drove the Mustang 160 kilometers per hour down a deserted highway with Van Halen screaming from the cassette player and into the wind. I parked on a trail by a pond and took off on my fastest run since retirement. I turned around 45 minutes into the run, when a crocodile climbed out of a swamp and started chasing me. I kept looking back and to the sides to see if another crock would jump out of the pond or a python would crawl out of the tall grass. I hopped into the convertible without opening the door and floored it. I was still puffing when I arrived back at the Eggers' house. The only change was that the tables were covered with paper tablecloths and the tailgate of Eldon's 1969 green pickup was being used as a buffet table for the overcooked feast prepared by Clare and her mother.

"Breathe, little brother," Mark said. "Breathe."

The dinner also was a homecoming for Clifford Eggers. Clare's only sibling sheared sheep on a farm 100 miles from Moose Junction. Eldon asked me if I didn't mind making his son a groomsman.

"I do mind," I said. "He can be an usher."

I carved into my rubber chicken and tried to ignore the old tires and radiator hoses hanging above our guests' heads and the gasoline smell that seeped from a rusted-out lawn mower. Mom asked me for the salad oil.

"Would you like Penzoil or Quaker State?"

Mark laughed. "Jonny, could you pass me the blow torch? I need to heat up my roll."

Clare nudged me. "Cut it out, Langenwanker."

I whispered in her ear. "If you want me to marry you tomorrow, you must promise not to call me Langenwanker."

"Maybe I don't want to marry you."

The conversation went to running and Clare's plans to go back to training after the baby is born. I said Clare has much potential and assured Eldon "I will be rooting for your daughter."

Everyone but Mom and Mark stopped eating and drinking and stared at me with disgusted looks. Clare whispered into my ear, "Honey, 'rooting' in Australian language means 'screwing.'"

Mark broke the silence. "The main thing will be finding her a coach in Texas."

"Ah, that will be hard, mate," Clifford said. "You'll never find one better than Darcy."

I stared at Clare. "Darcy?"

"Yes, Darcy."

"You mean Darcy Ellard?"

"Didn't I tell ya'? He coached me for 10 years in the Outback."

I must have turned Satan red or Jolly Green. Darcy Ellard, the same man who encouraged coaches to train me until I dropped and convinced Wooosh to drop its grass roots program and was known to sleep with his athletes no matter how old they were. I looked around at her father in his ridiculous hat, her mom sipping a cup of tea, and the hammers and monkey wrenches piled on the shelves of this garage-turned-dining room. I kept breathing and breathing until I was out of breath.

After the guests left and the dishes cleared, I motioned Clare to the garage and pulled the wooden door shut.

"I want to know one thing, Clare. And I want the truth. Is Darcy Ellard the father of your child?"

"What the bloody hell makes you say something like that?"

"I know his reputation and I know you were with him at Barcelona."

"I was with him. I wasn't sleeping with him."

318

"How do I know that? And don't throw that 'you just have to trust me' crap around again."

"Look, Langenwanker or whatever I'm suppose to call ya,' you're the bloody father of my child whether you believe me or not. If you don't, then don't bother showing up at the church tomorrow. "

Clare snuck out the garage door and marched into the house. I stood and stared at an oil pan Fiona had used for the gravy.

The next day, Saturday, January 23 welcomed the first rainstorm in Moose Junction in three months. A gray-haired lady at Christ Savior Church cranked music from *Chariots of Fire,* or something that sounded like it, on a poorly-tuned organ. The priest put on his vestments. The guests, most dressed more appropriately for a bowling alley than a church wedding, crammed into the small pews. Mark escorted Mom to the front row on the right. Clifford escorted Fiona to the front row on the left. The bride's father paced in the back of the church. The bride primped her dress with the help of the portly maid of honor.

Everyone was there – except the groom.

The guests glanced at their watches. Mark stared out the window of the sacristy. "Where *is* he?"

I had spent the night at the Crocodile Pub and slept in a motel room above the bar. I told Mark I wanted to spend my last night alone, and he gave me the Mustang. I ran for an hour up Kangeroo Hill, the only hill within 100 miles, the next morning and looked as far as I could see into the distance at the lightning bolts that struck the desert. I figured if I stayed up there long enough, one would strike me.

I sat on the hill in the pouring rain that dowsed my T-shirt and shorts, closed my eyes, and meditated. "Feel the feeling," I thought. "Feel the feeling."

I stood up, opened my eyes, and ran down the hill back to the Crocodile Pub. I poured back a shot of whiskey, showered, put on my tux, made the sign of the cross, and knelt on the side of the bed. "Oh God, please help me to do your will."

His will was for the highway to Moose Junction to be flooded and for a crocodile to park himself in the middle of the road. I pulled up to the church 10 minutes after the wedding was supposed to start. The organist plodded through "Endless Love" as I dodged puddles and lightning bolts and snuck in the side door and into the sacristy.

"Second thoughts?" Father Mulligan asked.

"More like third, fourth, and fifth thoughts."

Mark smiled. "It's show time." He pat dried my black jacket with a towel, straightened my white bow tie, and pinned a flower on my lapel. Mark practically dragged me out of that little room to the altar. Father Mulligan motioned to the organist, who played Beethoven's "Ode to Joy" – or something that sounded like it. I whispered in Mark's ear. "What the hell is that?"

"Don't know," he said. "But I'd ask for my money back."

The butterflies danced in my stomach to that dreadful tune as maid of honor Melody waddled up the aisle and met Mark at the altar. They bowed and took their places. I stared at the front of the Church at a woman in a white wedding gown and a man who looked like he had never worn a tie in his life. Fortunately, he wasn't wearing his hat.

As father and daughter started up the aisle to the organist's glass shattering "Wedding March," all I could think was, "What have I gotten myself into this time?"

Eldon escorted his daughter to the altar and took his place next to his wife. I took Clare's arm and faced Father Mulligan. After the readings, Father Mulligan spoke of a couple's devotion to each other and how love and family would keep them together.

"Love?" I thought.

Then Clare and I stood and faced each other. Father Mulligan asked me the question I dreaded all day.

"Do you Jonathan Christian take thee, Clare Elisabeth, to be your lawfully wedded wife, to have and to hold from this day forward, for richer for poorer, for better, for worse, in sickness and in health, until death do you part?"

I considered the eternal question that stopped time. The lightning quit, the raindrops ceased pounding the roof, and everyone stared at me as if the question was asked by Regis Philbin. I looked at Mark and the freedom he possessed and the freedom I was sacrificing. I looked at Mom and the tears that dampened her dry make up. I looked at the guests, mostly the Eggers' relatives and acquaintances who fanned themselves with church leaflets and couldn't wait for the free meal. I looked at Eldon Eggers and wondered why he wasn't holding his wife's hand. I looked to Father Mulligan to help me answer the question.

I looked at Clare's stomach, at her perfect pink nail polish and hands that gripped her sweet-smelling bouquet. I looked at the satin sleeves of her white dress and to the veil that separated me from the spark in her warm, trusting eyes. I looked a moment longer and took one last breath until time resumed.

"I do."

◆ ◆ ◆

Dick Schwartz walked into the conference room at *The Dallas Star* like he owned the place. In a way, he did.

His great-grandfather, R.W. Schwartz, was one of the co-founders of the newspaper in the early 1900's and its first managing editor. R.W.'s son and grandson succeeded him as managing editor. Dick Schwartz's father, Hayden Schwartz, hoped to keep the tradition going. But Hayden's only son flunked out of the SMU School of Journalism. The only position in the newspaper Hayden felt safe to employ Dick was assistant sports editor.

"Nobody reads the sports section anyway," Hayden said in the early 1960's.

Hayden made Dick the sports editor in 1972 on a promise that he let his staff run the department. When his father died of a heart attack in 1983, Dick forgot the promise and ran the sports department in whatever manner he saw fit. He fired legendary columnist Mo Madowski and replaced him with Marcia Vanderberg, a copy editor in the living section who never wrote a word in print in her life. Many of his hires were sports journalists in the image of himself – unschooled, untalented, and egotistical.

That's why as I sat there in my sport coat and tie and looked up from the padded seat to his Highness swiveling in his leather chair in front of his petrified assistant sports editors, I didn't think I had a chance at the position of sports fitness writer. Another reason was that Jeremy Roche, who was leaving as the fitness writer to work as a general assignments reporter in news, recommended me as his successor. Jeremy's choice had merit. I had worked as a sportswriter in Lubbock, Eugene, and Boston. I had spent the past 2 ½ years covering high school games for *The Star*, I was a world class runner, and I grew up and spent most of my life in Dallas. More important, I had to support a wife and a baby who was due in May. I couldn't keep free-loading off Mom with free room, board, and car rental.

But Schwartz didn't want anyone telling him what to do. He was the Scarecrow, Tin Man, Cowardly Lion, and the Wizard of Oz wrapped into one five foot, six-inch asshole. He had no brain, no heart, no courage, and no scruples. He hired his executive secretary from The Boob Trap, wore a three-piece suit and a gold Rolex, drove a Rolls Royce, and had a black toupee and side-hair that looked like he had painted with shoe polish.

I could smell Schwartz's after-shave from my seat, 15 yards away. I braced for what might be Schwartz's first question – Why do you think you would make a good fitness writer? Or what kind of columns would you write? Or what events would you cover? Schwartz swiveled forward in his chair, put his palms on the desk, and cocked his head toward me.

"So Langenslugger, I understand you were on a running contract with Wooosh. That means you would focus all your stories on athletes who represent Wooosh. Wouldn't you say that would be a major conflict of interest?"

I don't know who was more shocked at the question, me or the three assistant editors who adjusted their ties and prepared for a long, heated interview. "W-W-Well, Mr. Schwartz. I haven't run for Wooosh in two years and I retired from running in December. So I'm on no one's payroll."

I continued to bob and weave from Schwartz's jabs and hooks, questions unrelated to fitness or sports writing. The final question seemed to put me in position for the job. "Your resume says you went to Caprock State. My grandfather was a big fan of Grimsley Roeper. You know anything about him?"

"Yes, he was my great uncle."

I walked out of the conference room and received a back slap from assistant editor Larry Shaw. "Way to go, Langenslugger. That answer about your Uncle Grimsley may have sealed it."

Ten days later, I wasn't sure. Jeremy said among the applicants who followed me into the lion's den were an English Literature graduate who wrote a column for his college newspaper entitled, "To run or not to run, that is the question," an aerobics instructor who wrote a newsletter for her 16 clients, and a triathlete who never had a word published in his life.

I told Jeremy, "Certainly I can beat out the aerobics instructor."

"I don't know," he said. "Have you seen her legs?"

Clare was more nervous about the job prospect than me. It would take her six weeks to get her green card, and the only subject she pursued since age 16 was running. The wedding bill, the three-day stopover in Honolulu for our honeymoon, and the travel from Australia left us with $381.63 in our bank account.

"What in the world are we going to do if you don't get this job, Jonny? How are we going to afford to have a baby, much less take care of it?"

Instead of answering the questions, I answered the telephone.

"Hello."

"Langenslugger, this is Dick Schwartz. How would you like to be our new fitness writer?"

Within two days Clare and I had moved from Mom's house to the Crossroads West Apartments in the middle of Dallas and bought a 1984 fire engine-red Toyota Corolla. We had a second floor one-bedroom apartment with a study I would convert into the baby's room. The complex had a pool, spa, weight room, and a one-mile jogging path that looped two duck ponds and meandered through several adjoining apartment complexes. White Rock Lake was two miles in one direction, and Highland Park was two miles in the other direction.

"I retired too soon," I told Clare as we walked around the duck pond one afternoon. "This is the perfect place in Dallas to train."

"You always could come out of retirement," she said.

"You kidding? With a wife, baby, and a full-time job?"

"When this baby is born, I'm running back here from the hospital. I can't wait to fly around that bloody lake."

Clare said she had everything she wanted – the man she loved and living quarters with indoor plumbing. I just wanted out of the Outback. The "I do's" had been followed by a ham steak and potatoes meal swallowed whole by the guests and the father of the bride, who hurried home with son Clifford to watch the end of the cricket match. I danced with Clare, Mom, Mrs. Eggers, and Melody to the 60's tunes on Moose Junction's lone radio station. Clare and I cut the wedding fruitcake, drank a glass of champagne, and literally ran off into the sunset. We had changed into our shorts and sneakers and wrote "Just" on her T-shirt and "Married" on mine. We ran two miles in the pouring rain to the bus depot, where Mark had checked our bags before the wedding.

We jumped onto the bus and kissed in the backseat until we arrived at our honeymoon suite – atop the Crocodile Pub.

When we finally settled into our new Dallas apartment, I settled into marriage. I was falling in love with macaroni and cheese dinners for two, with talking to someone other than myself, and with playing mattress polo anytime I wanted and with the same partner. I was falling in love with my wife. Clare bought me a briefcase for my first day of work, gave me a kiss, and pushed me out the apartment door with, "Good luck, mate. It's a bloody jungle out there."

I expected to see the king of the jungle that first day, but only ran into his monkeys. That first day was more like a press conference. I couldn't write a sentence without being questioned by a frustrated jock-turned-beat writer.

"Why did you quit running?" college writer Brent Goldberg asked.

"If I could make a living at it and had nothing else to do, I'd keep doing it."

"What kind of sacrifices did you make over the years?" boxing columnist Rock Delberto asked.

"I figure I gave up about $250,000 in the 12 years I ran. That's based on the salary I would have received as a full-time sportswriter minus the little bit of money I earned during that time."

Darvis Mack, the track and field writer, said he covered the Olympic Trials in New Orleans. "I watched from the press box as you moved into third going into last lap and fade. My thought progression was like, 'This could be a column, this could be a column. Oh, wait, it's a note.'"

One writer wanted to know what to do about shin splints. A copy editor asked how he could train for a half marathon, and an agate clerk needed advice on what running shoes to buy. I had a 4 p.m. deadline on my first fitness column, and at 3 p.m. I didn't have a clue what to write. Somehow, at 3:59, my story was on the screen of my editor, Larry Shaw. I snuck out before he read the lead:

> *I did not have to go to the track or the pool or the gym to find subjects for my first fitness column for The Dallas Star. All I did was hang around the water cooler.*

The telephone rang as soon as I opened the door to our apartment. I made Clare answer it.

"It's for you, Jonny. It's Larry Shaw."

I put my finger to my lips. "Tell him I'm not here yet."

"I'm not going to lie for ya,' mate."

I grabbed the telephone. "H-Hi, Larry."

"Good column. Just had a couple of questions. You mention something about a fartlek workout. What is that?"

The editing session took longer than it did to write the column. Larry called back twice to check facts. A copy editor woke me up at 11:30 p.m. to make sure I had the correct spelling for plantar fasciitis. Someone should have edited Dick Schwartz's handwritten memo, which greeted me the next morning. "I was impresed with your first colum. Their were probably a lot of readers out their who were realy interested in it. You write good. I can see how you are related to Grimsley Roeper."

I showed it to Jeremy in the lunch room.

"That's Dick Schwartz."

"Wait, the guy is the sports editor of *The Dallas Star* and he can't write?"

"Can't edit either."

I sat with Jeremy at a corner table. "Hasn't he ever covered a game or done a feature?"

"Once." Jeremy bit into his turkey sandwich and told me about the time Schwartz showed up in the locker room after the Texas Rangers lost in the ninth inning to the Boston Red Sox. Jeremy was there to write a sidebar.

Schwartz wedged his way through the crowd of experienced beat writers and asked Texas Rangers' manager Colt Hudspeth, "Do you think replacing Nolan Ryan in the ninth inning in a tie ball game with a newly required relief pitcher was a bright idea?"

Hudspeth picked up a baseball bat from the rack behind him and pushed it into Schwartz's face. "Do you think sticking this all the way up your scrawny little ass would be a bright idea?"

Jeremy laughed as he thought about it. "Ol' Schwartz never stuck his face in another locker room again."

Schwartz didn't show up much in the newsroom either. He spent most workdays at the golf course or at a press luncheon, bragging about what a good team he has assembled in the sports department. He was especially high on his lead columnist Marcia Vanderberg, whose copy read more like a romance novel than a sports column. I read the lead of her current column to Clare over dinner:

Duke guard Terrell Minor slumped aimlessly on a chair along the sidelines of the A.L. Fulton Coliseum in the waning moments of his Duke Blue Devils' disappointing 83-60 loss to South Carolina on Friday night. He slowly, deliberately slid a snow-white towel over the sweat beads of his smooth, stern face, fervently hiding the tears of a night's frustration from his coaches, teammates, and fans who care about him more than he could ever possibly imagine.

Clare took the sports page out of my hands and walked toward the bedroom. "How much are they paying this bird to write this rubbish?"

"About a hundred thousand dollars a year."

"And what did you say they're paying you?"

"Let's put it this way. Don't look to move out of these 600 square feet anytime soon."

"I'll read the rest of her bloody fluff piece in bed. It'll help me get to sleep."

My first race coverage made me understand why Jeremy chose to relay his pen the week before the Fort Worth Marathon. Race Director Warren Tubbs decided to save money by doing the results himself. He looked at the starting line of the newly added 10K with his clipboard, pencil, and stopwatch and said, "Oh-h-h, shit-a-brick."

There was a person for every meter and they came through the chute 300 per minute. Race volunteers scrambled to write down the race numbers at the end of the chute. I figured Tubbs guessed at the times. I rode in the lead van and watched the marathon through the dirt-tinged back window. Twenty miles into the race, two Mexican runners battled up a big hill. Sweat dribbled down their grimaced faces. Their quadriceps contorted on their heavy legs. They gasped for air like they were trying to suck algae off the adjacent river. One runner looked like he was about to lose his breakfast burrito.

Clyde Kenworthy, who was covering the marathon for the *Fort Worth Daily Reporter*, looked at me. "You wish you were out there?"

I stared back at the two runners foaming at the mouth.

"No."

Winner Carlos Alcon and runner up Ysidro Hermanez were helped to the press tent. I asked, "So how did it feel after 26 miles, 385 yards of pounding to cross the finish line as the winner of the Fort Worth Marathon?"

The Mexicans looked at each other and shrugged. "Como?"

Clyde and I scrambled for an interpreter. When we returned, the Mexicans were gone. We went to the results center, where Tubbs was looking at a replay through the lens of a camcorder and trying to re-determine the order of finishers of the 10K.

"Grab a chair," Clyde said. "We are in for a long night."

At 10:30 p.m. I was driving my red Toyota 90 miles per hour down the DFW turnpike to explain why I had no results and no quotes to editors who had to explain the same to Schwartz at Monday's breakdown meeting. Braden Hancock, the Saturday night editor slammed his right hand on his desk. "Schwartz will read the newspaper over his Sunday coffee and donut in his Highland Park mansion and will see a blank where the results are. It doesn't matter why there were no results. It only matters that there were no results."

On Monday morning I was more worried about the results of our first sonogram. We had to wait until Clare was six months pregnant to see our child. That's how long parents without money wait on the no frills maternity list at West Dallas Medical Center. You also have a pot luck doctor. I took one look at our doctor and joked, "Didn't you win a marathon in Fort Worth on Saturday?"

"Como?"

Dr. Speedy Gonzalez, or whatever his name, told me that my wife and baby were OK by giving me a thumbs up sign. He was replaced by a bubblegum chewing radiologist, who looked like he served Boppers in South Dallas.

"You be wantin' to know the sex of your baby?" he asked.

"No thanks," Clare and I said in unison as we gazed at the screen.

"Finding out the sex would be like opening your presents before Christmas," I said.

Clare wanted a girl and would name her Simone. She said if the baby was a boy, I could name him. We cried and held hands as the images came up on the monitor. I imagined the fear the baby must have in that dark pit and the struggle to live long enough to see the light in the birth canal.

"That's our baby," Clare said.

"I hope so," I thought.

Eight months into the pregnancy, Mom threw a baby shower for Clare. We were given a crib, car seat, playpen, tons of clothes, and a baby jogger. We attended Lamaze classes and prayed daily for a healthy baby. My trust in Clare grew, mostly because no guy would be attracted to a woman with a stomach as big as a watermelon and a bladder the size of a watermelon seed. I understood what my friends were talking about at the bachelor party. I covered my first triathlon on April 17 at Clearwater Lake, south of Dallas. I stood on the bank and stared at the women competitors emerging from the cold water with their hard nipples outlined on their bikini tops. I couldn't help but notice how a wet brief can ride up a firm ass on a bike seat or how well-toned breasts can bob in unison with every stride.

I had to jump into the cold lake before I could interview the first-place woman. I returned to the apartment and asked Clare, "How long did the doctor say we had to wait until after the baby was born?"

The last month of the pregnancy caused irritability, edginess, and anger. It was also hard on the woman. Everytime the telephone rang at my desk in the sports department I expected it to be Clare telling me it was time. Instead, it was an editor calling me from across the room to ask what "PR" stands for or how far is a 10K or what's the difference between duathlon and biathlon. The only words I heard from Dick Schwartz came after some idiot wrote a letter to the editor that said my stories have nothing to do with Dallas. Larry Shaw sat down on my desk. Schwartz said you need to concentrate on the local angle.

I reminded Larry that the farthest I've strayed from Dallas was to Tyler, where Dallas runners dominated the 10K. Among my column subjects were a 57-year-old postal worker who had run a marathon in every state, a Jewish woman who wouldn't race on Saturdays, and a Navy pilot and masters' swimmer who dodged scud missiles over Iraq in the Gulf War.

"All of these people are from Dallas," I said.

"How about the story on President Clinton?"

"He was running through Highland Park. I interviewed a Dallas man who snuck through his secret service men to run with him. If I could just explain this to Schwartz-"

"Wouldn't do any good. He has a customer-is-always-right policy no matter how wrong they are. If you want to stay around here for a while, I suggest you learn two words."

"And they are?"

"Yes and sir."

I understood this as I stepped into the lead police car on Saturday, May 1. I rode alongside my tape recorder and Officer Joseph Lozario during the Run for Your Life 10K near downtown Dallas. The reports on Officer Lozario's radio sounded like they came from an attendant at a drive-through restaurant. About the only words I could understand as we led the running pack through the Dallas streets were, "Do you have a Jonny Langenfelder with you?"

Officer Lozario put the microphone to his mouth. "Affirmative."

"His wife called the race headquarters with this message. 'Meet me at the hospital.'"

"What does that mean?" the officer said.

"That means you need to pull over and let me out."

I didn't have time to wait for post-race interviews, and Dick Schwartz wouldn't understand why my race coverage was replaced by an ad for a penile enlargement. So I jumped into the race. I turned on my tape recorder and ran behind the co-leaders. Dalton Lambert surged away from Tony Rizzo at the four-mile mark and I went with him. I put my tape recorder up to his mouth.

"Why did you decide to make your move at this point of the race?" I asked.

"I'm kind of busy here," Lambert said, between puffs. "Let's talk after the race."

"Can't. My wife's having a baby."

Lambert tried to surge away from me, but couldn't. "OK. Rizzo's got a big kick, and this is my chance to beat the sonuva bitch."

I dropped back and ran alongside Rizzo. "How do you feel about your chances of catching Lambert?"

"Not good," he said. "I have a side stitch as big as cantaloupe and feel like I'm about ready to throw up."

"But Lambert fears your kick. Why don't you go after him?"

"Fuck off."

I waited at five miles for the first woman and ran her to the finish line with my tape recorder next to her mouth. I jotted down the top times from the timekeeper, sprinted to my Toyota, and sped to the West Dallas Medical Center. Clare was climbing out of a cab as I arrived. I helped her to the elevator, which we shared with an orderly and a dead body on a gurney.

"Going down, I assume?" I said.

"To the morgue" the orderly said. "I presume you are going up."

"To the labor room."

I did most of the work there. While Clare walked up and down the hallway timing her contractions, I batted out my story on the Run for Your Life 10K on my laptop computer. My lead:

Dalton Lambert outran a tough competitor, a nagging reporter, and a police car's faulty muffler to win Saturday's Run for Your Life 10K.

I attached my computer couplers to the telephone in the nurses' station, sent my story to the newspaper, and joined Clare in the delivery room. There were wires and monitors and nurses all over the room. I held Clare's hand and coached her breathing, which was about as heavy as Rizzo's. After two hours of panting and pleading, the nurse put Clare's legs in stirrups. I looked down at a soft, little head showing through her vagina. Doctor Justin O'Keefe arrived and looked at the proceedings. I looked at his running shoes.

"I don't know if I can let a guy wearing Wooosh delivery my baby," I said.

The doctor laughed. "I did the Run for Your Life 10K this morning. I heard some idiot reporter interviewed the top runners during the race."

Clare held my hand tighter and screamed as the top of a head emerged between her legs. Dr. O'Keefe ordered her to push. Her scream was interrupted by a ringing telephone. A nurse answered and handed me the telephone.

I pressed it against my ear. "Langenslugger. It's Bernie on the copy desk. I've got a question on your story about the Run for Your Life 10K"

"I'm kind of busy here, Bernie. Can I call you back a little later?"

"We're on deadline. What's that screaming?"

"That's my wife having a baby."

"Oh. Quick then. You wrote the winning time was 31:16 and results say 31:17."

The next scream Bernie heard was from me. "Who gives a shit? Go with 31:17!"

I handed the receiver to the nurse right before Clare's final scream of "Oh God, come get this baby!"

The baby's eyes followed the light out of the birth canal. Then came a nose, mouth, arms, stomach, and legs.

Dr. O'Keefe stated the obvious. "It's a boy."

The little fellow sat up for a moment, straddled the umbilical cord, and let out a little cry. I cried a little too. Dr. O'Keefe let me cut the cord. The nurses wiped off the blood and fluid, wrapped him in a cloth, and placed him in my arms. The tiny boy stared at the reflection in my eyes. I carried him to Clare, who cuddled him and kissed his forehead.

I turned around to the doctor, to the nurse, and to the world.

"I give you Miles Simon Langenfelder."

◆ ◆ ◆

It took a terminally ill man to tell me why I couldn't quit running, why I still enjoyed a lap of White Rock Lake or an out-and-backer on Rolling Hills Parkway no matter how hot or cold or how wet or windy.

Olin Sawyer's words spilled from his mouth onto my fitness column in *The Dallas Star*.

> *Running is a friend that's with you always and never asks a lot of you. Running is a love affair, a mythical thing. It encompasses so much. A minister tried to get me to go to church, but I told him I am as close to God when I'm running around White Rock Lake as I'm ever going to get.*

Lung cancer took away Olin's friend and left him too weak to find him again. Running, he said, made him quit smoking and gave him an extra 20 years, his best 20 years. The last words from the 68-year-old's interview I played over and over on my tape recorder were, "Keep running as long as you can and wherever you can. Don't quit. No matter what, don't quit."

I enjoyed running after retirement more than I did before it. There was no pressure, no worries. I ran as far and as fast as I wanted. If I felt like running for an hour or sprinting some 200's on the Forest Hill Track, I did it. If I didn't feel good or didn't have time, I didn't do it.

Running with a three-wheeled contraption called a baby jogger brought my family closer. I had carried Miles Simon Langenfelder from the delivery room to the nursery. I held his tiny, pink hand through every needle poke, every eye drop, every swipe of a wash cloth. The next morning's circumcision? I was there.

I bought him a birthday cake with a 0 candle. Clare and I sang to him, blew out the candle, and wished him a long, happy life. Mom, Mark, and The Stallion dropped by the next afternoon to wish him well.

"When are you taking him out for his first run?" The Stallion asked me.

"As soon as I put together that baby jogger."

That was in September of 1993, after his baptism and when I was confident I didn't have to stop every mile to change a diaper. Miles never seemed more happy or content than when he was with me on a run. He sat there, quacked like a duck, and looked at me like I was the best dad in the world. The baby jogger slowed me down enough to run with Clare, who was back training within a month of delivery. Clare breast-fed while reading Darcy Ellard's *Run like a Cheetah, III*.

"I can't wait to go out and smash all the bloody records in this town," she said.

Such fire in me, I figured, had been dowsed by 20 years of training and racing and the runners who confronted me every race I covered for *The Dallas Star* with the same question. "Why aren't you running today?"

"I'm retired" was never a good enough reason. One old fart beamed, "You could do it as a training run and win a trophy."

"I've got about a hundred trophies and twice as many medals all in a box somewhere in my mother's attic."

Nothing could get me back out there until that October afternoon of 1993, when I pushed Miles to the Highland Park Community Athletics Track. Tony

Rizzo, leader of the Hewlett-Hobart Fall Grand Prix Road Race Series, was limbering up for his workout. After I rolled by the start/finish line, I heard, "wimp." The next lap I heard, "pussy." Then I heard, "coward."

I stopped. "What's your problem, man?"

I turned around to see Rizzo sitting there in his Oakley sunglasses pulling his knee to his chin. "Just keep pushing your little cart, has-been."

"I'd rather be a has-been than a never-was."

Rizzo stood up and twisted his trunk. "Nah, Langenquitter, you're all washed up. Bet you couldn't break five minutes in a mile right now."

I pushed the baby jogger off the track and marched to lane one. "Start your watch."

I pressed my wristwatch as I lunged off the line and lifted a body, which hadn't run a hard mile in almost a year, around the blue rubber track. I hammered as hard as I could around every bend and down every straight with one thought, "I'll show this guy who's a has-been."

I crossed a finish line stared by Rizzo on one side and Miles on the other. I glanced at the number on my stopwatch.

"4:24.7."

I smiled at Rizzo, who looked up from his watch with his mouth open. I pushed Miles out the gate and under the bleachers until I was out of Rizzo's sight.

"Oh my God that hurt." The fire I thought had vanished was in my lungs. I heaved reddish-yellow mucous from my throat. I sat down for 20 minutes, before I pushed Miles and my aching body back to the apartment. The pain wasn't worth the satisfaction of annihilating Rizzo's challenge. But it was worth it to see Miles' eyes light up as big as quarters as I finished the mile. It was the first time he watched me run, and his smile told me he wanted to jump out of the baby jogger and run with me.

I knelt beside him and brushed his silky blond hairs with my palm. "You and I one day will run a lap together, and it will be memorable."

I returned to my jolly jogging, but still was fodder for skinny jokes. At halftime of the Forest Hill Homecoming football game I told another reporter, a scout, and Forest Hill athletic director Bum Pickens that in the year since I retired from competitive running I've gained only three pounds. Pickens stuck another piece of popcorn between his lips. "Hell, I've gained three pounds tonight."

Holly Ritzenbarger hadn't gained much weight either. I glanced back from a midfield post-game interview to see her walking hand in hand with her date out of the stadium. Divorce had changed her about as much as retirement changed me. Her butt fit never more firmly into her Jordache jeans. A gold necklace hung off her golden skin and rested on the white sleeveless sweater filled by her well-toned breasts. She probably still could do hand-springs from the 50 to the end zone.

As usual, I returned to the apartment at midnight to a mother and child cuddled in a bed once used as a mattress polo field. Clare's first excuse was it was too close to when the baby was due. Then it was too soon since the birth, then postpartum depression, and now Chapter 21 of *Run Like a Cheetah III*. I pulled the bookmark out and read this from Darcy Ellard.

> *Relationships, especially married relationships, can cause an athlete to lose focus on his or her goal. An athlete must think of himself or herself first and of their partner's needs second. The athlete must make it clear to their partner what the goal is and vigorously pursue that goal no matter how hard the partner resists.*

Miles' cry stopped my reading. I went into the bedroom and woke Clare. "Aren't you going to feed him?"

"You can, mate."

"I'm not exactly equipped for that."

Clare rolled over to the other side of the bed. "I've gone off breastfeeding, not good for my training. There's a bottle and a formula in the fridge."

The constant 2 a.m. and 4 a.m. feedings eventually caused an 8 a.m. argument heard by our neighbors. Clare was barely through the door after her dawn 12 miler, when I asked, "So you believe in Chapter 21?"

"Been reading my book behind my back?"

"I asked first."

Clare took off her shoes, lay on the living room carpet, and pulled her knee to her waist. "OK, I'll answer that by saying I believe in Darcy Ellard. He got me to where I am and his training will get me to where I want to go."

"To a divorce court like he and all the other runners he trains?"

Clare stopped her stretching and sat up. "What the bloody hell are you talking about?"

"The guy's telling you to turn your husband into your servant and abandon your child, for God sake."

"You're not my bloody slave," Clare said. "I never asked you to be. Who cooks your meals?"

"Some zit-face kid at Bopper Burger?"

"Then who does your laundry?"

"Some Chinese guy around the corner."

Miles' cry from the bedroom paused our argument. Clare picked him up, carried him to the lounge, and put him in his playpen. "You see what you've done, Langenwanker."

"I asked you not to call me that. Besides, you're the one who started it."

Clare took Miles' bottle from the refrigerator. "I'm the one who started it? You started in on me right as I came in the door. I'll do anything possible to make this work. I don't care what the book says."

"Fine," I said. "Then I'll call Mom and ask her to baby-sit Miles tonight, so you and I can go to dinner and a movie."

"Can't."
"Why not?"
"I have a speed session tonight."
I took the bottle from Clare and put Miles in the baby jogger.
"Where are you going?"
"To give you some peace and some time to read Chapter 22 – "My only friend is my Olympic medal."

I pushed Miles eight miles to The Stallion's house. He welcomed me to marriage, to pre-menstrual cycles, to obsessive-compulsive behavior patterns, to women who don't know what they want, and to finding out more about myself than I really wanted to know.

"I never knew I was such a possessive control freak until I got married."

The Stallion picked up Miles and bounced him on his knee. "Eventually, you'll learn all kinds of things about yourself."

The Stallion, Miles, and I watched the Dallas Cowboys whip the New York Giants and ate lunch before The Stallion drove Miles and me back to our apartment. Clare didn't say a word. She took her spikes and marched out the door. I took a shower and went with Miles to the evening Mass at St. Peter Claver. Father Yoksui – I nicknamed him Father Chop Sewy – concluded his sermon with a little joke.

"A man who gives in when he is wrong is wise. A man who gives in when he is right – is married."

I stopped by Blockbuster and Pizza Hut on the drive home, put Miles in his baby bed in the other room, opened a bottle of wine, and slid *Far and Away* into the VCR. Clare fell asleep on the sofa, and I carried her to a bed that finally was being put to better use the next night until the telephone rang. I reached over and answered it.

"Langenslugger, this is Bernie at the copy desk. I had a couple of questions on your fitness column on this guy running 50 miles on his 50th birthday. Why are you breathing so hard? You just come in from a run?

"Actually, Bernie, I'm in the middle of something. Can I call you back in say, two minutes?"

Clare laughed, and I'm not sure if she was laughing at me or my job. Who wouldn't laugh at a sportswriter who spent the Saturday morning of the Cluckity Cluck 10K riding through Dallas in the backseat of a convertible pace car next to a man dressed as the Cluckity Cluck Chicken or the next Saturday Morning's Founder's Day Five Miler in the backseat of a Model T pace car that ran over the lead runner. I spent 5 ½ hours of the Flatter Than a Pancake 100-mile bike race in Nowhere, Oklahoma with my feet propped up in the back of the pace van and drinking a six-pack. I looked up at the driver. "Yep, I get paid for doing this."

That night I relaxed with a pizza on my motel room bed and turned on the television for the 10 o'clock news. The anchorman led with "A 54-year-old man died today at the 10th annual Flatter Than a Pancake 100-mile bike race."

I threw my pizza slice back in the box. "Damnit, I can't even relax. Now I'll have to call the race director, the medical examiner, and then rewrite my story." The thought was followed by, "What an asshole I am. This guy died, and I'm mad about my pizza going cold."

I called Flatter Than a Pancake race director Murray Hess, who was equally perturbed he had to get out of bed to take my call. "You figure it's gonna happen sooner or later. We've had 50,000 riders in our 10 year race history and only one death. So I'd say that's pretty good."

Some readers questioned why my fitness column was in the sports section. To most Dallas folks, road racing was a bunch of people running through the streets without their clothes on. It was "that damn race that tied up traffic for half an hour." I felt their point was valid for about 99 percent of race participants, who entered with no chance or desire to win.

In late October of 1993 more than 10,000 women came to the Forest Hill Mall for the Women's Society of Texas 5K Run. The goal was to improve women's health by getting them out for a run. The race backfired. Only 150 women *ran* the distance. For the other 9,850 waist watchers, it was a march. The only time they ran was through the refreshments tent where they piled every energy bar, yogurt cup, soft drink can, candy bar, cupcake, and cookie they could find into a cardboard box and lugged it home. Their once-a-year run defeated the purpose and turned waist watchers' friends into whale watchers.

Clare celebrated her return to racing by taking command in the first 100 meters and winning by 57 seconds. My lead:

Clare Langenfelder ran in a field of 10,000 runners Sunday, but couldn't find anyone to run with.

Dick Schwartz's Monday memo:
"Langenslugger, you are no longer aloud to cover any raice your wife runs in."

I brought the memo to Larry Shaw, who edited it with a pencil but agreed that my coverage and Clare's running created a conflict of interest.

"What am I going to do?" I asked. "Clare wants to run all the big Dallas races? If I can't cover the races, I won't have a job?"

"Simple," Larry said. "Get a divorce."

Clare solved the problem for me. The next day she ran a workout at Forest Hill High School that included four sets of 20 bleacher sprints and an all out mile. She limped home with a golf ball-size lump in her calf muscle. I rolled a ball to Miles on the carpet as Clare rubbed ice on her calf, winced, and kept repeating, "Bloody hell."

"You must have gotten to Chapter 32," I said. "The Myth of Overtraining."

Clare couldn't run another step the rest of the fall. I ran enough for the both of us. After beating Rizzo's challenge with my life-threatening effort, I had decided to do other sports to quench my competitive desire. In November I signed up for the Crossroads West Apartments Over-35 basketball team. Ethan Hawksbury, Crossroads West manager and basketball coach, said the league was for fun.

"It's good to have a world-class athlete on the team," Hawksbury said. "You'll get your 50 bucks worth."

I missed a lay-up and was whistled for traveling in the first two minutes. Hawksbury motioned me to the bench for my replacement, some bald guy with a headband and a beer gut sticking out his cut-off gray T-shirt. He went to his knees every time he ran down the court. He obviously needed the workout more than I did. We lost that game 70-36 to Fire Station 1197. The second game Hawksbury recruited a tenant who played junior college basketball and had scars up and down both knees. The guy threw the ball up from three-point land every time he touched it and limped down the court like he needed another knee surgery.

With our team down 90-22 to the South Dallas Old-Timers in the fourth quarter, I started to go in for the guy with the Joe Namath knees. Hawksbury waved me off. I grabbed my sweats and waved good-bye.

"Where you goin'?" Hawksbury ran off the court and met me at the exit door.

"I didn't pay 50 bucks to sit my ass on the bench next to some fat, smelly bald guy."

In February of 1994 I went on my first ski trip, to Arapaho Ski Resort in New Mexico with the St. Peter Claver Youth Group. Fearing injury, I never skied while a competitive runner. One day on the slopes told me that was a good decision.

I dressed in long cotton underwear, Lycra tights, Polyprolene socks, wool sweater and gloves, Gore-Tex jacket, and toboggan hat, and still shivered in the cold Arctic-like breeze. I must have looked like an astronaut walking in moon boots toward the ski school. The instructor held me as I locked my boots into my ski bindings. Then I fell and took the entire class down with me. I fell on the rope tow, the poma lift, the T-Bar, and the learner's conveyor belt. I took off my skis, walked up the hill, and fell down four times as I attempted to ski down. I made it on my last attempt. But I forgot how to stop and crashed into the parking lot.

The next morning Brady, a wired-toothed teenager from the youth group, talked me into going with him on the chairlift to the top of the mountain. I death-gripped the safety bar and ordered myself, "Don't look down."

"You'll be fine, Mr. Langenklammer, once we get to the top."

I fell on my butt as I departed the chair lift. Brady went down the mountain like he was Jean Claude Killy. I crashed at least a dozen times, contorted my body in ways it's not suppose to contort, washed my body with snow, and knocked down a row of skiers waiting for the chair lift.

Brady retrieved my skis and placed them next to the snow bank that broke my fall. "You want to go up again, Mr. Langenklammer?"

"Yeah, sure."

Clare took up orienteering, after she re-injured her calf muscle while running in hiking boots in May, and talked me into it giving the sport a go. I knew I was in trouble when I got lost en route to the course. The meet director gave me a compass, a map with all sorts of weird looking lines and symbols, a punch card with more symbols, and a roll of toilet paper.

"I'll wipe with leaves."

"Wouldn't advise it," he said.

"Why not?"

"Poison ivy."

I set off like I was running a cross country meet, right past the first two controls. I backtracked through the forest and looked for 20 minutes, before I realized some joker must have stolen the control. I sprinted down a trail for the next control, took a short cut over a stream, slipped, and went face-first on a jagged rock. Blood poured out of the gash above my eye. A teenager ran by and didn't even notice.

I ran back to the start and told the meet director, "Don't let my son look at me. I must look like Frankenstein."

I patched my head with a bandage and returned to Fort Worth, where I covered a bull-riding event that night and fit in quite nicely with the competitors.

We had better luck with the map in June on the Langenfelders' 1994 summer vacation. We left for Boulder, Colorado after the funeral of Olin Sawyer, who succumbed to cancer and probably was back running on a cloud above White Rock Lake. We stopped by Grimsley Roeper's statue at Caprock State en route to the Rockies. We also went to my old Rutherford Hall dormitory and to the Tumbleweed Stadium track where I ran so many workouts. Miles crawled around on the red rubber, stood on the starting line in an effort to walk, and fell like I did on the ski slopes.

He smiled at me with rubber pellets on his smooth face and said, "Da-a-a-a."

We drove the Toyota to Boulder. At dawn the next morning, I laced up a new pair of Spyridons and ran along a mountain trail like I was floating on the mile-high air beneath me. As I rolled along in the perfect harmony of each breath and to the sun that lit the golden mountain, I realized there was no other sport that could give me such satisfaction or contentment.

As I neared the summit, I saw a distant child and a woman who drove to this pinnacle on a back road. The child recognized his "Da-a-a-a" and ran toward him like he was a long lost friend. I reached Miles just as he was about to fall, hugged him, and lifted him by his armpits above my head to a height that couldn't come much closer to God.

◆◆◆

Tony Rizzo finished with his arms raised and his fists clenched as he reached the pinnacle of his running career – a victory in the 1994 Dallas Turkey Day Race.

The *Rocky* music of "Gonna Fly Now" seemed to lift him higher and drowned out the applause of the spectators who cheered him through the chute and past a reporter. Sunglasses blocked Rizzo's eyes, and his ego kept him from saying to me anything other than, "Fuck you."

He bowed to the crowd, kissed the concrete, and spit into my tape recorder. He took a large Italian flag from a friend and ran into the distance, waving the flag and waving good-bye to me with his longest finger.

My story the next morning in *The Dallas Star* reflected Rizzo's triumph more than his tirade or his finishing time a world-class runner would do on a tempo run.

Tony Rizzo let his feet do the talking at the Dallas Turkey Day Race. They said, "We are quicker, stronger, and lighter than any of the other 24,000 feet that pounded the downtown Dallas pavement," in the wake of Rizzo's dominance during yesterday's 23rd annual seven-mile race.

The letter that Rizzo faxed to Dick Schwartz was less diplomatic:

Dear Mr. Schwartz:

Last week's story on the Dallas Turkey Day Race was another shoddy effort by your fitness writer. He writes about the race with quotes from the second and third-place runners and from the top three women runners, but none from the men's winner. This is because your writer is jealous of me and is threatened that I will soon replace him as the fastest runner ever to come from the Dallas area.

I laughed as I carried a copy of the fax to Larry Shaw's desk. "Did you read this shit?"

"I don't get to read any of your shit anymore," Larry said. "I've been demoted to high school editor.

"Then who the hell is my new editor?"

Larry pointed to the person standing behind me.

"Hi, I'm Rebecca Sikes. You're in big trouble, pal."

Rebecca led me to the conference room, where she sat her flabby ass on a chair and spread some letters to the editor on the table. One was from a man who wrote there should be more coverage of wheelchair athletes.

"There are three wheelchair athletes who compete in the Dallas area," I said. "I've written columns on all three."

Next was from a 68-year-old woman who finished second in her age group at the Harry Moss Run and was disappointed I didn't interview her.

"There were two people in her age group and 4,000 in the race. I couldn't possibly talk to all of them."

Then came the letter from a man who complained because "a black man won the Metroplex Half-Marathon and the picture next to the story was of a white woman."

"I write the stories. I don't take the pictures or decide which ones are placed in the newspaper."

Rebecca lifted her pen from her notebook. "You need to be more proactive in dealing with the desk people on what pictures they run in the paper or people will think you are a racist."

"If we'd run a photo of the man, then people would think I was a sexist."

"Well, you need to start writing stories about players from all races and all cultures. When did you last write a story about a Chinese player?"

"First of all, they are called runners, not players. Second, I don't know of any Chinese runners in Dallas."

"Maybe you should find one."

I renamed Rebecca Sikes, Rebecca "Yikes." Schwartz recruited her from the newspaper's research library, known as "the morgue" in newspaper offices. Yikes knew little about sports and nothing about running. I had to take orders from someone who when asked if she has ever run, replied. "Once, I did The Stairmaster."

On the Rizzo complaint I told her that I had written three columns on him and had a front page cover photo of him winning the Turkey Day race, even though his only comment was his right middle finger.

"Then gear whatever races he wins on him and write some more columns about him. How about a feature on him for next week's Dallas Marathon?"

"He's not running the Dallas Marathon. Besides, I'm already in the middle of a special piece on the 25-year history of the race. I've interviewed past winners, runners who have run every race, and I obtained some old photographs from the first race. I want to write a 50-inch story with vignettes from past participants."

"I don't think anyone would be interested in that. I'd rather just focus on one person."

I scrapped 30 hours work for a story on the 68-year-old woman from the Harry Moss Run. Virginia Rush had about as much to say as Tony Rizzo, and was less interesting. Yikes said she found the story bland and replaced me on the marathon coverage with the Texas Rangers' beat writer Cal Redden, whose story had no quotes and no race description. He thought the race organizers were supposed to bring the top runners to him. Cal's lead:

Runners from all over the country assembled for the Dallas Marathon yesterday under blue skies and cool temperatures. Clayton Edwards looked exhausted as he crossed the finish line as the winner of the 26-mile marathon.

I went nowhere near White Rock Lake that day. I went to Whispering Springs Lake and ran 12 miles on a forest trail that seemed hundreds of miles from the Dallas Marathon and an editor whose apparent goal was to get rid of me. The more I thought about Rebecca Yikes the harder I ran along rolling dirt trails that winded through the thick East Texas pine forest for presumably no one other than me and a lone mountain biker I blew past. I don't know if I reminded Yikes of an ex-boyfriend or what. But this was hate at first sight. Clare's answer as she cut Miles' hot dog at the dinner table was to find a job at another newspaper, perhaps even in Australia.

"Where, Clare? The Moose Junction Monthly News? Maybe I could cover crocodile racing."

Her next suggestion was more absurd. "Come out of retirement, train your butt off and make the 1996 Olympic Team. You finally can reach your dream, Jonny. Once you do that, you can get a job anywhere you want."

I rejected her magical idea as unrealistic. I had not raced in two years, and no way I could work 40-50 hours per week as a sportswriter, support Clare and Miles, and train at the level needed to make a valid attempt. Also, I finally was coping with my failure. The rerun of the 1992 U.S. Olympic Trials 5,000 final stopped playing in my brain. All that remained was a recurring school dream. I was a senior in college, which happened to have classrooms at St. Peter Claver School. I couldn't graduate, because I never went to this one class.

"The dream means there is something in your life you have yet to complete," Clare said. "The only way you will ever stop that dream, mate, is by making the Olympic Team."

"Or dying," I added.

Clare's hopes of making the Olympics faded in the midst of a recurring calf injury she claimed was caused by a lack of zinc. The real culprit was Darcy Ellard, whose run-until-you-drop program finally felled Clare. She caught me looking at her old training logs one night in bed.

"Hey, Langenwanker, those are private."

"Look at this shit. January 21, 1989. Eight kilometer run, 30 times sprint up sand dune, 5K for time, 6K warm down. Then you had a 1,500 meter track race the next day? No wonder why you ran 4:42 and finished last."

"That's because my bloody hamstring cramped on me. Otherwise I would have won it."

"Your hamstring cramped because of the ridiculous workout that jerk made you do the day before."

"Bugger that. If I could go back to the Outback and train with Darcy, I'd make the Olympics long before you ever would."

Paging through the logbook made me less interested in making the Olympic team. I was content on my hour runs around White Rock that began with Miles handing me my running shoes. I walked out our apartment door and looked at this little face in the living room window. When I returned an hour later, his face was still there. Miles met me at the door in his little Spyridon shoes, and I took him for a run around the trail that circled the ponds next to our apartment building. He ran every step with a smile, whether he fell or not. I don't know if he liked running, or just liked being with me.

I wished Clare showed half as much interest in being with me. Her sole focus was on curing her left calf muscle. She went to about every specialist in town. The orthopedist took x-rays. The podiatrist gave her orthotics. The chiropractor cracked her back. The masseur told her to lay on the table naked and said that the pain was coming from her butt. She never went to these quacks, especially the masseur, again. For Christmas I gave her a plane ticket to Flagstaff to see my blind healer, Malcolm Gould. I had suggested him before. But she had no faith in someone she did not know.

"How well do you know the doctors?" I asked. "Just because Doc's got a diploma on his office wall does not make him God."

Clare left the day after Christmas. I wish I could have been there to hear Clare screaming, "Bloody hell," as Malcolm exorcised the demon from her calf muscle. She returned on New Year's Eve, in time for my run from one year to the next. We bundled Miles in a blanket and put him in the baby jogger. He slept through the New Year, which brought fireworks and a healthy calf muscle. Clare kissed me along the way and told me the plane ticket to Flagstaff was the best present she ever received. That night she read Chapter 38. "There's no safe road to the Olympics." Three days later, Clare slipped on an icy bleacher on her first workout and broke her kneecap.

In early 1995 Rebecca Yikes was trying to break my spirit. I interviewed former Dallas high school runner Mitchell Burgess, imprisoned in Oklahoma for selling drugs while competing in college. I followed the three-hour interview behind the razor-wired fences with a 100-inch expose. Yikes browsed it and said, "I don't feel sorry him. I'm not running this."

She also rejected a piece about three women who each had a child with cerebral palsy. They were running the Houston Marathon in an effort to raise money for the disease. "Too sentimental," she said.

She probably would have killed my column on what it was like to be a retired runner, if she hadn't been on vacation. She returned in time to read Tony Rizzo's faxed letter in which he claimed the 4:24 mile I ran that day on the Highland Park Community Track was really a 6:24. Yikes said "the truth probably lies somewhere in the middle. Maybe 5:24?"

My feature leading to the Fort Worth Marathon was on Claude Winkler, who had run a marathon a week for 62 consecutive weeks. Yikes replaced it with a map of the race course and a fact box.

"A marathon a week – that's not such a big deal, is it?" she asked.

I shook my head. "Was Steve Prefontaine a great runner?"

"Who's Steve Prefontaine?"

I saw Claude after the marathon and explained why his story wasn't run. I wrote my race story in the media area and asked race director Warren Tubbs when the results would be done. "Bout half an hour."

That was good news, seeing that Yikes devoted an entire page to the marathon. Tubbs used a new computer system he said would "spit out the results faster than the time it takes to run a hundred meters."

I wrote a sidebar and asked Tubbs if the results were ready. "'Bout half an hour."

I ran for an hour along the Trinity River, ate a greasy hamburger and fries, and returned to Tubbs "'Bout half an hour," he said.

Tubbs must have been referring to how fast it takes a snail to run a hundred meters.

At 11 p.m. I stood behind Tubbs in the control room. He stared at his computer and scratched his forehead. "Now what did I call that dern file?"

Tubbs' oldest son, Leo, grabbed my arm and escorted me to the hallway. "My dad's brain is fried. Why don't you just take whatever results we have and get on out of here."

I drove to Dallas in a PR of 20 minutes with a disk containing partial results and a plan. I suggested to Bernie, the night editor, to run my race story and sidebar and partial results. I inserted Claude Winkler's time from the marathon into my feature on him and told Bernie to use it to fill the space meant for the other results.

After a mad dash that succeeded in meeting the midnight deadline, Bernie said, "I don't know what was more brilliant – your idea to run the Winkler feature or the Winkler feature."

Claude Winkler can't run down his block in Tuscola, Mississippi without someone yelling, 'Run Forrest, Run.' He can't eat anything other than pasta on Fridays, and he can't walk without a limp all week.

But what the 53-year-old Winkler can do is run a marathon every weekend, no matter if he has to drive his '73 Ford LTD to Ardvark, Alabama or Anchorage, Alaska.

I felt like I had run a marathon, when I went to bed at 2 a.m. I don't know what hurt worse at 7:30 the next morning, the telephone or the editor ringing in my ear.

"Who gave you the authority to run that story, and what the hell happened to the results? I got Dick Schwartz out of bed this morning to alert him on this."

I took two aspirin and a shot of Bourbon to pull me through an explanation to which Yikes responded. "No excuse. Your responsibility is to get us those results no matter if you have to write down all 10,000 finishers as they cross the line."

I would have quit then if it hadn't been for that cute woman in a bathrobe, hunting the real estate pages for her dream home or that little boy in his Texas Rangers pajamas, needing a backyard to run through sprinklers and play with his trucks. We saved enough money in two years to look for a house and enough money to buy one in June. I was willing to write whatever Yikes wanted me to write to keep Clare and Miles happy.

After March and April passed and Tony Rizzo continued his string of victories en route to the Dallas Runner of the Year Award, I ran out of adjectives for the word "great" and patience for someone calling me a chump after every victory. Recent letters to the editor came from runners who wanted to read about someone else. I respected their wishes after Big Ted's Twilight 10K. Rizzo won by two minutes, and his post-race interview was verbatim of his last three interviews:

"I felt really good today. I just went out and ran as hard as I could, and the good Lord blessed me with the strength to keep it going."

I asked him if he was getting bored with winning.

"No way, pal. I always like to win. But the problem is there is no one in this town who can keep up with me. They are either too afraid to race me or they don't have the guts to try and stay with me."

I led my story with Sheila Rosales, a Dallas native who rode 24 hours on a bus from Brownsville and arrived only 10 minutes from the start. Sheila overcame a 400-meter deficit in the final mile and outsprinted defending champion Nicole Summers in the final 30 meters to win in a course record 36:23.

The road from Brownsville to the start of Big Ted's Twilight starting line was bumpy and tedious but worth the thrill Sheila Rosales found at the end of her 700-mile journey.

That prompted Rizzo's Monday fax to the editor. The words certainly were penned by him, but signed by his buddy:

Dear Mr. Schwartz:

Langenchump's article on Big Ted's Twilight 10K was a disgrace to the running community. He writes about a woman who won by a mere two "seconds" and barely a paragraph about the man who won the overall race by two "minutes." Langenchump neglected the men's winner, because he hates seeing him in the spotlight and doesn't have the guts to try and knock him out of it. Furthermore, Langenchump is a racist. He doesn't want to write about anyone of Italian descent.

Yikes responded later that week with a photo spread and half-page feature on Rizzo, written by Marcia Vanderberg. Her story helped cure Clare's insomnia and uncovered why Rizzo was the lightest tanned Italian in America. He was adopted.

An alarm clock begs its owner to hit the snooze button before dawn Monday in the Spartan confines of a North Dallas apartment. Tony Rizzo rises sharply, diligently from the warm spring sheets, carefully ties his red and white sneakers, marches confidently out the door and onto the streets without a yawn and with one thought.

"I own these Dallas streets," he says. "Nobody, I mean nobody is willing to punish their body enough to beat me. I am the King, and all the other runners are the peasants."

The quote wasn't enough to show Yikes that Rizzo was full of himself. Two nights later a tornado struck south of Dallas and leveled Brinks, Texas. The next morning Yergo Slovinski from Yugoslavia rode through the town in the Tour de Texas Cycling Race and grabbed the overall lead. I wrote:

Yergo Slovinski thought he escaped his war-torn country until he dodged the broken tree limbs, roof shingles, and assorted debris that lined the path through Brinks and his glorious journey in stage six of the Tour de Texas.

Yikes sounded like the Wicked Witch of the West on a Sunday morning call that made me want to drop a house on her.

"You insensitive pig! It's one thing you neglect the top runner in town. Now you are making fun of this poor man's homeland. You have called his entire country a dump."

I pushed the telephone back to my ear. "Sorry, Rebecca. But are you aware of what's going on in Yugoslavia? You weren't planning a summer vacation there by any chance."

"I don't need your sarcasm. I am beginning to think Rizzo is right about you."

I was not going to let her comments ruin a special week. Clare found a perfect house, just north of Dallas. It had three bedrooms, a little study, a nice garden, and a large backyard. There was a large park down the street, where I imagined someday hitting baseballs and throwing the football to Miles. Friday, June 2, 1995 was the closing date, right after lunch with Larry Shaw at Kepler's Kafe. It was the first time anyone from the office invited me to lunch. I ordered a large turkey sandwich and fries and took a big bite. As I chewed, Larry talked.

"Jonny, this is very hard. But I just wanted to bring you here today to let you know that you are being replaced as the fitness writer for *The Dallas Star*."

I stopped chewing. Larry continued.

"We've decided we need a fresh approach. Marcia Vanderberg is taking over your beat until we find a replacement."

I swallowed the turkey and threw the sandwich on the plate. "Dad gummit, Larry. Couldn't you have told me that after I finished my lunch? Now I can't eat. Didn't Schwartz ever teach you guys how to fire someone?"

Larry smiled. "Sorry, Jonny, this is my first time. I'll try and do better next time."

I knew Larry was just the messenger, doing the dirty work for an asshole who didn't have the guts to do it himself. "Why did Schwartz send you, instead of Rebecca?"

"I volunteered. Besides, Rebecca wouldn't have taken you to lunch."

I arrived at the mortgage broker's office, where Clare sat in a light blue church dress and Miles played with his matchbox cars in the corner. Clare held a silver pen in her hand and stared at the legal papers on the broker's desk. I asked Clare to step outside the glass office. Moments later, the broker witnessed two people in tears. One comforting her husband for the loss of his dream job and the other comforting his wife for the loss of her dream house.

"What are you going to do now?" Clare asked as we unpacked the boxes in our cramped, little apartment.

The answer came the next morning on the starting line of the Dallas 5K Dash for the Dollars. Rizzo stood there in his black high-cut shorts and Wooosh Texas racing singlet. A victory would be his 10th straight, earn him a first-place prize of $1,000, and assure him the title of Dallas' fastest runner. The starter strolled up to Rizzo. "So how far you gonna' win by this time, Tony."

Rizzo adjusted his Oakley's. "Don't know. Two, three minutes. Whatever I feel like. Now why don't you walk your beefy butt back there, shoot your fucking little pistol, and get this thing going? I got things to do today."

The shot from the starter's pistol blasted Rizzo off the starting line and into his customary lead. He waved at the spectators along the 5K route in North Dallas. About a mile into the race Rizzo realized he was not alone. He heard someone breathing behind him. He looked down to see a ragged pair of white Spyridons running stride for stride with his brand new black Woooshs. He glanced back at the runner on his shoulder.

I smiled. "Your worst nightmare has just come true, pal."

Rizzo immediately surged, and I covered it. He pushed harder and harder the next mile. He looked back again. I winked. He hammered as hard as he could in the final mile. I stayed on his shoulder no matter how tired my rusty legs felt or how much my lungs burned. Around the final turn, Rizzo threw an elbow at my chest. I blocked it. I could see the finish line and the spectators lining the homestretch. I could hear the *Rocky* music. I looked at the sweat dripping down Rizzo's sunglasses, his gritted teeth, and his right shoulder tattoo that read, "Perfecto."

He stared at me running alongside him. "Make the first move." I said between breaths.

Rizzo sprinted hard, his knees pumping toward his chest and his arms lifting from his waist to his nose. Within a moment, a flash of Langenfelder whipped past him like he was running in place. I never slowed up until I reached the end of the chute. I grabbed the $1,000 check from the race director and jogged toward the parking lot until a woman waddled up from behind with a tape recorder from the 70's. I stopped long enough for Marcia Vanderberg to introduce herself as the fitness writer for *The Dallas Star*. Amazing, she covered running in Dallas for a newspaper where I worked for more than two years and didn't even know who I was.

She stuck the microphone to my dry lips. "So how does it feel to beat the great Tony Rizzo?"

I grabbed the microphone from Marcia's hand and grinned.

"No fucking comment."

◆◆◆

I stared at Steve Prefontaine that afternoon following the Dallas 5K Dash for the Dollars. His picture on the television screen illuminated my apartment living room and left the two of us, again, eyeball to eyeball.

The 20th anniversary of Pre's death was marked by a documentary called "Fire on the Track: the Life Story of Steve Prefontaine," which aired before the Prefontaine Classic. I watched for an hour as Pre grew from a boy to a high school record-holder to an Olympian to a man who stood up for his friends and fellow runners until that fateful night his car crashed into a rock on a winding hillside where he trained every week.

He died never realizing his dream of winning an Olympic medal. I wondered as I sat there that afternoon how I could sit here breathing comfortable breaths and not pursuing my dream. Was I too old? I don't think so. Off jolly jogs around White Rock Lake, baby stroller runs around an apartment pond trail, and an occasional glory days' romp of the Forest Hill track I whipped the fastest man in town in the best shape of his life.

Two-year-old Miles sat on my lap in our Crossroads West Apartment as I watched men I used to beat on the track at Hayward Field, where I trained and raced so many times. I turned to Miles as the winner crossed the finish line of the 5,000 meters in a time I could have shattered.

"Dadda go run?"

"Yes, my boy. Daddy's going running."

I ran every day that summer. I ran at the Pacesetter Sports All-Comers meets at the Highland Park Community Track, improving my mile from 4:16 to 4:12 to 4:09. I set a course record of 14:43 at the Sizzlin' Summer 5K Series around Wyndham Pond. I ran and ran without anyone but Miles knowing my intention. His bedtime story one night was the 1992 Olympic issue of *Track and Field News*. His face was lit by the pictures of the runners in the red, white, and blue from Barcelona, the flame that soared above them, and a photo of Centennial Olympic Stadium in Atlanta. I put my arms around Miles and slid our cheeks together. "One day will you come watch me run in the Olympics."

"Yes, Dadda."

Clare didn't know I ran the Dallas 5K Dash for the Dollars. She must have thought the grand I deposited in the bank was my severance check. I doubt anyone read that I won the race. The thrilling upset was hidden in the sixth paragraph of Marcia Vanderberg's race report, somewhere between "an army of runners infiltrated the North Dallas concrete in a sneaker-pounding salute to their beloved sport" and "a halo of pollen from roadside daisies submerged on the race course as the runners surged dutifully toward their desired destination."

Two months later, on our summer vacation to Northern Minnesota, I fulfilled a promise to Zac Groves of visiting the place he grew up and the wooded trails he traversed. Zac once told me this place was like heaven, so I figured he must be running through here everyday. Zac and I once ran the Prefontaine Memorial Loop. Nine years later, I was running the Zac Groves Memorial 10K. I didn't lie to Clare that August afternoon, when I left the home of Zac's brother Nathan. I told her the same as before every race in Dallas. "I'm going for a little run."

Clare decided to take a walk with Miles and stopped to cheer the runners at the halfway point. Miles pointed from his stroller as I charged from the distance, well in front of my nearest pursuer.

"Dadda run," he told his mom.

All I heard as I ran by was, "Nice 'little run,' Langenwanker."

Clare caught up to me as I jogged my warm down on a dirt road along the cemetery where Zac was buried. "So when were you going to tell me, mate?"

I stopped, wiped the sweat from my contact lenses with my shirt tail, and picked up Miles. "Tell you what?"

"That you are taking another shot at the Olympics."

"Quite a 'long' shot. Did you see my time today?"

"Bugger that. I saw you cross the finish line with the most content grin I've ever seen on ya.' Let's face it, Jonny, you're a runner. You love it just as much as your friend who is lying in the ground over there."

Clare was right. I had been in denial the past 2 ½ years. There was nothing better than the rush of adrenaline I felt when I whipped past Tony Rizzo. I enjoyed the pain in the final backstretch of those All Comers miles, when I felt like

I couldn't make the finish line but somehow did. I liked pounding mile after mile in Zac's Memorial Run, even though it felt like someone was hitting me in the head with a hammer. It felt so good when it stopped, and I had won the race.

I handed Miles to Clare and continued my warm down. I looked back. "Ain't got anything else to do."

Rebecca Yikes saw to that. Mom, who had been cutting out my columns and pasting them in scrapbook, called and asked why Marcia Vanderberg's mug had replaced mine. I told her I moved into an editing position.

"You always lie to your Mum? Clare asked as I steered the Toyota to Indianapolis.

"Not a lie. Every Thursday morning, I lay in bed with a pencil and edit Vanderberg's column on the newspaper."

"When are going to tell her?"

"Tell who what?"

"Tell your mum you're trying out for the Olympics again, Langenwanker?"

"When I'm damn good and ready, and how many fricking times do I have to ask you to stop calling me Langenwanker?"

"About as many times as I ask you not to swear in front of Miles. And keep the bloody car on the road?"

Another thing I remembered about running is how irritable I became before a race. I made Clare sleep with Miles in his bed at the Motel 6.99 the night before the Indianapolis Open Track and Field Meet. I yelled at her for steaming up our hotel bathroom, for waking up Miles from his nap, and for taking too long to eat her lunch.

"You're a real asshole before a race," she said.

"Never realized it before," I said.

"Never was married before."

I wasn't much nicer in the race that night at The Indianapolis Track and Field Stadium. I elbowed anyone who brushed my side, pushed the person in front of me for running too slow, and showed my finger to the guy who accidentally clipped my heels. I was a real jerk in the last four laps, leaving the field behind and winning the 5,000 meters by a straightaway. I took off my shoes just past the finish line and tossed them on the ground. Clare leaned over the railing with a little boy with big blue eyes and a smile.

"Dadda running," Miles said.

"Dadda winning," Clare said. "What's wrong, Jonny? Brassed off because you didn't lap everybody?"

I pointed at the huge lit numbers on the large scoreboard at the end of the track that read, "14:38.88."

"I don't care how hot and humid it is, I used to run that in my sleep. I can't believe I hurt so bad to run that slow. I'll have to run more than a minute faster to make the Olympic team next summer."

I waved at the press box. "The meet's over! Turn off the scoreboard! I don't want to see those numbers again!"

I ran a three-mile warm down and the numbers 14:38.88 still filled the scoreboard. I yelled again, "Turn it off! It's embarrassing!"

The numbers still lit the sky when I drove away and were still there three hours later when we returned from dinner. I looked at them in my rearview mirror.

"Gonna make that Olympic team, Jonny?"

"You better 'effing' believe I am."

The first person I sought in my Olympic attempt was Father Litzke. I hadn't meditated since the 1992 Olympic Trials. The Indianapolis race showed that my mind was rustier than my body. But Father Litzke didn't want to know about running. He wanted to know about my life. He sat in his chair in the candlelight. He must have been in his mid-80's now. But he looked the same. His soft voice, almost a whisper, calmed me even before the meditation. I told him about Clare and Miles, Dick Schwartz and Rebecca Yikes and Tony Rizzo, and my frustration at being fired from my fitness column.

"All this anger you have inside you is weighting you down, Jonny. You must release this torment inside you, if you want to reach your goal."

"Yes, father. How do I do that?"

"I want you to close your eyes and repeat after me. "Our Father who art in heaven, hallowed be thy name.""

"Our Father who art in heaven, hallowed be thy name."

"Thy kingdom come thy will be done, on Earth as it is in heaven."

"Thy kingdom come thy will be done, on Earth as it is in heaven..."

"...Forgive us our sins as we forgive those who sinned against us."

"Forgive us our sins as we forgive those who sinned against us."

Father Litzke paused long enough to let me feel myself breathe. Then he repeated,

"Forgive us our sins as we forgive those who sinned against us."

Father Litzke paused again and told me to join along to complete the prayer. "You can open your eyes now," he said. "This session is over."

It was the shortest and the strangest session, but the one that made the most sense.

Father's Litzke's F word was forgiveness. It released my anger and helped me see again. I needed to forgive Clare for stealing my freedom, Dick Schwartz and Rebecca Yikes for taking my job, and Tony Rizzo for being an asshole. But could Clare forgive me for getting her pregnant – as she claimed - and cooping her in a one bedroom apartment and keeping her from sand dune repeats and a coach with a chair and a whip? I returned home with a bottle of wine and a hug.

"I'm sorry, Clare."

"Sorry for what?"

I had my own F word in the months leading to the 1996 U.S. Olympic Trials. Focus. I assembled a team of supporters to help me take a run at my long-sought and almost forgotten goal. Clare started training too soon from her kneecap fracture and strained the ligaments. She took a sales clerk job at Pace-

347

setter Sports to help pay the bills.

Larry Shaw called and said I could cover high school football, basketball, baseball, softball, and soccer games on a freelance basis for *The Dallas Star.* "Anything but running," he said.

I called The Stallion, who laughed when I told him my plans. "I knew you couldn't stay retired for long."

I needed a sparring partner, someone with whom to grind out a few runs and track workouts. I found the only man who could keep up with me in Dallas, on a Sunday run along White Rock Lake.

"Hey there, Perfecto."

Rizzo turned his head and stared through his Oakleys. "Hey, Langenchump."

"That's Langen 'champ' to you, pal."

Rizzo spent the rest of the run talking about himself and complaining about the new fitness writer for *The Dallas Star.* "Can't believe they got rid of you," he said.

"Gee, I wonder why?"

I asked Rizzo what's wrong with former *Dallas Star* football writer Babe Golinski other than the fact he got the job because he missed a meeting, the first race he ever saw he covered, thinks a 5K is five miles, refers to some races as a 10K marathon, and wrote that the fastest 400 meter man in the world is Michael Jackson.

"His only subjects in his columns are participants who have cancer," Rizzo said.

After winning the Awesome Autumn 15K in a thunderstorm, Rizzo had asked Golinski if he would write about him in the next day's paper."

"Sure, if you get hit by lightning," Golinski said. "If you die, you might even make the front page."

I ran through the rainstorms and snowstorms and hailstorms and loved every mile of the 121 I pounded every week from October through January. I researched my old logbooks for a program that would set me up for the Olympic Trials in Atlanta in late June. Several times I took my tent and sleeping bag to Whispering Springs Lake in East Texas and hammered through the pine forest trails. Dark clouds greeted Rizzo and me on our first track workout at the Forest Hill track in mid-February. The Stallion stood on the starting line with a stopwatch. We tore off our sweats, and The Stallion told us to put them back on.

"What do mean?" Rizzo asked. "It's not even raining yet."

The Stallion stared at the lightning crackling in the distance and counted. "I studied meteorology in college. According to my calculation, the lightning will be on top of us in six to seven minutes."

"Fuck it, let's start the workout," Rizzo said.

I grabbed my sweats and walked with Rizzo to the parking lot. "No, this guy knows his shit – at least when it comes to the weather."

The three of us sat in The Stallion's pickup truck. Six minutes after The Stallion made his call, a lightning bolt lit up the track. "Oh, shit, that would have been us," Rizzo said.

"Too bad," I said. "You could have got your name in the paper,"

Rizzo led off the 'Round the Rock Relay, a low-key 3 X 5K event hosted by the Dallas Runners Club and my first race of the season, the first Saturday of March. Rizzo handed the baton to Clare, healthy but unfit after a four-month layoff. I waited next to Miles in the baby jogger until Clare showed in the distance, two minutes behind the leader of an all-male team.

"Dadda push me."

"No, Miles. You wait here when Mom comes."

Clare, who was passed by six men, handed me the baton and smiled. "Go Langenwanker!"

I launched from the exchange zone and glanced back, "Don't call me that!"

I breezed past the huffing and puffing runners of the all-male teams ahead of me and gained steadily on the leader. I went by him with 400 meters to go. He yelled, "Oh, you guys!"

I slapped Rizzo a high-five at the finish and went to shake the hand of runner-up anchor Conrad Morgan. He rejected it.

"What the fuck is your problem?" Rizzo said.

"Why don't you pricks go run in the Olympics, instead coming out here showing us up?" Morgan said. "The only reason you are any good is because you got talent."

I followed Morgan to the refreshment stand and grabbed a banana. "No, fella, the reason why we are good is because we train our asses off day and night, and I've been doing it for 24 years. Me and this guy are the fastest runners in town, and you're telling me we don't belong out here?"

I continued training my ass off day and night. Miles played in the long jump pit at the Forest Hill track, as Rizzo and I ran around and around it. Rizzo agreed to be the rabbit for the first 5K of the Texas Relays 10,000 meters, if I stayed away from the Dallas road races.

"You can be the fastest runner in Dallas," I said. "I'll be the fastest runner in the United States."

I didn't know what shape I was in as I stood on the Memorial Stadium starting line next to a guy who wore sunglasses even at night. I just wanted to run hard for 25 laps.

"How many laps for the 5K?" Rizzo asked.

"You don't run a lot of track races, do you?"

I told Rizzo to run as many laps in 69 seconds as possible.

He grinned. "I'm good at 69."

He proved it by hitting 69 on 12 successive laps in his racing flats and bringing me through the 5,000 in the same time I ran on the relay – 14:22. There were more spectators on the track than in the stands that cool Wednesday evening at Memorial Stadium in Austin. They watched a 38-year-old man run with the precision of a Swiss clock, clicking at exact intervals. The other runners let me lap them on the inside and cheered as I drove for the finish and the Trials' qualifying standard of 28:40.

I barely could hear the bell or the split over Rizzo, the rabbit-turned-cheerleader, who screamed from the infield, "Come one, Langenchump, you need a 65!"

The call sent me screaming down the backstretch and up the world's longest homestretch. I finished and looked through the sweat in my eyes to the scoreboard lit numbers, larger than the ones on the Indianapolis track. "28:39.83."

I stepped off the track and fell to the artificial turf. I closed my eyes and thanked God for steering me back to the track and a berth in my fifth Olympic Trials. I opened my eyes to Rizzo's grin. "PR," he said.

"No, I ran 28:04 in Paris nine years ago."

"No, I was talking about me. That was a 5K PR by 20 seconds."

I stayed in Austin the rest of the week, cruised around the Town Lake trail, then pitched my tent at Bennington State Park and hammered the rolling forest trails. I returned to Austin four weeks later to win the 1,500 meters in 3:46.3 at the Longhorn Open and then traveled to Vancouver for the Canada International Meet, where I raced three Kenyans with sub-13:20 personal bests. I was still breathing hard as I pressed the buttons on the pay phone just outside the track.

"Clare, I've got good news and bad news."

"What's the bad news?"

"I lost my first race since coming out of retirement."

"What's the good news?"

"I just ran 13:34."

My success baffled me. How could I take so much time away from competition and run so well and feel so good? The Stallion answered over a pizza the day of my return.

"You're more rested and not beat up as you would be if you had kept plugging away. You had a chance to clear your mind, and now you want it more than ever."

Also, I never lost my experience. I knew how to train and how to race. I knew how to push myself and how to pace myself. It was like riding a bicycle or playing a game of mattress polo. You never forget. I ran nine miles from our apartment to 2000 Hickory Lane the day before my departure to Atlanta for the Olympic Trials. Clare, Miles, and I sat around the table and feasted on Mom's pot roast and mashed potatoes.

"So how do you like your chances?" Mom asked.

I cut my meat without looking up. "What are you talking about?"

"The Olympic Trials. Are you going to make it this time or what?"

I chewed my meat and looked at Clare, who raised her hands as if to say, "I never told her."

"How did you know, Mom?"

"I was born 79 years ago, not yesterday. Look at you with your gaunt face and your bony ribs. You haven't looked like this since before the last Olympic

Trials."

I put down my knife and fork. "Sorry, Mom. That Olympic flame just keeps calling me"

Mom smiled. She joined the support team and came to the airport to wish me luck. I comforted Mom by telling her I decided to run only the 5,000 meters and not risk my life with a 5K-10K double in probable broiling conditions, like I did in Indianapolis in 1988.

The Stallion was there at the airport gate and so was Rizzo, who for the first time wasn't wearing his sunglasses.

"Jonny, I just wanted to say I'm sorry for what I did to you. I was a real ass wipe."

I patted Rizzo's "Perfecto" tattoo. I looked at a man who grew up not knowing his true father or even his adopted father, who abandoned him at age three. "Fuck it." I said. "Without you I wouldn't be standing here with a chance to finally realize my dream."

I looked at Clare, who never complained about losing her dream house or the money I spent to make the Olympic Trials. She never moaned about us being so broke that she and Miles couldn't afford to even drive to Atlanta to watch me run.

She kissed me on the cheek. "Do your best, Langenwanker."

I walked toward the gate ramp and turned around to see Miles holding a little American flag and standing alongside his Mom. I walked back, crouched down, and wiped the tear off his little face.

"Dadda go run?"

I stared into his blue eyes. "Yes, my boy. Daddy's going running."

◆◆◆

You ever go to a party wearing faded Levis and sipping a Bud, look around at stuff shirts you don't know wearing ties and drinking martinis, and wonder, "What the hell am I doing here?"

That's how I felt on the starting line of my 5,000 meters heat at the 1996 U.S. Olympic Track and Field Trials. I stared around at the 80,000 mostly empty seats of Atlanta's Centennial Olympic Stadium and then to the young men to my right and left and then to the nearest exit. I didn't fit in with runners with Army crew-cuts and barbed-wire tattoos around their biceps, an earring or two, and maybe a goatee. These kids didn't drink or cuss. They married their high school sweetheart, whom they proposed to over the telephone, and went to bed at dusk. They drank cappuccino in an outdoor cafe, drove a BMW, and never had a Coke or ate fast food.

The guy next to me in the baby blue UCLA singlet shook my hand and said, "Good luck, sir."

Then I realized that half the field wasn't born when I started running. They weren't around when JFK was shot or when man walked on the moon. They never owned a leisure suit or spoke into a CB radio or typed on a portable typewriter. I hadn't even used this new thing called the Internet. My roommate, steepler Alex Ingram, thought I was a track official. I told him I was running in my fifth Olympic Trials, ranked in the top 10 in the United States a couple times, ran the 20th fastest 10,000 meters in the world one year, and missed making the team to Barcelona by seven seconds.

"You're the fastest runner I've never heard of," he said.

What made me belong on that thin red layer of rubber carpet in that concrete sauna was the dream shared by the other 10 heat-one runners who simultaneously left the starting line at the bang of the starter's pistol. We all wanted to make the Olympic team.

My break from retirement allowed me to reunite with the butterflies that mass produced in my stomach overnight. I had forgotten what it was like to barf at the sight of breakfast flapjacks and spend all afternoon watching movie previews on my hotel room television. I thought, "I could be home playing baseball or flying a kite with Miles."

I used every bit of Father Litzke's magic to move my body from that bed to the track shuttle bus to the starting line. "Be in the moment," I thought. "Be in the moment."

The shot from the starter's pistol killed the butterflies. I filed into a pack that made me anything but intimidated. How could I fear runners whom I never had seen nor heard of before? I watched these rookies weaving in and out of the field, surging from first to last, passing in lane three on the turn, and simply running themselves out of the Olympic Trials. On one lap, the UCLA runner went from last to first and then faded back to where he started before the lap was completed.

I held my position at mid-pack and moved past the energy-wasted youngsters down the backstretch of the penultimate backstretch and into a lead pack of the four automatic qualifiers who separated ourselves from the non-qualifiers. I almost laughed in the homestretch as the three runners in front of me raced for the finish line, only wasting their energy for the final. I jogged the stretch and checked back to make sure there were no late surprises. While the three other runners shook hands with each other and consoled the others, I walked through the tunnel and talked to reporters as I munched an energy bar. While I warmed down and then caught the first shuttle bus back to the Peachtree Suites, they sat in the stands and watched the next two 5,000 meters heats.

I called Clare, who was watching the final lap of heat three on television.

"You looked good, honey" she said. "How did it feel?"

"Like taking candy from a pack of babies."

The only tactical error I made the night of my Olympic Trials heat was not yanking the telephone cord out of my hotel room wall. I answered the next morning on the fifth ring.

"Langenslugger."

"Yes."

"It's Dick Schwartz."

These were the first words the slime manure of *The Dallas Star* sports department spoke to me since my job interview. I sat up in bed and wondered, "What in the hell does he want?"

"Hot nuff for ya' last night, Jonny."

"Probably not as hot as where you come from."

Schwartz paused in an attempt to get my insult, but probably didn't. "There's a front-page column about your wonderful comeback in the Fort Worth paper this morning. I was just wondering why our paper got scooped."

"Don't know. Why don't ask your track writer? You know these post-race interviews are open to all credentialed reporters."

"No one here knew you were even running anymore. You write for us; why didn't you tell us, instead of making us look like a bunch of fucking idiots. And more importantly, making 'me' look like a fucking idiot."

I pulled the phone away and muttered, "It doesn't take much to do that."

"What?"

"As I recall, Mr. Schwartz, you sent one of your goons to fire me about this time last year. But thank you for giving me the incentive to take another shot at the Olympics."

Schwartz's inaudible mumbling told me he didn't know whether to thank me or kill me. "You better make that team, because I'm sending a reporter there to talk to you."

"You know what they say? If you want something done right, do it yourself."

"I'd give anything to cover these meets, but I'm the editor. I have to run this show."

"Nah, you never had the balls to begin with."

My phone slam ensured that I never would cover another game or write another word for *The Dallas Star*. Clyde Kenworthy's column in the Fort Worth Daily Reporter already had done that. Clare faxed a copy to the hotel.

Jonny Langenfelder thanked several old coaches and friends for a career that has consumed the last 2½ decades, after qualifying for the 5,000 meters final of the U.S. Olympic Track and Field Trials in Atlanta last night.

But if the 38-year-old Dallas resident finishes in the top three on Friday night to earn a return ticket to Centennial Olympic Stadium,

353

there is one man he will owe a special thanks. Dick Schwartz, sports editor of The Dallas Star, never timed Langenfelder's workouts or gave him advice on training or nutrition or the slightest hint of encouragement.

Schwartz simply slipped him the two words he has sent so many other sportwriters via messenger, scribbled memo, or garbled answering machine.

"You're fired."

My heat one effort around the Olympic oval had me fired up. I didn't know any of these guys and didn't care. This "I'll show these young whippersnappers how to run an Olympic Trials final" attitude carried me through the pressure cooker of the slowest countdown to show time in sports history. Ingram went home to his fiancee in Florida after his early exit in the steeplechase, leaving me with four white walls as my only companions.

My 5,000 meters final was like one of those corny television game shows. – "Make the Olympic team and you win a trip to see the Olympic flame and a burning memory that will last a lifetime. The tale of your miraculous comeback will be sent over the wire to thousands of newspapers whose editors will come calling with a full-time sportswriting position and an expense account.

"Miss the team and watch the flame flicker on the first flight out of Atlanta. Oh, but don't forget your parting gift – a certificate with your misspelled name that shows you participated in another bloody track and field trials."

I slept with that thought the afternoon of June 21st. Another five rings from the bedside telephone woke me up.

I grabbed the telephone without looking for it. "Clare?"

"Guess again?"

I rubbed my eyes and looked at the ceiling. "Not in the mood for a guessing game."

"It's Fubby Tuppernacker, the 'former' head track and field coach at Caprock State."

"Somebody wise up and finally fire your ass, Fubby."

"No, I retired from coaching and work in the athletic office. But I read a column in yesterday's Fort Worth paper about a sportswriter whose ass was fired."

"Yeah, so what do you want, Fubby?"

"I want to try and get you the job as the cross country and distance coach at Caprock State."

I sat up in bed and turned on my lamp. "I'm a sportswriter. What do I know about coaching?"

"A lot more than he does," I thought.

"You must know a lot about running by now."

"Yeah, but I want to write, and now is no time to think about my future. I've got sort of an important race in a few hours."

I lowered the phone until Fubby's faint call of "Langendorner?" lifted it back to my ear."

"What, Fubby?"

"How do you think you're gonna do tonight?"

I yanked the telephone cord out of the wall and turned off the light.

The next lights I saw were atop Centennial Olympic Stadium. They surrounded the 16 finalists who listened to their names echoing through the large arena. The only name I recognized was my own. I shook my legs and arms through the introduction of All American and All Conference performers in the red of the Wooosh Track Club, the green of Thunderbolt, the blue of Dazzler, and my yellow of Spyridon. I had the same shorts and singlet and the same spikes I wore in my last Olympic Trials final.

The guy next to me didn't seem to have a running club. He was a heat magnet in an all black singlet, knee-length shorts, and floppy black socks and with a cheetah emblem on the front of his jersey. He shaved his head and his tree-trunk legs, but left whiskers on his face. He hung round, bronzed earrings from each lobe and wrapped a red bandanna around his head. All he needed was an eye patch and a metal claw and he was Captain Hook.

He also had a down under accent and the biggest nose this side of the Outback.

"Good luck, mate," he said.

My reply, "Aye, Aye, Captain," was overwhelmed by this thought, "There's at least one guy I can beat."

The starter's pistol blast sent us onto the race course slower than blindfolded prisoners walking the plank. After a 4:35 first mile, I thought, "Am I in the 10,000?"

A bearded guy in red shorts and singlet answered that with a surge that made me think I was in the 1,500. He stretched us into a single file of chasers, drop-offs, and those holding on for dear life. I held on to the latter group and the slim hope that the brutal heat or the humidity or the insane surges would bring the dreamers and dopers back to reality.

With four laps to go, I glanced up at the huge Jumbotron to see where everyone went. I hung in there, not necessarily to make the Olympic team, but to finish the race. I questioned that decision to come out of retirement, to tell Dick Schwartz he had no balls, and to show up on the starting line. Sweat flooded my eyes so severely I couldn't see the number on the lap counter and couldn't hear the splits over the crowd's roar for the winning pole vault clearance. I was weak, tired, dehydrated, disoriented and still passing people. I heard the bell from atop the penultimate homestretch and went by three disintegrated runners as I started the final lap.

I passed two more runners on the backstretch and moved alongside Captain Hook around the final turn. His sudden surge forced me into lane two on the bend, and he held me off into the homestretch. I dug my blistered feet into the rubber and moved my arms and head faster than my aching legs. I definitely was in the moment – the moment of complete agony. Somehow I kept closing in on a blurry finish line, kept battling the man who perhaps could keep me from the Olympics. I closed so fast I almost ran into the back of a green singlet. I tumbled at the finish line, not knowing if was third, fourth, or eighth. Clare, Miles, and anyone else watching from the stands or their living room knew if I made the Olympic team before I did.

I sat up on the track, took a towel from an official, wiped my eyes, and stared at the distant Jumbotron. My 20-second wait for the replay of the finish seemed like 20 minutes. My heart beat faster than the stride that carried me to the finish. Finally, a runner in a red singlet emerged on the screen. He waved at the crowd and threw his hands up as he crossed the finish line. I kept staring at the colored screen that lit up the night. "Oh please, God. Oh please..." I whispered.

Then came a blue singlet and then a green and then me five meters behind in fourth place, a stride ahead of Captain Hook. I lowered my eyes from the screen and stuck the towel in my face, a moment that hurt most of all.

A pity clap from the stands distracted me from my devastation. I turned around to see Captain Hook jogging up the homestretch. I shook my head at the chap, who took the bandanna off his head and waved it to the crowd. I don't know if I was more demoralized to have finished fourth and one spot from the Olympic team or having to sprint so hard to lap a man whom I had not known was in the last place.

I turned my head to see the three Olympians hugging each other, taking group pictures for a row of photographers, signing autographs, and starting a victory lap with small American flags. I walked to the exit tunnel with Captain Hook, who patted me on the back and said, "Good race, mate."

"I was right," I thought. "I *knew* I could beat him."

PART VII

TUMBLING FORWARD

August 3, 1996

Centennial Olympic Stadium is lit by hundreds of floodlights and the Olympic flame as the 15 finalists for the 5,000 meters step to the starting line on a mild – by Atlanta standards – Saturday evening.

The multi-colored uniforms and spikes reflect off a television camera lens that sends the only light through a dark apartment in Dallas, Texas. I sit with my legs crossed in front of the television, the only item other than pizza crumbs not boxed and wrapped with packing tape. The sofa, beds, desk, dining table, and chairs have been moved to the U-Haul trailer outside the door.

The starter's pistol fire moves the runners off the line and me closer to the television screen. The runners strike the hallowed surface that will become the Atlanta Braves' outfield after the flame is extinguished. The next-door Fulton County Stadium, where Hank Aaron surpassed Babe Ruth with his 715th home run, will become a parking lot. It would take a gold medal from the only American finalist to match the roar Aaron created with his blast into the left-field bullpen 22 years before. The only uproar from the apartment comes when the network goes to commercial after Kenya's Tom Nyariki tows the field through the first three laps. I suffer through 6 ½ minutes of commercials that includes the Budweiser frogs and a preview of "Third Rock from the Sun."

"Come on!" I shout. "We're missing the whole fricking race."

The only change during the six-lap pause is the lead Kenyan. Shem Kororia has assumed command and is shadowed by American Bob Kennedy, a cue for NBC announcers Tom Hammond and Craig Masback.

"Kennedy is the news here in striking distance," Hammond says, "a rare occurrence for U.S. men in distance running."

"Shades of Steve Prefontaine," Masback says. "Twenty-four years ago at the Munich Olympics with four laps to go, it was Prefontaine who took the lead and started pushing the pace."

Masback continues pushing the microphone with a lap-long prattle about Kenyan race tactics, which makes me reach for the mute button. I stop to hear the crowd's surge for the bearded American record-holder, who takes the lead with two laps to go. I tune out Masback's recitation of running facts and figures and stare at the blue-clad runner steaming down the backstretch as Pre did in Munich. But Kennedy has no response to the move made by Burundi's Venuste Niyongabo with 500 meters to go.

The green-clad African launches himself through the final lap, leaving 1992 Olympic silver medalist Paul Bitok and defending champion Dieter

359

Baumann of Germany in his wake. Bitok, Morocco's Khalid Boulami, and Baumann close on Niyongabo in the homestretch, only to fall a few meters short. Kennedy finishes sixth, racing that Masback calls great, not gutsy. Niyongabo slaps Kennedy's hand and walks past the defeated Kenyans to the embrace of his coach and to the announcers' account of the winner's war-torn country.

"Over 100,000 people killed in tribal clashes over the last three years," Masback says.

"When they asked him his tribal affiliation, he refused to answer," Hammond says. "Perhaps, his victory in the Olympic 5,000 meter run could do a small part in uniting that country."

Their words and Niyongabo's flag-waving victory lap I have missed. I have run out the door, past the U-Haul truck, to a trail that loops a pond lit by a distant street lamp. I pound the black pavement with my Spyridon running shoes and shake my head with every spirited stride.

"I could have won that."

What were the odds a tumbleweed would blow across my path the same time Mac Davis crooned "Happiness is Lubbock, Texas in the Rearview Mirror" through my car speakers? The tumbleweed and an armadillo squashed into the road were signs that I was staring at Lubbock, Texas through my windshield.

All that was in my rearview mirror was my three-year-old boy, Miles Simon, in the backseat next to cardboard boxes wrapped with duct tape. Odds were I had left behind the dust storms, the ground hogs, the scent of cattle fields, and the graves of famous Lubbockites Buddy Holly and Grimsley Roeper the morning of Grandma's funeral in 1981. Except for a brief visit in 1994, the only time I drove near Lubbock I took the loop.

Clare, sitting in the passenger seat, sang along with Mac Davis and nodded her head in unison with the pumping oil rigs in the adjacent desert field. "Happiness is Lubbock growing nearer and dearer..."

"An Australian singing with a Texas accent, that's great," I said, as Clare continued her duet.

"You can bury me in Lubbock, Texas – in my jeans."

I turned off the radio. Clare smiled.

"I kind of like Lubbock," she said. "It reminds me of the Outback."

"All you need are a few crocodiles, snakes, and a kangaroo and you're home."

"And Darcy."

I cupped my hand over my mouth. "Screw Darcy."

"What did you say?"

I reckoned Clare already had. Certainly Darcy Ellard screwed me at the Olympic Trials. I looked into the rearview mirror again to see the final lap of the Olympic Trials and Darcy's pupil, a lap behind but taking me down with him.

I had exited Centennial Olympic Stadium alongside Shane Roarke, the dorky Captain Hook of a runner, through a dark tunnel.

"Bloody piss poor race," he said.

"Bad one, eh?"

"Can't figure it out. I felt great on my 18 miler yesterday."

That clue more than his next comment – "It's even hotter out there than the Outback" – and his Australian accent told me Darcy was his coach. Who else would tell his athlete to run for two hours before a big race and advise him to hold off runners in the homestretch even if he is about to be lapped?

Clare picked up her book off the dashboard and pointed to it. "That was straight out of *Run like a Cheetah.*"

"Did you say 'Run like a *Cheater*? '"

"Shane wasn't cheating. He was in the race."

"He was a lap down. What the hell was he running for – except to keep me off the Olympic team."

"How many times are you going to go back and forth over this guy keeping you off the bloody Olympic Team?"

I had been over and over it about two thousand times in my head and about two hundred on the video replay. I had been over it so many times I had lumps on my head from banging it into the wall. Roarke, an Australian who married an American and gained U.S. citizenship a month before the Trials, had cost me a berth on the Olympic team.

"For the one millionth time, Jonny, you don't know that," Clare said as I approached the Lubbock city limit sign. "Maybe he made you work harder and that brought you closer to the third-place finisher."

"For the two millionth time, the guy held me up on the turn. If he would have let me go, I could have caught the guy a stride ahead and finished third. All because of him and your idiot coach I'm driving into Lubbock right now, instead of parading into the Olympic Stadium for the closing ceremonies."

I wished I had never come out of retirement. It wasn't worth the pain of another heartache. I didn't run a step after the Trials. I had spent hours sending my resume and newspaper articles to sports editors around the United States. The only offer I received was from the *Voca Voice* in Voca Beach, Florida, where I would be covering minor league baseball. Ira Binkley, the Voice sports editor, called and said he was excited about working with a writer from *The Dallas Star.*

"This position pays eight dollars an hour," Binkley said. "But with your experience and vast knowledge of writing and sports, we are prepared to pay you nine dollars an hour."

I told Ira, I would think about it. Two seconds later, I said, "No thanks."

It was insulting and humiliating to know my journalism degree and 20 years of sports writing was worth only one dollar an hour.

I didn't know where to turn. Our apartment lease was up at the end of July, and we didn't have enough money to pay the $100 monthly increase on the new lease. I resorted to the original offer – the one from Fubby Tuppernacker.

Fubby had handed over the keys to the track and field office during Caprock State's indoor season. Buzz Bohamer was the perfect replacement, because he was the only candidate who would work for less money than Fubby and who knew less about track and field. Fubby suggested to Buzz that he hire me as the cross country coach after Buzz asked him, "Cross country – is that indoor or outdoor?"

I faxed Buzz my resume on the opening day of the Olympics. He called me back the next night. From the noisy background, it sounded like he was calling from a bar.

"Five Olympic Trials, huh?' he said. "Was that in track or cross country?"

"They haven't had cross country in the Olympics since Paavo Nurmi."

"Who?"

"Paavo Nurmi. The greatest runner in Olympic history."

"Oh. I was just kidding ya.' I know all about the 'Flying Dutchman.' Just come on out here and you can be an assistant coach."

The pay was not more than I was offered in Voca Beach. But I figured I could pick up some free-lance work from the *Lubbock Ledger*, and Clare could get a part-time job. Mom gave us a farewell brunch after Mass at St. Peter Claver. All my brothers and sisters and various nephews and nieces showed up for the brunch and to wish us luck and offer condolences on my Trials' disappointment.

I grinned as I carved into my link sausage. "Maybe I'll make it in 2000."

Mom wasn't grinning. "I'm being sarcastic, Mom. I'll be 42 and happily sedentary by then."

Mom sipped a glass of orange juice. "You have to go where the good Lord leads you, Jonny."

According to Mom, the good Lord led me to a Motel 6.99 in Lubbock the night of the Olympic closing ceremony. Our motel room's television set had more sparks shooting from the back than the fireworks sprouting on the screen. The next morning I met the new Caprock State Track and Field coach.

"Call me Coach Buzz."

Buzz stood up for less than a second to shake my hand. Then he fell back into his padded office chair and propped his cowboy boot-clad feet on his wooden desk. He barely could finish a sentence without spitting a wad of tobacco into the rusty Folger's Coffee can on his desk. Buzz had crowbarism written all over him.

"I could coach the distance runners by myself," he said. "I spent a lot of time observin' 'em from the shot and discus ring. The problem is they see me as a thrower and wouldn't trust the workouts I'd give 'em."

"I've learned a little about the sport the past 25 years. They'll trust me."

"But will they respect you?" Buzz spit into the can and put his boots on the floor.

"Just because you ran in five Olympic Trials don't mean you can coach."

"I'll do my best."

"If you don't, then you damn sure ain't the nephew of the Great Grimsley Roeper."

I shook Buzz's hand and felt a gob of tobacco grease on my palm. Then he gave me the bad news. My job was part-time with no benefits and only from September through May. When I asked where my office was, he laughed.

"You're a distance coach," he said. "You don't need no office."

I settled for a desk in a cubby hole in the track locker room, which also would be my home for the next three weeks. I told Fubby my predicament. He gave me a key and told me not to tell anyone.

"At least it's better than living in your car, Langendolfer. And you know what that's like?"

Clare and I unloaded our furniture from the U-Haul trailer into the track equipment room and made ourselves a home atop the foam jumping mats that were stored in the locker room-turned-three-year-old's paradise. Miles jumped up and down and from mat to mat for hours. It was the first time Clare didn't tell us off for jumping on the bed or climbing on the roof. The track locker room was located under Tumbleweed Stadium.

Clare got a job at Willy's Supermarket and asked for an advance that allowed us to move from the sweatbox into an air-conditioned apartment across the street from it. I could see Grimsley's statue outside our window and hear crackling of shoulder pads and coaches' whistles from the adjacent practice field. Miles' playground was a long jump pit, an artificial turf football field, an eight-lane Mondo track, and a pole vault runway – all overlooked by a three-story press box and endless rows of red and silver bleachers.

The last week of August was the first week of cross country workouts. I sat under Grimsley's statue and drafted my opening speech, which I rehearsed to myself.

"Four years from now, someone in this locker room will compete in the 2000 Summer Olympic Games. It will take more than talent. It will take dedication, discipline, and total devotion to this sport. If you do what I tell you, you will be looking at the flame in Sydney, Australia."

The next morning I marched into the track locker room to see 15 athletes who looked like anything but runners. The men were tall and probably spent more time in the weight room than on the track. The women had butts larger than their busts. The cellulite on their legs was covered by soccer-style shorts that hung to their knees. I turned around and walked to the door, where I was met by Buzz.

"Sorry, Buzz, I must have the wrong locker room. That must be the basketball team."

Buzz shook his head and spit a wad of tobacco on the concrete. "Nah, those are them."

I took a deep breath and went back in. As I was about to speak to the team, Buzz stepped in front of me.

"OK, ya'll listen up," he said. "We have a chance for a good cross country season this fall. But it will take a team effort from everyone. No one likes to finish last. You have to run hard and give it everything you got."

Buzz picked up a paper Coke cup off the floor and spit into it, before continuing. "This season I've found someone I think can help ya'll. He ran here a long time ago. His great uncle was Grimsley Roeper, whose statue you'll pass every day. I hope he can instill some of Grimsley's greatness into you guys.

"So here's Jonny Langen, uh – how do you say your last name again, buddy."

"Langenfelder, Jonny Langenfelder."

I started to speak, just as Buzz hacked another wad of tobacco into the Coke cup. I looked at all these faces of runners, many who weren't even born when I ran my first steps for Caprock State, and said, "S-S-Seven miles. L-Let's all go for a seven miler."

I figured in time they would learn I held the Caprock State 5,000 meter record for the past 19 years, ran in five Olympic Trials, and missed making the U.S. team by seven-tenths of a second. I dragged the men through seven-minute miles that left them gasping, heaving, and complaining. They wore shorts better suited boxers and said my "old fashioned" running shorts looked like underwear. I doubled-back to find three women walking, two jogging with Walkman's, and two who got lost without stepping foot off campus. I made all 15 runners do four-stride outs on the stadium turf, before they limped back to the locker room.

Buzz walked past me at midfield. "How they look, Langencoach?"

"Gonna be a long season."

I checked my old high school logbook from Coach Hightower and knew what I had to give these runners – LSD. The Long Slow Distance was the only way to make them strong enough to race 10,000 meters. At first, some couldn't even 'run' 10,000 meters. The rest of that first week I crammed them like cattle into the school equipment van and drove to the flat, dirt roads north of town. They ran six to 12 miles, based on their fitness level, back to campus. For variety and because of a southerly wind one day, I had them run from campus to the dirt roads. I ran the first three miles with the longest group to make sure they didn't go out too fast.

Two runners quit by the end of the first week and my top runner had his doubts. Hank Kirkland, the New Mexico state 800 and 1,600 meters track champion and all-state basketball player from the one-picture theatre town of Applerock, was recruited and coached by Fubby and happy to see him retire. Kirkland helped me move an old desk from the city dump to a locker room space that once housed the track team's washing machine and dryer. I also found an office chair and a small sofa at the dump. A football manager gave me some leftover artificial turf that I glued to the concrete floor. I put up my picture of Steve Prefontaine on one wall, a bookshelf on the other, and I had an office. I bought Kirkland and myself a cold Powerade from the outside Coke machine and we sat in my office.

"So you ran in the Olympic Trials?" he asked.

"I'm probably the only American to run in five Olympic Trials without making the team. I missed making the team by seven-tenths of a second in Atlanta. If this guy I was lapping hadn't held me up, I would have made it."

"Yeah, and if the queen had balls, she'd be king."

We each took a sip of Powerade. Then Kirkland asked. "We gonna have a time trial some time soon?"

"Why would we do that?"

"Fubby always had one the first week to see where we're at."

"I can see where we're at."

Kirkland took a swig of Powerade. I kept talking. "Think of me as Christopher Columbus."

"How's that?"

"He kept saying the world was round, and everyone thought he was crazy. Some of his crew members jumped overboard and others were organizing a mutiny. Those who remained faithful were rewarded by seeing the New World."

Kirkland downed the last drop, smashed the can in his palm, and smiled. "I'm with you, Coach."

I held workouts at 6:30 a.m. the first month of school to avoid the September heat wave. The headlights from my Toyota illuminated Kirkland's pickup, parked before the stadium gate, every morning. The others strolled into the locker room at 6:35, 6:40, 6:45, or not at all. Erin Macklin asked if I could give her a wake-up call.

I did the morning of our first fartlek workout. I pounded on her dorm room and told her to be on the Tumbleweed golf course, located across the highway from the stadium, in 10 minutes. She arrived in time for the workout briefing. I instructed the runners to sprint from the tee to the green, jog the next fairway, and then sprint from the tee to the green on the next hole and continue that for 18 holes. I sent the men in the opposite direction, running from green to tee. The seven women set off down the fairway on the 400-yard hole. When they reached the green, they kept sprinting. I chased them down somewhere in the middle of the course by a ball washer. None of the women knew what a tee or green was and all were too afraid to ask.

"It all looks green," Macklin said.

The next week the workout was four hill sprints up the par-five ninth hole, cross the bridge under the highway, to the grass practice fields and run two

800's. I started the men on their six hill sprints, so they would arrive with the slower women at the grass fields at the same time. The women reached the top of the hill on their fourth sprint just as the men completed their fifth. I jogged down the hill toward the start to find the women sitting on the fairway and casually changing from their spikes into flats.

"What the hell are you doing?"

"We don't want to jog on the concrete with our spikes," Macklin said.

"It's only 60 meters across the road."

"Hank told us to do it."

"Who's the coach, me or Hank?"

Or Buzz? At the first weekly press conference at Tumbleweed Steakhouse the head volleyball coach, soccer coach, golf coach, and football coach spoke to the media and answered their questions. When they called for the head cross country coach, Buzz beat me to the podium.

"We have a mighty fine lookin' bunch of runners this year," he said. "They've been workin' hard, puttin' in their miles. It's a young team, but I'm lookin' forward to watching them grow and getting better each week."

"This guy hasn't been to one workout and doesn't even know who's on the team," I thought as he kept jabbering on to reporters, who were too busy cutting their meat to take notes. "I realize I'm the assistant track coach, but I'm also the assistant cross country coach?"

Looking at the starting line of the season's first cross country meet, the Pampa Invitational, made me happy I wasn't listed as head coach. My women's team looked more suited for rugby than running. I told them to stick with the baggy shorts. The bun huggers looked like bologna wrappers.

Les Moore, the University of Amarillo coach, grinned. "Your team looks like a bunch of dikes."

"That's what we want at Caprock State," I cleared my stopwatch and re-turned the grin. "We want girls who'll slap each other high-fives before the race and say in deep voices, 'Let's go kick some ass!'"

"That's some pretty big ass," Les said.

The only advantage for the great wide hopes is that it was hard for oppo-nents to go around them. That didn't stop the Lady Tumbleweeds from filling the last six spots in the 20-runner race. My only success was Carmen Pirelli, the Lady Tumbleweeds indoor 5,000 meter record-holder who finished 12th in her first race in two years. Some butcher-turned-doctor cut into her Achilles and told her she needed another two years in rehab. Buzz limited her to two miles per day during the summer and told her not to run cross country. I got her up to 10 miles by the first meet. She was our only women's runner who wore spikes on the muddy Pampa Hills Golf Course. Macklin said she felt more comfortable in her 15-ounce, heavy-heeled training flats.

"If you felt more comfortable in army boots, would you wear those?" I asked.

Our male runners looked like giants compared to the University of Ama-rillo's Kenyans and struggled up the rolling four-mile course like it was a beanstalk. Amarillo took five of the first six places. Kirkland, wearing a Tumbleweed tattoo on his right shoulder, finished fourth to break up the sweep. We nipped Pampa for second in the three-team race.

Buzz watched the race from the driving range, where he smacked 150-yard worm burners with his Big Bertha driver. He arrived in time to tell a reporter, "We competed well for our first race. We'll keep working hard and improve with each meet."

Buzz turned and whispered in my ear, "How'd we do, anyhow?"

I attempted to psyche the team up on the warm up before the next week's Amarillo Invitational by telling them about the top flight Kenyans I ran against here. I explained that these Kenyans were younger and not as fast, because the NCAA no longer allows athletes in their late 20's and 30's.

My comment annoyed Troy Hesson, who at tiny Amberly High School lettered in every sport but cross country. "Then why don't you run, Coach. Show us how it's done."

Following a volley of "Yeahs," I jogged back to the finish area and borrowed spikes from a Lady Tumbleweed, who had the same size foot. I showed up bare-chested and in skimpy orange shorts at the start. My runners were so psyched they went out the first mile with the Amarillo contingent. By the two-mile mark I passed everyone on the team but Kirkland and worked my way through the Kenyans. I looked up at four miles and to the only runner between me and the finish line – Kirkland.

I cut the 80-meter deficit on the final mile, and Kirkland was struggling. My thoughts: "I could easily catch him. But this guy has never come close to winning a college cross country race. Why would I want to ruin the race of his life?"

I didn't gain another step on Kirkland, who was too tired to raise his fist in triumph. I helped him through the chute, and he bear-hugged me and pressed his sweat-soaked singlet against my bare chest.

"You're right, Coach. The world *is* round."

There were no more wins that fall, in cross country or football. Clare was demoted from supermarket checker to deli server. The *Lubbock Ledger* sports editor said they didn't hire stringers. Kirkland never came close to winning another race, and the women – all but Pirelli – were not getting faster. Only fatter.

Kirkland sat in my office after a workout and explained the "freshman 40," the average number of pounds a woman gains her first year in college.

"They have a starch explosion," he said. "They go from the good, wholesome sit-down dinners with Mom and Pop to the all-you-can-eat starchy, high-fat dorm food."

"Then why is Pirelli looking so fit."

"Because the other girls are eating all her food."

"If she's not careful, they'll start eating her."

Pirelli lived in an apartment with Jason, her long-time on-again, off-again crowbarism boyfriend. Jason had no degree, no job, and no personality. Jason must have had that charisma-bypass surgery. Pirelli didn't have much to say either. I tried to make conversation while massaging her sore Achilles one morning.

"So Carmen, how's your boyfriend, Jason, doing?"

Carmen hopped off the massage table, crying. "He's no longer my boyfriend." She walked out the locker room, leaving me and slow redshirt freshman "Fast Eddie" Hockler laughing.

"There's no crying in cross country," I said.

Pirelli and a change in conferences saved us from the conference cellar. The break-up of the Southwestern Conference in 1995 sent Caprock State into the Mountain Valley Conference with Northern California, Southern Arizona, Nevada State, the College of the Rockies, and several other outcasts. Pirelli finished fourth in the women's race, and both women's and men's teams finished fifth at the meet held on the Tumbleweed Golf Course.

I took only Pirelli and Kirkland to the NCAA Region VI Meet in Austin, where the top four finishers not on the top two teams qualified for the NCAA meet. Kirkland finished 38th, apparently saving himself to cheer Pirelli to a near-qualifying effort in the 5K race. She overcame a near career-ending injury, an abusive boyfriend, and a head track coach who advised her not to run that season to finish 10th place for All Region honors and only one spot from nationals. She started crying again in front of the hoarse, exhausted coach who sprinted from point-to-point to yell for his courageous runner.

"I never could have done it without you, Coach," she said, pushing her head against my red and silver sweat-top.

I left a message on Buzz's answering machine – he had stayed behind so he could watch the Caprock State football team get hammered 59-14 by the visiting Southern Arizona – and drove back to Lubbock. I walked to my dining table the next morning to Clare, Miles, waffles, sausage, and the Sunday *Lubbock Ledger*. The headline on the bottom of page 4C in sports read, "Caprock Runner Just Misses NCAA berth."

I read down to the paragraph that contained the only quote. "I knew all along Carmen could shake off her injury and have a great season, and I did everything I could to get her back in shape," said Caprock State Head Cross Country Coach Buzz Bohamer.

◆◆◆

The boos rang out the moment I stepped onto the green rubber floor of the University of Amarillo gymnasium. Nothing had changed in the 16 years since that night I won three events in the annual duel meet slugfest and carried the

Panhandle Pan Cup back to Caprock State. The 20 orange cones were set so close to the padded wall on the homestretch and the stands on the backstretch that only one runner could pass at a time.

The Kenyans weren't as old, experienced, or fast. But they were there. Also, there was the same graffiti – a bit faded, but still legible - on the bathroom wall, "Flush twice, it's a long way to Lubbock."

I waved at the booing crowd. Hank Kirkland waved also, but with only one finger. "Those boos aren't for you, Coach."

They were for the previous year's Caprock State team that had reclaimed the Panhandle Pan from Amarillo, which had kept it since the year after I left. Caprock won by one point after winning the mile relay by one meter. Fubby Tuppernacker grasped the Panhandle Pan and was carried out of the gymnasium on the shoulders of the Tumbleweed mile relay team. He announced his retirement the next day.

In 1997 the athletic directors from the two schools decided to make it a coed meet and combine the scores of men's and women's events. As if the atmosphere needed more intensity, a loud speaker blared, "Let's get ready to rummm-ble!" and the accompanying music for the runners warming up for the 1,000 meters. As I had instructed, Leon Colle landed an elbow across the chest of Amarillo's top Kenyan, Mike Sigei, at the first smoke sighting from the starter's pistol. I laughed at Kirkland's question, "Coach, couldn't he get disqualified for doing that?"

"You got a better chance of getting arrested in here than disqualified."

Sigei never knew what hit him and never recovered. Colle, a part-Indian who wore his dark hair slicked back and had a pony-tail, won by 20 meters to the crowd's whistles and howls that grew louder throughout the night. We led by one point with only the women's 3,000 meters and the men's and women's 4 x 400 relays remaining. Buzz Bohamer chewed his tobacco like a cow chewing cud.

"We got Pirelli and two fat girls in the 3,000 and ain't got shit for 400-meter runners." Buzz tried to spit on the track, but hit the toe of his left cowboy boot.

"Don't worry, Buzz." I said. "I've got a plan"

Carmen Pirelli took off on the 3,000 like *she* was running the 400. The fat girls, Emma Pomeroy and Justine Cowin, beat the Amarillo runners to the first turn and ran side by side – or rather, wide by wide – down the backstretch. Emma and Justine filled the narrow track and thus blocking the Amarillo girls. The roly-poly runners sprinted around the tight turns and held their position. Any attempted pass resulted in an Amarillo runner butt-checked into the wall. The boos grew louder as the race went on and hit a crescendo after the Lady Tumbleweeds' 1-2-3 finish to clinch the team victory. Emma and Justine carried triple-winner Pirelli and the Panhandle Pan out of the gymnasium into the Caprock State equipment van-turned-distance runners' transport. I was out of Amarillo before our anchorman finished the relay.

I made a pit stop at an all-night convenience store, before cruising back onto the highway. Behind me I could hear my runners sitting on the floorboard, munching sandwiches and opening cans. I heard Kirkland and Colle sipping and shushing.

"You guys don't think I know what's going on." I looked in the rearview mirror to see them hiding cans between their legs. "Think I was born yesterday?"

There was quiet for 20 seconds and then an eruption after my next question. "Well, are you going to pass me a fricking beer or what?"

My runners poured their beers into the Panhandle Pan and took turns sipping from it as we sang along to my tape of Don McLean's tribute to Buddy Holly. "Bye, bye Miss American Pie. Drove my Chevy to the levee, but the levee was dry. And them good ol' boys were drinkin' whisky and rye..." Then I told them Buzz had been using the pan as a spittoon.

We stopped for a team leak 50 miles from Lubbock. The women snuck into the bushes, while we flooded a cow pasture. I looked over at Fast Eddie Hockler, whom I barely could see finishing his business in the near pitch-black field. "Hockler, if you shake it more than three times, you're playing with it."

We beat the women to the van and drove off. They chased us for 400 meters, before I slowed down to let them jump through the side door.

"Macklin," I said. "That's the fastest you've run all night."

I dropped everyone off at the locker room and joined them at 1 a.m. at the Sawdust Tavern. Hesson met me at the door and led me to a round wooden table, held by Colle.

"You ever been here before, Coach," Troy Hesson said barely loud enough to be heard in this noisy establishment.

"Twenty years ago. Back then, it was called "Disco Dick's.""

"What's disco?"

Kirkland arrived with a pitcher and a frosty beer mug he filled immediately for me. "Where you been, Coach?"

I talked over some-kind-of rock music and bar chatter from drunken college kids no longer allowed to smoke in this bar. "I had to clean out the van. It smelled more like a brewery than this place."

"I wouldn't worry about it, Coach," Kirkland said. "They don't pay ya' enough to fire ya.'"

He was right. Buzz was making $38,000 per year. Sprint coach Lincoln Brown was making $28,000, and I was making $8,000. Kirkland continued filling my mug and me in on what I didn't know.

He said Brown, Fubby's long-time assistant who everyone called "Pappy," often fell asleep after pressing his stopwatch at the start of the 100 meters. "He's so old he was declared dead a few years ago," Kirkland joked. "We just prop him up in the front seat of the van to take on trips."

Buzz didn't have much more coaching experience than me. He played third-string nose tackle on the Caprock football team, majored in fun machine, and qualified for the 1989 NCAA Championships in the shot put.

"He made it by the length of his little dick," Kirkland said. "Then he fouled on every throw at NC's."

Buzz worked in the oil fields for a few years and returned to Lubbock to marry his high school sweetheart, have a kid, and finish his P.E. degree. He was a volunteer throws coach, when he became the interim coach.

"No one knew who he was," Kirkland said. "Not even the throwers. The athletic director told him if he didn't break any NCAA rules during outdoor season, he would be the head coach."

"Did he coach anyone?"

"He tried. The best workout he ever gave us was what he wrote on the board one afternoon. It read, 'Do what you need to do.'"

Kirkland said the longest run he had the 5,000 and 10,000-meter runners do was four miles. The board-stiff one-ton running shoes made their feet feel like bricks and the static-stretches turned their muscles into guitar strings. He had Hesson running three times 800 meters in 2:03 with a 20-minute sun bathe in the stands between each. His philosophy was after running that fast, the pace for the 5,000 would feel like a jog. Hesson led the first mile of the 5,000 meters at the 1996 Mountain Valley Conference Meet and then jogged to a last place finish.

"Buzz said he hired me, because you guys didn't have confidence in him."

Kirkland filled my glass again. "Coach, the reason Buzz hired you is because we all threatened to transfer if he didn't hire somebody or anybody who knew more about the sport than that lard ass."

Kirkland helped me to my red Toyota at closing. I made it back to my apartment that smelled of bologna and pimento loaf from Clare's work-shift at Willy's Supermarket Deli. I smelled like the Sawdust Tavern. I woke up a few hours later to an orange sunset and little fingers pulling on my beer-stained Caprock State sweatshirt.

"Dadda, I want beckfast."

Miles looked blurry. That was probably from the hangover. "Where's your momma?"

"Riding."

I looked out the window at snowflakes and roads turned into a sheet of ice. I staggered into the living room to see Clare's bicycle, helmet, and Clare missing from the living room.

"I'll make you waffles, pal."

Clare's new passion, the triathlon, turned me into a house-husband. She rode five hours Sunday mornings, swam an hour at dawn every weekday, and ran for as long as her battered legs would carry her every weekday night. She biked to and from Willy's Supermarket every day she worked.

Her injury rash made her realize she no longer could run like a cheetah. By taking up the triathlon, she still could train like one. "I've had to cross-train so much the last three years that I've accidentally become good at biking and swimming," Clare said, as she soaked in a warm bubble bath after her long ride.

I handed Clare a cup of hot herbal tea. "I imagine there are many fast swimmers in the Outback."

"Why is that?"

"Crocodiles."

I received a rare chuckle from a wife, whom I rarely saw awake in the winter of 1997. She would go straight from the pool to work and return to the apartment just in time for me to go to afternoon workout. I made dinner while she ran and made recruiting calls while she ate. She went to bed after dinner and set her alarm for 5 a.m. On her off day, Saturday, I was at a track meet. I felt sorrier for her than me. I figured I was making four dollars per hour, but at least I was enjoying it. I felt like I was back in college. My runners and I ran around campus, throwing snowballs at cars and each other and ran off campus, streaking through the drive-through tunnel of Barney's Beer Barn. I controlled the men's and women's track workouts by training with the runners.

Clare, hoping to escape from the supermarket deli, applied for retail and office jobs with only rejection letters from employers who balked at hiring a foreigner. I wrote for her a mock letter of application for an administrative assistant's position at Caprock State.

Dear person who does the hiring:

I moved here five months ago and need a job to support my bastard child and deadbeat husband. All I could come up with is a job at a supermarket deli, where my Hispanic manager, who speaks no English, thinks he's fricking Saddam Hussein. I've come close to chopping my fucking hand off on a meat grinder and I get propositioned every night by some fat butthead who orders three pounds of moldy bologna.

Anyhow, about this bloody job at Caprock State. I can peddle papers better than the next guy. Just give me an office, an expense account, and free lunch and I will be the best damn administrative assistant that ever walked the Caprock State campus.

I have experience and references, but who gives a shit for this job. All you need to know is that I have never been in prison, I'm not a lesbian, I'm not on drugs, and I don't have a tongue ring or a tattoo of a snake's dick running down my leg.

Sincerely,
Clare "Gimme A Fricking Break" Langenfelder

Clare laughed at every sentence but the first. It insinuated I didn't believe after four years of marriage that Miles was my biological child. I wanted to believe it, but that speck of doubt lingered and haunted me. I could not afford a paternity test. Even if I could, I couldn't bear discovering that Miles was not my child and that Clare didn't love me as much as she said she did. The thought of anyone screwing my wife, even in those months between Germany and Dallas, enraged me. I dreamed one night that Darcy walked into my apartment with a doctor's certificate proclaiming him Miles' father and then took the little boy away, kicking and screaming.

I woke up in a cold sweat and rushed to Miles' room. I slipped under the covers, held him in my arms, and whispered, "I'll never let you go, Miles."

Miles' eyelids peered open. He put his little hands around my neck, and kissed my cheek.

"I love you, Dadda." Then he went back to sleep.

Miles was the glue that kept Clare and me together, though her triathlon training and my newfound coaching career seemed to be tearing us apart. I only had enough energy for the athletes who rounded a track and the little boy who played in the long jump pit while I timed them.

Coach Langenfelder's runners sat around him in the track infield to hear him speak of the dedication it takes to become a winner in athletics and in life. They sat before a dry erase board in the locker room to see him diagram a track and explain the workout. They hung around his office after workout to listen and laugh at the tales of the sport that took him to Europe and back. They partied with him the night he brought April Jennings, prize recruit and state champion 3,200 meters runner, to the apartment shared by Kirkland and Hesson. They took turns with their coach bouncing quarters into a beer mug, shared a beer bong, and ran a naked mile on the dark dirt roads. Jennings said she had never been to a better party on all the campuses she visited.

She signed with Baylor.

My runners also suffered with me on the track trips organized by a to-bacco-chewing crowbarism dressed up like a coach. At least Fubby put us up in a Motel 6.99. Travel, Buzz-style, was a charter bus that left Lubbock Saturday at 6 a.m. and returned from Dallas or Fort Worth or Austin or El Paso or Albuquerque before dawn Sunday. Buzz expected my runners to perform their best after being crammed for six hours by the back of a metal seat and one of his lard butt discus throwers. I spent Saturday afternoon of March in the SMU bleachers waiting through 23 heats of the 100 meters to finally watch Kirkland and Colle run 2:01 for the 800 meters. They both complained of back stiffness. I escaped the track during the 27 heats of the 200 meters to have The Stallion drive me to 2000 Hickory Lane, where Mom sent me back to work with a sack lunch and a kiss on the forehead.

I returned to watch Emma and Justine's battle for last place in the women's 5,000. Hockler, who finished last in the men's 5,000, and I bet Mom's ham sandwiches and his Coke on the last place finisher in the women's race. We barely noticed Pirelli lapping the two twice. She had to go to lane three to do it. We focused on the two slowest runners in the meet. Emma, Hockler's pick for second-to-last, surged to a 30-meter lead with four laps to go. But Justine caught her on the last lap and sprinted by in the homestretch to beat Emma and 20 minutes by a butt cheek. Mom's sandwiches and Hockler's Coke saved me. Buzz told the bus driver to bypass the hundreds of fast-food joints along Highway 20 and had him stop for dinner of stale corn chips and Twinkies at midnight at Elmo's 24-hour Gas and Grub outside Abilene.

The next Monday I sat in Buzz's office behind the framed desk photograph of his wife and two-year-old daughter, Clarissa. He said he didn't want to take me or any of my runners to the Texas Relays.

"Arkansas would kick the shit out of our guys," he said. "Won't look good for recruiting."

"Sort of a *Catch 22*, Buzz," I said. "You're saying they have to have experience to run in the Texas Relays. But the only way to get experience is to run in the Texas Relays. Besides, what are the recruits going to say if we don't even show up."

The last comment and the need to find 400-meter runner Terrance McCray a relay on Friday night convinced Buzz to bring Hesson, Colle, and Kirkland for the distance medley relay. He also wanted me to go, so he wouldn't have to drive the van.

Arkansas walloped my runners. But our 9:54.35 for eighth place was the fastest a Caprock team ran since I anchored the DMR. They celebrated at the Austin Motor Lodge with pizza and the case of beer I promised if they broke 10 minutes.

I would have preferred pizza and 20-year-old runners to the annual Texas Relays Bar-B-Q for the coaches and officials atop Memorial Stadium. It was an excuse for no talent good ol' boy coaches like Buzz to stuff themselves with beef, chicken, and sausage soaked in Bar-B-Q sauce and pour Schlitz Malt Liquors into their flabby bellies. The same coaches whose runners I wasted in my college days were the same ones at the Bar-B-Q in their designer golf shirts embroidered with their school affiliation. They looked the same but with gray and less hair and more wrinkles and weight. For Fubby, the Texas Relays Bar-B-Q was more important than the Texas Relays. These weren't just his fellow coaches; these were his hunting buddies. He bragged about his plan to use his early retirement to begin his world-wide hunting expedition in the summer.

I escaped Fubby and the glory day mongers and sat in the quiet of the upper-deck bleachers. I looked over the track where I won the state mile, qualified for my first NCAA Championships, and captured the 10,000 meters a year before to qualify for my fifth Olympic Trials at age 38. Fubby interrupted my pleasant reminiscence.

"Langenflacker?" Fubby sat beside me and pointed to the finish line. "I remember that time you passed out after the distance medley. We all thought you were a goner."

I wanted to go back to the motor lodge. But Buzz and his fellow crowbarisms, throws coaches dressed up like coaches, stopped at a check-your-guns-at-the-door strip joint called "Hootersville." Buzz pissed in the parking lot with his buddies and marched into the club. "I want to get drunk and see somethin' nekked," he said.

I hoped Buzz was too drunk to see strippers of three generations stroll past our table and too wasted to remember what this happily married family man yelled at them.

"Honey, as long as I got a face, you got a place to sit!"

Buzz told his friends "I am rude, crude and socially unacceptable" and proved it by pulling a hefty stripper onto his lap. She asked him what kind of girl he is looking for. Buzz gulped a beer and looked at his buddies. "Darlin,' I 'm lookin' for a nice, sweet, innocent young girl – who likes to swallow."

The other crowbarisms laughed as the stripper smiled, pecked him on the cheek, and walked back to the stage. "You goin' for it, Buzz?" a crowbarism coach asked.

"I might."

"Man, if you don't fuck that, you're crazy."

Buzz looked at the only person at the table not laughing. "Come on Langenwusser, take out a few dollar bills and get you some poon-tang."

"I'm married, Buzz."

"So am I. But just because you're married don't mean you can't look at the menu."

Before Buzz ordered dessert, I left the animals in their cage and ran six miles back to the motor lodge at 3 a.m. I drove a hung-over Buzz and his dead-ass-last shot putter and discus and hammer throwers back to Lubbock the next afternoon. I was never happier to slip back under my comfortable sheets with Clare and serve Miles his Sunday morning waffles.

Clare competed in her first multi-sport event the following Saturday, at the Buffalo Lake Triathlon. She was lucky there weren't any crocodiles. Clare was the last person out of the lake and flatted in the transition area. She didn't have to worry about being penalized for drafting, but she did manage to catch a jogger on the run.

Miles met his mom at the finish line with a cheek kiss. I had a grin.

"What happened, sweetie?" I asked.

"Bad transition," Clare said.

"You mean from the swim to the bike?"

"No. From running to triathlons."

My focus transitioned to the Mountain Valley Conference Track and Field Championships at Wyoming State. My runners reached peak form by mid-May, ready to score enough points to keep us out of the conference cellars in the men's and women's divisions, enough to give Buzz some job security. The crucial workout for the middle distance runners came the Saturday morning following the final school exam. Hesson and Colle arrived with hangovers. Kirkland arrived on crutches. He said he sprained his ankle on his eight-miler Friday afternoon.

"And you celebrated by getting drunk with Hesson and Colle?" I threw my clipboard, and my runners watched it bounce off the turf. "Here it is five days before the biggest meet of your lives, and you guys go out and get fucked up."

I ordered Kirkland into the locker room and to wait until I finished dragging the others through the track workout. I marched into the locker room.

Kirkland propped himself on his crutches in front of my desk. "Coach, the trainers said I have to keep my foot in a boot and can't run for three weeks."

I yanked the crutches from his armpits and dropped them on the floor. During the next two hours I had Kirkland limping, walking, and then jogging across the locker room carpet no matter how much he screamed or grimaced. He wobbled on a board, did toe raises, turned the ankle in a circular motion, and put a death grip on the massage table as I rubbed his ankle with my knuckle. He walked out without crutches and with orders to soak his swollen, purple ankle in an ice bucket and apply a Chinese herbal lotion.

On Tuesday, Kirkland sprinted up and down the track yelling, "I can run! I can run!"

He proved that in Wyoming with his personal best 3:52.3 for second place in the 1,500 meters. Pirelli, whose personal problems I sorted out on the 14-hour van drive from Lubbock simply by listening, finished second in the women's 3,000 and fourth in the 5,000. Hesson was third in the steeplechase, and Colle was fourth in the 800. Even Hockler scored a point in the 10,000. All nine of my runners, including Emma and Justine, ran personal bests. My male runners scored 20 of the team's 28 points, and Pirelli scored 13 of the women's team's 21 points. Both teams finished ninth in the 10-team fields. Buzz's throwers didn't score a point.

I walked off Wyoming State's green track that sunny afternoon in quiet solitude. But all I heard in my head were cheers.

◆◆◆

A rush of wind swept past me that August afternoon of 1997 as I ran around the Caprock State campus. It was so fast and furious that I knew it wasn't a dust devil – also because the flash was black, not orange.

I had run around this campus at least a thousand times without anyone passing me. That's why I stared at the graceful stride clipping through the soft grass and immediately knew he wasn't from around here. Maybe he was visiting from South Dallas, East L.A., or Harlem. Maybe I had stumbled upon the greatest running find in Caprock State history. I chased the mystery man, but the harder I ran the faster he drifted away. He faded off the horizon as I reached Grimsley's statue in full atomic breathing.

I caught my breath and walked into Buzz's office. He welcomed me back from my summer in Dallas, while chewing tobacco and tacking a poster of

Olympic shot put champion Randy Barnes on the wall. I told him about this incredibly powerful athlete who flew past me on my run.

"Must have been Gabriel," Buzz said.

"Gabriel?"

"Gabriel Onderaki, the Kenyan I signed."

The words "Kenyan I signed" didn't seem to sink in until Buzz stuck the final tack in the wall and spit into a metal awards cup. "There, does that look straight?"

Pretty crooked, really, for Buzz to sign some Kenyan behind my back. I didn't ask for a Kenyan. Didn't need one, didn't want one. They were the bad guys throughout my career, the ones who stole our scholarships and our victories. Now I had to train one?

"I imagine he'll train himself," Buzz said. "That's what those guys like to do."

That's not what I did as a coach. I had a "my way or the highway" attitude and I didn't care if the runner was from Nairobi or New Mexico. Gabriel came from Cloud County Community College in Nowhere, Nebraska. He ran in the shadows of even faster Kenyans his two years there, and we got him because no one else recruited him. CCCC coach Milo Mogenberg, one of the crowbarisms who accompanied us to Hootersville during the Texas Relays, called Buzz and asked if he wanted him.

That was recruiting Buzz-style. That's also why Gabriel was the only runner we signed that year. Buzz told me to leave the recruiting to him. I learned a valuable recruiting lesson – never bring a distance recruit to meet Buzz. I introduced April Jennings, the state champion 3,200 meters runner, to Buzz. He poured peanuts into a root beer bottle and swigged it down, while bragging how we traveled by charter bus. The guy didn't realize this girl was recruited by colleges that travel by charter "plane."

"It gets scary sometimes on those icy roads traveling back from a meet at all hours of the night," Buzz said. "I always say a prayer before we leave the track."

Another lesson is never bring a recruit into our locker room. Parents shrieked at the idea of a coed locker room. Their children shrieked at the stench of toilets cleaned once a semester and at the rats, crickets, and monster roaches scurrying across the tattered puke-stained carpet. How can you conduct a serious recruiting interview with rat droppings on your desk papers?

The rats – rodents and runners – returned to the locker room late that summer. The good news about the 1997 cross country season was everyone was back. The bad news was everyone was back. The only exception was Carmen Pirelli, who asked Buzz to appeal on her behalf to the NCAA for a sixth year on a hardship case.

"You can only ask so many favors of the NC two-A," he said that first day in his office. "What would happen someday if our star quarterback wanted a sixth year?"

Buzz didn't respond to my answer. "We don't have a star quarterback."

Buzz probably would make a concession for Erin Macklin, whom he called "the incredible edible." He followed her around like a dog with a boner and said under his breath, "Honey, you can shit on my Post Toasties any morning."

Hank Kirkland, Troy Hesson, and Leon Colle were now juniors and Fast Eddie Hockler was a sophomore like Emma and Justine. I'm not sure how long Macklin had been taking up space in the limited clean air in a locker room that should have been condemned. Somehow, she showed Buzz just enough flesh to stay on scholarship. "I don't know about the scholarship," Buzz told me as he slid his wedding ring up and down his finger. "But I'd like to give her a 'full ride. '"

Everyone – including a few new crawl-ons – showed up on time for our first workout, except for our star Kenyan. Gabriel arrived in full sweats in the middle of my opening address. I spoke slower to make sure Gabriel understood my English. I turned to the dry-erase board and wrote "seven miles and six 100-yard strides."

"Do you understand, Gabriel? Today we will be running seven miles and six 100 yard strides."

Gabriel smiled. "What the fuck, Coach? You think I am right off the boat, man."

Gabriel sounded more Jamaican than Kenyan. He later explained that his junior college roommate was a Jamaican sprinter who tried out for his country's Olympic bobsled team. We took off on our seven-miler around campus and through the beer barn. Gabriel wore his sweats in 90-degree temperatures. We ran tight-lipped in a tight pack until Fast Eddie Hockler turned to Gabriel. "Ever seen a grown man naked?"

Gabriel laughed harder than anyone else. "Yeah man, we ran naked in Kenya."

"Couldn't afford clothes?" I asked.

"No, man, always running away from jealous husbands."

Gabriel ran away from everyone at the season-opening meet in San Angelo. He had a 300-meter lead at the first mile mark. Even the pace four-wheeler had trouble keeping up. The driver looked at me on the side of the course. "Can he keep this up?"

"What do you mean? He's just getting cranked up."

Gabriel lapped a guy en route to his two-minute winning margin on the two-lap 8K course. We would have won the meet had the officials scored it on overall time. Instead, we lost by a point to TCU. The women's team, the most well-fed cross country squad in the state, came last by a point. I couldn't understand how women who ran so much could gain so much. Kirkland explained one afternoon as we stomped crickets that invaded my office through an air conditioner vent.

"They *don't* run that much," he said. "You know that eight-mile loop that goes under a highway overpass at four miles?"

"Yeah."

"Coach, not one of them girls has ever been to that bridge."

Kirkland said the women cut through a cow pasture at two miles and connected with the road that led back to campus. He said the eight-miler wasn't even four and proved it by spray painting these words on the concrete pillars that held up the bridge: "Fat girls run fast" and "Coach L. kicks ass."

No woman responded back at the track where I asked them if they saw anything unusual on the bridge.

"Told ya,' Coach," said Kirkland, as he scraped white paint off his hands.

Clare noticed the graffiti on her four-hour bike ride the Sunday she announced her intention to compete in an Ironman Triathlon. I cut Miles' waffles while she took off her cycling helmet, shoes, and gloves. "You almost drowned on an 800-meter swim in a lake. How do you expect to swim six times as far in an ocean?"

"I'll start with the New Zealand Ironman. They swim in a big lake."

"Think you can ride six hours on a bike?"

"Not a problem. Just more training."

"And a marathon, Clare? You can't run a 10K without breaking down. And we got no money. You'd have to swim the Pacific Ocean to get there."

Clare strapped her cycling gear back on. "You're not very supportive of me, mate."

"I made you waffles. I look after your son."

"He's *our* son, Jonny. How many times do I have to remind you of that? You always refer to him as your little boy or your little buddy. When are going to call him son?"

I put my hands over Miles' ears. "When I truly believe in my heart and without the slightest doubt, I will call him son."

Clare took a waffle and left with a door slam. Her fitness fanaticism at least got her out of Willy's Supermarket Deli and into a health club called "Move Your Buns." She worked as a fitness trainer, mostly keeping grandmas and horny old men from falling off the treadmill.

I wished the women runners at Caprock State had a fraction of Clare's commitment to fitness or her body. My women runners scheduled classes or jobs or social events during workout. Justine said she couldn't work out one day because of a pulled left hamstring. Then she limped away from my office, while favoring the wrong leg.

My saving grace was a Kenyan who went undefeated in the first four meets. I started training with him, because I was the only West Texan who dared to keep up with him. Gabriel was looking at winning conference, qualifying for the NCAA Cross Country Championships, and making "All Kenya." Then he came down with a cold. He missed a week of training and still coughed as we boarded the plane for Northern California. I told him to avoid all dairy products and junk food. I should have told him to avoid Erin Macklin. She carried a bag of chocolates and dished them out to her teammates by the palm-full.

I went for a run at dawn the next morning. While the other schools' runners were waking their bodies up with a short jog, mine were asleep. I pounded each hotel room door six times before a weary-eyed runner answered in a pitch-black room. Everyone lumbered to the vans, except Macklin. I opened her door with her roommate's key and found her bed flooded with chocolate candy wrappers. Macklin was still under the covers at 9 a.m., which was 11 a.m. Lubbock time. She lifted her head from her pillow and spoke with a croaky voice. "I don't want to run today."

Neither did anyone else. Fast Eddie Hockler was in last place after the first 100 meters and stayed there. Kirkland, Hesson, and Colle weren't much farther ahead. I told Gabriel to go out slower, because he was recovering from his cold and because the figure-eight course through the forest was confusing. He went out in a 4:32 mile and led the field by 30 meters. He looked at me on the side and said, "Where do I go?"

I lifted my hands. "I don't know."

Gabriel faded in the last mile and was passed by Irishman Neville Flannery of Salt Lake State in the last 800 meters. I carried Gabriel from the finish line chute and into the van. He said, "I feel like shit, man."

Our men's team finished seventh. Then it got worse. The loudest starter's pistol I ever heard couldn't wake my girls. They wandered around the course like they were on a morning jog. I sprinted past Kirkland and Hockler, who were warming down, and said, "This sucks."

I never looked at the cards that had their finishing place written on them. I ordered the Tumbleweed joggers to run back to the hotel and meet me in my room.

Their laughs and giggles upon my entry did not improve my mood.

"That was a disgrace this morning." My opener silenced the room. "I thought it might be a problem getting you around the course, but I couldn't even get you out of bed. Then you desecrated that course with your lackadaisical attitudes. The competitors who whipped your butts today were up at dawn. They commit themselves to the sport, never miss a workout, and sleep on the floor if that's what it takes to be a champion. Unless you start focusing on this sport, we'll continue getting DAL."

Hockler broke the silence. "What does DAL stand for, Coach?"

"Dead Ass Last."

I took Gabriel to the NCAA Region meet in Austin and left wondering if he understood as much English as he claimed. I told him to go out slow and not take the lead on the hilly 10K race. He went out in 4:28 the first mile, eventually surrendering the lead to five Arkansas runners and the final NCAA qualifying spot to Norwegian Knut Kvetland of LSU in the final 400 meters. I handed Gabriel his sweats outside the finish chute. "What happened, Gabriel?"

"I fucked up, Coach."

What I learned most from the 1997 cross country season is that I needed runners. I called every decent high school senior runner in Texas and New Mexico and sorted out those who might be interested in becoming a Tumbleweed. I hung the phone up on the cocky prep who said he narrowed his choices to Stanford, Arkansas, Colorado, and Wisconsin. I slammed it down on the book scholarship-offered nerd who said he was deciding between Caprock State and Lubbock Baptist College. Another 18-year-old boy walked into my office and said he was looking for a full scholarship. "What's your best time?" I asked.

"Five minutes."

"For the mile?"

"No, for the 1,500."

I advised him to consider a junior college or a Division III school. He kept going on about how great he was and how he deserved a scholarship until my patience hit the finish line.

"Look buddy, I've got six fat girls who can run faster than you, and *they* don't even deserve a scholarship."

The most promising recruit was El Paso's Fernando Shirvana, the state runner-up in cross country. Fernando came for a visit and said he wanted to study music. We walked around campus, and I asked him what he scored on his SAT.

"Six-fifty."

"Was that math or verbal?"

It was both, leaving him 400 points shy of the required university entry and me wondering why I was showing him the music department. A lady professor asked Fernando if he could read music.

I pulled her aside, "Ma'am, he can't even read."

The only promising female I recruited was Nikki Lancaster, Oklahoma's Class B 3,200 meters champion off a farm somewhere above the Panhandle between Texas and Kansas. Nikki's decision was between Caprock State and Oklahoma A&I.

"Oklahoma A&I offered me a full scholarship and ya'll only offer a half," she said over the telephone.

I leaned back in my office chair and pushed the telephone to my lips. "Nikki, do you really want to run track in college."

"Sure do."

"Then why would you consider signing with a school that doesn't have a track team. Oklahoma A& I only has cross country."

Nikki woke Clare and me up with a 3 a.m. phone call a few nights later. Clare handed me the telephone.

"Coach, I just wanted to tell you I have decided to sign with Caprock State."

"Great," I said. "But couldn't you have committed a little later in the morning."

In 1998 I focused more on the athletes I coached in the present than on those I might coach in the future. I had them running hills and fartlek in January and February and the track in March. We took aim at the Texas Relays, where we would assault Arkansas and my school record distance medley. The team of Kirkland, McCray, Colle, and Onderaki ran a school indoor record 9:52.7 in Norman, Oklahoma. I accompanied the Kenyan on the long track intervals. Ten days before the Texas Relays we ran a hard 700-meter loop of the practice fields around Grimsley's statue and then 400 meters to the track for one lap. We did four sets and hit the 400's in 59.6, 60.3, 60.2, and 58.9.

"You're in fucking good shape, Coach," Gabriel said on our warm-down around campus. "Are you running some track races this spring?"

I laughed. "I'm retired."

"How old are you, 32, 33?"

"Try 40."

"No fuck. Why don't you run masters' races?"

"And run against a bunch of old farts with one foot in the grave? No thanks. Running 14:30 doesn't thrill me."

"Aren't you at least curious how fast you can run?"

"Not in the least."

Clare was more into competing than me. She entered every swim or bike or run event that came to Lubbock. She reneged on the Ironman and concentrated on the shorter Olympic distance races. I wanted us to have a child, one I could be certain was mine. But that couldn't happen until Clare gave up her ridiculous Olympic dream. I had a better chance of making the Olympics than she did, and I was retired. There was another reason we couldn't have a child. You had to have sex, first. Clare could swim, bike, and run all day. But she had no energy for a simple game of mattress polo. Anytime we started kissing on the sofa after a late-night movie, Clare ruined the mood with another fantastic flashback of the great Darcy Ellard.

I looked at Miles the next morning as I dressed him for church. "Would you like to have a little brother or sister someday?"

"Someday, daddy. But right now you're like my big brother."

It was a big week for my distance medley relay runners, who cruised through 12 times 300 in 43 seconds on Monday. Colle, Kirkland, and Onderaki slapped hands after finishing the last one while gasping for air.

I was met in my locker room office on Wednesday afternoon, April 1 by the usual rat poopies and shocked looks on the faces of Kirkland, Hesson, McCray, Onderaki, and Hockler.

"You guys gonna tell me what's going on or do I have to guess?"

"Colle's in jail," Kirkland said.

"What do you mean Colle's in jail?"

Kirkland launched the story of how Colle, already on probation for unpaid speeding tickets, drove his 1993 black Camaro 100 miles per hour around the Lubbock loop until he heard a police siren. Then got it up to 120 and led police on a 30-minute chase through Lubbock. It ended about 2 a.m., when Colle crashed his Camaro into a Fotomat.

I stared at the runners and smiled. "April Fool's."

The runners didn't even grin. "It's true, Coach," Kirkland said.

I thought about it for a minute and then rushed to the Lubbock Jail. The judge had denied Colle bail, leaving us without our top 800 man for the Texas Relays and possibly the rest of the season. I was permitted a visit. I sat behind a plastic glass window next to a telephone. Colle appeared on the other side of the glass in his light blue jail fatigues and rolled up sleeves. We picked up our telephones simultaneously.

"Kind of a wild night last night, Leon?"

He smiled, scratching his dark whiskers. "I've had wilder, Coach."

Leon said his attorney was working on getting him out in two weeks. I gave him some fartlek work he could do in the jail yard and some push-ups and sit-ups he could do in his cell.

"I'm sorry about this, Coach. I knew you were really counting on me for this relay."

"You can never look back, Leon. Only ahead. Just make sure you get your shit together once you get out of here. You can inspire a lot of people and do something with your life. But you can't do it in the slammer."

Hesson ran in Colle's place. His 1:56 leg kept us out of contention and well-off the school record pace. Buzz wanted to kick Colle off the team and off campus. I talked him into giving him a second chance.

"Look at this way, Buzz, Colle will be the only competitor at conference with a striped uniform and the number 02457936."

Buzz spit into his office trash can. "But how fast can he run while pulling that ball and chain?"

Colle was released from jail, but not from Texas. His parole officer permitted him to go to the Mountain Valley Conference Meet at Southern Arizona only if I promised to look after him. I should have handcuffed him and released him only long enough to run his non-qualifying 1:56.8 in his 800 meters heat. He must have been too busy making license plates to run at the jail. He jogged to the nearest barstool and was joined by other non-scorers Kirkland, Hesson, Hockler, and all my female runners. Justine kept bugging me all weekend about what tactics she should use in her 3,000 meters. "What difference does it make?" I said. "You're gonna finish last."

My last hope was Gabriel, who finished third in the 1,500 and begged me to let him lead the 5,000 final from the outset. I grabbed him by his singlet on the starting line. "Don't take the lead until I wave my red cap."

Gabriel must have felt imprisoned by the large pack. He looked at me as they passed the two kilometer mark, and I shook my head. At the 3,200 mark he held out his hands as if to say, "What the fuck, Coach?"

With 1000 meters left and three runners remaining in the lead pack, I took off my cap and waved it. Gabriel took off like he was running the 400. His 58.5 lap gave him a 60-meter lead that doubled by the time he crossed the finish line in his winning time of 13:58.3.

Gabriel hugged me just beyond the finish line. "I just have one regret, Coach."

"What's that?"

"That you weren't in the race, so I could have kicked your fucking ass."

My regret was allowing Colle on the plane. Gabriel, Kirkland, and I were relaxing with a beer at the bar, when a woman rushed over to our table.

"Your buddy just stole my purse, while I was playing pool."

The woman said she saw the thief walk in with us and couldn't have described Colle more adequately. "He had well-tanned skin, wore a purple Hawaiian shirt, and had a dark pony tail."

The three of us looked at each other and said in stereo, "Never seen him."

We found Colle outside, wrestled him into the rental van, and made him cough up the purse.

"I'll give ya' the purse, if you let me drive," he said.

"Yeah, right," the three of us again said in unison.

Colle sobered up by doing a 4 a.m. skinny dip. Hotel security arrived. No one claimed him.

I didn't unpack after arriving back to my apartment. I traveled to Austin on a scouting and nostalgia trip to the Texas High School Track and Field Championships, the final meet to be held at Memorial Stadium. Seventy-four years of track and field memories were not enough to keep the football fanatics from replacing the track with a few extra thousand seats within spitting distance of the sidelines. A new track was being built next door on top of a parking garage. I sat in the stands and watched the mile winner run four seconds slower than the 4:12.5 I ran to win it 22 years before. I watched the final mile relay and everyone leave the stadium one by one and each light extinguished.

I walked into the dark exit ramp, shined a flashlight on my little crack under the stadium, and re-entered the stadium. I jumped over the railing and jogged, alone, around 'my' track. I ran strides on the infield. Then, as my final farewell, I stripped into shorts and laced up the spikes I wore to win the state meet.

I started my watch and tore around the orange track with no one to race but my shadow. Twenty-two years before, I was watched by 22,000 spectators and seven competitors who wanted to beat me to a finish string. Now I ran on a rubber cloud with only my shadow and the ghosts of Texas Relays and State Meets past to applaud my effort. The more I hurt, the harder I ran. The harder I ran, the more wonderful it felt. This was the track where I won, almost died, and so many times revived my Olympic dream. No one again would pound this lane of Earth.

I charged down the final backstretch, around the curve, and into one last dash of the world's longest homestretch. I finished arms raised, staggered a few steps, grabbed my knees, and looked at my glow-in-the-dark watch.

"4:12.5."

53

No word was spoken for three hours of desert driving toward the 1998 Mountain Valley Conference Cross Country Championships at the University of Sante Fe. The seven male passengers sat on the vinyl seats of the Caprock State van studying, sleeping, reading, or looking at roadside cactus. Then two simple words ignited accusations, denials, threats, and an inquisition.

"Who farted?"

Hank Kirkland's question brought chaos and confusion. Some runners held their noses, others whipped open the windows, and everyone shouted, "Ohhhhh, that stinks!"

Most fingers pointed to Fast Eddie Hockler, the usual culprit on such long journeys with a solid reputation for a foul extraction of an SBD. Silent, But Deadly.

"I didn't do that one. I think it was Hesson. He had baked beans for lunch."

"Not me," Hesson said. "I took a shit right before we left. It came from the back. I think it was the Kenyan."

"No way, man," Gabriel said. "I only eat bread and rice. Mine don't smell like that, anyway."

"Smells like one of Colle's to me," Kirkland said. "Did you shit in your pants again?"

"No," Colle said. "I think it came from the front. Coach?"

I had one hand on my nose and the other on the steering wheel. "Don't look at me. I think the smeller is the feller."

All fingers pointed to Kirkland. "He who smelt it dealt it," Hockler said.

Finally, a confession. Kirkland smiled.

I didn't mind them stinking up the van. I just didn't want them stinking up the University of Santa Fe cross country course. Certainly, my job situation stunk.

Clare was growing restless the more we outgrew our small apartment across from Uncle Grimsley's statue. Buzz expected me to coach and recruit on a four-figure salary and with a limited number of scholarships. He poured his scholarships into regional qualifiers in the shot, discus, and pole vault and borrowed off the football team, sprinters who couldn't run farther than the 40. I couldn't find another Division I college job anywhere else, even with the experience of five U.S. Olympic Trials. I had to prove I could coach, and my near-last place teams in the Mountain Valley Conference proved nothing. Clare came back from the mall one afternoon in late August with this idea.

"Why don't you make the Olympic team? Then you can coach anywhere you want."

The suggestion, as always, was absurd. But this time it gave me goose bumps. On every run around the Caprock State campus I fantasized either about making a previous Olympic team or the upcoming one. I came back to reality at Grimsley's statue, where I finished my solo runs, and at the sofa where I looked at the shopping bags at Clare's feet.

"Where's Miles?"

Clare's mouth opened, and she turned whiter than a virgin's wedding dress. She couldn't talk, so I talked for her.

"You left him at the mall?"

I was out the door on the first nod. I drove faster than Colle did on April Fool's and parked the red Toyota on the Caprock Mall sidewalk. I ran through the Saturday mall traffic faster than Emmitt Smith went through a field of tacklers. I didn't count how many people or shopping bags I knocked over or how many store windows I glanced through. I ran up escalators and between shoppers going in the opposite direction. I looked everywhere and asked seemingly everyone if they saw a five-year-old boy wearing a red T-shirt with the silver printed letters, "Little Tumbleweed."

Then I stopped, sat down on a bench, closed my eyes, and caught my breath. "Let's see, if I was a five-year-old boy lost in a mall, where would I go? To the toy store? To a police officer? But how about if I was Miles?"

Within a micro-second I was sprinting for Hill and Dale's Sporting Goods. Dale Hill, the store manager, said Clare was talking to a triathlete and Miles was in the back putting on track shoes. "I never realized she had left him here."

I sprinted back to the Toyota, pulled the parking ticket off the windshield, and sped back to the apartment to call in a missing person's report to the police. I opened the front door to Miles licking an ice cream cone and watching Sesame Street. I hugged him like I had never hugged him before.

"How on Earth did you get here?" I asked.

"A great big bus, Daddy," he said. "I ride it until I see Tumbleweed Stadium. Then I get off and walk home."

I wiped the ice cream off Miles' face with my fingers, put him down for a nap, and returned to Clare at the dining room table. I disregarded the handkerchief soaked by Clare's tears.

"So who was the triathlete you were flirting with, Clare?"

"What triathlete?"

"The triathlete in the store that was so fascinating that he made you leave your five-year-old son stranded in a mall. Or did you just have one massive brain fart?"

More tears, one from the right eye and then the left, streamed down Clare's face. "You bloody asshole. You don't think I feel bad enough without you reminding me how lousy a mother I am?"

Clare slammed our bedroom door. The next door I closed was on the confessional at the Caprock Campus Catholic Center. I told CCCC pastor Father Gino, who still performed his 30-minute miracle Masses with a stopwatch in his pocket, what happened and told him how sorry I was that I treated my wife that way.

"You can tell me and God you're sorry. But there is someone more important who needs an apology."

I stopped at Caprock Florists on the way back to the apartment. The lady at the desk said, "The usual, Mr. Langenfelder."

For the cross country season just about everyone and everything returned, including the crickets. They glued themselves by the thousands to the outside wall of the locker room and found their way through the air conditioner vent. I found twice as many crawling on my desk and chair when I walked in for a 6:30 a.m. Monday workout. I stomped a few hundred into my turf floor, which was a mistake. The odor of dead crickets overpowered the stench of the toilets which had not been cleaned all summer. I marched to Buzz's newly carpeted office after workout and told him about my uninvited guests.

Buzz didn't look up from his computer game and jelly donut. "Don't worry. The rats will eat them."

Heath Himmel, the facilities manager, was more concerned. Caprock State was hosting the University of Houston in the season-opening football game, and the track locker room was being used as the visitors' locker room. Himmel had the campus fire department blast the critters off the outside wall and hired an exterminator to fumigate my office. He even called pest control to kill the rats. On Friday morning not a cricket or a rat was seen anywhere near the locker room. The toilets and sinks had been cleaned, the shower tile scrubbed, and the carpet vacuumed.

Himmel called me into his office after the Friday morning workout and held a dust buster in his hands. "Why did you guys go in the locker room this morning?"

"Let me think, Heath. Because it's *our* locker room?"

"Wrong. It's the University of Houston's locker room, and they'll be here in two hours. I want you to vacuum every piece of grass off that floor."

I returned the following Monday at 6:30 a.m. to a locker room trashed with crumbled athletic tape, smashed Coke cans, foot powder, toilet paper scraps, half-eaten sandwiches, candy bar wrappers, and potato chip crumbs. A rat that survived the holocaust ate through a rubber trash can and used my desk as a Port-A-Potty.

I looked around as my runners waded through the debris to their lockers. "Looks like Houston lost."

"That's not the worst of it, Coach." Kirkland picked up a soiled jock strap with a javelin. "Caprock doesn't have another home game for three weeks."

A welcomed edition to the locker room was Nikki Lancaster. The Oklahoma farm girl was everything her new teammates were not – skinny, dedicated, determined, and fast. She turned the locker room into an incestuous cesspool. She spent more time at Kirkland and Hesson's apartment than she did in her dorm room. Colle also was on what they called the "Nukki Tour."

On long runs on the dirt roads Hesson often asked, "Which one of you guys is going to get some 'Nukki' tonight?"

Nikki didn't discriminate. Jumpers, throwers, hurdlers – she did them all. Everyone, but Hockler. Fast Eddie didn't want to screw her. He wanted to marry her.

He sat on the little sofa in front of my desk and asked how he should go about getting a date with "Miss Lancaster."

"Miss Lancaster?" I sat up in my chair. "From what I've heard, you don't date Nikki. You do Nikki."

"Call me old-fashioned, Coach. But I want to lose my virginity on my wedding night."

Hockler had my ideals, when I was his age. I told him he should call Nikki and ask her out. I told him about Holly Ritzenbarger, and how I regretted never having the guts to dial her number.

"What happens if she turns me down?"

"Then she turns you down. Just take the next bus. If you don't call, you'll spend your whole life wondering."

For the team's sake, Kirkland and Hesson helped Hockler's cause by telling Nikki what a great guy he was. Hockler was a right wing, conservative, church-every-Sunday, early-to-bed, early-to-rise, no profanity or alcohol kind of guy, and his running mirrored his existence. He never went out fast in fear of blowing up, a strategy that prevented him from becoming anything but a mid-packer. His stubborn approach we feared could cost us a conference title. Hockler was our fifth man.

"If we can just get him drunk and laid," Kirkland said, "we can get him out of that conservative mode."

I ran with the team every morning and night and sprinted back and forth across the golf course in timing the men's and women's workouts. I figured I had a better workout than them. Colle suggested I ride a golf cart.

"Too slow," I said.

Hockler accompanied Nikki to the Caprock State Homecoming football game but failed to treat her as the screw-on-the-first-date kind of gal she was. He said goodnight with a chicken peck kiss on her cheek and returned to his dorm room and watched a movie.

Gabriel, Hockler's roommate, was not impressed. "Man, you can't get no booty off no T.V."

After Kirkland's gas excretion and eventual disclosure en route to Santa Fe, Hockler talked the next three hours about his Nikki crush. He and his dream girl ran the course together the afternoon before the conference meet and ate dinner at their own table.

Kirkland glanced at them from our table and then back at Hesson, Colle, and me. "Tonight's the night, fellas."

Kirkland spiked Hockler's ice tea with Everclear while he went to the restroom and sent Nikki to Hockler's room at 10 p.m. Gabriel slept on a roll-away bed in Kirkland and Hesson's room.

Nikki finished eighth the next day, leading the women's team to fourth place and its best conference team finish in school history. The starting gun for the men's race was followed by my loud scream of "Get out! Get out! Get out!" that seemingly echoed off the distant snow-capped mountains. They all obeyed but Hockler who went out like he was running an 80K, instead of an 8K. I sprinted back and forth across the course and yelled "Hockler, get your ass up there!" with no effect. Gabriel led from start to finish. Kirkland, Hesson, and Colle finished three abreast in tenth, 11th, and 12th and then waited through 47 other finishers before Hockler crossed the line not even winded.

Hockler sat up front on the van ride back to Lubbock. I finally broke his silence two hours down the road. "So what happened?"

"Don't know, Coach. I just had a bad race."

I turned my eyes from the steering wheel for a split second. "I mean with Nikki."

"She dumped me."

"What happened?"

"She came into my room and sat on my bed. I took her hand, looked into her eyes, and told her I loved her."

"Then she got up and walked out, right?" I shook my head. "You idiot. Never ever tell a girl you love her. I don't care how long you've been going out. I've been married for 5 ½ years and I don't even tell my wife I love her."

Colle, who had been eavesdropping, consoled Hockler. "That's rough, Eddie. I hope you at least got a blow job out of the deal."

Our men's team followed a third-place conference finish with a ninth-place at the NCAA Region VI meet in Austin. Gabriel battled with the Arkansas runners and finished second, becoming the first NCAA qualifier from Caprock State since I made it in 1979. I trained all week with Gabriel and challenged him to beat my best NCAA finish of 48th place. We hammered a 14-miler at Wuffalo, sprinted 18 fairways from tee to green, and tapered with some easy runs on the dirt roads.

Buzz took the credit – of course – for the team's improvement, for Gabriel's NCAA qualifier, and tagged along to nationals. He put himself up in a suite at the meet headquarters hotel in Iowa City, Iowa and made Gabriel and I share a room. Buzz spent the weekend watching ESPN and dined from room service, while I ran Gabriel around the course and took him to the pre-meet banquet. Buzz didn't even go to the race. "Too cold," he said, watching a truck-pulling contest on the big screen television in his suite.

Gabriel wore ski gloves, a toboggan hat, a wool sweater, and long johns under his Caprock State sweat suit for warm up and was so cold I had to tie his shoes on the starting line. My final instructions were to go out in the top 50 in the 250-man race and gradually work his way through the field on the brutal 10K course. "My only regret is that I'm not out here running alongside you."

Gabriel bounced up and down and rubbed his hands together. "I would kick your ass, Coach."

389

I stood 800 meters from the starting line amidst a five-deep crowd along the roped course. Using binoculars, I zoomed in on the runners charging off the line like battle-charged warriors at the faint crack of a starter's pistol and a crowd's roar. I had no problem finding Gabriel in the running herd. He was leading.

He didn't hear – or tuned out – my command to "slow down!" He led for 6K, before fading quietly into the running masses. He led them out and was herding them in. Finally, at 8K he finally heard me. I yelled, "Come on Langenfelder, you can kick Onderaki's butt!"

That was the prod needed for the battle-weary Kenyan, who passed two runners and held off three others in the homestretch. I met him along the chute with his sweats.

"Coach," he said, shivering. "That was not fun."

At the end of the chute he was handed a finish place-card that put a smile on us both.

"Forty-seventh," he said. "I told you I would kick your ass."

Gabriel went to Kenya for the Christmas holidays. Clare, Miles and I went to 2000 Hickory Lane. On Saturday, December 12 I attended a pre-race party for the Dallas Marathon at the White Rock Sailing Club. The first person I bumped into was Tony Rizzo, who slid a cold Coors Lite into my palm.

"Langenchump, we need you for my marathon relay team tomorrow. One of my guys got sick."

"No way, Rizzo. I just got into town, and I have absolutely no desire to get up at dawn tomorrow morning and run a fricking road relay. I'm 41 now. I'm not into it."

After I drank the beer, I told Rizzo, "I'll think about it." After two beers, I said, "Maybe." After six, I said, "Hell yeah, let's go for it."

Six hours later, I was back at White Rock Lake in a Team Perfecto singlet waiting for a baton on the third leg – from the 20K to the 30K mark – of a four-leg relay that started at the same time as the marathon race. Clare dropped me off, and I told her to meet me downtown at the finish line. I would cruise through my 10K leg and hop on the press truck, which was doubling as the marathoners' pace vehicle. I saw the press truck in the distance and two runners, neither holding a baton. Four more runners and four minutes passed before my teammate Monty Franks handed off with "sorry" instead of "stick." I learned later that Monty got lost on the way to the lake and was five minutes late for the arrival of the lead-off man.

If I couldn't catch the press truck, I had no ride to the finish and would miss watching the end of the marathon. That thought propelled me around the lake and past the marathoners like they were race cones. I finally caught a glimpse of the press truck a mile from the exchange zone and ran like I was trying to catch a train. I caught the lead marathoner 20 meters before handing off to Rizzo. I stopped my watch, but kept running until a photographer pulled me into the press truck.

I sat on the truck's flat bed in a flush of red and holding my gut and spitting.

"Pretty fast leg," said Randy Dugan, the former horse racing PR man who was the fifth running columnist at *The Dallas Star* since my dismissal. "What was your 10K split?"

I looked through the sweat on my contact lens to the light shining off my watch. "The numbers read, "28:54."

"Don't know. Forgot to start my watch."

I feared Dugan might write about it. It might get back to Mom, who had just turned 81. She might think I was going for the Olympics again. I also didn't want Clare to know. She would start nagging me again about trying to make the Olympics. She would say, "If you make the team, you'll kill those bloody recurring dreams about being back in school."

Clare was having her own dreams as the clock struck 1999. I was away from that warm bed in my old room on a five-miler up and down Rolling Hills Parkway on my 24th annual run from one year to the next. The run on that dark, quiet road lit by a few midnight fireworks brought back memories, good memories, of my youth. Of those 141-mile weeks and life with freedom and no responsibilities. Of life with a single focus aimed toward making the Olympics. Mom greeted me, as she did back then, at 2000 Hickory Lane with a warm smile and a hug. She sat with me at the dinner table, while I dunked my glazed donut into a cup of hot chocolate. She told me that every night for the past 24 years, she has prayed the rosary from one year to the next.

I bit into the donut and returned Mom's smile illuminated by a dim lamp.

"There is something I want to tell you, Jonny. This might be as good a time as any."

"What's that?"

"I saw a doctor a few weeks ago, and he found a lump on my chest. He had it removed."

I lifted the donut and watched the hot chocolate drip into the cup. "W-W-Was it benign?"

"Malignant, Jonny. I have cancer."

I closed my eyes, dropped the donut into the cup, pressed my elbows onto the table, and covered my face with my sticky palms.

"That stinks."

My tears smeared the ink Mom used to write me a letter in late March. She told me how the chemotherapy made her hair fall out, destroyed her appetite, and left her so weak she barely could get out of bed to throw up in the toilet. But that's not why I was crying. It was from the words in the next paragraph:

I am very proud of you, Jonny, my youngest and most precious son. You seem to never give up on anything, no matter how severe the obstacles. You have a lovely wife and a charming, well-mannered little boy. You are such a good family man, and a strong, secure husband. Above all, you have stayed close to God and have never let anything come between you and your family.

That part of the letter hurt most, because it was so bloody untrue. What kind of "family man" goes out drinking with 21-year-old college kids or misses his little boy's kindergarten play to recruit some disinterested high school punk or spies on his wife in hopes of catching her in the throes of an adulterous affair.

My distance runner's recruiting day began with Buzz's speech in the Tumbleweed Lounge, where he went off on a tangent on why the Caprock State athletic teams sucked in recent years. He failed to mention the biggest reason – because the A.D. kept hiring know-nothing do-nothing coaches like him. A campus tour started at Grimsley Roeper's statue. Hank Kirkland explained the Grimsley legend.

"If a virgin ever graduates from Caprock State, Grimsley comes crumbling down."

I raised my hand. "Actually, he fell the day I graduated."

Kirkland grinned. "Yeah right, Coach."

The recruiting day ended with a pizza and keg party at Kirkland and Hesson's apartment. When I arrived with the pizza, recruits Ryan Fergus and Garth Willoughby already were wasted. Fergus said he could drink Colle under the table.

Kirkland laughed. "Colle can drink more whisky than you could drink beer."

The recruits were throwing up in the bushes along the patio after two shots. Anyone not passed out by midnight went to the Sawdust Tavern for the Annual Tumbleweed Wet T-Shirt contest. Half the contestants were from our track team. Erin Macklin looked better in pink panties than baggy running shorts and won $100 for third place, igniting my call from the crowd.

"I want 10 percent! I want 10 percent!"

I crashed on the Kirkland-Hesson sofa and dreamt of Fergus' mother, screaming at me for getting her son drunk off his ass. I woke up to two hungover recruits. "Coach?" Fergus said. "That was the best damn party I've ever been to. I'm signing with Caprock State."

"It was quite memorable," Willoughby added. "Count me in, too."

I had a noon breakfast of Alka-Seltzer and Kirkland's questions.

"Coach, what's your wife gonna say when you come strolling in this afternoon?"

"Nothing. I called her last night from the bar on Hesson's cell phone. I told her I was too drunk to drive home and I was crashing at your place."

"Your wife really trusts you."

"She either trusts me or she doesn't care."

I trusted Clare 99 percent, but that one percent was driving me crazy. How could I be sure she didn't take a pit stop on her five-hour bike rides? Clare looked sexy in her tight triathlon suit, especially right out of a cold lake. How many of those bonehead triathletes were hitting on her? She often arrived home two hours after an event. How about at work? The Move Your Buns Health Spa is the biggest pick-up spot in town. I imagined Clare sitting in the sauna and wearing nothing but a towel next to Chip, that new blond hunk of a manager she always talked about. Too many nights went by when she arrived home at 10 p.m. from a health spa that closed at nine. And how about all those telephone calls I answered to a dial tone?

Maybe it was Darcy Ellard or some other bloke. My imagination got the best of me. I interrogated Miles on his Mommy's whereabouts when I returned home from the Arkansas Indoor Meet. I went through Clare's purse and the trash, where I hoped to find a note or a receipt or anything that linked me to my wife's lover. I drove the route Clare said she was riding Sunday morning and found her, alone, pumping her well-toned legs on the pedals of her racing bike. I picked up the telephone at 2 a.m. one morning to discover Clare talking to her brother in Australia.

Then one Thursday night I put Miles to bed and jogged three miles across campus in my gray cotton sweats to the health club. I hid behind a dumpster in the dark parking lot and waited for Clare. Finally, there she was walking alongside Chip, the manager, to our red Toyota. Clare said, "I'll see you tomorrow, Chip" opened her door, started the car, and drove off.

Suddenly, I realized, "I have to beat her home."

I dashed down the road, through traffic, and between campus buildings. My route was direct. Clare had to drive around campus and through seven traffic lights. My hope was she would stop at each light or for gas. I sprinted past Grimsley's statue in full atomic breathing and made the apartment complex just as she steered the Toyota into the parking lot. I hid behind the dumpster and waited for Clare to walk into our upstairs apartment. I pulled myself up on the balcony, climbed along a ledge, opened our bedroom window, and slid stomach-first into the apartment. Seconds later, Clare entered the bedroom to find her husband under the covers, sound asleep. The fake snore must have convinced her.

I turned my attention from spying to coaching in the spring of 1999. I set my sights on a conference track and field title and didn't care that the other two coaches each made $20,000 to $30,000 more than me without doing any coaching. The throwers, jumpers, and sprinters eavesdropped on my daily inspirational talks. The 400 meter runners threatened to quit if I wasn't allowed to coach them. Pappy, the aged sprint coach, often napped during their workouts.

I also fixed athletes by using the techniques blind masseur Malcolm Gould taught me. I cured pulled hamstrings with a well-placed elbow, strained knee ligaments with the circular motion of a knuckle, and lower back spasms with a well-planted heel. I had my athletes training in racing flats, ordered them to warm up in sweats, and cut their ridiculous static-stretching exercises to prevent recurring injuries. My methods kept the athletes out of a training room, where they took a number behind the football players and eventually were sent to a luke-warm whirlpool or a melted ice bath. Justine Cowin asked a trainer, who wrapped an ice pack around her sore shin, what was wrong with her leg. The trainer said he had no clue.

Justine tore the ice pack off. "If you have no idea what it is, then why are you putting ice on it?"

I fixed Justine's shin splints in one rub. Such stories eventually reached the trainers, who ordered Buzz to bar me from treating the athletes. Buzz called me into his office while woofing down a foot-long meatball sandwich.

"We don't want you treating the athletes," Buzz said.

"Why, are the trainers running out of customers?"

"Insurance." Buzz wiped meatball juice off his chin with his thumb and licked it.

"You could make an injury worse, and the athlete could sue. Then we'd both get fired."

"Why would an athlete sue me, if I fixed him?"

"Do it, Langendorker, or I'll kick your ass out of here."

I found it difficult taking orders from a crowbarism who spent much of the track budget on a team pig roast in Tahoka, a charter bus for the one-hour ride to Plainview, and a hotel suite on the day-trip to the San Angelo Relays. He bought running shoes from Dewey's Discount Shoes Source, because of their two-for-one special. My runners returned them and used the money to buy Spyridons out of a running shoe catalogue. At the Caprock State Invitational, Buzz and his "Uhhh, I feel good today" shot putters carried the high jump mat across the track and the path of the 800 meter runners, who rammed into it like it was a blocking dummy.

I still treated injured athletes in the locker room with another athlete guarding the door, and hollering "incoming!" when Buzz approached. My apartment turned into a revolving door of athletes wanting a rub or encouragement. Clare made me buy a cell phone to keep athletes from calling the apartment. "I'm not your bloody personal secretary," she said.

I continued pacing my runners through their workouts and played the rabbit role in several races. Gabriel had left for Kenya over the month-long Christmas break with a goal of qualifying for the NCAA meet, but returned fat. I asked Kirkland on a warm down how someone could gain so much weight on rice and bread.

"Gabriel said he didn't run a step the five weeks he was gone, Coach."

"How can go to Kenya and *not* run?"

He didn't want to run in America either. I went to his dorm room one Saturday afternoon and asked him how his 17-miler went. "Haven't run yet, Coach."

"It's 4:30, what the heck you been doing all day."

I ran that 17-miler with him around a street-lit campus. A steady diet of such long runs in snow, dust, rain, or shine and long track intervals sorted him out for the 1999 Mountain Valley Conference Championships at the University of California at Norwalk.

The last hard workout was eight 400's with a one-minute interval. The four seniors – Onderaki, Kirkland, Hesson, and Colle – psyched themselves up for the workout by rubbing their hands on the cleat of Grimsley's statue. Then they asked me to join them. We traded leads on each 400, urged each other to keep up, strained for the line, huffed and puffed between sprints, and finished five abreast on the eighth straight 400 meter in less than 62 seconds.

We slapped each other a high-five. "We're ready boys," Kirkland said.

I could see fire in their eyes as they marched to the Cal-Norwalk track that Thursday night, May 13 for the first day of the Conference Championships. Kirkland and Hesson each won their 1,500 meter heats, and Colle eased up for second in his 800 heat. My three 400 meters runners – Terrance McCray, Quincy Sims, and LaMarcus Roe – qualified comfortably for Saturday's final. The six runners and I, spaced 57 meters apart at the track's edge, screamed every lap for Gabriel, the 10,000 meters leader, and Hockler, the 10K trailer. We turned our attention to Hockler after 6,000 meters, where Gabriel separated himself from the lead pack with a 67-second lap. Everyone else died, but Hockler. His conservative approach finally paid off, as he finished with his arms raised in seventh place. He jumped into the arms of Gabriel, who had passed Hockler on his victory lap.

"Get the fuck off me, man," Gabriel said.

We returned to the Pacific Palms Motel, where I found Buzz at the bar with three other conference throws coaches. "How'd we do in that 10,000, Langendoper?"

"Gabriel won it, and Hockler was seventh. That's 12 points."

"Where were you, Buzz?"

"At the dog races. We're goin' to a titty bar later on. Want to join us?"

"No thanks."

Buzz tossed some beer nuts into his mouth. "If my guys come through in the throws, we should get fifth or sixth this year."

Buzz was in that bar the next night, while Hesson was finishing second in his 3,000 meters steeplechase debut. He also missed Nikki Lancaster's school record 17:09 for third in the women's 5,000 meters.

I awoke on Saturday, May 15, 1999, the 23rd anniversary of winning the state high school mile, and went for a 10-miler along the beach at dawn. I bounced on the sand along the ocean's roar and waves that carried the tide across my toes. The sun eventually gave way to the twilight of the Cal-Norwalk track stadium as Gabriel, Kirkland, and Hesson toed the line for the 1,500 meters final. I huddled them and told them to close their eyes and take a deep breath. "Feel the feeling. You are strong and you are powerful. Feel the feeling."

I returned to the stands and called the race in my head. "OK guys, look for the smoke. Good. Now stick right behind the leader and run close to the rail. That's it. Now just wait for the homestretch."

Gabriel struck first, at the top of the homestretch, bursting past Northern California's Trey Woolsey. Kirkland followed, and Hesson caught Woolsey at the line for a 1-2-3 Tumbleweed sweep. Gabriel (3:48.9), Kirkland (3:49.8) and Hesson (3:50.6) recorded personal bests. The 24 points moved us from eighth to fifth in the team standings. I raised both fists and shouted, "Yes! Yes!"

The race ignited the team as twilight gave way to stadium lights. Colle won the 800 in 1:50.7. McCray won the 400 in 46.3, leading second-place Sims and fifth-place Roe and moving the team into third position. I knew this was a magical night, when Erin, Justine, and Emma scored in the women's 3,000. Nikki finished second in 9:56.2, another school record.

Gabriel and Kirkland came to me before the 5,000. "I'm fucked, Coach," Gabriel said. "I don't know if I can do this."

"That makes two of us," Kirkland said. "And Hesson threw up three times after the 1,500."

I put my arms around the three seniors and walked them through the infield. "Gentlemen, this is a night you will remember the rest of your lives. It's one you will tell your kids and grandkids. You may never run another race. So give it everything you got. Just one last time."

My three runners sat at the back of the pack and looked about to fall off it. But they hung in there, no matter how much their faces contorted and their heads rolled from side to side.

"Be tough!" I shouted.

In the final mile they worked themselves into the lead pack of seven runners. They must have heard my hoarse voice from the 200 mark. "Come on, Tumbleweeds! Hang in there! You can do it!"

Gabriel did it with two laps to go, launching a long drive that took him and his shadow away from the field. Kirkland and Hesson were still sixth and seventh with 200 meters to go, but somehow found renewed strength and flew past their rivals in the homestretch. Kirkland crossed the line in second, and Hesson fifth. They kept each other from falling to the rubber track. I stayed on the other side of the track. I didn't want them to see their coach crying.

The announcer interrupted with the team scores heading into the final event – the 4 x 400 relay. "First place, Southern Arizona, 115 points. Second, Caprock State, 114 points..."

Southern Arizona, the defending team champion which won every sprint and hurdles event but the 400, walked to the start of the final event with the top two finishers in the 200, the 400 hurdles winner, and the third place finisher in the 400. My four runners – Roe, Sims, McCray, and Colle – knelt, held hands, and prayed. Colle, who was paroled for this meet only a year before, jogged the homestretch and pointed to me in the stands. "This one's for you, Coach."

Southern Arizona blasted out of the blocks and into a 30-meter lead and held it into the third leg. McCray, who was supposed to anchor, switched with Colle and pulled even with Southern Arizona on the final turn of the third leg. Colle took the baton on the final leg and sprinted into the lead, only to lose it on the backstretch. Runners, throwers, and jumpers lined the infield on the homestretch and lane eight and woke the neighborhood with their deafening hollers. I jumped up and down on wooden bleachers and screamed, "Come on, Colle!"

Colle, teeth gritted and pony tail flopping, pulled alongside the Southern Arizona runner in the homestretch. They ran side by side, stride for stride, strain for strain, until Colle dove for the finish line a half-meter ahead. He was dog-piled by every man, woman, and coach on the Caprock State team. The school waited 100 years to celebrate a conference track and field title, and we made up for it. Buzz was so excited he swallowed his tobacco.

We took a team victory lap and hoisted the large trophy. Gabriel won a plaque for the high-point man with 30 points. We scored 124 points, and all but 18 came from my athletes. Then the call from the press box for "Men's Coach of the Year" – "Buzz Bohamer."

A little "boo" rang out from the Caprock athletes, who carried me on their shoulders and threw me in the steeplechase pit. Later that night, I loaded the van with beer-drinking runners, jumpers, and throwers and headed for a beach bar that served us alcohol and cigars until 3 a.m. We finished with a dip in the Pacific Ocean and arrived at the hotel for a 4 a.m. dip in the hot tub.

Buzz, who probably had opted for a titty bar or the ESPN re-run of the National Truck Pulling Championships, didn't say a word as we loaded the airport shuttle a few hours later. The chatter inside the bus was more about the post-meet party than the meet. As we waited at the gate for our flight to Lubbock, Buzz spit his entire glob of tobacco into a Coke can and placed a bulldog stare within inches of my face.

"Langenshitter, give me one good reason why I shouldn't fire your *fucking* ass right here and now!"

Every athlete heard Buzz take down his four-figure per year salaried coach, who had won him a conference title.

"What the *fuck* were you thinking, taking these athletes drinking and smoking God-knows-what last night at the beach? I could your hear your *fucking* voices all the way from the lobby, when you came in!"

I lost eye contact and stared down at Buzz's cowboy boots. I couldn't talk, only listen to someone who often took his throwers to Hooters after the meets and reportedly passed out the previous month at Hootersville after the Texas Relays Bar-B-Q. I realized anything I said would bring about my immediate dismissal. When he was done, I said, "S-S-Sorry, Buzz. I have no excuse. I promise it won't happen again."

I shook his hand, "I-I-I just want to help these young men and women."

I sat in the back of the plane, as far away as possible from Buzz. Kirkland gave me a ride from the Lubbock airport to my apartment. "Don't worry about it, Coach," he said, as I opened the door of his red pick up. "Everyone on the team knows who the real Coach of the Year is."

While I unpacked my bags, Clare packed hers. We had distanced ourselves from each other the past few months with my coaching and her triathlon training. What did Clare think our marriage needed? More distance. She was traveling to Australia for her brother's wedding and to spend time with her parents, whom she had not seen since we were married. Eldon Eggers said he could not come to America, because the only cheap flights were during cricket season.

Clare zipped up her bag. "This will give you some time, alone, with your son, whether you believe he is your son or not."

She flew to Australia about the same time I registered 27 runners into the Tumbleweed Distance Camp. For three days I ran the high school kids around campus, analyzed their strides, lectured them on injury prevention and race tactics, and showed them a film on the life of Steve Prefontaine. At Rutherford Hall the boys stayed on one side of the dorm hallway and the girls on the other. Miles and I had a room in the middle. I read Miles to sleep and ordered the campers to bed at 10 p.m. the first night and left to set up the lecture hall. I returned at 2:30 a.m. to find them walking up and down the hallway.

"Coach, what are you doing up?" one boy said.

I pointed him to his room. "No, the question is what are *you* doing up?"

The next morning three sets of parents came to pick up their daughters and yell at me for running a disorganized camp. The girls told me a 15-year-old boy snuck out and bought beer. I spent the next two nights sitting in the hallway all night, making sure no one left their room. I figured the 17-year-old boy in room 403 wanted to screw the 16-year-old girl in room 416. They kept cracking open their doors, looking toward each other down the long hallway, and hoping I would leave or fall asleep.

I thought, "This guy probably is going to screw this girl. But not on my watch."

I had five hours of sleep in three nights, gave the campers back to their parents, cleaned up their mess in the dorm, and returned to my apartment at 2 p.m. with the promise to Miles that I never would organize another distance camp. I put Miles down for a nap and then collapsed in my bed. The ringing telephone woke me five minutes later. I stretched my arm to the bedside table, and pulled the phone to my ear.

"What's up?"

"Jonny, it's Caty. Mom's in the hospital. Can you come right away?"

◆◆◆

55

Watching Mom die was not near as bad as seeing her that night at White Rock Medical Center. In six months she aged 20 years. Her cheeks were sunken, her arms and legs were skin and bones, her wrinkles ran down her neck like contour lines, her hair – what was left of it – was as white as her hospital sheets, and she was so pale I thought I had arrived too late.

Eighty-two? Mom looked like 102. I walked out and checked the name-plate on the door to make sure I had the right room. It gave me a moment to compose myself. The only thing that hadn't changed was her eyes. They sparkled an ocean blue as soon as I sat next to her. I held her bony hand and rubbed my right thumb back and forth across her forehead.

Mom sounded like she was fighting laryngitis and paused to catch her breath between every sentence. "You look as skinny as a rail, Jonny. What's Clare been feeding you? Don't tell me you're trying out for those Olympics again."

I smiled. "You're the one who looks like she's training for the Olympics. What do say we go for a quick run around the lake?"

She kept smiling at me, but I had a hard time looking back. "Jonny, my precious boy." Mom said that over and over in that croaky voice until she fell asleep. I walked out of the hospital, which was adjacent to White Rock Lake. I strolled along the shore in the darkness, sat on a vacant boat ramp, and sprayed tears into the murky water for 45 minutes.

I had arrived in Dallas six hours after Caty's telephone call. I somehow had driven six hours to Dallas without falling asleep at the wheel of my red Toyota, which wasn't much better off than Mom. A 15-minute catnap at a rest area between Sweetwater and Abilene and playing two hours of "I spy" with Miles, kept me awake. I called Caty on my cell phone. She suggested I bring Miles to 2000 Hickory Lane, where she would look after him while I visited Mom.

"You are in for a shock," Caty said, after I dropped off Miles and backed out of Mom's driveway. "She doesn't look too good."

Nothing Caty could have said would have prepared me for that. I returned to 2000 Hickory Lane at midnight, slipped into my old bed with Miles, and hugged him until I fell asleep. I awoke at noon to the wonderment of whether I had dreamed what I saw the night before. The reality returned, when I returned to the hospital. I think Mom aged another year. I went to the nurse's station and asked for Mom's physician, Dr. Lloyd Sizemore. I found him drinking coffee and eating a large cinnamon roll in the staff lunch room.

"What did you say your name was again?" Doctor Sizemore, who diagnosed Mom's cancer and then referred her to the cancer doctors, sounded more like a Texas rancher than a Dallas doctor. The flab hanging over his belt told me he didn't know much about nutrition.

"Langenfelder. You have been my Mom's GP for the past 20 years?" I wanted to add, but didn't, "the doctor who gave her a clean bill of health every six months and waited until she was coughing up blood before you decided to run some tests and hand her over to a specialist."

I followed Sizemore back to the nurse's station, where he looked at Mom's chart and shook his head. "Looks like that cancer spread like wildfire. What a shame."

The only shame for him was that he was losing a patient who helped pay for his Highland Park mansion and Mercedes. I walked back to Mom's room, where they had just served lunch – beef stew, lima beans, and lime Jello.

I took the tray off Mom's lap. "I would rather die than eat that," she said. "Me too."

I paced the room and thought about this disease that weakened Mom's body but not her spirit. Hospital rounds were killing her as rapidly as the hospital food. I didn't want Mom to die in a cold white-walled room next to some geriatric getting an enema.

"Mom, do you want me take you home?"

"The doctors ordered me to stay."

I grinned and took Mom's hand. "Do you want to go home?"

"Yes, Jonny."

I ran a lap around the lake at dusk, smuggled Mom's suitcase to my Toyota, and waited for the 10 p.m. shift change at the nurses' station. Then I picked up Mom from her bed and carried her down the quiet hospital corridor and into the parking lot. Mom felt like a bag of bones, not much heavier than Miles. It probably was the cleanest break in hospital history.

The telephone rang at 8 a.m. the next morning at 2000 Hickory Lane. I ran from my upstairs bedroom to the downstairs kitchen and got there by the third ring. "This is Doctor Sizemore. I would appreciate it if you would return my patient to the hospital as soon as possible."

I paced the kitchen tile with the portable telephone, while eating a banana. "First of all, she is no longer your patient. Second, what are you going to do if she refuses to go back? Give her the death penalty?"

"Listen here," Sizemore said. "Your mother is a very sick woman."

"No shit, Sherlock." Then I hung up.

I walked back to Mom's room. She stared out her bedroom window at the sun breaking through the clouds. "How do you feel this morning, Mom."

"Very comfortable, very peaceful. I can't tell you how good it feels to wake up in your own bed."

I was warned that cancer patients can become demanding, irritable, and unreasonable in their final days. Mom, as sick as she was, never complained. She thanked me for feeding her, bathing her, giving her medicine, and praying the rosary with her. For 41 years, she taught me how to live. Now she was teaching me how to die.

God, I felt, often came between Mom and me. She seemed too busy going to church or helping at an orphanage to come watch me run. She suggested that my drive for success only would keep me off the path to heaven. Now, at last, God had brought us closer than ever before. She listened to how my life had taken a downward spiral, of how Caprock State refused to give me a full-time salary, of how Clare left the country indefinitely. Mom grinned. "The Lord said he would show us the way. But he didn't say it would be easy."

Then she winked. "I'll put in a good word for ya.'"

Miles painted a picture of his Mom, Dad, and himself standing alongside a house with the sun shining above it. I taped it to Mom's bedroom wall. Miles kissed her goodnight. "Please get well, Gran-ma. I need you to play ball with me tomorrow."

Mom sent me to bed with this, "Be good to your children and show them the way. One day you will have to turn them back to God."

Mom woke the next morning to see her son and grandson throwing a tennis ball around the backyard, just as I had spent my youth. I found the old ball trampoline Dad made for me and set it up for Miles. I walked to Mom's room, where she was sitting up in bed and staring out the window at Miles. "He reminds me so much of you, Jonny."

Mom's condition grew worse the next few days. She refused to take anything for the pain, which made it almost as painful to watch. My brothers and sisters visited, but said they couldn't bear to see Mom go through this. Matthew suggested I bring her back to the hospital.

The words under the date Wednesday, July 12 of Mom's bedside religious calendar read, "Our little time of suffering is not worthy of our first night's welcome home to heaven."

Mom lay in her warm bed and gasped for breath. Her rosary was clutched to her hands and her fingers held the final bead. The sun shone through the curtains and illuminated the framed Jesus Christ picture Mom awoke to every morning. The birds chirped outside the window but could not wake the woman who smiled daily at their song.

I held Mom's hand, rubbed her forehead, and told her I loved her. Her breaths came slower and slower the next two hours. I prayed the rosary and asked God to take care of her. Just as I thought God had taken her, Mom's eyelids cracked opened. She stared at the Jesus picture with a joyful glaze so magnificent she must have seen God.

She took a long breath, lifted her head off the pillow, and said, "The light, Jonny. The light."

Mom's head fell back and slumped to the side. The rosary beads dropped from her hand.

Mom no longer was with me. She had a first-class, non-stop ticket to heaven and left me holding a lifeless, hollow hulk of cold flesh and bones. My tears wet her white nightgown as I brushed her fine white hair with my finger tips.

I finally let go and walked out the front door. I was astounded to see cars motoring down Rolling Hills Parkway, the letter carrier delivering the mail, and Mr. Shelton mowing his front lawn three doors down. Somehow, I expected life to stop at least for a few minutes. But time went on. The police came to declare Mom dead. My brothers and sisters arrived, each sobbing and hugging each other and saying they wished they could have been with her. The coroner wheeled Mom's covered body to his hearse and drove into the distance. I didn't wave, because I knew Mom wasn't there.

I didn't cry anymore either. I did enough of that on the boat dock that night. I was relieved Mom no longer had to suffer and that she achieved her life-long goal. I would miss her, but I knew she was with Dad and in a place free of corruption, terrorism, injustice, and taxes. Outside of her children and grandchildren, Mom didn't have many guests at her funeral Mass at St. Peter Claver Church. She had outlived most of her friends and gave most of her spare time to God.

Miles never asked where his grandma went, not even after they lowered her casket into the grave beside the grandpa he never met on the cemetery hill overlooking Rolling Hills Parkway. Miles told me in the limousine on the way back to Hickory Lane that he had awoke in the room above Mom – at about the time of her death - and saw her spirit shooting through his ceiling.

As my brothers and sisters wept and drank coffee at the dining room table after the burial, I went for a 10-miler along Rolling Hills Parkway. When I returned, they were still weeping and drinking coffee. A ringing doorbell dried their tears. Joel Bickler of First Republic Realty must have read Mom's newspaper obituary. "Ya'll selling the house?"

Matthew pointed Bickler back to his car. "When and if we do, I guarantee you we won't go to First Republic."

Mom didn't leave us much to do. She had given most of her belongings to charity and even paid off her funeral expenses in advance. She had allotted $1,000 to pay for her coffin and suggested in a note we go to Caskets R Us, where the day after Mom's death a man in a plaid coat had greeted us like a used car salesman. He showed us his "Summer Sizzler Sale" and all the different models and options in the showroom.

As he paraded us by each casket with my sisters, I whispered to my brothers. "He's telling them, 'Now what's it gonna take to get you into this coffin today?'"

"Maybe he will let us take one out for a test drive," Mark said. "Here, hop in."

"Let's ask him if he has any used models," Matthew said.

"What's that one in the corner with all the dirt on it?" Luke said. "Must be a repo."

No pun intended, but we died laughing at Caskets 'R Us. The laughter eased our suffering and brought us together. Two nights after the funeral, as we loaded the remaining furniture from 2000 Hickory Lane into a U-Haul truck on the front lawn, Mark painted the front hallway. A police officer assumed we were burglars and crashed through the front door.

"OK, I want to see some ID here," he said.

Mark stopped brushing. "Yeah, officer, I thought I'd paint the place before I robbed it."

The house was emptied, painted, cleaned, and ready to go on the market by the end of the week. We held a farewell party the night Mom's lawyer, P.J. Stillwell, read her will. As expected, Mom gave 10 percent of her money to the St. Peter Claver Parish and several catholic charities and the rest to her children. Unexpected, she said the house must not be sold within one year of her death. Then to everyone's surprise, Mom left me Grandma's house.

"What house is that?" I asked.

"The one north of Lubbock," Matthew said. "The house you most likely were conceived in."

I looked at Maggie. "She owns that house?"

"Grandma willed it to her," Maggie said. "Mom rented it out for the past 18 years for the income they needed to pay for their retirement. It was a beautiful old house, but it's probably a run-down shack by now."

I grinned at Miles, knowing I was finally a homeowner. "Now it's *my* run-down shack."

I went for a run along Rolling Hills Parkway at dawn the next morning, ate waffles and sausage with my brothers and sisters, packed my bags and Miles into the Toyota, and drove back to Lubbock. Miles couldn't wait to see his mommy again. Every billboard we passed, he asked, "How much farther, Dad?"

We arrived at the apartment to a mailbox full of letters and an answering machine full of messages, but no Clare. She sent a postcard from Moose Junction, saying she was having a good time and she missed us. In her one telephone message, she said she was having a good time and she missed us. Three weeks and many TV dinners passed without a word from Clare. One afternoon as Miles and I tossed a baseball back and forth in front of Grimsley's statue, a woman ran across the road to us. Miles yelled, "Mommy!" He ran to her and hugged her.

Clare picked him up and walked toward me.

"How's your summer been, Jonny?"

"Fine."

"How's your mum?"

"Not so good. She died last month."

Clarence the Angel of *It's a Wonderful Life* fame said, "Each man's life touches so many others. When he isn't around, he leaves an awful hole."

Clarence just as easily could have been talking about a woman – my mother, in particular.

I never knew how much Mom meant to me until she was gone. She was the link that kept our family together, the ear that allowed us to vent life's frustrations, the voice that gave us comfort, the light that allowed us to see God.

Clare suggested I fill the void by trying for the Olympics, one last time.

"And for the last time," I told Clare, "I'm too old. Besides, Mom wouldn't want me to."

Clare walked over to the sofa and put her hand on my shoulder. "You're Mom is longer with us. I don't think she would mind."

I pushed Clare's hand away and stood up. "I would have to be pretty bloody down and out to want to go through that heartache again."

"I'm giving it a shot," Clare said.

Clare visited Darcy Ellard at his hidden Outback training post during her trip to Australia. He gave her some ointment, probably off a dead crocodile, that cured her leg miseries. The mention of his name infuriated me. "The best way to stay injury-free is to stay away from him," I said.

"Not a chance," Clare said. "He's sending me a schedule as a build-up to the Australian Olympic Trials."

"The postage on such a package with the miles and miles of bullshit workouts would cost a fortune. It might be cheaper just to fly there and train under the Almighty Darcy Ellard."

Clare tied her running shoes, started for the door, and said just before she slammed it, "If you're going to keep being such a bloody asshole, I might take you up on that."

While Clare was running, I was drinking. Miles started first grade that August of 1999, which allowed me to fill my mornings with a campus 10-miler and afternoons with a happy hour at the Sawdust Tavern. The running more than the drinking helped me sort out my life.

I wanted to move out of this shoebox of an apartment and into Grandma's old house, which was now *my* house. It was only a 25-minute drive north of Caprock State, and a more gorgeous area than I remembered. It was the first time I had been there since Grandma's funeral in 1981. Tall oak trees lined the street and a creek meandered through the well-groomed park near the house. There was a new playground for Miles and miles of rolling dirt roads for me and his mom. I called it an oasis in the middle of the desert. Clare called it a slice of heaven and was amazed I hadn't taken her there before.

I turned my sarcastic smirk at Clare as I coasted the Toyota along the street toward 1721 Lucas Lane. "I didn't realize Mom owned this house and that she was going to shrivel up and die of cancer and leave it to me in her will."

I stopped the car atop the cracked driveway and stared at the house.

"Is that it?" Clare asked.

"Unfortunately, yes."

Miles leapt out of his car seat and opened the door. "Cool, it looks like Herman Munster's house."

The white wood-framed house had been painted puke yellow. Clare and I walked to the front door through paint peelings and weeds that were taller than the once-white picket fence. Miles climbed the large oak tree, the only part of the property that didn't seem to be falling down. Window screens lay on the front porch next to the fallen old swing I once sat as a baby for hours with Grandma. We dodged broken, rotted boards on the porch floor and cobwebs to reach the front door.

"You can't judge a book by its cover," Clare said.

In this case you could. I wanted to know whodunnit to my childhood sanctuary. The rusted front doorknob fell off after I twisted it. Clare and I waded inside through the wallpaper and paint that fell off the foyer walls onto the tarnished wood floors. I pointed in silent horror at the oak banister that lay on the stairs and the carpet that was covered with cat and baby pee, food crumbs, and who knows what else. I followed Clare like one of the evil spirits I figured wrecked the place through a kitchen with cabinets falling away from the walls and a backyard-turned-weed jungle. I couldn't bear to go into the bathrooms. The only frame left hanging was the "Home Sweet Home" picture Grandma embroidered for the living room.

The place reeked of cigarette smoke and rotten meat. I wondered if Grimsley was buried in the basement.

"So what do you think, Clare? Should we bulldoze it or burn it?"

Clare stared at the Home Sweet Home picture. "I think we should live in it."

"You kidding? Only a ghost would want to live in this place."

On the drive back to Lubbock, Clare wondered out loud how much it would cost to fix the place up. Miles asked if I could build him a tree house. I tried to figure in my head how much money I could get after I demolished the place and sold the land.

The only house on a pigsty par with 1721 Lucas Lane was Conrad Nolecky's trailer home in Wichita Falls. My first thought on my recruiting visit the previous March was that it must have been hit by a tornado. The first words from Conrad's mother was, "Excuse the mess, we got hit by a tornado a few weeks ago."

Mrs. Nolecky asked if her Class 4A state cross country runner-up son was expected to attend workout if we gave him a scholarship, if she should write her son's first and last names on his underwear, and if he needed a passport to attend a meet in New Mexico. Mr. Nolecky arrived home from work from the steel mill, sat on the sofa, dropped his booted feet on the coffee table, turned on the television with his remote, ordered his "old lady" to toss him a beer, and didn't say a word to the coach who was offering his son a scholarship.

Conrad Nolecky showed up for the first cross country workout at Caprock State in running shoes his mother bought at a grocery store. I asked him to take them off. He had glued four-inch thick sponges inside the shoes "to protect me from the road." I tossed the shoes in the trash can, and gave him an old pair of mine until we ordered new ones. I dragged Nolecky through that first run, a seven-miler that made me wonder if our men's team would beat any conference teams that season. Everyone had graduated but Fast Eddie Hockler, who returned for his final season with a steady girlfriend.

Buzz only allotted me 1½ scholarships for the entire cross country team. Ryan Fergus and Garth Willoughby would have to run for free beer. Caprock State was Marco Barrero's fifth college. He asked why we were only giving him $1000. I said, because that was the amount we agreed upon and listed on the letter-of-intent he signed. Also, I was the only coach desperate enough to take him. He called my office the day before the first workout and said he wouldn't be here until later in the week, because he had to help his brother pack for the Marines.

I stomped a few crickets. "Marco, if you don't show up tomorrow, you don't show up at all."

Marco was the only runner not awed by my Caprock State records that had survived for 22 years, by my appearance in five Olympic Track and Field Trials, and by the knowledge that I had met Steve Prefontaine. He walked into my office after the seven miler and slouched into a chair he dampened with the sweat that ran from his beaded necklace down his bony chest.

"Coach, what would you say if I did my own workouts on my own time and just show up for the meets?"

I spared Marco the Christopher Columbus speech. "I would say to walk into the parking lot, start your car, get the hell out of here, and never sit your greasy ass in my chair the rest of your life."

The others heard my voice and my message. No one, including Marco, missed a practice session all fall. No one flinched at an eight-mile time trial at Wuffalo, hill repeats on the golf course, or 14-milers on flat, see-forever dirt roads. Even the women's team returned with a commitment to winning. Emma, Justine, and Erin Macklin looked almost as fit as Nikki.

My runners were "too" fired up for the opening meet at the University of Amarillo golf course. They used up their energy doing the "Tumbleweed Cheer" on the starting line. Nolecky went out with the Kenyans and hit the wall at two miles. He staggered past me 800 meters from the finish line. Buzz walked up with his five-iron and suggested I pull him off the course.

"If I yank him now, it will take the paramedics 15 minutes to get here," I said. "He can stagger down the hill to the finish, where he can get immediate attention."

Nolecky's final time for the five-mile course was listed at 37:41. He had passed out with his right hand on the finish line. But all runners were wearing on their shoelaces a computer chip that recorded their times. Nolecky's computer chip didn't beep until trainers carried him across the line 10 minutes after he passed out.

His collapse cost us the win. The first words when he came to were, "Sorry, Coach."

"Don't worry about it, Conrad," I said. "There's always another race."

I trained with my college runners every morning, and trained and drank with my ex-college runners every night. Gabriel Onderaki hit the U.S. road circuit and raced somewhere in the country every two weeks. We often started and finished our Thursday run at the Sawdust Tavern, where we met Hank Kirk-land for $3 pitchers.

The more we drank the more Gabriel argued that he could kick my ass in a race. "I was ninth at Falmouth, man. Ninth." Gabriel said. "I haven't finished out of the top 10 in a road race yet."

I poured Gabriel a beer. "Then why can't you break me on an eight miler at Wuffalo?"

Kirkland intervened. "Once and for all, why don't you two guys go out to the track right now and settle this?"

Instead Gabriel and I competed at darts, arm wrestling, and beer chugging. I was too drunk to remember who won.

I hoped the drinking would take my mind off –who I termed after the fourth round – "that lying, cheating bitch." Clare dropped Miles off at school every morning and then disappeared until she picked him up every afternoon. Often when I called the Move Your Buns Health Spa, Clare was at lunch or not even scheduled to work. Kirkland volunteered to follow Clare one morning before his 9 a.m. class. He said he lost Clare in traffic as she sped north past the loop "like a woman on a mission."

I also found a scrap of paper with the name "Clint" and a telephone number scribbled on it in the Toyota's glove compartment. Clare several times hung up the telephone when I walked into the apartment. One day she said she was going to the Caprock Mall. I checked the odometer before and after she left. It registered 41 miles. The mall was only six miles away. Clare spent even more time away from me in October, often making me pick up Miles after school. He did his homework in my office while I trained my runners. We tossed the football back and forth on the Tumbleweed Stadium turf after workout and ran a lap or two on the track.

Miles sat down with me on the finish line after a two-lapper. "Daddy, did you run in the Olympics?"

"I almost made it a couple times."

Miles grinned, looked at the stands, and then hugged me. "When you do make the Olympics, I promise I'll be there."

"I promise you will always be with me, Miles."

Then I took off from the starting line as Miles yelled, "Marks, set, go!"

Miles was the light in my otherwise dark existence. Buzz continued call-ing himself the head cross country coach even though he never attended a practice and was overheard saying to his throwing grunts, "The only sport more boring than cross is country."

A Buzz quote in the *Daily Tumbleweed*: "We have such a young team this year I don't even know some of the runners' names." That's because he hadn't even met most of them.

I applied to other universities, whose track coaches weren't interested in hiring an "assistant" cross country coach. Instead of hiring someone who "ran" in the Olympic Trials, they hired someone who "read" about the Olympic Trials.

I continued my out-and-back runs from the Sawdust Tavern, where I left my cell phone one night. I returned the next night and asked the barmaid for it. She said she hadn't seen it. I asked her to look, and she pointed at me. "Read my lips. Your cell phone is not here!"

I called my cell phone from the pay phone next to the rest rooms and heard it ringing and ringing under the bar. The barmaid handed it to me, "Here smart-ass."

It rang again two hours later, when Kirkland and I were finishing our second $3 pitcher. "Coach, it's Hesson. I'm at a titty bar called, Va-Va-Va-Voom, about 30 miles south of Lubbock. You and Kirkland gotta come see this."

"I don't do striptease joints anymore."

"Coach, really man, you need to come down here."

Kirkland and I drove to Va-Va-Va-Voom and dodged the Harleys and piss puddles to the entry. Hesson met us at the door and pointed to the stage. "Coach, you recognize her."

I didn't at first. That's because I never saw Erin Macklin naked. Here, she was called Sheeba, and I never realized she was so limber. The person I did recognize at first was the man stuffing a dollar bill into her G-string and whispering into her ear. That would be Buzz Bohamer.

The moonlighting job explained why Macklin always was the last one dragging in for morning workout. But it didn't explain why, after several years as Sheeba, she would quit the team five days before the conference meet. I sat in my office chair and stared at her frown. "Erin, you are the number two runner and a senior on a team that could win a conference title. You've worked so hard to get here."

All Macklin said as she stuffed a handkerchief in her eyes and walked out of the locker room was, "I know, Coach. I know."

Buzz denied having anything to do with her departure. He also refused to help organize the Mountain Valley Conference Cross Country Championships at the Tumbleweed Golf Course. I was so busy setting up the course, coordinating volunteers, and compiling entries I barely had time to fire up my team, spy on Clare, or sleep.

I awoke to a sunny sky on my 42nd birthday, October 30, 1999 and to Nikki Lancaster running away from the field in the final mile of the women's 5K race. She was the first women's conference cross country champion in Caprock State history. The basketball player I found to replace Macklin finished a respectable 64th, but cost the women the team title.

I huddled the men before the Men's 8K conference race. "You guys remember all those early morning workouts, all those hill repeats, all those Wuffalos? Now let's put that work to use."

They broke the huddle with Nolecky saying, "Let's get after it, you guys."

My guys demonstrated the best display of team running I ever drew up on a dry erase board. Our top five ran together behind the lead pack of 10. They kept pushing each other, talking to each other, encouraging each other. I sprinted from point to point yelling, "Teamwork! Teamwork!"

Marco sacrificed his shot at the individual title by laying back and helping his teammates. He waited until the final mile to unleash a long drive that placed him fourth. He turned around in the finish chute to see Fergus in seventh, Willoughby in eighth, Fast Eddie Hockler in 10th and Conrad Nolecky in 12th. The greatest performance by a Tumbleweeds' cross country team added up to 41 points and the first conference cross country championship in Caprock State history. We had done it with three freshmen, a transfer, Fast Eddie Hockler, and 1 ½ scholarships from a blubber-butt track coach who considered the sport a nuisance.

I slapped my runners high-fives and tens and stood behind to watch them hug each other, a moment that made 3 ½ years of 6 a.m. wake up calls and dust storm driving worth every lousy penny the school paid me. At the awards ceremony Harlan Prescott, the Mountain Valley Conference commissioner, called the top 10 runners in the men's and women's races to the deck of the Tumbleweed Clubhouse and handed them their All Conference plaques. My Tumbleweeds were joined by their three teammates for the presentation of the men's team trophy.

Then Prescott called the winner of the Mountain Valley Conference Men's Coach of the Year.

"Buzz Bohamer!"

Buzz spit out his tobacco, walked to the deck, shook the commissioner's hand, and accepted the plaque. He patted my runners on the back and smiled for a group photo. I stood there and watched this prick with his arms around a plaque and my runners he barely knew or cared about. If someone had lit a match, I would have exploded. Hockler shouted down from the deck, "Coach, don't just stand there like a doofuss. Get the camera out of my bag and take our picture."

I didn't pick up a camera or a race cone or a finish line flag. I drove to the locker room and transferred everything, including my Prefontaine picture, from my desk to a large brown box. As I headed for the door, Buzz walked in with the team trophy and his Coach of the Year plaque.

"Where ya' think I should hang my new plaque, Langendumper?"

I dropped the box on the floor. "First of all, it's Langenfelder. Jonny Langenfelder. As for the plaque, you can hang that on your big fat ass."

Buzz sat the trophy and plaque on a locker bench. "What's your problem, we just won a conference title."

"We? We?" I shouted as my heart pounded out of my red and silver Caprock State sweatshirt. "Who the fuck is we? You don't come to one fucking workout in 3 ½ years and you have the audacity to accept the coaching award?"

Buzz grinned and put his hands on his hips. "Yeah, I guess I do."

I picked up the brown box and started for the door.

"You whining piece of bird shit," Buzz said. "Look at the name plate on my office door. It says, 'Buzz Bohamer, Head Track and Field *and* Cross

Country Coach.' All you got on your office is a pile of rat shit that spells out '*Assistant* Track and Cross Country Coach.'"

"Well, now I'm the *former* Assistant Track and Cross Country Coach." I opened the door and turned around. "By the way Buzz, cross country never is run indoors. And Paavo Nurmi, the greatest runner in Olympic history, was called the 'Flying Finn,' not the 'Flying Dutchman,' you ignorant lard butt, crowbarism. Uhhh!"

I could hear Buzz's voice as I marched toward the parking lot. "Consider yourself fired, Langen – whatever the fuck your name is! You'll never live up to your Uncle Grimsley!"

I drove to the Sawdust Tavern, sat alone at the bar, and ordered a bottle of Southern Comfort and a shot glass that I raised to my lips with a shaky hand. I staggered out of the bar an hour later, singing "Happy Birthday, Langenloser" to myself. I drove around the Lubbock loop three times in a failed attempt to sober and cheer up, before I went to my apartment. Clare greeted me with, "Where the bloody hell have you been, Langenwanker?"

"And Happy Birthday to you too, Clare. And why the fuck didn't you come watch the meet?"

"I was getting ready for your birthday. I have a big surprise for ya,' mate."

Clare walked out with a blindfold that I snatched off her. "I don't want a blindfold, I don't want a surprise, I don't want any stupid gifts, and I don't want a cake with 42 fucking candles!"

Clare held her nose. "I think you've had 42 shots of whiskey."

I took a bottled beer from the refrigerator and sat on the sofa. Miles walked in with a picture he drew of me running in the Olympics. I wadded it up and threw it against the wall. "And I don't want any reminders of me missing the Olympic team!"

Miles ran back to his room crying. I slouched there in a maniacal daze with dagger words ready to explode from the unguarded floodgates. "What is your bloody problem?" Clare said.

"The problem is I'm 42 years old. I don't have a job. I don't have any parents. I don't have any friends. I don't have any money. I drive a car that has done more miles than I've run. I live in piece of shit apartment. I have a little boy who I doubt is my son, and a wife who hates my guts, worships some lunatic coach in the Outback, and has spent the last three months fucking around on me!"

Now Clare started to cry. "Jonny, you're drunk. You're saying things that don't make sense. Why don't you tell me what's wrong?"

I pushed Clare away and fired the beer bottle at the wall. The crash was not as loud as my voice.

"I don't want your sympathy! I don't want your help! I don't want you!"

"Oh, Jonny," Clare said. "You're scaring your son."

"He's *your* son! Your bastard son! Why don't you take him and all your shit and go back to Australia and out of my life where you belong!"

Clare ran back to our bedroom and shut the door. I went back to the Sawdust Tavern.

I woke up early the next morning on a floor that must have been colder than my mother's grave. I looked up at Grimsley's statue, where I must have collapsed en route to my apartment. A campus tour guide was explaining the statue to a group of high school seniors. "This is Grimsley Roeper, the greatest athlete in Caprock State history."

I helped myself to my feet, picked up the brown-bagged whisky bottle beside me, and burped.

"And that my friends," the tour guide said to his chuckling audience, "must be the campus drunk."

The campus drunk lumbered across the street to his apartment, trying to unclog the events of the previous day. In my drunken haze, I wasn't sure if I had said all those things to Clare or dreamed them. The answer came when I opened the door to a beer-stained wall, broken glass, and Miles' wadded-up picture. All of Clare's belongings were emptied from her drawers and closet. Miles and all his toys and clothes and even the little U.S.A. track and field uniform he intended to wear on Halloween had disappeared. The suitcases were nowhere to be found.

The tears that never came to Mom's funeral finally arrived. Another woman in my life – and a little boy – were gone.

The freezing West Texas wind that almost blew over Grimsley Roeper's statue on New Year's Eve night of 1999 didn't disturb the passed-out runner lying amongst the ruin of his apartment and his life.

Unpaid bills and eviction notices lay on the dust-filled carpet. TV dinner trays and their gnawed chicken bones and dried gravy were stacked on the kitchen table next to the empty milk cartons and boxes of Wheaties and Cheerios. Egg shells and orange juice cartons sat on the kitchen tile beneath the overflowing garbage pale. Three blankets that were wrapped around the runner's bony frame and a pillow stuffed in his whiskered face sheltered him in a place left cold by an impatient landlord and a woman and child who burned in his memory.

It was 52 minutes until midnight and I didn't mind sleeping, or even dying, through the New Year. I just lay there in my bed, alone, in the darkness with Bob Seger's song from my clock radio to keep me company:

Seems like yesterday
But it was long ago.
Clare was lovely; she was the queen of my nights.
There in the darkness with the radio playin' low.
The secrets that we shared
Mountains that we moved
Caught like a wildfire out of control
Till there was nothing left to burn and nothing left to prove

And I remember what she said to me
How she swore that it never would end
I Remember how she held me oh so tight
Wish I didn't know now what I didn't know then

Against the wind
We were runnin' against the wind.
We were young and strong
We were runnin'
Against the wind...

I wasn't sure if it was the wind or someone knocking on my door, 48 minutes until midnight. It might have been the landlord trying to kick me out before the end of the 20th century or a crowbarism sent to break my legs for not paying the gas bill. The shrill voices made me realize it was not the wind.

"Coach! Let us in! It's cold as shit out here!"

I struggled from the bed to the door without unwrapping myself from my layers of warmth. Three shivering runners entered my dwelling with a case of Lone Star, pretzels, and running gear. Hank Kirkland, Troy Hesson, and Gabriel Onderaki looked at me and laughed.

"Coach, you look like a taco," Kirkland said.

"Pretty shitty looking taco at that," Hesson added.

Gabriel rubbed his gloved hands together. "Damn, Coach, it's colder in here than it is outside."

I took their beer and put it on the kitchen counter. "What are you guys doing here? I thought you'd be at the New Year's Eve party at the Sawdust."

"We came to join you on your 'Run from one year to the next, '" Kirkland said. "Except this year, we'll be running from one century to the next."

"Isn't this like you're 25th straight year?" Hesson asked.

I took a beer from the box, pulled the tab, and took a swig. "It would have been."

They stared at me as I detailed the grim events of the previous two months. Within 12 hours, beginning with the Mountain Valley Conference awards ceremony on my birthday of October 30, I had lost my job, my wife, my little boy, my car, my money, and my apartment.

I had followed the blow-up with Clare with a Budweiser at the Sawdust and a whisky bottle from Mario's liquor store. I drank and drove the Toyota on the dark dirt roads south of town until I crashed into a telephone pole and cut my head on the windshield. I somehow staggered six miles back to campus, where I passed out in front of Grimsley's statue in the early hours of Halloween. All this came back to me the next morning after I discovered Clare and Miles missing. I rushed to the parking lot and couldn't find my Toyota. My head wound reminded me my car had been totaled.

I stuck a bandage on my head and ran seven miles to the airport, where a baggage handler recalled a woman and a boy matching Clare and Miles' description and pointed to the sky. "I believe they was on that there plane."

I looked into the sky with the wonder of where in the world that airplane was taking them and whether I would see them again. An Eagle Airlines travel agent told me Clare bought one-way tickets to Sydney via Dallas. I asked for the next flight to Dallas, but my credit card became overdrawn with Clare's purchase. I attempted to rationalize on my run back to the apartment. "That's all right, she never loved me anyway. She just wanted a father for Miles. She's better off with Darcy, and at last I'm free to go after Holly."

I left my apartment the next three weeks only to run or buy beer and food. I never returned to the locker room and to the runners who betrayed me. I later heard that Buzz drove them to the NCAA Region VI Meet in Austin, got lost, and parked a mile from the start. The men didn't have time to remove their sweats and training flats and finished last. The women's team was disqualified, because Buzz forgot to give them their race numbers.

By Thanksgiving, which I celebrated with a bowl of turkey noodle soup, I was down to a few hundred dollars Clare left in the checking account. I didn't have enough money to pay rent. Selling Grandma's old house would give me three options. I could use the money to find Clare and Miles in Australia, start a new life as a ski bum, or pay for my funeral in advance.

I ran 20 miles from my apartment to the house, where a real estate agent was to tell me how much I could get for the dump. I ran down the tree-lined street and through the park until the sight of the house stopped me in my tracks. I thought it was a mirage as I barely noticed the cobblestone driveway beneath my running shoes.

The front lawn had been cut and edged. The white picket fence had been repaired and repainted. Fresh dirt and flowers were planted in the garden. The house was painted white with light-blue shudders and looked like a cover for *House and Garden.* I twisted the glimmering front door knob that opened to the smell of varnished wood floors, new Berber carpet, and soft gray paint. I wandered past the sparkle of a spotless kitchen and bathroom counters and cabinets and a polished banister that looked ready for Miles to use as a slide. The living room, dining room, and bedrooms were just as immaculate. The backyard grass looked as soft as a major league infield. Grandma's embroidered "Home Sweet Home" picture hung next to the fireplace, which was stacked with wood and set to bring even more warmth.

I didn't have to read the birthday card on the mantle piece to know why Clare had been sneaking around for three months. This explained why Clare wasn't at work when I called, the people who hung up when I answered the telephone, and the rapid deduction of our savings account. The name "Clint" I found scribbled on a piece of paper was probably a plumber or a carpenter. Clare's gift wasn't the shack she made into a home. It was the love she so desperately wanted to show me. I read the card anyway. She wrote it the morning of my birthday, probably right after she put the final polish on the wood floors.

Dear Jonny,

Sometimes it is hard to for me to express how much I love you and how much I have wanted a home for you and our son. I can see us very happy here. I see us celebrating Thanksgiving and Christmas and Easter and Birthdays and Mothers and Fathers Day. I can see you playing ball with Miles in the backyard, while I'm making the Sunday morning waffles.

I know this sounds corny, but it's the life I've always dreamed of. I once told you I would follow you anywhere. I hope this home proves I meant it.

Love always,
Clare

Rex Bradshaw, the real estate agent, entered the living room as I wiped my eyes. "Cute little house," he said. "We can make a few bucks off this place."

"You ain't making a dime," I said. "I'm not selling it."

I vowed only to return to my home with Clare and Miles. But how could I find them in the Outback without the money to travel there? I realized there was only one way to get to Australia.

The unrealistic journey to the 2000 Summer Olympics in Sydney had faded into a December depression that drowned me in bills, alcohol, and absolute loneliness. I wrote Clare a letter, sent it to her parents house, and waited everyday for a reply. None came. I reached a 121-mile week on Christmas Day and hadn't run a step since.

I looked at my runners, who didn't blink an eyelash of sympathy.

"Get your shoes on, Coach," Kirkland said. "It's 18 minutes until New Year's."

"You guys go ahead. Start your own bloody tradition."

Gabriel stopped the other two from going out the door. "I know what this is," he said, pointing at me. "You're afraid of the cold wind, of slipping on the ice, of not being able to keep up with me. You're a pussy, Coach. I always knew I could kick your ass."

They barely opened the door before one word closed it.

"Wait."

At seven minutes until midnight four runners bundled in sweats, gloves, and toboggan hats ran into a merciless wind and onto a campus path we had beaten with our sneakers every day for the past 3½ years. I explained that the finish of this five-miler would end at Grimsley's statue, and at the stroke of the year 2000 I threw in a surge that shook everyone but Gabriel.

Kirkland and Hesson's inebriated version of "Auld Lang Syne" faded in an overdue match between a prodigy and his protégé who both disappeared into the night. Gabriel went past me as I slipped on a turn, but I pulled even down the long grassy stretch in front of Rutherford Hall. We pumped frozen air from our lungs and ploughed through a blustery wind that seemed to blast our faces no matter what direction we raced. Still, the 40-mile-per-hour gusts went unnoticed and the "Happy New Year" shouts from passing motorists went unheard. This was a duel. It was America vs. Kenya. Experience vs. Youth. Life vs. Death. Gabriel almost broke me with an all out sprint next to the journalism building, about a mile from the statue. But I clung to his pace like I was holding onto the ledge of a skyscraper. The harder I breathed, the faster I ran. The more I hurt, the stronger I became.

I barely could see the statue through the darkness and through the sweat that dripped into my contact lenses. Gabriel went as hard as he could and opened five meters, then 10, then 20. He looked back for a moment to see his lead cut from 20 to 10 to five. Something inside me, probably the flame that often flickered but never extinguished, propelled me past the Kenyan. I never let up until I reached Grimsley's statue and then climbed it.

Gabriel climbed also. We sat on either shoulder, panting and spitting and coughing the fire from our lungs. Gabriel threw off his gloves and extended his moist right hand. "You're back, Coach."

I grabbed his hand firmer than our last arm-wrestling match. "Darn right, I'm back."

Gabriel, Kirkland, and Hesson helped me pack my things that night. They drank their beers and passed out on the living room floor. I finished a 12-miler and decided my option before they woke up the next morning. I was going back to Dallas one last time to train like I never had before up and down Rolling Hills Parkway. I couldn't live in my refurbished house alone, even if I wanted. It was too close to the bill collectors, who already had put a lien on the property.

I called Matthew, the executor of Mom's will, and begged him to let me stay at 2000 Hickory Lane. He said, "Nobody's in there. You can do it, but on July 12th you're out. That's the day the place goes on the market."

"Fine," I said. "That's the same day I leave for the Olympic Trials."

I left Lubbock the next morning on a Trailways Bus and with all my belongings in the same Samsonite and duffel bag I brought to college. I left behind an angry landlord probably unsatisfied with the tattered bed and sofa I abandoned for the unpaid rent and my runners who gave me hope. An hour down the wind-swept highway I closed my eyes and relaxed to the song that continued through my headphones.

The years rolled slowly past
And I found myself alone
Surrounded by strangers who I thought were my friends
I found myself further and further from my home.
I guess I lost my way
There were oh so many roads
I was living to run and running to live
Never worried about paying or even how much I owed
Moving eight miles a minute for months at a time
Breaking all the rules that would bend
I began to find myself searching
Searching for shelter again and again

Against the wind
There's something against the wind
I felt myself seeking shelter
Against the wind...

The chilled wind that howled up and down Rolling Hills Parkway that third night in January didn't have a chance against the runner in full-body Polypropylene. He attacked the breeze with the passion of a warrior blitzing into his final battle. He pumped his hand in triumph at the finish, the curb that so often welcomed him to 2000 Hickory Lane.

I did not run alone that winter, no matter how cold, windy, wet, icy, or dark. I ran with the thought of my estranged wife and little boy who were somewhere sweating on an Outback trail that couldn't be farther from me.

My old running route felt the same, despite more traffic and buildings and condominiums alongside it. My boyhood home felt nothing like it. The floors, the walls, the stairs, and the rooms were the same. But, without Dad propped on the sofa and watching his John Wayne movie and Mom lying in her bed and praying the rosary, it had become just another shelter. The house had no heat, no telephone, and no furniture. I slept in a sleeping bag in my old room and taped Miles' picture of his happy family and the sunny home on the empty wall, next to my picture of Steve Prefontaine. I spent my non-running hours meditating, napping, watching my 13-inch black and white television set, and formulating a plan that would put me on the Olympic team and on an airplane to Clare and Miles. The final dollars in my bank account were budgeted for the raw fruits and vegetables that became key ingredients on an eat-to-win diet.

I lived a simple life, but not without the worries and temptations stricken to mortals. Only so many breaths could keep my mind off Clare and Miles. I dreamt one night that I woke up and Clare was downstairs making waffles for

Miles and me. When I woke up for real, I ran downstairs to only a dark kitchen. The next day I received a letter from The Stallion from his new house in Tyler. I had asked him if he could use the Internet to find my wife. The Stallion said he did a search – whatever that meant – for "Clare Langenfelder" and came up with nothing new. Then he searched "Clare Eggers" and found a road race she ran in early February in Darwin. The Stallion sent me a copy of the results. Clare's time and placing proved she was nowhere near making the Olympics, and her return to her maiden named showed she had no intention of returning to me.

I channeled my anguish into the Cotton Bowl 8K on the first Saturday of March. The race, which toured the State Fair grounds and nearby Swiss Avenue mansions before finishing at the 50-yard line of the Dallas Cowboys' former field, confirmed what I already knew. The previous 3 ½ years of runs around campus, along the dirt roads, up and down Wuffalo, and around and around the Caprock State track with my runners had kept me fit. I was training without realizing I was training. My only timed efforts, the 4:12.5 mile solo in the darkness of Memorial Stadium and the 28:54 10K chasing the Dallas Marathon press truck, kept me fresh and hungry. I beat Gabriel on my 25th annual run from one year to the next only two weeks before he ran 28:20 in the Tampa 10K road race. I hadn't missed a beat, as my easy 23:46 win at the Cotton Bowl proved.

After the race announcer called "Jonny Lingenfracker" to the stage for his first-place trophy and champagne bottle, I looked into the crowd at a blonde woman waving at me. Holly Ritzenbarger looked better in her 40's than she did in her teens. She told me over a post-race Powerade that she still was happily divorced and had thought a lot about me over the years. I gave her my marital status, and she asked me to her house for dinner the following Friday. Holly left the race course with a wink. "Maybe we can play a game of twister."

For a second, I thought she was going to say polo.

After 25 years of that love-at-first sighting, I was having dinner with my high school dream girl. This gorgeous woman wove through my life and my career and never seemed that far away. I finally was taking a giant step closer to discovering what I had missed all these years.

What I missed more was a berth on the U.S. Olympic team. Despite the recent success, doubt lingered on how a 42-year-old man without a real race in almost four years could consider himself a contender for an Olympic quest he twice abandoned. The Stallion surprised me with a visit the next day. He took me to lunch at the same Bopper Burger we went after the Dallas Marathon in 1992.

"You're never too old." The Stallion slurped his chocolate shake and then recited some old-timers' facts and figures, a hint that he had been watching too many cable sports shows. Nolan Ryan, at age 44, recorded two no-hitters and 203 strikeouts during the 1991 season. Hale Irwin won the 1990 U.S. Open at age 45. A.J. Foyt finished ninth in the 1992 Indianapolis 500 at age 57.

I took a sip of water. "But who was the oldest person to win an Olympic medal."

The Stallion smiled. "Oscar Swahn, a Swedish shooter. He won a silver at the 1920 Antwerp Games at age 72."

I sought someone older to convince me I deserved to make the Olympics. I hadn't spoken with Father Litzke in years. I figured he was either dead or senile. I ran 20 miles to St. Francis of Assisi Catholic Church north of Dallas the following Tuesday. I reached the church out of breath and lumbered past a hearse and street-parked cars and into a funeral Mass. The people in dark suits and dresses wiped their eyes to an organ hymn that echoed off the wooden casket. I sat in the back pew and watched a 90-year-old priest walk as if on air to the pulpit. His words resonated not from his mouth, but from his soul.

"Death does not discriminate from old or young, black or white, good or bad, healthy or weak. It can call upon us in our prime or in the last stretch of old age. It is life's great mystery, understood only by the light at the end of a dark passageway."

Father Litzke sounded nowhere near death in a eulogy delivered in the calm voice of a great orator. He comforted the large congregation for the loss of a high school football coach who died of a brain tumor. He talked of the man's passion for his sport and of his ability to make his players continue in the final grueling moments of the fourth quarter. Father Litzke continued.

"He was the light that paved their way to success. Just when you think you can't run another step, make another tackle, throw another pass, that's when you find a new strength, a burst of energy that keeps you going until the final gun. God's power suddenly is revealed to us at our weakest moment and shown to us through a forceful spirit that drives us to our ultimate glory."

I followed Father Litzke back to his apartment after the Mass. His face lit up, especially after I told him I ran 20 miles just to see him. He gave me a cup of tea and we sat in his den, illuminated by the light from a drawn shade. I took a sip and stared at the tea leaves. I told him how my life had fallen apart. I started to tell him about the cursing, the drinking, the fornicating, the racial slurs, the friends' feelings I must have hurt, the countless women I humiliated, and the explosion that led to Clare's and Miles' departure. But he interrupted.

"Do you remember the prayer you said the last time you were here?"

"The Lord's Prayer."

"What was the line I had you repeat twice?"

"Forgive us our sins as we have forgiven those who have sinned against us."

I paused for a second to consider this – I had forgiven others, but I must forgive myself – and then I wept.

"Your sins already are forgiven and forgotten, Jonny. They exist only on an unconscious level. You must rise above your past, if you want to see God."

Father Litzke was delighted to hear of my comeback. He smiled when I told him I didn't know if it was possible at age 42.

"Forty-two is a number, a concept. When you run, you don't think about how old you are. You focus on running, on each breath, on each stride."

My thoughts then turned to the man in the coffin next door in the church. Father Litzke told me of the man's humility, of the athletes he inspired, and of a life he left fulfilled.

"How old was he, Father?"
"Forty-two."

I finished my 10 miler along Rolling Hills Parkway the next Friday. I showered, shaved, and slapped my neck with cologne. I walked with my champagne bottle to Holly's house, across the street from our old high school. I followed her perfume scent to a candlelit table, where she served a scrumptious Caesar salad and tomato and basil soup to the light jazz from her living room stereo. Hannah, her 14-year-old daughter, was at a slumber party.

We finished the champagne and retired to her bedroom, which had a mirrored ceiling and bedside candles waiting to be lit. Holly went to the bathroom and returned in a black negligee and another dose of perfume. She kissed me on the cheek, lay on her bed, and motioned me toward her.

"Care to join me, Mr. Langenfeller."

I looked at Holly from her pink-painted toenails to her dark, false eyelashes and grinned. "Thank you for a delightful evening. I'm going home now."

Holly sounded as if this was her first rejection along these bedposts. "Are you sure?"

"Yes, very sure."

My 25-year erection had been deflated over a one-hour dinner conversation in which Holly had detailed how Coach Rogey, her "piece of dog dirt" husband, cheated with every cheerleader on campus, the numerous suitors who had entered her revolving bedroom door, and her latest pursuit of a pyramid sales scheme. She never asked about my life and interrupted every time I started to talk about the Olympics. But I would have left anyway. Clare's departure gave me permission to love someone else. But Clare was the only woman I wanted to love. The longer I was with Holly, the more I yearned for my wife.

As I exited Holly's house for the first and last time, she confirmed the self-centeredness I never saw through a teenage crush. "You running in some masters' meets this summer?" she asked.

That's where the runners who lined up for the 5,000 meters at the 2000 Texas Relays thought I belonged. The University of Texas lad next to me with the tongue ring, night-time sunglasses, and the shoulder Longhorn tattoo patted me on the back. "Hey there, Pops. Don't forget to move out to lane two when I lap you for the third time."

I thumped his tattoo when I lapped him late in the race. I finished second in 13:52.16 and then spent three days on the Bennington State Park Forest Trails. My tent and I hitched a ride back to Dallas with the SMU track team, and I drove an auto-driveway station wagon to the Mt. Sac Relays in Los Angeles.

I needed a 28:40 to stay on the road to Australia, and the calm, cool conditions and fast rubber made the ride less bumpy. I worked my way through a field of 47 runners, most so young I could have dated their mother. I never looked at the lap counter. I never listened to the lap timer. I just ran for the sake of running until a bell rang. Then I sprinted like I was running a 400 in my youth past two runners on the final curve. Not even a sudden homestretch wind gust slowed me down en route to my fourth-place finish. Three days and 1,500 driven miles of an auto-driveway SUV later, I found myself back on Rolling Hills Parkway and on the Olympic trail. My 28:07.35 shattered the world masters record, ranked as the world's eighth fastest time of the young season, and qualified me for my sixth U.S. Olympic Track and Field Trials.

I earned a round-trip ticket to the Dot Com Track and Field Classic in Palo Alto, California two weeks later and parlayed it into a third-place finish and another masters' world record. My 13:36.42 in the 5,000 meters gave me a double-or-nothing shot at my Olympic dream.

Age, as Father Litzke suggested, is a mere concept blown away by the soul of a runner in search of his home. I continued up Rolling Hills Parkway stride for stride with the sound of my breath and the Bob Seger tune that swirled about my mind:

Well, those drifters days are past me now
I've got so much more to think about
Deadlines and commitments
What to leave in, what to leave out

Against the wind
I'm still runnin' against the wind
I'm older now and still runnin'
Against the wind...

The beeping of a heart monitor at St. Agnes Memorial Hospital in Sacramento, California was like the countdown to my Olympic dream. "If someone doesn't unhook me from these wires," I thought, a few hours after my 10,000 meters final at the U.S. Olympic Trials, "you might as well hear one long monotonous beep."

This incredible comeback effort had continued with the best training of my life leading up to the Olympic Trials in Sacramento. I lived the ultimate Spartan lifestyle at 2000 Hickory Lane. I ran at dawn and dusk and ate, meditated, did push ups and sit ups, prayed the rosary, and volunteered as a baseball coach at the St. Peter Claver Orphanage. It was the only way I could concentrate on my goal without thinking about my wayward wife and little boy and how much I missed them. I focused on a top-three finish at the Olympic Trials and a plane ticket to Sydney, Australia. It was the only way I could bring my family back. I dedicated every workout to Clare and Miles. Every run along Rolling Hills Parkway and every workout around the Forest Hill track brought me closer to them.

My last workout on the Forest Hill track was the first workout Coach Hightower put me through on that track 25 years before – 220's, with a jog across the field. My last run came during my family's "Farewell to 2000 Hickory Lane" party on July 12. I stuffed my Prefontaine picture and everything I owned into my Samsonite and duffel bag and loaded them into Mark's Mazda Miata. I told Mark to meet me five miles down Rolling Hills Parkway, just past the cemetery where Mom and Dad were buried, and then drive me to the airport for my flight to Sacramento. This was my way of saying good-bye to Rolling Hills Parkway. "Once I step off that curb," I told Mark, "I'm never looking back."

I took one last tour of 2000 Hickory Lane – the backyard where I learned to throw a baseball, the living room where I watched Pre run in the Olympics, the dining room where I announced I was joining the cross country team, and the front lawn where I argued with Dad about my moonlight running. I walked into my bedroom and took Miles' picture off the wall. I folded and slid it into my running shorts and marched downstairs and out the door.

Matthew stood with a "For Sale" sign ready to be stuck into the front yard like a dagger into the heart. My other brothers and sisters and nieces and nephews hugged me and wished me luck as I touched my toes, took a breath, stepped off the curb, and ran into the distance.

The next big breath I took was on the starting line of the 2000 Olympic Track and Field Trials at Sacramento State's Hornet Stadium. A quick look at my competitors made me wonder if I was in the Olympics. I must have been one of the few American-born runners in the 10,000 meters final. The announcer read the entrants like he was naming the members of the U.N. "Achmed Khalami, formerly of Morocco. Suleiman Narui, formerly of Tanzania. Jose Gamez, formerly of Mexico. Silvano Aguerro, formerly of Argentina." The only name he had trouble pronouncing was mine.

I made a mental note, "I must tell Gabriel his best chance to make the Olympics is to marry an American."

The opening lap, 63.5 in a stadium temperature of 83.5, was Olympic material. I expected Haile Gebrselassie to pass me any second. I somehow hung on to the American Record pace that severed the pack through splits of 4:18 for the 1,600 and 8:43 for the 3,200 meters. We kept pounding the rubber track in the night. It was like each man put a hand on the stove, and the last one who took his hand off won. By 6,000 meters I lost track of the time, but not the leaders. Narui and Khalami broke from the field, leaving a single file battle of attrition for the coveted third spot. I moved into fifth and fourth and then took over third, when Hunter Wheeler dropped out with 10 laps to go. Suddenly, I no longer was running in the Olympic Trials. I was running through a dark desert that seemed as wide as Australia. Clare and Miles were on the other side of that desert, a thought that kept me upright and in third place.

Four laps from the finish, Clare and Miles started fading from me. I took water and a wet sponge from a backstretch table, but the picture wasn't any clearer. Narui and Khalami were gone and so were Clare and Miles. I surrendered third place with two laps to go. The rest was a blur of runners going by and an announcer's slow-motion call blending into the crowd. I don't remember finishing or riding in a blaring ambulance to the hospital. I awoke a few hours later with an I.V. in my arm and surrounded by tubes and wires and a beeping heart monitor. I still wore my yellow Spyridon singlet, shorts, and spikes. I looked up at the nurse.

"Did I make it?"

"Make what?"

"The Olympic Team."

The nurse smiled. "Just be glad you made the finish line."

I took it as a "No," which Dr. Orville Neisbaum confirmed. He said I suffered from heat exhaustion and would be held overnight for observation and tests. I awoke feeling fresh and rejuvenated from the I.V. I put my bare feet on the carpet and started changing into my sweats until Dr. Neisbaum entered my room, while reading a chart.

"Not so fast," he said. "There are some abnormalities in your heart rhythm. We need to run some tests."

"Just as long as I'm out of here for my 5,000 meters heats in two days," I said.

Neisbaum made no promises, only tests. I remained in the hospital for two days of poking and prodding and wired like I was the million-dollar man. I refused a stress test. "Why don't we do this, Doc? Let me run my 5,000 meters heat tonight. If I don't die, then I'm all right."

"Can't do it," Neisbaum said. "I can't be responsible for you having a heart attack and dropping dead out there."

"If I don't run this race, then I might as well be dead."

Dr. Neisbaum put the wires on me and a guard on the door. But he forgot to put a lock on the window. When Neisbaum made his 7 p.m. rounds, my bed was empty. I was on the starting line at Hornet Stadium.

Only my hospital bracelet made me look like a heart patient in my 5,000 meters heat. I cruised in at 13:44.91 to finish fourth and easily qualify for the final, which would be held four nights later. I escaped the white coats to the Olympic Training Center in Squaw Valley. There, I found fresh air and mountains that reminded me how far I had climbed in the past six months. On the top peak I envisioned Clare and Miles. I returned via rental car that carried three other escapees from the Olympic Trials' pressure cooker to Sacramento's Park Towers Hotel on the Friday morning of July 21.

My wake up call for the night's final was a clanging telephone and a familiar voice through the ear piece.

"Langengooper?"

I sat up on the bed, turned on a lamp, and rubbed my eyes. "Hello, Fubby. Finally back from your hunting expedition?"

"I'm calling from a pay phone at Hornet Stadium. In case I don't see you, I just wanted to wish you good luck."

There was a pause, and then Fubby continued. "How do you think you're gonna do?"

I took a deep breath and released a few butterflies. "I am going to make the Olympic team."

I didn't see Fubby as I walked to the starting line at 9:05 p.m. But I did see 12 of my former Caprock State runners, bare-chested and standing across a row of backstretch seats with red and silver painted letters on each belly that spelled out "Langenfelder."

Then they serenaded me with the song we sang returning from the Amarillo Indoor Meet a few years before. "Bye, bye Miss American Pie, drove my Chevy to the levee, but the levee was dry. And them good ol' boys were drinkin' whisky and rye..."

I softly mouthed the final words as I neared the starting line, "Singin' this will be the day that I die."

I saw a few other familiar faces in the stands and heard Kirkland's voice, "You can do it, Coach!" above the crowd's rustling.

I had to do it. I had nowhere else to go, nowhere else to turn. This, my 14th Olympic Trials race in 20 years, was my last. It's impossible to hitchhike to Sydney. It was Australia or bust. I ran a final stride around the turn as the announcer read off the 16 finalists and their list of accomplishments. I tried not to listen to the butchering of my name or the pity clap I received for being introduced as the masters' world record holder in the 5,000 and 10,000 meters. I'm sure that threw shivers into my competitors, some whose personal records were tattooed to their shoulders.

As the starter raised his pistol and the television cameras zoomed in and I dug my spikes into the hard rubber, I did not think of Clare or Miles or the consequences of the next 13 ½ minutes. I simply breathed and remembered the last words Father Litzke told me, "Blessed are the single-hearted, for they shall see God."

What I saw after the starter's pistol fire launched me off the starting line were 15 other runners and their shadows rushing for the first corner like greyhounds trying to catch the bunny. The rabbit on this cool crisp evening was 10,000 meters Trials winner Narui, who was rumored to be setting the pace for his finishing kick-challenged training mate Leyton Downy and dropping out at 3,000 meters.

I did not listen to split after split, just breath after breath. The faster I breathed, the faster I knew we were running and the sooner I knew I couldn't keep up. The pace was as relentless as a West Texas wind. As the number eight lit off the electronic lap counter, Narui, Downy, and NCAA champion

Quinn Harper had gapped the field. I turned my attention from the three leaders, focused on the sweaty singlet of the 15th place runner in front of me, and regrouped. I knew that of the three breakaway runners, the pace-making Narui was slated to drop out and thus leaving the final Olympic spot for the trail pack.

I passed the faders during the next three laps and worked my way into the four-man chase group. I felt strong and confident. I thought, "I'm going to Sydney."

The thought was erased at the 3,000 meter mark, where Narui was expected to drop out. He didn't, not even after Downy and Harper went by him with four laps to go. Narui clung to their heels. They maintained a full-straight lead over a chase group, whose victor would gain nothing but resentment for a greedy African.

I kept feeling my breath and telling myself not to panic. Time was running out, but I knew any sudden surge this far out would be fatal. I only could hope Narui would drop out or pass out. I filed into fifth place over the next lap and followed Gamez, who made up no ground on the runaways. The number three flashed from the lap counter and then two. I was still in fifth and tiring and struggling to hang on to Gamez and dwindling hope. The bell that clanged for the three leaders I heard faintly over the crowd. I barely could see them through the sweat I feared would soon turn to tears.

Then it happened. Harper and then Downy pulled away from Narui, who looked over his shoulder like the scared rabbit he had become. I hurled my body past Gamez into fourth at the start of my gun lap and went after the Tanzanian-turned-American, who looked back twice more on the backstretch. Narui was the length of an Air Australia 747 ahead of me as I hit the final 200 meters. I sprinted with every ageless muscle in my fiber around the final turn, even though Narui seemed no closer.

Something possessed my body as I hit the homestretch and chased third place like it was my train leaving the station. I could not feel the clamp that grasped my calf muscles or the blade that pierced my hamstrings. I ran like the wild animal I had become. Narui looked back two, three, four times and with the fear that radiated from his dark eyes and propelled him toward the finish line. The closer I got, the harder I ran, and the faster the finish line came. My opponent looked back one last time as I neared his shoulder. I threw my chin upwards and chest forward into a final, desperate gasp through an unearthly zone of crowd hysteria, camera flashes, dreams, doubts, and the ultimate lean for an imaginary string.

The noise faded as I leaped at the air and onto a red rubber cushion that broke my fall. The next sound I heard was a beep.

PART VIII

OUT, BACK...
AND BEYOND

September 30, 2000

Fifteen pairs of eyes focus on the starting pistol beneath a myriad of lights, television cameras, and more than 100,000 spectators in Stadium Australia. The 5,000 meters final at the 2000 Olympic Games in Sydney shines off television screens world-wide to millions of viewers.

School children in Dallas and Berlin and Tokyo and Nairobi are drawn to the light and the 15 men about to begin a journey that will test their courage, their stamina, and their will. The men are dressed in the green of Ethiopia and Morocco and Australia, the white of Algeria and Germany and Japan, the maroon of Qatar, the red of Kenya, the blue of Ukraine, and the red, white, and blue of the United States.

Television commentators Del Hayes and Marv Lenzi pan the line of world-class runners and fill the momentary silence with a final thought. "A fast pace favors the Africans," Lenzi says. "But a slow, tactical race gives anyone a chance for a miracle."

The Olympic flame soars into the night sky without notice from the runners, who step to the starting line upon the starter's call of "On your marks!" The runners crouch in unison to the command of "Set!"

Within a micro-moment, each runner's career passes before him. The Ethiopian, Falemu Tegassi, remembers racing his brothers home from school barefoot through dirt fields in scorching heat. The Ukranian, Dmitry Fesserov, thinks of the snow that seeped into his boots on training runs along frozen farm roads that led to seemingly nowhere. The Moroccan, Said Bulami, recalls the footprints he left on the sand along the shores near Casablanca.

The American takes a breath, closes his eyes, and returns to one morning in his youth. He is wearing a white V-neck T-shirt, blue-jean cutoffs, black high-tops, and a hero who floats across his eyes. He runs down a quiet, undulating road and approaches a sun's light he will follow for the next 28 years.

I open my eyes and surge from Rolling Hills Parkway to the red rubber track of the Olympic Games. I make the sign of the cross, plant my Spryidon spikes, and launch myself off the line at the first spark from the starter's pistol.

The race begins.

59

All I heard when I awoke at St. Agnes Hospital in Sacramento was the beep of a heart monitor. All I saw were plain, white walls and a familiar face.

"Langendubber?"

I shook my head and tried to make the face go away. I opened my eyes, but it was still there. "If I'm dead, I hope I'm in Purgatory."

"Why is that?" said the man with the goofy hunting cap.

"Because I see two of you."

Fubby Tuppernacker spoke very slowly, which only made my dizzy head hurt more. "Langengooper, you fell down at the finish line of the Olympic Trials, hit your head on the track, and was knocked unconscious."

I sat up on the hospital bed, scratched my head, and stared at Fubby. He stared back.

"I never realized it before, Langenfluffer."

"What's that?"

"You are the spitting image of Grimsley Roeper?"

The name clicked my memory back. I remembered sprinting down the homestretch like a wild man and diving for the finish line. What I didn't remember is if I had gotten there before or after my African-turned-American competitor. Dr. Orville Neisbaum interrupted the thought. He walked into my room, while reading my chart. "Mr. Langenfelder, I have good news and bad news."

"Give me the bad news first."

Neisbaum paced the room. "The bad news is you're on the 12th floor, so this time there is no way you can escape the hospital."

"The good news?"

"You suffered only a slight concussion, even though you slipped in and out of consciousness through the night. You should be able to start training for Sydney by tomorrow."

Neisbaum's bedside manner restored my memory to full and watered my eyes. I didn't need to watch the Olympic Trials' tape I would play on the television in my hospital room 27 times during the next 24 hours. I could remember my arms flailing in front of me and my chest edging in front of Suleiman Narui as I dove for the line. The glory of the moment gave way to the continued hope of finding my wife and little boy.

I turned to Fubby, whose face was now singular, and peered out the window to the blue sky.

"What time is it?" I asked.

"It's 8 a.m.," Fubby said. "You woke up for a second in the ambulance, took off your spikes, and then slept through the night."

I never had been admitted into the hospital since I was born and now I had been in twice within seven days. Fubby comforted me with more good news. Buzz Bohamer was fired as the head track and field and cross country coach at Caprock State University, after Erin Macklin threatened a sexual harassment suit against the university. According to Erin, Buzz told her if she wouldn't sleep with him, he would tell everyone she worked as a stripper. That's why Erin quit the team. She agreed to drop the suit and give up her moonlighting job, if Buzz was fired and that she be permitted to compete one more year. The entire team signed a petition, which Fubby distributed, to make me the new head coach.

"Making the Olympic team should help your cause," Fubby said. "You should call the athletic director first thing Monday morning."

That night, Hank Kirkland organized a congratulations/get well/good luck party in my hospital room. They brought balloons, cards, and banners all with the Olympic rings printed on them. They all came to pay their respects. Hesson, Colle, Gabriel, Fast Eddie Hockler, Fergus, Willoughby, Nolecky, Marco, Justine, Emma, Nikki, Carmen Pirelli, and my 400 meter contingent of McCray, Sims, and Roe. I received congratulatory faxes from Bart, Mitch the Bitch, Funky Joe, Stub, Louis Cannoli, Ray, Bobby Mac, Rizzo, The Stallion, my brothers and sisters, and Coach Hightower.

My college runners talked about me like I wasn't even there. Colle spoke of how I came to visit him in jail. Carmen said I gave her the encouragement to run again. Fast Eddie Hockler thanked me for the advice on dating. They all raised whatever they were drinking. Kirkland offered the toast.

"To Jonny Langenfelder – a wonderful coach, runner, writer, father, husband, counselor, and friend. We will follow you, wherever you go."

"Here, Here," they said, clinking their glasses, cups, and cans.

They each knelt down beside my bed to wish me farewell and a safe, successful journey to Australia. I told them I would be thinking about them. That night as the white walls turned pitch black, I wondered if all the miles and sweat had been worth it. The answer had come not only in the Olympic berth, but in the birth of a running career that would allow me to change the lives of those around me. I did not realize how many people I inspired until that night. Those I inspired will go on to inspire others.

But the two people I cared for the most were somewhere in the Australian Outback with the thought that I no longer loved them. My Olympic goal was not only to win a medal, but to win back my family. I figured it might take a medal and the media exposure that would come from it to convince them how deeply I cared for them.

Dr. Neisbaum released me the next morning from St. Agnes Hospital. "The X-rays of your brain showed nothing," he said with a grin.

"Gee thanks, Doc."

"Seriously, you have to be careful not to sustain another head trauma. You can only have so many concussions. A real bad one could be fatal."

I had one when Mom dropped me as a baby and another in my car accident in 1976, on my collapse at the 1978 Texas Relays, and when I was hit by the pickup in January of 1988. I often hit my head against the wall after a bad race. I never told Neisbaum about any of that in fear that he may not sign my medical release to the U.S. Olympic Committee. "I'm not planning on playing for the Dallas Cowboys after the Games, Doc."

I watched the last day of the Olympic Trials and called Gerald Grainger, the Caprock State athletic director, the next morning from my hotel room in Sacramento. Before I finished the last syllable of my name, Grainger made me an offer – $48,000 per year, full medical and dental benefits for the family, a leased van, Buzz's old office, and a large equipment, travel, and recruiting budget.

There was a long pause on my end of the telephone. "Coach Langenfelder, do you need some time to think about?"

"I've thought about it, Mr. Grainger. I have just one question?"

"And that is?"

"When do I start?"

Caprock State's new head track and field and cross country coach caught a ride with a track official from Sacramento to Eugene, Oregon, where the U.S. Olympic Committee paid for athletes' room and board. I had a dormitory room that overlooked Hayward Field. One last time I was running in the footsteps of Steve Prefontaine.

I felt like he was running alongside me on Pre's trails, up and down the Hendrick's Park road where he died 25 years before, and around and around the track. We made great training companions, especially since my 13:21.9 at the Olympic Trials equaled his personal best. It was just me and Pre. The other athletes were racing in Europe, a trip I couldn't afford or wanted, or pounding the road race circuit. I figured it better to let them race themselves out and go to Australia – or Oz, as everyone called it – fresh and in the shape of my life.

I reached 101 miles my first week and followed with two weeks of 121's. Then I ran my first track workout on Thursday, August 17. I did three times two miles with a four-lap jog interval in 8:45, 8:46, and 8:42. As I powered around the final turn, the thought was clear. I am going to stand on the top step of the awards' platform after the 5,000 meters finals with a gold medal around my neck, put my hand on my heart, and hear the national anthem as the American flag waves in front of the Olympic flame. I imagine that's what Pre thought as he geared for Munich on this same track. The thought was clearer after three more weeks of five miles of intervals twice per week and a Saturday 20 miler. My final test was a two-mile time trial on Monday, September 10. I waited until 9:30 p.m., when there was no wind or heat or people. Just me and a shadow I called Pre.

A full moon lit our way around the track we both had toured so many times and at a pace that made Pre work to keep up. The numbers on my glow-in-the-dark watch split 62, 2:05, 3:08, 4:11. The Hayward Field stands were empty except for the ghosts who pounded the wooden bleachers and chanted, "Pre! Pre! Pre!..."

I couldn't shake Pre through splits of 5:14, 6:17, and 7:20. So I surged at the bell and drove hard down the backstretch in a late-ditch effort to break the gutsy bugger. Still, he was there as I hit the final turn and raced me stride for stride in the homestretch. The closer the finish line came, the faster I pumped my arms. Pre ran me all the way to the line and we leaned together. It was a dead heat, as the numbers 8:19.4 on my watch lit the night.

The next morning I said good-bye to Pre to Hayward Field to Eugene and to the United States. I could not have prepared better. I was on my way to Australia, halfway around the world, to find a family and a flame I had searched for what seemed an eternity.

◆◆◆

60

I would have taken a tornado to Oz if one had been available the morning after my tumultuous 42nd birthday. Instead I endured 10 months of excruciating workouts, two life-threatening Olympic Trials' races, and Sunday mornings without waffles and my family for a first-class charter flight from Los Angeles to Sydney.

I had explained my situation after making the Olympic team to USOC teams' manager Allan Stein, who offered advice but no early plane ticket. "Why don't you just e-mail your wife and kid, tell them you're sorry, and to come home?" he said over the telephone from his office in Colorado Springs.

Only if it was that simple. Clare and Miles were somewhere in the Outback, which seems to make up about all but about five large cities and the beach in Australia. I remembered my college coach Rupert Wade telling me that Darcy Ellard likes to move his runners around, so they can train in seclusion without distraction. A walk-about could take months. I only had two weeks. Stein said that my visa, like that of most the other members of the U.S. delegation, went from September 14 until October 2. The opening ceremonies were on September 15, my 5,000 meters heats were on Wednesday, September 27 and the final on Saturday, September 30. That left me 11 days to find my needles in the Australian desert.

What I needed was a Munchkin to show me the yellow brick road, a scarecrow to protect me from the wicked witch, a tin man to escort me to the wizard, and a cowardly lion to point me in the right direction. The wicked witch, in this case, was Darcy Ellard. He brainwashed my wife into thinking he was her way to happiness and a spot on the Australian Olympic Team or at least a spot in the limelight of a major marathon or an Ironman Triathlon. If I could find him, I'd melt him.

Our charter flight touched down at the Sydney International Airport without a bump. I felt much pride walking off the airplane through flag-waving greeters with the greatest runners, swimmers, boxers, wrestlers, and rowers the United States had to offer. I would not only be competing for myself, but for my country. We were roomed by event at the Olympic Village. My 5,000 meters teammates Leyton Downy and Quinn Harper slept on the bunk beds and gave me the double bed in the separate room.

"Seniority?" I asked.

"No," Downy said. "We figure at your age you must snore like a warthog. Besides, we might pick up some Russian babes. We'd offer you one, but the USOC doesn't hand out Viagra."

I told them I came here to run and find my family and that I wouldn't need the bed again until after I returned from the Outback. I explained that I couldn't call Clare's parents, because they didn't have a telephone. I figured they wouldn't tell me or even knew where Clare and Miles were. "Sure you want to be touring the Outback so close to your 5,000 meters heats?" Harper said.

"Do I have a choice?"

I weaved through the mass of foreign dialects in the athletes' dining hall, trying to find someone who might know where Darcy was hiding my family. Australian marathoner Duncan Conway laughed at my question. "Darcy doesn't have any athletes in these Games, mate. Everyone in this country knows the guy is a bloody idiot."

I made up for whatever sleep I didn't get on the charter flight and awoke the next morning to a large suit bag with my name on it. At 5 p.m. that evening, after a track workout with my roommates, I was wearing the contents of the bag. I stared in the mirror at my navy blue blazer, white shirt, beige slacks, white brim hat, and red, white, and blue tie.

"You look like a million bucks," Downy said.

"Feel like it," I said. "Sure beats that all-brown Bopper Burger suit."

Four hours later, the U.S. men's 5,000 meters trio walked down a tunnel of Stadium Australia with hundreds of other like-dressed male athletes and women in their red blazers and blue skirts. We waited in the dark behind the eight–man contingent from the United Arab Emirates. Then, the moment I had awaited 28 years.

We followed our flag bearer to the light of a stadium that was filled with more than 100,000 cheering and hollering spectators and their flashing cameras. I paraded around the red rubber track and before rows of television cameras. I whooped it up with American athletes anywhere from a foot smaller to a foot larger than me and waved my little American flag to no one in particular.

For one momentous lap, I didn't care how long it took me to arrive here or that the team handball player in front of me said he only took up the sport the previous summer. I walked stride for stride alongside camcorder-wielding professional athletes who made a million dollars per year and alongside archers who didn't make a cent.

We took our places on an infield of athletes representing 199 nations and wearing every color of the rainbow. I listened to John Farnham and Olivia Newton-John sing "Dare to dream," IOC president Juan Antonio Samaranch deliver his Olympic welcome, Head of State Sir William Deane declare the 2000 Summer Games open, and the Olympic hymn and oath. The huge Olympic flag was carried in by past Australian Olympians.

Then there was silence as we awaited the Olympic flame. No one knew who would carry it into the stadium or who would light the huge cauldron that would be elevated to the highest point of the stands. The stadium lights were turned off.

A figure emerged from the tunnel and lit the dark stadium with his high-held torch as the crowd cheered in a crescendo. The orchestra played "Waltzing Matilda" and the announcer introduced the famous torchbearer "Nineteen Fifty-Six Olympic Marathoner – Darcy Ellard!"

In an instant, all the joy I felt turned to hatred for this arrogant bastard still running like a cheetah into his 70's. This asshole responsible for making me run 20 repeat 880's up a Lubbock hill in the rain, for keeping me from a shoe contract and an important European race, and for filling my wife and so many other promising runners with so much crap from his ridiculous over-training books was carrying my Olympic flame. Why did he deserve this honor and all the recognition? All he did was crawl on his hands and knees to make a finish line.

I stood by the start/finish line and zoomed my eyes in on this smug lunatic, waving at the crowd from the top of the homestretch. My anger intensified at the thought that he could be Miles' father and holding my little boy and Clare in some Outback shack. As he approached, Downy hollered in my ear. "Isn't that the old fart who's fuckin' your wife?"

The rage shot out of my ears. As Darcy closed in on the start/finish line, I lowered my head and lunged at his knees. The old man toppled over my shoulder and fell back-first to the track with a "Uhhh!" Darcy popped up and continued running. I was helped up by two large security officers, who escorted me to the nearest exit.

I couldn't believe I had tackled the Olympic torchbearer. It happened so fast. It was like someone took over my body, and I was watching him do it. The security officers put me in a holding cell. I banged my head against the bars.

"Way to go, Langenloser," I thought. "You've come all this way and don't even get to see the lighting of the cauldron. You won't get to run in the Olympics, and you won't get a chance to find Clare and Miles. They will put you on the first plane back to America, for sure."

I pleaded with the Stadium's head of security, Officer Ian Barker. "Look, man, it was an accident. Somebody pushed me onto the track. I didn't mean to do it."

"Don't believe ya.'"

Barker said media officials told him the incident did not appear on American television, because they were showing the Dream Team at the time. He said the crowd thought it was part of the festivities, perhaps re-enacting Darcy's Olympic crawl.

Barker scratched at his whiskered chin with his dirty fingernails. "The only way to know for sure if you tackled Darcy Ellard is to ask Darcy Ellard."

I waited for 30 tense minutes, before Barker returned with the verdict. Barker put the key in the cell door and let me out. I clasped my hands in a praying pose and held them to my lips.

"What did he say?" I asked

"He said, 'No worries, mate. '"

The next morning, instead of being on a plane to America, I was on a bus en route to the Outback. I used the $800 of Australian per diem money to fund my rescue mission. I recalled all the places in the Outback Clare had talked about and took trips to those little one-donkey towns. I asked at the pubs and stores, if they saw any runners in the area.

"I believe all the running blokes are in Sydney," said a pissed Aussie at the Snakeskin Pub.

I also showed him a picture of Clare and Miles. "Who's the good-looking bird?"

"My wife."

I traveled from desert to desert from Queensland to Western Australia without seeing or hearing about a single runner. I took an Outback adventure tour. The bus driver said, "I can show you a crocodile, a kangaroo, a Kuala bear, or a python But I don't know about your wife and kid."

After six days, I had seen enough cactus and sand and creeks and brush. I started back to Sydney, where I would appeal to Australian television and newspapers. It was a long-shot, but I thought maybe I could convince them to air or publish my story. Maybe a headline like "U.S. Olympian desperate to find family" could generate a response from viewers and readers.

On Friday, September 22, or whatever day it was – it's easy to lose track in the Outback – I woke up from a nap on the bus somewhere in the Northern Territory. I looked out the window and hollered "Driver stop!"

The driver hit the brakes. Passengers smashed into the seats in front of them.

"Bloody hell," the driver said.

I walked to the front and pointed to a dark-skinned man running down a dirt path. "That might be one of Darcy's boys."

"No, mate. That's an Aboriginee. He's probably out hunting for food."

"But look. He's wearing Wooosh running shoes."

The driver pulled over and let me and my backpack out. I ran the man down about a mile down the path. I talked to him like he was from Pluto.

"I am looking for a group of runners, who train with Darcy Ellard. Can you stop and try to talk to me?"

"Bugger off, mate. I'm trying to finish my 35K."

The man wasn't running like a cheetah, but I knew he must be one of Darcy's boys. I couldn't run any farther with the heavy backpack. I walked and followed the Aborignee's footprints 5K to a campsite of runners and worn sneakers hidden by tall trees and sand dunes.

The Aboriginee greeted me with a handshake. "My name is Jama. I'm sorry I couldn't talk back there, but my coach doesn't like me to stop on the run."

"Chapter 47," I said under my breath.

I showed him the picture of Clare and Miles. Jama studied it for a few seconds. "You must be Jonny."

"Yes. Where are they?"

"Sorry, mate. Clare left yesterday. Went back to Moose Junction."

"Darn," I said with a fist pump. "When's the next bus?"

"Monday, and no use hitchhiking from this place. The bus is the only vehicle that ever drives down that road."

Jama and I sat back on a fallen tree and shared a pot of tea from water he boiled from a small campfire. He said Clare came to the training camp off and on since November, sometimes with Miles, sometimes without him. This time she was alone. He said I was all Clare talked about, and she didn't have much to do with anyone else.

"She trained for a marathon, but her heart wasn't in it."

Miles, he said, talked about me constantly and how his daddy was going to run in the Olympics, without even knowing I had been training my butt off. He said Miles built, in the sand dunes, an Olympic Stadium, complete with a track and the Olympic cauldron. He put some twigs in there and lit the flame.

"He used his two little fingers to pretend it was his daddy running around the track," Jama said. "He hollered, 'Marks! Set! Go, Daddy!'"

My wait for the bus allowed me to catch up on some sleep and training. I ran a 12K up a steady winding incline called "Darcy Hill" and floated down it like I was on a cloud. I spent the nights staring at a sky that had more stars than a planetarium.

"I can see how runners like training out here," I told Jama.

"It's good," he said. "But it's no place for a family man or woman. Clare was a lost soul out here."

The next day I intended to find her soul and take it and Miles back to civilization. The bus ride was only 3 ½ hours to Moose Junction. The Eggers' house was a swift 3 ½ minutes for a man with a backpack and an apology.

Eldon Eggers was right where I left him, in front of the television set and watching his bloody cricket. Fiona Eggers sat at the table, right where I left her, drinking a cup of tea. Eldon didn't move his head from the light. He just pointed to the back room.

I opened the door to a dark room, illuminated only by the light creeping through the tattered orange curtains, to a woman crying into her pillow. I sat on the bed, put my hand on her shoulder, and kissed the back of her neck. She sat up and gazed at me as if to say, "Can it be true?" She put her arms around me, squeezed me, and cried some more.

"Oh, Jonny, I am so sorry."

I kissed her forehead. "No, my sweet Clare, this was all my fault. I was a bloody fool and didn't realize it until I walked in and saw all the hours you spent transforming my house into our home. I never dreamed anyone could love me that much."

I told Clare what I had to do to find her. She kissed me on the cheek and smiled, "I told you that you could make the Olympic team, Langenwanker."

"I love you, Clare."

"I love you too."

I looked around the room. "So, where's my little boy?"

Clare started crying again. She looked like she had been crying all day and like she hadn't slept or showered in days. "Jonny, I don't how to tell you this."

"Tell me what?"

"Miles. He's disappeared."

I sat there and stared at the dark, empty walls.

Clare said she had returned to her parents place from the Outback to find Miles' clothes, his suitcase, and his toys gone. He cut several Olympic articles out of the newspaper and magazines and walked out the door. Eldon asked him where he was going. "To watch my daddy run in the Olympics," he said.

"I reckoned he was having me on,'" Eldon said. "How bloody far could a seven-year-old boy go?"

Miles, we knew with his boundless energy and adult-like resourcefulness, could go as far as Sydney or even Lubbock. He and Clare often hitchhiked to her Outback training centers' less remote areas. Miles made 400 Australian dollars in Moose Junction by collecting beer cans and cashing them in for the deposit money and $300 from a summer lemonade stand he set up alongside the building of a new road. He never spent a penny of his allowance in Lubbock. He always said he was saving it for something big.

Was it for a ticket to the Olympic Games or a ticket to Lubbock? Clare said she checked the bus station and everyone in Moose Junction and nearby deserts and called every police station from Moose Junction to Melbourne to Sydney. But there was no sign of him. The local authorities weren't much help. The only people who went missing in Moose Junction showed up hungover in the bushes. We took the bus to Wallonby Creek and spent the day and most of the night, asking if anyone saw him. Frantic, yet exhausted, we gave up around midnight and took a room above the Crocodile Pub. It was the same room we spent our wedding night, the same night we found our way back to each other. I held Clare's warm naked body through the night. At dawn, she took my left hand. "Jonny, you're still wearing your wedding band."

"I never took it off."

Clare flashed her left hand and the diamond ring I slipped on her finger at DFW airport. "Me neither."

Clare said she never received the letter I sent. She said she went to the Outback to find herself. What she found was how much she needed me and how much she didn't need or want anything to do with Darcy Ellard.

"The guy is a bloody idiot," Clare said. "He would show up about once a month, make us run a hundred sand dunes, and wrote me a ridiculous *over-training* schedule he considered for about two minutes. When I left the last training center, I left for good. Why didn't I listen to you?"

"Actually, I'm thankful for Darcy," I said.

"How's that?"

"Without him, we probably never would have met."

We made love again, and I told Clare I never would let her or Miles go again. "Does this mean you finally will start calling him your son?" she asked.

I didn't answer.

Not long after I drifted back to sleep, Miles stood at the foot of my bed with a huge grin. I extended my arms and then woke up. My arms were extended, but all that was there was the bedpost. All that was real were the tears.

Over a hot bowl of porridge in the Crocodile Pub at dawn, I unveiled my plan to Clare on how to find Miles. "First, pray and pray very hard to my mom and dad in heaven. My fingers already are sore from gripping the rosary beads yesterday.

"Second, I have to go back to Sydney and win the Olympic gold medal."

"Just like that, huh?"

"Yes, just like that. I have to. That's the only way to get my story told. It would get as much media attention as Michael Johnson taking a dump or Marion Jones shopping for lingerie. Someone is bound to have seen Miles and report in. I don't have enough time on my visa to check under every rock in Australia and I can't waste any more energy and sleep on worrying about what crocodile or Australian Outbacker has him.

"Third, you go back to Lubbock and see if he somehow turned up there. Maybe he talked someone into escorting him onto an airplane. Your mom and dad can send you a telegram if he turns up back here."

I envisioned Eldon on the sofa with that hat with the corks and the empty phone jack on the wall. "He doesn't exactly have e-mail does he?"

Clare smiled. "I will be waiting for you at home."

"Home?"

"Home, Coach Langenfelder. As in 1721 Lucas Lane."

"If I come there, would you make Miles and me some waffles?"

I took the first bus out of Wallonby Creek to Sydney. The expected arrival of noon on Wednesday, September 27th would allow me a pre-race nap at the Olympic Village. But the bus suffered a flat tire and then a broken fan belt and didn't pull into the Sydney bus terminal until 8:10 p.m., 90 minutes before my scheduled 5,000 meters heat. I ordered the Arab taxi driver to stop and wait for me at the Olympic Village, where I dropped my backpack and grabbed my U.S.A sweats and singlet and shorts and spikes and race numbers. I sprinted back to the taxi and pointed the driver to Stadium Australia. "Step on it!"

I changed into my running gear – spikes and all – and pinned my race numbers to the back and front of my singlet in the backseat of a taxi. The Arab driver with sweat dripping from his turban fought his way through what he called, "Olympic Traffic." He arrived at Stadium Australia at 9:20 p.m. I threw whatever money was left in my wallet on the front seat and rushed out the door.

I ran from gate to gate showing my credential to ticket takers who directed me from gate to gate. At 9:35, five minutes before the heats, I hurdled a turnstile, stiffed-armed a ticket taker, slugged a security guard, knocked over spectators and their popcorn, and ducked into an entrance. I ran down the stairs and hopped over the rail to the track, where I outsprinted two more security guards to the laughter of a capacity crowd and to the starting line of stunned world-class runners.

I was met there by the starting line official and security's head man, Ian Barker. "Not you again," Barker said.

"Sorry I'm late," I said to the starting line official as I tore off my sweats. "I got caught in a traffic jam."

The official handed me two numbers to press on the sides of my shorts and pointed Barker off the track. I took a deep breath, made the sign of the cross, and thanked God for getting me there. Then the starter fired his pistol. My Olympic career began.

During the next 12 ½ laps I discovered the best way to prepare for an Olympic race – spend 11 days in the Outback looking for your wife and little boy and arrive via taxi only moments before. This makes sure you don't over-train or spend too much nervous energy thinking about the race. The effort of running from gate to gate and of striding away from security proved the perfect warm up. I never felt more loose or relaxed in a race. I followed the leaders around the Stadium Australia track for 11 ½ laps. I sprinted into the lead on the final backstretch and held off several challengers in the homestretch to win the heat and automatically advance to Saturday's final. It was the easiest 13:30 5,000 meters I ever ran.

Now I had three days to recover for the Olympic final. As I exited Stadium Australia I smiled, knowing my next exit could be as the Olympic champion. I had the brains, the heart, and the courage. All I needed was a little luck.

Dressing for the Olympic 5,000 meters final was a time travel through a career that spanned 28 years, 11 countries, and three continents. I remembered the oversized Bishop Callahan jersey I slipped over my skinny chest before my first cross country race in 1972, the Forest Hill singlet before the 1976 state mile, the Caprock State shirt at the NCAA Track and Field Championships in 1980, the Wooosh vest in Geneva in 1987, and the Spyridon uniform before the final of my six Olympic Trials' appearances.

But this race ritual on Saturday, September 30, 2000 took the longest. That's because this race was my last.

I stuck safety pins through race number 1225 and pinned it to the navy-blue front of my singlet. I turned the singlet over and pinned another number 1225 to the red back of the jersey. I pulled it over my head and tucked it into my red, white, and blue shorts, while primping the sides to make sure the shirt was unwrinkled. Next came a U.S.A. T-shirt, sweats, socks, and yellow and white Spyridon training flats. I combed my hair, rolled my underarms, brushed my teeth, checked the mirror, and knelt over the bed in my room at the Olympic Village. I clasped my hands together, closed my eyes, and whispered.

"Dear God, Thank you for giving me the talent and the tenacity to overcome all obstacles and make the Olympic Games. I pray not that I win a medal tonight, but that I run to the absolute best of the ability you have given me. I pray also for Miles Simon that, wherever he is, he is safe and that, if it is your will, that he find his way back to us. Amen."

I made the sign of the cross and marched out of my room, down the hallway, and toward the conclusion of my Olympic dream.

My pre-5,000 meters heat adventure had baffled my roommates, Leyton Downy and Quinn Harper, who failed miserably in the next heat.

"I don't get it," Harper said. "I slept in a comfortable air conditioned room for 11 days, while you slept on a bus in the Outback. And *you* are the one going into the final. How do you explain it?"

"Desire," I said.

They probably would have made the final too, if it meant getting their little boy back. You don't realize how much you can love a child until you have one or until you lose one. Miles was not lost in a mall, this time. He was lost in a massive country of 20 million people. To find him, you don't just stick "lost: little boy" posters on a few corner telephone poles. You have to put the word out over the airwaves and through the newspapers.

I was escorted to the interview room after winning my 5,000 meters heat. But the only question a reporter asked me was, "Have you seen Maurice Greene around here anywhere?"

The next day in Olympic Village media room I approached Marv Lenzi, who did not remember me from the 1980 or 1984 Olympic Trials. "I'll run it by the producer," he said, stuffing a hot French fry into his mouth. "But we only have so much airtime, and there are too many touchy-feely stories out there like this already. What sport are you in? Yachting?"

I could live without a gold medal, but not without Miles. I couldn't go back to Clare empty-handed. Miles would be as good as gold. But I knew, as I marched out of the Olympic Village, what I had to do to have my story told. Bronze or silver wouldn't do it. I needed gold for this 1A headline – "Forty-two year-old runner finds Olympic gold, now looks for his little boy."

Such a feat, I knew, was unimaginable. I had the slowest personal best in the field. Four runners had dipped under 13 minutes, and the fastest time was 33 seconds better than my best. All I could hope for was a funeral procession – a slow, tactical race that would come down to the final lap and who wanted it the most. No other runner in the field needed a gold medal to get his little boy back. You can measure a runner by his height, weight, VO-2 max, and his PR. But you can't measure the size of his heart.

My heart was beating out of my singlet as I sat my warmed up body in a control room inside the massive Stadium Australia 20 minutes before the final. I looked down at the green carpet floor and then into the eyes of my competitors, who looked just as worried as me. The officials gave us our side numbers, marched us down the dark tunnel, and stopped us 30 meters from the entrance. I lay on the side, propped my legs on a hurdle, and breathed. I thought about Mom and Dad, Uncle Grimsley, Coach Hightower, Zac Groves, Malcolm Gould, Father Litzke, Clare, Miles, and Steve Prefontaine. "This," I thought, "must have been exactly what Pre felt in Munich."

I breathed deeply and visualized the race until the gun lap, when someone tapped me on the shoulder.

"Excuse me, mate. Are you Jonny Langenfelder?"

I looked up at a teenage messenger with a Games credential and an envelope with my name on it. He handed me the envelope and said he was told to deliver it to me. I pulled a piece of fax paper out of the envelope. The only word and numbers on the page were "Luke 17:21." I stood, gave the messenger back the paper and envelope, and asked for his pen. I wrote, "Luke 17:21" on my race number, just below my heart.

Then we broke through the darkness of the tunnel to the light of the stadium and its 100,000 spectators, who cheered as we marched to the starting line on a cool night warmed by an Olympic flame that towered above this great mass of humanity. I did not stop to look at the flame, only at the red rubber path that could lead me to glory and my little boy. I removed my sweats and dropped them into a basket on the side of the track. I did a stride, alone, 50 meters to the middle of the curve and walked back to the starting line, where my competitors poised for the race introductions. The only name I listened to was the runner in lane seven. I was welcomed by a voice that echoed off the stadium walls and applauded by the spectators, who anticipated a memorable race.

"From the United States, Jonathan Christian Langenfelder!"

The final name was called, and the television cameras were positioned for the start. All that remained was for a man to press the trigger on the starter's pistol he gripped in his right hand and held above his head. I closed my eyes one last time, breathed, and whispered. "This one is for you, Miles."

I left the starting line as soon as the smoke left the starting gun and ran straight to the back of the pack. Ahead were 14 runners of about every color, size, nationality, and religion. We thumped our spikes into the rubber and blew nervous breaths out our lungs. I lifted my knees in cadence with the long, flowing stride of the blue and gold-clad runner in front of me. We passed the finish line, a lit digital race clock, and the number "12" on the electronic lap counter.

Around the turn and down the backstretch, I heard a number that gave me hope,

"Sixty-eight!"

The sluggish pace only alarmed one runner, who surged to the front and gapped the field. I stayed in the back of the pelotin, certain the wayward leader would be reeled in. The slow, methodical procession continued, and I did not have to listen to the hollered splits to know how slow it was. It felt slower than any race I had run during the past eight years. It was exactly what I wanted.

I sat in last place and waited, as the others mixed it up in the pack, jostling in and out and wasting their energy. I ran along the rail, not running a step farther than the prescribed distance and free from the pushing and shoving and cursing that only made the others lose focus of the ultimate goal. The early leader was caught by the pack after four laps. The pace quickened the next mile, but not at a velocity that could drop me off the back. I stayed with the plan and focused on a singlet in white or yellow or maroon or blue, or whatever colored wind-block happened to be in front of me.

I listened to my breathing and felt my toes touch the rubber Earth. I was running not to win a gold medal, but only for the sake of running. I never felt stronger.

We passed the finish line and a lit number "4" on the lap counter. The pack was growing restless. Elbows were used as weapons in the turbulent stream of runners. Some pushed and shoved and forced their way in and out of the pack. Still, I ran last, content to teach my competitors a lesson in race tactics. The pace quickened with each lap, and I felt never-more powerful as we passed the number "2." The world watched as I charged from last to eighth on the backstretch, raced around the turn, and surged past three more runners at the top of the penultimate homestretch.

The crowd cheered my arrival to the front group. I looked ahead to the lap counter with the number "1" and the clock's numbers flashing into the night. I was gliding on an air cushion and ready to sprint away from the field with a boundless burst. As I moved to the end of the stretch, a wet elbow from an Ethiopian pierced my side. I lost my balance, and my foot collided with a Moroccan's shin. Someone shoved my back with such great force that there was no way I could keep myself upright.

As the bell was ringing, I was tumbling. A mass of bodies and rubber heels flew over me and scourged my flesh. Runners' spikes dug into my palms, and my head struck the metal rail. I lay there, bleeding from my hands and head and without anyone coming to my aid. I lost consciousness and to the runners who roared down the homestretch to take gold, silver, and bronze.

I slipped into a peaceful dream and to a path that led me out of darkness. I ran from Rolling Hills Parkway around White Rock Lake and the Caprock State Campus, through Pre's Trails, up Heartbreak Hill and along the tracks of Memorial Stadium, Hayward Field, and the European track circuit. I kept running through the clouds, alone, until a tiny voice brought me back to Earth.

"Get up! Get up!"

I figured this was my inner soul beckoning me to finish this final race. Then I felt a tug on my arm and heard the voice again and more clearly, "Get up! Get up! Come on, Daddy, get up! Marks, set, go!"

I opened my eyes and through the sweat was the blurred face of a boy in his little U.S.A. Track and Field uniform. I had fulfilled my promise to run in the Olympics. Somehow, as he promised, Miles Simon had come to watch me and, now, to help me finish. He had ventured through the desert of Australia, past police, stadium security, and track officials to be by my side.

He pulled me from the rubber slab and held my hand as this weary, beaten and bled body started running again. Together, Miles and I ran around the turn and past the screaming crowd that exhorted me to the finish. The last lap of my career was slower than the first lap of my career. With Miles' help I struggled onward and reached the top of the homestretch. The finish looked a mile away, and I barely could see it through the blood that dripped into my contact lenses.

Still, we continued toward the finish line and the mob of television and still cameras that gathered behind it. Miles hollered over the crowd noise. "Come on, Daddy! Not far to go! You can do it!"

I held Miles' hand tighter and gathered his energy on a homestretch that seemed steeper than Heartbreak Hill. I ran slower and slower but kept running until my aching chest leaned across the finish line. The numbers on the lighted finish line clock stopped at "17:21." I bent over and grabbed my knees. Then I threw my arms around Miles and hugged the tears out of us.

Our eyes reflected off the camera lenses that sent our moment around the world. I picked up Miles and carried him through the media herd to the stadium exit at the far end of the homestretch.

Then, as I walked off the track toward the tunnel, I gazed upward with wonder and delight at the Olympic flame that shot its powerful sparks into the heavens and illuminated the Earth. The glorious flame swallowed us with every step and lit our path with its awesome power. I kept walking toward this magnificent light that gave me strength, peace, and life.

Miles wrapped his arms around my shoulders. "Where are we going, Daddy?"

"Home, son. We're going home."

Breinigsville, PA USA
01 December 2009
228411BV00001B/232/A